BET ON THE BLACK

Mike had lost it. At some level he knew that and didn't care.

He leapt the trench, running ahead of the Keldara, M4 tracking right and left and automatically engaging targets of opportunity, round after round cracking straight through a screaming mouth, behind fierce-slitted eyes, rounds cracking past him, ducking and weaving as some part of his mind anticipated shots.

Combat psychologists had determined that there were four broad states to humans in relation to combat: white, yellow, red, and black. Some warriors, the most highly trained, could enter into black and function. By definition, they were some of the most deadly persons on earth. In black, the fighter's reactions were superhuman. A fighter who could ride the wave of the black could, would, never miss.

Mike was in the black. Time was slowed for him to such an extent he could see the bullets flying from the Chechen AKs seeming to glide through the air towards him.

He had reached the Chechen line but the fighters in front of him were having a hard time even lifting their weapons with dead bodies falling around and on them.

Some detached portion of him watched as the butt of the M4 shattered on a Chechen face. The barrel bent across the side of another's head, wrapping into a half U and the impact.

The axe came up. The axe of the Kildar and Mike struck down and across, shattering a skull, up to slash through a neck, down to take off an arm.

The air was filled with a mist of blood, the sacrifices falling slowly, so slowly.

Baen Books by John Ringo:

Unto the Breach

JOHN RINGO

UNTO THE BREACH

This is a work of fiction. All the characters and events portrayed in this book are fictional, and any resemblance to real people or incidents is purely coincidental. This book has no connection to reality. Any attempt by the reader to replicate any scene in this series is to be taken at the reader's own risk. For that matter, most of the actions of the main character are illegal under US and international law as well as most of the stricter religions in the world. There is no Valley of the Keldara. Heck, there is no Kildar. And the idea of some Scots and Vikings getting together to raid the Byzantine Empire is beyond ludicrous. The islands described in a previous book do not exist. Entire regions described in these books do not exist. Any attempt to learn anything from these books is disrecommended by the author, the publisher and the author's mother who wishes to state that he was a very nice boy and she doesn't know what went wrong.

A Baen Book

Baen Publishing Enterprises
P.O. Box 1403
Riverdale, NY 10471
www.baen.com

ISBN 10: 1-4165-5535-8
ISBN 13: 978-1-4165-5535-3

Cover art by Kurt Miller

First Baen paperback printing, April 2008

Distributed by Simon & Schuster
1230 Avenue of the Americas
New York, NY 10020

Library of Congress Cataloging-in-Publication Data: 2006023925

Printed in the United States of America

10 9 8 7 6 5 4 3 2 1

Pages by
Frank Aguirre at Hypertext Book and Journal Services
hypertext1@gmail.com

Acknowledgments

There was a bunch of people I had to get research help from on this one. As usual, Ryan Miller and Mike Massa contributed to technical operational help as well as well as HALO training details. As founding members of RingTAB (the Ringo Tech Advisory Board), they have put up with much.

I'd like to thank Christopher Austin, former member of the Army High Altitude Rescue squad, for really professional input on the mountaineering portion. My experience in mountaineering is decades past, and techniques and equipment have, ahem, changed considerably. It turns out serious mountaineers hardly ever wear leather boots and wool sweaters any more . . .

Retired Master Sergeant Sean Fleenor contributed helpful smacks to the head over weapons-use while failing to convince me not to issue the Keldara beer.

Lieutenant Colonel Dave Grossman, author of *On Combat* and *On Killing*, sent me an incredibly detailed proofread of an early version of this manuscript. Among about a billion other things, he pointed out that Ranger School was longer than I remembered. In addition, both of his books were seminal to several aspects of this novel. *On Combat*, especially, is highly recommended to anyone who is in the business of regularly or occasionally bringing violence upon others.

James Cochrane, husband of my coauthor Julie, and Emil "Praz" Praslick, of the Army Marksmanship Training Unit, supplied helpful advice on long-range shooting about which I previously knew virtually nothing. (Much as I write about it, I'm a "broad side of the barn" shooter.) I'll add that James, on the spur of the moment, took over a necessary four-hour drive when I was so sleep-deprived from writing I was babbling. The fact that I didn't die in the midst of writing this novel is probably due to James and Julie. Thanks.

As usual, any mistakes are mine.

Last but not least, I'd like to thank my daughters, Jennifer and Lindy, for accepting "Daddy's under deadline" as a reason for my almost total mental absence over the last couple of months. Hoowah.

Prologue

"Working late, Doctor?" Boris asked, yawning and glancing at the scientist's identity card.

Dr. Tolegen Arensky nodded, trying not to appear nervous. "One of my samples is done cooking; I have to test it when it's fresh."

"Better you than me," Boris replied, handing the ID back and making a note on his log-sheet. "If I ever have to pass the doors of even Level One, it will be too soon, yes?"

"The day we have to call security into the quarantine zones is the day I quit," Dr. Arensky said with a weak smile. "I barely trust our research assistants in there, no offense."

"None taken," Boris replied with a shudder, pressing the solenoid under his desk. At the sound of the all-clear buzzer the overwatch, observing the entry room from a remote security station, opened the sliding steel entry door and Dr. Tolegen Arensky started the last hour of his tenure in Russian biological research.

He passed through another metal door, nodded at the sleepy guard on the far side and turned right towards his office. If he had turned left he would have quickly confronted a third steel door and the various processes required to enter Quarantine Level One. Since he generally worked in Level Four or even Five getting to his primary labs was a daily chore.

Staying in the outer "nonquarantine" zone of the hexagonal building, he passed seven office doors, all on his right and representing by their names and title plates descending levels of power in the institute. His own was the seventh. Any sample, of course, would be cooking away in Level Four—nobody did any more research in Five since the "incident" nearly ten years ago—but he hoped that the guards would be their usual efficient self and ignore that.

He went past his room, however, and stopped at the very end of the corridor. There was one more door there, a janitor's closet. He entered the janitor's closet and removed some bottles of ancient and dust-covered bleach from the third shelf on the left. From under his bulky winter coat he removed a vaguely pyramidal object and stripped a coating from the flat underside, revealing a sticky tape. He pressed the object against the wall, then very gently unscrewed the tip of the object, which was cylindrical. On the base of the screw device was a plastic plug with a round plastic tab jutting from it. He grasped the tab and pulled, removing the plug with a vaguely "pock" sound. As he did a blue LED on the other end of the cylindrical device began to blink. He carefully screwed the cylinder back into the device and then placed the plastic plug in his jacket pocket.

That done, he proceeded back to his office.

As he entered the room, which was not much larger than the janitor's closet he'd just left, he removed his heavy outer coat and fur hat, hanging them on the coatrack by the door, then followed them with his suit coat and donned his lab coat. After a moment's thought, after actually turning to his desk, he paused, removed the lab coat and redonned his suit coat. After another moment's thought he removed the heavy jacket and fur hat from the coat rack and placed them on his desk.

The office was small, barely adequate to fit his desk, a safe in one corner and a filing cabinet. It was also spartan. On the desk was a lined pad, a pencil and a framed photograph. On the back wall was a picture of the current Russian president. A slight discoloration around the frame indicated that there had once been a larger picture in the same spot. It also indicated how long it had been since the office was painted.

He picked up the briefcase that was already in the room, set it on the desk and opened it. Turning to the safe, the combination for which the facility administrator did *not* have even if the idiot thought he did, he dialed in the combination from memory and opened it. Inside were four steel containers. Smuggling them to his office had taken the better part of two nerve-racking months but getting them out of the building was impossible; everything leaving was searched with otherwise abnormal efficiency.

Which was why he was here at three o'clock in the morning.

He opened the briefcase and slitted the containers into the pre-cut slots in the foam rubber inside. He then removed ten CDs from the safe and carefully arranged them on the face of the foam rubber. He started to close the case then paused and picked up the framed picture on the desk. He looked at it for a moment and then carefully removed the picture itself, sliding it into the briefcase before closing and locking it.

His preparations complete, he centered the briefcase on the desk, sat down on his hard wooden chair and steepled his fingers in front of him. After a moment he looked at his watch. He would continue to do so every nine seconds, unthinkingly and really unseeing, for the next three minutes and forty-seven seconds.

At the same moment Boris was questioning the doctor on why he was arriving to work at three in the morning, on a narrow road nearby a delivery truck was stopping at a police checkpoint.

Police checkpoints were so ubiquitous, and greedy, in the Confederation of Independent States, the former Soviet Union, the only surprise on the part of the driver was to find one at this time of the morning at such an out-of-the-way spot. However, based upon their standard police car and there being only two of them it was probably a roving patrol that had chosen a side road to "raise some revenue." If they were on the main road it would be obvious and they'd have to cut their watch supervisor in on their take. Out here nobody was going to notice.

The driver braked to a stop and pulled out his license and registration, slipping a ten-ruble note between them. He'd put it in an expense report and probably be paid back, eventually. Argenia Pharmaceuticals could afford the bribes; they were after all a part of doing business in Russia. They were so common, they weren't even considered bribes. Given the way that *all* public servants were paid these days it was almost reasonable for the cops to increase their salaries in this way. But they could be god-damned greedy about it.

"License and registration," the officer said as the driver rolled down the window. There was another officer on the passenger's side, waiting patiently. Not common but not unknown. Generally they were both on the driver's side so that the partner could be sure of the take.

"Please step out of the vehicle," the policeman said, stepping back and gesturing. He also hadn't pocketed the money.

"Why?" the driver said. "I'm not drunk."

"I need to ask you a few questions," the policeman said, waving again with is left hand and placing his hand on the butt of his service pistol. "Out of the truck!"

At this the passenger-side door was yanked open and the officer on that side grasped the driver's mate, pulling him down to the road.

"Okay, okay!" the driver said, raising his hands then lowering them to open the door and climb out. "What's the big deal?"

"To the side of the road," the policeman said, sternly. "Hands above your head."

"Fine, fine, whatever," the driver replied, shaken. "What is all this about?"

The answer was a cold sensation in the back of his head and then blackness.

The "police officer" slid the silenced pistol back into the rear waistband of his perfect uniform trousers and looked at his watch. As he lowered his hand, a man wearing coveralls identical to the driver's, right down to the Argenia Pharmaceuticals badge on his left breast, walked out of the woods carrying a body bag. He unrolled it next to the body and then the "driver" and the "policeman" lifted the driver's body into the bag. The "driver" zipped it shut and then the two lifted it and carried it to the rear of the panel van.

When they got there six men in heavy battle dress were already there, opening up the back door. Four of them boarded and caught the tossed bodies, rapidly stacking them on the shelves lining the side of the panel van. The remaining two were carrying weapons, coveralls and body armor. As the bodies were being stacked one of the policemen slid on the coveralls as the two porters handed off their burdens to the four stackers in the van. The second stripped off his police uniform, revealing the uniform of a Federal Security executive underneath. He was handed a heavy jacket, a fur hat and correct equipment for his position. When the "policemen" were dressed, all four climbed into the now crowded panel van.

Three seconds after the door slammed, the panel van started rolling again. From braking to a stop until moving the van had been in place for two minutes and twenty-seven seconds, three seconds ahead of plan. The "driver" considered this and reduced his speed by one kilometer per hour. It wouldn't do to be there early.

A rubber boat crunched to a stop on the shingle of the island and the six men in black immersion suits and body armor spread out in three teams of two. Each team had one man carrying a dual-tubed Russian RPO-A disposable rocket launcher while the second carried an SV-98 sniper rifle. Each man was wearing night-vision goggles and ran through the darkness as if he had done it a thousand times, easily avoiding the many large rocks that littered the beach.

One of the teams paused and took a knee as the team member carrying the sniper rifle pulled a heavily weighted device from his belt. The device was, essentially, a tomahawk with a heavy head. The "front" side of the head was a razor-sharp axe blade. The "back" side was a hammerhead.

After a moment there was a crunch of shingle as a sentry stepped off a worn trail and started walking to the east, away from the crouched team.

The team sniper stepped forward silently, placing his feet carefully to prevent the shingles crunching and pausing to let the wind carry the slight sounds he was forced to make away from the sentry. This silent, but rapid, stalk brought him to within an arm's length of the sentry in less than a minute. As soon as he was within reach he brought the axe, which had been held up over his right shoulder the whole time, down and across from the left, burying it slightly sideways at the very top of the sentry's neck. Leaving the axe in place, he caught the falling body and lowered it to the ground, then gestured to the trail and followed the rocketman up.

Just over the slight rise to the north was a hexagonal building, guarded on its vulnerable rear by three heavily armed, and armored, bunkers. . . .

As Dr. Arensky was screwing a blue blinking cylinder into a pyramidal device, the regular morning delivery from Argenia Pharmaceuticals pulled to a stop at the outer gate of the facility.

The outer gate was on a narrow causeway that led to the mainland. The hexagonal facility was on a small island in Astrakhan. The only ways on and off were by helicopter, boat or across the narrow, kilometer-and-a-half, causeway.

"Where's the regular guy?" the guard asked, blinking. It was breezy as hell on this guard post and he'd been huddling in his unheated shack trying to survive until he saw the headlights. Being out in this whipping wind wasn't his idea of fun, either.

"Drunk? Sick? Quit? I dunno," the driver said, unpleasantly, handing over an Argenia ID and manifest stating that he was Ivan Sorvoso, Argenia Pharmaceuticals Employee Number 54820, and that Ivan Sorvoso, Argenia Pharmaceuticals Employee Number 54820, was the correct driver for the vehicle on this day for this load of biological chemicals, precursors and testing samples, inventory enclosed. "All I know is I got called at damned midnight for this shit. So I'd like to be done and gone as soon as possible."

"Fine by me," the guard said, but studied the documentation carefully. He was new and motivated, which was why the old guys had stuck him on the outer guard shack. That way the little snot wouldn't be grumbling all the time about them being asleep. He nodded after a moment's careful perusal and handed the documents back. "All in order," he said, stepping back into his guard shack and pressing a solenoid to raise the heavy metal pole across the road.

Without so much as a wave the truck jerked to life and headed towards the vast hexagonal building ahead.

❖   ❖   ❖

As the panel van pulled away from the guardhouse the three sniper/rocket teams reached their pre-attack points. Each of the sniper members pulled out a periscopic night-vision device and checked the bunkers. Each was manned, with lights on in the interior. Tactically, they should have been red or blue but over the years the various users had substituted white bulbs so the bunkers stood out like neon signs. It also meant that the users would be effectively night-blind.

Almost simultaneously, although separated by eighty yards, the three snipers snapped their periscopes down and picked up their rifles.

As the sentry was being taken down, four of the eight entry specialists in the panel van slid off as it passed the front doors. The reason for the hexagonal shape was purely security; the hexagons made it possible to fit more area in while maintaining a reasonable number of external cameras. A rectangle had less internal area, a circle created too many "blind" areas.

Unfortunately, the excellent theory had run into far too typical Russian inefficiency. The front cameras, in fact, left precisely that dead zone to the left of the front doors. The eastern camera pointed slightly outwards as did the western. This was supposed to be covered by the two cameras over the door, but those left a solid gap, about six meters wide, along the wall. The team of four crouched in that gap for a moment as the lead checked his watch. Then he nodded and waved one of the armored and masked figures forward.

The figure, the "policeman," drew his silenced pistol again and fired one round. The shot took out the right-hand camera and he darted forward, reaching into a pouch. From it he extracted a small device and, quickly unplugging the left-hand camera's port, he inserted the device and replugged the assembly into it. He stepped back and extracted a small PDA and looked at it for a moment. Then he hit a button on the PDA, turned his head and nodded.

As the snipers snapped down their periscopes a new vehicle appeared out of the woods of the distant mainland.

"Busy night," the guard muttered, stepping out of the shack and slapping his mittened hands together to try to get some feeling in them.

"This is a restricted area," the guard said, as the passenger slid down his window.

"I have a pass," the man said.

The guard had no time to react to the sight of the silenced muzzle.

"Camera four is out," the intercom announced to Boris on his lonely vigil at the front desk. "And five just flickered. Go check it out."

"Got it," Boris sighed, picking up his walkie-talkie and trudging to the front door. He slid his card through the reader, a newfangled innovation in his opinion and totally unnecessary, and opened the door. The last thing he saw was the masked figure in front of him.

"Security, this is Boris." The radio crackled with static and was half unreadable.

Markov set his bottle of vodka down and belched, then pressed the microphone button. "Yes? What is wrong?"

"The plug came undone again in this damned wind," Boris said. Or Markov thought he did, the reception was terrible. "There, how is that?"

The screen for the right-hand door camera flickered for a moment and then came to life. After a moment Boris stepped in view by the door. His head was down and covered by a heavy fur hat with the flaps down, but from the way his uniform was blowing it was reasonable wear for the out-of-doors.

"I'm going in," the guard said, sliding his card through the reader.

As the panel van backed up to the loading dock the new car accelerated down the causeway. The car's former passenger was now standing in place of the guard, wearing the same style uniform and markings.

"Teams," the driver said into his microphone.

"Team One, place."

"Two . . . place."

"Three, place."

"Go," he said, quietly, sliding to a stop in front of the main doors.

The back doors of the panel van crashed open and the single external guard had just enough time to wake up from a vodka-induced haze and see the four heavily armed attackers before he died. Two more shots and both cameras were out.

"Boris" opened the front doors and drew two pistols. One shot took out each of the internal cameras and then he stepped to the side as the entry team trotted past. The lead of the team slapped a ring of thermal entry plastic onto the steel door while another slapped a breaching charge in the center. All four of the entry team turned to the side, covering their eyes with their arms, as the plastic was ignited. There was a moment of searing white and a sharp "crack" and clang as the refractory steel was first burned through and then slammed backwards by the breaching charge.

At the side door the identical assault had opened up the loading area. Both teams were in.

A moment later an alarm began to shrill.

At the sound of the alarm Dr. Arensky sighed and pulled a small device out of his side pocket. He pulled a pin from the device and then pressed the only button on the face. There was a distant "crack" and all the lights went out: on the far side of the wall in the janitor's closet was the main electrical breaker for the entire building.

At the first hoot of the alarm, which had been right on time according to their internal clock, the three rocketmen stood up, tracked in on the narrow slit openings of the bunkers and fired, all within the span of a second.

The U.S. Marines in Iraq had recently started to use a "new" thermobaric rocket system against the insurgents. It was only "new" to the Marines, though: the Russians had been using it all the way back to the Afghanistan War.

Thermobaric, often incorrectly called "fuel-air," rounds used heat ("thermo") and overpressure ("baric") to create a devastating explosion. Early thermobaric rounds *had* used "fuel" as their delivery medium, spreading a gas over a wide area before detonating catastrophically. Newer systems, such as the rocket being used in this instance, used a specialized "slow-fire" solid explosive that, as it exploded, continued to carry molecules of the explosive along its blast front which, in turn, exploded.

This created massive overpressure inside of the bunkers, instantly killing everyone within, blasting off the reinforced rear doors and tossing body parts and chunks of machine gun out through the narrow engagement slots.

Immediately after they fired, the snipers peeked up beside them scanning for targets. There were two potential reactions that the internal defense team could take. They could respond to the bunkers being hit or to the attack on the inside. In the event of attempted reinforcement of the bunkers . . . there were the snipers. . . .

Team Two, the side-door team, blew down the cargo door on the side and turned immediately to the right. The internal door here was only wood, and the lock blew off at the blast of a shotgun. As the door thudded open the lights went out. The alarm continued to shrill but only spotty emergency lighting, red and dim, came on throughout the facility. The team waited patiently, however, for what was about to occur as shotgun blasts, regular as clockwork, began to boom down the corridor.

Team One, the front entry team, spread out. Two team members started down the hallway to the left, two more to the right. As each team came to a door, the lead placed his shotgun against the lock, pulled the trigger and then stepped back. The trail then stepped forward to toss a head-sized device into the room and the cycle was repeated.

The right-hand team did the same, moving down the corridor to Dr. Arensky's office then passing by.

As the two teams spread out, the driver of the sedan strolled into the main corridor and turned to the right. When he reached Dr. Arensky's office, as the right-hand team reached the end of the corridor and tossed a device into the janitor's closet, he knocked on the door, three times, with pauses between.

The door was jerked open as Dr. Arensky struggled into his heavy outer coat, the briefcase in his hand.

"This is madness," the doctor said, sputtering.

"You do have it, though, yes?" the man asked. He was tall and broad with gray-shot black hair and a tanned face lined by much time out-of-doors.

"I have it," Dr. Arensky snapped, lifting the case.

"Let us go, then," the man said, lifting his arm to look at his watch and then nodding as a sharp crack sounded down the corridor. The crack, and flash of light, was followed by a series of rapid, short bursts of fire. Seven in all. "Our ride is on the way and we don't want to keep them waiting."

He waved down the hallway as the team of two men, one of them "Boris/Policeman," walked to the door. "Boris" casually tossed his last packet in the room and the two followed Arensky and the broad man out the front door.

From out of the cloudy sky, which was now drifting snowflakes downward, a Panther helicopter dropped, twin to the one dropping to the rear of the facility. The team boarded silently, the broad man and "Boris" simultaneously pushing Dr. Arensky into one of the seats and buckling him in. When they were done, and in their own seats, the rest of the team was in and secured.

The broad man looked at his watch and nodded as the helicopter lifted into the sky.

"One minute forty-seven seconds," he said across Arensky to "Boris." "Very good time, Kurt, very good." He pulled a device similar to the one that Dr. Arensky had had out of his pocket and extended an antenna. When he depressed the plunger the entire administrative section of the Russian Institute for Agricultural and Biological Research disappeared in a blinding flash. The concussion slightly rocked the rapidly ascending helicopter.

"Very good time indeed."

Chapter One

"Fuck me."

Mike Harmon, aka Michael James, aka Michael Duncan and currently Mike Jenkins or "Kildar," was thirty-seven years old, brown of hair and eye, medium height with a muscular build and a face that, while slightly handsome, was also so "normal" that he could pass as a local in just about any Indo-European culture from the U.S. to northern India. That trait, and an almost prescient talent for silent-kill, had earned him the nickname "Ghost" while on the SEAL teams. After sixteen years as a SEAL, most of it spent as an instructor, he had found himself unable to readjust to team life, gotten out and gone to college. Since then his life had taken so many weird turns that he had ended up as a feudal lord in the country of Georgia. With a harem, no less. Oh, and with every terrorist on earth searching for his head. Which was why he never used the name "Ghost" or "Harmon" except around a very few, very close, friends.

Mike was sitting on the summit of Mount Sumri, drinking in the cold, heady air of the high mountains and just taking a look around. He'd taken to climbing the mountain every few days as a way to get exercise and some time away from his various duties.

The Keldara called it "Mount Raven" for the flocks that gathered on its slopes. It was the highest peak of the many surrounding the valley and the birds apparently liked the viewpoint. So did Mike: one of the reasons to climb it was to take a look around.

As he'd been examining the mountains to the north, a source of constant low-grade anxiety, a flash of movement caught his eye. The hills had small herds of deer, wild pigs, mountain goats and even a few wolves. But this shape was different. Low-slung, slow-moving and . . . predatory.

He steadied the binoculars by resting his elbows on his knees and engaged the digital zoom. The picture tended to pixellate but he could zoom to a hundred times normal view magnification at the maximum. He zoomed it out to about seventy times and then controlled his breathing instinctively, trying to catch the shape again.

It was a tiger. A young male Siberian if he wasn't mistaken. Which was just flat impossible. The last tiger in the Caucasus Mountains had been killed off nearly a century ago. The Keldara still had a few preserved skins, but that was the only remnant. And the nearest breeding group of Siberians, which were themselves threatened with extinction, was, well, in *Siberia. Eastern* Siberia, which was about as close to the Caucasus as Southern California was to Nova Scotia. There was no *way* a tiger could have just walked all the way from Siberia.

But the evidence was there before his eyes. He wasn't about to dismiss it. Even if it *was* impossible.

The tiger only remained in sight for a moment then disappeared over the crest of the ridge. It was as if it had come into sight just to say: Hey! Yo! Here I am!

"Cool," Mike whispered. But he made the decision, immediately, to keep quiet about it. There was no way he was going to mention the sighting unless other evidence turned up. Nobody would believe it. Oh, they'd be polite enough about it. He did, after all, employ or, basically, "own" just about everyone he met on a day-to-day basis.

While he couldn't be said to "own" all he could survey from his lofty aerie, he did control it. The valley below, the valley of the Keldara, he did own. He had bought the valley, and the caravanserai that came with it, more or less on a whim. He had gotten lost and found himself in a remote mountain town with the strong possibility of being stuck there all winter. Since the only available living quarters, an unheated and bug-infested room over the town's sole bar, were less than pleasant, he had needed someplace to stay. And, frankly, he was tired of traveling. So, thinking that he could always sell the place if he had to, he had "bought the farm," mostly for the caravanserai, a castle-like former caravan hostel. The "farm" was in the valley below, a fertile high-mountain pocket valley about five miles long and two in width stretching more or less north to south.

The farm came with tenants, the Six Families of the Keldara. The Keldara were, at first, a pretty mysterious group. They were said to be fighters but on the surface they were much like any similar group of peasant farmers Mike had encountered in over forty other countries.

The valley also came with problems. The farm had been terribly neglected for years and the Keldara still used essentially dark ages equipment: horse- and ox-drawn plows and hand scythes. They threshed the grain by running oxen over it. The farm manager was a blowhard who had all the farming and management skills of a rabid badger. And the Keldara had little or no motivation to improve things.

Mike had solved that problem early on by finding a new farm manager, a former Keldara who had been university trained as an agronomist and then "exiled" from the Families for challenging the farm manager's authority. The other fix was just throwing money at the situation: he had bought new equipment, tractors, combines, chainsaws and everything else a modern farm needs. With modern seeds, fertilizers, herbicides and farming techniques, the direct farming aspects were coming together. The fields below were yellow stubble from the largest bumper crop any of the Keldara had seen in their lives. The harvest festival scheduled for tomorrow was going to be a happy event.

The other problem, though, looked to be more intractable. Right over the mountains to the north was Chechnya, where the Russians were fighting an ongoing insurgency that had continued without relief for over fifteen years. The Chechen resistance used the Pankisi Gorge, less than sixty miles from where Mike sat, as their primary basing area. It was technically part of the country of Georgia, but Georgian forces, limited in number, under-trained and under-funded and with other serious problems to handle, didn't even consider trying to contest it with the battle-experienced and well-armed Chechens.

The battles spilled over to the region of the Keldara. The Chechens used the area as a transshipment point, sending drugs and kidnapped women out to be sold or traded for weapons and ammunition and bringing the ammo and weapons back. The constant trade was a source of anger on the part of the Russians, who regularly threatened the area with outright invasion.

The Chechens didn't just wander through the area. They often extorted food and girls from local farms or, in some cases, raided and burned them. Whole towns had been raided within the last few years.

It wasn't the best security situation in the world.

Mike's response was simple: Turn the Keldara retainers into a militia. He had, in his time, seriously pissed off every terrorist on earth. If he was going to be right next to Chechen Central, he wanted some shooters at his back. He hired a large number of trainers from the U.S. and Britain, shipped in top-quality gear and set out to turn the "simple farmers" into a group capable of, at the very least, securing their own homes and his.

The Keldara had a hundred and twenty males available between the ages of seventeen and thirty. Mike's goal was to turn them in to a decent company of militia, period. He wanted them to be able to maneuver against an enemy force while the younger women, who were trained in positional defense, held the homes. That was it.

What he found out, as the training progressed, was that the Keldara were far from "simple farmers." They took to military training as if they had been born with rifles in their hands. Enthusiastic didn't begin to cover it; he realized, quickly, that he had unleashed a monster.

The reason for their response trickled out, slowly. He still wasn't sure he knew the whole story. But one part he found out even before the training began: the Keldara were not "true" Georgians; they were a living remnant of an ancient elite force called the Varangian Guard. The Varangians were Norse, mostly from Russia, hired by the Byzantine Emperors as their personal bodyguards.

In the Keldara, the fierce warrior spirit of the Viking was a present-day reality. They had to survive as farmers, but at heart they were reavers and warriors that sought death in battle so that they could ascend to their heaven: "the Halls of Feasting," Valhalla. They masked as Christians but practiced their ancient worship of "the Father of All," Odin, in secret. Their preferred weapon was the axe and they trained with axes as seriously as they learned to plow.

They *were*, in fact, born with a weapon in their hand. When a Keldara male was born, one of the ancient battle-axes the Fathers kept—axes handed down over literally millennia—was placed in his hands and the hands closed over the great hilt. The first thing they learned to grasp was a weapon.

The Keldara had always had a lord and that person had *always* been a "foreigner," a mercenary who was not of the government that controlled them. Often they had been northern European adventurers, knights, cavalrymen, wandering bravos; over the ages the position and weapons had changed but not the pattern.

There was even a name for the person: Kildar.

Mike was but the latest in a long string of foreign mercenaries who had arrived, trained the Keldara in the latest innovations in bringing harm to an enemy and then used them to bring that harm.

That was fine with the Keldara. They just went on. As long as they had their beer, and incredible beer it was, and someone to kill in the name of their Kildar and for the glory of the Father of All, they were happy.

They were called by the locals, and even the Chechens, the Tigers of the Mountains. Simply saying those words to rural Georgians caused them to make the sign of the evil eye and shy away.

Mike swung the binoculars around the valley, idly wondering what the world would bring to the Keldara next. Chechens had come and been defeated, the Keldara being then right off their first day on the range. Another mission in Albania had started as a lie and been made truth by their burning spirit. The toxic result resided in the vaults of the caravanserai, a troubling burden he tried his very best to forget.

He looked down at the homes of the Keldara, low stone buildings with slate roofs, and caught sight of a group of Keldara militia sitting outside their barracks, working on weapons and taking in the remaining light of the mild late-fall day. They seemed . . . happy. Why shouldn't they be? It was a nice day, they had weapons in their hands and, for the moment, nobody was trying to kill them. Of course, they looked even more happy when people *were* trying to kill them and they were responding in kind.

Where, he wondered, would the Keldara descend next, following their Kildar a-viking to bring fire and axe and ruin?

"I saw it, I tell you."

Sion Kulcyanov was eighteen, just. Tall and more slender than the "standard" Kulcyanov, he had the Kulcyanov bright blond, nearly white, hair and blue eyes. He was considered probably the most handsome of the Kulcyanovs, with a squared chin that had a slight cleft, high Scandinavian cheekbones and eyes with a very slight epicanthic fold. His blue eyes were the most notable feature, though. "Striking" was the term that men usually used. "Piercing" was another. Women outside the Keldara girls normally just sighed.

Sion did not consider himself particularly handsome. And among the Keldara he really wasn't. Oh, he was better than the average, perhaps the best-looking among them. But the Keldara, male and female, were invariably so good-looking that people had a hard time believing it. He might be the "best" but in his general age group there were at least twenty guys that most women, internationally, would count as a "ten" for looks. And the low end was probably Shota, the great dumb ox, who would count as an "eight" in any normal society. A dumb eight. But an eight nonetheless.

Sion's eyes might have looked nice but they had other assets. He was possessed of vision that was normally reserved for birds of prey. Far-sight was the term. Where other men had to use binoculars he simply . . . peered.

In America, with his phenomenal reactions, high intelligence and incredible eyesight, he'd have been a shoe-in for fighter-pilot training.

In the Keldara he was spotter for the top team sniper, Lasko Ferani.

With his relative youth, few of the militiamen were much older but few younger, and his anomalous position, his status wasn't the highest in the militia. Which was why he found the present argument slow going.

"The tigers have been gone for years," Efim Devlich said, shaking his head. The machine-gunner was somewhat old in the teams at twenty-seven and well regarded. So his argument held more weight. "And there aren't any anywhere around here. So, tell me, Pee-Boy, where did it come from and why hasn't anyone else seen it?"

Sion had four kidneys, a not unusual, if unrecognized, mutation among the Keldara. It, perhaps, explained why they could drink so much beer without notable effect. That and the fact that they were given weak beer while still nursing. But one result of four kidneys was a tendency to have to urinate more often than normal. Sion had never quite lived down an accident he'd had when he was six.

"Well," Sion answered, dryly, "it might be because I can see better, yes?"

The group chuckled and nodded. Just as everyone knew that Sion had peed his pants during Sunday Church when he was six, they also knew his eyesight was phenomenal.

"Well," Efim said, shrugging, "I'll believe it when I see it. Or hear it. They roar, you know, just like lions. We will know the tigers have returned when we hear their roar. Now, it's time for dinner. I would suggest, though, that you keep this to yourself, Sion. Perhaps, if there was a tiger, he did not want to be seen. Not yet."

"I will," Sion said, shrugging. "But one day, Efim, you will hear the roar. Then you will know: the tigers have returned."

Mike opened up the side gate of the harem garden and made his way through the dark yard, limping slightly. The path up the mountain was enough of a ballbuster but finding his way down, in the dark, was always tricky. The late-summer blooms filled the air with a heady fragrance but he was concentrated on just making it to the back door. There was one spot on the trail that, no matter what he did, he slid. It was tough enough getting up, a slick portion of worn granite at about a sixty-degree angle. There were a few finger- and toeholds on the way up, but coming down in the dark the best bet was to just slide it. This time he'd done just that, taking his ruck off and letting it follow him down in a barely controlled slide. Fortunately there was a wide wedge of overlying sandstone at the end of the section of granite and he and the ruck had arrived in one piece. If he'd slipped very far to the right, though, it was a fifty-meter fall to the next more or less flat spot.

Very few of the windows were lit, which made making his way through the garden more a matter of memory than sight. Although the Keldara had ended up pulling more than two dozen girls out of the Balkans slave trade, Mike wasn't about to bring them all back as part of his "harem." They had been brought to the caravanserai, but only temporarily. He'd set the harem manager and Vanner on finding a spot for them, and the two of them had tracked down a parochial girls' school in Paraguay of all places that was willing to take them. Mike had also offered the girls currently in the harem the option of going and two of them had left.

He knew that most of the girls would be getting ready for bed as he walked in the door so he didn't expect to see anyone in the circular "common room" but Anastasia was sitting on the settee, reading a book.

Anastasia Rakovich, his harem manager, was twenty-six, long-legged, blonde and beautiful with the most perfectly "blue" eyes Mike had ever seen. She was, however, "too old" to be in the harem of an Uzbek sheik that had "given" her to him. Mike, suddenly faced with having a harem of girls from the local area, had gone to Uzbekistan looking for someone like her. Well, he'd sought a manager. A young lady that spoke seven languages, trained as an accountant and manager and an extreme sexual masochist had been a bit of a surprise. As had her approach to the harem.

She had pointed out that the harem was for far more than sex. The girls of the harem were supposed to act as counselors, people on whom Mike could dump the problems and stresses of being, effectively, a feudal lord.

She admitted that it was going to take her a while to train the girls, but in the meantime she herself fit the bill perfectly. When Mike had a problem, he had learned to not hesitate talking to her about it. When she had suggestions, they were generally very good, especially when it was about handling people. And when she didn't even understand what he was talking about, she would still listen carefully and help him to fully "verbalize" the problem. All in all he decided that Anastasia had been one hell of a catch.

"Good place to read?" Mike asked as he negotiated the door. The rucksack was a standard Keldara combat ruck, Swiss-made with integral bracing, multiple sections and all the rest of the modern bells and whistles. But it wasn't the easiest thing to get through a door.

"The light is good," Anastasia said, flowing gracefully to her feet and clapping her hands. Petro, the son of the groundsman, came through the far door immediately. "But I was, in fact, waiting for you, Kildar. Petro will take your rucksack. I will have Tinata come up to your room with a light supper after your shower."

"How long have you been waiting?" Mike asked, helping Petro, who was barely fifteen and overwhelmed by the heavy-ass ruck, to get the mother on his back. The boy's knees barely sank; he was strong for his age. But he would have had a hell of a time getting the hundred-and-fifty-pound ruck off the floor.

"About five minutes," Anastasia said, smiling. "Not long."

"I hate to think I'm that predictable," Mike replied, rolling his shoulders. "I'm not a person who should be predictable. People can use that, you know."

"I think that you are only predictable to those who love you and know you well," the harem manager said, smiling. "And I know you well. Now, go take your shower and by the time you are done Tinata will be ready with supper."

"Just as a question," Mike said, "why Tinata?" He had to admit that the comfortable and placid Tinata was a good choice. He wasn't really up for complex conversation at the moment. All he wanted was to get something to eat and maybe a quick screw, then get some rest.

"Because she is right for you, now," Anastasia said, shrugging. "I don't question your military decisions or understand them."

"And I shouldn't question yours, huh?" Mike said, grinning. "Okay, Tinata it is."

Chapter Two

Mike swung up onto the gelding and settled into the saddle.

He'd ridden when he was a kid and sort of enjoyed it but until he'd moved to the valley he'd given it up for over twenty years.

However, due to the pressure of circumstances, the Rite of Kardane being the circumstances, Mike had decided that learning to ride again was a good idea. Reality was that horses were flighty, smelly, cantankerous creatures. But chicks dug them and the Rite was really about the lady, not the Kildar, in Mike's opinion.

Since relearning, though, he'd started to ride a good bit. It was a reasonable alternative to driving around in an SUV when he was checking out the farm. He also preferred to use a horse for the Keldara's various ceremonies and festivals. It just . . . fit better, somehow.

The Keldara were embracing aspects of the twenty-first century with enthusiasm. On the shoulder of the hills to the south was a new brewery that, while archaic-looking on the outside, was as advanced as anything to be found in Europe or the United States. Computerized temperature controllers and hydrometers, automated bottling systems, the works. In the bowels of the caravanserai, young ladies who a year before had been hand-weaving cloth for clothing and hand-sewing same were using computers to analyze voice intercepts, running satellite communications gear and managing one of the most advanced battlefield networks to be found in the world. And those ladies weren't just punching buttons; they were learning the basic theory behind the systems, how to fix them, how to troubleshoot, how to repair. Programming and debugging. Cracking and counter-hacking.

Most of the real "smart-work," Mike had to admit, was done by the women. The men . . .

The Keldara men had also embraced aspects of the twenty-first century. The team members at least. But the *aspects* they'd embraced made him want to shake his head. Oh, they were just fine with thermal imagery scopes, vibration trackers and such. But show them a circuit diagram and they tended to scratch their heads.

On the other hand, put an Xbox controller in their hands . . .

But the reality was that in their souls, the Keldara were still very medieval, even barbaric. Give them a generation or two and they might go soft. Might. They'd survived Mongols and Ottomans, Russian tsars and Communism and still kept their soul. They'd just have to see what the internet was going to do to them.

For now, the seasonal ceremonies remained so true to an ancient core that, somehow, turning up in a Ford Expedition just didn't seem . . . right.

On the other hand, there was the matter of dress. Mike had one really . . . uhm . . . fancy riding outfit. Fancy was the only way to describe it. But he reserved that for the Rite of Kardane. Otherwise he preferred to dress, and ride, Western.

Thus he was wearing a pair of jeans, nice ones admittedly, and cowboy boots—okay those were about six hundred bucks—to the festival. Everyone else would be in their "Sunday Go To Meetin'" clothes so he'd be slightly underdressed. But anything was better than that damned riding costume for the Rite.

He tucked the reins into one hand and gave the gelding his head. He knew he didn't have to kick or otherwise suggest the Braz Curly get going. The gelding *liked* going down the hill to the small hamlet of the Keldara. The younger girls of the Keldara tended to pamper him to the point where getting him to *leave* was the hard part. Irana Tsar—or, as Mike preferred to call him, "Dumbass"— was *really* popular with the younger girls of the Keldara. They all wanted to mount Illyria—the "gray" palfrey that was currently eating hay in the stables—one day and follow Irana up to the caravan-serai.

That *damned* Rite. Mike wished he'd never heard of it. He *really* wished he hadn't worked so hard to make it "special." Dumbass was getting fat from being plied with special cakes, apples, sweets and anything else the girls could filch to feed the pig.

Mike reined in on the road down. The road from the caravan-serai was steeper than any similar road would be *allowed* to be in the U.S., very nearly a nine percent grade. It was easy enough to ascend on a horse, you just leaned forward. Going down, through, was tricky. There was a technique for taking a grade like that fast, one that Mike hoped he never had to try. He could ride, he wasn't a horseman. There's a difference.

Dumbass, though, had gotten used to the grade and handled it easily. He wanted to trot—cakes and brushing were waiting—but Mike kept him to a walk.

There were two switchbacks on the drive—each positioned to be swept by fire from the caravanserai—before it reached the main road. The main road was fairly flat through the valley, winding along the west side past the caravanserai. Going north it passed over the mountains and eventually swept west over some nasty passes to Tbilisi. The drive was kidney-pounding once you left the valley. Mike had actually driven improvements, all paid out of his own pocket, up to the pass to the north. But that was as far as he was paying for. After that he had to put up with the road. It was horrible but one of these days he was going to get a damned heli-copter.

To the south the road ascended first to the town of Alerrso, a pretty small town of about five hundred souls, then farther up to a pass that led to the southern plains of Georgia. Tbilisi was accessi-ble in that direction, as well, but a bit farther. And the roads were no better.

Not far south from where the drive met the road was the downslope to the homes of the Keldara.

The latter were on a slight terrace on the south side of the val-ley, not far from Alerrso in direct line and at about the same level as the main road. However, Mike had to first descend to the valley floor then climb back up to get there.

The drive from the road to the houses was graveled, but well maintained. It was far better than any of the roads in the mountains outside of Mike's control. The Keldara had their own gravel pits and ensured that all of the gravel roads in the valley were maintained in top order.

Mike had considered paving some of them but it didn't seem worth the bother. Since he'd brought in heavy equipment, the Keldara's workload had dropped so much that maintaining the roads was good "busywork" for the older men and the team members when they weren't on deployment cycle. Pretty much every day one of the Keldara men would be out grading them or a group would be laying down new gravel. It was ritual at this point.

The valley had one "major" river, about fifty feet across at its broadest, and five or six, depending on how you counted, streams that joined the "river."

One of those streams had been dammed, by a former SF engineer Mike brought in, and now provided hydroelectric power to the Keldara and the caravanserai.

During spring they could flood rather badly, which was why the road, and the houses, were somewhat elevated. The river was glacier-fed and the streams in spring would bulge with meltwater. That was good and bad. Flooding bogged the valley for a few weeks every year, requiring replacement of bridges that got swept away and general fixing of the fields. But the floods also brought silt, rich with nutrients, the reason that the valley was so fertile.

Hell, the way the weather looked they might flood tonight. The sky was overcast and strong winds, at times low gale force, were ripping through the region. The forecast, though, said that rain would hold off until about midnight, by which time most of the Keldara would be under cover.

When he hit the road, Dumbass started to shake his head. He wanted to *go.*

Mike gave him his head and the gelding broke into a canter almost directly out of the walk. Mike was fine with cantering, it was a pretty smooth gait, but he drew the line when the horse tried to gallop. Galloping was for horsemen.

Many of the Keldara were already gathering in the broad, flat, area in front of the houses. Mike was pretty sure that the original reason for the higher ground there was a palisaded camp. There were even traces of a defensive ditch in front of the terrace. The open area would have been a marshaling area.

The Keldara used it for much the same reason, now. That was where the tribe gathered for the minor portions of festivals. That was where the kids ran screaming through the crowds and, in this case, people gathered to sample food.

The women of the Keldara prided themselves on two things: their beer and their cooking. Already trestle tables piled with special foods had been set up in the area and everyone was sampling the wares. Which meant there were plenty of young teen girls in the area, carefully ignoring their male counterparts. And Mike had been spotted as soon as he left the gates of the caravanserai.

So when Dumbass came cantering up the road into the area, Mike sawing on the reins to slow him down before he trampled some kid, he was immediately swarmed.

"God, girls!" Mike said, grinning against his better nature. "Give me a chance to at least get *off* the damn thing!"

The girls were a swarming mob, dressed in bright blouses and black skirts. The Keldara kept some very strict customs about dress which told an informed observer a lot. Girls who had had their first period wore *"dhimmi"* scarves, a legacy of Islamic occupation under first Magyar tribes then the Ottomans. Girls who were "available" wore their hair in braids. Girls who were married wore their hair unbraided.

Younger girls, those who hadn't hit puberty, didn't wear scarves. Younger ones, their hair was generally pulled back but unbraided. The older ones, though, mostly wore braids.

Mike tossed his reins to one of the girls with a *dhimmi* scarf and braids and slid off the horse.

"Don't overfeed him!" Mike said, sternly. "He nearly got colic the last time! You don't want to kill him, you know."

"Yes, Kildar," the girl holding the reins said, bobbing in a curtsey. She had blonde hair and bright blue eyes. And, as always with the Keldara, was just fucking beautiful. Okay, so maybe the Rite wasn't *all* bad.

Mike made his way through the mob as politely as he could, trying to avoid brushing against breasts or being groped. The Keldara were very strict about sex but there were some very odd aspects. If they could get away with it, if they thought nobody would notice, if, for example, they were surrounded by other girls who shielded the act from the elders and who wouldn't tell, the girls in the *dhimmi* scarves would grope him in an instant. And they had *very* strong hands.

They also weren't above giving the Kildar a little tease with a quick brush of a breast against his arm. Or back or any other part of his body they could reach.

Mike finally broke through *that* throng and then hit the kids. He'd taken to carrying hard candies with him whenever he went down to the valley and he gave them out to the children. Sometimes he was pressed for time and all but the youngest understood. But when he had time he handed them out.

"Gregor, that's Stasi's," he said, pulling back a sweet and giving it to the younger girl by the boy's side. He handed Gregor one, next.

Generally, he could just hold the sweets out in cupped hands. The Keldara kids had learned not to grab more than one, to let the younger ones go first. It had taken a while, but Mike had been firm and patient. By now the older kids tended to teach the younger the rules, sometimes with a slap on the hand or the back of the head.

The kids also didn't drop their wrappers. Mike had instituted the almost purely U.S. and Western European concept that "littering is bad." The older Keldara still had trouble with the idea but the kids were learning. A child that just dropped his wrapper on the ground was, like as not, not going to get a sweet the next time around. Mike sometimes had trouble with names, there were nearly six hundred Keldara all told, but he rarely forgot a face.

Once the kids had their candy, Mike dropped the last few pieces into his pockets and looked up into a pair of blue eyes so deep they were very nearly purple.

There was one girl of the Keldara who, *dhimmi* scarf or no, didn't braid her hair despite being all of fourteen. It fell long and fiery red past her shoulders in a titian waterfall. Heart-shaped face and slightly Tartar eyes and that incredible blue.

"Hello, Katrina," Mike said, smiling faintly. "How have you been?"

"Actually, not that bad," Katrina said, walking up to stand far too close to him and looking up at him out of those huge, beautiful, eyes. "I'm working up at the brewery these days."

The reason Katrina wore her hair unbound was simple. She, against every order, prohibition or curse, considered herself Mike's primary partner. The Kildaran was the term. The fact that Mike had never laid a hand on her, that Anastasia effectively held that position, that Mike had stated he wasn't going to have anyone with the moniker "Mrs. Jenkins" or children with that last name as potential hostages, didn't particularly matter from her perspective. She'd set her sights high and she wasn't taking them off the goal.

"Glad to hear it," Mike said, trying not to gulp.

Katrina was the first Keldara he'd ever met. He'd gotten lost in a snowstorm headed for a ski resort in northern Georgia. Lost, in the middle of a blizzard, damned near out of gas, he'd almost hit a figure struggling down the road. The female, at the time he'd thought her an old woman, was carrying a bundle of sticks and wrapped up against the cold. He'd offered her a lift home and not really seen her face or figure until he entered the House Devlich.

Despite the difference in age, despite all the differences, Mike had to admit there was something that really got him about Katrina. Oh, there was plenty of lust there and a good bit of infatuation on both sides. But Mike hadn't felt this way about a girl in a long time, if ever. Call it chemistry. In a few more years he'd have to make up his mind what to do about it. In the meantime, he tried very hard to keep his distance. But he wasn't going to back up just because the girl had closed to a few inches.

"I've started working directly with Mother Lenka," Katrina said, smiling secretly. "She is teaching me much of her magic."

"Well, you're the one to do that with," Mike said, frankly grinning. "You and Lenka are two of a kind."

Mother Lenka was the Keldara brewmistress. All of the Houses had their own brew but, hands down, Mother Lenka, who like Katrina was of the Devlich Family, was the best of an amazingly good lot.

Lenka was a Russian war bride, originally from St. Petersburg. A force of nature, she was never willing to describe what role she had been in, exactly, prior to marrying Fredrik Devlich and returning to the valley to live out the rest of her days. Given her foul mouth, generally lewd approach to life and absolute bloody-mindedness, though, Mike was willing to bet she wasn't displaced aristocracy. The term "whore" came to mind.

But she had carved a niche for herself in the Keldara, a position of respect equivalent to or even higher than the House Mothers.

All of which were reasons Mike had chosen her to run the new brewery. That beer was designed for sale and export. The first batch had just hit the American market and it was receiving rave reviews. Mike wondered what the drinkers would think if they knew the Keldara considered it less than third-rate.

"You think so?" Katrina asked, tilting her head to the side. "And is that a compliment or an insult?"

"I think it's a compliment," Mike said. "A sort of sideways one. I don't think that Lenka has had the happiest life."

"Should life always be happy?" Katrina asked, her eyes still pointed at his face but now looking past him at some other place. "The world is a wheel, cycles upon cycles. Winter and summer, night and dark, good and evil, all spiraling together. Without pain there is no pleasure and without sadness no joy. All of life is a circle of balance on the wheel." She shook her head and looked at him again. "Sorry. I . . . I guess . . ." She looked down, clearly ashamed. The Keldara were, by and large, a pretty rock-headed lot when it came to philosophy. Katrina was not, by any stretch, considered a "good" Keldara.

Mike liked the Keldara for about a billion reasons. But that particular rock-headedness was not one of them.

"Don't apologize," Mike said. "There are some pretty good technical thinkers among the Keldara but I think you're just about the only true genius. Genius is never easy to live with. Especially in a place like this. I know you want to be Kildaran but if I have my druthers you'll get shipped off when you're eighteen to someplace like the Sorbonne or Princeton to get turned into a nice little liberal."

"Very funny," Katrina said, shaking her head. "Look at what happened to the last Keldara to go to college."

"He came back to be the farm manager," Mike replied.

"I don't want to get an agronomy degree," Katrina snapped back, just as fast.

"No, I think you're more the liberal arts type," Mike said. "Semiotics, maybe?"

"I've read some Foucault," Katrina said, shrugging. "Not interested. I think one rock dropped on his head would have adjusted the whole concept of relativism."

"Where in the hell did *you* get a copy of Foucault?" Mike asked, surprised.

"Out of your library," Katrina said. "I think it's Colonel Nielson's though. It was filled with notes, most of them consisting of foul-mouthed diatribes."

"Yeah, that'd be Nielson's," Mike said, chuckling. The former War College instructor had very little patience with anything that smacked of "baffling with bullshit." And people had learned not to say words or phrases like "politically correct," "Marxist" or "trans-national progressives" around him unless they'd brought a chair, a lunch and some sort of poncho to keep the spittle off.

"Well, then, you can go to Texas A&M and hang out with the Aggies," Mike said. "You should get a kick out of that."

"I don't want to go to college," Katrina said. "I want to be Kilda-ran. It does not require a college degree. The only training I need is from that blonde witch you brought in from Uzbekistan."

"Oh, yeah, you two would get on like a house afire. Every been in a house that's on fire, Katrina?"

"I actually get along just fine with Anastasia," Katrina said, bat-ting her eyes at him. "Who do you think gave me the book?"

"Katrina!" Father Devlich shouted, striding over. "Quit pester-ing the Kildar!"

Father Devlich was tall and broad with gray-shot red hair clipped above the ears and off the collar. Practically the definition of "rock-headedness," he had been landed a "daughter" that was his functional opposite. Perhaps it was the reason that he seemed to be perpetually angry.

"It's quite all right, Father Devlich," Mike said, smiling at the man. Of all the Fathers, Devlich was, hands down, his least favor-ite. And the feeling was mutual.

"Kildar," Father Devlich said, nodding. "It's just that the elders are waiting."

"I will be there momentarily," Mike said. He was, after all, the fucking Kildar. If he wanted to talk to a pretty girl, the elders could damned well wait. On the other hand, Father Kulcyanov was in the group and the old soldier didn't deserve to be ignored. "Katrina, we'll talk later. But you're not in the running for Kildaran. That's final. Not any time soon. So do good work for Mother Lenka. Get your education down, too. Okay?"

"Oh, I will," Katrina said, licking her lips. "A very *broad* education, yes?"

"Oh, my God!" Mike said, shaking his head and walking over to the cluster of elders.

"Katrina, I swear by the Father of All . . ." Father Devlich ground out.

"You swear *what*, Father?" Katrina asked. "That you will beat me? That you will deny me food? That you will have me shunned? That you will cast me out and send me to town? You've done all of those but send me to town and the Kildar has forbidden that for any girl of the Keldara. I do my job at the brewery, do it *well*. And I will be Kildaran, bringing honor to the Family. Be it in a year or ten years, I *shall* be Kildaran. And as to the Father of All, blessings be upon his eye, you know that I now follow the other way. So cursing me by the Father is a weak threat, Father."

"Very well," Father Devlich said. "You feel that you are a woman grown? Then I give you into the hands of Mother Lenka. Let her handle you."

"I have been for three years, Father, and you know that," Katrina said. "I have been in the hands of Mother Lenka since I came of age. At this point, I am very close to being her designated Heir, Father. More status to the House, yes?"

"Much peace be it to you," Father Devlich said, contemptuously. "Great honor, yes. The Goddess is so honored, no one will speak Her name. Her Priestess does not speak of Her except in the dark of the moon and the stillness of the cave."

"She holds Her hand upon the Wheel," Katrina said, smiling and looking into the distance. "It is She who brings the Spring."

Chapter Three

"Father Kulcyanov," Mike said, bowing to the elder.

Although not the oldest Keldara Father—that would be Father Ferani—Father Kulcyanov was the elder held in the highest honor. A highly decorated war veteran of WWII, what the locals called the Great War, the man was tall and broad but much of what was clearly formerly great strength was wasted by age. He must once have been as huge as Oleg, Mike's primary team leader, but age had shrunken him.

He still, when he summoned it, had a commanding majesty. He was currently wearing a black broadcloth jacket and fine wool trousers but Mike suspected that later in the day, as ceremonies approached, he would don the tiger-skin mantle of the high priest of the Keldara.

"Kildar," Father Kulcyanov replied, raspily. "You honor us with your presence."

"I am honored by the Keldara," Mike said. "But I'll admit I wasn't briefed on this day. I hope I'm not chopping wood again."

The first season ceremony Mike had participated in had been the Rites of Spring, a twenty-four-hour-long festival that might be the most authentic spring rite left in the world.

Part of that festival involved cutting several types of trees for a great bonfire. They had to be cut over one night, starting near dusk. Only a special axe could be used and it wasn't well suited for the task, being one of the ancient battle-axes of the Keldara.

Mike had ended up, through a desire to bond as much as anything, one of the designated woodcutters. What was worse, after the woodcutting and moving the logs up to the ceremonial area he'd been expected to participate in feats of strength and agility.

It was an annual ceremony to determine who was the best of the Keldara. Mike had realized that too late but, unfortunately, his competitive streak, which any SEAL has in full measure, kicked in. He ended up effectively winning the contest, even the bull wrestling. He'd refused the honor of being the winner, though. The position, the Ondah, was one of high honor in the Keldara and Mike wasn't about to take that from the, in all honesty, second place, Oleg.

His argument was that the Kildar *should* be the best of the best but that Ondah was a position reserved for the Keldara.

The entire ordeal, though, had been as exhausting as a day in Hell Week. He wasn't interested in repeating his previous triumph. If he could. The Keldara were in high training at this point. Mike wasn't sure he could win if he had to do it again.

The summer festival had been another day straight out of a storybook. Held on the longest day of the year it was a straightforward Lammas festival with the exception that the Keldara held the "bringing of light" portion in spring.

"Not today, Kildar," Father Ferani replied, grinning.

At "somewhere around seventy-five" Father Ferani was the eldest of the Fathers of the Keldara, short for his race and shrunken from age. But he was one of those men that, as they aged, seem to harden like old teak. Like Father Kulcyanov, he was a veteran of the Great War, one of the handful of Keldara to return alive. But unlike Kulcyanov, he had spent most of the war in a supply depot well behind the lines.

He was one of the Fathers that Mike got along with very well. Mahona was in that category as was Makanee. Father Shaynav still treated the new Kildar with caution, being a bit hidebound when it came to change. Father Kulcyanov simply went along with the changes of the Kildar but was always cautious, always watching, always considering *exactly* where the line might be that impropriety set in. Strangely enough, from Mike's perspective of "impropriety," it was Father Kulcyanov who originally suggested the Rite of Kardane.

Father Devlich simply hated Mike's guts. He was the first Father Mike had met the night Mike returned Katrina to her House in the middle of a blizzard. Whether from the impropriety of a man being alone with one of his "daughters" or just because he was a bloody-minded bastard, it was Father Devlich that always presented obstacles, who carped and worried about all the changes.

"During this morning we will simply gather and enjoy the fruits of the harvest," Father Mahona said. Mahona was medium height and heft with short-cropped blonde hair shot with gray and a graying beard. "In the afternoon, the brewmistress will choose which crop of barley is suitable for the beers of the House. The young men will then cut the field. For this ceremony we prefer to do that by hand."

"Of course," Mike said, nodding. Mike fully recognized that this was as much a religious ceremony as a get-together. It was a hell of a windy day to harvest, though. He hoped that wouldn't fuck things up. He was pretty sure that if the ceremonial harvest was screwed up, all the grain and fat livestock in the world wouldn't make the Keldara happy.

"And there is the bonding of Gretchen and Kiril," Father Mahona added, grinning.

"Of course," Mike repeated, trying to smile politely. That *damned* Rite. "What's that consist of, exactly?"

"The Mothers bring them to Father Kulcyanov," Father Mahona said, shrugging. "In front of the Six Families. They are promised to each other formally in front of the Families. That is, really, it."

"I don't have to do anything, do I?" Mike asked.

"Not today," Father Mahona said, grinning more broadly. Everyone knew of Mike's ambivalent position on the Rite. "I believe that would be tomorrow, yes?"

"Wood has already been cut for the fires," Father Makanee said, politely changing the subject and pointing to the dun. Father Makanee—just about the youngest of the elders, being in his low fifties—was medium height with brown hair and eyes and broad shoulders. "We will hold the Harvest Feast on the dun. Given the night, though, I suspect we will break up shortly after. Rain, maybe snow, is on the way."

The dun of the Keldara, Mike was pretty sure, was a drumlin, a remnant of the glacier that had carved the pass. When glaciers carve their way through mountains they dig up masses of rock. Much of it is then pulverized into soil called loess, a super-fine soil that can form clays or, when plants get in it, becomes some of the richest soil in the world.

As the glaciers retreated, through, they dumped their loads of soil and rock. Rivers running through the melting glaciers tended to form it into humps that could be hundreds of feet high in places.

The dun was about a hundred feet high and three times that at the base. Not the largest drumlin in the world by any stretch of the imagination but pretty darned big.

"I can smell it," Mike said, nodding. "And the forecasts say the same. Hopefully, it will hold off until midnight. Are the winds going to interfere with the harvest?"

"It will be as the Father of All chooses," Father Kulcyanov said. "But for now, Kildar, the Mothers request that you sample the fruits of the harvest. Be at ease."

"I am, Father Kulcyanov," Mike said. "I am among my people. And I see one that I should greet," he added, looking past Kulcyanov at a bald head by the buffet table.

"Figure you'd be anywhere there was free food and beer," Mike said, picking up a plate.

"Hey, Ass-Boy," Adams said, taking a bite out of a lightly spiced chicken leg.

Former Master Chief Charles Adams was Mike's tactical second, a right arm for Mike when the bullets were flying. They'd known each other since both were SEAL candidates in BUDS and both had survived the utter horror of Class 201, now an infamous SEAL legend. But when Mike had gone off to be a SEAL trainer Adams had stayed on the teams.

Tall, bald and blocky, Adams had divorced his fifth wife shortly after Mike contacted him, looking for trainers. Although it had, at the time, been a temporary contract, Adams had stayed on. At this point, Mike couldn't imagine doing a mission without him.

Adams was also just about the only person in the world, outside of a very select group in Washington, who could connect the

"Kildar" to a mysterious figure who had broken up a major terrorist plot and, worse, killed Osama Bin Laden by practically shoving mustard gas down his throat. Adams had been the team chief of the SEALs who dropped into that madhouse to extract the kidnapped co-eds and a vaguely defined "independent" who had found and rescued them. He'd found a very old friend, one he'd pretty much lost touch with, just about shot to ribbons.

"Ass-Boy yourself," Mike said, ladling some beets onto his plate. "Enjoying yourself?"

"Except for the weather," Adams said. "I hope everyone recognizes that there's a fucking storm on the way."

"Everybody's fully aware of that," Mike said, getting a sudden chill. "I hope it holds off for a few days, anyway."

"It's going to hit tonight," Adams said, looking at him quizzically.

Mike blinked and shook his head.

"Yeah," he replied, confused. "I knew that. I don't know *why* I said a few *days*..."

"Sniper right," Kiril Devlich said, ducking for cover. Kiril Devlich was just eighteen, medium height and heavy of body with jet black hair, blue eyes and broad cheekbones. One of the SAW gunners in Sawn's team, he had been born and raised in the valley of the Keldara. He had had the axe placed in his hand in the birthing bed, he bore the scars of judgment from the year he came to manhood and had participated in his first Ondah contest only the year before. Today he battled for honor and glory and, of course, the flag.

"Got it," Hadar Makanee said, calmly. The Team Sawn spotter was acting as sniper today. "Tango down. Go."

Kiril darted forward, hunkering down behind a rock then tossing a grenade over the rock towards where the enemy had been previously emplaced. There was a screeching sound over the radio and his armor-clad opponents burst from cover, ducking as the frag grenade went off.

"Tango down," Darin Shaynav said. He had taken a rear position and was covering Kiril's flank with a heavy battle rifle. "Two tangos moving right."

"Tango down," Hadar said. "One more..."

Kiril rolled around the left side of the rock and then came around in circle. The green clad enemy was just ducking around the rock, looking for him.

"Tango down," Kiril said, putting a three-round burst into the enemy's back.

"I've got the flag," Darin said, coming out of the green base. "Not much sense even bringing it back to ours."

"Engagement . . . terminated . . ." a deep voice announced and the green players suddenly started getting to their feet.

"That fucking sucked," one of the green players said in a high voice. "We had you pawned, what the fuck did you do?"

"They cheated!" another of the green players said. "Cheaters!"

"We sucked you into a simple deception scheme," Hadar said. He'd taken the teleport down to the ground level and now walked out of the fort carrying his sniper rifle. "We made it look as if the center was open. And you fell for it."

"You sound funny," the first green player said. "You're not from around here, are you?"

"If you mean the United States, no," Kiril said, chuckling. "And we do this for a living. You're not bad, for noobs . . ."

"Noobs?" the green player screeched as the scene faded out.

"Making fun of babies, Kiril," Hadar said, setting down his controller and taking off his headset. "It's beneath you."

"My name is Kiril Devlich," Kiril said in a deep voice. "And . . . I . . . Hate . . . Babies!" He set the headset on the Xbox, still half giggling.

"You'll have babies of your own, soon enough," Roan Makanee said. He normally carried one of the M240s but had taken a submachine gun in today's operation. He'd also agreed to act as bait, sacrificed as, supposedly, the only "defender" in the center of the attack route. The others had been arrayed and concealed to the side and had easily ambushed the less experienced green players. "Well, the *Kildar's* baby."

"Oooo, *cheap* shot," Darin said. "Two points."

"Well, you *might*," Hadar said, looking at his watch. "If you make it to your handfasting."

"Oh, holy shit," Kiril said, scrambling to his feet. "I completely forgot!"

"Kiril, Kiril, you're going to be late to your own funeral," Darin said as the boy pounded out of the door to the barracks. "I suppose, though, that we should go along and lend moral support."

"Why?" Hadar asked, picking up his headset. "We are *training*, after all. . . ."

"Who brings this girl before me?" Father Kulcyanov boomed.

"I, Mother of the House Mahona," Mother Mahona said. She was holding Gretchen's left hand. Standing behind her was Mother Silva, Gretchen's "Body Mother," the woman who had borne her seventeen years before.

Gretchen Mahona was five feet ten inches tall with gorgeous blonde hair and a figure that made men want to follow her around like little puppy dogs. With high cheekbones, blue eyes and a beautifully heart-shaped face, she was one of the most traditionally "Nordic"-looking Keldara. Mike suspected that she had hellacious legs as well, but since she always wore a skirt it was hard to tell. There was no question about her upper body, though. Even the baggy Keldara blouses couldn't conceal that.

It was shortly after noon and the whole clan was gathered in front of the houses, watching the ceremony. A circle of pine branches had been laid on the ground and the two groups stood within them, presenting the two young people for Father Kulcyanov's blessing.

"Is she pure?" Father Kulcyanov asked.

The Keldara set big store by virginity. At least to a point.

"She is. On my oath as a Mother."

"Is she free of defect?" Father Kulcyanov asked.

"She is. On my oath as a Mother."

Mike realized that he'd never been to one of the bonding ceremonies. That question begged a dozen others. But if Gretchen had any defects, he'd never noticed them. Okay, so maybe the Rite wasn't all bad.

"Is she fit to bear child, to bring forth warriors and wives, to be a Mother of Tigers, to honor the Keldara?"

"She is," Mother Mahona said, fiercely. "On my oath as Mother Mahona."

"Bring to me the boy," Father Kulcyanov said, looking at the Devlich contingent.

Mother Devlich stepped forward, holding her son's hand.

Kiril looked nervous. Any teenage male would hate being forced to hold his mother's hand in public. Being called a boy wasn't the greatest, either. And he'd nearly missed the thing, arriving at the last minute at a dead run. And from the direction of the barracks, by the looks of it. Playing Halo again. The boy needed to get out more.

"Who brings this boy before me?" Father Kulcyanov asked.

"I, Mother of the House Devlich," Mother Devlich said. Short and dark, she was as calm and pleasant as her husband was an asshole. Given that they'd been bound in a similar ceremony, possibly without any input from either side, Mike thought that it had to be an interesting marriage.

"Is he a warrior?" Father Kulcyanov asked.

Mike had to snort. The most important thing about the girls is that they be virgins. The most important thing about the guys is that they be warriors. He looked across the crowd at where Stella Kulcyanov, recently married to Vil Mahona, one of the team leaders, stood holding her husband's hand. Tall, slender and as beautiful as her husband was handsome, the girl had unshed tears in her eyes. Oh, they were tears of happiness. But Mike remembered the girl's smooth handle on commo, feeding him only the information he really needed to know, during the bloody chaos of the Lunari extraction, and had to wonder why the first question for both groups wasn't the same.

Next to her was Jessia Mahona, the mortar team leader. Tall with long brown hair and . . . well, one fricking *huge* chest, she wasn't nearly as smart as Stella but Mike would take her at his back any time. He'd wondered recently, given her status, if he should bring her into his household. Now probably wasn't the best time to ask but he could understand her less than thrilled reaction to the events.

"He is. On my oath as a Mother."

"Is he free of defect?"

"He is. On my oath as a Mother."

Same question. Mike felt there was an itch there he needed to scratch.

Various societies in history had had "tests" at birth to determine if a baby was pure. Inbreeding, especially in a group like the

Keldara, was always a problem. Oh, with the Keldara the problem of fathers covering their daughters didn't seem to be an issue. But it was a very small gene pool with minimal outside input. Mother Lenka was the only outsider Mike knew who had entered the society in generations.

Inbreeding meant that the normal "spread" of breeding, the famous "bell curve," tended to turn into a sort of "U" on a graph. At one end were exceptional specimens. And the Keldara *were* exceptional specimens.

What Mike had never wondered, until now, was where the normal and anticipated "defectives" you'd get in a *normal* population were. Much less one with a restricted gene pool. There were no Down's syndrome Keldara, no hydrocephalics, none of the usual birth defects you'd expect. Okay, Shota was pretty moronic. But he wasn't Asperger's, autistic or the rest of the alphabet of potential birth defects.

He suddenly got the feeling there was a lot buried in that one little question.

"Is he fit to start a child, to start warriors and wives, to be a Father of Tigers, to honor the Keldara?"

"He is. On my oath as Mother Devlich."

Father Kulcyanov took the two young people's unrestricted hands and placed them together.

"Kiril Devlich, do you give your Promise to Gretchen Mahona, save only that agreements can be reached between your two Families?"

"I do," Kiril said, grinning hard. He suddenly looked sideways directly at Mike and grinned harder. Then his head snapped back. "I do!"

"Gretchen Mahona, do you give your Promise to Kiril Devlich, save only that agreements can be reached between your two Families?"

"I do," Gretchen said then swallowed, nervously. "I do." She was nervous but she was also glowing. Then she looked over at the Kildar and smiled.

Yeah, the Rite with Gretchen wasn't exactly gonna be awful.

It wasn't time for the next major ceremony, the Choosing, yet, so Mike grabbed a mug of beer and wandered.

There were several contests going on but Mike avoided them. He'd be called in as judge and he had no clue how to judge most of them. The Keldara had a number of games based around pebbles and throwing sticks that he just couldn't follow. Some of them were like marbles but so complicated they made his head ache. Others were easier, most of the young men were throwing axes and that he could figure out easy enough. He still avoided it. He'd participated in an axe-throwing competition, once, and done well enough. But he also knew most of it was luck and he wasn't going to try his hand again.

But, by golly, a deputation was catching up to him. He paused when he noticed Father Kulcyanov and the rest of the Fathers approaching. What this time?

"Kildar," Father Kulcyanov said, nodding and gasping for breath. The old guy was looking particularly worn today. Mike hoped he'd make it through the ceremonies okay.

"Father Kulcyanov," Mike replied, nodding back.

"I will let Father Mahona speak to this," Father Kulcyanov said. "It is complicated and . . ."

"I understand," Mike said, nodding back. "And takes air."

"Which I will much need later," Father Kulcyanov said, nodding at Father Mahona.

"Kildar, we have a request," Father Mahona said, nervously. "We wish to . . . to do a ceremony that we have not done for some time, the Beatai Leanah."

"The ceremonies of the Keldara are their own," Mike said, blinking. "Why did you stop doing it?"

"None of us were alive the last time the Beatai Leanah was performed," Father Mahona replied. "But it was stopped in the late Tsarist period."

"Does it involve human sacrifice?" Mike asked. "That's about the only thing I'm not going to go for."

"No, Kildar," Mahona said.

Mike had asked the question in dead seriousness and it was returned the same way. Which meant there probably *was* a ceremony they had somewhere in memory that *did* involve human sacrifice.

"But it is the ritual slaughtering," the Father continued, clearing his throat. "As you know, at this time of year we need to start slaughtering the animals that we don't wish to keep through the winter. This is a ritual that . . . starts that process."

"You do it up on the dun?" Mike asked. "You're going to have to just haul it all down again."

"Some," Father Kulcyanov said. "Some is burned there, some is left for the ravens."

"Most is kept," Father Mahona said. "It is considered special, used in specific dishes."

"Kildar," Father Makanee said, taking a deep breath. "It is a very . . . bloody ceremony."

"Slaughtering generally is," Mike said, frowning.

"Somewhat bloodier than that," Father Makanee replied. "You . . . might want to change."

"I've got other clothes," Mike said, blinking. "But this sounds familiar, too. Every year the Gurkhas have a ceremonial slaughter of animals. One member of the individual tribe or unit, carefully chosen, does the slaughtering. Nobody but the Gurkhas, and their British officers, are allowed to witness it."

"Then we will perform the Rite," Father Kulcyanov said, nodding. "There are none in this valley who I find it ill to be present at the Rite, but I . . . recommend that some not attend."

"I can't imagine who," Mike said, dryly. "But why don't I suggest to Anastasia and the girls that they retire early."

"That would be best, Kildar," Father Mahona said, thankfully.

"It is time for the Choosing," Father Kulcyanov said, looking over at a similar deputation of women who were headed towards the barley fields. "We should go."

"After you," Mike said, gesturing the Fathers forward. "I will be along shortly."

The rest of the Keldara were headed towards the Choosing but Mike grabbed one of the young boys who was running in that direction.

"Ivar," Mike said, dredging up his name. "Go find Colonel Nielson, the master chief and Vanner and make sure they meet me at the Choosing."

"Yes, Kildar," the boy said with a gap toothed grin. "I shall."

"Good lad," Mike said, releasing him. He'd already spotted Anastasia. Some of the harem were mingling with the Keldara girls but a few were clustered around her. Good.

Mike made his way through the throng to the harem manager who was heading for the Choosing.

"Stasia," he said, smiling as he touched her arm.

"Kildar," Anastasia said, smiling back. "You have been keeping to yourself."

"I've been avoiding deputations," Mike said. "But a couple caught up with me. One concerns the ceremony this evening. I . . . strongly recommend that you and the girls not attend."

"We are not welcome," Anastasia said, nodding. "I had been surprised that we were permitted at the other festivals. We should leave."

"That's not it," Mike said, shaking his head. "It's a purely . . . It's a blood sacrifice. Animals, I'll add. But it's probably going to turn your stomach, and the girls'. The Fathers made it a recommendation. It's based purely on that. Don't go before the Choosing."

"Very well, Kildar," Anastasia said.

"In fact," Mike said, taking her arm, "I think we should *both* go to the Choosing. Together."

"That would probably be appropriate," Anastasia said, smiling. "By the way," she added as they made their way through the crowd, "I got a glimpse of your next Kardane girl. And you are bothered by this Rite why?"

"I'm still wondering that myself," Mike admitted, sheepishly. "But I can't think that it's a good thing. I have to have these guys at my back. I can't imagine that one day one of them *isn't* going to get pissed about the Rite."

"They seem to take it very well," Anastasia said. "I mean, that is unusual but not unknown. There are other societies that practice similar rituals."

"Yeah, but it still bugs me," Mike said as they got to the stone wall of the first barley field.

Mother Lenka led the deputation of Mothers. She wasn't one of the Family heads but she *was* the acknowledged mistress of brewing among the Keldara so it wasn't exactly surprising.

The Mothers were wandering in apparently random order through the field, fingering the heads of barley and occasionally picking some of it and tasting.

"I have no idea how long this takes," Mike said. "But it's probably a *long* time."

"We have time," Anastasia said as the Mothers gathered on the far side of the field. They had their heads together, fingering handfuls of barley and apparently discussing it. Mike suspected they were just making a big show.

Mike sensed someone walking up behind him but didn't turn around.

"You were looking for me, Kildar?" Vanner said.

Patrick Vanner, a stocky, blonde, crew-cutted former Marine intel geek, handled commo and intelligence. He'd started off as a linguist, ended up in intercept then analysis and finally communications security and eventually spent time working with the NSA. A whiz with any sort of electronics, communications or information technology, he filled the role of both commo officer and intelligence officer. Since he spoke more languages than Mike could count and was "into" cultures, he thought Vanner would really enjoy this evening's ceremony, bloody or not.

"I need to talk to you, Adams and Nielson," Mike said, turning around. "We'll wait until they're all here." But he could see both of the other staff making their way through the crowd.

Colonel David Nielson, USA, retired, slim, medium height with black hair gone gray and piercing green eyes, was a former infantry and civil affairs colonel, the only "professional" officer in the group. He fitted in as sort of chief of staff. Nielson juggled the operations and training schedules when things weren't "hot," relieving Mike of the tedium of paperwork that was anathema to him. When things *were* hot, and they often were, Nielson managed the battlefield conditions—made sure there was supporting fire, argued with any higher, got the ammo forward—while Mike went forward to lead. He was a maniac for training but admitted that he wasn't quite as happy doing the tactics.

Chief of staff, XO, whatever, he handled the details; Mike led.

The Mothers had headed for another field so Mike waved for the group to follow.

"There's a ceremony this evening," Mike said.

"The Samman Latract," Vanner said. "This is their version of the Night of the Dead. But I've been picking up on another one. The Beatai Leanah I think is what I'm catching. I've been brushing up on my Gaelic since McKenzie was here and I think the first is something like 'Calling the Dead' or 'Waking the Dead.' The second one . . . I think it's some type of sacrifice."

"Give the man a cigar," Mike said as they reached the second of six fields. The fields were not designated for any particular Family but the Keldara tended to do things in sixes. "It's a blood sacrifice, the beginning of the winter slaughtering. They haven't done it in a *long* time. And it's supposed to be pretty bloody."

"Like the . . . What's that Gurkha rite?" Nielson said.

"The Dushera Festival," Vanner said. "Biggest guy in the regiment cuts off the head of a bull with a big kukri. If he succeeds, it's good luck for the year. If not, bad mojo."

"I think so," Mike said. "We'll see. I've asked the girls to head back to the caravanserai, since I don't think they want to get too splattered."

"The top of the dun *isn't* all that big," Adams said, nodding. "Carotid blood does have a tendency to spray everywhere."

"Thank you so much for that image, Master Chief," Anastasia said, politely.

"And *that*, my dear, is why it's suggested you not attend," Mike said, grinning.

"And so I shan't," Anastasia replied. "I think some of the girls would take it just fine, but we'll all retire when the group heads up the hill."

"Then it's agreed," Mike said as the Mothers finished checking out another field. "And off to another field we go."

Chapter Four

Mike hadn't realized that they'd check all six fields but they did. Then, still standing in the last one, they held a meeting that involved a bunch of arm waving. Mike was surprised that Mother Lenka, who usually had an, often foulmouthed, opinion on anything was standing listening to it with her arms folded.

The whole tribe had gathered around the last field, waiting to find out which would be chosen. Some had been gathering handfuls of the grain that nodded over the stone fences, arguing amongst themselves, and Mike was pretty sure he saw some surreptitious betting on which field would win.

Mike was surprised, though, when he saw the harvester headed towards their position. He was under the impression the field for the Keldara's beer was to be harvested by hand. But it was headed their way, driven by the farm manager, Genadi.

As the harvester neared, Mother Lenka waved to him and imperiously pointed at two fields. There were some mild groans in the crowd and Mike saw Sawn, one of the team leaders, collecting money.

As the harvester, which could rip through the five-hectare fields in a few minutes, began to harvest the definite losers, the Mothers went back through the other fields.

"This is taking forever," Adams finally muttered. "I'm gonna go get a beer."

By the time Adams got back, Genadi had started on two more fields that didn't make the cut. The Mothers wandered back and forth between the final two and finally met near Mike's position. This time there didn't seem to be any argument, just a lot of nodding.

"The barley is chosen," Mother Lenka shouted, very formally, holding up her arms. "Let it be harvested."

Six young men, followed by twelve of the younger unmarried women, entered the field. The men were carrying scythes and working their shoulders, clearly preparing for the harvest. The girls were just giggling. Gretchen was among them and she broke off with Nikolai Mahona, one of the machine-gunners from Oleg's team. Mike didn't know the girls as well as he did the guys but he was able to pick out enough names to figure out that the teams were broken down by Families. Six families, six teams.

"It's a race," Vil said, coming over to lean on the fence by the Kildar.

"Hey, Vil," Mike said. "We needed some cultural explanation."

Vil was tall, slim and dark of hair. Very handsome as all the Keldara were, he looked just a tad like Omar Sharif.

When he first formed the militia, Mike had, with some "help," chosen six of the younger Keldara to be the team leaders. He hadn't realized just how carefully he had been steered until later. The six team leaders were the acknowledged heirs of the Families, the men who, when it was their time, would almost certainly be the Fathers of each family.

They, in turn, had chosen their team members in a process that reminded Mike of teams being chosen in school. He'd insisted that the teams have members from every House, spread as much as possible, so that if one team was badly damaged in a battle no one Family would bear the brunt. But, naturally, the team leaders had chosen people that they were most comfortable with. What had resulted were six distinctly different teams. Oh, each could do any basic job, but they each had specific vocation, a set of skills that leaned to one use or another.

Oleg was a big, "bull forward" guy and he'd chosen big, "bull forward" people for his team. If you needed something flattened, Team Oleg would do it best. Sawn Makanee was one of the more thoughtful Keldara and he'd chosen people who, like him, were a tad more intellectual. They talked about international politics and philosophy rather than beer. Oh, they could flatten stuff, too, but they would rather figure out if it really *needed* to be flattened. And so on.

Vil was a rapier to Oleg's battle-axe. His team specialized in raid and ambush, hit and run, maneuver and feint. He had the faintly aristocratic air usually associated in old movies with British fops. But Mike would rather have him on a raid mission than any two of the other team leaders. And the guy was strong as hell; Mike had seen him lift twice his own weight in unwieldy rock.

"When we used to do *all* this stuff by hand," he continued, waving around the valley languidly, "the Chosen field would be left for last. The field is then harvested by six teams, chosen from unmarried men and women. When the last stalk is cut we make a sort of puppet which we call the *sanbahn*."

"Old woman, probably," Vanner said.

"That's what we call it, yes," Vil said, smiling faintly. "More books, yes?"

"Yep," Vanner said. "Gotta love 'em."

"The *sanbahn* is carried up the dun," Vil continued, pointing to the hill, "and at the end of the ceremony it's thrown in the bonfire. Then we get down to the real purpose of the whole thing which is drinking all of last year's beer we possibly can. Can't have old beer hanging around, can we?"

"Who carries the *sanbahn*?" Mike asked.

"Oh, the oldest girl of the losing team," Vil said. "Why?"

"Just wondering," Mike said, glancing over at Vanner and shaking his head as the intel guy started to say something.

Mother Lenka had reached the point where the six teams waited, the other Mothers leaving the field, and now raised her hands. She looked at each of the men then dropped her arms.

The harvesters already had their scythes back and swung downward as one, cutting a swathe then stepping forward. As soon as they were clear the girls moved forward, gathering up armfuls of the grain and binding them in their own stalks.

To shouts of encouragement, and in some cases derision, from the Keldara the six teams raced down the field.

"Nikolai is going too fast," Vil said, gesturing to the machine-gunner. "Mahona is likely to lose."

"He's ahead of two of the other teams," Adams argued.

"I know Nikolai and while he has plenty of strength and lots of strength in his legs, he doesn't have much stamina for this sort of thing. He'll start tiring about the last third. Bet you a hundred rubles he comes in second to or dead last."

"You're on," Adams said.

But, sure enough, as they got into the last part of the cutting, Mike could tell he was flagging. His cuts were getting ragged and he, twice, had to overcut to get all the grain. That put him second to last and Georgi Makanee, who was last right up until the end, managed to cut his stand just as Nikolai was raising his blade.

"Halt!" Mother Lenka called. She'd gotten behind the team towards the end and now walked over. "Mahona is last," she cried.

"Nikolai's in for it now," Vil said. "Oh, not as bad as the *caillean*, but he'll be teased a good bit. And now Gretchen will be the *ogbahn*, the carrier of the *sanbahn*." He frowned at that.

"And that means?" Mike asked.

"Oh, nothing," Vil replied. "Nothing at all."

"Come on, Vil, give," Vanner said.

"Well," Vil said, frowning. "It's said that the *ogbahn* can never be the *sanbahn*."

"The *sanbahn* is a puppet made out of straw," Mike said. The last sheaf had been cut and Mother Lenka was already binding it into the figure. Mike shivered suddenly in the chill wind. You could smell the storm approaching.

"It also, as Mr. Vanner so astutely pointed out, means old woman," Vil replied. "It's the term for . . . someone. An old woman." He turned and looked at the Kildar, frowning still. "It means Gretchen will never be old. If you believe in that sort of thing."

"Of course she'll never be old," Vanner said after Vil had wandered off. "She used to be sacrificed."

"Yep," Mike said. "A sacrifice to the old gods. The daughter of spring given to the god of the dead, the god of the underworld."

"That's terrible," Anastasia said. "I can't believe anyone would perform human sacrifice!"

"Oh, not these days," Mike said. "Probably. But it used to be really common, even up to the time of the Romans. They got rid of most of it, after *they* gave it up. And that was by a vote of the Roman Senate not long before Caesar was born. They were the ones who stopped the sacrifices in Gaul, France now, and Britain. The Germans took longer. And even the Romans kept it up in some remote areas, right up until they started to become Christians. And the Russians only stopped around the time of the Mongols when Christianity finally had a firm hold. *Outside* Europe it was common right up until the colonial period. Given how . . . traditional the Keldara are, I figure they probably stopped around the same time as the Russians. Say . . . the 1300s."

"They wouldn't . . . start again?" Tinata asked. She'd been listening avidly.

"No, they won't," Mike said. "First of all . . . times have changed. I don't think *they* could stomach it. Second, I'd put a stop to it if I even suspected it. But the choosing of the caillean at Beltane or whatever they call it, and this thing with the 'old woman' and the 'young woman,' those are all vestiges of human sacrifice. Be glad they only sacrifice animals now."

"They're headed to the dun," Vanner pointed out.

"Well, then, we are headed for the caravanserai," Anastasia said. One look at the gathered harem girls stifled the beginnings of protest. "I leave it up to you to ensure that your Kardane is actually *alive* tomorrow, Kildar."

"Guaranteed," Mike said, giving her a peck on the cheek. "And . . . you might make sure there are some clothes ready in the foyer. I suspect that we'll have a bit of blood on us when we get back."

"Kildar," Father Kulcyanov said, as the Keldara began to gather at the base of the dun, "I would ask a favor of you."

"Anything I can do," Mike said. The old soldier had smoothed things over a lot and Mike knew it.

"We must Feed the Dead," Father Kulcyanov said, sighing. "But I am aged. I have all I can do it make it up the hill and chant the words. I would ask you to take my place as Eater for the Dead. One of the other Fathers could do as well but . . . You are the Kildar."

Mike smiled and nodded, his face blank. He wondered if that meant *he* was really supposed to be high priest. Pass, thank you.

"I hope you won't mind if I ask a few questions," Mike said. "I've learned, through painful experience, to ask about the hidden details of Keldara rituals."

"Kildar," Genadi said, coming up at his elbow, "there is no hidden trap. You must simply . . . eat your way to the top of the hill. Father, indeed all of us, will chant the dead. A girl will be by your side carrying a big platter filled with all good foods. Another will be by your side, carrying beer. At a certain point in the chant, you will take a sip of beer or eat some of the food. You take a bite of the food and then throw the rest to the side. You take a sip of beer and then pour some upon the ground. I will warn you, however, that we circle the mound three times. I hope you stopped eating a while ago."

"I think I can do that," Mike said. "As long as I don't take big bites."

"Thank you, Kildar," Father Kulcyanov said. He lifted his eyes to the mountains and then nodded. "Soon, we will begin."

The Keldara had gathered near the trail up the dun, a winding beaten-down path that was reinforced with slabs of rock. It might have been a bad day for a festival but Mike was pretty sure it was a great night for a ceremony like this one.

The Keldara called the night Samman, very much like the Celtic Samhain. For them it was the time of ending, when the spirits of winter rose, the night when the unquiet dead could walk free. Many of the Keldara had made masks for the evening, most out of woven barley straw. Samhain was the origin of the holiday called Halloween in the U.S. and England but hadn't always been about children gathering candy. It was a time when the summer was dying and winter's power rose, a time to battle the power of death and the old gods of evil and darkness. The masks were designed to frighten away spirits as was the chanting, dance and songs.

Father Ferani walked through the throng, carrying a large wooden case. Father Kulcyanov took a massive battle-axe from the case, turning to the trail and holding it in front of himself, upright in a two-handed grip, the head at the level of his nose, as if in salute. Then he looked to the sky again, clearly checking the light level, and gave a great shout:

"*Ay, Samman seaol Latrach! Uraim Na Mair Imakt!*"

With that the drummers began tapping on their drums, a slow, syncopated rhythm as Father Kulcyanov began ascending the hill.

Behind him walked Gretchen, carrying the barley effigy of the "Old Woman." Stella and Lydia appeared at Mike's elbows, quite suddenly, and Lydia nudged him to fall in next.

"Each third time that Father Kulcyanov says 'Imakt,'" Lydia whispered, handing him a shallow bowl of beer, "drink or eat then pour the rest on the ground. Try to get it off the path for the Father's sake."

The bowl was fired clay, with a handle on either side. Mike had read of one similar somewhere, probably in *The Golden Bough*. He took a sip and tossed the rest to the side, narrowly missing Stella.

"Careful, there," the tall brunette said, grinning and handing him an oat cake.

Mike took a bite out of the cake and tossed the rest down the hill.

"This seems awfully wasteful," he whispered.

"The dead are hungry," Lydia shrugged, handing him the refilled bowl. "Would we fail to feed our honored dead?"

Mike took a sip at the appropriate point in the chant, poured it out a bit more carefully, then looked over his shoulder. All the Keldara had formed up in something like a conga line. At the front were six drummers, keeping the pace. The rest were repeating the refrain of the chant and on the "*Latrach*" they'd stamp down, hard. The whole massive hill rumbled with it.

"Wake the dead, indeed," Mike said. Bite, toss. "Father Kulcyanov normally eats, too?"

"Someone feeds him," Stella whispered. "But it's so hard for him to keep in time, now. And when the cake is dry . . ."

It was all Mike could do to keep up with the eating and drinking; he couldn't imagine leading the chant as well. But the two girls kept him supplied in time and he kept up with the group, eat a bite, toss, drink a bit, pour.

But even eating a "bite"—and they got smaller and smaller—and drinking a bit—and the sips got to where he was barely touching his lips—he had a hard time managing the entire climb. By the time they got to the top it was full dark, the wind howling, and he was more than a bit drunk. And, oh yeah, stuffed to the point of throwing up.

The turf on the top of the dun had been carved into seats and the two girls led him to one on the north side, directly behind where Father Kulcyanov was standing and still leading the chant. Gretchen, with the barley figure, was on the east, Mother Lenka with a flagon of beer was on the west and, as the group gathered, still chanting, Oleg appeared out of the darkness on the south. He was bare-chested in the cold and probably appreciating the roaring bonfire in the center.

Mike's senior team leader was a bull of a man, standing over two meters and broad of body with flax blonde hair cut into stubble. He looked, at that moment, very much like a Viking of old.

". . . *Imakt!*" Father Kulcyanov roared, stopping the chant by raising his axe over head, still vertical. "The time has come. Let the Rite begin!"

He turned to the right and, marching in the goose step he had undoubtedly learned as a young man in the Red Army, walked to Oleg's position.

"Do you accept the responsibility of *dummart*?" Father Kulcyanov roared. "Do you stand ready to face the Gods?"

"I do," Oleg answered.

"Then face the Gods in the name of the Keldara!" Father Kulcyanov said, handing over the axe.

He goose-stepped back, completing the circle, then raised his hands.

"Father of All, look down upon us!" he bellowed, holding his hands to the sky. "We bring food for your Son that he might bring back the spring!"

There'd been a lowing of cattle as he was marching back, and out of the darkness they were led. Most were being led by the team leaders but they had a lot of help. The cattle were oxen, steers that were used for carting until Mike had brought in tractors. These had been fed-up, stalled was the old expression, and were fat and ready for the slaughter.

Vil was leading the first one, holding a pole that was attached to the ring through its nose, and two more Keldara males followed with nooses in their hands.

"*Ay, Samman seaol Latrach! Uraim Na Mair Imakt!*" Father Kulcyanov started to chant, still holding his hands up.

The whole group joined in as the two Keldara fixed the loops around the ox's back legs and held it in place.

On the second repetition of the chant, at the ". . . *Imakt,*" Oleg struck downwards, severing the ox's broad neck in one massive cut.

Blood from the stricken animal sprayed across the nearest spectators, who were on their feet chanting and stamping. The entire group let out a cry as one of the Keldara girls slid a basin under the slaughtered beast's neck, catching as much of the blood as she could.

Another of the oxen was brought out of the darkness, taking up the western position by Mother Lenka. Again it was held in place by three men as Oleg slashed downward. Another group of Keldara, this time including Adams, was splashed by the blood.

On the south, Vil had been handed the basin filled with blood and with a cry splashed it in a circle, starting towards the fire and raising a fragrant smoke like cooking beef, then out over the Keldara.

Mike was standing, now, but he was fighting what was going on around him because the Keldara, normally incredibly reserved, were descending into hysteric frenzy. The drums, the chanting, the stamping feet, was turning into a giant dance of ecstasy, fueled by the blood rite they had been denied for so long.

Pavel had collected the blood on the west and he sprayed it into the fire and through the group, liberally dousing Mother Lenka, who raised her hand to taste of it, letting out a scream that sounded very like orgasm.

Now it was Mike's turn and Sawn was leading this ox, who was fighting as hard as he could to get away. Oleg had come around the fire, his body covered in blood, eyes wide and staring, and Mike winced as the axe came down.

It was like getting hit by a water from a spray nozzle on a hose. As the ox twisted in death it sprayed the whole group, which went absolutely frantic. The bucket of blood from Sawn wasn't really necessary.

On the east it was Yosif and he made sure to liberally douse Gretchen, who was pretty wide-eyed since all she could do was stand there holding up the effigy. She hadn't gotten into the frenzy because she couldn't but she had a very strange look on her face. It made Mike wonder exactly how long ago the Keldara had stopped committing human sacrifice. She looked . . . fixed on the fire. As if psyching herself to be thrown into it.

A fifth bull was slaughtered on the south and a sixth on the north, splattering Mike again, and then Father Kulcyanov shouted something Mike for the life of him couldn't catch and people picked up both Mother Lenka and Gretchen and carried them towards the fire. The group was so frenzied Mike started forward; he could see Adams moving as well. He wasn't sure either one of them could stop the hysterical Keldara before they tossed the two women in the bonfire but he was *damned* well going to try.

But at a cry from Father Kulcyanov, the effigy was thrown into the fire by Gretchen to another scream from the crowd. It was covered in blood so there was another smell of steak being overcooked.

Both Mother Lenka and Gretchen were dropped, rather unceremoniously, and the drums broke into a different rhythm. Father Kulcyanov stepped back, looking as worn as Mike had ever seen him, and settled onto one of the turf benches, holding his chest.

There was still a big pot of beer by Mike's seat, courtesy of Stella, who was now dancing around like a mad thing, covered from head to toe in blood, so he picked it up and poured some, holding it out to the old man.

"Thank you, Kildar," Father Kulcyanov wheezed. "I think this may be the last year I can do the Rites."

"Which will be too bad," Mike said. "Because you do them very well."

"It must be a warrior," the old man said, taking a sip of beer and catching his breath. "One who has taken lives and seen the face of Fir. There are, were, so few left. I held on . . ."

"And you've got a whole new crop," Mike pointed out. "I'd hate to skip a generation, though. Talk about that another time. Do you have anything else you need to do?"

"No," Father Kulcyanov admitted. "Except figure out a way to pry Culcanar out of Oleg's hands before he kills someone with it."

The ceremonial axes of the Keldara were named and Mike now recognized the axe *he* had wielded in the spring festival. The damned thing was a monster, a real man killer.

Mike looked over at the team leader, who was apparently doing some sort of an axe dance and was pretty much out of it, and winced.

"Let somebody else handle that," Mike said. "Me, maybe. I can stand in, right?"

"Yes, Kildar. I'd appreciate it."

"Well, this looks like a party for the youngsters," Mike said, standing up and gesturing to Adams and Nielson. He couldn't find Vanner for a minute then spotted the intel NCO. He was covered in blood, dancing with one of the female intel specialists, and completely out of it.

"Get Father Kulcyanov down the hill," he said to Nielson. "Ass-Boy, you and me got a job."

"What?" Adams asked, trying to wipe some of the blood off his face. "When you said it would be bloody . . ."

"Yeah," Mike said, licking the back of his hand. Tasted like raw steak. "See Oleg?"

"Yeah," Adams said, uncomfortably.

"We gotta get the axe out of his hands."

"Oh fuck."

"I'm not going to track this shit through the caravanserai," Mike said, looking at the doors. He had a rather nasty cut on his arm he was ignoring. Pain is weakness leaving the body. Nobody was dead and that was the important thing. The next time, though, he was going to sit on the south and pry the damned thing out of Oleg's hands right after the last sacrifice.

"Fuck it," Adams said. "It's late. We just strip right here and head for the showers." The master chief was unscathed. Well, except for a few hairs that had been cut *slightly* shorter when he ducked the axe. Given that he was damned near bald . . .

"Works for me," Mike said, pulling off his shirt. "And we'll just burn the clothes."

"I think some of the Keldara were starting to strip when we left," Adams said. "They probably had the same idea. Damn, these pants are *stuck* on!"

Mike walked into the great room of the caravanserai, holding his blood-soaked clothes under one arm, and paused, froze really, at the sight of Daria and Anastasia playing chess.

Daria Koroleva was Ukrainian, blonde and nearly as beautiful as Anastasia with, if anything, a better figure. She had been kidnapped into the sex-slave trade in the Balkans where Mike had rescued her from a snuff house. Since she was a trained secretary, and he'd needed somebody to keep up with the administrative side of the mission, he'd dragged her along. And when he offered her a job she'd jumped at it. They'd been lovers from time to time as well. There really wasn't much there but lust and some friendship but she was a great administrative assistant.

The two were both frozen, wide-eyed. Since they'd both seen him naked he could only presume that it was the blood.

"It got a little messy."

"I can see that," Anastasia replied.

"So we thought we'd just go take a shower," Adams said, walking past.

"Good idea," Daria said, tittering.

"So, I guess I'll see you two tomorrow," Mike continued, heading to the stairs.

"Okay," Anastasia said. "Try to keep from tracking things up too badly."

"I will," Mike said. "Oh, and Anastasia?"

"Yes, Kildar," the harem manager said, her hand over her mouth but the smile in her eyes.

"Could you make sure that before the Rite *Gretchen* has had a bath?"

Chapter Five

"You look perfect," Anastasia said, picking a bit of lint off of Mike's shoulder.

"I look like a fucking fruit," Mike replied, frowning. "This getup . . ."

"You always say that the Rite is for the benefit of the young lady," Anastasia said, playing with a curl of hair. "Not for you. And ladies like it when you dress up."

"I know that," Mike said, fiddling with the *God*-damned lace ruff. "But, *God*, I hate this!"

The Rite of Kardane made virtue of necessity. The Keldara had long had the custom of dowry. Dowry was a poorly understood function of many early societies. The first year or so of marriage was a tough time for a new couple and women just had less economic worth in agricultural societies than males. Among other things, they spent a great deal of time pregnant and less able to do work. Dowry was a response to this, providing the young couple with a starter fund.

In the Keldara, dowry was set at the approximate income of the male for one year. When it was first explained to Mike, the sum of five hundred rubles or equivalent in materials seemed laughably small. But it was a function of how very poor the Keldara had been before his arrival.

The issue had first come to light in regards to Lydia and Oleg. Lydia's family simply did not have the available cash, at that time, to pay her dowry. Mike, therefore, offered to just grant them the funds. Lydia was a fast-coming intel specialist and Oleg one of his top team leaders; just handing them the cash, more, seemed like a natural action.

However, the Keldara also had a hatred of debt that was deep and abiding. Thus Mike simply handing them the money with, in his eyes, absolutely no strings attached was out of the question. A debt of honor would remain. In a way the Keldara were more stuck on honor and propriety than Japanese *giri* and *gimu*.

There was, however, one clear alternative: The Rite of Kardane. In Western Europe, the term was "droit du seigneur."

In most feudal societies, the very bodies of the "serfs" were owned by the lord. And many lords required that the first person to "open" a virgin be themselves.

The Keldara may have been tenant farmers, may have had various overlords over the years, but calling them "serfs" must have always been a stretch. But the pressure must have been there. The Ottomans, for example, were big on virgins. So were the Tartars, who had clearly been in the area. Hell, the Russian tsarist lords rarely left a lady "pure" for her marriage bed. However, at some point they had made a "virtue" of both problems; in return for a young lady's "virtue," she would be gifted with her dowry.

When Mike finally understood what they were saying he nearly had a heart attack. While Lydia was a . . . well, a fucking hotty, the guy he was going to be leaving to sloppy seconds was . . . his top team leader. Oleg was going to be at his back with a weapon *a lot.* Not to mention being a fucking ox. Pissing him off was very low on Mike's list of things to do. And Mike couldn't imagine "the Rite of Kardane" not pissing him off totally and permanently.

Oleg, however, had been fine with it. His biggest worry was that Mike would turn them down. Mike got along with the Keldara incredibly well, they even had similar senses of humor which was unusual, but sometimes they could blindside him.

He had, therefore, reluctantly agreed to the "Rite." However, he put several stipulations in place. If he was going to do this he was going to do it right.

First, he insisted that she be given some classes. Riding horses for one. But he also insisted on, as he put it, "other riding classes" conducted by Mother Savina, his housekeeper, and Anastasia. He also insisted that there be a little ceremony. He wasn't going to just yank her up on the horse without any "by your leave" and ride off. Among other things it got way too close to where some of his demons lurked.

On his part he did his best to make the night special and the dowry much more reasonable than the cost of a good pair of jeans. Lydia had walked away with about four thousand dollars, plus five one-hundred-ruble notes, a pearl necklace and matching earrings.

The result, once Lydia let loose some of the juicier details, was that the unmarried females now considered the "Rite" a *Right.* They wanted their evening with the Kildar, damnit, and the dowry had *nothing* to do with it anymore.

Anastasia had added a few details to his original plans. Mike had to agree that they were *popular,* but he didn't have to *like* them.

Which was why he was dressed in a pair of polished riding boots, a short, tight, dark green velvet horseman's jacket that made him feel like a waiter, a silk shirt with a ruffled front and skintight velvet pants.

A waiter, hell, he felt like a God-damned *gigolo!*

"I would rather face a thousand deaths . . ." he muttered, turning to the door of the caravanserai.

"Don't give me that," Anastasia said, grinning. "We're talking Gretchen, Michael Whateveryourrealnameis."

"Yes," Mike said, looking at her for a moment. "There is that," he added, grinning.

"Just remember to take your time," Anastasia said, picking at another bit of lint. "Be a good boy."

"I'll *try,*" Mike said. "Now you need to go."

"Yes," Anastasia said with a sigh. "I have a date as well. But if you need any help . . ."

Mike rolled his eyes and strode out the door.

Petro was holding Dumbass' reins and bowed as the Kildar came down the steps followed by Anastasia. He also had a lack of expression that bordered boredom. At this point he no longer had to try not to grin. The first three or four were grin-making, after that, well . . .

"Thank you," Mike said, mounting then taking the lead rein of the palfrey. "Now scat. You've got duties as well."

"Yes, Kildar," Anastasia said, finally grinning.

The pouring rain of the night before had led to a cooler day but clear as a bell. The sun had just set, it was what the military called "early evening nautical twilight" and Mike referred to as "blue time." He wanted to arrive at just full dark and visibility was already a bit bad so he took the road down carefully. But he had to admit it was a beautiful evening for riding.

Dumbass was getting used enough to the routine that he didn't try to canter. This wasn't a run where he was going to get oat cakes and apples. This was work.

Mike ignored the fire burning on the dun. It was smaller than the Samman bonfire but, to someone who knew the processes and practices of the Keldara, an announcement of a ceremony of a different type. A group of young men were clustered there, one of them Kiril.

There was a younger Keldara female waiting by the door of the Mahona House when he arrived. Mike had requested that the minimum possible males be involved in the Rite and now getting the horse-holding duty was a perk among the younger Keldara girls. That way they got to peek without any fear of retribution.

The girl was smiling fit to burst but he just nodded at her sternly. Taking a breath, he pulled down the front of his jacket, strode to the door of the house and pounded on it sharply.

The door was opened by Father Mahona, who nodded at the Kildar.

"I request the privilege of entering the home of the Mahona," Mike said.

"This roof is yours, Kildar," Father Mahona replied from within. "These walls are yours. This home is yours to enter."

Everybody at this point had the Rite down pat.

Everyone had been cleared from the main room of the House leaving only the principals: Mother and Father Mahona, Father Jusev the Orthodox priest and Gretchen.

Anastasia had designed the wear for the Rite. While giving the girls some very graphic instructions, "theoretical" sex education in its true form, she had them measured. A renowned clothier in

Paris custom-made the outfit Gretchen was now wearing. It was white but it didn't look in any way like a wedding dress. Covered in seed pearls, the front was a deep V that, in Gretchen's case, was almost too much of a good thing. The girl was threatening to spill out. The skirt stopped well above the knees revealing for the first time that Gretchen, yeah, had one *hell* of a set of legs. My God did she ever. Long, shapely and tapered, they were works of art. On her feet were a matching pair of white high heels, also decorated with seed pearls and rhinestones.

The outfit was an invitation to rape and, to the Keldara, beyond scandalous, which was why Mike limited the number of people present to the bare minimum. He knew that the younger girls were probably peeking from every corner they could find, but he'd sworn not only vengeance but revocation of right to be in the Tigers for any young male who took a peek.

Having been a young male, he was pretty sure they were ignoring him. If he'd been as sheltered as the Keldara boys, he'd have given his left *nut* to see Gretchen in that dress. All the "bother" of the Rite of Kardane went straight out of his head and he knew he was embarrassing himself if anyone looked at the front of the very *very* tight, *unpleasantly* tight, pants.

"I am come to take my rights as the Kildar," Mike said, sternly, looking Father Mahona in the eye.

"The right of the Kildar is acknowledged by the Keldara and the Family Mahona," the elder replied. "The Kildar is reminded of his duty to the future family."

"I acknowledge my duty," Mike said, turning to Father Jusev, the priest. "I have come to take my rights as the Kildar."

"The right of the Kildar is acknowledged by the Church," Father Jusev said. "The Kildar is reminded of his duty of teaching," the priest added, dryly.

Father Jusev was an older priest, one who had started when the Soviets were at their height and a few of the priests from Tsarist times were still around. Back then you had to be *committed* to become a priest; it was a good way to get sent to Siberia. And there wasn't any such thing as a "liberal" Orthodox; back then the only people willing to profess a faith in a God who was communism's bitterest enemy were the true believers. Those guys didn't tend to be "new-age."

Thus when the subject of the Rite had been brought up with him the first time, he'd just nodded. Not only was he aware that it was a tradition amongst the Keldara, it was a hell of a lot better than the way the tsarist lords generally treated it. Heck, the commissars hadn't been lily-white by any stretch of the imagination. And then there was the fact that the Kildar, while he didn't attend services much, was by several orders of magnitude his biggest contributor. He wasn't going to tell him that this was "sin" and that it would violate any future marriage compacts in the eyes of the Church. Not a guy who paid the tithes the Kildar did and, by the way, owned the local cops and had a hundred and twenty dedicated shooters who knew where to find a backhoe.

"I acknowledge my duty," Mike said, turning to Mother Mahona. "I come to take my rights as Kildar." His tone in this case was much less stern.

"The right of the Kildar is acknowledged by the women of the Keldara," Mother Mahona said then winked. "The Kildar is reminded of his duty of gentleness."

"I acknowledge my duty," Mike said, then turned to Gretchen, dropping to one knee with difficulty in the tight pants and bowing his head. "My lady, I am come to crave a boon of you, one night of gentleness. May I have my time as is my right?"

"You may, Kildar," Gretchen replied. She was clearly happy, her smile revealing deep dimples, but nervous as well. "May you remember your . . . duties in all things." She stumbled a bit on that line but all in all it was pretty good. He had designed the ceremony so that the young lady, who was going to be worrying about other things, had the least to do.

"I shall," Mike said, standing up and taking her hand. "I shall return with this daughter of the Keldara when the sun rises," he said, looking at the three. "I shall render my duty as tradition fits and no shame is had in this Right."

"No shame, only duty," Father Mahona said.

"No shame, only duty," the priest intoned.

"No shame," Mother Mahona said, winking, "only pleasure."

Mother Makanee had thrown that line in at the first ceremony and, despite Mike's quiet protests, it had remained.

He tried not to sigh.

❖   ❖   ❖

"You've seen the place, of course," Mike said as they walked in the front of the caravanserai.

"I've been up here on cleaning duty," Gretchen said, looking around with interest nonetheless. "But I've never been in your quarters."

"Then I guess I'd better show you those."

Mike had had a small kitchen installed off of his bedroom. It was separated from the bedroom—which was more like a small suite with a king-sized bed, sitting area and desk hardly filling it— by a three-stool bar counter. The counter had been set for two in china and silver. There were two candles burning and a long-stemmed rose in a vase.

When they entered, Gretchen just craned her long and shapely neck around for a quick look, as if determining she knew where everything was, then walked over and perched on a stool at the bar.

"You girls talk too much," Mike said, smiling and taking off his jacket. He donned an apron to keep any splatters off his shirt and trousers then pulled a bottle of champagne out of a bucket of ice. He opened it expertly, none of this silly blasting the cork into the ceiling, then poured a glass for Gretchen and one for himself. "Cheers," he said, clinking glasses with her.

"Eyes of the Father," Gretchen replied, then took a sip. "That *is* nice."

"So are you," Mike said, smiling. "All of the Keldara women are beautiful, but I've never seen one that looked so incredible in that outfit."

"I think you said that to Stella," Gretchen replied, but still smiled.

"Did not," Mike said, frowning. "Did I? Besides, I hadn't seen *you*, yet."

"So who is the prettiest Keldara girl?" Gretchen asked, tilting her head to the side.

"That's a dangerous subject on a night like tonight," Mike said, walking around the bar to the cooking area. He'd had that built onto the back side of the bar so he could talk with the lady while he was cooking.

All the ingredients were laid out; thank God at least he didn't have to prepare them. But he had to stop and think for a moment, looking them over.

Part of his regime in regards to the Rite was that it was a date. The Keldara girls did not date. Their husbands were chosen for them and they went to them from their father's arm, very much in the original tradition. Outside the variable of the Rite, they were supposed to be virgins. Oh, some weren't—Spring Festival was a time when some things went on that were generally overlooked. But they certainly did not date.

Mike, when faced by the necessity of the Rite, decided that it was going to be a date. The best date he could possibly manage. Of course, there was no real question how the evening was going to turn out, sexually. The girl in question was going to get laid, will she, nil she. So far it had always been "will she" but Mike was dreading the day that it was "nil she."

Mike had been on a lot of dates in his time. And he'd been a "bad" date occasionally, but rarely in the last ten years or so. It was a social dance and had certain rules that had to be followed. There should be food of some sort, light if the evening was almost certain to include sex. There should be conversation, also light for the most part. Various "romantic" aspects had to be observed. And if the male wanted it to be a "good" date for the female, he had better get her to talk about *herself* for the most part and make sure she wasn't playing serving girl the whole evening. If he wanted it to be good for the lady, he had to pay *attention* to her needs. And, generally, one of those needs was a day off from her "traditional" roles.

Women, even in modern societies, were traditionally viewed as the housekeepers. Especially so amongst the Keldara. Keldara males could barbecue but few could really cook. So, for the evening, Mike took over the cooking duties.

"You like Katrina the most," Gretchen said.

Mike wasn't going to look up to see what expression was on her face. He was busy trying to remember how to cook Shrimp St. Jacques.

One part of the Rite he was starting to have trouble with was the meal. He'd decided, early on, that every girl should have, at the least, her own "special" meal. But this was about his fifteenth "Rite" and he was starting to run out of easy dishes. His skills were mostly focused on the stovetop, stir fry and the various French equivalents. At this rate he was going to have to learn how to cook Lobster Thermidor or Chateau Briand.

"Actually, Gretchen," Mike said, still not looking up as he started the pasta, "while I like Katrina, my *physical* tastes are somewhat elsewhere. If I was asked to describe my dream girl she'd be, oh, tall with long shapely legs, a firm stomach, good, high, firm breasts, a pretty face, blue eyes . . ." then he looked up into hers and smiled, "and blonde hair."

"Liar," Gretchen said, shifting a bit in her seat and trying not to smile.

"*Au contraire,*" Mike said then considered for a moment. "On the contrary. That describes my dream girl. Well, she could be somewhat shorter and more rounded, that has its attractions. But the breasts, eyes and hair remain."

"So I guess you like what you see?" Gretchen said, shifting again to lean sideways. She'd meant for it to be coquettish but one of her breasts damned near slipped out of the not particularly restraining dress and she straightened, pulling at the edges of the dress modestly.

"I like it very much," Mike said, trying to give the impression he hadn't seen as much of that lovely *lovely* breast as, in fact, he had.

"But that also describes Daria and Anastasia," Gretchen pointed out.

"Neither of whom, my dear, were virgins when I met them," Mike said, bluntly.

"What is it with men and virgins?" Gretchen asked, sharply.

"Do you really want to know or are you just finding something to be unhappy about?" Mike asked. He was busy getting the alfredo sauce ready but he looked up again, curiously. Gretchen was acting quite the handful and he wasn't positive why.

"I'm sorry, Kildar," Gretchen said, looking down. "I apologize."

"Don't," Mike said, stirring in the parmesan cheese. "I've never been particularly happy about this . . . rite myself. As I've made plain many times."

"You don't like breaking in virgins?" Gretchen asked. "What, you don't want to bed me? Didn't you just say that I'm your ideal girl?"

"Yes, and I meant it," Mike said. "But it's supposed to be something the lady enjoys, not rape. And right now I'm getting the impression you're less than happy. I think at me but I'm not sure."

Gretchen looked away again and then sighed. Mike was trying very hard *not* to look at her body but the sigh was impossible to resist.

"Kiril is downstairs, isn't he?"

"Oh, so that's it . . ."

Kiril closed his eyes as Anastasia ran her hands down his body.

She had turned up out of the darkness at the fire on the dun, as she had since the first Rite, and taken him up to the caravanserai.

Mike thought that *both* parties should be "aware" when they came to the marriage bed. As it was his job to please Gretchen and teach her what pleased men, it was Anastasia's to do the same for her mate. Both were careful, however, to stay away from their actual interests which leaned, no hurled, in the direction of whips, chains and as much pain as possible. Mike to inflict, Anastasia to absorb.

"This is not the first time you've been with a woman," Anastasia said, sitting down on the bed next to him.

"No," Kiril admitted.

"So *many* lost their virginity on the Balkans trip," Anastasia said, smiling. "Before that all of you were virgins. Since . . ."

"So, you really don't have to do this," Kiril pointed out. "I mean, I'd love to, but . . ."

"Do you think I don't enjoy it?" Anastasia said, grinning. "For years in the hareem all there was was Otayar and you don't want me to describe what a *thrill* it was lying with an old fat man who cared only for his pleasure. But part of my purpose is to teach you how you can please your wife, not just to take your mind off of other things."

"I really don't need my mind taken off of that, actually," Kiril said. "I'm probably more okay with the Kildar being with Gretchen than . . . anybody. Including, I know, the Kildar. I'm just saying, if you don't want to . . ."

"So thoughtful you are," Anastasia said, running her hand down his body again. "But I do want to. It has a special thrill, yes?"

"I . . . yes," Kiril replied as there was a knock on the door.

"Who in the . . ." Anastasia said, her face reflecting fury as she stood up and walked to the door of the suite. Yanking it open she was confronted by the Kildar, holding an obviously embarrassed Gretchen's hand. Gretchen was pulling at her dress front, trying to cover more skin and looking *anywhere* but at the two people in the room.

"Kildar?" Anastasia, in English, raising one eyebrow. "I take it the Rite is going somewhat Wrong?"

"You are one of the few people I know that can change languages just to get in a pun," Mike said, stepping past her and closing the door, which was soundproofed. "Kiril! Come here!"

"Yes, sir!" the young man said, snapping to attention and practically marching over. He, too, was trying *very* hard to not look at his fiancée.

"Gretchen knows where my quarters are," Mike said, putting Gretchen's hand in his. "Get to it girl," Mike added, slapping the girl on the butt.

"Kildar," Gretchen said, pleading in her eyes.

"I like rape just fine, but I don't do it," Mike said, his face hard. "You two. Upstairs. That's an order. I don't care if you do anything or not, but if Kiril misses this opportunity, he's over the line between hardcore and stupid. Nobody will know but the four of us." Mike looked at the two of them, both wide-eyed and frozen, and sighed. "You'll have to cook your own dinner."

"I don't know how to cook that!" Gretchen practically wailed. "I'd never seen a shrimp before in my life!"

"There are other ingredients," Mike said, softening. "Go."

When the two stunned youngsters were gone, Mike looked at Anastasia.

"So, doing anything this evening?" he asked.

Chapter Six

Gretchen stood, just looking around the small kitchen filled with devices she had no idea how to use, then picked up the Kildar's apron and put it on over her beautiful dress.

"So what happened?" Kiril asked, picking up the glass of champagne and sniffing at it. He took a sip and swirled it around in his mouth before swallowing. "This stuff doesn't half make your nose tickle, does it?"

"I don't know," Gretchen said, opening the unfamiliar refrigerator and looking at the contents. It was very well stocked for a spare kitchen. She looked in the freezer and recognized meat. She could probably do something with meat. Suddenly, she started crying.

"I didn't want *this* to happen," she said, sniffling.

"Well, it did," Kiril said, taking another sip of champagne. "Nice dress, by the way."

"It wasn't the Kildar, it was me," Gretchen said, looking over at him. "I just couldn't . . ."

"I guess I can understand that," Kiril said. "I mean, sort of. But I thought all the girls wanted the Kildar?"

"Not that you idiot!" Gretchen snapped. "It . . . I . . . It . . ." She stopped and shrugged.

"Oh," Kiril said, setting down the glass with a clink that was the only sound in the room. "So . . . You did all this because you didn't want me with Anastasia?"

"And did you want me with the Kildar?" Gretchen asked, angrily.

"Yes," Kiril answered, expecting an angry reply.

"Do you have a reason?" Gretchen said. "I do, I was just angry you were with that woman. Now . . ."

"You do?" Kiril asked, confused. "I mean, since the Kildar, okay, some of us have been thinking about our traditions, trying to pin down *why* they are. He started it, always asking questions, trying to *understand*, not just do things automatically. So some of us have been thinking about it and discussing it, quietly. And we think we've got a handle on Kardane, but . . . You already do?"

"Yes," Gretchen replied, "but that is all I can say. It is part of . . . woman's rites."

"Oh . . . shit," Kiril said, his face suddenly white. "The . . ."

"Goddess," Gretchen said, nodding. "Kiril, I *must* lie with the Kildar this night. But I have failed. I will be shamed if I do not. I . . ."

"Oh, damn," Kiril said, working his jaw. Guns he'd face, but not the vengeance of the Priestess. Not being able to marry Gretchen was the *least* of it. If she angered the Priestess, she'd almost assuredly be cast out, Kildar or no Kildar. He, too, might face the wrath. Oh, they hadn't done the full Goddess Rites in a *long* time, but he didn't want to be the person to break the trend. "Gretch, there's only one thing to do, then . . ."

"Oh, Jesus Christ," Mike said, lowering the whip at a knock on the door. Anastasia had indicated the need for a seriously hard whipping and for once he wasn't holding back; the whole thing with Gretchen had been incredibly frustrating. He hadn't had a date go that bad in *years*. And, okay, he hadn't looked forward to the Rite that much in a long time, either.

"Mff, mgh, mff?" Anastasia asked through the gag.

"How the *hell* should I know?"

How long were they going to wait? Oh, the hell with it.

Mike walked to the door and opened it, shielding the view of the interior, and the whip, from whoever was at the door.

Technically he shouldn't have been here at all at this time. This was *really* going to screw things up. He wasn't sure how bad, but *bad*.

He snatched the door open: "Wha . . ." He paused at the sight of Gretchen and Kiril and took a deep breath. "Yes?" he said ground out as pleasantly as he could.

"Kildar, the Rite must be completed," Kiril said, holding out Gretchen's hand. "Please, Kildar, let's just . . . try to start over." He'd clearly rehearsed the words and gotten through them without really taking in what he was seeing.

Gretchen wasn't saying much, she was just blinking.

Mike had changed clothes. He was wearing a skintight black leather cuirass, a leather g-string, chaps and a spiked leather collar.

Mike was tempted to do many things, swear, burst into laughter . . . but what he did was just nod.

"I'm going to need a few minutes," he said. He looked at Gretchen and shook his head. "Gretchen, go await me upstairs. Kiril . . . front room."

"Yes, Kildar," Kiril said.

Mike shook his head and walked around to look at Anastasia.

"Think I should take the whip with me?" he asked.

Anastasia thought about it for a few seconds then nodded her head affirmatively. Very affirmatively.

"Think the kid's up to this?" Mike asked waving around at the temporary bondage scene.

Anastasia shook her head, ruefully, in the negative.

"Yeah, I agree," Mike said, frowning. "Good strong arms but then there's the safety briefing and negotiation and all that time Gretchen's waiting upstairs getting more and more nervous . . ." He grinned evilly. "Okay, here's a question. Want him to at least *see* you like this? That would be humiliating, right?"

Anastasia shook her head hard and Mike started to grin then stopped.

"Hell," he said, pulling the gag out of her mouth. "We're out of scene. Are you clear enough?" Serious bondage tended to get so many endorphins running in the submissive that it was very much like being drugged, one of its attractions for those who had the tendencies. For those who didn't it was simply painful.

"I'm clear," Anastasia said. "We had barely gotten started. While I would actually appreciate the humiliation, you know how I am, I don't think it would be good for *him*. While I'm pretty sure the Keldara are more or less aware of your interests, I think that having it thrown in his face wouldn't be good."

"Damn, for a miserable little bitch of a sub who's all tied up, you're thinking pretty clearly," Mike said.

"I thought we were out of scene?" Anastasia said.

"Your nipples still got all crinkled up, which was the point," Mike replied. "Okay, let's get you down."

Getting her down took less time than getting everything put away. But when Anastasia started putting her clothes on, Mike stopped her.

"I'm giving you to another man this night," Mike said, roughly. "He will come in here and have his way with you. Don't bother with any of the cutie training him, he's here to take you and you will pleasure him well or you will answer to me."

"Yes, Kildar," Anastasia said, breathing hard.

"Await him on your knees," Mike said.

"Yes, Kildar."

It was the best he could do for giving her a good evening. It would have to do.

Mike left the whip behind but kept the bondage gear on. The hell with it.

Kiril popped to attention as he entered the front room, trying very hard to not look at how Mike was dressed.

"Kiril, I've got a question for you and I need a straight answer," Mike said. "Do the Keldara talk about my sexual . . . adventures?"

"Yes, Kildar," Kiril said after a long pause.

"About my interests?" he asked.

"Yes, Kildar."

"And is it clear that Anastasia *shares* that interest?" Mike asked. "And that I don't, normally, let it interfere in the Rite?"

"Yes, Kildar," Kiril said on surer ground. "Both. That Miss Rakovich . . . shares your interests and that you don't . . . do that sort of thing during the Kardane."

"Well, Miss Rakovich, as you put it, is very put out. She was looking forward to an evening of 'who's a bad harem girl?', given that the Rite had gone so awry, and now she doesn't get to have one. Straight question: Do you lean that way?"

"Straight answer, Kildar: No, sir. I just don't have that much interest in that sort of thing. That is not a . . ."

"I didn't take it that way," Mike said. "I've had more sexual experiences than you've had hot breakfasts. But I've got a problem. Anastasia, who needs a certain amount of being called a little bitch and a slut and a bad girl to keep her sunny disposition and incredible efficiency, is now in the position of *not* getting that when she expected it. So your orders, Kiril, are to get in there and do your very damned best. Don't ask her if anything is okay. If you want to do *anything* to her except hit her in the face or something that is clearly unsafe such as choking or, notably, gagging her, then go in there and do it. Don't ask, don't even call her by name. Just do whatever you want and call her bad names. That's interesting, isn't it?"

"Yes, Kildar," Kiril said, his eyes wide.

"Good," Mike said. "Now I have other things to do and so do you. And I *promise* to treat Gretchen with as much care as I possibly can. But I want this made quietly but *abundantly* clear. The ladies who are involved in the Rite from here on out had better know, up front, that they are going to go through with it and not panic at the last second because their *boyfriend* is satisfying my harem manager when I *can't*. In case you guys hadn't figured it out, part of the whole thing with *you* getting laid is that *I'm* with another girl and Anastasia *isn't* getting laid. The harem girls don't bug her. The Kardane girls bug the ever living *hell* out of her. So while I'm *cooking*, you guys had better get it through your heads that you're my stand-in. Is that *clear*, Keldara?"

"Clear, sir!" Kiril barked.

"Now get in there and do your best," Mike said. "I'm going to just sit here and let your future wife *sweat* a little longer!"

It was about thirty minutes later when Mike yanked open the bedroom door and walked in. He was still wearing the dominance outfit.

Gretchen was sitting on the couch, her knees pulled up, hands wrapped around them, looking very very nervous. She'd also, clearly, been crying.

"Starting all over is out," Mike said, walking over to the stovetop and looking at the pots and pans. "This alfredo is ruined.

Just totally *ruined*. The shrimp is starting to look a bit off, too, and you *really* don't want to go eating an off shrimp . . ."

"Kildar . . ."

"I should be the adult about this," Mike continued, cutting her off and refusing to look at her. "I'm the one with all the experience. I am, in every way, the adult here. Hell, you're barely legal where I come from. But what I am is pissed. Everyone knows I've been pretty down on this whole Kardane thing ever since it started. What happens in the Kardane is legal grounds for *murder* in Texas. I like virgins as much as any guy. But not when they're the fiancées of people who stand behind me with guns. And I was just managing to take out my frustrations about it when I get *doubly* frustrated. So, tell me, Gretchen, where does that leave us?"

"Kildar, I just don't know," Gretchen said, sniffling.

"As far as I'm concerned, it means we're done for the night," Mike said, turning towards her and crossing his arms. "Because right now, if we had sex, the term would be 'grudge fuck,' meaning I'd be taking out my frustrations on you. Which is the last thing you need for your first sexual experience. So you hop in bed and try to sleep and I'll go find one of the *many* other rooms in this place to bunk."

"Kildar, please," Gretchen said, shaking her head. "Don't do that."

"Because it would doubly shame you?" Mike asked, shaking his own. "I had that one trotted out on me one time already. When I suggested that Lydia just spend the night up here. Doubly shamed, once for being 'with' the Kildar alone and twice for being found wanting. Right now, Gretchen, dear, I'm not sure I *care*. I did mention being pissed, right?"

"Kildar, please," Gretchen pleaded. "*Please*, for Kiril if not for me, lie with me this night. You can just take me as you wish. You can rape me as you would. You can do anything to me you wish. Beat me, strike me, take your anger out on me in any way you would care to. I *deserve* it. I admit it. But you *must* take me this night!"

Mike blinked. He knew a sub that wanted to be abused when he saw one and he knew the opposite. This girl wasn't being submissive, she was just willing to do *anything* to "lie with him this night."

The anger blinked off in a second as he realized he'd just stepped into ground that he didn't understand. Lovers' quarrels, those were all well and good. But this was some sort of much larger issue. Cultural, yes, assuredly. But something else, deeper and stranger. He could smell it. Like looking in a placid field and knowing it was mined.

He walked over to the couch and sat down next to the girl, far enough away to not be terribly threatening but close enough that he could really watch her reactions. And while when he arrived she had been nervous, she was now frightened. He was pretty sure that it wasn't her begging to be hit that had changed things, either. Gretchen had the full measure of the Keldara physical bravery; she'd take a punch and keep on going. And likely punch back, harder. Whatever was bothering her was something that slipped in through other doors.

"Why?" he asked, quietly.

"Kildar, I would be doubly shamed," Gretchen said.

"We covered that," Mike said. "Why? Really why?"

"I cannot say," Gretchen replied. "May not say."

Keldara had the same dichotomy of meanings and Mike knew the language well enough at this point to catch it.

"You are not allowed to say," Mike stated.

"Yes."

"Okay," Mike said, nodding. "How about charades?"

"Pardon me?" Gretchen said, blinking in puzzlement.

"Uh, the Alligator game."

That was the local name for charades and while the game was old in the West, like bowling it was just catching on in the former Soviet Union.

"Wave my arms and you guess the words?" Gretchen said, finally smiling again. "No, I think that won't work, either."

"Then give me something," Mike said. "Because I'm starting to realize that I might have been screwing up all along."

"No, you have not," Gretchen said, sliding over to grab his hand. "Kildar, the way that you accomplish the Rite is a joy. I am *sorry* that I was so stupid. I was more than willing, *am* more than willing, to come to your bed. Beyond the Rite, what you have made of it is wonderful. I am sorry."

"Then give me something," Mike said, nodding. "I accept your apology fully and equally apologize for not handling things better. But I need some idea of why you're so terrified of me *not* taking you tonight. Anything."

"Kildar," Gretchen said, swallowing. "I . . . Kildar, the Kardane is a *Rite*. It is . . . It is a Rite of our religion. It is part of our Mysteries."

"Of the Father of All," Mike said, puzzled.

"No," Gretchen said. "Kildar, I'm afraid if I say more it will be worse than if you reject me. Please, Kildar, you must not speak of this, must not ever give any idea that I spoke of it to you. Not even this much."

"*Not* of the Father of All," Mike said, musingly. "I'd bet not of Fir, Lord of War, either. Nor of . . . No, I'd bet Balor falls in there, somewhere . . . It's a woman's Rite."

"Kildar," Gretchen said then sighed. "Your damned books. Others have read them at this point so we realize that our mysteries are not so mysterious."

"It is always the Kildar," Mike said, wonderingly. "And the Kildar is always a foreigner; that's part of the definition. A foreign warrior. Probably a good one. A woman's mystery. Heh. I bet any 'Kildars' that didn't measure up didn't last long, yes?"

"Please," Gretchen said, frowning.

"God *damn*," Mike said, grinning. "That prize bull that Father Makanee asked me to import. Out of stock from America. It was expensive as hell but Genadi agreed that it was important. The local stock was too *inbred*."

Gretchen was now looking at the floor, her hands clenched in front of her.

"I'd wondered how come the first three girls I lay with *all* came up pregnant, apparently by me," Mike said, wonderingly. "It's because they were 'put to stud' when they were at the most likely point to *catch*. I'm the Keldara's damned prize *bull*, aren't I? And all the Kildars before me. Age upon age, century upon century, the best soldiers of each generation, adding to the pool . . . You people have been breeding yourselves as warriors for *centuries*!"

"*And* they have to be good-looking," Gretchen said, sighing. "Pure of form and . . . un-ill. That is, they cannot be of bad blood. What is now called genetic illnesses. If they are, the Keldara avoid breeding with them or, if they cannot, the women kill them, usually with poison, or the children are aborted. The Mothers know of ways to do both. I only found out when I was presented with the Rite."

"Son of a bitch," Mike said, shaking his head. "I just don't know what to say."

"Nothing," Gretchen said, looking up pleadingly. "Please. You will say *nothing*. If the Mothers find out that I said as much as I have . . ."

"Oh, your mysteries are safe with me," Mike said, grinning. "But if I'm to be the local stud stallion, will you squeal like a mare being bred for me?"

"Oh, Kildar," Gretchen said, laughing in relief. She slid over into his arms and tucked her face into his neck. "I will do that if you wish. But what I'd really like . . . I have been a very bad girl. Could you spank me? But not more, please?"

"Oh, I think that can be arranged," Mike said, burying his face in her hair. She'd clearly been stressed, he could smell it on her. But she also had put on a perfume, something like apples. It was just begging for a bite. "But now I wonder if my pattern for this thing is a good idea . . ."

"You mean this?" Gretchen said, sliding off the couch and getting on her knees. She ran her hand across the g-string and started to undo it. "So far, so good. Let's not break tradition."

His member was fully engorged when she pulled the g-string down. Between the anticipation, the frustration and, hell, the tits, he was about as ready to burst as he'd been in years.

Anastasia gave good classes but he wondered where Gretchen had been practicing. She ran her tongue down his dick just once then slid her mouth over it and began to fellate him. And, damn, she was good.

The girl had to have been practicing. You didn't get suction like that naturally; the jaw and mouth muscles weren't normally exercised that way. But she had purely unreal suction and immediately fell into a slow rhythm of up and down stroking, thumb and finger laced around his dick just right, no teeth, just lips, going in time with the mouth, slowly speeding up . . .

Mike normally had pretty good control but this time he couldn't help it; he came in her mouth so hard some of the cum must have squirted all the way down her throat.

Gretchen choked, slightly, but kept sucking, getting every drop. Then she pulled back, swallowed and ran her hand, lightly, down under his balls.

"Is that what you were worried about, Kildar?" she asked, smiling. "Did that take the edge off?"

"What were we fighting about?" Mike asked. "That was . . . exquisite. *You* are exquisite."

Gretchen had brought a refilled glass of champagne over and she took a sip, swished it around her mouth, swallowed and repeated. Then she slid up next to him, still fingering his dick, and tucked back into his shoulder.

"Tell me the truth," she whispered. "Do you really like me that much?"

"Ask yourself this question," Mike said. "I know the girls talk. Did any of them get me off that fast?"

"No," Gretchen admitted in practically a purr. "Can we see if I can get you off as fast other ways?"

"What about you?" Mike asked, sliding his hand up under the dress and tickling at her nipples.

"You always worry about us," Gretchen whispered, breathing in his ear, lightly. "Now you know. We are here *for* us. For ourselves. I need you, now. I need you inside of me. I need you to be in me, filling me and coming in me. I want it inside of me and on me. I want to be fucked, fucked hard. I want you to fuck me and fill me and come on my beautiful breasts. Will you do that for me, Kildar?"

Mike was usually pretty good about recharge time. But that had been some sort of a record. He was stiff as a board.

Normally this was the point where he got really graceful and controlled, making sure that the girl with him either came before he did or, better, at the same time. But he was beyond thought at this point.

He reached up and tore, rather than unbuttoned, the single button that held the dress up and ripped it down, burying his face in those lovely breasts. He dragged the girl off the couch and onto the floor, pushed up the silk skirt, ripped off the lace panties and took her, hard.

And she was ready, not just moist but actively wet, and tight. God she was tight and hot. And they were perfectly sized. "Bigger is better" only goes so far. Mike wasn't Long Dong Silver but he was "upper average." Some of the Keldara girls had, Lord bless them, been a bit too small for him. Not Gretchen. As the fairytale went: Just right. Just tight enough that he *knew* he was filling her, fully.

The hymen ripped without notice by either of them and as he filled her she screamed, not squealing like a mare being covered but *shrieking* in pleasure and agony and fulfillment. Screamed like a tiger princess being taken by her striped mate.

Those beautiful long legs came up and wrapped him in yards of silk and flesh as her fingers dug into his buttocks and she pumped against him, rocking with every thrust and shrieking in joy.

Mike realized, immediately, that she wasn't just having fun, she was coming for all she was worth, one continuous orgasm that had started as soon as he filled her. Making a women really *feel* was his greatest desire, whether pleasure or pain. And Gretchen was unquestionably feeling, wrapped in an ecstasy of Biblical proportions. He turned his brain off, gloriously, for once in sex, just turned it off and pounded as hard as he could. No coy games, no positions or different strokes, no who pleases who, just lost himself in glorious skin and hair and smell and that exalted rapture of every sense filled to overflowing. . . .

Chapter Seven

"Caravanserai Kildar . . . No, I'm sorry, Colonel, the Kildar is *unavailable . . . Colonel, sir, I recognize that, but he really is very very unavailable . . . For some time, sir . . . Sir, I absolutely cannot do that, the Kildar's orders are very specific in this regard . . . Yes, sir, as a matter of fact that is the only person that he said could be put through . . ."*

"Caravanserai Kildar . . . *Say again?* . . . Yes! . . . Yes, sir . . . *Immediately, sir. Yes, Colonel Pierson made that plain but . . . I must warn you, sir . . . Yes, sir . . ."*

Mike opened his eyes at the dawn light, looking at the girl, no the *woman*, by his side. She was lying with her beautiful blonde head on his shoulder an arm and a leg thrown over him possessively.

Both were naked, their clothes scattered across the entire suite. A pair of chaps dangled from the bar. The lovely dress, somewhat the worse for wear, lay on the floor by the door. A single stocking was across one of the sconces on the wall. A white shoe was at the head of the bed.

A quart container of chocolate mousse was on the floor of the kitchen in the middle of one *hell* of a mess. More marks of mousse led a winding trail, via the bar, the couch and the floor in several places to the bathroom.

Mike was, frankly, afraid to look in the bathroom.

He could move pretty easily, which was odd. When he lay in one position for very long he tended to stiffen up, badly. Then he looked at the clock and realized he'd been asleep for *maybe* thirty minutes.

He licked his pinkie and wiped some chocolate mousse off her cheek, wondering if he should warn Kiril *never* to give this girl chocolate, then poked her in the side.

"Hey, you, wake up," Mike said. "The dawn's a-breakin' and birds a-singin' and all that."

Gretchen's eyes flew open, momentarily confused, then she looked up at him.

"Let's do it again," she said, rolling over on top of him and rubbing her breasts on his chest. "And again and again and again . . ." she continued, leaning forward to rub them in his face.

"I . . ." Mike said, only to have whatever he was going to say muffled by a nipple. Oh, hell, he didn't have anything to do today . . .

The phone rang.

That should *not* have happened. The phone did *not* ring during the Rite of Kardane God *damnit*! The phone did *not* just . . .

It rang again.

"Shit!" Mike said, rolling over. If the phone *did* ring . . .

And it was the God-damned secure phone! It went through the communications section. They *knew* better than to put anyone through to him unless it was an absolute emergency. For *him*.

"What?" he shouted as soon as he had the headphone on. Fuck checking the scrambler, he just didn't *care*.

"Mike, it's David," President Cliff said. "I know that I've caught you at a bad time. I apologize. However, when they wouldn't let Colonel Pierson through, I found it important enough to call direct."

"Yes, sir," Mike said to the President of the United States.

Fuck. Gretchen was already hunting for her clothes. By rights, the Rite should be over. He was just going to have to saddle up his horse and take her back and never ever . . .

FUCK!

"I need you to come to D.C. and see some people," the President continued. "Colonel Pierson will call your staff and arrange the details. If there's time, and opportunity, I'd love to have you over to the House."

"I look forward to it," Mike said.

"In fact, why don't you just *plan* on staying here?" the President said. "Why get a hotel room when you've got friends in town? Pierson will arrange a cover."

"Yes, sir," Mike said, trying to clear his head. About thirty seconds before he'd had a gorgeous tit in his mouth. "I'll make sure everything is arranged."

"Great," the President said. "And, again, I'm sorry for having to break in."

"Not a problem, sir," Mike said, watching the naked seventeen-year-old coming out of the bathroom with an armload of clothes. "No problem at all. Put it out of your mind."

"I'm going to D.C. for a day or so," Mike said as he polished off the last of his eggs.

Mike had passed around the word that he'd like most of the staff to be at breakfast for an "informal brief." It wasn't by any stretch the sort of staff the American military would recognize, fitting the conditions rather than making an American "staff" fit them.

Nielson now had the title of "colonel" back, although it was very unofficial. For that matter, Adams was a "master chief" and Vanner a "sergeant." The Georgian government did not *officially* recognize anyone's military status except Mike's, and even that was under a *very* old law that had been "put back on the books." However, both of them had dealt with Georgian officers and NCOs in the last few months and even those carefully briefed on their equivocal status had treated them exactly as they'd have treated NCOs and officers of equivalent rank in the Georgian forces. Actually, with *more* respect. Over the summer, several Georgian National Guard units had trained with the Keldara and come away with their heads on a platter.

The Keldara had built a reputation as first-class mountain infantry and if their "command structure" was a little irregular the Georgian military—faced with an ongoing low-level insurgency in

Ossetia, and Chechen control of hundreds of miles of Georgian territory—was not going to look a gift horse too closely in the mouth. The Keldara had shut down the Chechens in their sector and held the back door. That was good enough.

Mike sprung his surprise at breakfast. It was the best time to get everyone together without putting too much emphasis on things.

"I'd wondered what the call was about," Nielson said. He took a sip of coffee and pursed his lips. "A job?"

"Looks like," Mike replied. "Something delicate and 'right up my alley.'"

"Which means you're gonna get your ass shot off," Adams grunted.

"More or less exactly what I thought," Mike replied with a grunted laugh. "Stasia, you up for a quick trip to D.C.? I don't think I'll be staying long but you can probably squeeze in some shopping."

"I don't have a visa," Anastasia temporized.

"I'll pull some strings." Mike paused and considered her carefully for a moment. "If you don't actually want to go you don't have to. But I promised I'd take you traveling if it came up. This is traveling."

"I would like to go, Kildar," Anastasia said, swallowing nervously. "But I hope you are around most of the time."

"Where we'll be staying I'm sure we can find someone suitable to show you around," Mike said, cryptically. "Trust me. You'll enjoy yourself."

"Thank you," Anastasia said.

What was being cautiously ignored was what Anastasia, in her rare joking moments, referred to as "every harem girl's friend": agoraphobia. Anastasia had gone from her parents' small farm to a harem. There, with the exception of occasional trips to nearby Samarkand, she had spent over ten years immured in virtual purdah; the walls of the harem had become her world. When she was bartered away to Mike in return for future "favors" he had made clear that, from his point of view, she was a free agent. He had also promised not only to introduce her to visitors—she had been more like a mobile piece of furniture in the meeting he had attended at the sheik's home—but to take her traveling. However, she had a very real fear of the chaos to be found outside of controlled surroundings. Intelligent, balanced, speaking seven languages, she could barely bring herself to go to Alerrso, population 3,000, within sight of the caravanserai, practically owned by Mike. Wandering around the District of Columbia on her own would be unlikely.

"Thanks," Mike added. "That works. I think we're done until I see what's up. But I've got the feeling they need, or want, more than me. Make sure the teams are up and ready to go."

"Am I going?" Vanner asked. "I mean on the op?"

"Don't know until we know what it is," Mike said.

"Well, if I do," Vanner added. "Can I get a gun this time?"

"Mike, one more thing," Nielson said after the others had left the table.

"Yah?" Mike asked, contemplating how much he was *not* looking forward to this trip.

"I finally tracked down a humint guy," the colonel said. "Sorry it took so long."

Mike pulled his mind back from D.C. for a second and considered that. Earlier in the year, as it became obvious that he had to think about more than just the Chechen threat, he'd asked Nielson to start looking around for a "human intelligence"—humint—operator. Right now, other than picking a few things up in the village and using Katya for insertions, they really didn't have a humint side at all. And they needed one. They should have built a network among the Chechens long before this; the fact that they didn't have one had been eating at him. And, frankly, he'd been willing to think "big" on the humint side, depending on money. So far he, personally, had been in ops ranging from the U.S. to Siberia and most places in between. He wasn't sure he could create an "intelligence agency," but he was willing to give it a very serious shot.

"Go," Mike replied.

"Well, I thought it would be easy," Nielson said, grimacing. "Did you know that during the Clinton Administration the humint side in the Agency got cut by right on the order of ninety percent?"

"No," Mike said with a grimace. "But it doesn't surprise me. Al Gore's 'reinventing government.' They cut a *bunch* of government employees, but they all seemed to come out of DOD and intel. I swear, every damned day I find another reason to lay 9/11 at Clinton and his ilk's feet."

"Anyway, with that many people on the street I figured I could find somebody *good* pretty quick," Nielson said. "Until recently, though, no such luck. Most of them have put up the cloak and dagger and weren't willing to go out in the cold again for *any* money. And some that were . . . well, let's just say that some of the people that got cut needed to be."

"Nature of any bureaucracy," Mike replied with a grin. "Let's not get big enough to be called a bureaucracy."

"But I finally found one guy," Nielson said. "Or, rather, he found me. Only name I've got is Jay. At least, that's the name that anybody knows. First I got sent an encryption code for e-mail then an e-mail out of the blue. He had heard I was looking, is sort of interested and had checked *us* out before calling."

"Wonder what he found out?" Mike asked.

"I dunno," the colonel said with a grimace. "He's . . . pretty close to the vest."

"Go figure."

"I checked *him* out, though, as well," Nielson continued. "As well as I could. As I said, maybe somewhere in Langley there's a file that has his real name on it. But he's a known player under 'Jay.' Very well known."

"That could be bad," Mike said with a frown.

"If he ever used the same name twice, except with higher, it might be," Nielson admitted. "But the guys I contacted that knew him, or knew of him . . . Well, among other things, I couldn't get a fixed description. He was, variously, blonde to black hair, every eye color you could name, pudgy to skinny as a rail, no chin, big chin . . . You get the picture. And these are people who have met him in person. Ever heard about the CIA switching around the men's rooms and women's rooms sign in the KGB headquarters?"

"No, but it sounds like a pretty good laugh," Mike said, smiling.

"Yeah, well, he had a piece of that," the colonel said, shaking his head. "In the intel community, he's what spec ops would think of as a Son-Tay Raider."

The Son-Tay raid was one of the most magnificent failures in history. It was a large-scale raid, very late in the Vietnam War, intended to recapture a large number of prisoners of war from the

North Vietnamese. It had been meticulously planned, expertly per-
sonneled and perfectly performed. The only problem being that
when the raiders reached the objective, the prisoners had already
been moved. They, nonetheless, slaughtered the guards with precision and "stacked them up like cord-wood."

Son-Tay Raiders were legends in the spec-ops community. The
failure had been at a much higher pay grade than anyone on the
op. They had performed a difficult mission flawlessly.

"That good," Mike said. "Okay, if the mountain's not going to
come to Mohammed . . ."

"He said he can meet anywhere in the D.C. area with at least a
day's notice," Nielson said, raising an eyebrow.

"Get ahold of him," Mike replied. "Arrange a meet."

"Will do," Nielson said, standing up. "If that is all, Kildar? I have
a previously scheduled meeting with Flopsy."

"Get out of here, you old goat," Mike replied with a grin. "But
keep me updated."

"Will do."

"Captain Hardesty," Mike said, walking up to the door of the
Gulfstream.

"Mr. Jenkins," the pilot said. "I swore the last trip was going to
be the last, you know."

Mike regularly chartered with Chatham Aviation, a small but
select group out of England. And about half the time there were . . .
issues. The first time he'd flown with Hardesty, a former RAF Tornado pilot, he had had to change names, twice, turned up with
quite a bit of blood on him at one point and casually instructed the
pilot, during a trip to Paris, France, that he might want to "deploy
the plane a bit away from Paris, probably southeast given the
winds . . ." a day before it was revealed a nuclear weapon had
almost gone off in the city.

But the last trip had really beat all. That time "Mr. Jenkins" had
requested a "somewhat larger jet . . . about enough to handle a
company of infantry . . ." and had turned up with forty heavily
armed retainers and a string of what could only be described as
"ladies of the evening" in tow. The armaments, ranging from pistols to rocket launchers, had been casually but rapidly stowed in
the cargo compartment and the group boarded somewhat hastily.

As if, for example, they were being chased. And on takeoff Hardesty had been pretty sure he'd caught a tracer flying by his windscreen. He'd seen a few in his time. But whoever was, possibly, shooting was pretty bad because they'd managed to miss an entire 737.

However, things had gone from bad to worse during a petrol stop in England. The English government had grounded his aircraft pending "inspection," an inspection he was not looking forward to given the contents of the cargo hold, then several very senior members of the British government had boarded. Whatever was going on, however, had been resolved and they eventually got on their way. He'd sweated American customs but, as it turned out, the "inspection" on arrival in the U.S. had been less than cursory. Given that he had a hold full of weapons and ammunition, what was a clearly a tactical team, a bunch of hookers and *none* of them had proper visas . . . Obviously the BCIS was slipping.

The experience had not been the happiest of his life. And he was not interested in a repeat.

That being said, generally flying businessmen around was . . . unsatisfying. Oh, it paid well enough, but it was a bit like being an aerial bus driver. Not quite like flying a Tornado balls to the wall down a Balkans valley filled with flak.

Flying "Mr. Jenkins" around was rarely boring. Bit too exciting at times, but rarely boring.

"No issues this time," Mike said, grinning and slipping by him to board the aircraft. "Cross my heart. Just a quick trip to D.C. then back."

"And Miss Rakovich," Hardesty said, not deigning to comment. "Beautiful as always."

"I did not think you'd remember me," Anastasia said, dimpling prettily and nodding as she boarded. Her only previous flight had been on either this Gulfstream or one identical to it, with Hardesty piloting.

"I could never forget a lady so beautiful in both face and spirit," Hardesty replied. "If we're all loaded?" he continued, checking where the Keldara had been putting the bags in what he referred to as the "boot."

"Think so," Mike replied. "Only two rocket launchers and hardly any explosives at all this time."

"You are pleased to jest," the pilot said. "I've got a flightplan filed for D.C. Winds may be against us over the Atlantic but otherwise smooth. Flight time of about twenty hours, mind."

"Works," Mike said. "I'm gonna flake out most of the trip."

"And Miss Rakovich," Hardesty added. "I will endeavor for a smooth takeoff and climb-out."

"Thank you," Anastasia said, buckling herself in. She had rarely flown and did not enjoy the experience. Especially any "unexpected" movement.

"Off we go again," Mike said, taking her hand as the engines started.

"At least this time I've got *some* idea what is going on," Anastasia said. "And are we going to 'play' again?" she continued, coyly.

"Oh, a bit more than the last time," Mike said, smiling but not looking at her. "Definitely. I'm not sure a blow job counts for the Mile-High Club. I want my stamp."

Anastasia continued to hold his hand as the plane taxied to the runway and then took off, at which point her hand clamped like a vise. True to his word, Hardesty was taking it smooth and easy. A Gulfstream, as lightly loaded as this one, could point darned near straight up and Hardesty *loved* to fly at the edge of the envelope. But he also was both professional and considerate. If Mike, who apparently didn't care, was the only one on board they'd have taken off like a fighter climbing out of a bombing run. With Miss Rakovich on board, he took it easy.

Anastasia, nonetheless, kept her eyes tightly closed and hand clamped until they were at altitude and flying smoothly. Then she took a breath, opened her eyes and released her death grip.

"You really don't *have* to travel with me, if you hate it that much," Mike said.

"I want to," Anastasia said, shrugging. "I want to *see*. But I fear as well. I won't say I'll get over it but I'm not willing to let the fear stop me."

"Oorah," Mike said, quietly, smiling at her. "Take not counsel of your fears."

"Yes," Anastasia said. "And on that score . . . I want to talk to you about . . . Gretchen."

"Oh, Christ," Mike said. "I thought the harem manager wasn't supposed to get jealous."

"I am not jealous," Anastasia said, evenly. "But . . . You're acting different. I can tell something happened. Beyond the slight . . . issues that occurred in the middle of your encounter. *I* have noticed. I'm not sure how many others."

"It was the chocolate mousse that gave it away, wasn't it," Mike said. "I'd never waste chocolate mousse unless I really cared, right?"

"How badly are you affected?" Anastasia said, refusing to take the bait.

"Oh . . . pretty badly," Mike admitted. "Pretty damned badly. Pretty fucking badly. Pretty much head over heels in love with one of my team members' fiancée."

"I was afraid of that," Anastasia said. "How are you going to handle that?"

"Not much choice, really," Mike said. "I just go on. Kiril and Gretchen get married. They have one of my kids. I try very hard not to treat her, him or it any differently than any three other Keldara. I just . . . try to forget."

"You won't," Anastasia said. "There are other . . . ways."

"Sure," Mike said. "I could ask the Fathers to dissolve the bonding. I could throw my Kildar weight around and have her. No question. Then I'd stomp all over their damned culture and piss off a bunch of men with guns, one in particular. Kiril is as smitten by her as I am, you know. I, frankly, don't know where Gretchen stands."

"I didn't have time to investigate that myself," Anastasia said. "I suppose we'll find out when we get back. There is . . . another way. David and Bathsheba, yes?"

King David was best known for creating the first rule of gunfights, "always bring a gun," by defeating Goliath with a range weapon while poor Goliath was armed only with an over-large knife. But he was very nearly as famous for falling in love, more like lust, with one of his soldiers' wives, Bathsheba, then sending said soldier, one Uriah, to the front lines so he'd get offed. While bringing a gun to a gunfight was the sort of thing Mike would *always* do if he could, the latter . . .

"Fuck that," Mike said, blanching. "No fucking way. I'd rather piss the Keldara off honestly than dishonestly. They'd see right through that. No, I need to just keep keeping on. I'll get over it."

"Seeing Gretchen day after day, year by year?" Anastasia asked.

"Hey, she'll get old," Mike said, smiling with only his mouth, his eyes closed and his jaw flexed. "Probably gain weight. Tits will sag. I'll get past it. In time." He closed his eyes and shook his head. "Say about a century."

"Yes," Anastasia said, her hand creeping downward. "I'm sure you will. But if it happens at all, I know only one thing to speed it."

Mike tried not to shake his head in chagrin. He truly *was* in love. Probably for the first time in his life. It was true that that sort of thing could hit like a lightning bolt. But it was, also, apparently true that a stiff prick has no conscience.

Chapter Eight

"Where is my daughter?" Arensky said as the van drew to a stop.

"Nearby." The man who had been "handling" him had not been introduced and had not offered a name. He just told Arensky where to go, or more often simply grunted and pointed. "And if you'd like us to send you some pieces it can be arranged. Or pictures of her being raped by a dozen men. Out. Into the building. Don't look around. Don't make eye contact if anyone is nearby. Just get out and go in the door."

Arensky's face tightened but he did as instructed, picking up the briefcase containing the "samples" and exiting the van. The "building" was shabby, made of roughly dressed stone with a slate roof and small, wooden-shuttered, windows. The interior was dark since the shutters were closed. There was a trickle of light coming in from around the shutters and it took his eyes a moment to adjust. When they did his face tightened even more.

"Ah, Dr. Arensky, come in."

"Sergei," Arensky replied, walking to the table in the center of the room and setting down the case. There was the table with a couple of rickety chairs, two metal beds without mattresses and a gas camping stove. Other than that the room was bare. "Where is my daughter?"

"In a nearby town," Sergei said, calmly. "She is unharmed, guarded by my men, tended to, I might add, by local women. Frightened, but I have assured her that as long as you cooperate she will remain unharmed. And I so assure you. I will arrange for you to talk to her, briefly, very soon. Not in person, you understand. We have, now, to wait. You will wait here. She will wait there. When the transfer is completed she will be moved to where you are going."

"So she can be used against me by your employers," Arensky spat. He started to take off his coat but refrained; the room was colder, it seemed, than the out-of-doors. Much colder than the stuffy van.

"My contractors, yes," the man said.

"Sergei, this is madness," Arensky said, again, with desperate resignation. "What is in there . . ." he added, pointing to the case, "that is death as you cannot possibly imagine. If that gets out, if these Islamic black-asses *use* it, it is the end of the world. Not only their enemies will die, you will die, everyone you know will die. The fucking *world* will die."

"Everyone dies," Sergei said, standing up from the chair. "Everyone dies eventually. Societies die. Species die. The weak make way for the fit. If it is mankind's time to die, then die it will. Besides," he added with a grin, "I've been inoculated. And so have all of my men."

"Inoculation doesn't *work* with this," Arensky said, slumping into one of the chairs. "Nothing does. And it *lingers*."

"For what I am being paid for this job, I can retire to a remote island staffed entirely by willing women," Sergei replied, shrugging. "I can restart the human race single-handed. Every man's fantasy, yes? Gregor will see to your needs," he added as the morose guard entered the room. "And in time, if you're very good, you can hear that your daughter is well."

"Madness."

Mike had to admit that he was ready to get out of Georgia. He enjoyed the various perks of being "Kildar" but he also missed modern civilization. He'd been "deployed," as he thought of it, for over a year. It was time to get back to the World.

But as he considered the traffic outside the window he had to admit there were more benefits to being in Georgia than he'd remembered. Tbilisi could get some traffic jams, but nothing like D.C. And he was going to have to put up with all that protocol bullshit and probably ritual dick-beating.

The car had been waiting for them at the airport, a discreet government luxury four-door, like a thousand others in the city. A "ride-along" had met them at the exit from security, handled the bags and whisked them to the car.

There wasn't anything they could do about the traffic, though.

"Anastasia, honey," Mike said, looking at his watch. "I'm running on short time. I've got a meeting at the Pentagon in about an hour. Given the traffic . . ."

"Should you go directly there?" Anastasia asked. "I will be fine."

Mike suspected that was true. A person doesn't get dropped off at the White House and then just get left. *Somebody* would make sure she went where she was supposed to. If she looked as if she was wandering, at the very least the Secret Service was going to step in. But that was the *last* thing he wanted to happen.

"No, I'm going to the House," Mike said. "I'll make sure you're settled. But I'm going to have to do that as quickly as possible and then scoot."

He knocked on the divider, not knowing quite which control worked it, then leaned over the seats.

"Okay, I need some cards laid down," Mike said. "Secret Service or just drivers?"

"DOD secure transport," the rider said.

Fuck. Mike wasn't sure what that meant.

"I know diddly about your group," Mike said. "But I've got a problem and it's a secure issue . . ."

"Your cover is Mr. Michael Ford," the rider said. "A businessman currently working a start-up business in Georgia and a former fundraiser for President Cliff. Also a personal friend from long back, something about baseball." He reached back and handed Mike a folder. "I was wondering when you were going to ask."

Mike flipped through the documents and nodded.

"Thanks," he said. "My brief on this was lousy."

"You're welcome, Mr. Ford," the rider said. "We're going to be driving you to your next destination. Given the traffic, you're on short time for the meet at the White House. I'll ensure that Miss Rakovich has an escort but I'd suggest that you cut any conversation at the House as short as possible. And for your general comfort level, I'm former CAG, the driver is a Green Beanie and from your utter cluelessness and tan I'd say either SEAL or Recon."

"Glad to finally be back in the warm," Mike said, chuckling as the divider went back up.

They rolled up to a side entrance to the White House and the rider got out to open Mike's door.

"Your luggage will be taken care of Mr. Ford," the former Delta said. "You've just got time to shower and change if you need to."

"Love to," Mike said. "Even a Gulfstream gets kinda rank after a twenty-hour flight."

Mike took Anastasia's arm and led her to the door where he was greeted by an aide and two uniformed Secret Service. He did the ritual dump of keys and spare change then walked through the scanner followed by Anastasia. He'd left all his knives and guns behind, much to his chagrin.

The aide nodded to them as soon as they were through the security screen.

"Mr. Ford," the man said, smiling and shaking Mike's hand. "Miss Rakovich? I'm Thomas Johnson. I understand you are in a hurry so I'll show you to your rooms. I'm aware that Mr. Ford has a priority meeting but the First Lady would like to talk to you for a moment before you leave."

"Of course," Mike said. "I'd love a shower, though."

"Not a problem, sir," the man said. "We installed plumbing back in the early 1900s."

Mike was surprised at the size of the room. He'd only ever stayed in Camp David which was cramped enough, but this room wasn't much bigger than one of the harem girls' rooms at the caravanserai.

But then he had to think that the White House was built back in the days when large rooms weren't made unless they were ballrooms. In summer, big rooms were not much cooler than small and in winter they were impossible to heat. Ballrooms were kept warm in the "season" as much by dancing bodies as by the roaring fires.

The service, though, was first rate. Somehow, the White House staff had managed to get their bags up to their room, unpacked, everything put in drawers or hung up and toiletries in the bathroom, before they'd gotten to the room. And probably every bit of it had been swept by the Service for threats.

"Honey," Mike said, shaking his head, "you need to be taking notes."

"I am," Anastasia said, clearly just as impressed. "I wonder if I can hire anyone away."

"I'm getting in the shower," Mike said, stripping off the clothes he'd been wearing since yesterday.

"I'll do your back if you'll do mine," Anastasia said, unzipping her dress.

"I'm not sure that's a good idea," Mike said. "But what the hell. Pierson can wait."

"It's not Colonel Pierson I'm worried about," Anastasia said. "You're supposed to meet the First Lady."

"*We* are going to meet the First Lady," Mike said. "So do your makeup *fast*."

The shower had, alas, involved a minimum of grab-ass and Anastasia *could* dress and put on makeup fast when she had to.

So in no more than thirty minutes they were back out of their room, Mike in a suit and carrying a briefcase while Anastasia had changed into a different dress, this one a light blonde color just a shade darker than her hair.

"This way, sir, ma'am," Johnson said. "The First Lady is in the Green Room."

"Amanda," Mike said when they walked in the room.

The Green Drawing Room was originally used by Thomas Jefferson as a small intimate dining room. Sometime in the early 1800s it was restructured and refurbished into a parlor for relaxed, personal meetings and renamed the Green Drawing Room by John Quincy Adams. With walls lined by green silk, beautiful paintings and an Italian marble fireplace, it was one of the most favored rooms of many of the First Ladies over the years.

"Michael," the First Lady said, smiling and shaking his hand then giving him a hug. "It's so good to have you in the House at last. You really shouldn't stay away so much."

"It's Washington, ma'am," Mike said, shaking his head. "I really shouldn't come here at all."

"Nonsense," Amanda said. "And this must be Miss Rakovich."

"Ma'am," Anastasia said, shaking the First Lady's hand. "It is a pleasure to meet you."

"And you," the First Lady said. "I know that Michael has to go to an appointment and I won't keep him longer. But you are my guest and I'd like to talk for a bit if you don't mind. I know you've been flying for a while so if you'd prefer to rest . . ."

"I'd love to sit and chat, ma'am," Anastasia said, smiling. "I got some sleep on the plane. Quite a lot, actually."

"Then, Michael, I look forward to seeing you when you get back," the First Lady said.

"Yes, ma'am," Mike said, wondering just how bad this was going to be. The First Lady grilling his harem manager could be very bad indeed. "I look forward to it as well."

"Please," the First Lady said, gesturing for Anastasia to sit in one of the antique chairs.

"Yes, ma'am," Anastasia said, easily. The door opened and a small, thin black lady came in with a tea service.

"I made the assumption that tea would be acceptable," the First Lady said, nodding at the maid in thanks and pouring for both of them.

"Yes, ma'am," Anastasia said.

"Please call me Amanda," the First Lady said, smiling. "Ma'am and First Lady grow tiresome quickly and I consider Michael a friend. Sugar?"

"Then could you call me Anastasia?" Anastasia said. "Or even Stasia if you wish. Two lumps."

"Stasia it shall be," the First Lady said, proffering the cup. "Russian? Or perhaps Ukraine?"

"Russian, Amanda," Anastasia said. "But I hardly remember it. I left when I was twelve."

"And then?" the First Lady said, sipping her tea.

"Uzbekistan," Anastasia said, picking up her own.

"You waited until I took the first sip," the First Lady said, smiling. "Where did you train?"

Anastasia paused and then set down her cup.

"In a hareem," she replied. "I was married, an arranged marriage, to a sheik in Uzbekistan at the age of twelve."

She had expected at least mild shock. The First Lady just nodded and took another sip.

"Not *exactly* what I'd expected, but close," she said. "I would say something like 'I'm sorry' but that doesn't quite cover it, does it?"

"It's not really that bad," Anastasia admitted, picking up her tea again. "I was raised on a small and very poor farm. Given the conditions, then, and my looks, I would probably have ended up as a prostitute if I hadn't been noticed by one of the sheik's scouts."

"But far outside my own experience, and therefore fascinating," the First Lady said. "For one thing I had not expected that harems trained quite so precisely in manners."

"I was, among other things, Sheik Otryad's hareem manager," Anastasia said. "I was given advanced training. But there is a good bit of what can be called 'manners' to being in a well-run hareem. It is not all about . . . that. It is about creating a quiet and comfortable place for the sheik to retreat to."

"Now *that* I can understand," the First Lady said. "One reason that it's wise for presidents to have a really *good* spouse is to create that refuge."

"Yes, for Presidents that would be *vital*," Anastasia said, nodding vigorously. "The pressures of such a position are very nearly killing. They need that one place where there is no pressure, where they know that they are accepted just as they are. That is the true purpose of the hareem and I have the *hardest* time *explaining* that to anyone. It sometimes drives me nearly to distraction, yes?"

"I believe I touched a nerve there, Stasia, sorry," the First Lady said, grinning. "But I think you are good for Michael as well. He has some of the same problems, I think."

"Yes, he does," Anastasia said, calming. "In a way he has no one that tells him what to do but there are so many politics, yes? He has to keep his Keldara on his side. He must deal with the Georgians and the Americans and the Russians, friend to all but never so close that any own him. I try to give him that quiet place. But even there he puts so many pressures on *himself* sometimes I want to tear my hair out. He is so . . . *American*."

"That he is," the First Lady said.

"I am sorry to be so strong," Anastasia said, shaking her head. "I am not normally like this."

"I tend to cause people to talk," the First Lady said. "It is one of my talents. Very useful in politics, I might add."

"Where is your place?" Anastasia asked. "Where do you go for comfort?"

"Oh, books," the First Lady replied. "And David. We are very good for each other. And I think you are good for Michael. Michael *Ford* this time. It's always so cloak-and-dagger."

"I think that the idea is that if his normal name ever comes up in connection with something, no one will connect it to the White House."

"That is to be hoped," the First Lady said. "But I've wanted him to come to the House for some time. We had him at Camp David, of course, but he's never made it to the House. Of course, officially, I don't know *why* he was at Camp David. Or why my husband thinks that he walks on water. But it was rather easy to determine, given the timing."

"I would not know," Anastasia said. "I have only known him as the Kildar. The years before . . . ? I know he is American. I surmise, from his friendship with Master Chief Adams, that he was in the Navy commandoes, the SEALs. Other than that I know very little. I know not to ask."

"Smart girl," the First Lady said, leaning forward and patting her on the leg.

"And that explains," Anastasia said, smiling.

"Yes, it does," the First Lady said. "That was why I made sure someone passed the word that I wanted to meet Michael's 'assistant.' But I'll say that that is no longer the reason. I like you, Stasia. I like you very much. *Mi casa es su casa* as we say in Texas."

"*Gracias, Señora,*" Anastasia replied, smiling. "*Usted es bien amable.*"

"*¿Usted habla español?*" the First Lady said, smiling back.

"*Sí,*" Anastasia said. "*Dominé en español. También Deutsche, Russkiya, Arabi, Français y Uzbek.*"

"And English," the First Lady said.

Anastasia just shrugged and held up one hand, palm up.

"I'm glad we've met," the First Lady said. "David holds him in such high esteem, I felt it was vital that he, and you, come to visit."

"I'm just his assistant," Anastasia pointed out.

"If you were just his assistant, Stasia, the protocol recommendation would have suggested two rooms," the First Lady said. "But I am glad to meet you. I wanted to know who the woman was in his life." The First Lady paused then smiled. "Or should that be 'women'?"

"Oh, most definitely 'women,'" Anastasia replied. "But for the purposes that you mean, the woman that he looks to for most such things, that would be me."

"There are arrangements into which, I have learned, it is unwise to pry," the First Lady said, smiling disarmingly. "Has coming out of the harem been difficult? Do you find it hard to deal with cities and people?"

"Very," Anastasia admitted. "I can attend a formal function with ease. But put me on the street of even a small town, much less a city, totally on my own and I am at a loss. I am to do shopping while we are here. The Kildar has given me a credit card with . . . too much money available on it. What I did not wish to tell him is . . . I have never used a credit card except online. I can barely haggle with the merchants in the small town near where we live. It is all very confusing. A new world. One I want to enter, to enjoy, to understand, but, yes, it is hard. Even frightening."

"When were you planning on going shopping?" the First Lady said.

"I'd hoped to do so this afternoon," Anastasia said. "I had hoped that Michael would be back but he has another appointment this afternoon, after his meeting. We are definitely committed to spending the night, but given the urgency with which he was summoned, I doubt we will have more time. So I think I'll need to go out on my own."

"Not to be borne," the First Lady said, firmly. "Amelia Weston."

"Pardon me?" Anastasia said.

"Even if Michael was available, men rarely enjoy shopping," the First Lady said. "And they're *never* good at it unless they are gay. So. Amelia Weston is the wife of General Weston, commander of the Military District of Washington. Which should mean, frankly, that she is the compleat bitch. But she's not, she's a very gracious lady of the old Southern school. Hard as nails, mind you, but very gracious as long as no one is trying to stick a knife in her or General Weston's back. I will call her, we've become friends, and ask her to take another friend shopping. She knows just where to go."

"Thank you, ma . . . Amanda," Anastasia said, blinking.

"You are *most* welcome, Stasia."

Chapter Nine

"Mr. Jenkins?" the major said as Mike got out. Mike was carrying the only the briefcase he'd ever owned. He kept it just for such occasions. The calf-leather case had come from the same haberdasher's as the suit and said "I'm a rich and powerful asshole" in full operatic splendor.

"What day is it?" Mike asked, pulling out his passports, checking them to find the right one and handing it to the MP.

The MP smiled slightly as he checked the name against his roster and nodded as he checked it off.

"You're cleared, Mr. 'Jenkins,'" the MP said, handing over a visitor's badge with his name and a very bad picture already on it.

"Major Pauley," the officer said, sticking out his hand.

"I read it on your nametag," Mike said, shaking his hand. "Sorry I'm so grumpy; I hate visiting this place."

"You ought to try working here," the major said. "You don't know what hate is until you've been stuck here for a couple of years. But we'll try to make you feel at home. This way, sir."

One of the reasons Mike hated the Pentagon was that it was one of the few buildings that could cause him to lose his spatial awareness. It was like the place was some sort of intentional puzzle, designed to get people lost. And it happened to him again; they'd only been walking the corridors—which were literally infinite if you considered they were concentric pentagons—for five minutes and he was totally lost.

Finally, though, they arrived at another MP post, the fourth they'd had to clear, beyond which was a small door marked "Office of Special Operations Liaison."

Mike had never actually visited the office that "controlled" him, to the extent that he was controlled at all. He'd spoken to various officers besides Pierson over the years, but he'd only ever *met* Pierson.

He wasn't sure what he'd been expecting, but this wasn't it. The main room was filled with cubicles, most of them overflowing with papers, most of which had "Top Secret" cover sheets, and all manned by officers. With the exception of the MPs outside and a couple of very senior NCOs who appeared to be pushing even more paper than the officers, the place was staffed with nothing but O types, and major was the lowest rank Mike saw.

To a former petty officer it was a wonder the place worked at all.

Pauley led him past the ranks of cubicles to the far end of the room where there were three offices and a small conference room. Mike wondered how they had staff meetings; there was no way to fit everyone in this room. He also wondered how secure the damned area was; there were none of the trappings of secure rooms about either the office or this conference room. It appeared to be very standard construction. He'd seen more secure rooms in a battalion headquarters.

Mike sat down at the conference table and cooled his heels for a couple of minutes, internally grousing. Right about now . . . he'd probably be taking one of the girls to bed come to think of it. Depending on what time it was in . . . Yep.

"Sorry to make you wait, Mike," Pierson said, opening the door and sticking his head in. "Wander with me?"

"Sure," Mike said, getting up and following Pierson back down the line of cubicles.

"I'd have met you outside but it's the usual clusterfuck," Pierson said. "We just got tasked with briefing the OMB on SOCOM budgeting and procurement. Since that's as far out of our usual line as you can get, we're all hopping around like fleas on a skillet. And then we got *this* dropped in our laps."

"I guess I get to wait to find out what *this* is?" Mike said.

"Yep," Pierson said, grinning as he turned into the main corridor.

They walked down the corridor a short distance and turned inward, as far as Mike could tell.

"The deal around here used to be 'who's closer to the E-ring?'" Pierson said, making another couple of turns. "These days, being *on* the E-ring makes you important. But after that it's 'how deep are you?' Which means, how close are you to the Tank and the other really secure rooms?"

"So, how deep are we?" Mike asked, raising an eyebrow.

"In just a second," Pierson said as they made their way through another checkpoint and entered a stairwell, "we're going to be about as deep as you can get. Of course, it's in bullshit. But even deep enough bullshit has an allure."

"I can tell I'm going to love the fuck out of this," Mike said. "Aren't I?"

"Absolutely," Pierson said, grinning evilly.

The stairs opened onto a very short corridor and *another* damned checkpoint at which Mike had to fish out his, totally false, passport in addition to his visitor's pass. But on the other side of the checkpoint they entered a shield room. It was the real deal, full Faraday cage, soundproofed, no electronics in or out, with hard-eyed guards with wands to ensure same.

Three men were already waiting in the room and Mike could tell that, yes, he was going to love the fuck out of this mission. All three were in suits, but unlike Mike they wore theirs as if they were daily clothing. Including the guy who looked like a tennis pro that Mike pegged as Agency. And not the covert-ops side, this guy was "old agency," the group that gave the OSS the moniker "Oh, So Social." Northeastern liberal WASP, one each. Bred with a silver spoon in his mouth, which was why he had to keep his teeth clamped all the time. The other two were pure "GS": civil servants. They could have been anything from Agency to NSA to . . . Office of Management and Budget. A bureaucrat was a bureaucrat was a bureaucrat.

"Mr. Jenkins," Pierson said, waving at Mike.

"Pleasure to meet you, Mr. Jenkins," one of the bureaucrats said. "I'm Mr. Mannly."

"Pleasure to meet you," Mike said, shaking the man's hand perfunctorily and sitting down.

"Mr. Jenkins," Bureaucrat Two said, sliding a folder across the table. "We have detected what could be called a business opportunity."

"I don't work just for money, guys," Mike said, darkly. "And I have plenty. So let's cut the horseshit fast or I'll just go home. Got it?"

"Got it," Mr. Mannly said, his forehead wrinkling. "The situation involves the Pankisi Gorge . . ."

"I told the Russian military attaché," Mike replied, starting to stand up, "and I'll tell you. The Pankisi is Georgia and Russia's problem, not mine. See you—"

"Sit, Mike," Pierson said, waving at the chair. "Seriously. Listen."

"Shit," Mike said, sitting back down. "I do *not* want to take the Keldara into the Pankisi. They're not ready by a long shot."

"Understood," the colonel replied. "But listen anyway."

"This is all your fault, anyway," Pierson said. "You remember that Russian you picked up just before the Balkans op?"

"Mikhail or something," Mike said, frowning. "What did we ever do with him?"

"I love your prisoner management technique," Tennis Pro said, shaking his head. "While you were gone some of your people called Colonel Pierson and asked him what to do with the guy. He had no earthly idea, so he called us. We got him to the Russians, who bled him dry and got everybody on the trail of this mission. Boss?" he added, looking at Mannly.

"This is a picture of Dr. Tolegen Arensky," Mr. "Mannly" said, sliding a pic across the table. It had been taken from a distance with a telephoto by the looks, maybe digitally enhanced. Dr. Arensky wasn't much to look at, short, dark, balding, graying and fat with long sideburns that made him look vaguely like a hobbit trying to look like Elvis. "Dr. Arensky is a Russian scientist who recently dropped off the radar screen. We thought, at first, that the Russians had just taken him fully 'black,' but then sources indicated that they were looking for him as well. About the same time, technical means picked up the Chechens talking about a weapon that would win the war for them in one blow. The intercept actually used the word 'worldwide jihad.'"

"That's a phrase," Mike pointed out. "Even in Arabic."

"So you're an Arabic expert?" Tennis Pro asked.

"I can hum the tune and dance a few steps," Mike replied. "What does this have to do with me? And why the Pankisi, which is a bitch and half of an area. I mean just the environmental conditions suck, not to mention the fact that it's crawling with badguys with guns."

"We've been able to build *some* humint contacts among the senior mujahideen," Tennis Pro said in a pure Cambridge accent. "It hasn't been easy, but we get information, finally. The information that we got is that Dr. Arensky is providing the Chechens with three backpack nukes in exchange for sixty million euros in cash, bearer bonds and gems."

"Woohooo," Mike said, whistling. He suspected that "Tennis Pro" was better than he looked; he clearly was part of the team managing the Al Qaeda penetration. "That's an ugly scenario. But backpack nukes . . . aren't exactly backpack. Not the Russian ones. They're in a damned big container, if I remember correctly. Two containers."

"Not anymore," Mannly sighed, sliding a picture across the table. It was of a small tubular device with a ruler for scale. "That's what we're looking at. Not huge yield, about ten kilotons, but . . ."

"But that's the same size as Hiroshima," Pierson pointed out. "And the damn things are easy to smuggle."

"So this Russian scientist is selling the *Chechens* nukes?" Mike said, incredulously. "And the go-betweens are in the Russian mob? Last but not least: Sixty mil isn't chump change to the muj. I smell a rat. Is it plausible?"

"The Chechens didn't have that kind of money," Bureaucrat Two said. "So they have contacted senior Al Qaeda to try to raise the money. They have finally done so and the trade is scheduled for a month from now. In the Pankisi, which is their most secure area."

Okay, that placed Bureaucrat Two. Some of the discussion had to have been electronic and he was from the National Security Agency, the group that handled electronic intercepts and analysis. It had once been so secret it was called "No Such Agency" but had come a bit more out of the closet in the last couple of decades. They still were very low profile, but very very good.

"The Georgians can't or won't get troops into the area," Mr. "Mannly" said. "And they freak out if Russian troops violate their border."

"Can't," Mike said, definitely. "They've tried and gotten handed their ass every time. And I think Svasikili would probably turn a blind eye to Spetznaz over this. Spetz *might* be able to penetrate."

"They won't," Pierson said, unhappily. "We asked. At the highest level. Nor will they let *us* take care of it."

"Did you ask about this thing in particular?" Mike asked, frowning. "Svasikili is not, in my experience, that much of an asshole."

"No, just to let us quietly send some spec ops into the Pankisi," Mannly said. "Or let the Russians go in. We were willing to let the Georgians have all the credit if it worked and we'd go black if it went south."

Which made "Mannly" the CIA case officer managing the investigation. There were various covert-ops groups that "Mannly" could use for this mission, but clearly they'd been ruled out. Probably at the level of the White House. The problem would be inserting and extracting them without the Georgians even knowing they were there. Things were too touchy in the area to piss off the Georgians. Among other things, they had gotten close to the U.S. over the Russians for various reasons. And what with one thing and another, nobody wanted to drive them back. Whether it would be worth it over nukes was a question much higher than Mike's pay grade.

"And they didn't bite," Mr. "Mannly" said. "But we just happen to have the precise rendezvous point and time," he added, removing a CD crystal case from the folder and sliding it across the table.

Mike looked at the CD as if it were a snake, then picked it up.

"Two questions and a comment," Mike said, flipping the crystal case open and looking at the unmarked CD inside. "First the comment: There's a reason that I created a tiddly little militia in the first place. It's called 'security.' Who's going to watch the store while the Keldara are gone for from a week to a month?"

"This shouldn't take a month," Tennis Pro protested.

"I wasn't asking *you*," Mike said, looking at Pierson.

"We can do Rangers again," Pierson said. "The usual company. Good enough?"

"That should do. Now for the questions: Was this discussed at a higher level? Specifically, at a high enough level?"

"Yes," Pierson replied, definitely. "It was."

"Question two: What's my take?"

"Standard recovery on a nuke is five mil," Mannly said. "If you recover the full shipment, the vig is twenty-five mil."

"Okay," Mike said, blowing out his breath. "I hate to sound mercenary but this is going to cost like crazy; that will do nicely. Nice to have never met you, gentlemen."

"The shipment of copra is ready for delivery," Rashid said, slipping into a chair.

The coffee shop in Docklands—a recently gentrified section of London—was a multi-ethnic stew of "traditional" English, islanders, Africans and every version of "brown" from Hindu to pale Berber North Africans. It was set close to a major financial district, and most of the patrons wore business clothes, but a few college students from nearby UEL in distressed chic added color. As did the occasional flash of "native" dress.

Two vaguely Arabic gentlemen in business suits were hardly out of place.

Mohammed Al-Kariya looked up from his laptop and tapped pudgy fingers together thoughtfully.

"Allah is benevolent," he replied. "The copra is first quality?"

"Impossible to tell until we examine the shipment," Rashid replied. "I have the proper reagents. They were difficult to obtain. But I found them."

"As Allah wills," Al-Kariya breathed. "The umah shall be secure. Forever. The payment side is arranged, all as agreed. Arrange the transportation. With all due care."

"Copra?" The technician leaned back in his chair and looked around. "We got a code-link for copra?"

"Situational," the analyst across the van said. "Could be anything. He's bloody happy, though. Hard to tell with Kari-Lad but he is. Whatever it is it's big. And Rashid is not one of his usual middlemen. Says he mostly works with KLA and sometimes the Chechens."

"I hope *somebody* has a clue," the tech said, spinning back around and fiddling with the filter on the shotgun mike. "Because I'm sodding *clueless.*"

Mike took a sip of his mocha and then flipped a page without looking around.

He wasn't sure if it was good tradecraft or lousy, but he was, as instructed, sitting at an outside table at the Perk's Coffee Shop on North Fairfax Street in Alexandria, Virginia, reading a book called *Spy Dust* about intelligence operations and methods during the Cold War.

As far as he could tell from the book, the tradecraft was lousy. On the other hand, he didn't expect the KGB to come arrest him. Or the FBI for that matter.

"Mr. Jenkins?"

Mike looked up and nodded as the businessman sat down. Nice suit, good shoes, *great* tie. Middling height, thin, ascetic face, brown eyes, light brown hair. Could be anywhere from forty to sixty. He looked like a thousand other guys wandering around Alexandria. The eyes really got caught by the tie. Bright yellow. Silk, for sure. Probably Thai. And one purchased overseas. Not the sort of thing you could pick up even in an expensive shop in the U.S.

"Mr. Jay?"

"Just Jay, please," the man said with a winning smile. "And may I call you Mike? Or would Kildar be more appropriate?"

"Mike works," he replied. "The whole Kildar thing is a little strange."

"Not really," Jay said with a shrug. "An international security specialist needs shooters. I understand that the Keldara are coming along nicely. I suppose you could hire Gurkhas, but the really good ones are getting very expensive these days. But I understand that Vanner isn't getting the job done."

"Not the way I'd say it," Mike said with a frown. "Vanner's sigint. I need humint. Vanner is probably at your level on sigint or very close. Less of a rep, admittedly, but he's *very* good."

"I accept the clarification," Jay said. "I take it, though, that if I work with you I won't be working for him."

"No," Mike said. "I'm not even sure exactly how a chain would look. I'd suggest that you two work it out. Frankly, I'm sure that there are plenty of times Vanner would prefer somebody with more experience around. But try to work *together*. If you start working at cross-purposes we'll have a problem."

"Agreed," Jay said. "Payment?"

"Hard to say," Mike replied. "I can give you a salary number if you wish, but what I think would work better is to just say: Tell me what you want. That is, besides your salary, you're going to have expenses. I'm not going to nitpick those. All I ask for is results. You tell me what kind of money you need and if I can't afford it I'll lay out my books and show you why. I'm running a very expensive operation. I make quite a bit of money on ops, enough to run it so far, but there's an upper limit. However, I'd put the upper limit on a million a year. I'd prefer that you tell me what you want to get paid, but understand that that is part of the budget. And if you don't use it all, that's fine too. I'm not going to ask why you paid some guy twenty grand. You're not doing this for the money, anyway, or I wouldn't be talking to you. You're doing it for the fun, the excitement, the professional challenge and because you're a patriot."

"I am, am I?" Jay said with a slight smile. "You're sure."

"Yeah, I'm sure," Mike replied.

"Very well," the man said, smiling more broadly. "What are the parameters? Be aware that there are reasons D.C. hates humint. For one, it's slow. You have to take time building networks. For another, it's uncertain. You're depending upon what people tell you. People lie. Everyone lies all the time and *especially* in the intelligence world. So I may get a piece of information that looks good and it will be terribly wrong. For a third, any intel is a two-edged sword. If you use it, you're often going to burn a source. That, in fact, was why I quit. I got tired of the State Department under our last president using my intel in negotiations and burning my networks."

"You ought to hear Vanner some time when he's going on about Clinton revealing we had OBL's satellite phone number and were listening in every day. I mean, the guy called his stepmom every damned day he could. And naturally she wanted to know what he was doing to further the jihad. And then our lovely president goes and talks about it on *national TV.*"

"And, of course, there was the Chechen attack because the Russians revealed you were intercepting their calls," Jay said, nodding.

"You have good sources," Mike replied. "You going to stay out in the cold or you want to come to Georgia?"

"I wouldn't necessarily say that Georgia is in the warm," Jay replied.

"You'd be secure," Mike pointed out. "As secure as anywhere forward and arguably more secure than here. You're also going to need support. I'm not sure how much the Keldara can do along those lines, but they're there. I don't know what *kind* of support, exactly," he added, holding up the book, "but I keep realizing how much I'd depended on support staff back when I was working for Uncle Sam."

"But there's that long damned drive to the airport," Jay pointed out, smiling very slightly and quickly. The smile was just with the lips, not the eyes, and come and gone so quickly it was almost invisible. "However, I understand that the perks are great."

"I'm eventually going to get a helicopter," Mike said. "I don't like the drive, either."

"Oh, yes, now *that* would be covert," the man replied, snorting. "But your comment about support staff is germane. I don't suppose they sew?"

"All their own clothes," Mike said, nodding.

"I'll need to get some stuff to set up a shop," Jay replied. "Initial outlay may be high."

"I've spent better than four million outfitting the Keldara," Mike said with a grimace. "Higher than that?"

"Uh, no," Jay said with another fleeting smile. "I see a vast number of issues, however. I know just about every skill or task related to supporting my job. Except some of the more esoteric chemistry. However, passing those skills on will require time on my part."

"You want another body?" Mike asked.

"Again, no," the man replied. "I know a number of people who could provide support but none I would care to actually put my life in their hands. For the time being, I'll simply provide my own when necessary. There are professionals, as well, I can call upon for individual items."

"How's your Rolodex?" Mike asked. "Those tend to get out of date fast."

"For the technical items it is, in fact, up to date," Jay said. That smile again. "There are even a few . . . associates, a very few, on it that were not burned during my tenure or after I left. Notably in Iran and Syria. I'm not sure I can reactivate those networks, but I can look into it. Alas, I haven't anyone on the Chechen side. Those I had were all rolled by either the Russians or, in two cases, the Chechens. Okay, I just wanted to check you out in person. I'm in. Three hundred kay for me. And budget up to a million a year. I'll try to keep it much lower than that. Most of the time it will be well under. Works?"

"Okay," Mike said, shrugging. "I'm planning on going back tomorrow if you want a ride . . ."

"I'll make my own way," the man said, standing up.

"I'd be surprised if you didn't know this," Mike said, frowning, "but the valley is in a Georgian military controlled zone. You can't just waltz in and out. There are a slew of checkpoints to get through."

"Excuse me?" Jay said, the smile reaching his eyes this time. "Exactly *why* are you hiring me?"

"Oh," Mike replied. "Brain fart. Good point."

"I'll see you in Georgia," Jay said, walking into the shop.

Mike just had to do it. He sat out in the Alexandria sunshine for the next two hours, flipping through the book and not really reading while keeping an eye on the only entrance. But Jay never reappeared.

Chapter Ten

"At a certain level, there is no such thing as a storefront; the people it pays to shop with simply do *not* advertise."

Mrs. John J. Weston was a spare woman in her late fifties, much shorter than Anastasia. She seemed to never hurry, but made her way through the crowds like a lioness parting gazelles. People simply, instinctually, stepped out of her way.

Anastasia was simultaneously trying to take in the city, trying not to get overwhelmed and simply *absorb* Amelia Weston. She hoped that by the time she was a hundred she might have half the grace and just amazing *aura* the woman exuded.

Mrs. Weston was definitely not "Amelia." The First Lady, despite the fact that they were clearly friends, referred to her in person only as "Mrs. Weston." That was fine by Anastasia; having to call the wife of the President of the United States "Amanda" had nearly killed her. She was much more comfortable with Mrs. Weston. She was not going to *think* of telling her, but Mrs. Weston reminded her, very much, of the first manager of Otryad's hareem she had served under, Salah. But Salah with a cosmopolitan background.

Samarkand? That had been a lovely stationing. Mrs. Weston named shops that Anastasia *knew*, and a list of shopkeepers, by name, that she only vaguely recalled. Details of meals and meetings in a calm, unhurried voice.

Tbilisi? Only for a short time when the General, capital letter, was an envoy. Lieutenant Colonel, then. Still Soviet, of course. Pleasant town but . . . gray. She understood from friends who wrote her that it was much more gay now.

No name dropping, no one-upping, no "well, when the General was running arms negotiations for the SALT II Treaty . . ." No, all the mentions were small things to put Anastasia at her ease, to make her feel as if she had found a friend, a confidante. A highly formal one but a friend nonetheless.

In a hundred years . . . maybe.

"You have to know where to go," Mrs. Weston said, nodding at the bellman of what looked very much like a sprawling hotel.

"And here is where to go?" Anastasia asked. "This is a hotel, yes, Mrs. Weston?"

"It is indeed," Mrs. Weston said. "The Watergate of infamy and legend. But it has some places worth visiting as well. David has his hair cut here. All Good Republicans do."

"I am unfamiliar," Anastasia said. "I apologize."

"Oh, water under the gate, my dear," Mrs. Weston replied. "But quite famous."

The lady made her way to a back elevator, nodding to various people who obviously knew her, and chose the fourteenth floor.

"It helps," she said, "if you think of it as a very large souk. I have to make the assumption, you will forgive me, based on the First Lady's request, that you have not done significant travel in cities."

"I have not, Mrs. Weston," Anastasia admitted. "I think you have seen more of Samarkand than I have. And Tbilisi, for that matter. I have not even been in the souk very much. Only twice that I recall."

"Hmm, hmm."

Anastasia wasn't sure exactly what "Hmm, hmm" meant but she suspected that a very sharp and cosmopolitan mind was putting some clues together.

They exited the elevator and turned down the corridor, stopping at a door that looked very much as if it went to a hotel room or possibly suite. It had a number but below that was a discreet brass plaque that simply said: G. Groome, Clothier.

Mrs. Weston didn't bother to knock. She just opened the door and swept in.

"George," she said to a gray-haired black gentleman. He was seated on a chair looking at a ledger, wearing a striped silk shirt and exquisite wool trousers held up by bracers. "It's been simply ages."

The room *looked* a good bit like a suite, albeit the living room, and was tastefully and expensively decorated. Anastasia was taking more notes.

"Mrs. Weston," the man said, smiling and revealing very white, very straight, teeth. "As I live and breathe."

"George, I have a bit of a problem," Mrs. Weston said, pulling Anastasia forward. "This is Miss Rakovich from Georgia, note that's the country, George, not the state. Her friend, a Mr. Ford, is visiting the House. Only in town for a day. Old friend of David's or something. *No* decent shops in Tbilisi as you know and his wardrobe's gotten quite threadbare. *Hawaiian* shirts if you can believe! The staff is simply *clucking*."

"I understand," George said, throwing a wink to Anastasia.

"So Miss Rakovich and I would like a spot of tea," Mrs. Weston said, walking to the divan, hand on Anastasia's arm. "And perhaps you could show us what London and Paris are messing up this year?"

Mike arrived back at the White House in a taxi. He paid the driver then went up to the side gate. This time he was careful to have the right passport ready.

"Mr. Ford," the uniformed officer said, nodding.

"I've got a bit of a problem," Mike said, taking back the passport. "I can't recall exactly how to get to my room, I don't know where my girlfriend has gotten to—the last time I saw her she was about to get grilled by the First Lady—and I need a shield room with a computer that can run a PDF file."

"Why don't I call an escort?" the officer said, trying not to grin. "And Miss Rakovich left about an hour ago in the company of Mrs. Amelia Weston, wife of General Weston, the MDW commander. I believe they were going shopping."

"Why am I not surprised?"

❖   ❖   ❖

Mike slid the CD into the computer and opened the single PDF file. It contained photos of the seven known or suspected players on the operation as well as an estimate of opposition forces.

The Chechens had about three hundred fighters in the area, organized in another "battalion" like the one the Keldara had wiped out a few months back. The leader was Commander Bukara, another of the organizers of the Beslan attack as well as others on the Russian heartland. The Russians seriously wanted his ass but had never been able to localize him. It was probable that he'd be at the rendezvous. If Mike could bring back his head the Russians would be very happy.

Person of interest two was Mohammed Al-Kariya. He was a money man for Al Qaeda with fingers in various sources of supply. He was technically "white" although he was on the State Department list of terrorism supporters. Nobody had ever pinned anything on him, though, and the Europeans let him come and go. His "white" identity was as an international banker and fundraiser for "Muslim Charities."

Mohammed had required Muslims to support the poor and thus it was the duty of good Muslims to donate to charities. A large number of Muslim "charities" however were funding channels for international terrorism. The money traveled mostly through a closed banking system among Muslim groups that was surprisingly hard to crack. But plenty of it got to Al Qaeda and similar groups. And Al-Kariya was one of the main men handling it. If the Chechens wanted *that* much money, he was going to be around keeping an eye on it.

Al-Kariya was, to say the least, heavy-set. He wasn't going to be running very fast.

Then there was Arensky. The data on him was surprisingly sparse. He'd gotten a Ph.D. from Moscow University back in the Soviet days and then disappeared into the Soviet and then Russian "Advanced Research Agency." ARA was something like America's DARPA, a clearinghouse for various high-tech research projects. What bothered Mike was that as far as he knew, ARA didn't play with nukes. That was under an entirely separate agency and the two rarely interacted. And although it said that Arensky had gotten a Ph.D. the document didn't say in *what*.

Arensky had a daughter, Marina, who had apparently disappeared with him. Twenty-two, blonde, green eyes. Pretty thing. But not a security issue on the op.

Arensky was probably going to have security with him. The number-one probable provider was Sergei Rudenko. Former Spetznaz colonel, fifty-three, and started under the Soviets. Described as "tall and broad" with gray shot black hair. The photo was from his official dossier and Mike mentally added "seriously cold eyes." Russian mobster but not a member of any particular group, known hitter. He had a group of former Spetznaz that he picked and chose from for missions. There would be at least fifteen to twenty of them. Mikhail had been one of his usual guys, which was what had made the first connection.

Another "person of interest" was one Kurt Schwenke. Often worked as Rudenko's second-in-command. Former East German Stasi specializing in "wet work." Got into the game late but made something of a name for himself in his brief period before the fall of East Germany. Forty-seven. There was a photo but it was old and had the notation that Schwenke was "an expert in disguise and deception." The list of kills, culled from the Stasi archives found after the fall of the Berlin Wall, was impressive as was the variety of techniques from pistol to sniper to small explosives. Wanted by Germany for "crimes against humanity" and by just about every government in Europe for that matter; he was tied to most of the former Western European communist terrorist groups. He'd been around. Like Mike himself, he was an expert at infiltration and silent-kill.

The Al Qaeda guys would have their own security and then there was the Chechen "battalion." The Keldara had tangled with them once, but it was from prepared defenses. Unless he got brilliant, that wasn't going to happen this time. The correlation of forces was adverse.

If he had full support, say a B-52 loaded with JDAMs or a Specter gunship, this would be dead simple. But using just the Keldara it was going to be tough.

Not as tough, however, as simply getting into the Pankisi. The last Georgian control post stopped nearly sixty miles from the site of the rendezvous. And it wasn't a straight sixty miles; the area was nearly vertical alpine mountains. The Chechens had patrols and logistics groups moving all through the area so even flying in would be tough. The closest they could get was maybe thirty miles from the rendezvous. Then they'd have to hump in, hit the site and hump back out. It was hard enough to carry food for a thirty-mile hump through that sort of terrain: carrying ammo, weapons and commo was going to be a stone bitch.

Where'd they put those mules from the last Chechen supply train they'd hit?

If they brought mules they'd raise their profile significantly. However, they could probably mask as a Chechen train. That had an upside and a downside. There *were* Spetznaz working the other side of the border, covertly. They were likely to get hit by "their" team. And the Chechens had control teams on the routes in the area.

Okay, he knew a group that had the helos to get them into the area. And they could handle the mules; the Keldara weren't that far from their farmer roots. The last thing they didn't have was good intel on the area around the rendezvous. But he knew how to get that, too. It would mean a preliminary covert insertion and some way to set up short-range commo. But that could all be arranged. Come to think of it, Vanner was airborne-qualled.

Mike started to grin evilly.

"Did you have a good day, Stasia?"

The dinner was the definition of "intimate." The room was, like most in the White House, small, and was tucked away in a corner of the East Wing. The only diners were Mike, who had seen his "assistant" for about three minutes since he'd left, Anastasia, the President and the First Lady.

Mike was still having a hard time figuring out which fork to use.

"Both good and interesting," Anastasia said, cutting a bit of her salad and taking a small bite. "Mostly because of Mrs. Weston."

"Didn't I tell you Amelia was a treasure," the First Lady said.

"A force of nature," the President added. "There don't seem to be many like her, anymore, present company excluded."

"I must exclude myself, Mr. President," Anastasia replied. "I thought many times, today, that if I live to be a hundred I *might* come close to being Mrs. Weston."

"I think I need to meet this lady," Mike said, smiling.

"You'd probably get along well," the President said. "She's far more steely than she generally lets on."

"You should hear her talk about the first attack on the Embassy in Mogadishu," the First Lady said. "The Embassy Marines beat it off, with some help from the Embassy staff and . . . others. The general being then a military attaché he was in the thick of it."

"And according to General Schnorer, so was Amelia," the President added. "On the roof with a sniper rifle taken from a wounded Marine. I understand your meetings went well, Mike."

"Yes, sir," Mike said. "Well enough."

"All the issues resolved?" the President asked.

"More like in the process of being identified," Mike admitted. "But it's doable. Marginally."

"If it was easy, we wouldn't be talking," President Cliff noted, smiling.

"The difficult we do immediately," Mike responded. "The impossible takes a little longer."

"Take all the time you need," the President said. "As long as you make the train."

Mike shook the hand of the pilot then stepped out of the Blackhawk. Petro was already there, grabbing bags from the crew-chief. Of course, with what Anastasia had bought, the kid couldn't carry it in one load.

"Lemme get that," Mike said, hefting both of his bags as well as one of Anastasia's and the big case he'd bought to carry her purchases. And apparently *most* of them were going to be shipped. Shit. He was seriously getting heavy in the clothes department.

"I told you not to let her go shopping," Adams said, grabbing bags as well. "What's up?"

"Command room," Mike said. "Combat staff. Daria. Thirty minutes."

"Got it," Adams replied.

"We got ourselves one colossal fuckup in the making," Mike said, sighing.

Adams, Vanner, Nielson and a somewhat nervous Daria were gathered around the staff table, all of them wondering what was up.

"Methinks I hear distant musketry," Nielson replied.

"Not so distant," Mike said, rubbing his eyes. "The Russians, the mob in this case, are selling nukes again. And this time to the Chechens."

"Get out," Vanner said. "Why in the hell would the Russians sell the *Chechens* nukes?"

"Money?" Mike said. "Sixty mil in this case. We recover them, we get twenty. There are supposed to be three. I hope even NSA can count that high. It's not something you want to diddle with. A nuke here, a nuke there . . . The problem is time and location. We know the time but it's just a couple of weeks away. And we've got minimal intel. I'm planning on sending Katya in to get some more, but that has problems, too. And getting there . . . it's right in the middle of the Pankisi."

"Gods," Adams said, rubbing his eyes. "We could walk there in a couple of days. Drive there . . . about the same time as getting to Tbilisi. That is . . ."

"If there weren't a few thousand Chechens in our way," Mike said. "We can't use any of the regular passes or trails. They're all watched."

"High," Nielson said. "Way high up. Don't take the low passes. Hell, in some cases don't take passes at all, go right across the shoulders of the mountains. Serious alpine. Winter's already started up there. It's close here. It's gonna be a bitch."

"More or less my thinking," Mike said. "Daria, darling?"

"Yes, Kildar?"

"Order climbing gear from Arctic Outfitters in Alaska," Mike said, sliding over the list he'd made up on the way back. "We're going to need everything from soup to nuts. Clothing, crampons, ice axes, the lot. Express ship. Make sure they know we need it now and I don't care how much it costs. Charter a plane if you have to."

"Yes, Kildar," she said, making a note on the list. "I'll match this to the Keldara teams. But you've got two sets of female gear. Who?"

"That's up to Vanner," Mike said, turning to the intel specialist. "Katya's going to need commo. Her implants are short ranged. Which means sending in a commo team in advance."

"Well, it's the same problem, isn't it," Vanner pointed out. "Getting there. I mean, the girls are strong and I think they could make the walk. But they're going to need the gear, first. Getting there ahead of Katya, or even ahead of the teams to pick up intel, that's going to be tough."

"Sure would, if they were walking," Mike said. "I seem to recall you mentioning you were airborne-qualified. Ever done any free-fall?"

"Kildar . . . ?" Vanner said, warily.

"See, jumping in makes *so* much more sense," Mike replied, grinning.

"Oh, you have *got* to be out of your mind," Vanner said, his eyes wide.

"I *like* it," Adams said with an evil grin.

"Daria, another list," Mike said with just as evil a grin. "Five sets of high-altitude jump gear. Parachutes. Freefall trainer. The works." He slid over another sheet of paper and grinned, again. "I've actually got both lists on files. I'll get them to you."

"Good news," Adams added. "He's a fully trained HALO instructor. Got *thousands* of jumps. Jumpin' fool."

"Great," Vanner said. "*You* go."

"You know why I can't," Mike replied. "Two of your best commo girls, at least unmarried ones. I'll assign a couple of shoot-ers for security. And then we start training. Piece of cake. All you have to do is fall. You can *fall*, right?"

"All the way to the ground," Vanner said with a sigh.

"It's fun," Adams said. "You'll love it. Oh, prebreathing sucks and I imagine that the DZ is probably going to be a little small. Then there's all the problems of where, exactly, ground level is and winds in mountains and . . . Actually, it's going to suck. Glad it's you and not me."

"We gonna try to use any special weapons or techniques on this?" Vanner asked, ignoring the master chief. "With the support we're getting we could probably get *anything* from the U.S. government."

"I don't think so," Mike said after a moment's thought. "Trying to integrate special weapons at this point would really set us back. Let's go with conventional approach. But, out of interest, what were you talking about?"

"There are some interesting sound weapons that are being developed," Nielson said. "And the new thermobaric system the Marines are using."

"Too much overkill on that for this mission," Adams said. "Those things are used for flattening houses."

"Be useful for interdiction," Mike said. "But it takes coordination from what I've read. You have to penetrate the wall of the structure with a standard rocket round and then put the thermobaric through the hole. That is if you don't have a window as a target."

"How fast can we get some?" Adams asked. "I can set a few of the Keldara to training on them. Run everybody through, but Shota's shown a real knack for the Carl. Which is good given how big it is."

"I'll check into it," Nielson said, making another note.

"First thing is to call all the troops in," Mike said.

"Already done," Nielson said. "It will take about another day for Team Padrek to get back to pickup points."

"Get with the Georgian military," Mike said. "I'd rather that they not get back worn out from humping. See if you can get helicopter support to pick them all up."

"Will do," Nielson said, making a note.

"Call General Umarov," Mike said, referring to the Georgian military chief of staff. "I don't want any petty bullshit getting in the way. He should be up on this, if he's not, wake him up."

"Will do," Nielson said.

"Vanner, we need to get the insertion of Katya as a high priority."

"Will do," Vanner said. "You're seriously planning on inserting me?"

"I'll even let you have a weapon," Mike said, grinning. "Set up the insertion on Katya as soon as we get the data dump from Chechnik and you run through it."

"Will do," Vanner said. "Does *Katya* know she's being inserted?"

"That's my *next* meeting," Mike admitted, grimacing.

Chapter Eleven

"You wanted to see me, Kildar?"

Katya was, if anything, more beautiful than Anastasia and in the same mold, blonde, blue-eyed with a slight Tartar tilt. Great tits and a fine ass, delicious lilt to her voice and hips that swayed in a way that was truly extraordinary. The blue eyes could look as innocent as a child's but she had long before discovered that Mike saw right through her. So the eyes he looked into, now, were as cold and dead as a shark's.

"I need another insertion mission," Mike said, waving her to a chair. He'd considered doing some chitchat but it usually was pointless with Katya. "Into the Pankisi. The vig is fifty thousand dollars. We need eyes on the ground."

"One hundred," Katya said. "Up front."

"Ten up front," Mike said. "Sixty on completion. If you do as well as Albania, a forty bonus. You did a damned good job in Albania. If you sit on your ass and just feed us intel, seventy total."

"I nearly got my ass shot off in Albania," Katya said, scornfully. "Your perfectly planned mission was a disaster. And all for a whore."

"No mission survives contact with the enemy . . ."

Katya had revealed a very definite chip on her shoulder over the Albanian op. As she put it: "Nobody ever came to rescue me."

She'd been horribly abused in the process of being broken in as a hooker. Whether that had caused her current mental condition or if it had been there before, she was now as sociopathic as anyone Mike had ever met. And she actively enjoyed killing people, especially men.

To make matters worse, in preparation for the Balkans op the U.S. government had offered some very advanced "upgrades," upgrades that even their own agents had been unwilling to have installed. Katya was now, arguably, the first generation of a sort of science fiction super-assassin. She had an internal system to dump combat chemicals that sped up her reactions and caused a "slow-time" effect, video and audio connections built right into her brain and poison glands connected to her long, and sharp, nails.

Mike, and all the rest of the men in the house, were now absolutely unwilling to sleep with her. Not that Katya cared; she found the situation amusing.

"How am I supposed to penetrate Chechan units?"

"Try to figure out a way," Mike said with a shrug. "Be your usual helpful self."

At that, Katya let loose one of the few real laughs Mike had heard out of her. She was about as helpful in the harem as a snake, which was why Mike had been spreading her around to keep her busy. When she was busy, and interested, she wasn't nearly the problem she was when bored. But she was never really "helpful." She'd do a job until she mastered it to her satisfaction and then start causing problems. Vanner pulled her out of intercept after she started calling up the Chechens she was supposed to be monitoring and taunting them.

Mike sometimes thought that her natural spot was psychological operations. Or maybe the Mafia. Hopefully "Jay" would be able to ensure her functionality at the very least.

"Very well," Katya said, still chortling. "I will go into the lion's den, again. And for the bonus I will try to be very helpful. I'm going to need you to get me some more 'medications.' I used up most of my stores in Albania."

"Will do," Mike said. "Can I ask you a question? You're still hanging around. I'm, frankly, surprised. Why?"

"Because I am learning much here," Katya said, cold again. "From Anastasia I am learning languages, accounting, business.

From Vanner I am learning electronics, computers and programming. He has even shown me some hacking and I am working hard on that; I like it very much. From you and Adams I learn combat skills, yes? Now there is Jay, who is teaching me so many new skills. When I feel there is nothing left to learn, then I will leave. But in the meantime, you feed me and keep a roof over my head while I learn. You even continue to pay me a stipend. And then there are these occasional 'jobs' which pay quite well. Why should I leave? Yet."

"The usual goes," Mike pointed out. "If you're burned, we'll try to extract you. Try rather hard I'll add. We owe you that. You may not consider yourself part of the team, but I do. But if you burn *us* . . ."

"Run far and fast," Katya said, smiling coldly. "This, also, I am learning. How to run far and fast."

"Come," Mike said at a knock on the door of his office.

He looked up from his computer screen, rubbing his eyes and frowning. He was doing more reading than doing these days and it was killing his eyes. He was afraid he was going to need glasses soon.

The man who came through the door was dressed like any of the Keldara, if a bit short for one. One of the older guys, not one of the ones on the teams. Gray-shot beard and mustache, getting the "beer gut" that some of the older Keldara had. But when Mike rapidly ran a file of the faces of the Keldara, he couldn't place him to save his life. He figured he'd play that off. It wasn't like he could remember *all* the Keldara.

"You know," Jay said, walking over and flopping onto the chair in front of the desk, "if I was an assassin you'd be *so* dead right now. You've got lousy security."

"I'll keep that in mind," Mike replied, leaning back and trying not to let his surprise show. "Good trip?"

"Fair," Jay said. "First class as far as Prague. It got a little rougher after that."

"I can imagine," Mike said. "Can I show you around or do you already have the whole place mapped out?"

"I will say that your security on whatever is in the basements is better than getting to your office," Jay replied. "Doors are solid and the guys you've got on them weren't fooled. I've seen the rest. Nice harem quarters. Who's the blonde?"

"Well, the basement is where *your* shop will be," Mike said. "So maybe I ought to show that to you. And depending on which, the blonde is your sole 'employee.'"

"Oh, great," Jay replied. "If ever I saw one stone psychopathic bitch of a killer . . ."

"That would be Katya," Mike said with a laugh. "You *can* handle that, right?"

"Oh, yeah," the intel specialist said. "I *like* psychopathic bitches. It describes every girlfriend I've ever had."

"Intel room here," Mike said, nodding at the Keldara guards. They were regarding Jay with puzzlement in their eyes. They *did* know every single Keldara. "Commo room across the hall. Head-quarters in a larger room at the end. Other way there are four more or less empty rooms and two sub-levels. There are two remaining really good apartments upstairs, although the view is of the mountain. Pick which mountain view you prefer."

"Any problem with getting one down here?" Jay asked, walking down the corridor and opening up one of the doors of the "more or less empty" rooms. More or less empty because they still had some left-over trash from the Soviet occupation. "An apartment I mean?"

"I don't think so," Mike said. "Kind of . . . claustrophobic."

"Yeah, but very secure," Jay replied, opening up another door. "Can I get better doors and locks?"

"Your budget," Mike said.

"What's the sub-basement like?"

"There's a reason we call it the dungeons."

"I'll stay here."

"Come on in the intel shop," Mike said, opening up the door. The door was soundproofed and the corridor immediately filled with the sound of printers and computers running at max.

"Vanner, this is Jay," Mike said, waving the sergeant over. "Just . . . Jay."

"It's actually just an initial," Jay said, shaking Vanner's hand. "Just the letter."

"Very James Bond," Vanner replied, warily. "You're the humint guy."

"'Spy' works," Jay said. "And I checked you out. You have a very good rep."

"Thanks," Vanner said. "Can I ask with whom?"

"Admiral Kinnison. We've got history."

"How's his dog?" Vanner said, nodding.

"Cat," Jay replied. "Ginger tabby named Halsey. Died. Cancer. About six months ago. And JC was in a car wreck with her kids. They all made it but she got really banged up. Grandkids were okay. Well, Bobby broke his arm but I signed the cast and he was grinning at the time. Jim's had a bad year. You should write him. I'll give you his e-mail address."

"Thanks," Vanner said, blinking.

"We straight?"

"Straight."

"Jim said you were good with micro. I'm a gadget guy when I can use them. Are you going to have time?"

"Some," Vanner admitted. "If it's really complicated, we might have to shop it. I've got two sources."

"I've got more than two," Jay said. "But I'd prefer to keep it in-house. We'll manage. I ran across a new microwave design . . ."

"I'll just go tell Anastasia that we're going to have a guest," Mike said. "She'll take care of your housekeeping arrangements. Daria handles budget, I'll speak to her as well."

"Thank you," Jay replied. "What would you like me to do next?"

"Just hang out," Mike said. "We've got a mission in the planning stages. Vanner's going to be very busy. You're going to have to develop and do most of your tasking on your own. But that's why I hired you."

"What about the blonde?"

"Katya will be on the mission," Mike replied. "I'd bring you in on it but it's a snap-kick. I don't see an insert point for you."

"Understood," Jay said. "Well, I'll just pick Vanner's brain for a bit until Anastasia's up to speed and then start with my self-tasking. I'd like to talk to Katya about her mission, if you're okay on the need-to-know."

"Works," Mike replied. "Just ensure she's got her mission face on when she's out the door. Vanner, as far as I'm concerned, Jay has choice on his need-to-know. If you have issues, bring them up with me."

"You're very trusting," Jay said, frowning slightly.

"You were vetted by good people," Mike replied. "I can't, won't unless something comes up, second-guess that. In for a penny and all that. So . . . if you are afraid something will be compromised, don't ask."

"Yes, Kildar," Jay said. That smile again.

"Who's the visitor?" Nielson asked as Mike was headed to his office. "The Mother Savina came in asking *me* who he was."

"That was Jay," Mike replied. "You found him. I almost want to say 'You keep him.' The guy gives me the creeps. I'm pretty sure I still don't know what he actually looks like. If he burns us, there's nobody really there."

"He's as good as they come," Nielson pointed out. "And very much a patriot. As long as we don't screw the U.S. . . ."

"Let's hope we never have to," Mike said. "I'd prefer not to myself. You were just asking about him?"

"No," the colonel said. "I just got word. A Colonel Erkin Chechnik, Russian Army, is on his way to see us. I was told you know him."

"I do," Mike said, shaking his head. "Russian spook. Pretty good. Pretty much Pierson's equivalent; briefs the president on Russian black ops. He's probably going to brief us on the Russian side."

"More or less what I guessed," Nielson said. "So . . . You wanna talk?"

"About what?" Mike asked.

"Gretchen," Nielson said, raising an eyebrow. "And you. And Kiril."

"How about just saying I didn't like this entire Kardane thing from the beginning," Mike said, shrugging. "I've got it handled. I'm not going to do a King David on Kiril, I'm not going to lay another hand on Gretchen."

"And you are . . . where in there?" Nielson asked.

"How about 'I'm not going to lay another hand on Gretchen, damnit to *hell*'?" Mike said, grimacing.

"Been there," Nielson said. "Prior to my wife dying I had some
. . . encounters with other ladies. All by agreement with my wife.
The agreement was I could screw around as much as I liked, as
long as I didn't fall in love. And then . . ."

"You fell in love," Mike said, sitting down and listening.

"I did indeed, laddy," Nielson said, leaning back in his chair.
"Lady named Sharon. Very much a lady. I was to be her first. Very
strange circumstances. I actually passed on the honor. She later
found other men, none of them particularly good for her. We
eventually lost touch, half by purpose. But . . . She's still there in my
heart. And Gretchen?"

"It fucking sucks," Mike said. "I've been married but I never felt
this way about a girl, ever. I never believed in love at first sight and
it wasn't even that. It . . . I don't know. It just snuck up on me."

"And clobbered you over the head," Nielson said, nodding.
"That is the reality far more than 'love at first sight.' A friend, a
companion, someone you knew casually and then one day . . .
Wham! All of a sudden, they're something different. Any idea how
Gretchen feels about the situation?"

"Not sure," Mike admitted. "The Kardane girls . . . generally
have a pretty good time. But it was an unusual encounter in both
directions. I haven't really spoken to her since and . . ."

"And you're the Kildar," the colonel said. "Big attraction right
there. It would be hard to be sure what she actually thinks. I'm not
sure that even if she was as honest as she could be that it would be
clear what she really thinks. For General Kildar's Ears Only, I think
that Kardane is a damned bad idea. I haven't said anything but . . .
you don't screw the wives or girlfriends of your subordinates.
Period. The Keldara take a different tack on that but . . . It's just
been a damned bad idea. This is only one of a dozen reasons why."

"Thought of all that," Mike said with a sigh. "But right now we
have other things to think about. The whole thing with Gretchen,
and the Kardane, needs to be tabled for the time being. Bigger fish
to fry."

"Such as the Russian," Nielson said. "I'm surprised that he's
coming in person. No read at all on why?"

"Only that it can't be good. I've never seen Chechnik turn up
when things are going well."

❖   ❖   ❖

"Erkin, what a pleasant surprise."

Mike hadn't seen Colonel Chechnik in about a year, not since the Paris mission. But he hadn't changed much. The Russian intel officer was short and broad as a house. Also somewhat ugly or at least unintelligent looking. He looked more like a member of an Olympic wrestling team than a highly qualified intel officer. Mike was sure that he'd used that to his advantage more than once.

"Mikhail," the colonel boomed, clasping Mike close and kissing him on both cheeks. "Or should I call you Kildar, now?"

"Mike will do," Mike replied, grinning. He'd arranged a formal reception line for the visiting Russian and now waved him farther into the foyer of the serai. "May I introduce Colonel Nielson, my operations officer?"

"Colonel Nielson," Chechnik said, shaking his hand. "I read your paper on IED patterning as they related to street crime incidences in Iraq. A very interesting premise."

"I had to think of something," Nielson said, nodding. "And my original paper was rejected."

"And what was that on?" Chechnik asked, smiling quizzically.

"The utility of crucifixion as a means of control," Nielson replied, smiling thinly.

"I think we need you in the Russian Army, Colonel," Chechnik said, smiling in much the same way. "We could use you in Chechnya."

"My field operations number two, Master Chief Adams," Mike said, shaking his head.

"Master Chief," the Russian replied, shaking hands again. "I've only been able to see a portion of your confidential files, but I must ask a question: What in the world does your first team nickname, 'Ass-Boy One,' relate to?"

Both Adams and Mike flinched at that and Adams shook his head.

"Colonel, I doubt that you have the stomach for the full horror of that story," Adams said. "But if you have to know, you'll have to ask . . ." He suddenly stopped and shook his head. "Ask someone else."

"Sergeant Vanner, my intel specialist," Mike said, moving on rapidly. What Adams had nearly said was "Ask Ass-Boy Two" referring to Mike. However, if Chechnik knew *that* team name, then he also had access to Mike's *other* team name, Ghost. And since "Ghost" was known as the man who had broken up the Syrian operation, and thus drawn the ire of virtually every terrorist on the face of the planet, Adams had nearly handed Chechnik a piece of information worth both money and power.

"I sincerely apologize for the lapse in our own security," Chechnik said, shaking Vanner's hand. "The leak to the Chechens has been closed."

"That one," Vanner said. "But you ought to know that at least one of your people has been having regular sat-phone contact with Kamil Resama. All we're picking up are the externals, some sideband waves and scattering, but whenever that one phone, coming from your Stalin Base in Subya, starts sending, Kamil's phone's duration is dead on for receiving quite a few of the calls."

"I'll keep that in mind," Chechnik replied, stone-faced.

"Last but not least, my manager of internal matters, Anastasia Rakovich," Mike said. He'd promised Anastasia that, unlike under her former employer, she'd get introduced and not treated like a piece of furniture.

"The picture in your file does not do you justice, Ms. Rakovich," Chechnik said, bowing over and kissing her hand.

"I have a file?" Anastasia asked, raising one eyebrow.

"You've had a file since you became the harem manager for Sheik Otryad," the colonel replied. "It has simply been moved up in precedence since you've become the Kildar's."

"Oh," Anastasia said, her face blank.

"It is a pleasure to meet you all," Chechnik said, nodding to the group. "I hope that we can talk at length sometime soon."

"Meaning that right now you'd like to talk at length with me," Mike said.

"Alas, yes," the colonel replied. "If you don't mind, I would like to have the talk in private."

"Not at all," Mike said. "Guys, I'll see you later."

Chapter Twelve

"Sit," Mike said, collapsing behind his desk. His office was in one of the older parts of the serai, with thick stone walls and no windows. Vanner had checked it for emissions and it was damned near as good as a professional secure room. That was probably because of the high olivine content of the local stone. Mike still had it swept once a week and Vanner had insisted on "touching up" with some impossibly expensive paint. The stuff was a nice light blue but apparently it was opaque to transmissions.

"What's on your mind? And are you an emissary from Vladimir?" he asked, meaning the president of Russia.

"Among others," Chechnik replied, sighing. "In fact, it was I who convinced the president, and others, that I should come. I have some information that you need about your mission."

"So give," Mike said, frowning.

"Yes, that is the problem," the colonel replied, sighing again. "Kildar, Mikhail, I believe that you are an honorable man, a man of your word."

"He said, just before ripping the honorable man off," Mike said.

"Nonetheless," Chechnik said. "I must ask you this. I cannot give you the information unless you agree that you will not, in turn, give it to your government or the government of Georgia."

"Oh," Mike replied. "I *could* go for that, but it depends. Does this information have serious strategic or tactical bearing on the United States?"

"Unfortunately, yes," Chechnik said. "But my masters have determined that they are unwilling to share the information with the Ami." The Russian paused and grimaced. "It has to do with an area that the Americans have chided us on. In my opinion with good reason. But it . . . this situation is extremely embarrassing for our government. And we can only take so much embarrassment. That thing with Paris last year, my God, the ripples are still refusing to settle. Then the Albanian thing that you turned up!"

"Every government had problems with that," Mike pointed out. "That's why it's stayed so damned quiet."

The Albanian op had turned up a load of files on a sex ring that had "honey-trapped" dozens of officials in nearly as many countries. The worst part about the honey-trapping was that the officials, ranging from minor military officers all the way to the British home secretary, had abused, raped and even killed the prostitutes involved. The files were still sending very quiet shudders through more than a dozen governments, including every major world power. And in the end, Mike had ended up holding all the originals. The thought on that went something like this: None of the governments trusted the others with the information. But somebody had to hold it. Mike was the easiest to wipe off the face of the earth if it came down to cases.

The DVDs, paper files and hard drives were buried in the basement of the caravanserai. The information in those documents was power in a very real sense; one person privy to it had referred to it as "the blackmail equivalent of a nuclear weapon" with good reason. But it was a dangerous power that Mike intended to invoke as cautiously as possible and only in an extreme situation. It was a power that could topple governments. If he used it, he was going to be immediately targeted by some very pissed off, and hugely powerful, people.

Mike was far less worried about the Russians, for example, than the Japanese yakuza. Some of the files referred to actions of senior Japanese businessmen. They'd all, at this point, committed suicide, even if some of them had to be helped with the knife. But the

Japanese would not care for the loss of face if the information surfaced. Nor the French, Chinese . . . The list was very long.

"Yes, but most governments are not still recovering from the embarrassment of one of their nuclear weapons almost vaporizing Paris," Chechnik snapped. "If this got out on top of everything else . . . Please, Mikhail, I must have your word. If your mission is successful, let us hope to God, even then I hope I can persuade you to keep the exact nature of this secret."

"That's a hell of a lot to ask, Erkin," Mike replied. "What's so damned important? I mean, yeah, nukes are a big deal. But we already *know* about those."

"Dr. Arensky is not carrying nukes," the Russian replied, softly.

"Then what the hell *is* he carrying?" Mike asked, just as softly.

"Your word."

Mike sat back and looked at the Russian for a long time. The colonel was a professional intelligence officer with a long track record. He'd been in a lot of hairy situations from what Mike had gleaned; he hadn't always been a desk officer. But as Mike watched, a bead of sweat formed on his forehead and started to trickle down.

"You've got it."

"Dr. Arensky is not a nuclear scientist," Chechnik said, leaning back in his chair with a sigh. "He is our premier expert at biological *and* chemical weapons."

"Biological," Mike said, softly.

"Dr. Arensky walked out of the Biological Weapons Research Facility with four vials of weapons-grade smallpox."

"WHAT?!" Mike shouted, then clutched his head. "How in the FUCK!?"

"The security on our facilities has . . . much to be desired, yes?" Chechnik replied, shrugging. "This material was kept in Category Five quarantine, the very highest level. It was surrounded by guards. Everything in and out was carefully controlled. As far as we can determine, he moved it out slowly. First from Cat Five then to Cat Four and so on. The missing material was not discovered until after he left. 'Left' does not cover it. The offices of the facility were destroyed by a special operations team that took down the entire guard force. *Then* we did a very thorough survey of the materials and, lo, the smallpox was missing. Only that. And it was the *only* sample of that particular, particularly vile, weapon."

"Jesus Christ," Mike said. "Smallpox. That shit is *nasty*. And you go and let him waltz out with . . ."

"Yes, it is nasty," the Russian said. "Also eliminated from the face of the earth. But this is not just *any* smallpox. This was developed very late in the Soviet era, when genetic technology was fairly advanced, far enough advanced that our scientists could really begin to tinker, yes? They made a breakthrough, then. May I lecture?"

"Go ahead," Mike said, sighing.

"There are three strains of smallpox," Chechnik said. "Standard, hemorrhagic and macular, you understand this? Standard has about a thirty percent death rate, but it has a slow onset. So if you are inoculated against it, only those with very weak immune systems die. Often inoculation will stop onset even in those showing symptoms. Hemorrhagic and macular are quite different. They strike very very fast and kill even faster. And almost everyone who gets them dies. The one clinical study showed ninety-four percent for hemorrhagic and one hundred percent for macular, each with over a hundred cases."

"So this is, what? Hemorrhagic or macular?" Mike asked.

"Wait," the Russian replied. "It is worse. The problem with hemorrhagic or macular as a weapon is that they are infectious only for a very short period of time. Then the carrier dies and is no longer spreading them. From a bio-weapons standpoint, that is termed a 'sub-optimal carrier.' Standard, in many ways, is better *because* the onset is slow."

"You figured out a way to spread it out," Mike said, tonelessly. "Or you upped the fatality level of standard."

"This is a modified form of macular, the very most deadly," Chechnik said, nodding. "The infected person lives for up to five days while being infectious and then dies, nearly one hundred percent of the time. And that is even if they have been given the vaccine. There is no vaccine, no antidote, that will save anyone who is infected. If this gets out, it will kill the whole world. Your writer Stephen King wrote a book, yes, *The Stand*. This is Captain Trips. At most a few thousand people left in the whole world. That cannot even restart the human race. And it was modified to be very . . . latent. That is it will survive for a long time even if there is not a host. It will wait for years if necessary to find a host."

"You evil motherfuckers," Mike whispered. "You couldn't just destroy it, could you? We turn our nukes away, you turn your nukes away, but you keep this . . . this fucking doomsday device? Why?"

"We see as one on this," Chechnik said, shrugging. "Vladimir swears that he was unaware of this weapon, but I don't believe him. However, if you recover it . . ."

"If I *recover* it it's going straight to the U.S.," Mike said, savagely. "I don't know if *they'll* destroy it or not . . ."

"No," Chechnik said. "Please. This is exactly what we cannot allow."

"What? You think I'm just going to give it *back*?"

"No, I don't expect that," Chechnik said. "No one expects you to give it back, although I have been assured that if you do we will destroy it."

"Right," Mike scoffed. "Just like you did for the last, what? Twenty years?"

"But Dr. Arensky knows the proper protocols for destroying it," the Russian continued as if he wasn't listening. "He will show you how to destroy it. You must recover Arensky, alive."

"I'm tempted to put a bullet through his head," Mike snarled.

"Don't," Chechnik said, shaking his head. "Arensky is very much a victim in all of this."

"Huh?" Mike replied, frowning. "More stuff you haven't told us?"

"Arensky is a good man," Chechnik said. "Yes, he works on biological and chemical weapons. But he has come up with more cures, more defenses, than assaults. He also is a . . . a universalist, yes? He thinks of his country first, but then of the good of the world. He prefers playing the defense, yes? You have people in your own military who work on these things. Are they all evil?"

"So why'd he defect?" Mike asked. "And take this shit with him?"

"Probably his daughter," Chechnik said with a sigh. "He dotes on Marina. We now believe that Marina disappeared well before Dr. Arensky. It is probable that she was kidnapped and used to force him to do this. Arensky is also a genius in the entire field. He is expert on chemical and biological production methods. He even has much knowledge of details of nuclear weapons production. We believe the smallpox was only the tip of the iceberg. He took disks with him with details on various forms of weapons production, including nuclear. We believe that he is being traded to a major country. They probably were the funding source for this operation. One assumes that they can continue to use Marina as a method to force him to assist them in their WMD efforts. And the smallpox is probably not for use. Some country, Iran, yes? They will get it, prove that they have it, and hold it to prevent the Americans from taking action against them. Mutual Assured Destruction, yes? If you overthrow the mullahs, they destroy the world."

"Your security is a nightmare," Mike said. "You know that, right?"

"We are aware of that, yes," the Russian said with a frown. "In this case . . . we are aware of this, yes. We are, as they say, working on it."

"Work faster," Mike replied. "I'm getting tired of cleaning up your messes for you. The Keldara are *not* prepared to handle chem-bio. Hell, we haven't even trained them on MOPP gear!"

"If this gets loose, it won't matter," Chechnik said, shrugging. "But the vials are in very sturdy containers. As long as those are not breached, and you cannot do that with a rifle or even an RPG, then everything will be fine. He took containers as well. They are about ten centimeters high and eight across and made of steel and depleted uranium, yes? You cannot even penetrate one with one of your Barrett sniper rifles. But you must recover Arensky, yes? It would be good if you could recover Marina. Then destroy the vials and this nightmare is over."

Mike thought about what was being asked of him for a moment and then shrugged.

"I'm going to do this anyway," he said, carefully. "And I don't want to sound mercenary. But . . . Bob pointed out that if I recovered nukes, I'd get the vig on those. If you guys don't even want me to tell the U.S. what I got . . ."

"How are you going to get paid?" Chechnik asked.

"That and . . . They're going to want to know what I got," Mike pointed out. "If I turn up empty-handed, there are going to be lots of unpleasant questions."

"We will give you three nukes," Chechnik said. "If you destroy the smallpox and . . ."

"Keep my mouth shut," Mike finished for him.

"Yes."

"So . . ." He started to chuckle and just couldn't stop for a second. "So what you're telling me is that you're going to *hand* me nuclear weapons? Atomic bombs? Da Big Ones?"

"Well, we're pretty sure you won't *use* them," the Russian pointed out. "And then you can sell them to the Amis and everyone is happy. Also, they will be very *small* nukes," the intel officer added with a grin.

"Four," Mike said. "For this op, I'd better be paid a pretty penny. And it's not like you don't have a shitload lying around."

"Now *that* was mercenary," Chechnik said, frowning.

"I've got a very high overhead," Mike replied. "Welcome to capitalism."

"Four," the intelligence specialist agreed.

Mike suspected by the quick capitulation that he could have gone higher. But, hell, he was going to get that damned shipment even if it meant expending every last Keldara and *no* payment. On the other hand, if the Russians stiffed him they weren't going to like the repayment. That assumed that he wasn't being handed *another* bill of goods.

"We will get the nukes to you, here, as soon as you send word that the material has been captured and eliminated. The Georgians have agreed to let an American team pick them up. We can sneak the nukes in easily enough."

"Got it. Do I need anything special to destroy this stuff?" Mike asked.

"There are various ways," Chechnik said with a shrug. "But I would suggest carrying some carboys of acid. Very strong acid."

"Great," Mike grumped. "Just what I need to be carrying on a combat op."

"Katya," Anastasia said with a slightly malicious smile, "this is Mr. Jay." She'd called Katya into her office to introduce the Kildar's newest associate.

"Just Jay, please," the man said, looking the girl up and down. "Just . . . Jay."

"Hello, Jay," Katya said, looking the apparent Keldara up and down. She was smiling and ducking her head, coquettishly. "I'm Katya. How are you?"

"English, please," Jay said in British-accented English. "Anastasia, could I borrow your office for a moment?"

"Certainly, sir," Anastasia replied, getting up and going to the door. "You two have fun."

"Could you say that for me again?" Jay said, walking up to the girl and starting to circle her from just beyond arm's reach.

"Who are you?" Katya asked, still smiling pleasantly. "And could you stop circling me? It's making me nervous."

"Then you need to learn to use more than your eyes to track me," Jay replied. "Say it again. In English. I will choose the language, you will reply. And you are my padwan, and I am your Jedi master. You may call me Jay."

"I do not have a master," Katya said, somewhat less coquettishly. But it was in English.

"Well, in this case, it's an honorific," Jay replied. "And we'll need to work on the accent. You should be able, at your age, to learn to turn it on and off. After nineteen, for some reason, it becomes nearly impossible. *Sprechen Sie Deutsch?*"

"*Nur bisschen,*" Katya said. She'd taken to looking straight ahead rather than following him in his circling.

"Definite accent there," Jay said in Russian. "Try something a little longer."

"*Gottverdammte teilzeit schmierfink,*" Katya said, smiling pleasantly.

"Yes, we're definitely going to have to work the accent out," Jay continued, ignoring the rather odd curse. "There are only three major remaining regional dialects in German. At least in Deutschland. Austrian and Swiss German are slightly different. We'll see how many you can absorb. And Arabic, well, there are so many variants of that it's funny."

"I can't pass in Arab countries," Katya said, lifting up her hair. "Blonde, see?"

"There are some blondes to be found," Jay replied. "And there's this thing I don't think you've ever heard of called 'hair dye.' Oh, no, I take that back. You're not nearly as light a blonde as you would like to appear. Closer to dishwater than platinum, babe.

Your dye job's showing through at the roots. Nice touch making sure the carpet matches the drapes, though."

"You're a spy master," Katya said in English, dropping the coquettishness.

"No, I am a master spy," Jay replied. "There is a difference. A spy master runs multiple spies but is not necessarily a good spy. A master spy is a master spy. Part of my job will involve training you. Part of that will be teaching you to see what is really in front of you instead of what you want to see. There are two main purposes to that; reporting accurate information and developing the ability to recognize and assimilate every detail of a culture so that you can disappear into that culture in an instant. You'd like to learn to disappear in an instant, wouldn't you, Katya?"

"Yes," Katya admitted.

"So I'm not going to threaten you with anything but this," Jay continued, leaning in from behind so he was right by her left ear. "The moment that I think your attention wavers, the moment that you don't give me every particle of your being, I will simply stop teaching you. When you know it all, feel free to leave. Please. Because it will no longer be worth my time and I will no longer waste my time. There will be no threats, there will be no warnings, there will be no appeal and there will be no more lessons. Do you understand me?"

"Perfectly," Katya replied.

"Then let us begin . . ."

Mike had arranged a meeting with the rest of the command group after the private meeting. He could tell that Adams, Nielson and especially Vanner were alive with curiosity about what had been discussed. But he was still trying to figure out how to handle the information so he ignored their curiosity.

"Baseline," Mike said as soon as the group was assembled in his office: "I trust Colonel Chechnik with any information we give him. On the other hand, he's also required to report it to his superiors. And since we got burned by leaks in the Russian military one time, you can ask him any questions you'd like but we're not giving him our mission plan. You okay with that, Colonel?"

"Perfectly," Chechnik replied.

"So, besides what you gave me, which is not open for discussion at this time, why are you here?" Mike asked.

"My job is to find out what you need to improve the likelihood of this mission's success and then get it to you," Chechnik said. "I have the full support of the Stavka as well as the office of the president. We want these nuclear weapons stopped. But we ask that it be quietly."

"Also, Arensky is no longer to be considered a bad guy," Mike noted. "And we need to raise the profile of recovering his daughter. It's now believed that she was kidnapped to force him to defect with the . . . materials."

"Okay," Nielson said after a moment's pause. "You realize you just said we're going to have to do a split mission. And it was already hairy as hell."

"I'm aware of that," Mike said. "For various reasons I'm going to handle the side with Arensky and the WMD. Adams will lead the strike team to try to recover Marina. Katya will duplicate the Balkans op: localize to secure. So what do we need, want or desire from Colonel Chechnik."

"Sucks to be a hostage," Adams said, repeating a common SEAL mantra. In most hostage-rescue training missions, the "hostage," invariably a dummy dressed as the hostage, was killed either by the rescuers or the holders.

"Try to make it suck less," Mike said. "Anything else?"

"Well, I could use some better satellite intel," Vanner said. "Specifically, better than one-meter scale shots for the entire area."

"You need them for map generation, yes?" the Russian officer said. "Would maps be better? We have high-resolution maps for the area."

"You do?" Vanner said. "I've been looking for maps for forever for this area."

"What do you think our Spetznaz use?" Chechnik replied. "We can get you topographical maps, in raw DTED or imagery, if you wish. Also the satellite photos. And we can provide real-time satellite tasking during the mission."

"I was going to ask Washington for that," Mike admitted. "I'd like a Predator on station in support."

"I have been made aware that the U.S. is willing to supply such support," Chechnik replied.

"Christ, talk about cooperation," Adams snorted. "Am I the only one that's having weird reality distortion here?"

"I've seen it before," Mike admitted. "Once."

"Paris," the Russian said, nodding. "Yes, when one of our nuclear weapons becomes, as you Americans say it, 'in play,' we become very cooperative."

"We need everything you have on the players," Nielson pointed out. "And the order of battle with data on individuals down to small-unit commanders. If you have it."

"Of course," Chechnik said, opening up his briefcase and sliding a DVD onto the tabletop. "All of what we have is in here. It is everything that my office was able to find, at least. As with your American intelligence agencies, there is often something out there that one group knows that the rest do not. But I swear this is everything that the president of Russia could put his hand on in less than a week. It is in Russian, but I understand you can handle that."

"One thing that might or might not be in there," Mike said, musingly. "We need the name of a slaver that works the area. Preferably one that's not terribly brutal. I'd prefer one that if he has a good worker doesn't punch her around just to show her who is boss."

"I only reviewed the information," Chechnik said, cautiously. "And it focuses on the military groups in the area. I'm not sure what it has about the sex-slavers. Some of them are both, of course."

"Everything you can get in a couple of days," Mike said. "We are getting on short time for this op. And *that* request for info stays very close to the chest, understood? You don't even pass it to Vladimir. Just inside your group on a need-to-know basis."

"I will do it," Chechnik said.

"I think that's it for now," Mike continued. "Colonel, we have a lot of planning and prep to do for this mission. I hope you won't find it remiss if we cut this short. I'd appreciate it if you'd stay for dinner and overnight. I can have Anastasia show you around the area. I'd do it myself but I'm going to be pretty busy."

"Of course," Chechnik said. "I will leave you gentlemen to your business."

Chapter Thirteen

"Okay, Ass-Boy, why's he really here?" Adams said as soon as the door was closed.

"I'm still assimilating that," Mike said, looking at the wall. "Among other things, I had to promise to not tell the U.S. government what he told me to get their cooperation. And that goes for you guys, too. I'm willing, not happy but willing, to go along for the time being. But . . ."

"How serious is it?" Nielson asked. "I won't ask *what* it is, but how serious?"

"Not sure I can say even that," Mike replied. "But there's a reason that I'm taking the mission to recover the WMD and Arensky. I know the Keldara will keep their mouths shut."

"Well . . ." Vanner said, uneasily. "I hate to say this, but at this point, American and all that, my primary loyalty is here. If you think we should keep this from the U.S. government . . ."

"I'm pretty sure I should be on the phone to Washington right now," Mike said. "And I'm going to call them and ask them for a special tasking in case we fail. Put it that way."

"Special tasking?" Adams said. "You mean you want them to bomb the area if you can't get the materials?"

"Sort of."

✧　✧　✧

"This is rather unusual, Mike," the President said over the video connection.

The secure room in the U.S. Embassy, Tbilisi was a windowless shield room. But it had a video connection on the securest possible system connected to the American military communications system. Mike simply didn't have time to go to Washington for the conversation; this was the best compromise under the circumstances.

"I agree Mr. President," Mike said, looking at the other connections. The secretary of state, the former NSA, was on one of the screens, the secretary of defense on another. "And thank you for your time. But this was something that only you could decide upon."

"Go ahead," the president said.

"Yes, sir," Mike said, trying not to swallow nervously. "I have been given some additional information by the Russians. However, I was given the information on the agreement that I would *not* pass it to the American government."

"So why are we here?" the secretary of defense asked, angrily. "And how the hell could you agree to that?"

"Because Colonel Chechnik said I needed it," Mike said. "And because I hope that I can convince you of something very serious without, in fact, divulging the information."

"Do *we* need the information?" the secretary of state asked.

"Probably," Mike replied. "I'm playing a very hard game here, balancing a wire that's damned thin. I will say that if my mission succeeds you probably don't need it anymore. It will be history. And if I fail, well, that's why I'm here."

"Mike . . ." the president said, then paused. "Mike you've done a lot of good things for your country, for the world. I'm not about to sit here and question your patriotism. But I have to wonder about judgment."

"So do I, sir," Mike admitted. "But if my judgment was incredibly hot, I never would have made it to Syria."

"Point," the president said, grinning. "What do you want?"

"I think it's what we all need, instead," Mike replied. "I'm going to insert the Keldara, and an agent, into the area then attempt to intercept the transfer. One of the items I don't feel bad about passing is that the Russians now think that Arensky is being forced by the terrorists. His daughter was probably kidnapped to get him to go along. That means we're now trying to intercept the shipment, rescue Arensky *and* his daughter. With a very small force. The only thing that matters, though, is the shipment. In the event that we are unable to secure the shipment, I'm asking that you task a nuclear weapon to take it out."

"You want us to drop a nuke on Georgian territory?" the secretary of state said, evenly.

"Yes, ma'am," Mike replied. "Here is my thinking on this. The Georgians are aware that there may be a passage of a weapon through their territory; that's why I have the mission. If there is a nuclear event, we can say that it was a detonation of the package due to the terrorists. Just like the Bahamas. Put up a B-2 on station with a steerable special munition. If the package goes into play, if we fail, the B-2 takes out the package. It looks as if the terrorists set off the nuke rather than have it fall into our hands. I'd also like to request Predator tasking in support."

"Mike . . ." the President said, then paused again. "How far do we let it run?"

"Nowhere," Mike replied. "Hit it the moment it goes into play. Right then, right there. If I am still in play and on site, I will specifically request it."

"That's your own position," the secretary of defense pointed out. "Close *counts* with nuclear weapons, Mike. I'd hate like hell to have a nuke in play, but I'm not sure it's worth taking *you* out. We've got strategic room to stop it."

"Sir, as I said, I have information that you do not," Mike replied. "My . . . judgment is that if we cannot absolutely secure this weapon at the point at which we know it is going to be, that a special munition be used to ensure that it does *not* go into play. And it has to be a special munition. It *can not* be a standard munition. That would be worse than not hitting it at all."

"You said 'weapon,' not nuclear weapon. It's not a nuke," the secretary of state said definitely. She had cut her teeth on Soviet disarmament negotiations and knew WMD backwards and forwards.

"Neither confirm nor deny," Mike replied with a death's-head grin.

"I'll get back to you on this," the President said, looking at his own monitors. "With either a yes or no. If it's a no, it's a definite no. Who's going to coordinate for the Predators and such? That we can guarantee."

"I'll work that through our CIA liaison," the secretary of defense said. "Based upon Mr. Jenkins' recommendation, though, you have my assent and recommendation. His argument about the cover story is a valid point. We can blame it on the terrorists. And if he is willing to nuke his own position, and his own people, to stop this 'weapon' then he has thought this through carefully."

"I'm not worried about blame," the President said. "I'm worried about killing a friend."

"Don't, Mr. President," Mike said. "Make that the last thing on your mind. Because no decision you've *ever* made is as important as this one."

"Minuet?" the President said, as soon as Mike cut his connection. "You have a clue what he is talking about I'd guess."

"I think the Russians let a biological out of their labs," Minuet said, thoughtfully. "An infectious one and deadly. That is his point about not using a standard weapon. As standard weapon would have the possibility of breaking containment and spreading the biological. A nuke will sterilize the area."

"That's what the Russians don't want us to know," the secretary of defense said, angrily. "I can see why. Those *stupid* bastards."

"And if Mike wants to keep his relations with the Russians we can't let them know that we even guess," Minuet pointed out. "However, we don't know that that is actually what is going on."

"Explain," the president said.

"It is probably accurate," Minuet pointed out. "But it is what Colonel Chechnik knows or has been told and then what he has chosen to tell Mike. Probably he was told we're looking at some sort of infectious biological. Mike, from his SEAL training, is well versed in biologicals. If it were, say, anthrax, he would not react this way. However, he is also a well-known personality within a small group. The Russians may have anticipated his reaction and told him it is a nasty bio-weapon so that he would, in turn, scream to us for help. They may be simply interested in ensuring that Dr. Arensky is taken out of play. A nuke would certainly do that."

"For now, I am giving provisional authority," the President said, tightly. "But when this mission goes down, I want all three of us up and alert. I am going to have to make moment-to-moment decisions on release. Ensure that all the communications are in place for that."

"Shota, I want you to listen to me *carefully* this time," Adams said, trying not to sigh.

Shota was probably the biggest Keldara there was and just about the most massive guy Adams had ever known. He was even bigger than Russell, the former Ranger who had been a trainer up until he went back to the World. Shota was over two meters in his stocking feet, broad as a fucking house and most of it slabs of heavy muscle. The guy had shoulders that, literally, filled a door. Unfortunately, while not all big guys were dumb, Shota typified the stereotype. At least Russell had had two brain cells to rub together. Not more than two, mind you, he was a Ranger, after all. But two. Shota would be a perfect point guy for entry if Adams could ever teach him to count as high as *five*.

"It's really really easy," Adams said, slowly. "You go through the door and take *five* steps. Not four, not six. Definitely not *one*. Understand? Five. Count them with me. One . . . Two . . ."

"One . . . two . . . three . . . f . . ." Shota said, his brow creasing.

"Okay, try it this way," Adams said, turning him to parallel the wall of the shoot house. "Walk with me. One . . . two . . . three . . . four . . . five steps."

Shota nodded and looked around. "I stop here? Room's over there?"

"No, you'll be *in* the room," Adams said. "Just do the steps again. One . . . two . . . three . . . four . . . five! Got it, do it again . . . One . . . two . . ."

Adams had him take five steps, his weapon forward, over and over again. Then he had him trot it. Finally, he was pretty sure the big ox had got it.

"Okay, now we're going into doctorate territory," Adams said. "You point your shotgun at the lock of the door. When I give you the word, you blow the lock off. Then you *kick* the door open. When it's open, *then* you take your five steps, got it?"

"No," Shota admitted.

"Follow my actions," Adams said, pointing his M4 down as if at a doorknob. "Follow me." He ran through the sequence seven times with the massive Keldara following his moves. He'd ensured Shota's weapon was unloaded before they started so he even had him dry-fire.

"When you get to the end of your five steps, *then* you look for valid targets. What's a valid target?" They'd drilled this one mercilessly in training, so Shota got it right off.

"He got a weapon in his hand," Shota said. "You shoot the guys with the weapon."

"In your sector," Adams added.

"In my sector," Shota said. "I do my sector. Oleg, him do his sector."

"What *don't* we shoot?" Adams asked.

"We don't shoot no girls," Shota said, carefully but fast enough it was clear he understood. "'Less them got weapons. We don't shoot no kids, even if them got weapons. We don't shoot no men not got weapons."

"By George, I think you've got it," Adams said. "Okay, troops, let's load 'em up and try this! Through that door at a run!"

"The Keldara are a fascinating people," Jay said.

He and Katya were parked on a wall watching the small Keldara village. Both were dressed in local clothes and to a casual observer blended in. Jay was not a casual observer. As Katya reached a hand up to fiddle with her top he held up his hands with index fingers making the sign of a cross as if over a grave.

"You're dead," Jay said. "You *are* a Keldara woman. You have worn those clothes your whole life. There is no reason to fiddle with them. Very few women will adjust anything in public unless they are very uncomfortable with the clothing. Street whores will, I'll give you that. And if you're at a formal-dress dinner with a large number of women unaccustomed to formal dress, you *must* fiddle from time to time. And walk badly in heels. Very important. Walking badly in heels, if you normally don't, is a very difficult skill to learn. But you are not playing the part of a street whore or a female more accustomed to jeans than gowns. So you're dead."

"Yes, but I *can* play the part of a street whore," Katya said, bitterly. "I have that down to an *art*."

"As the Kildar has the bluff warrior down to an art," Jay sighed. "Because he lives it. But you cannot play a Keldara woman, yet, nor the slightly different version you'll find in Chechnya. And you *must*. This is the first part you must learn if you want to survive this mission."

"Why?" Katya asked. "I go in, find the target, do what I can to prevent her being taken out and then we extract with the strike team."

"And if anything goes wrong?" Jay asked. "The strike team gets intercepted? The mission is blown? Your cover is blown? What then? You're out in the cold, honey. And they're looking for a blonde whore."

"Lots of blonde whores," Katya pointed out.

"Then you know it all?" Jay asked, carefully.

"No, I do not, O master," Katya replied. "Enlighten me, O font of wisdom."

"Sarcasm I can take," Jay said. "Mulishness I can't. You are out in the cold. The enemy is looking for a street whore. You cannot, yet, become a man in an instant. Who do you become?"

"One of the local women," Katya replied. "They speak Georgian and Russian."

"Can you mimic the accent?" Jay asked.

"Oh, yeah, sir, that I can," Katya said in a provincial southern Russian.

"But you are not *them*," Jay said. "You are not a teenage girl, frightened of these problem men all around. Probably raised Eastern Orthodox but surrounded by Muslims who consider her not much more than a whore because she doesn't wear a burka. At least her head will be covered. Flinching and skulking to get to market and back to the farm without being beaten or robbed or raped. Born on a farm, hardly seeing a town her whole life. Not even knowing what sex or rape really is most likely unless her father or uncle has broached her on a long winter night. Just that she can't have either one happen or she'll end up as . . . a street whore. You were born in a city, weren't you?"

"Yes," Katya said. "How did you know?"

"Ask me again in two or three years," Jay replied, watching with interest as several of the elders of the tribe gathered outside one of the houses. "But you won't have to. Orphanage. First sexual experience there when you were . . . ten? The guy who ran the orphan-age, the 'orphan master.' Somewhere in Siberia. Not Novy Birsk but close. Killed someone in the orphanage. Made it look like an acci-dent. Probably not even someone who had hurt you, just someone you knew you could kill and get away with it. Tossed out at thir-teen or possibly just sold straight to your first pimp. Shuffled south and east towards the Balkans. Left here because the whoremaster in town couldn't find anyone stupid enough to buy you, no matter how pretty. Picked up by the Kildar as a necessity and he made a virtue out of it by using you as a spy. But he's just another user to you, isn't he?"

"How?" Katya said, softly.

"Again, ask me in about ten years," Jay said as the elders filed into the house. "But if you've been my pupil for that long, and you won't be, you won't need to ask. I doubt you'll stay for more than a year more. If, when, you go out on your own, if you keep studying in about twenty years you will know. If I can get you to even mimic a Keldara in six months, really mimic, so I can find no flaw, cut six years off that time. Either one. But I'm not sure you'll ever be good enough. You're missing one very vital component for being a really good spy."

"What?" Katya asked, confused.

"Empathy." Jay said, looking at the house then up at the cara-vanserai. "Very important to a spy. Empathy gives you the ability to read below the surface. To see not only what is there but what is hidden."

"There is no way to hide it," Mother Mahona said. "She is smit-ten."

"As is the Kildar," Father Ferani said. "Which is a pity."

"I have always felt that this Kildar was . . . not good," Father Devlich said. "He is not true Kildar."

"He has proven his worth again and again as a provider and as a warrior," Mother Makanee snapped. "The Kildar must, by rights, have both strength *and* the Soul of Battle. The Soul, though . . ."

"Makes them vulnerable," Father Kulcyanov wheezed. "I saw it in many of the best of my commanders. But it is what makes them the best. Without the Soul they are brainless bulls, unfit to lead a squad much less the Keldara. As much as we need the strength and spirit that the Kildars bring, the Soul has always been the hardest to find. This is a true Kildar. Whether he can manage to survive his trials, though, that is another question."

"He is weak," Ferani argued. "This . . . infatuation proves it."

"What of Kiril in all this?" Mother Devlich asked.

"If need be, Kiril will be sent forth," Father Kulcyanov said. "But I do not believe this Kildar will force that necessity. He has honor, this one. Strength, fierceness, honor and the Soul. It is a rare combination."

"A weak combination," Father Ferani said. "You will see. Every man has his weakness."

"Just because you have them, does not mean the Kildar does," Father Devlich said. "Some of us can keep our hands off other men's wives."

"Baaaaa," Father Ferani replied.

"Do *not* start that again," Mother Kulcyanov snapped. "Either of you. We must wait and see. If it is necessary, Kiril will be sent forth. We will speak to Colonel Nielson and ensure that he is sent to a proper place for a trained warrior. This is Tradition."

"Agreed," Father Devlich said, nodding. "Kiril is young. He will survive and even prosper. And a Keldara as Kildaran . . ."

"Oh, yes, leave it to *me* to break it to Katrina," Mother Ferani said, shaking her head.

"Katrina will be the least of our worries," Mother Lenka said. She was not usually included in such councils. She knew why she was here for this one. "If you send Kiril forth and present Gretchen to *this* Kildar, he will probably send you *all* forth. Bide your time. The final toss is yet to be played in this game."

"Okay, I've briefed you on this," Mike shouted over the roar from the freefall simulator. "Now I'll show you."

The vertical wind tunnel was a fairly massive structure. Mike had had one hell of a time getting one in any sort of short time frame; they usually were built in place over a couple of months. As it was it had taken three precious days, and damned near a half a million dollars, to get it to the valley of the Keldara. And that didn't include the Georgian military heavy lift chopper that brought it from the airport.

Designed to be loaded on a trailer, the system was hardly state-of-the-art. The enormous sound generated by the older-style trainers had become an issue in all developed countries so they were going relatively cheap. If you could call two hundred thousand dollars cheap.

But it was the one that Mike could get, in a hurry, cash on the barrel, no questions asked. So it was what he had to work with.

The system included a catwalk that led to a wide platform. The catwalk and platform were supported twenty feet in the air. Under the platform was a heavy-duty fan, a wind generator. Around the platform, which was heavily padded, was a steel cage in case the "flyer" got lifted too high or off to the side. In the middle of the platform area was a ten-foot hole through which the wind entered.

The whole thing, fortunately, had fit in an Russian Antonov heavy lift aircraft. Mike had had to rent time on the private aircraft for the lift, which was hardly cheap. But with the generator he could speed up the training of the insertion team to the point that they'd be *marginally* qualified for one hairy damned mission in time.

Besides Vanner, he'd chosen Julia Makanee and Olga Shaynav, two of his best radio operators. To backstop them there were two Keldara "hitters." The five were his charges for the next week. He had exactly seven days to get them not only HALO-qualified but *comfortable* with the idea. The standard military course was *five* weeks, not one. And on any conceivable mission that the U.S. military would send green HALO jumpers on, they'd be accompanied by trained and experienced personnel. In this case, the *entire team* would be green jumpers.

Given that a few people *always* balked at actually jumping out of a perfectly good airplane, that was going to be interesting. He'd considered picking a few standbys, just in case one of the group was absolutely unwilling to actually jump or couldn't handle the training. But he really didn't have anyone to spare.

He'd used the three days to advantage, giving classes in freefall maneuvers, having everyone practice body positions while lying on their stomachs and going over the theory of freefall, steerable parachutes and HALO. The classes had run from early morning until he could tell that everyone's brains but Vanner's were cooking.

Now it was time to start working on freefall techniques. He wanted all five to be comfortable with that before their first jumps; he just didn't have the time for tandem training.

Everyone was wearing jump coveralls, which were easier to train in. The coveralls were loose but Mike had to admit that Oleg and Julia still looked hot. Mike looked around at the group, grinned and then jumped into the rushing wind.

The enormous force of the wind picked him up out of his leap and lofted him up to about head-height. He hung there in a box-man position, arms and legs spread, then used his fingers to carefully spin in place, without moving out of the wind. He was pretty rusty—his last freefall was more than two years ago—but the moves were coming back pretty quick.

"What's this position, Jeseph?" Mike shouted.

"Box-man, Kildar!" the shooter replied.

"Exactly, full box-man," Mike said. "Now, if I pull my arms and legs in . . ." he said, matching actions with words, "I sink. That will mean you fall faster. Olga! Why would you want to do that?"

"I'm lighter than the men," the girl shouted back. "I might have to speed up to maintain formation!"

"Right!" Mike yelled then assumed another position, the quickly snapped out of it as he started to fly out of the windstream. "What was that position, Jeseph?"

"Delta!" Jeseph shouted back. "Useful for dropping fast and short, fast, maneuvers."

"Got it!" Mike yelled then got back in the box-man position, but with his hands out of position. Suddenly he started moving away from them, slowly. "Julia! What's happening? What's happening?!" he shouted as if panicked.

"Kildar!" the girl shouted back, nervously, then stopped, grinned and shook her head. "Slide? Yes? You try to scare me!"

"Slide," Mike said, reconfiguring to get back in the middle of the windstream. "When you use this at first, you're *going* to slide! I'll be shouting instructions at you on how to stop sliding. But you'll go back and forth, side to side," Mike said, adding motions to the explanation. "But even if you get thrown *all* the way out!" He moved his arms outwards and was suddenly thrown backwards out of the windstream, hitting the padding hard and then rolling to his feet. It was an effort, but he needed to demonstrate. "You'll be fine! That's what the padding is for! Besides, when you start you'll have on a harness," he added with a grin. "Vanner! You're up."

"Urrah!" the Marine shouted. "Let's *do* this!"

Chapter Fourteen

"Master Chief?" Greznya said as Adams was walking out of the shoot house. He looked ragged and she wasn't sure if now was the best time but the intel was very hot.

"Go," Adams said, stripping off his balaclava and taking a deep breath. "Christ. I swear shoot houses take a year off your life every time you go in one. If it's not the propellant fumes it's the gaseous lead."

Greznya Kulcyanov was twenty, old for a Keldara girl to be unmarried, with bright blue eyes and red hair. She had been one of the first girls to join the intel section and when Mike had finally instituted rank for the "intel girls" was immediately appointed NCOIC with a rank of team sergeant, the highest NCO position among the Keldara.

"Yes, Master Chief," the girl said, dimpling prettily. "We have a new download from Washington. They've gotten ground penetrating shots of the buildings in Gamasoara as well as the two buildings near the agreed meeting place. There is no guarantee that Marina is in any of them, but . . ."

"But it's good intel," Adams said, rubbing a bright red mark on his cheek that looked something like the imprint of a gun barrel. Greznya could tell that it was fresh and couldn't imagine where he'd gotten it. "Can you convert . . . ?"

"I've already converted the shots into two-dimensional maps of each of the buildings that are probable for holding the hostage," Greznya said. "However, Creata has an interesting idea. She is pretty sure that she can create 3-D imagery for Unreal for some of the buildings. That will give an internal map of the building that we can load into the game packages. We could even run scenarios with it. Perhaps when we find where Marina is, if Katya can . . ."

"We're looking at nearly a week for insertion," Adams said, rubbing his chin. "Do it if you have time. Good work. I need to look at those maps as soon as I'm done with reviewing this exercise."

"Very good, Master Chief," Greznya said. "I'll have them in your office by the time you get back."

"Okay, now let me go speak to the children," he said, turning back to the entry team. "SHOTA, WHAT THE FUCK DID YOU THINK YOU WERE DOING? FIVE! FIVE, FIVE, FIVE! NOT FUCKING *ONE!*"

"Okay, Julia, hold that," Mike yelled over the wind noise.

A couple of days' hard training and the group weren't exactly masters of the air, but they had the basic moves. They'd all managed to learn to hold position in a box-man, maneuver slightly from that position and work in a delta, with the arms tucked in for more rapid descent and maneuvering.

Now it was on to tougher processes.

"Bring your arms in front of your face, carefully," Mike said. "Now, check your direction and distance."

At least Mike had managed to get top-line electronic equipment. Each of the team was outfitted with a GPS based navigation system. Punch in a GPS coordinate and it would give them current altitude and a direction and distance to the target.

Julia slowly brought her arms in front of her face and then glanced at the GPS.

"That way," Julia said, gesturing to her right with her chin. "I'm at ten thousand AGL." She referred to Above Ground Level. Height above sea level doesn't matter to a parachutist; the only thing that matters is height above what you're going to smack into.

"I'll give the distance as two kilometers," Mike said. "Okay, slowly rotate in that direction. Rotate a bit, check position, rotate a bit, check position. Carefully. Don't worry if you overshoot, just rotate back."

Julia followed the directions, occasionally bobbling in the air and sliding to the side but always getting back in position. It was hard work, fighting the blast stream the whole time while trying to keep in position three-dimensionally. But finally she was lined up.

"Do a ground check," Mike said. "Can you see the ground?"

"You said the weather report said clear," Julia replied. "I can see the ground."

"Do you think you have the DZ in sight?"

"I have the DZ," Julia said. "I think so. It's right *there*," she added, pointing to a mark Mike had made on the wall.

"Could be the wrong DZ," Mike pointed out. "Wouldn't be the first time. But you don't have a lot of margin for error; most of the area is vertical. It's the only potential landing spot you've got if you don't want to be kissing a cliff."

"It's the right DZ," Julia replied, grinning. "I recognize it from the satellite shots."

"Good," Mike replied. "Check your teammates, now. Where are they?"

"Most of them are below me," Julia said, looking around. "Even Olga; she's been putting on weight."

"Have not!" Olga yelled.

"Okay, slide over so you're clustered, but don't get too close. You don't want their airstream interfering with yours. Do a ground check. You're off course to the left. What's happening?"

"Wind shear," Julia said. "I correct."

"Check your GPS," Mike said. "Your distance is now one hundred meters to the DZ. You are at four thousand AGL."

"How did I get there so quickly?" Julia said, confused.

"You tell me," Mike replied, raising an eyebrow.

"The wind," Julia said after a moment. "It's pushing me across the DZ."

"Three thousand AGL," Mike yelled. "You're going to be popping any second. What do you do?"

Julia's mouth opened and closed for a moment and then she shrugged.

"I don't know!"

"Out of exercise," Mike said, waving her to the side. The Keldara girl slid sideways in the airstream until she was at the edge of the tank and then slid off into Mike's arms.

"It wasn't really your call to make," Mike admitted. "But . . . dropping is strange. You think you have all the time in the world and then all of a sudden you're *out* of time to make decisions. Vanner, your team is overshooting the drop zone. Enough that you're not going to be able to paraglide back to it. What do you do?"

"Rotate the formation into the wind," Vanner said, quickly. "Go into a delta-track and head as much into it as possible. It increases our rate of drop but increases our horizontal velocity. I trade height for distance."

"Good enough answer," Mike replied. "And that is the answer to Julia's question as well: You follow your team leader. That's why he should be lined up at the bottom of the stick. He is responsible for ensuring that you all get close enough to the DZ that you can all make it. Even if you think he's wrong on his approach, *you follow your team leader.*

"What probably happens is that you miss the drop zone," Mike admitted. "If the winds are that high, that they push you that fast during the drop phase, you're going to be all over the map in the paraglide phase. Where you're dropping, most of you are probably gonna kiss a cliff or slam into a mountainside. In which case, Vanner, you're going to have four or more out of your team with broken bones or worse. Who takes over if Vanner is killed?"

"I do," Julia said.

"Right, then Olga. And if both of them are out?"

"I take over," Jeseph admitted. "But I'm not as up on the commo end."

"Set up the commo, report in and then do what you can to hold on until I can get someone in to replace and support you," Mike replied. "We *will* get somebody in there, I promise. But you have to be ready for worst case. Worst case is you disappear into a black hole from my side. Worst case for you as well, but second worst is serious injuries in multiple on the drop. Keep an eye on your height and distance . . ."

Mike paused as the door to the simulator opened and Nielson stuck his head in the door.

"Kildar, got something, can't wait."

"Okay," Mike said. "Crap. Vanner, take over. Just work on positions and air-feel. I'll be back . . ." He looked over at Nielson and raised an eyebrow.

"Not soon," Nielson said, frowning.

"What you got?" Mike asked as soon as he was out of the simulator and the ensuing racket was somewhat quieter.

"We've got a problem with the helo transport," Nielson said, his upper lip twitching angrily. He probably didn't even realize he had that tick, but Mike knew when he was really REALLY pissed and the retired colonel was *definitely* pissed. People dying pissed.

"The Georgian government is balking at letting us use that heavy lift company we used in Albania," Nielson said. "Guess why."

"No guesses," Mike said with a sigh. "They're Russians."

"Bingo. I just got off the phone with General Umarov. They're, barely, willing to let us use them to lift us part way in. But the group *can not* be used inside the Pankisi military zone. They can neither be used to extract us *nor* for dust-off of wounded. No entry. Period."

"What the fuck do they want us to do?" Mike snapped. "Walk out? With our wounded? We *are* going to take casualties on this one."

"I, as calmly as I could, asked the general the same question," Nielson said, his lip really going now. "And he suggested that he speak with the Kildar."

"Actually said it that way?" Mike asked, trying not to grin.

"Yep," Nielson replied.

"Okay," Mike said, shrugging. "I guess I go put on my Kildar hat."

"General Umarov," Mike said, leaning back in his chair. "How good to speak with you again."

"And you Kildar," Umarov replied, his voice a bit taut. "I'm sorry I had to disturb your training schedule: I understand it is rigorous."

"More so, lately," Mike said with a sigh. "I think we need to talk but I'd prefer not over the phone. However, time is tight. Is there any way you could free up a bird so I'm not on the road four hours in each direction? And, of course, some of your time which is also precious."

"Of course, Kildar," Umarov said. "I'll have it dispatched immediately."

"I'll be ready," Mike said. "We have an LZ set up, now. Down by the Keldara houses. I'll be there."

Mike opened up his closet and contemplated. He'd never had so many clothes in his life. Not only had he, perforce, gotten suits, variously graded depending on who he was meeting with, Anastasia had been shopping for "informal" wear for him. He contemplated the array, reached for his second-best suit, then his best suit, then reached all the way over to the side and pulled out a set of digi-cam.

This wasn't his field wear, though. This was the set of "dress" digi-cam he'd set up more or less on a whim. Modern "developing country" militaries had started to treat camouflage field uniforms as if they were dress uniforms. This probably came from the habit American generals had of almost always appearing in field uniforms. An American general, though, would only wear a couple of his qualification badges, name and branch tags and a shoulder patch on a plain, if well-pressed, digi-cam or BDU uniform.

Filtered through the medium of culture in developing countries, though, and you ended up with something different. The worst had to be "Syrian Commandoes" who had a purple camouflage uniform that would make a peacock go "OH MY GOD!" And, of course, it had to be bedecked in medals otherwise nobody would realize you were a general, right?

Mike had realized at some point he was going to have to tread a fine line. While there were times he was going to have to wear a cammie uniform for more or less "official" reasons, as a SEAL he had a problem. When SEALs wore field uniforms they *might* have a nametag. Otherwise they tended to be pretty bare. For one thing, everybody on the team knew who you were and what you'd done so you didn't have to cover the damned uniform in qualification badges and geegaws. You were a SEAL, who cared if you'd gone to another school; BUDS was all that mattered. And you didn't have to wear some stupid subdued SEAL badge. You were on the team. Ergo, you'd passed BUDS. Point, set, match.

But if he turned up in a set of sterile cammies, that would send the wrong message. It all came down to politics, something he'd hoped never to have to play. But in his current situation, it was a daily grind.

So he'd set up a set of "dress" cammies, most of it stolen lock-stock-and-barrel from the U.S. Army.

On the right and left shoulders were the snarling tiger face that was the Keldara patch, the left shoulder because he was, by God, a member and the right because he had, by God, been in combat ops with them. Over the left one was his Ranger badge from that extended version of hell: a fraction as bad as Hell Week but nine times as long. Under it was a U.S. flag because he was, by God, still a U.S. citizen. He'd found a subdued SEAL badge and that was on top of his qualification badges. Below that was his HALO badge flanked by Pathfinder. He could put on airborne wings if he wanted, master jumper given the number of times he'd jump-mastered drops.

Figuring out which to put on the Velcro patches had been hard. He'd sat down when he was contemplating the uniform and tried to figure out how many schools he'd gone to, on the side, that would qualify for badges on an Army uniform. In the end he realized that he could basically cover the damned thing. Sometimes he put on the Marine Sniper badge instead of Pathfinder, sometimes he switched both out for Sapper or for SCUBA, having cross-trained in all of them. Hell might as well put on French Commando school, which was a joke so bad it should be run by Cub Scouts, or Special Boat Squadron, which was one kick-your-ass motherfucker of a school that should be outlawed under international treaty.

SEAL instructors were supposed to be "broadly and comprehensively trained," said so right in the documentation. And their schools budget was huge, comparable to an entire Army division. In every department of the government budgets were the same: Use it or lose it. So the SEALs, especially the instructors, tended to spend two-thirds of their time training and the other third . . . burning off budget. It was amazing how many courses you could pack in in a sixteen-year career that had covered most of the time the U.S. was at relative peace.

The toughest part had been figuring out the branch tape and nametag. In the end, the branch tape, where it would say "U.S. Army" or "U.S. Navy" or whatever, simply read "Mountain Tigers" in Georgian. The nametag simply read: Kildar.

He looked at the suits, looked at the dress cammies and tossed the latter on the bed. Sometimes you just had to dress for success. Politics. What the fuck had he done to earn politics?

Mike got out of the Expedition and was surrounded by a smaller than normal contingent of children. From the looks of it most of the older ones were up in the hills picking tiger berries.

It was the time of year that the "secret ingredient" in Keldara beer reached full ripeness. Some of the shrubs had been planted to harvest for the brewery but they hadn't matured enough to provide more than a pittance. There was less than a week when they were ripe and for the Keldara the picking was an all-hands evolution. With the preparations for the mission, they had to be hard pressed to have enough bodies. From the looks of things the kids, down to six or so, had been sent up into the hills.

"Dimi," he said to one of the few of the younger children he recognized. "I need you to find someone to drive the truck back. Can you do that?"

"Yes, Kildar," the boy said, tucking the sweet in his cheek and dashing off.

Mike had about finished passing out the candy when he heard an indrawn breath and looked up into Gretchen's face.

"Ah, Gretchen . . ." Mike said, clearing his throat. "I don't suppose you know how to drive an Expedition?"

"Yes, Kildar, I do," Gretchen said. She was carrying a baby and looked positively beatific despite the thoroughly pissed expression on her face. "But there is only one adult here for each Family to watch the children."

"I don't think all the girls up at the castle are fully . . ." Mike stopped and thought about it. "Yes, they are. Damnit. We need more Keldara," he added with a grin.

"Here they are," Gretchen said, gesturing to the children. "Pick the one to drive the car."

"Pass," Mike said. "I'll pick it up when I get back." He paused and frowned. "I hate to be . . . How you doing?"

"I am fine, Kildar," Gretchen said. "Except for having twenty brats to keep an eye on."

"How come you got stuck with the duty?" Mike asked.

"Some of the teams are training in the same area as the berry picking," Gretchen said.

Mike had to process that for a second then shook his head.

"And if I was going to be doing anything with my little spare time it would be checking on the teams," Mike said. "Not coming down to the houses where I might run into you? And if I'd picked anyone but one of the little kids to go find a driver . . . They'd have found *anyone* but you, right?"

"Did I say that?" Gretchen said, relenting. "It is . . . good to see you."

"Same here," Mike said, flexing his jaw. "Care to let me in on any of the Mysteries surrounding this? I take it there has been . . . talk."

"Much," Gretchen said. "And, of course, I'm the last to be informed of any of it. Well . . ."

"Except for me," Mike said. "What have you heard?"

"Let me see . . ." Gretchen said, tapping her finger on her lips. "The Kildar is honorable and will not violate the contract between myself and Kiril. The Kildar is human and therefore can only be expected to violate it. I should be sent away, so as to prevent the offense. Kiril should be sent away, there is a group called the . . . Legion Etran . . ."

"The Foreign Legion," Mike said, translating it into Keldara. "Over my dead body."

"And then I would be Kildaran," Gretchen said, shrugging.

"Anybody ask you what *you* want?" Mike asked. "I know nobody has asked *me*."

"It is not the Keldara way," Gretchen said, shaking her head. "The Keldara's fates are chosen by the elders, not by themselves. Our spouses are chosen, our lots in life. I was picked for neither the intelligence teams nor the mortars. I am one of the few women of my generation who is not contributing, directly, to the teams."

"Why?" Mike asked, frowning. "You're not exactly . . . dumb."

"Thank you *so* much for the compliment!" Gretchen snapped.

"That wasn't what I meant and you know it," Mike said. "Why weren't you . . . You are, in fact, quite bright. You'd make a good contribution to the intel section. What am I missing?"

"I am . . ." She paused and frowned. "The Mother of a Family is not necessarily married to the Father. There are some in the Keldara who are spotted for . . . other needs. Stella . . . Stella and Lydia, yes, I could see them being Mothers. But it is less likely with Shariya, who is promised to Yosif . . ."

"Shariya *is* a mortar girl," Mike said, frowning. "One of the ammo bearers . . . She's . . ."

"Sweet," Gretchen said. "Also very simple. Yosif, on the other hand, is very smart and capable. He is the man most likely to be the Devlich Father when his time comes but . . ."

"Shariya wouldn't make a good Mother," Mike said. "So . . . you're getting married to *Kiril* who is a Devlich so you transfer to *that* Family . . ."

"And I train as a Mother," Gretchen said, shrugging. "Instead of, you know, something fun or *exciting*. And I get to take care of the babies."

"Except *that* is so that you wouldn't meet *me*," Mike said, shaking his head. "I'm sorry. I appear to have really fucked up your existence."

"And have I had no effect on yours?" Gretchen asked.

"If you hadn't, would any of this be going on?" Mike replied at the sound of rotors in the distance. "Spread the word, quietly. The Kildar is going to be a very good man. He can look you in the face and walk away. He can watch your children grow. He admires Kiril and hopes the best for both of you. Nobody should be sent away. Except these children because there is a helicopter about to land on them."

"Yes, Kildar," Gretchen said, frowning slightly.

"I don't think we talked, did we?" Mike asked as the helo descended.

"I don't think so," Gretchen shouted. "But I wish we could . . ."

Chapter Fifteen

"General Umarov, good to see you again," Mike said as he was ushered into the general's office by an aide. He hadn't had to wait, which he took as a sign. A sign of what, he wasn't too sure.

"And you, Kildar," the general said, walking around his desk to shake Mike's hand. He gestured for Mike to take a seat, ordered coffee and did everything but check to see if Mike needed a blow job from the secretary.

It was going to be bad.

"How are Galiko and the kids?" Mike asked. Mrs. Umarov had passed away before Mike arrived in-country. Galiko was their sole child. She was married to a captain in the Georgian National Guard and they had two children that the general doted upon.

"All are well," Umarov replied, nodding. "I will send them your regards."

"Please do," Mike said, taking a sip of coffee. He'd actually become a pretty big tea drinker but since he was American it was assumed he'd prefer coffee. It wasn't bad, by Georgian standards. "General, we need helicopters to get this plan to work."

"In that you and I agree," Umarov replied with a sigh. "But there are . . . problems."

"Politics," Mike said. "Is it that they are Russian? I don't, off the top of my head, know of a group *besides* Birusk Flying Services that can, and will, pick up a company of infantry and take them anywhere *close* to where they might be shot at. And Birusk is *not* Russian government, any more than I am U.S. government."

"And again, you and I agree," Umarov said, shaking his head. "Others do not."

"What others?" Mike asked, blanching. "General, this is no insult to your armed forces but we *have* to keep this information very confidential!"

"That is not a problem," the general said, making a placating gesture. "It is, as you would say 'very tightly held.' But the president and the defense minister *had* to be told of what was going on, you know that, yes?"

"Of course," Mike said, nodding. "I cannot disagree at . . . Oh, crap. The defense minister?"

Vakhtang Gelovani was a strong Georgian nationalist who had risen to the rank of major in the Red Army before the fall of the Soviet Union. Of course, that had been over a twenty-five-year period. Ethnic Russians had controlled the upper ranks of the Red Army even under Stalin, who was a Georgian. Anyone non-Rusk rising above colonel was exceedingly rare. He clearly felt that he should have been a general and it was rumored that for that reason he hated and despised all things Russian.

From Mike's perspective, the reason he'd never made general was that Gelovani would barely tie his own shoes. The man was a classic case of "active/stupid" if Mike had ever seen one, a micromanager who had a strong tendency to choose *exactly* the wrong course of action and enforce it on subordinates. And then, as often as not, blame them for the failure.

The fact that he was frequently bruited as a possible successor to the current president, who while not great was head and shoulders over Gelovani, was good reason to contemplate the stupidity of settling down in Georgia. And Mike had heard quite a few rumors about clashes between Gelovani and Umarov. Given that Umarov *wasn't* an idiot, Mike didn't find that surprising.

"I will neither confirm nor deny that the defense minister has raised objections," Umarov said, grimacing. "I will however say that the president has also stated his objections."

Which meant that the president did not want to give Gelovani an excuse to paint him as in the pocket of the Russians. Even over a black op. Of course, Gelovani would not *care* that it was a black op if he went babbling about it to some group of faithful or supporters.

Taking Gelovani out was looking better and better.

Mike lowered his face and rubbed his forehead for a moment then looked up.

"Okay, then can I have *Georgian* helicopter support? You've got a couple of Hips and those Blackhawks from the U.S. I don't know if we can make it in one lift, but . . ."

"No," Umarov said with a shake of the head. "And that is *my* objection, solely. We have very few helicopters. Not only are most of them busy, most of the time, but the loss of even one, and there *is* a good chance of losing one on this operation, would be . . . very bad. Unlike the U.S. military, we could not hide the fact that we'd lost one or *where* we'd lost one. Given that, it would be apparent that we'd lost it to the Chechens or at least in operations against them. Call it 'face' if you will, but with everything that is going on in this country, making it truly apparent that we cannot control actions in that area would be very bad, politically. Let me ask: Would you prefer that Gelovani replace me with one of his hand-picked cronies?"

"No," Mike said, grimacing.

"If we lost a helicopter in this operation, I would grade that as 'likely,'" Umarov said placidly. "Also, the loss would be a *capital* loss to my military, both in the loss of the helicopter and the *pilots*. We would have to send our very best pilots, yes? And we have very few who are of the caliber you would need. I would be, in your American phrase, eating my seed corn if I lost them. We guard them very preciously, the helicopters *and* the pilots. I cannot justify using them in an operation with this great a risk factor."

"So that gets me back to square one," Mike argued. "I *have* to have helicopter support. If I don't use it, I'd have to have already left to do the whole thing on foot. I *need* birds to get me in striking distance. And I *really* need dust-off. We're going to take casualties. I'll walk out if I absolutely have to, carrying the damned items if I must, but I'm not going to do this mission if I have to pack my wounded out on litters. Not."

"I have argued the same," Umarov said, holding up a hand to forestall an angry rebuttal. "I have also managed a small, not large enough, compromise. You may use the Russian company to fly to your drop-off point. I got that concession because I pointed out, as you did, that you could not do the mission in time without having already started your 'hump,' yes? But they cannot enter the Pankisi military controlled zone, absolutely not. That is from the president. And they must enter on a controlled route, pick up your forces, drop them off and then leave."

"So no pick-up and no dust-off," Mike said, angrily. He took a deep breath and then thought, hard. "What if . . . Look, I need dust-off and I need some helo support in the background. Among other things, both the U.S. and the Russians are very interested in retrieving Dr. Arensky, alive."

"So I was informed," Umarov said, nodding. "But, frankly, I had not put together that he, and his daughter, would have to walk out. Not a very pleasant trip."

"We're planning on something on the order of Hannibal's March across the Alps," Mike pointed out, sourly. "No, not a pleasant trip. High elevation, low temperatures, nasty terrain. It's going to be hard enough on the Keldara. I can't imagine getting an out-of-shape scientist and his daughter through it. But I'm *really* worried about getting casualties out of there. I need a helo. And I have an idea."

"Go ahead," Umarov said, nodding.

"What if they weren't Russian and they weren't temporary hires?" Mike asked, putting a plan together just ahead of his words. "I've been saying that I need a helicopter, and some pilots, for quite some time now. So . . . I get a helicopter and some pilots. Possibly two helicopters and some pilots. And *they* are my support."

"I presume you're talking about American or European," Umarov said carefully. "Can you get them? On short notice? And that will be willing to do this mission? I could see a pilot that was willing to fly back and forth to Tbilisi, yes? But to fly on this mission?"

"I don't know," Mike replied honestly. "But I can try. If I *can* get them, can I use them?"

"I am not sure what you mean," Umarov said lightly. "You wish to get a helicopter for transportation, yes? They will not be armed, this is a simple business transaction, a bit of paperwork. I'm sure it would entirely escape my notice, I'm not sure why you even bring it up."

"Gotcha," Mike said, nodding. "Well, then, I think that's settled. And I need to make some very fast phone calls."

"Don't let me slow you down," Umarov said, nodding. "But since you mentioned this simple business transaction, I'll make a few phone calls, for a friend, and make sure that all the paperwork is . . . smoothed out."

"I appreciate it," Mike said, knowing that the Georgians could be byzantine, and greedy, in processing such paperwork. He'd grease palms if he had to, it was a standard part of doing business in the region, but the fewer he had to, and the faster they worked, the better. The chief of staff knew just what butts to prod to get them in gear. "I'll be going, then. Give my regards to Galiko and Captain Kahbolov."

"I shall," the general said. "I'll also note that if I *was* to send a group of highly qualified pilots, one of them would have to be my son-in-law. But, no, that is not why I declined."

"Pierson."

"Bob, it's Mike," Mike said, sighing over the secure sat phone. He could barely hear the colonel over the sound of the rotors from the helicopter but, on the other hand, short of a very capable and sophisticated intercept that could crack U.S. satellite transmissions, he wasn't going to be overheard. "We have a situation. No, we have an issue. No, we have a mission killer."

"Helicopters," Pierson said. "I was going to call you. We already got the word."

"The Georgians are *not* going to let me use my Russki friends for anything more than lift into the nearby area. I'm not going to have dust-off, I'm not going to have support and I can't exactly evac Arensky and his kid through those fucking mountains."

"They're also not going to let *us* do it," the colonel replied. "That has been discussed. Not at 'the highest levels' but at a level high enough that it's damned firm."

"I'm not going to stick the fucking Keldara out on a limb over some jackass' bigotry about Russians," Mike said, bitterly. "But there's one slender loophole. I can buy my own god-damned bird and hire my own god-damned pilots out of my own god-damned pocket and as long as they're not Russian I can use them for 'noncombat' missions. Including into the Pankisi zone."

"So you need pilots," Pierson said. "And birds."

"I'll get my own birds," Mike replied. "The Czechs make a very nice Hind variant that is available off the shelf with a high-altitude package. And not only does it cost *way* less than a Blackhawk, most of the parts are compatible with other Hind variants. But I need pilots. ASAP."

"We're not an employment agency, Mike," Pierson replied with a humorous tone.

"You are if you want me to do this mission," Mike responded with absolutely no humor in his voice. "I need pilots. I'm up to my ass in alligators and so are all my people. None of us have time to go looking through the want ads. I haven't slept in three days. I don't have time to be having this conversation. I need two highly qualified and technically excellent pilots in recent training who can cross-train to a Hind on short notice and are willing to go in harm's way for a sizable cash bonus and love of the thrill. I'd prefer no dependents. As Umarov pointed out, the risk of this mission, to everyone including me, is high. That includes the pilots. I need them on a plane within the next two days. Call Anastasia to make the travel arrangements. And I don't care who you have to know, blow or glow, I need them *now* or this mission is a scrub. I am totally fucking serious. I *will* scrub this mission and the President can then consider . . . other options."

"Oh," Pierson said, thoughtfully. "In that case, I'd better start making some calls."

Kacey flipped through the mail angrily.

"Junk mail, bill, bill, *overdue* bill . . ."

Kacey J. (Jezebel) Bathlick, formerly Captain Kacey J. Bathlick, USMC, was five foot four inches tall and weighed in at a respectable one hundred and thirteen pounds, as of that morning, after her morning run, according to the bathroom scale. With brown hair that reached to just shoulder length and brown eyes, she had generally been described as "solid" in her officer evaluation reports. That is because nobody was going to put "stacked, packed, hot and ready to rock" on paper.

"Face it, Kace, we're gonna have to find a job." Tamara opened the refrigerator and removed broccoli, onions and red peppers. "I mean, we're talking 7-Eleven time here."

Tamara Wilson, also formerly Captain, USMC, was not incredibly taller than Kacey, standing just a bit over five feet seven inches. However, with noticeably longer legs and torso, she seemed to positively *tower* over her longtime friend. She also had brown hair and eyes and her grading officers had often found themselves at a loss to describe her in militarily acceptable terminology. "Erect of carriage" was usually what the reviewers settled upon. That was because, in the case of her male reviewers, they felt that forms covered in drool with incoherent phrases like "Yowhzah!" and "Babe-a-licious!" would not have told the review boards much.

When, as had often happened until recently, the two were sharing a cockpit, units sometimes came to blows over who got to fly in the bird.

"I can't believe we didn't get hired with Blackwater," Kacey said, tightly. "They're *screaming* for pilots."

"Male pilots," Tammy noted, starting to chop up the vegetables. "They do *not* want to be the first company to have a female civilian killed in action. Wouldn't look good on CNN."

"Which means that everyone else who needs pilots in the States should be screaming for women," Kacey noted. "So why aren't we getting any calls?"

"It's only been two months," Tammy pointed out. "And we really didn't start hunting until we got back from the islands. Of course, we *thought* somebody would be banging down our door but . . ." She paused at a knock on the apartment's door. "Okay, now that would be too . . ."

Kacey looked through the peephole and turned back to Tammy. "Military. Army. Major."

"Pro-face," Tammy said, nodding.

"Yes, Major, what can I do for you?" Kacey said as she opened the door.

"Ms. Kacey Bathlick?" the major asked. "Captain Bathlick?"

"Up until a couple of months ago, yes," Kacey said.

"And is Ms. Wilson present?" the major asked. He was black, medium height and heavy build. Kacey had done an immediate check of his uniform and she suspected that there were some ribbons missing from his dress greens. But there *was* an SF patch on his right shoulder to counteract the Military District of Washington patch on the left. And he was wearing the "Tower Of Power":

Ranger, SF and Airborne tabs stacked. No CIB but a two-year Pentagon service badge. And his highest medal was an Army Commendation Medal. Either this guy was a washed-out Green Beret who had been shuffled off to Washington after being found "unfit for combat" or he was deliberately understating his experience and leaving off merit badges. From his look it was probably the latter. Which in the five-sided Puzzle Palace was . . . weird. Everybody wore every possible doodad so they could look more military than Napoleon.

"Yes, I am," Tammy said, walking over while wiping her hands on a towel. "Pleasure to meet you Major Stang. What can we do for you?"

"I was told . . ." the major said and then paused. "Could we do this somewhere other than the doorway?"

"Of course," Kacey said. "Sorry." Of course, he could be a rapist dressed up like an Army major, but he had all the badges in the right place, which would be unusual for a "wannabe." And between herself and Tammy they could probably handle him, weight lifter or no. Tammy had been studying karate since before she was really walking well. Kacey's fighting style was a bit more eclectic, running in the direction of beating the hell out of people she didn't like.

She stepped back and then to the side so that she had him flanked as he entered the room. The brief, amused, glance over his shoulder told her that he'd noticed, knew why and found it both tactically correct and funny.

"Take a seat if you'd like," Tammy said, smiling.

"Nah, I'll be quick," the officer said, dipping into his blouse pocket and pulling out a slip of paper. It appeared to be cut out from something, possibly an e-mail. "I was told that you two are looking for a flying job, preferably as a matched set."

"Yes," Tammy said, frowning but taking the paper.

"I'm also told that you were very pissed off when the Marines pulled you both out of combat slots," the major added. "That's the name of a guy who needs some helo pilots, yesterday. He's not in the U.S., though, the country of Georgia. But he doesn't have the time to come to the States and do an interview. So he's willing to pay appropriate pilots five grand just to fly out there and interview, as long as they don't dawdle. The flip side is that while it's intended to be a permanent gig, he needs them for a mission that . . . well, that involves a certain amount of risk. The pay, I'm given to understand, will be commensurate."

"He's a merc?" Kacey asked. "The U.S. government is death on mercs."

"Mercenary, security specialist, the U.S. government hires out a lot of stuff these days," the major said with a shrug. "I have it on very good authority that this is one of the good guys. I will mention that the U.S. government is, effectively, being his hiring and screening agent for this. I'm not here on my own, I'm on government time."

"That's odd," Tammy said.

"Yes, it is," Stang said. "But I get a lot of odd jobs. I'll add that while you're not covered by the UCMJ or USC 18 on this, I'd *appreciate* it if you didn't pass on the fact that you were contacted, and in this way. More to be the point, Uncle Sam would appreciate it. I don't know what's going on, so don't ask. All I was told was go tell you two and get your answer on whether you'd go interview."

"He's going to pay five grand just to fly out and *interview*?" Tammy said. "That's not a signing bonus. That's just to interview."

"And your transportation," Stang said with a nod. "If you say yes to the interview, we'll have you on a plane headed towards Georgia, and I quote as fast as you can pack end quote."

"What's the mission?" Kacey asked, taking the paper from Tammy and glancing at it. All it had on it, though, was a name, "Michael Jenkins," and a number. She did recognize that it was a sat-phone number, though.

"I have no idea," Stang admitted, grinning. "I will say, though, that some very senior and connected people have been running around lately like there's a monkey gnawing on their neck. And we're not expecting an IG inspection in simply ages."

"So who do you . . ." Tammy stopped at his expression and grinned. "Classified?"

"Got it in one," Stang said. "If I told you I'd have to find a place for the bodies."

"So do we call this guy or what?" Kacey asked.

"Got a cell phone?"

"Yes."

"Call him on the way to Washington National?"

❖   ❖   ❖

"You look all in, Master Chief," Mike said, sitting down to breakfast in the kitchen. The coffee was already on the table and Mother Griffina was frying up the eggs. Life was good. Some sleep would be nice.

"So do you," Adams said. "When's the last time you slept? Never mind. I *gotta* use Shota for entry. Every single other position is *tasked*. And they all require more sense than blowing a door, then taking five god-damned *steps*! The way I got it set up, all he has to do is this simple task. The guy has at least learned to shoot, and what to shoot and what not to. But he can't seem to get the concept that just because there are bad guys in the room, he *still* has to take *five steps* to clear the door."

"Sucks to be you," Mike said, taking a sip of coffee. "Try teaching HALO to a bunch of newbies in a *week*. Not to mention all the other prep for this damned mission. On the other hand, it's going pretty good. First real jump today."

"You know you don't have to be busting your ass as hard as you are," Adams said. "Nielson can handle some of it."

"I have reasons to stay busy," Mike pointed out.

"Being all bleary *before* a mission isn't good for anybody, *boss*," Adams pointed out. "Or are you talking about your latest slash?"

"You're so eloquent about these things," Mike said.

"Nielson is eloquent about these things," Adams said. "I'm from the Teams, remember? The list starts: My wife, sure . . ."

"My toothbrush, maybe, my knife, never," Mike finished. "And you've been through *how* many of those wives?"

"Enough that I'm glad to be out of the States," Adams admitted. "They can get my pension but they can't *touch* what I'm making over here."

"Then let me just suggest that you're out of your league, Master Chief," Mike said with a sigh. "Except, maybe, on one question: Think I should talk to Kiril about this?"

"No," Adams said. "I already did."

"Thanks," Mike said.

"I told him you weren't nearly the cockhound everybody made you out to be. Hell, you hardly knew where to put it. There was no way that Gretchen was going to go for a guy as bad in the sack as you are."

"Let me repeat my thanks," Mike said, chuckling.

"He was really weird about it," Adams said, frowning. "Resigned, maybe. He just said that his fate would be decided. What's this I hear about him being sent off?"

"Isn't happening," Mike said. "They're talking about sending him off to the Legion and me hooking up with Gretchen. I'm putting my Kildar boot on that. He marries Gretchen."

"Ain't like you're short on pussy," Adams admitted.

"Eloquence, thy name is Ass-Boy," Mike said. "But, to reiterate, pussy is not the issue. However, changing the subject, we may have helo pilots."

"That would be great," Adams said, nodding. "We're seriously fucked without pilots. I mean the bad kind of fucked. Not the fucking Gretchen kind of fucked."

"Pierson said that quote some candidates end quote are on the way," Mike said, shaking his head at Adams' aside. He knew the approach, it was the specialty of the Teams. Call it "tough love." As in "go cry in somebody else's beer." On the other hand, Adams didn't actually have to deal with the management of the Keldara's morale. "So, so far the rest of us are on track. Sucks to be you, though," he added with a grin.

"You want this girl alive or not?" Adams grumped.

"Be nice," Mike said, taking another sip. "That's why I detailed you to it. But the most important thing is getting the package. And that means getting eyeballs on the target and into commo with Katya."

"She in place, yet?" Adams asked.

"Should be."

Chapter Sixteen

The first thing Dmitri told her was: "You're going to need to change clothes."

Katya didn't see what was wrong with her clothes. She'd carefully chosen them based on her cover as a new hooker in the trade: hip-hugger jeans, a tight, low-cut blouse, black patent-leather high heels and a fake fox coat. All of the clothes were well worn, the coat actually a bit ratty. Most of what she had packed in her small bag was the same.

"The Chechens, well . . ." Dmitri had sighed and shrugged. "They move the whores, they use the whores. But if you look like a whore they're going to make your life hell."

Katya didn't know what Dmitri's connection to Russian intel was. The one thing she'd insured was that he did not know she was "connected." Another agent had handed her off to him without any suggestion she was working for Russian intel. What she had come to realize was that he was an expert in the trade. He'd treated her with polite disinterest, not even trying to cadge a freebie. And he knew all the guards at the crossing points. So by the time they reached Gamasoara she'd changed.

Full-coverage sweater, slightly tight but not even vaguely sexual, a skirt she'd picked up on the road that hung to well below her knees, flats, the hardest to find. Her makeup was dialed way back. She looked . . . drab.

Looking at the women of the town, many of them in Islamic *dhimmi* scarves that covered their hair and ears, skirts that went all the way to the ground and heavy coats that gave little if any indication of their figure, she had to admit she looked more the part.

"You're not going to get as much for me looking like this," Katya pointed out.

"The buyers know what they're looking at," Dmitri replied as they pulled into the town. "This isn't a market, it's a trading point. You know you're headed for Turkey on this route, right?"

"Yes," Katya said then shrugged. "Turkey or Europe, what's the difference. A whore is a whore."

"With your looks you'd do better in Europe or the East," Dmitri said, then shrugged in return. "But if you want to go to Turkey, that's nothing to me. I already have you contracted to Georgi Torshin so I'll just drop you and be gone."

Dmitri pulled the antiquated Lada to a stop in front of a coffee shop and gestured at the door. "Last stop. For me, anyway."

Katya was glad for the rest. The roads to Gamasoara had been atrocious and the Lada had apparently lost all of its springs decades ago. She felt as if her teeth had been rattled loose by the long journey. But they were finally at the area of operations. Now to see if she could find the target.

She got out, grabbed her bag and, head down and posture slumped, followed Dmitri into the café. She still was cataloguing her surroundings. The café had a small stream behind it and a patio to one side. In fact, it was practically identical to the one in Alerrso. However, the design was so common in this region it wasn't particularly surprising.

The town was a bit larger than Alerrso, maybe ten thousand people. She wasn't sure *what* the local industry was but it didn't appear to be booming. Most of the people in the town seemed to be selling things to each other, most of it old and worn. There were two food vendors on the street and they didn't seem to be doing much business.

The interior of the café was hot and stuffy, the windows and doors closed against the late-fall chill. All of the patrons were male and most of them watched her as Dmitri led the way to the back of the room. They had the look that said "Islamic" to her, automatically. She had never really understood how you could spot an

Islamic, or an American or a European, immediately. Jay had explained some of it to her. Islamics followed certain laws that affected their dress and demeanor to a degree most of them didn't realize. For example, when you had to regularly take your shoes off for prayer it just made more sense to step down on the backs so you could slip them on and off like slippers. But when you did that you had to shuffle as you walked or they'd slip off. Thus Islamics tended to shuffle their feet and take small steps.

There were a thousand such minor cultural clues about personal behavior and body language that subconsciously, to most people, screamed what culture a person derived from. The job of a spy, or an actor, was to learn them and copy them slavishly.

"I will see where Georgi has gone to," Dmitri said as soon as she was seated. "He is usually in here this time of day. Talk to no one."

Dmitri went to the counter that served the café and it quickly became obvious that something was wrong. Not quite an argument but Dmitri was clearly unhappy when he came back to the table.

"Well, there is a problem," he said with a sigh as he sat down with two cups of strong coffee. "Georgi is dead."

"How?" Katya asked, wide-eyed. She was playing the biggest innocent a new whore might be and wide-eyed was the right reaction to sudden news of death.

"Heart attack," Dmitri spat. "There is a man called Yaroslav has taken over his business. He will come."

"Do you know him?" Katya asked, nervously. Again, the nervousness was right for the character. Of course, there was some true nervousness to it. Things were going wrong, which was always bad for a mission. The intermediary, Dmitri, and the primary, Georgi, had been carefully chosen. Georgi normally held his "girls" for a few weeks, setting up someone to move them to further down the line. He also was reputed to be easy with his girls' time as long as they brought in a few rubles while they were waiting. Katya *needed* that time, and the freedom, if she was to have any chance of finding the target.

"No," Dmitri replied. "He's a sweetmeat vendor, of all things. When Georgi died he bought all of his stock. He's trying to unload it now, but is willing to buy some more."

Katya didn't bother to ask where a sweetmeat vendor got the money to buy a string of whores. Obviously he was more than a sweetmeat vendor.

Yaroslav, when he finally made it to the café, turned out to be a pig. The man was short and grossly obese. If she had to service him it was going to have to be from on top; the man would crush her otherwise. He wheezed his way across the café and collapsed in the chair, which creaked ominously, then leaned back, interlacing his fingers across the top of his huge belly.

"She is pretty," Yaroslav wheezed. "But I already have too many girls. I cannot afford to pay more than a thousand euros . . ."

Katya had gotten used to it a long time ago and now that it wasn't, at some level, real it was easier. But it was never fun to be bartered over. Fucking men treated women like a piece of meat to be dickered over.

Finally a price of five thousand euros was settled on and Yaroslav hoisted himself to his feet.

"I will return with the money," he wheezed, stopping to breathe deeply at the effort to get to his feet. "I of course don't carry that much on me. I will return. Soon."

"Well, if you decide to run you won't have much trouble," Dmitri said, bursting into laughter as soon as the door to the café shut.

It was much the same thing Katya had been thinking but she just shook her head.

"I won't run," she said with a shrug. "What do I have to run to?"

Besides, she had a mission to complete. There were men to screw over and, with luck, a few to kill. Why should she run?

"This is . . . where you . . . will be sleeping," Yaroslav wheezed, gesturing at the room.

It wasn't . . . yes, it was. This was definitely the worst place she'd ever been bedded down in her long career as a whore. The stone building was one large room, about the size and general shape of the Keldara homes, but open and filled with beds lining the walls. The beds were springs, no mattresses, and the room was unheated. Cracks in the walls let in drafts that were virtually gales in themselves. The floor was packed dirt, so stained with unnamed fluids and garbage that it brought a new meaning to "dirt."

Arguing or complaining had never gotten her anywhere, though.

"Is there a blanket?" she asked, meekly.

"I will try to find you one," Yaroslav said. "I am doing this practically out of the goodness of my heart. When my good friend . . . Georgi died his ladies were left with no protector." He paused to breathe deeply and wiped at his eyes as if there were tears. There weren't. The pause indicated that he'd had to dredge the name of his "good friend" from unsure memory. If he wasn't such a slob, Katya would have suspected him of offing a competitor just to buy up his stock at a discount. "It was from the goodness of my heart that I took you girls in. I will have no complaints as to the quality of the lodgings."

"I'm not complaining," Katya said, hastily. The man might be a pudge-monster, as the Kildar would put it, but he could still probably smack the hell out of her. And in her current cover, all she could do was try to move so it didn't hurt *too* much. She'd have to take the punch with barely a flinch.

"All the other girls left yesterday," Yaroslav said, puffing. "I had hoped to return to my simple life of a sweetmeat vendor. Then you were dropped on me. So you must make the best of it until I can find someone to take you on to Azerbaijan." Pause. Wheeze. "There may be some blankets the girls left behind." Pause. Wheeze. "Check the cupboard. I must return to my moneymaking ventures. I do not have time for this."

"Yes, sir," Katya replied. "Should I work?"

"Of *course* you should work!" Yaroslav thundered. "There is little enough money to be made in this town, I cannot afford idle hands, or pussies in your case. Get out there and make my money!"

"Yes, sir," Katya said, smiling nervously. She so wanted to give *this* prick a heart attack.

"I may have another job for you, besides on your back," Yaroslav admitted, more gently. "Not that it pays anything but nothing in this town does. The Chechens have a woman they are keeping. They, of course, cannot defile themselves with dealing with her. They had hired one of the girls to tend to her needs. Perhaps you can do that."

Katya kept her face puzzled but let nothing else showed. But what went through her mind was: *It can't be that easy.* There was only one girl that could possibly match that description. Surely she wasn't being handed the fucking target on a platter.

It was that easy. Fuck.

It was Marina Arensky. From what Katya could see past the blindfold anyway. And the small scar on the chin was a dead give-away.

The girl was tied to a chair, a padded one Katya noticed, blind-folded but not gagged. Nonetheless she was silent as if she *had* been gagged.

The men holding her weren't Chechens, either. They were Russians and if she hadn't been on this mission for a specific reason she would have wondered what Russians were doing in a Chechen-held town. There were quite a few of them, too. The building was much larger than the barn for the girls with several rooms off a corridor. The doors of most of the rooms had been open as she and Yaroslav passed and there were men, heavily armed, in all of them.

Marina was held in a room at the very back of the building. It backed on a rock wall; there was no entrance at the rear and no windows. Conceivably the assault team could come through the wall if they used enough explosives. That wasn't for her to figure out, though. All she had to do was look around as they walked through and make sure the video was going to the, unfortunately small, memory chip installed in her skull.

"This is the new girl," Yaroslav wheezed. "All my other girls I had to sell. I will sell this one as soon as I can. Then we are done."

"We don't need her for long," the man said. He was a cold one, Katya could tell. About 175 centimeters, cold gray eyes, slim face. She ran through the dossiers she'd been shown and tried not to blanch. Kurt Schwenke, the former Stasi agent and terrorist. She was going to have to be *very* careful around this man. He was a trained agent, which meant that anything she did out of character was going to give her away. She instantly decided she was going to switch roles as soon as Yaroslav was gone. Just enough that Schwenke would catch it. It was a fine line to run. She had to show her hard side without in any way making him think she was an agent.

"I go now," Yaroslav said. "She will work for you. She is very biddable."

After Yaroslav had waddled out of the room Schwenke walked around her, looking her up and down.

"Biddable?" the German finally scoffed. "Is he blind?"

"Most men are," Katya said, coldly.

"I am not, bitch," Schwenke stated, stopping in front of her and then slapping her, hard.

With the change in demeanor Katya could have, would have, avoided the slap as much as possible. She couldn't have used a trained block, that would give too much away. But she could have lifted her arms, turned away, flinched, something.

If she'd had time. The man was faster than a snake. All she could do was spin away from the powerful slap and try to remain conscious.

She found herself on the floor, propping herself up with her hands and trying to breathe just before a boot crashed into her side.

"I am not," Schwenke said, just as coldly. "So let us not play games, yes? What are you?"

"A whore," Katya said, curled on her side. "I was born in an orphanage in Novy Birsk. I was raped by a man like you when I was eight. If I could press a button and kill every man on earth I would. But I know better than to cross you. Good enough?"

"Perhaps," Schwenke said, kicking her. "And perhaps too pat. Why are you here?"

"Because I killed my last pimp," Katya spat. "Veniamin was a bastard. But he has friends. He knew too many of the men in the Balkans trade and too many in Russia. If I stayed, I'd be as dead as the pig. Turkey, though, there I could disappear. So kill me or beat me or fuck me, I don't care. But if you piss me off too much, you'd *better* kill me."

Schwenke paused and then laughed. Shrilly.

"Better bitches than you have tried to kill me," he said, still chortling. "But I like your spirit. Feel free to try. We can make a game of it, yes? You try to kill me, I try to kill you. Nothing obvious. Shooting you, beating you to death with a lead club, these would be too easy. Fun but too easy. Poison? Do you know poisons? I know thousands. Shall we play the poison game, bitch?"

"Teach me a few and I'll gladly give you a blow job that will curl your toes," Katya said. It was pure honesty and that shone through.

"Perhaps," Schwenke said. "Perhaps. But you would probably not enjoy bedding me. I am a master of pain."

"I have been hurt," Katya said. "Plenty of men have beaten me."

"Who said anything about beating?" Schwenke asked. "I prefer to simply give them a little cocktail. That way they scream and scream in pain as I fuck them. Then the pain passes and they are so *grateful*. Until I brew the next cocktail. I make them watch as I prepare the syringe. They begin to scream before the needle even touches them. Would you like to scream?"

Katya was stunned. She'd run into some real bastards, absolute sadists, as pimps. But this guy was just fucking *nuts*. More around the bend, if possible, than Katya herself.

"I've screamed until I was hoarse, plenty of times," Katya said. "But if you'd settle for fake screaming and just teach me your recipe, I *promise* you won't know the difference."

"Oh, but I *would*," Kurt pouted. "But for my recipe, would you take my little cocktail? Voluntarily?"

"I don't know," Katya temporized. "How much am I getting paid? I'll fuck you for the recipe. For the pain . . . seven hundred euros. And Yaroslav doesn't find out. For that much pain I'm not going to cut in the pimp."

"What a *delightful* child you are," Schwenke said. "We'll talk about it, yes? In the meantime, you've been hired for other reasons."

"Who's the bitch?" Katya asked. "Your newest playtoy?"

"No," the German said. "Alas, I'm not permitted to play with her. Not as long as her father cooperates. She stays in the chair except for two exercise periods each day. That is when she craps or pisses or whatever. Her hands are never untied. Her feet are shackled whenever she is out of the chair. You have to feed her, get her to the latrine, get her on the pisser. The men are not permitted to talk to her. You will only talk to her as little as possible. If any of the men try to see her, to touch her or rape her, you will report it to me. They won't, though. They know the penalty. They start with my little cocktails. At night she lies in the bed. She must be shackled then, as well. You will shackle her and then return to whatever pisshole you call home here. I will check to make sure they are tight. In the morning you return. If I am unsatisfied by the tightness of her bonds the night before we will have another little chat."

"I won't let her go," Katya said, chuckling. "I'd just as soon watch her raped."

"You don't want to know why we are keeping her?" Schwenke asked.

"I assume for ransom," Katya replied with a shrug.

"Ah, and such a ransom," Schwenke said. "You will not ask her her name. If I find that you discover her identity, you will be killed. I may play with you first, but you will definitely be killed. She does not want you to be killed, I'm sure, so she won't tell you. But if you piss her off enough, she can kill you by simply mentioning her name. She did so to one of the girls who was . . . unkind to her."

"I will be kindness in itself," Katya promised. "What if she is a problem?"

"Then bring it to me," the ex-Stasi said. "Here you are, the two of you trapped like a proton circled by an electron. Unable to escape each other short of the death of either. Or, of course, she being moved on. So I would suggest that, despite your nature, you become the very best of friends."

"Hello, ladies," Mike said, looking around the room. "Thanks for staying up until the middle of the night to meet with me."

"You are very busy, Kildar," Mother Ferani said. "We are at your disposal."

"Here is the situation," Mike said, gesturing at the pile of recently received steerable chutes. "As you know, a team is being inserted by advanced parachute techniques to set up a radio center. I've got all I can do just training them to minimal standards. And we all want Julia, Olga, Jeseph, Ivar and Pat well trained. But that will require that, towards the end of training, they do multiple jumps per day. The master chief and I are the only qualified parachute packers in the area. I won't have the time to pack thirty chutes a day. That's the six of us doing five jumps per day, which is what I'm shooting for. Somebody is going to have to pack the chutes."

"Us," Mother Ferani said, her eyes wide.

"Yes," Mike replied, simply. "These days either specialized members of the military who *use* the chutes, riggers they're called, or the users themselves generally pack the chutes. Because the very lives of the users depend upon them being packed *right*. On the other hand, I don't have the *time* to train the team on HALO *and* packing. Nor do they have the time to do their own packing even if I did.

"However, four of the Six Families are represented on the jump. And a mother, sister or cousin of each of the team members is represented here. If they cannot trust their own mother, sister or cousin, who can they trust? Anyone who really feels they are not prepared to hold the lives of their son, brother or cousin in their hands after this training can opt out. There are actually about twice as many of you as I need. There's a reason for *that* too, but I won't get into it. However, if you don't think you want that responsibility, you can opt out. *After* you're trained."

"Very well, Kildar," Mother Ferani said. "We are at your command in things such as this. And I find it to be an honor."

"Great," Mike said, tiredly. "Let's get started. But just one thing I'll add: It's pretty apparent that the Keldara are going to get used for more and more 'special' missions. And the Keldara don't seem to mind, even when there are losses. So it makes sense to make sure they're all as prepared as possible . . ."

"You're going to extend the training," Liza Mahona said from the group.

"After this mission is over I'm going to institute unit-wide training in airborne and HALO techniques," Mike said with a nod. "We'll work on SCUBA later."

"What is SCUBA?"

Chapter Seventeen

Kacey yanked back the door of the Blackhawk and stepped out fast, carrying her flight bag in one hand and a carry-on in the other. Tammy, similarly encumbered, followed fast behind but paused to wave to the crew-chief and slide the door shut.

Their greeting party was a middle-height man dressed in casual clothes, more or less ignoring the rotor wash, and a bigger guy who had a look that Kacey somehow tagged as "local" wearing a digi-cam pattern she'd never seen before. The guy in digi-cam was wearing a sidearm of some sort in a fast-draw holster. It might have been an H&K USP, but Kacey wasn't enough of an expert in sidearms to be sure. The odd thing about the local took a second to sink in: He was so damned good looking it was scary. He looked like he could have stepped off a Hollywood set but she was sure he was a local.

The landing area was a farm in a valley just about surrounded by really high mountains, pretty prosperous with some new tractors working the fields and an SUV or two in sight. But the houses looked pretty much like the ones she'd seen in the Kurdish area in Iraq: dressed stone and slate roofs. They looked like they *might* have electricity.

"Captain Bathlick?" the casually dressed man asked. "I'm Mike Jenkins. Thanks for coming out here just to talk."

Up close it was clear that, while casual, the clothes were not cheap. The black comfortable shoes had that look that said "Italian leather," the pants were exquisite and the golf shirt looked as if it was silk. He'd fit right in at a Palm Beach golf course. But just as she thought that, she heard a crackle of gunfire over the sound of the spooling-up rotors. It was the crackle that said "ranges" though, to her ear, not "firefight."

"That would be me," Kacey replied, setting down her case to shake his hand. The local immediately grabbed her case and the nearly matching one from Tammy and trotted over to the waiting Expedition. Jenkins quickly shook Tammy's hand as well and then gestured at the Expedition.

"Let's get out of the rotor wash," Mr. Jenkins yelled, heading for the SUV. He got in the driver's seat after waving them to the back. Once they were in he turned around and grinned. "Welcome to never-never land. I'd give you the cook's tour, but I'm pressed for time. We'll talk, then you can tell me to stuff it or look around and make up your mind."

"Can we get a vague idea what we're here for?" Tammy asked.

"I've been asked, as a favor, to do something for the U.S. government. And the government of Russia. And the government of Georgia." Mr. Jenkins put the SUV in gear and headed up towards the road. It was only then that Kacey noticed what could only be described as a Turkish castle straight out of *Arabian Nights* up on the ridgeline. "To do that favor, I need at least two helicopter pilots. The rest can, has to, wait."

"The U.S., Russia *and* Georgia?" Kacey asked, leaning back in her seat and looking around. Most of the people in the valley were in "local" clothing but here and there there were more people in digi-cam. A couple were carrying sub-guns, M4s, on friction rigs. Most of them Kacey still tagged as "locals" but a couple had a look that she knew made them Western military. Not sure how to say the difference but it was there. But they clearly weren't an SF team, they looked more like "security specialists." What in the fuck was going on? "I guess we should at least stick around long enough to find out why."

"Oh, yeah," Mr. Jenkins said, opening up the center compartment and pulling out two envelopes. "Your 'I'm willing to travel' money." He held the two envelopes over his shoulder as he steered onto a winding road that looked damned near vertical.

Kacey quickly snatched the envelopes so he'd have his hands free to drive and handed one to Tammy. She didn't want to count it, it seemed rude, but it sure felt like what five thousand dollars should feel like. It was heavy. Bills could be paid and that was good. Whatever came from the "interview." It sounded like Jenkins would be willing to hire anyone who could fly. That meant they'd have to be interviewing *him*.

The castle turned out to be their destination. There was a curtain wall with some really huge doors on the gate and an interior keep, she'd guess that was what it was, that had been converted into a house. Again, it looked *really* Turkish; Ottoman was probably the right term. It had a couple of little towers like minarets on it, at least.

"In case you're wondering, this is my house," Mr. Jenkins said. "And farm. The people who work the farm are called the Keldara. The full explanation of the Keldara is a long discussion. We'll have to shelve that one, too, for the time being. If you'll follow me, your bags will be taken to your rooms."

"We'd like to keep our flight bags with us," Kacey said, uneasily.

"If it makes you comfortable," Mr. Jenkins said, smiling. "But they're only going to your room. Whether you take the job or not you'll probably prefer to stay overnight."

"Okay," Tammy said, handing over her flight bag with a shrug. She still had a purse. "Lead on."

Kacey gave up her flight bag somewhat more reluctantly but then followed the two into the house.

The first thing she noticed wasn't the decor, it was the women. There were three rather good-looking teenage females in school uniforms in the front room of the castle. All three popped to their feet as Mr. Jenkins walked in and giggled; then one gabbled at him in what was probably the local language.

Jenkins replied shortly, but in a friendly tone, then turned to Tammy and Kacey.

"These young ladies are Tinata, Lida and Klavdiya. They would like to make your acquaintance."

"Of course," Tammy said, grinning and walking over to shake hands. "Hello."

"Hello, I am pleased to meet you," one of the girls said, very slowly in English.

"Thank you," Tammy said, nearly as slowly. "I am pleased to meet you, too. What is your name?"

"I am Klavdiya," the girl said carefully.

"Hello, Klavdiya," Tammy said, smiling. "I am Tammy."

Mr. Jenkins said something briefly in the other language and the girls then cut the greeting shorter. When the ritual was all over, he waved the two pilots towards the back of the castle.

"To be brutally honest, the girls are members of my harem," Jenkins said without looking over his shoulder to gauge their reaction. "And, no, none of them are over eighteen. The story of how I ended up with a harem will . . ."

"Have to wait," Kacey said, snorting. "I can tell there are a lot of stories here. But if you're trying to shock me, or Tammy, we're pretty much unshockable."

"Good," Jenkins said, reaching a heavy wooden door and gesturing them into the room. It was set up as an office but there were no windows and only the one door. The first word that came to Kacey's mind was "cozy." There was a nice fireplace, logs currently unlit, on one wall. The second word that came to mind, though, was "secure." Bugging it would be hell except maybe through the fireplace. There were a couch and three overstuffed chairs arranged on one side in a "seating area," a desk and advanced desk chair. No filing cabinets, though. Mr. Jenkins grabbed one of the overstuffed chairs and swung it around so he could face the couch and waved them to it. "Sit, please. I know you've been doing a lot of sitting, but I've got to go back to teaching HALO as fast as I can and I'd like to get this over with."

"And that's another one that begs the question 'what is going on?'" Tammy said.

"Before I get to that, I need to lay out a few ground rules," Mr. Jenkins said. "Obviously what I do isn't covered by U.S. security regs. So I can't throw that at you. But if you're going to talk, in the military or out, you talk. From what I've been told, you're very good at keeping your mouths shut. It's one of the requirements I laid on the people I set to finding me some pilots. I didn't expect females, frankly, but I don't really care, either. I've got females going much more in harm's way than you'll be. I've got a green intel team that's going to be doing their cherry combat drop with nothing *but* green jumpers on their team into nasty terrain in the middle of absolute Injun Country. Two of them are female. So you can see that I don't hold your sex against you. I'll use whatever tools come to hand. In this case it is, potentially, you two."

"We don't talk," Kacey said. "But I take it the U.S. government doesn't want this talked about, either?"

"Not a bit," Mr. Jenkins said, leaning back. "This is as black as it comes. So black they can't even use their black-ops boys. The term is 'deniability.' I don't work for the U.S. government, they just occasionally let me know about issues that need attending to. If I successfully attend to them, I get some money from that."

"Enough to maintain your own army," Tammy said with a snort.

"Enough to train, build and so far maintain it," Mr. Jenkins said with a slight grin. "So far."

"That's expensive," Kacey said, regarding him closely. "So are helicopters and pilots."

"I only get called in on very expensive operations," Jenkins said with a shrug, then leaned forward and locked his eyes on first Tammy's eyes and then Kacey's. "So here is the deal. I have to take my team into Injun Country, which is surprisingly close but also very hard to get to. I have helo transport for part of the trip but for political reasons that is as far as it can go. Once in Injun Country I'm going to need helo support. I'm going to definitely need evac for two people of interest. I'm probably, almost certainly, going to need dust-off and probably resupply. The LZs might be warm, they might be unknown or they might be hot. I'm going to need pilots who really don't give a rat's ass; they're going into the LZ if they're asked. I don't say 'told to' I say 'asked.' If one of my teams is on the horn screaming for ammo or dust-off, I need pilots who are going to be willing to take the same risks as the rest of us. I need pilots who have balls, in your case ovaries, the size of mountains. Because every single person I've got has those size balls or ovaries. And because otherwise, well, I hope it was a nice trip but you *don't* want to be associated with me."

"Okay," Tammy said, half wonderingly. "That's an interesting proposition."

"I hate to ask this," Kacey said. "But I was raised to be practical..."

"I'd like you as permanent, or semi-permanent anyway, additions," Jenkins said, leaning back again. "The vig is two hundred fifty grand per year and combat bonuses. The bonus on this mission is fifty grand. If you don't make it, a half a mil goes to your beneficiaries. And let me be clear, there *is* a chance you won't be around to spend the money. There is a chance that I won't be around but there are other people to cut the checks."

"You're going on this op?" Tammy asked, still with that vague sense of wonder in her voice. Kacey could comprehend it; she felt like she'd stepped through the looking glass ever since the visit from Major Stang.

"This mission is tight any way you look at it," Jenkins said, shrugging. "I'm taking everyone I've got, including me. It's . . . very hairy. This area is going to be secured by a Ranger company in our absence."

"Well, the money's right," Kacey said, shaking her head. "But you've really got to work on your sales pitch."

"I'm not out to pitch you," Jenkins said, shrugging. "I want you here because you *want* to be here, because you love flying, because you love flying right at the edge of your ability and are hard, cold motherfucker combat fliers. I was told that was what you were, that you bitched unmercifully when the Marines pulled both of you off line duty and that you'd had serious experience in hot, hard, nasty flying conditions so you knew what you were going to be missing. I *need* that. But I don't want you here if you've lost that edge or you're not really what you seem."

"Well, we both ditched a bird in the Caribbean and that was about as hot, hard and nasty an operation as you could ask for," Tammy said with a chuckle. "I'll add that the bird going down *really* wasn't our fault. There were . . . extenuating circumstances."

"Oh, crap," Jenkins said, really leaning back and then grinning, hard. "Wait, were the extenuating circumstances a nuclear blast?"

"I can neither confirm nor deny . . ." Kacey started to say and then really *looked* at him. "Oh My Fucking God."

"I said I get paid well," Mr. Jenkins said with a grin. "And that's because I usually get my ass shot off and I'm very attached to it."

"That *was* you," Tammy said, really grinning now. "I figured you for dead; I've only seen that much blood one other time and that guy didn't make it even with a medic and a defibrillator in the bird. He wasn't unconscious and strapped into the seat of a cigarette boat."

"I'm a hard person to kill," Jenkins replied. "As any number of dead people can attest. I'll go ahead and add, since it's really germane and I've got to trust such sterling characters as yourself, that we're on the same track. Three or four Russian nukes. They're being traded to the terrorists, through the Chechens, for a sizeable sum. We have a location and time of the transfer. But it's *right* in Chechen territory. There's also a scientist, probably working under duress, involved. We need to get the nukes, the scientist and his daughter out, all in more or less functioning order. And, of course, this time keep them from detonating. I've got a hundred and twenty shooters and the Chechens have about four hundred, that we know about, in the area. From your POV, they have heavy machine guns, 12.7 millimeter and *possibly* some MANPADs. No solid evidence on the MANPADs but it's the way to bet."

"That is kind of adverse," Tammy said, shaking her head. "Blackhawks will take a fair amount of damage, but not a whole hell of a lot, trust me."

"Oh, that's one thing I forgot," Jenkins said. "We're not using Hawks, we're using Hinds. That's why you were chosen. You both did a transition stint with the 6th ACS. Frankly, I was delighted to get someone Hind-qualified."

The 6th Air Commando Squadron was an Air Force unit that flew several non-U.S. helicopter systems, including the Hind-D, a Russian attack helicopter. Unlike U.S. attack helicopters, however, it had a crew/cargo area in the rear that could carry five personnel plus a crew-chief or be reconfigured for aerial-ambulance duty. The Hind was heavily armored and generally referred to as a "flying tank." During the Afghan wars the quote used about the Hind by the mujahideen was "We do not fear the Russians, but we fear their helicopters."

Kacey started to reply and then couldn't help bursting into a half-hysterical laugh.

"What?"

"I'm getting Hinds," Jenkins said with a shrug. "They're cheaper than Hawks, more robust and I *can* get them, fast. Two birds are being retrofitted in Czechoslovakia, sorry, 'the Czech Republic' at the moment for high-altitude conditions. If you agree, and I'll give you the rest of the day to think it over, you're on a plane tomorrow for the C.R. You'll go to the factory, refresh and then, in the company of a couple of the company's pilots, ferry them back here. That will give you just enough time to brief in on the details of the op, get used to the local flying conditions and then do the op. We're on short time here."

"Look, you already *said* this was going to be tough flying," Tammy said, exasperated. "And you're talking about birds we've got no *time* in! We *transitioned* two years ago! I can barely recall where the controls are laid out!"

"You're going to be ferrying them over a thousand miles," Jenkins said, shrugging. "*Practice.*"

"There's . . ." Kacey said, then paused. "We'll have to think about this. But there are a few things that *any* helo pilot is going to need in this sort of situation."

"Go," Mike said, leaning back.

Kacey suddenly realized that despite the strong appearance of focus and animation this guy was *tired.* Desperately tired. He didn't show it much, but something about the way he leaned back told her he hadn't been getting much sleep lately.

"We need ground crew," Kacey said.

"The Czechs are supplying a crew initially," Mike said, nodding. "I'm not sure if they can teach the Keldara women everything they need to know. They're going to be very much starting from scratch and I'm even running out of labor on that side. I may end up hiring some outside personnel. But for this mission you're going to have a supplied Czech ground crew, the team leader at least speaking good English."

"Well, we're going to need a *good* crew-chief," Kacey said. "What the Air Force calls a flight engineer. Somebody familiar with the birds. More familiar than we are would be best."

"That's going to be harder," Mike said with a sigh. "If you know anybody hireable I'll hire them, gladly. And if you can't find somebody, if I have to I'll tap the Uncle Sam well again. I'd prefer you find them. If you take the job and head to CR you'll be taking a sat phone. Feel free to use it extensively. Get two. You realize that it might become necessary to solo fly on one or more missions."

"Solo," Tammy said. "On a hot mission?"

"Two birds, two pilots," Mike said, stone-faced. "But I won't tell you to. If the moment comes you'll just do it. Or I've got the wrong pilots."

"Pierson."

"Colonel, this is Major Fowler in USAF Missions Tasking."

"Go," Pierson said with a sigh.

"Sir, your office has placed a tasking on us for two C-17s to loft a Ranger company to the country of Georgia and perform an airborne insertion."

"And we've got a high-level tasking number on it," Pierson said. "What's the problem?"

"The problem, sir, is that we're flat out of birds for that period," the major replied. "Sir, you can go through a general or the USAF chief of staff or the president, but the problem is that the tasker is in too quick of time. We don't have birds we can redeploy that fast that aren't on equal high-level taskers."

"Major, that was a JCS-level tasker," Pierson said, confused.

"Sir, you can look at my board if you'd like," the major said. "We shot this around for quite a while *because* it was such a high tasker. But you're talking about six days' time and most of our 17s are deployed over in the AOR. And if we turn two birds we're going to fail on equally high-level taskers. Sir, we're scheduled out two *months* not two weeks. Bitch about not having enough lift or whatever you'd like, sir, I fully agree. But we're out-tasked at the moment. The only birds we could recall would be on the Azerbaijan relief missions and I note that you've already taskered one of our birds from that."

"Time to pound your nuts flat and find me two birds," the colonel said.

"Sir, I already got out the brick," the major said with a sigh. "You're not the first person I've had this conversation with today, just the highest tasker. We did come up with an OTB idea, though."

Pierson, who thought of himself as a master, even if he hated to admit it, of Pentagonspeak, locked up on "OTB" then managed to parse it. "How 'Out-of-the-Box'?"

"Sir, we can fly them commercial to Ukraine. The Ukrainians finally have those new AN-70s which are essentially identical to

C-130s from a jumper's perspective. They fly and drop about the same, they just carry a bunch more troops."

Pierson rolled that one around in his head for a moment. It had a certain allure but a dozen problems jumped up immediately in his mind.

"Ukraine is registered as a friendly country, not allied," Pierson said, musingly. "They're going to want to get paid for the bird time."

"There's a coding for payments for air time to friendly nations," Major Fowler replied. "We already checked. The problem from our perspective is that their aircraft aren't mission-certified. The AF mil attaché in Ukraine is a former cargo pilot. I contacted him off-record and he says that he's seen enough of their ops to be able to do a prelim cert but he's not sure he could full cert them for airborne ops. He doesn't have a problem with them being able to *do* airborne ops, the cert paperwork is pretty complex, though. There's a way around that, though."

"Don't keep me waiting, Major," Pierson said, dryly.

"For TS ops, and I note that this op has a code-word class over the confidential attached to the op, there's a point at which we can skip the cert requirement due to mission confidentiality."

"That sounds like following the letter while violating the spirit," Pierson said. "I *like* it."

"Yes, sir, I thought you might," the major replied with a chuckle. "But here's a stranger one, sir. Brace yourself."

"Go."

"How about a press release? 'Elite U.S. military force uses Ukrainian Air Force for training operation.'"

"Major, you just noted that this operation is TS code-word," Pierson pointed out.

"The drop, though, is Confidential. We can get low-level permission to open it to the PIO with certain mission data left out. We think it would be good press and the Ukrainian government would probably appreciate it. They've got problems with Russia and showing that *their* planes can carry American special ops . . ."

Pierson really had to pause at that one. The major in tasking didn't realize, because that side of the mission was totally black at a very high level, to just *what* extent it might tweak the Russians.

"Major, begin the tasking but final authority is probably going to have to come after consultation with higher," Pierson said after a moment's thought. "Certainly the press release will have to hold. I'll get back to you. But get working on the tasking and I'll get back on the rest."

"Yes, sir," the major said, deflated. He clearly was enjoying playing at that level.

"Major, I'm not just being an asshole," Pierson said. "There are parameters to this mission, the reasons that it is code-worded at such a high level, that may be risked at a higher level by some of these actions. The truth is, I'm not qualified or knowledgeable enough to decide. But I can contact those that can better eval the risks and rewards."

"They want to do *what*?" the secretary of state said.

"Mike needs the Rangers to ensure security and for a *maskirova*," Pierson said, sighing. "Rangers or somebody like them. I'd actually considered Polish GROM commandoes, but that was just too complicated to set up. So the Rangers are going. But then SOCOM noted that the entire company is just about out of jump pay status due to deployments, one of the reasons they're back in the States besides to get some down time. So we were going to throw a jump in as a sweetener and to keep them on status. But we are tasked out for birds. I double-checked that one and we really *are* flat tasked out. There are actually a couple of ARNG units we could call up for it, but they're out of cert on airborne ops and damned near undeployable or they'd be tasked. So that left looking outside the box. Which means the Ukrainians. They have indicated a willingness, hell an eagerness, to do a drop with our Rangers. But then I got to thinking about how the Russians would react, given what the op is all about . . ."

"Vladimir Putin is going to be livid," the secretary of state said. "We've been treading very carefully on military contact with the Ukrainians because the situation is so delicate. And this jumps right past half a dozen normal steps. The press release . . . Brilliant. Just brilliant."

"Yes, ma'am," Pierson sighed. "We'll just fly them commercial to Tbilisi, then. Mike has ammo; they can draw on him. The mission won't be all that long and by the time they're on their way back we'll probably have taskable birds so they can get their jump in . . ."

"Colonel, at what point did I indicate that I *don't* want Vladimir Putin livid?" the SecState asked. "You were right to bring this to my attention. Here's what we'll do . . ."

Chapter Eighteen

As soon as the door closed to the office, Kacey shook her head.

"That man is insane," she muttered. "Totally, completely and utterly insane."

"Yep," Tammy said, still in that strange voice. "So insane that he'd swim ashore on an island overrun by terrorists, kill them all and still come rescue us and the Marines with a boat. Even though he looked like a colander at the time."

"Sure, but that doesn't mean I want to attach myself to his coat strings," Kacey said, biting her lip. "I mean, he survives but what about the body count *around* him. Doing this sort of shit for SAR, with FAST, that's one thing. God and country and all that. But we're doing it for money, Tams. Is that worth getting our ass shot off?"

"Okay, great," Tammy said. "We say 'no thanks,' take our show-ing-up bonus and head back to the States. Wait on one of our many solicitous phone calls. Eat high until the money runs out and then get a job at the 7-Eleven. What are we waiting for? Sounds great. Get a cat."

"Very funny." Kacey was allergic. "I'm *serious*, Tammy. *This* is serious. I mean, so we don't get a flying job. We're both Naval Academy graduates. We don't *have* to work at the 7-Eleven."

"Sure," Tammy said, her eyes wide. "You've got a creative writing degree, I've got one in English lit. You write them and I'll critique them and we'll make a mint."

"Oh, God," Kacey groaned. "The guy's obviously American military of some sort, although you notice he didn't mention what sort. But if he's got a harem, he's bound to have a bar. We'll find it. You get drunk. I'll watch."

"I'd rather check this place out," Tammy said. "It's *really* cool."

"You're in love," Kacey said. "Mystery and romance and castles in the sky. As always, I've got to keep you grounded."

"Which is just what we're both going to be if we don't take the gig," Tammy pointed out, walking down the corridor. "First we find the harem girls. They'll lead us to *somebody* who speaks English. I mean, they've been taking classes."

"Pillow classes," Kacey snorted but she followed.

When they got to the front room, though, the cluster of girls had disappeared. Tammy was standing with her hands on her hips when the front door opened and a big bald guy in digi-cam, clearly directly off the range from the smell, stepped into the area and paused, looking them over.

"Oh, Christ, not more harem girls," the man muttered in an annoyed tone. "That boy's got a *serious* problem."

"Fuck you, asshole," Kacey snapped back.

"We're *not* harem girls," Tammy replied at the same time. "We're *pilots*."

"Pilots?" the man said, his eyes flying wide in joy. "We've got pilots? Halle-fucking-lujah! We've got PILOTS!"

"Not yet," Kacey said, angrily. She was still pissed about the harem-girl crack. She also wanted to know more about the "harem." She was hoping, at a certain level, that it was a joke but she suspected it wasn't. "We're still considering it. Carefully."

"Oh, well, in that case you definitely want the job," the guy said, fulsomely. "The living conditions are great, the food's excellent, the beer's outstanding and the pay is awesome. What more could you ask?"

"I don't drink," Kacey said. "And a guarantee that we'll survive would be nice."

"Nope, can't do that one," the guy admitted. "Can't guarantee *I'll* survive. But the missions are worth it and the people are top-notch. If you end up taking the Valkyrie ride you'll be in plenty of bad company. We *will* guarantee that."

As he said that a side door opened and an absolutely beautiful woman walked into the foyer. Kacey wasn't kinked that way but she knew fucking beautiful when she saw it. Neither she nor Tammy were slouches in the looks department, but this lady put them both to shame. She looked like a supermodel. Blonde, blue eyes, low to mid-twenties, stacked and an absolutely gorgeous face. She was wearing *a lot* of makeup but so artfully applied it looked almost as if she wasn't wearing any. Blue, probably silk again, pant-suit that looked as if it was a Paris original. And graceful as hell. Probably Russian at a guess, definitely not American. She reminded Kacey of a young duchess character in an old movie. The lady had that look about her, like Zsa Zsa Gabor when she was *young*.

"Master Chief," the woman said, nodding. "I see you have met our visitors." Her English was impeccable but there was a definite Slavic accent. "*I zee you haff met our vizeetors.*"

"Christ, I hope they're not just visitors," the "master chief" grunted. "We are *screwed* without pilots."

"We're still considering," Tammy said, much more gently than Kacey. "And we haven't been introduced."

"Ah, this is my fault," the woman replied. "I was supposed to be your tour guide but I expected your meeting to be longer. I am Anastasia Rakovich, the Kildar's administrative manager. This is Master Chief Adams, late of the United States Navy Sea Air and Land commandoes, the Kildar's field tactical manager. Master Chief Adams, Captains Bathlick and Wilson, late of the United States Marine Corps."

"Who's the Kildar?" Tammy said at the same time as Kacey said: "SEALs?" and Adams said: "You're *Marines*?"

"I am given to understand that they have combat experience with the United States Marine Corps," Anastasia said, answering the master chief first. "The Kildar is Mr. Jenkins. It is his title. I will explain. And, yes, Master Chief Adams is a former SEAL as they say. I understand that 'ex' is looked upon poorly."

"Yeah, we've got experience," Tammy said with a snort. "We pulled your boss out of the drink one time. Or . . . Well, he sort of pulled *us* . . . It's complicated."

"You're the two that crashed that helo in the Carib," Adams said with a snort. "Oh. Great. I take it all back."

"We took a short-range EMP blast, you moron," Kacey snapped. "What the fuck were we supposed to do without goddamned engines? We were lucky to set it down light enough most of the FAST made it off!"

"I was yanking your chain," Adams said evenly. "Anybody that's willing to fly *towards* an LZ that has an active nuke on it gets my vote. You guys want a beer?"

"I'd prefer tequila," Tammy said, happily. "But I'll settle for beer."

"This isn't beer you settle for," Adams said. "This is beer you kill for."

"I was going to show them around, first," Anastasia pointed out.

"I'd say take the cook's tour," Adams admitted. "This is a pretty interesting place. And I really need a shower. To answer your unspoken question, Anastasia, no, it is not going well. I think that Shota's mother dropped him on his head as a baby. I asked her, point-blank, if she had and she said she had not. But apparently he had a hard time finding his way out when he was birthed, so maybe it's prenatal."

"You asked a woman if she'd dropped her son on his head?" Tammy asked, amazed.

"Yeah, but you'd have to understand the setup here," Adams said. "It wasn't even a particularly unexpected question. Shota's well known among the Keldara. Big as an ox and just about as dumb. Really good shot with a Carl Gustav, though. I think I need to just switch him out but if I can get him to learn to count as high as five he'll be awesome for door-kicking. I mean, he'd kick down a bank vault. But, God, he's dumb."

"Well, we'll go take the cook's tour," Tammy said, "while you're having a shower. Then I'll get you drunk and pry all your secrets out of you."

"The day a woman can out-drink me I'll turn in my trident," Adams said, chuckling, but then his face cleared. "Except this one bartender at Danny's. But that girl was a fucking *pro*. I saw her drink a whole platoon under the table one time. That's a professional. Admittedly, one without a functioning liver, but a pro nonetheless. You guys go take the cook's tour, I'm gonna go grab a shower and try to figure out a way to teach Shota to count as high as five. I mean, if they can teach monkeys sign language, I should be able to teach him to count to five for fuck's sake. Maybe a little rhyme or an advertising jingle . . ."

The former SEAL wandered off, muttering.

"Where would you like to start?" Anastasia asked, lightly. "Or are you fatigued from your trip? You could rest. Jet lag is very debilitating."

"I don't, honestly, know what time my body thinks it is," Tammy replied. "This is an interesting place. Ottoman?"

"The caravanserai was extensively renovated by the Ottomans, yes," Anastasia said, walking over to one of the carved buttresses that held up the ceiling of the room. "But the original work is believed to be from the period of the Byzantine Empire. These buttresses have faint markings that are indicative of Byzantine construction. You see here the faint indications of lacework patterning which is a Byzantine motif and the gouged-out portions were probably crosses which the Ottomans, or other Islamics, removed. And much of the lower stonework shows signs very similar to Roman construction, which the Byzantines used extensively for their castellation. The serai was probably rebuilt at least once under the Byzantines. The next clear work is Ottoman but the period between those two holders, probably close to a thousand years, is unclear."

"Oh," Kacey said, looking at the patterns. Lace did seem to fit the bill. She'd have to take the manager's word on that being "indicative of Byzantine construction." She knew about zero about architecture and not much more about the Byzantine Empire. "I've got one question. No, I've got a billion questions. Could you start at the beginning?"

"In the beginning was the Word," Anastasia said, lightly. "But I think you mean something closer in time. Let us sit, this will be somewhat long."

"Good," Tammy said. "I could do with some groundwork here. I'm pretty confused."

"A moment," Anastasia said and disappeared through the door she'd entered by. After a moment she came back out with another young lady who walked off in the opposite direction. This one was *really* young, fourteen if she was a day and wearing the same "schoolgirl" outfit as the harem girls. Which raised other questions. The earlier girls had been . . . okay, "old enough." Not old enough in the States to be fucking a guy in his thirties, but "old enough" for a developing country, whatever the liberals at home would wish. That one looked as if she should be playing with dolls. "Martya will bring some drinks. I wasn't sure what you'd like so we'll have tea and if that doesn't suit your tastes there are others."

"We can get it ourselves," Tammy protested.

"You could and in some conditions you will," Anastasia said, nodding. "But there are servants in the house for a reason. I will try to inform you, brief you, sufficiently that you can have a firm overview of what you are potentially joining. That will take time. If you are fetching drinks that interferes. When you are entirely free with your time you can choose to fetch or be fetched for. But the servants are there for a *reason*. The Kildar does not have *time* to get drinks for himself, cook for himself, do his laundry. His time is much better spent managing the resources of the valley or, as he puts it, 'killing people and breaking things.' This is, among other things, what pays for our surroundings. The girls are in free-study at the moment and, thus, not particularly busy. I asked which of them was least busy and Martya said she was. Given that she is intelligent and quick at her studies, she could be bored trying to act like she was studying or fetch us a drink. Which is the better use of her time?"

"You just used up more time explaining that than I would have getting myself a Coke," Tammy pointed out as Martya reappeared, accompanied by an older woman, bearing a couple of trays.

"Yes, but it is *part* of your briefing," Anastasia replied. "I hope you enjoy tea. Since we were taking this time to be acquainted I asked Mother Griffina to prepare tea."

"Tea" turned out to be in the English manner, which mean a hearty snack as well as the drink. There were croissants, scones and various other baked delicacies to accompany. The total covered the table.

"Pour, Martya," Anastasia said, sitting back in her chair.

"Miss Bathlick? Cream or sugar?" Martya said, carefully but clearly.

"Sugar," Kacey said, blinking. She'd been practically dragged to the airport, cleared customs without a visa, thrown into a Blackhawk piloted by a local and now she was having an English tea in an Ottoman caravanserai, complete with harem. It was a bit much to take. "Two lumps."

Martya picked up the lumps with a pair of silver tongs, placed them in the cup then poured tea in, placed a small spoon on the saucer and handed the whole collection to Kacey. The movements had been as smooth as a dance, clearly practiced.

"Miss Wilson? Cream or sugar?"

"Sugar," Tammy answered, smiling. "Two lumps." She paused and then glanced at Kacey before blurting, "And cream!"

Kacey tried not to chuckle. Tammy was the health nut of the two of them, at least in certain ways. Kacey didn't drink and Tammy did, which was one divergence. The other was that it was *Tammy* who had the big sweet tooth, not to mention things like cream in her coffee and tea. At least in part to make up for it, Tammy was always pushing vitamins and, otherwise, healthy eating.

"Miss Rakovich? Cream or sugar?"

"Both, please," Anastasia said. It was clear that Martya knew her preferences, she'd already been reaching for the tongs, but just as clear that you weren't permitted to *assume* in this particular dance. Kacey suspected that at a later time, Anastasia was going to grade Martya on her performance.

Kacey realized as she watched that Anastasia *never* wasted a chance. Martya, who was "intelligent and quick at her studies," was being given an opportunity to hear English being used in casual dialogue and practice her social skills. And she and Tammy were being presented by a remarkably calm and well-balanced teenager who was, nonetheless, a member of a fucking harem. Two birds, maybe more, with one stone. Talk about a fucking pro.

Then she really thought about it. Adams was the classic SEAL master chief, a total pro at "killing people and breaking things." They didn't have to "ooh-rah!" about their time in service; they just had to say "I'm a SEAL master chief." Pro. The men she'd seen in uniform weren't swaggering around with their guns. They were clearly on some mission with a purpose. They might not be pros, yet, but they were going there with a purpose. And "Jenkins," if that was his real name, well, he was a guy who had walked onto an island with over thirty armed terrorists holding it, walked off it having killed every one and survived the resulting nuclear blast. Pro.

She suddenly let out a mental breath she hadn't realized she'd been holding. She was dealing with *professionals*. Experts. Since she'd gotten out of the military, and most of the time *in* the Marines, she'd had so little opportunity to deal with really expert professionals she hadn't realized how much she'd missed it. And this harum-scarum hiring procedure had scared something deep in her soul, because it didn't seem *professional*. But the whole movement had been greased. She and Tammy had moved from one prepared position to the other. She wasn't even sure what the visa entry requirements *were* for Georgia; there had been a polite man at the airport who had whisked them past customs and into a car, driven by a polite and professional English-speaking driver that had the look of "distinguished persons protection" all over him. That driver had brought them to the bird, which was flown by guys who, while not at her and Tammy's level, were good, competent, bird drivers.

It also said something about their being hired. If that was the caliber of people that "Jenkins," the "Kildar," surrounded himself with, then he obviously considered them in the same league. That was actually a bit daunting, but she wouldn't be a pilot if she really was challenged by it. She knew *she* was a fucking pro. And so was Tammy. It would be nice to work with competent people again.

The dying part would suck, admittedly, but she'd just have to make sure she didn't.

"Now that we are settled," Anastasia said, "I will tell you a bedtime story, yes? It is the story of how the Kildar came to be the Kildar."

"I'd assumed he was knighted or something," Tammy said, smiling at the small joke.

"No, he simply bought the farm," Anastasia said, smiling in turn. "The idiom has been explained to me, yes? It is a euphemism for dying. What happened was that he got lost. Very simple, no? And he found the Valley of the Keldara. He was looking at possibly being caught here all winter; the snows are very bad and the roads . . . not so good. So he inquired about someplace to stay. There were no rooms for let so it was suggested that he consider buying the farm of the Keldara. That was a large item, but he did so. I have never asked him *why*, but he bought the farm."

"Which is?" Tammy asked. "I mean, how big is the farm?"

"The entire valley," Anastasia answered, taking a sip of tea. "It is a very large farm."

"I can actually guess where he got the money," Kacey said, sarcastically. "It turns out we've met before. When he set off a nuke in the Caribbean."

"I have heard something of this," Anastasia said. "He is . . . quite extensively scarred. He does not flaunt them, you understand. But I sometimes ask 'Where is this from?' Sometimes he will tell me something. 'That is from my Caribbean vacation. Fortunately the hair grew back.' I later pick up that he was shot and a nuclear weapon was detonated. Others . . . he does not answer. Or he says 'Here and there.' Yes, he has made his money from 'killing people and breaking things.' Sometimes he finds someone that needs killing, something that needs breaking, and then he informs the appropriate government that their problem has been erased. And they pay him money for solving their problems. Sometimes governments tell him about a problem. And when he solves it for them, they pay him money. They do not tell him, 'There is a man named Boris. He lives on such and such a street.' Unless this Boris is such a bad man that he is worth millions of dollars and he is somewhere they cannot reach. What is the reach of the United States, yes? What is the reach of Russia? But the Kildar can reach where they cannot."

"I get the picture," Tammy said. "Freelance James Bond."

"Including the women, yes?" Anastasia said and then really smiled. It turned out that she had dimples, the perfect bitch. "He has a hareem, yes. But he could have a hareem anywhere, I think. He is very much all man, but not stupid in bed. Very not stupid. I will explain about the hareem in a bit, but I must add that recently, due to some other things I will not talk about without his specific permission, he had to find somewhere for a fairly large number of . . . call them 'fallen women.' He did so, a school in Paraguay, and paid for them to go there and for their education. Since he had this school available he asked the girls who were in the hareem if they wished to leave. Two did, one who was younger than he was willing to broach and another who . . . well, she did not have any interest in sex at all. I then, at the Kildar's insistence, pressed the other girls for why they wanted to stay. And they were definite about wanting to stay. All of them said that they liked it here and 'why should I go to some school where I will be forced to hide cucumbers from the kitchen when I have the Kildar?'"

"Gotcha," Tammy said, chuckling.

"I tell you this not to . . . pander for the Kildar, you understand?" Anastasia said, for the first time hurriedly. "But so that you can feel more comfortable with the situation. The Kildar is . . . How was it said: Neither fish nor fowl nor red meat. He is in a condition, a situation, for which there is no American custom or rule. He has to find his own middle ground in everything. I think, had things not happened the way they did, he would have just used local prostitutes for his needs. But . . ."

"He saved my life," Martya said, quietly. "Perhaps I would not have died, but my *life* would have been gone. For that I owe him everything. But I would leave but for one thing: In one more year I can also have the Kildar. For that I would give much. Shana was barely thirteen, too long for her to wait. And she told me that she was scheming of ways to get back when her time was up."

"Martya was part of a group of girls from the local farms and villages," Anastasia said. "She and the others had been sold to, or in one case kidnapped by, the Chechens. The Chechens made the mistake of also stealing a Keldara girl. The Kildar killed them for their mistake. But he then had seven girls with no place to go. Their families did not want them back. So they had nowhere else to go. The Kildar was unable to find a school for them at the time so he brought them into his household as concubines. They are not whores, they serve only the Kildar. And in more ways than sex and fetching and carrying, but that is too complex a subject for today. Know that they are all volunteers and while *your* society considers them young, in *this* society they would mostly be already married. The fact that they were not was what caused them to be as the saying goes 'sent to town.'"

"That had to be tough," Tammy said, looking at Martya.

Kacey thought that was either Tammy being brain-dead or the understatement of the year.

"It was," Martya admitted with what Kacey thought was remarkable calm. "But things turned out very well. I have learned enough of American attitudes and lives to understand that you may not think that. Know that, for me, this is a very high honor. I am from not far from here, I have even seen my parents and forgive them for what they did. I understood it at the time and now I understand some of the cultural and economic underpinnings, yes? But while I am not Keldara, the Keldara influence a wider area than they knew. The Kildar was a legend, like your King Arthur, yes? 'Things would be better if the Kildar was here. The crops would grow better, the sun brighter, the winter shorter, all the children would be more respectful of their elders.' And now the Kildar is returned and things *are* better. The money he brings in helps, but so does the *hope*. Everyone sees how things are going for the Keldara and hope for similar changes in their own lives. People are much more reluctant to sell their daughters so that they have enough money to survive the winter. There is more money everywhere. The Keldara are gone so often that many times they have to hire laborers to take their place. The Kildar treats women as special, even though he has a harem. Much more special than they had been in this society. So other men wonder if they should treat their women better. He 'leads by example' even when he knows it not. Things are *better*. And I am one of his women. That makes my status, in this society, much higher than if I had married any of the potential men around my farm. Much higher than my mother's. My family, who *sold* me, now have a higher status than they could even dream. Because their daughter is one of the women of the Kildar."

"I think that should adequately cover the issue of the hareem," Anastasia said, smiling again and showing those damned dimples.

"I'm . . . bemused," Tammy said. "But, yeah, I think it covers it. With one teensy-tiny question on redirect. Martya, you said that you only had to wait a year to . . . I guess be 'broached' as Anastasia put it, by the Kildar. How old *are* you?"

"The Kildar put the 'cutoff' at sixteen," Anastasia answered for her. "Martya is fifteen. She only looks a bit younger because she tries so very very hard."

"And I love to tease him," Martya added, grinning. "I like to bend over so he can see down my shirt, quite innocently, of course.

I want him to want me so badly that I get him as a birthday present, like a new pair of earrings. Unfortunately, I never needed braces."

"I won't *even* ask about that," Kacey said. "Okay, so he bought the farm and shot up some terrorists and got a harem. Where do the Keldara come in?"

"The Keldara have been around . . . for a very long time," Anastasia said. "The Kildar believes that they first came to the valley as guards for the caravanserai during the Byzantine period. They show signs, cultural holdovers, that indicate that they were part of a group called the Varangian Guard."

"Holy shit," Tammy gasped. "You're serious?"

"Don't get the reference," Kacey said. "Who were the Ferengi or whatever?"

"Varangians," Tammy said, chuckling. "Although the root of both names . . . Oh never mind. The thing is they were Vikings that were guards of the Byzantine Emperors, an elite force. But that was fifteen hundred years ago or so. I can't believe there's *any* remnant."

"The Kildar believes that this is the case, nonetheless," Anastasia said. "There are old songs that have been partially translated that indicate that this is so. But all records have, of course, been lost over the millennia. They have been the tenant farmers of the valley from before the records we've found from the Ottoman period. They also, however, supplied fighters to the Ottomans including for the local area and the caravanserai. The Ottoman Empire was, of course, made up entirely of 'foreigners' but in the case of the caravanserai it has always, in our studies, had a foreigner as the commander. Under the Ottomans they came from all over the far-flung empire and even from non-Ottoman Europe. Under the Tsars they were almost invariably European adventurers, mercenaries that worked for the Tsars. And the holder of the caravanserai has been called 'The Kildar' from at least the time of the Ottomans. It is probably held as a motif by the Keldara and picked up over time. The Keldara were not entirely Norse, at least according to the songs. They appear to be a mixture of Norse and some Celts from Ireland or Scotland."

"Now, even *I* recognize that as an odd mix," Kacey said.

"But mixed they are," Anastasia replied. "And they have managed to hold on to a warrior tradition even under various empires. Now, of course, the Kildar is an American, the masters of the current world empire, yes? An elite warrior of high training, currently for hire, very much in tradition. He is their perfect Kildar, their Arthur returned to bring the Keldara back to their glory. They don't just follow him, they worship him as if he was one of their odd old gods, for they are only very superficially Christian. I am surprised there are not secret shrines to the Kildar," she added, chuckling.

"Well, that's got to be kind of heady," Kacey said, a tad bitterly. "I mean he's got women throwing themselves at him and his 'retainers' worshipping him. Sucks to be him, right?"

"I will let you make up your mind about that as time goes by," Anastasia said, tilting her head to one side and regarding the pilot calmly. "I will try to give you a hint as to what 'sucks to be him' as you put it. One of your presidents, I was told, had a plaque on his desk that said: 'The buck stops here.'"

"Harry Truman," Tammy replied, nodding. "Your point?"

"When you were in the Marines, you were given orders to go here and do this," Anastasia said. "And the people giving you orders were given orders all the way up to the President. You simply followed those orders; you did not live with the responsibility of their effects. With the Kildar, where does the buck stop?"

"Oh," Tammy said.

"He is very attached to the Keldara and he is a man who cares about not only his people but, in a way, the whole world," Anastasia said, gently. "And even the slightest mistake could destroy all he has built either through violence or politics. Consider that burden upon your own shoulders then look around. Does a hareem and a nice house compensate for that?"

"Lasko, a moment of your time," Mike said, his head ducked through the door of the armory.

Lasko Ferani was the oldest member of the Mountain Tigers. One of the Keldara's designated "hunters" before the arrival of the Kildar. Now, he was still a hunter, but of men, the acknowledged leader of the Keldara team snipers.

He was medium height and whip-cord thin, and Mike was never sure how old he was. At a guess about forty, but he looked about seventy from years of hard outdoor work. Lasko was no runner, as had been proven several times, but he could go all day long with a ruck on his back and had that maximal sniper requirement: he could stay incredibly still for literally days on end waiting for a shot.

Mike had introduced him to the world of computers after the Albanian mission and given him a credit card to order gear. Snipers, owing to the nature of their mission, used highly irregular gear compared to regular infantry. Lasko had learned just enough written English to read the posts on sniper boards and begin exploring the world of gear, then started ordering. Some of the stuff he discarded after testing it but Mike didn't mind and had made that clear. He wanted the Keldara snipers professionally outfitted with gear that really *worked*. And the final determinant of what did and did not work was Lasko.

But Lasko's approach to webboards was the strangest Mike had ever seen. One time Mike had walked past when Lasko was online and just had to pause. He'd seen him three times that day and each time Lasko was just sitting in front of the computer, not doing a damned thing. Just . . . sitting, one hand on the mouse, the other on his thigh, perfectly still.

"Okay, Lasko, what are you doing?"

"Waiting for someone to post," Lasko had answered, coldly.

Mike had visited sniper boards like Sniper.com before and noticed that there were very few "regular" posters, most of them pretty clearly not operational snipers. The regulars were always posting and chatting and debating about techniques or equipment or what their dog had eaten that was really disgusting.

But then you'd see the occasional really bizarre post. It would go something like:

Afghan Sniper: Eagle 415.
AirborneSnipe115: Good.
SFSnipe22: Strap weak.

And so on.

Lasko finally made it all clear and Mike had a sudden mental image of serious operational snipers, all over the world, sitting there waiting for the first guy to make a move. When a sniper faced another sniper, the first one to move was the dead man. He could see it clearly now: Dozens, hundreds, of hard faces waiting for the guy who made the first mistake.

Snipers were natural lurkers. That was Lasko in a nutshell.

"Aircraft's coming in at 2230 day after tomorrow," Mike said when they'd stepped outside. He handed Lasko a slip of paper with coordinates on it. "Six LZs. That's where we're inserting. The pilot is the chief of staff's son-in-law. Now you know."

"I've got it," Lasko said and nodded.

"Recon only," Mike pointed out.

"Taken care of, Kildar."

That was what he liked about Lasko. Tell him he was going to go sit in place for a week, looking at a hopefully empty field, and he was positively happy. Not *quite* as happy as with a field full of targets and a full magazine, but close.

"Colonel, this is an advisory on an upcoming mission."

Lieutenant Colonel Peyton Randolph, commander 1st Battalion 75th Infantry (Ranger), hated video-conferencing and wished the geeks that invented it had been stillborn. Why not just use a simple telephone? It wasn't like anybody looked you in the eye. They were always looking down at the monitor!

"Yes, sir," he said, sitting up for the call from the SOCOM weenie. He'd been told he was getting a call from some Pentagon SOCOM bureaucrat and to just "do what you're told." Instead of staring at the stupid monitor, though, he looked right at the camera set on top.

"Your Bravo Company is going to be going over to the country of Georgia to train with some mountain infantry over there," the colonel said. "Because Bravo Company is jump-short they'll jump insert but the jump will be purely administrative; the DZ will be in a secured area. The catch is that they're going to be using third-country transport due to current transportation shortages. The good news is that they're going to be able to add an Antonov to their jump sheets and we'll see if we can arrange Ukrainian jump wings as a bonus."

"You're shitting me," Randolph said, chuckling. "Maybe I ought to strap-hang."

"Well, if you *do* you'll have to find your own way back or stay in-country for a couple of weeks," Pierson sighed. "Air Force is *really* tasked out. The Bravo Company commander will be given further orders but those are code-word classified. The mission may entail engagements but it is not believed that the risks on the operation will be high."

"I just hope we're not helping the Georgians beat up on the Ossetians," the commander said. "That's pretty much an internal matter, Colonel."

"The area they are going to has some threat from the *Chechens* but is outside the Ossetian area," the "Pentagon weenie" replied. "And the orders are from higher so who cares? Ours but to do or die and all that. This is only an advisory. But please recall your personnel at this time; we're getting on short time for this."

"Will do," Lieutenant Colonel Randolph said and finally looked at the monitor. To his surprise the Pentagon weenie was looking at him out of it.

"Tell them good luck and good hunting," Colonel Pierson replied. Then the monitor went dead.

Kacey put down the dash-one for the Czech Aeroframe Corporation Hind-J "aerial ambulance" and rubbed her eyes. Dash-ones were *the* manual for an aircraft, discussing not only design and engineering but flying characteristics. They were the pilot's bible and she and Tamara had been doing their best, with a lot of assistance, to practically memorize them.

That Kildar character hadn't been joking about "cramming." The Czech instructors were being paid to shove as much knowledge of the Hind-J into them in as short a time as humanly possible. And her head was about to explode.

The J variant was significantly different than the D variant they'd flown lo these many years ago. It had an additional supercharger on each engine for high-altitude operations, an oxygen system, pressurized flight and crew compartment and various other bells and whistles. It also had replaced a lot of metal parts with composites, reducing its base weight a good bit. But what was seriously different were the engines, modified Bells built by the

Czechs on contract that were thirty percent more powerful than the originals while being a tad lighter and smaller. That was good, in general, since the Hind-D was a bit of a pig in the air. Essentially, it was an entirely new aircraft as or more capable than the Russian Mi-35. But that also meant the aircraft had different flight characteristics. The ground training portion of the transition was about over. Since the one thing the Czechs did not seem to have was a good simulator for the craft they were going to be taking their first "familiarization" flights tomorrow. And she didn't want her eyes bleary for that.

But she had one thing to do before she went to bed.

The Kildar had, as promised, supplied them with a satellite phone. It was a desktop model, sort of bulky but capable of not just telephone connection but video and a limited internet pipe. For that matter, there was a whole set of controls that had something to do with a scrambler. Where the "Kildar" had gotten military grade scramblers she wasn't going to ask, but given their mission it wasn't too weird.

She didn't need any of that, though, all she needed was the phone.

"Calling Chief D'Allaird finally?" Tammy asked, setting down her own dash-one.

"About that time," Kacey said, dialing the number she'd finally managed to find in her address book. "Hopefully he hasn't already left for work."

"Hopefully he's *awake*," Tammy pointed out.

Kacey listened to the phone ring then pick up.

"837-4159. How may I help you sir or ma'am?"

Damn. Good to see some things hadn't changed.

"Mr. Timothy D'Allaird? This is Air Force Bureau of Personnel. This is to inform you that you've been selected for a recall tour to points in the AOR. Further information will be arriving by mail at your home of record. Are you still resident at—"

"Kacey, is that you?" the voice said. "God, damn, girl you almost gave me a heart attack!"

"Hi, Chief," Kacey said, grinning. "How they hangin'?"

"Still one below the other," D'Allaird said. "To what do I owe the honor of a call from Miss Snot-Nose?"

"Oh, all sorts of reasons," Kacey said. "So, how's the wife?"

"Divorced these last two years," D'Allaird said. "Which is why I'm working about sixty hours of overtime a week. You'll understand if I need to get ready for work. I'm with that comedian guy; next time I think about getting married I'll just buy a house for some woman I can't stand."

"Why aren't you contracting?" Kacey said, quizzically.

"I got *really* tired of the sandbox," D'Allaird said. "Tired enough I'm willing to work *lots* of hours to avoid it. I keep asking . . ."

"Business call, honestly," Kacey finally admitted. "I know someone who needs a contractor. Aircraft engineer. *Not* in the sandbox. But I'll also be up-front that whoever takes the job has to be Hind-qualified and aware that it may involve getting their ass shot off. The flip side is that the money is good and so are the conditions."

"Where?" D'Allaird asked.

"You did hear the part about getting your ass shot off, right?" Kacey asked.

"And let me guess who's flying the bird: the Bobbsey Twins."

"The same," Kacey admitted.

"Well, now I *got* to go," D'Allaird admitted. "If for no other reason than to keep you two out of trouble. I mean, does this place *have* a brig?"

"Hey, we weren't going to go to the *brig* over that," Kacey said.

"Yes we were," Tammy replied, not looking up from her manual.

"The most was going to happen was off flying status for a while," Kacey protested.

"Tammy doesn't think so," D'Allaird said. "And I keep asking . . ."

"The country of Georgia," Kacey replied. "Out in the boonies but nice facilities. A general contractor. I have the feeling it's a good idea to keep a bag packed. I'm not sure of the pay for you, but they're paying *us* great and we said we had to have a chief, a good one. We actually need two. We may be flying solos. And it's Hind-Js."

"The new Czech bird," D'Allaird said with a whistle. "Sweet. I've been reading up on the specs. I'm in. I've been wanting to get my hands on one of those. Screw these damned Lynx and Rangers, I'm sick to death of Lynx and Rangers."

"Hope you've got a passport," Kacey said. "I'll have somebody contact you about travel arrangements. And keep an eye out for another body."

"Male or female?" D'Allaird asked.

"Makes no diff," Kacey said. "The guy who's hiring us, a Mr. Jenkins also called 'The Kildar,' doesn't seem to care. But whoever it is had better be open-minded. The arrangements are kind of . . . odd."

"Better and better," D'Allaird said. "I'm tired as hell of same old. I'll be waiting for the call."

"See you soon, Chief," Kacey said, cutting the connection.

"Another lamb to the slaughter," Tammy said. "This thing is either sweet as hell or the Czechs let their marketing department write the dash-ones."

"Marketing departments *always* write the dash-ones," Kacey said. "Tomorrow we just get to find out if it's an *honest* marketing department."

"Power up, softly, softly . . .?"

Kacey didn't know if the Czechs had intentionally supplied one cute as hell instructor pilot or not, but Marek Kalenda was hot. Older than she usually liked, probably pushing a very in-shape fifty, but still hot. Nice voice, too. Resonant. Of course, it would help if she paid attention to flying.

"Good, hold it," Marek said. "Feel her. Nice isn't she?"

"I'm only at twenty-three percent power," Kacey replied. "This thing is, if anything, *over*-muscled."

"There is no such thing as too much power in a helicopter," Marek said. "I was asked when they were looking at the new Bells if, perhaps, that was not too much power for the Hind. No, I told them. What is that American show, the man is always saying 'More power!'?"

"*Home Improvement*," Kacey said with an unseen grin. The Hind, unlike Hueys and Hawks, was a tandem rig. The pilot sat back, the co- or gunner sat forward. Currently, Marek was forward. "Tim Allen."

"Yes, more power," Marek agreed. "That was also a command. Bring her out of ground hover if you please. Slowly."

Kacey poured on more power without disturbing any of the other controls. She, of course, had to tap the rear-rotor controls to keep the aircraft straight, but otherwise she kept it "as is" with the exception of power. The helicopter went straight up with only a slight side-to-side yaw as she got the feel for the rear rotor.

"Very nice," Kacey said. "I'm at forty percent. And out of ground effect, unless I'm much mistaken."

"Yes, but of course we are empty," Marek pointed out. "At height, with a full load? You will be pushing the redline. But I will tell you something that is not in the dash-one, yes? I have force tested this bird and engines. The redline on the engines is conservative. You have about twenty percent more power when you are red. But you must yank the engines after the mission, yes?"

"Twenty percent's a lot of power," Kacey said. "Why'd you do that?"

"Because we have some customers who, shall we say, are not as professional as you," Marek said with a sigh. "If some son of an Arab sheik goes down we like to be able to point out that he was not supposed to redline the aircraft's engine continually. Better still if he has the smidgen of sense to only touch the redline and still survive. At absolute full power the engines *will* eventually fail. But for an emergency . . . the power is there."

"Good to know," Kacey said.

"Now that we have taken this time for you to feel the bird *and* prove you can talk at the same time, you may push forward slightly on the stick. Your bird, ma'am."

"My bird," Kacey replied, pushing forward on the stick and increasing power to the engines unconsciously. She started to grin as the bird slid forward like it was on greased rails and lifted into the air. The mass of the Hind had always made it fly like a pig and they usually didn't hover for shit. Now, with the overpowered engines, it was like driving a *really* nice sports car, one of the ones that hugged the road like a limpet. Smooth didn't begin to describe it. "Oh. My. God."

"I thought you would like this, yes," Marek said with obvious satisfaction in his voice. "We at Czech Airframes *like* satisfied customers. Satisfied customers are repeat customers."

"Oh, I'm satisfied," Kacey said. "This bird can *fly.*"

Chapter Nineteen

"USAF Flight 1157," Second Lieutenant Kevin Ferlazzo said when the "incoming satellite call" light started blinking on his console.

USAF Flight 1157 was a MC-130 Special Operations (Electronic) aircraft from the 47th Squadron out of Moody Air Force Base in Valdosta, Georgia. Flight 1157, crew of five, was currently on a compassionate mission delivering relief supplies to Azerbaijan, motoring along on cruise control over the nation of Ukraine, which from thirty thousand feet looked *a lot* like Kansas. A recent earthquake had left dozens of mountain villages in Azerbaijan devastated and cut off with winter oncoming. About half of the cargo consisted of cattle feed donated by the American Cattleman's Association. The rest was general relief supplies including MRE-style "relief meals," tents, blankets and clothing.

Lieutenant Ferlazzo, the flight engineer of the aircraft (and as he thought of it "designated receptionist"), hadn't planned on becoming a relief worker when he'd graduated from the United States Air Force Academy and he wondered about the efficiency of using a top-of-the-line, state-of-the-art, special-operations, electronics-warfare aircraft that cost $8,000 per hour to run to deliver hay bales. However, nobody but *nobody* asked a second lieutenant what he thought except his mother.

"1157, this is Four-Seven Actual. Put the 1157 Actual on. Then get off."

"Roger, sir," Lieutenant Ferlazzo said, hitting the hold button and switching to intercom. "Pilot, Four-Seven Actual wants you." He didn't ask the pilot if he wanted to take the call. Unless you're in the bird's pisser or a declared emergency, if the squadron commander calls you say "Yes, sir!" and pick up the horn.

Captain Richard C. "Casey" Moore sat up out of his half doze and looked at the co quizzically. "Okay, what did you do now?"

Casey Moore was twenty-six, brown of hair and eye, just below medium height with "an erect carriage and firm demeanor." Said so right on his Officer Evaluation Reports. That's because his various squadron commanders hadn't wanted to say "who is a wise-ass that likes to tease parajumpers until an incident occurs." Among other things, he was one hell of a C-130 driver and it wasn't like anybody ever got *hurt*.

Without waiting for an answer he hit the accept button. "1157 Actual."

"1157 Actual, Squadron Actual," the squadron commander replied. "Divert Tbilisi Military Airfield for refueling and pickup of quote Friendly Nation relief workers end quote. Coordinate with military attaché, United States Embassy, Georgia, Colonel Randolph Mandrell. Transport of relief workers classified Top Secret Ribbon Blade. Obtain vocal orders Colonel Mandrell re Operation Ribbon Blade. Colonel Mandrell has full operational control 1157 in re Ribbon Blade. Do you copy?"

Casey blinked for a just a second and then stared at the windshield as if looking for divine aid.

"Four-Seven Actual, 1157. Copy divert Tbilisi Military Airfield, contact Georgian mil attaché, Colonel Mandrell re pickup of Friendly Nation quote aid workers end quote. Pick up classified Ribbon Blade. Operational details via mil attaché. Mil attaché has operational control. Verification code, over?" He easily recognized the squadron commander's voice and the orders were coming over an encrypted satellite link. But he also knew that if he didn't verify, Four-Seven Actual, who was a real prick, would jump his ass.

"Verification, code Four-Delta-Five-Niner."

"Ferz," Casey said, hitting the hold button. "I need a verification on order changes, Four-Delta-Five-Niner."

"Yeah, confirm," Ferlazzo said after a moment. "It's an updated code."

"Four-Seven Actual, 1157. Verification confirmed. Diverting to Tbilisi at this time."

"Roger, out."

"We're going *where*?" the co-pilot asked. Captain Jim Sanderson was a regular co-pilot for Casey but not because Casey trusted his driving. Quite the opposite. In fact, he sometimes suspected that Casey dragged him around the world on one weird-assed mission after another purely to take his monthly pay at poker.

And in that he would be right. He also was a great pawn to use in Casey's ongoing low-level war with the entire para-jumper corps. When Casey knew they were hunting a hostage, say because somebody had casually walked off with one of their damned gnomes, he could usually arrange for the co to be in the "wrong place at the wrong time" to get picked off by the PJs. Hell, better than giving up his nav.

The 47th was a "multi-mission" squadron. They had a variety of transport aircraft ranging from Beavers to C-17s with multiple variants and a group of pilots that were just as eclectic. Most of the pilots were cross-trained in special-operations missions; however the squadron, since it wasn't a dedicated special-ops squadron, tended to do mostly grunt hauling work. But, because it wasn't listed as a primary trash-hauler squadron they weren't first on the list for that, either. In fact, in the increasingly overtasked cargo air-craft field, it was the one squadron that had a relatively low opera-tional tempo. That meant that the pilots could get more training on more different missions than most of the overtasked squadrons. Even the spec-ops squadrons had a hard time digging up HALO drop qualified crews; the 47th had seven including Flight 1157.

"Tbilisi," the navigator said. Captain Cassandra "Cassie" Phil-lips could have been Casey's sister. Five foot five, brown of hair and eye, there was even a slight facial resemblance. But features that were handsome on Casey came out as beautiful on Cassie. "Capital of the country of Georgia. It's not far off our flight path anyway. If we hadn't tanked in Kiev we'd have had to land there and tank. Come to heading one-three-zero. Tbilisi Military Control is on fre-quency 1957. Notation says that it's closed to unauthorized birds, though and 'limited English.'"

"Oh, joy," Casey said. "Co, freq."

"Roger," Jim said, leaning forward to switch the radios.

"Just another day in paradise," Casey said, taking the plane off of auto-pilot and banking slightly to the left. "Oh, somebody ought to tell the load master we're picking up some passengers."

"They can sit on the hay bales," Cassie said.

"How's the company?" Captain Jean-Paul "J.P." Guerrin asked the first sergeant as he came into the CP.

"Pissed," First Sergeant Michael Kwan replied, shrugging. Kwan was a short-coupled Chinese-American with eighteen years and a bit in uniform. He'd started off in the 82nd Airborne, transferring to the Ranger Batts when he was a staff sergeant. He'd spent the next fourteen years doing the "Ranger Thang" all over the world. Nobody but his very *very* close friends dared use his early nickname, "Gook," to his face. "They'll get over it. But they're getting pretty damned sick of the sandbox. They'd been looking forward to some time on River Street."

"Aren't we all," the CO said. "The good news, what I have so far, is that we're not *going* to the sandbox. We're going to Georgia, the country just to avoid confusion, and doing some training with a local mountain infantry group. That's all I have right now, but feel free to spread it around. Mountain ops, about like New York this time of year. Pack snivel gear even if we're not going to use it. There is a threat in the area; the Chechens move around in the same mountains. Current plan is an airborne op into a secured DZ that's where we'll be basing. I'm told there are basing facilities."

"So it's a training op?" Kwan asked. "Rumor was that we were dropping hot." Carrying live rounds instead of training ammunition.

"We are," Guerrin said with a grimace. "*Good* training. Either somebody wants to see if we can really do it or the Chechen threat is worse than anticipated. I'll do an op order this evening at 1730. Birds will be at the airfield at 0430, civilian. We're flying to Ukraine."

"And then?" Kwan asked.

"That's apparently still being debated by higher," J.P. replied. "We're *going* to Georgia. How is still up in the air. So an all-nighter and a long flight with who knows what at the end."

"We can sleep when we're dead," Kwan said, grinning. To be a Ranger for twelve years you had to positively *enjoy* misery and Kwan was a legend on that score.

"Tbilisi Military Air Field this is USAF Flight 1157, C-130, requesting clearance and approach." Casey switched to intercom and looked over at the co. "Now to see if they speak English."

"Better than that landing in Indonesia," Sanderson said, shuddering. "He was damned positive he spoke Eeengeesh."

"USAF Flight 1157, Tbilisi Military Air Field Control." The voice was accented but fully understandable. "We have you are cleared to land Tbilisi Military Airfield Runway Zero-Niner. Turn to heading Zero-Five-Five and descend to Angels Eight, descent ratio one five meters per second. Conditions overcast at Angels Three to Angels Seventeen. Visibility below Angels Three seven kilometers. Civilian jet aircraft your vicinity at Angels Five, heading one-two-seven, five kilometers, direction zero-five-five. Note all pertinent flight advisories."

"Cass?" Casey said, taking the bird off autopilot

"They're bringing us in from the east," Cassie said, looking at the flight advisory bulletins. "Not only is there a note about potentially hostile activity in that general direction, you're going to have to come in over some mountains then drop it down hard. You wanna look?"

"Co has the bird," Casey said. "Maintain bank to zero-five-five, descent ratio fifteen meters per second."

"I have the bird," the co said, taking the controls.

"The security area is way off to one side," Casey said after a second and a slight lurch from the plane. "The descent over the mountains is pretty steep but nothing much. *Nasty* approach, though. But that's it, thanks, Cass."

"You got it," Cassie said, taking the chart back.

"Commander has the bird," Casey said then glanced at the instruments.

"You have the bird," Jim said, leaning back and crossing his arms.

"Fifteen meters ratio," Casey said after a second, sighing and reducing the bank. "One five, Jim. *Definitely* not three zero."

"Understood, sir," Jim said, his face blank. "Sorry, sir."

"Not as sorry as you would have been," Casey said with a sigh. "Look at the LIDAR."

Jim took his eyes off the glide ratio indicator and looked at the terrain tracking infrared laser system then blanched. A quick glance out the window revealed, even through the heavy clouds, a mountainside flashing by.

"Use caution when approaching the edges of the air," Casey said, pompously. "And how can these be defined, Jim?"

"Ground, water or outer space," Jim said, hangdog.

"Because it is very difficult to fly a plane in all three. Even harder to fly through mountains, Jim. You would have been very disliked by what remained of the crew."

"Commander, this is the load master," a female voice said somewhat nervously over the intercom.

"Go," Casey said, grinning.

"Sir, did we nearly just hit a mountain? Because I can see some out the window. And they're . . . kinda close, sir."

"Not at all," Casey replied, his eyes glued on his instruments. "We were just looking for mountain goats. Wait! There's one, out the right side!"

"Really? Where?" the girl asked happily.

"*Man*, she's easy," Casey muttered. "Ooooh, sparkly!"

Lasko stepped out of the door of the helicopter and took a knee as Sion Kulcyanov stepped out next to him. Both paused and scanned the nearby woodline through their NVGs as the blacked-out chopper lifted into the air. The helo turned out to be piloted not by the chief of staff's son-in-law, who was instead the co-pilot, but by the commander of Georgia's helo squadron. The crew-chief was one of the seniormost NCOs in the Georgian National Guard.

General Umarov was taking as few chances as possible on this mission being blown owing to leaks.

Lasko didn't let that worry him; that was the Kildar's problem. His was making sure that the landing hadn't been observed and finding a good spot to overlook the *actual* LZ, which was about ten kilometers away.

"Clear right," Sion whispered.

"Clear left," Lasko said, switching to thermal for a second view. There was a distant rumble of an aircraft in the distance but otherwise the night was silent. "Deer at ten o'clock. Bedding. Right."

"Moving," Sion said, standing up and heading for the woodline.

They had all of tonight and tomorrow to reach the LZ and get a good overlook point. Which was about how slow Lasko liked to move. Sitting perfectly still was better, but ten kilometers in a day or so was close enough.

Chapter Twenty

"Jim, the idea when landing is that you're going slow enough that you can actually *stop* before the runway does," Casey said, making his way past the hay bales towards the rear doors of the fuselage. When he'd been a kid his family would go visit his mom's parents on their farm in the summer. He'd never expected his aircraft to smell *exactly* like Grandpa's hayloft. On the other hand, that hayloft had some really nice associations, so it wasn't all bad.

"Sorry, sir," Jim said, stone-faced.

"I think Tbilisi control just thinks we're idiots for not asking for *two* touch-and-gos *before* we landed," Casey continued. "I'm really hoping they aren't thinking the truth, which is that *one* of us, and I won't say which of us because I'm kind, is unable to land a C-130 if his life depends on it."

"Sir, were we planning on two touches?" the load asked as the two officer approached. The load master, Sergeant Lisa Griffitts, was a short, pretty blonde that, to his great chagrin, brought up all *sorts* of associations with haylofts in Casey's mind. Unfortunately, she was a subordinate and, thus, very much off-limits. Even if there *were* all these convenient hay bales stacked in the hold.

"Absolutely," Casey said, nodding. "Certification stuff."

"Oh," Lisa said, nodding. "So it *wasn't* that Captain Sanderson couldn't find the ground?"

"Look! A doggie!" Sanderson said, pointing out the window.

"Actually, that's an Alsatian, sir," the load master said, not turning around to look out the porthole. "And the guy controlling it is part of a security contingent that just surrounded our plane."

"Really?" Casey said, bending down to look out the porthole.

"Really, sir," Lisa replied. "And not a mountain goat to be seen."

Before Casey could reply there was a banging on the troop door.

"I guess we need to see what they want," Casey said.

Lisa opened the troop door and, at the sight of an American colonel, dropped a step-ladder out.

"Where's Captain Moore?" the colonel said, swarming up the ladder.

"Captain Richard C. Moore, sir!" Casey said, saluting. He didn't *quite* snap to attention but close enough for an Air Force pilot. "Commander Flight 1157."

"I'm Colonel Mandrell, military attaché for the embassy," the colonel said. "Get your crew down here, Captain. I've got a briefing to lay out and this is as secure as we're going to get in Tbilisi Airport. And we're going to be joined in about five minutes by some other people. They'll be in on the briefing. Drop your ramp; they're bringing on some gear. About nine hundred pounds plus five personnel. You're probably going to have to dump some hay."

"Yes, sir," Casey said, blinking at the abruptness mostly. "Sergeant Griffitts, if you could . . ."

"Done, sir!" Lisa said, practically popping her heels together. "Drop the ramp and alert the goats, sir!"

"Goats?" Mandrell asked.

"Nickname for the crew, sir," Jim said quickly.

"I'm *so* not going to ask," the colonel muttered.

"Okay, let's get this done," Colonel Mandrell said, then paused. "Issues, Captain?"

Casey was trying not to stare. But the group of "relief workers" was . . . a little odd. As was their "gear." Two were big, unsmiling men, clearly locals, who looked more like bandits in a movie than relief workers. Especially the movie part; both were at least as handsome as he was and that pissed him off.

On the other hand, the two ladies with them more than made up for it. Youch! Lisa was hot, Cassie was hot, these two put *both* of them to shame. They were, clearly, locals also, in black skirts and colored tops that looked like they'd come right off a National Geographic cover. But . . . Oh. My. *God*. Hot. His brain would have been stuck on hay bales if it wasn't for the last person in the group.

The last guy was shorter than the men and damned near shorter than one of the women but stocky and clearly in shape. Erect frame, with the look of having recently left the military and Casey would put odds on Marines or something "elite" in the Army. Hair cropped on the side, glasses and . . . Okay, he *had* to be an American. Only an American would go around in a Hawaiian shirt and shorts with Birkenstocks. At least in Tbilisi. Admittedly, the temperature had come up a little, but, still . . .

"No, sir!" Casey responded, looking at the "gear" that had been loaded, which was a huge *fucking* mass of black ballistic nylon bags. Some of them had been *really* heavy and from time to time there was a clink or two of metal on metal while loading. The two big locals had done it with the help of four more that must have been related. The four hadn't even said goodbye, though, just dumped the stuff on the deck, piled into a couple of SUVs and driven off without a word. In fact, the entire loading had been in silence. "Just thinking about redistribution of the materials, sir!"

"Bit more complicated than that," the colonel replied with a sinister smile. "Let me get your basic mission orders out of the way then I'm gone. Before I begin, you're all TS cleared so I won't do the spiel. But this mission is classified Code Word Ribbon Blade. Ribbon Blade is a sub-classification under Ultra Blue. I personally *hate* the new classification system but what that means it that you *cannot* discuss any actions under Ribbon Blade with anyone who asks you up to and including the Joint Chiefs of Staff. The term Ultra Blue itself is classified Confidential and Ultra Blue information can only be declassified by the President of the United States or persons so tasked to declassify Ultra Blue information. Are you clear on this? Let me make it very clear. This is not a mission you can bitch about in the O Club. It is not a mission you can tell your squadron commander about or the wing commander or even the chief of staff of the Air Force even if directly asked. Even with other persons that you *know* are cleared under Ribbon Blade. The only person you can discuss this mission with are the President or his designated representatives. I'm going to give you some specific information then I'm going to *leave*. All further information will come from this gentleman," Mandrell concluded, pointing at the guy in the Hawaiian shirt. "Are we all clear on this? Load master? Are you clear?"

"Yes, sir," Lisa replied, swallowing. "Top Secret, sir. Don't talk about it."

"Try not to *think* about it," Mandrell said. "Lieutenant Ferl . . . How do you pronounce your name, Lieutenant?"

"Fur-laz-zo, sir," Ferz replied. "I understand, sir."

"Captain Phillips?" he asked Cass.

"Understood and comply, sir," Cass replied.

"Pilots? Is this clear?"

"Yes, sir," Jim replied.

"Absolutely, sir," Casey said. "Do we ask names?"

"Go ahead," Mandrell said. "But here's the mission. These people are not going to Azerbaijan. You will take off with them then proceed through normal HALO depressurization procedures. Vanner here," he said, gesturing at the guy in the Hawaiian shirt, "will give you the insertion point. You will calculate the drop point and altitude and so drop them. *Then* you go to Azerbaijan and your regular mission. Is this clear?"

"They're a HALO team," Casey said. It was not a question, more a statement of unbelief.

"If it makes you feel any better," "Vanner" said, "we're not all that sure of the answer to that question."

"I'm done," Mandrell said. He shook "Vanner's" hand and then the other members of the team. "Good luck."

"Thank you, sir," Vanner said. The two men just nodded but the females both said "thank you" in clear if accented English. Delightfully accented.

"I'm gone," Mandrell said, stepping to the troop door and opening it without help. "Captain, get this done."

"Will do, sir," Casey replied. "Sergeant Griffitts, close the door."

"Yes, sir," Lisa replied.

"I'm Pat Vanner," Vanner said when the door was closed, shaking Casey's hand. "Former Marine, former other things, presently what my boss calls an 'International Security Specialist.' The ladies are Sergeants Julia Makanee and Olga Shaynav and the men are Corporal Jeseph Mahona and Private Ivar Ferani of the Keldara Mountain Militia. Julia and Olga speak English. Jeseph and Ivar sort of understand some but they don't talk much anyway." He pulled a piece of paper out of his breast pocket and looked around. "Who's the nav?"

"I am," Cassie said, taking the paper. It had a set of coordinates on it.

"That's where we'd like to land," Vanner said with a grin. "It's at twelve thousand feet above sea level, mind you. Captain," he continued, looking at Casey, "we'd like to get partially rigged before you take off. Then, of course, we'll have to depressurize. There's nothing in your materials that's going to have trouble with that, is there?"

"No," Casey said. "I'll have the load master rig the oxygen."

"Okay, I guess we're good," Vanner said. "Is there anything?"

"No, sir," Casey replied, bemusedly. All this hay . . .

"Sergeant, actually, Captain," the "security specialist" said. "Then I guess we're good. Is there anywhere the ladies can get into their uniforms?"

As the aircraft crew started to disperse and the Keldara started getting the gear out of the bags, Vanner let out an entirely mental sigh. There was nothing that could take apart a small team like this like lack of confidence in their boss, that being him. He thought he'd handled that little interplay professionally, but he *desperately* had wanted to go "*Look, Captain, Colonel, we've never done a HALO jump for real before. You probably know a lot more about it than we do. HELP!!!*"

Which wouldn't have been good on any number of levels. Tempting but not good. It was all about psychology. In part, he thought, through the help of the Kildar he had maintained the illusion throughout training that, while he was as inexperienced as any of the rest of the team, HALO and, hell, the whole damned mission, was no big deal. "*Sure, we'll get it done. Yawn.*"

Which wasn't what he felt at all. First of all, he was afraid of heights. He'd never realized, though, what "afraid of heights" meant until that first time in the door of the plane. Looking out the window of an airplane at thirty thousand feet was one thing.

Standing in the open door of one was another. He'd played off being totally frozen, but he knew the Kildar knew it. And he was fully aware of the synergistic effect of stress. One stressor was minor, two stressors weren't just cumulative, though, they multiplied each other. Add enough stressors and you hit a break point in *anyone*. The only question was how many stressors it took. And right now he was dealing with a crapload. Including wondering where his break point was.

At that thought he gave a small smile and shook his head. Talk about over-analyzing.

"Something humorous, Sergeant?" Julia asked.

"If you have the right sense of humor, *everything* is funny," Vanner said, grinning. "And the current situation is hilarious. Get with that blonde girl that was down here. She's the equivalent of a sergeant, not an officer. She'll know where the bathroom is. You can change in there."

"Where are *you* going to change?" Olga asked. She and Julia had gotten out their uniforms, standard Keldara "sterile" digi-cam, and were starting to pull out the various bits of clothing and gear that were necessary to survive riding in an unpressurized, unheated, plane for several hours as they depressurized.

"Right here," Vanner said, starting to unbutton his shirt. "So you'd better get going."

"Is a question permitted?" Julia asked, holding up a hand.

"Always," Vanner replied.

"If we were American women doing this mission, where would we change?"

"Woosh! Good question," Vanner said. "Depends on the situation. If there were base facilities and stuff then in private. But there are plenty of times when women and men have to get undressed around each other in the field. Especially if they're in a hurry."

"It is as I thought," Julia said, undoing the ties of her blouse and stripping it over her head. "We are in a hurry, yes? So let's 'get it on.'"

"Julia Makanee!" Jeseph snapped as Vanner's mouth dropped. Of course the latter was unnoticed by anyone, including Julia, who was fixedly concentrated on her task.

"Shut up, Jeseph Mahona," Julia replied, reaching for the ties of her skirt. "First of all, I outrank you. Second, we don't have time for your complaints. Now start getting undressed. We have an insertion to make."

Vanner's brain kicked in just enough for him to want to point out that both "get it on" and "insertion" had dual meanings but paused and started taking off his clothes.

"Move, Jeseph, Ivar, the lady's right: We don't have the time to play nice," Vanner said. "But just one thing: What happens on the mission . . ."

"Stays on the mission," Olga said, starting to take off her own clothes. "Unless it's really funny and doesn't violate OPSEC. It's not like we talk about you lying with that Slovak whore in Romania, Jeseph."

"Hey!"

"I am hereby classifying all aspects of this mission that have cultural complications TS code-word material," Vanner said, pulling out his "snivel" gear.

The "snivel" gear, in reality high-altitude climbing gear, was a necessity not an option. Due to the altitude they were going to have to jump from, they would first have to ascend slowly to prevent decompression sickness, the "bends" more famous in SCUBA diving. And while the day presently at Tbilisi was a more or less comfortable sixty-five degrees Fahrenheit, by the time they got to fourteen thousand feet, much less the twenty-three thousand they were jumping from, it was going to be below freezing.

"Would that code word be 'Peeking Fly'?" Olga asked with a slight giggle, opening up her own bag.

The reason for the heavy gear they were changing into was twofold. First they were going to be jumping from way up high where it got very fucking *cold*. But HALO gear wasn't normally as heavy as what they would wear. The fact was that very few teams dropped into 14,000-foot mountains in the beginning of winter. And while it was sixty-five today in Tbilisi, that was a fluke. There was a nasty front on the way in, arriving early in the evening and continuing into the night. They would be jumping just before it reached their AO and almost immediately in one of the first snowstorms of the year in the high mountains. Between the temperatures on the jump and the predicted temps in their insertion area, well below zero *Fahrenheit* by midnight, they had to dress for success.

"I guess I should have briefed you guys on this sort of thing," Vanner said, apparently ignoring the comment and continuing to change. "One of the little cultural things to it is that nobody comments. Nobody. The guys don't ogle, the women don't giggle, they don't trade barbs about relative physical merits. Not at the time. Later, maybe, they might make some passing comment. But at the time you act as if it's no big deal. Don't take that as a slap, by the way, it's just information. Now, teams that have spent *a lot* of time together and 'seen' each other a lot, and there's a lot of trust, that's different. Then they joke. But not without the understanding and trust."

While he'd been talking, Vanner and the rest had been "getting it on." First came thin, slippery, polypropylene socks. The polypropylene would wick moisture away and, by adhering to the feet and not slipping, prevent or reduce blistering. Next were light polypropylene long johns and long-sleeved top made by Spyder gear, rolled down over the socks. Next were Smartwool socks and a polypropylene mid-layer top tucked into Keldara field pants. Then the "farmer-john" insulated bib, boots, Keldara field blouse, body armor and over the whole thing an insulated down parka. Each had a balaclava, presently pulled down, and would don a helmet on the way up. If their faces got too cold, there was an additional "gator," a circular neck warmer, that could be put on and pulled up over mouth and nose. Heavy gloves would later be slipped on over the blouse sleeves but under their parkas.

"Got it," Julia said, standing up. She was the first one dressed and had gone from one very svelte hottie to something that looked like the Michelin Man. "But if what happens on the mission stays on the mission . . ."

"There will be times," Vanner noted, unzipping his jacket and opening up his body armor to get some circulation. "Spring festival. The elders and kids have gone to bed. People are talking about their part of a mission. 'Oleg, you were over on Vasho Street so you didn't see when Jeseph really screwed up . . .' Jeseph will say something like 'At least my nipples are the right color . . .' Everyone will go 'Oooo, zinger!' And then everyone who *needs* to know and can *understand* will know. If they've got questions about under what conditions Jeseph saw your nipples, they'll ask, quietly. Or they'll already have heard. You keep it low-key or it doesn't work at all. Feel free to pass that on, by the way."

"Julia, sorry," Jeseph said, zipping up his boots.

"Not a problem," Julia replied. "What's that term the Kildar uses?"

"Culture shock?" Olga asked, tucking in her T-shirt.

"I was thinking more of cultural conditioning," Julia said with a grin. "But 'shock' works. Sergeant Vanner, are we close enough a team for a *little* joking?"

"Maybe," Vanner said.

"In that case, Jeseph's hung like a bull," Olga said, grinning. "Ivar's not bad, either."

Chapter Twenty-One

Lasko eased forward through the screen of low bushes with all the speed and daring of a snail.

The ridgeline overlooked LZ 1, the Kildar's LZ, which was a small upland clearing, probably the result of a recently silted up pond, at about three thousand meters above sea level and some forty miles from the valley of the Keldara.

The trees in the region had already begun to shift to upland coniferous, primarily firs, instead of the deciduous growth found down in the valley. The understory was thigh-high heather, tough, wiry and prickly as hell.

Lasko ignored the tugging of the heather and the bits scratching at his face as he brought up the thermal imagery sight with geologic speed. Lasko was capable of moving faster. He'd proven that several times. But he much preferred moving at about the speed of growing grass.

A long, careful, scan with the thermal imagery scope showed nothing hostile in or around the LZ. The LZ was away from the major routes the Chechens used and well away from the few farms in the region so there was no particular reason anybody would be there. Unless the Chechens were staking out good LZs on the off-chance the Keldara were going to start flying in.

So far, it didn't look that way.

Lasko looked over his shoulder at Sion and made an oval motion with his hand, indicating that this was where they were going to construct the hide. Then he started, ever so slowly, removing branches of heather. Removing vegetation was an art more than a science; for the sniper it resembled a form of bonsai. The vegetation had to appear as if it had naturally broken away or grown into that form. It could be tied down with small bits of vegetation colored string, broken away at the base or even propped up by another plant. Anything that looked natural. In the three cases where he simply *had* to break a branch off, he removed it right at the "trunk" and then wiped dirt onto the broken spot. Nothing could give the indication that someone or something had been ripping up vegetation.

As he did this, Sion had started on the hide. Since they were going to be there for a few days, this would be a full "bunker" hide position, a small underground shelter. Very small, about the size of a two man tent. Whereas any infantryman in the world, given that the enemy was nowhere around, would have stood up and begun stuffing the shovel in the dirt and tossing earth around, Sion was slowly and painfully learning to be a sniper at the very core. He was still stomach down, his German entrenching tool only half extended, lifting up shovelfuls of dirt and carefully placing them on a tarp.

By morning the two would be tucked away in a hide that didn't have much more signature than a rabbit hole. They would spend the rest of the time, until the flight arrived, living there. They would eat, sleep, pee and crap in the hole. Fortunately, the Keldara had provided them with American MREs so they wouldn't be doing much of the latter. Nothing jammed you up like MREs especially if, as Lasko had done, you left behind all the fruity stuff.

"Ivan Ivanovich!" Mike said, shaking the hand of the man descending from the Kiowa helicopter. The Kiowa was a new addition to the Georgia's expanding aircraft fleet.

"Kildar." Ivan Ivanovich "Son of Ivan" Markovsky was a former Russian army helo pilot who had turned one beat-up Hip transport into an international heavy lift company over the course of ten or so years. Mostly the company supported oil production around the world—Ivan's motto was "no job too remote"—with some paid assistance for disaster relief and other missions where people were willing to pay through the nose to move a large volume of heavy cargo somewhere that roads didn't reach. His most famous job was lifting an entire mammoth out of the frozen tundra of Siberia and transporting it nearly a thousand miles to the nearest railhead.

However, those operations more or less "paid the bills." Markovsky's other operations, those that most certainly did *not* make the press, were where he made his real money. Markovsky was honest about being the purest of mercenaries. He didn't care if he was carrying American black ops or Al Qaeda. The only group he would *not* support was the Chechens and that was probably because his pilots, almost all Russian, would balk.

He also was very closemouthed. Mike had never tried to pump him but others had. If he talked to Al Qaeda nobody had ever been able to find out. He seemed to be an "honest" mercenary in that way. Mike was never sure whether to admire him for that or not, but he was more than willing to *use* him for it. And because Markovsky had proven that he was one of those mercenaries that recognized that "loss is part of the job." In Albania Markovsky had lost an entire helo, and crew, and had two more shot up. He'd just taken his pay and agreed that it was bad luck. Admittedly, the loss costs on the contract had been huge but Mike had gladly paid them; the pilots on every portion of the op had been as good and brave as any he'd ever seen.

"I understand that there are political issues with this op?" Markovsky said, as they walked to the house. The pilot had come down on the caravanserai's helo pad, which was on Mike's old firing range, just beyond the harem garden.

"The Georgians won't let me use you for the whole op," Mike said. "Only for the insertion period. And you have to fly a narrow route to and from. Sorry."

"Given the way that Vladimir has been pushing all the CIS countries, it is not surprising," Markovsky said. "I am starting to run into such problems elsewhere. It's a pain but what can one do?"

Mike led him to the office and then turned on the projector on his computer. The projector flashed the map of the insertion area up on a whitewashed portion of the wall.

"Six teams, six LZs," Mike said. "One Hip per LZ. You got them?"

"I may have to substitute two Panthers for one of them," Markovsky said, musingly. "Depends on if one of my Hips gets out of the shop first. But I have the lift."

"Insertion will be night and full tactical," Mike said. "The Georgians require that you either enter through a narrow corridor and pick us up here then do the op or go to Tbilisi Military, tank there, then do the op. Your choice."

"I'd prefer to tank at Tbilisi military," Markovsky said. "If we have to tank in Russia we'll be all the way over in Krasnodar. I'd have to bring tanks for the turn. And I don't want to FAARP here, if possible."

"Actually, by then we'll have the beginnings of a helo-port here," Mike said. "I'm bringing in two of my own choppers to support the op. Czech Hinds. I can get the fuel here for sure. What about aborts?"

"That was why I wasn't sure about all the Hips," Markovsky admitted. "I'll bring a spare but if one of them goes down, then it will be the Panthers. If you're going to have actual ground support, I'll tank here."

"That works," Mike said, grinning. "I won't even charge you for the fuel."

"Why, thank you," Markovsky replied.

"Keep the coordinates of the LZs close until the op," Mike said, sliding over a file. It contained details about the LZs as well as maps. He deliberately didn't mention the reconnaissance teams. He trusted Markovsky but trust only went so far. "Please get with Nielson on details of refuel, support and payment. Usual terms?"

"That's fine," Markovsky said, looking at the contents of the folder then closing it and standing up. "I'd ask why you're only flying a few miles, but . . ."

"Training mission," Mike said. "Just getting the troops acquainted with air ops."

"Which is why you are using me and not the Georgians, yes?" Markovsky said, smiling slightly. "Have a good training mission."

"Well, I'll say it will be good training," Mike said. He'd checked the long-range weather forecast. It was going to be *very* good training.

✧   ✧   ✧

Vanner unplugged consul hose from his AIROX VII connector and switched to the bail-out bottle on his gear, waving to the team to switch at the same time.

The pre-breathe had been a pain in the ass. A necessary one but a pain all the same. They had to stay continually on the supplied oxygen or they'd get the bends when they started breathing much thinner air all of a sudden. The O2 flushed the nitrogen out of their system but it wasn't the most fun in the world. From as high as they were jumping they had to stay on it for an hour, minimum.

Because the oxygen was at lower than normal air pressure, he'd had a feeling the whole time like he wasn't getting enough air. It was a claustrophobic, strangling sensation that had bugged the hell out of him.

Worse, in a way, was the sweat that formed inside the mask. It tickled like hell and he desperately wanted to pull the mask away and wipe at it. But if he did that, everybody would have to start the pre-breathe all over again. One gulp of "real" air reset the whole thing.

"Pain in the ass" didn't begin to cover it but now it was show-time.

The load master stood in front of him and reached down to her waist, miming pulling something forward. All the cute had disappeared behind the oxygen mask, helmet and heavy clothes.

Vanner, for the third time, checked to make sure that the chute was "armed" and the safety pin had been removed from the AAD. In the event that a jumper was knocked out, either by the O2 failing or from some impact, the Airborne Arming Device would automatically open their chutes at seven hundred feet above ground level.

Now, in the case of the team, that was adjusted to 700 AGL above their planned DZ or right at thirteen thousand feet. If the jumper was unconscious he or she probably wasn't going to hit anywhere *near* the DZ. And almost everything *around* the DZ was higher than the drop zone meaning that they were probably still going to splat into the ground at a high rate of speed. It also, mostly, was vertical. He'd pointed this out to the team and also pointed out that not passing out, for any reason, nor failing to track to the DZ nor failing to pull their chutes on time were all very good things.

Frankly, Vanner had on the ascent come to the conclusion that the Kildar—he barely could *think* of him as "Mike Jenkins" anymore—was insane. The Kildar, whoever he really was, whatever he'd done before he turned up in Georgia, was clearly highly trained in HALO. He had, after all, trained them and done it in record time. Which means he *had* to know what a shot-in-the-dark insanity it was to send five totally green HALO jumpers and drop them into some of the worst conditions ever created by man for airborne operations: alpine mountains with a drop zone the size of a postage stamp. Just fitting all five of them onto it was going to be interesting.

Vanner tried to show none of that as he lurched to his feet and waved to the other four.

The lurch was necessitated by their gear. Besides their clothing, bulky and heavy enough, they were all wearing combat harnesses, their chutes, helmets and oxygen masks and last, but most certainly not least, their rucksacks, which were slung forward and down, making it nearly impossible to walk. The long, and heavily packed, rucksacks dropped very nearly to the ground in the case of the two women. They simply *had* to be helped by Jeseph and Ivar as the fivesome shuffled towards the ramp.

Currently the ramp was still up and that was just fine by Vanner. It had, however, been cracked to depressurize the cabin and the sound of the rushing wind filled the interior of the aircraft, making verbal communication, already difficult with the oxygen masks, impossible.

Which, of course, was what hand signals were for.

Vanner slapped the front of his harness and then gestured for the two pairs to check each other's equipment. He carefully ensured that they followed the memorized checklist then had Olga check his. As well as any of them could tell, everything was good to go.

Equipment checked, they shuffled towards the rear of the bird as the load master, who was suited up in a similar manner but tied off with a safety rope, lowered the ramp.

This occasioned even more roaring but very little actual wind movement. Vanner had expected the strong circulation they'd experienced during training but the air inside the bird was strangely calm. He could only think it was due to the entire rear of the plane being open instead of just side doors.

Vanner paused at the edge of the ramp and looked over at the load master. She, in turn, pointed to the red light mounted by the door which was solid. Blinking meant more than five minutes from the drop. Solid meant less than five.

The load master gestured with her right arm straight out, palm up then bent it and touched the top of the helmet. Thirty seconds. Time to move to the ramp.

Vanner shuffled forward as Olga grabbed the top of his chute from behind. The entire party then followed, shuffling towards the edge of the ramp but bound together in case one of them slipped.

The load master had moved to the base of the ramp on the far right and was now on her stomach, looking down and forward. She hit the ramp with a closed fist then raised it. Stand by; the DZ was in sight.

Green light.

Vanner stepped forward and then threw himself outwards. Strangely enough, it was easier than it had been in training. Part of that was because it was dark. There was nothing to give perspective; even the clouds below them were far enough away they didn't *look* like clouds.

Fear of heights is all perception.

He took a box-man formation and counted to ten then looked over his shoulder. Everyone was out, with Olga and Julia delta tracking to get in better position. The team was spread out in more or less a V formation. Nobody was trying to hold a solid position, just trying to both keep out of each other's airstream and keep an eye on Vanner.

Which told him it was time for a position check. He looked at his GPS and banked right, towards the DZ. Another check over his shoulder and everyone had followed the turn, still keeping spread. He went back and got a better fix on their position and the position of the DZ then had to wonder. They had been slightly north. They were still slightly north but closer, in vertical they were barely two hundred meters north. He wasn't positive, but he thought they'd moved about thirty meters in a thousand feet of drop.

Which meant there was, like, *no* wind. Which didn't make sense. There was always wind at altitude. *Always.*

The clouds below obscured the DZ, which was really gonna suck. He didn't know if they even broke at all; they could go all the way to the ground. They seemed kind of broken though . . . As he thought that, they broke up enough so he could see the DZ. And it was right *there*, the tiny silver of the stream shining in a brief flash from the moon.

They were right on top of it, there wasn't any wind. Something was *bound* to go wrong!

He took up a creep position, though. They might overshoot just a bit. He looked back and signaled with his thumbs to creep back then checked his position again. The clouds were breaking up a bit more and the DZ was like looking at a darkened sat shot. Everything was there.

He signaled to stop the creep, checked their position, checked the team—still with him—and then looked around. The cessation of wind finally made sense. To their north there was a wall of clouds. Sometimes in advance of a front, just before it hit, the winds dropped to absolutely nothing, even at altitude. "The calm before the storm."

Of course, that much "calm" often meant one hell of a storm.

He looked back and realized that the ground was suddenly rushing at him, seemingly faster than a train. And there were mountains all around, by trick of optical illusion apparently rocketing into the sky. He signaled for the team to spread out, waited one second and then pulled.

After he felt the canopy open, right on time, he looked up, grabbed the control toggles, did a quick check and then looked around. Five chutes, one, Julia he was pretty sure, just opening. She'd pulled so that she was barely four hundred feet off the ground by the look of it. Damned close. High altitude, low opening indeed. But even as he watched she banked east and then north, lining up for a landing. Banked and lined like she'd been doing it her whole life. She'd barely corrected before she back-filled and her feet touched the ground. He saw one side of the chute flutter away as she popped her riser then she was waddling off to the side, getting out of the way, in no more than two seconds. Olga came in right behind her.

Damn, he had good people.

But it looked as if their fearless leader was going to be the last one down.

"What the fuck, over?" Adams said as his head peeked around the door of Mike's office. "I thought *I* was working late."

It was nearly three AM and Mike was sitting in front of his computer peering at it as if it was a snake.

"Route planning," Mike replied distractedly. He clicked the mouse and then snarled, clicking again. "There's no way that the Keldara can plan their own routes through the mountains. So I'm having to flip between these topo maps Vanner made and the actual satellite shots to find the best route. Even with planning software it's taking forever. You realize most of the ground we're going to cover has never been explored in known history."

"Point," Adams said. He used OpsSoft regularly, but the sort of detail Mike was doing was out of his league.

"I'm doing this on the nights I'm not training or supervising packing," Mike continued, exasperated. "There's just *shit* in the way of every single insertion route. Cliffs, scree . . . The Keldara hump these mountains but we've never trained them in real mountaineering and I can't expect them to tackle a Class Five slope. I'm not even sure they can do a Class Two. And every time I find what looks like a good route, there's *shit* in the way that I can see on the satellite views but doesn't show on the topos. Then I gotta back up and find another way. I'm getting about one done a night. I've got three more to go. We've got five days left. Do the math."

"The math is that the mission commander is going to be totally wiped at the beginning of a tough mission," Adams said.

"The ladies are off packing duty so I've got all five nights," Mike pointed out. "If I can get these three done tonight and the next two days that's two nights of rest. I'll be mission capable. But *fuck* this is frustrating."

"Get some rest . . ."

"If you haven't got your health . . ." Mike continued. "Yeah. I will. You just make sure the teams are dialed in. I'll be there with bells on. And solid routes."

❖   ❖   ❖

". . . And set the autopilot," Marek said over the intercom. "There. Now we can go to sleep until we reach Bratislava."

The Hinds had been outfitted with auxiliary fuel tanks slung under the dual pylons. With those and the improved engines they had a range of a bit over a thousand kilometers. Plenty of range to reach L'yiven Ukraine after flying partially over Southern Poland. And at 310 kilometers per hour cruising speed, it was going to be a bit over three hours to get there. Have lunch, refuel, back in the bird, repeat as necessary. Two and a half days to get to the Valley of the Keldara.

Two and a half days, and two nights, mostly alone with Marek. Crap.

"I think I'm going to stay up," Kacey replied, smiling. "Just in case any big birds decide to hit us."

"The intakes are armored," Marek said with a grin in his voice. "It will take more than a goose to crash one of these."

"How about a Cessna?" Kacey said. "Nearly hit one of those one time. Guy was in a no-fly zone. No civilians, anyway. He nearly got taken down three ways, me, a SAM site and an F-16. They eventually had me fly back and explain to him that he needed to land. I don't think he even got jail time. I hope they at least pulled his license."

"I had actually wondered if you wished to work the bird a bit more," Marek said. "Your employer is, after all, paying me for instruction time even now."

"Love to," Kacey replied, taking the Hind off autopilot. "My bird. I need as much stick time as I can get."

"I take it you mean flying," Marek said. "But, yes, there is no such thing as enough 'stick time.'"

"Especially this time," Kacey said, raising an eyebrow at the comment. So far Marek had been so *sans peur* an instructor pilot he qualified for the endangered species list. "When we get back we have to go straight into ops. High altitude, most of it night, most of it tactical. Training ops with the Georgian military."

"You're kidding," Marek said, seriously. "You are very good with the bird but . . . That is not easy flying. I take it you told your employer to blow it."

"Actually, I said 'Yes, Kildar,' saluted and flew to the Czech Republic," Kacey replied.

"For a training operation?" Marek said, sarcastically. "He wishes to buy two new helicopters, and training for new pilots, so soon. And I would have thought *you* had more sense."

"I do," Kacey said. "Marek? Let's just fly the bird. I think we need to get Tammy and Dominick on the horn and do a little follow-the-leader."

"I agree," Marek said. "Slowly at first, though. Later I will show you just what this bird can do. Perhaps we play hide-and-seek, yes?"

"What, you planning on hiding?" Kacey said, making sure the intercom was off.

Chapter Twenty-Two

"Sergéant Vanner," Jeseph said, his voice pitched low, "I have found a hide point for the jump gear."

"Good," Vanner said, bent over Ivar's ankle. The shooter was the only one of the five who had managed to find a bad spot to land, a rock he hadn't seen until the last moment. It looked like it was only a sprain, but it was a bad sprain and they really needed to unass the DZ. Fortunately, Vanner had just gotten done wrapping it. "Julia, you, Jeseph and Olga get started on caching the gear then catch up with us. We're going to get off this DZ. I'll help Ivar."

"I can walk," Ivar said, his face working with pain.

"Yep, and you're gonna have to," Vanner said, raising his voice against a rising wind. He really had to work for the air. They'd taken drugs to help with altitude sickness but it didn't make the air any thicker. "*With* your ruck. I'll just be trying to take some of the weight off. Jeseph, give me a hand getting him up and the ruck on his back. Then we'll move out. Follow the route on your GPS. We're moving to point 478. We'll set up camp somewhere around there. And *hurry*. That storm's nearly here."

"Yes, Sergeant," Jeseph said. The wind threw his parka hood up and he pushed it back, looking around nervously. "This storm is going to be bad, Sergeant. I can smell the snow."

"*Don't* lose us," Vanner said. "Walk in through the beginning of the snow if you have to. I've got the dome tent, worse comes to worst we can all bed in there."

"Fortunately, it's all downhill from here," Vanner said as they crested the ridgeline. Getting the Keldara up from the small valley that had shielded the DZ from observation had been no joke. "There's some rocks I spotted on the sat map for a possible assembly area. We'll take a hide there."

"I am not sure which is worse," Ivar said, wincing and grabbing at one of the spindly fir trees that covered the slope. They were right up at the woodline, and the ground was already covered by a thin dusting of snow. Some of it had melted away but there were plenty of patches to slip on in shadow. And they were hard to see with the night vision goggles. Unfortunately, the clouds preceding the storm had already arrived and the night was black as pitch. NVGs were a necessity.

"Uphill," Vanner said.

He paused and let the Keldara lean on one of the trees then picked up the thermal imager he'd left hanging around his neck and swept the slope below. He'd gotten over the crest as fast as possible and now hunkered down to make sure they were alone in the area. He saw a couple of heat forms, but they had the look of animals. He didn't see any heat coming from the cluster of boulders and that was the important part.

"Let's move," Vanner said, taking Ivar's arm again.

The Keldara shuffled forward at his maximum safe speed and they began their creep down the ridge.

"Almost there."

"Careful cresting the ridge," Jeseph said. "Go across low and sideways. Less silhouette."

"Okay," Julia said, sliding forward.

She could barely see anything in the night-vision goggles. The lenses had gotten fogged and then frozen so she was looking through a distorted foggy picture. For that matter it was starting to snow, big, thick, flakes. Something about the wind, though, the smell and the size of the flakes told her that it was about to storm like mad. They needed to get to shelter, fast. She slid on a patch of snow and went down on her butt just as she reached the far side of the ridgeline.

"Damn."

"Up you get," Jeseph said, lifting her and the pack. "No lying down on the job. That's for after your wedding night."

"Like you'll ever know, Jeseph Mahona," Julia said, quietly, but she let loose a half-stifled giggle.

"Take a knee," Jeseph said. "Face east. Olga, west." He pulled his thermal imagers out and looked down the slope. "There's the sergeant. They made good time." He paused and looked around some more. "Nobody else."

"Then let's . . ." she said just as a gust of wind caught them. The wind tore the words out of her mouth it was so strong and in a second Jeseph, only a meter or two from her, disappeared in a wall of snow.

"Julia!" Jeseph screamed.

"Stay there!" Julia yelled back. This wasn't just a snowfall, this was a blizzard, one of the fast-moving ones of the early winter. The snow might all thaw tomorrow but tonight it was going to drop a ton. And they were caught in the middle of it. She had been living in these mountains her whole life but she'd *never* been this far from any shelter as she was right now. One of her cousins had been caught out in a storm like this and died. They had to get to Vanner and get some shelter set up. Or, possibly, just set it up right here, she wasn't sure which. She suddenly realized, to her horror, that the decision was hers.

She shuffled in the direction she remembered Jeseph being in and felt his body through the thick gloves. At that range, even through her fogged glasses, she could see him.

"Olga?" she shouted in his ear.

"There!" Jeseph said, pointing then looking through the thermal imagers. "Yes, there!"

"Go!"

Olga had hunkered down and waited. Smart girl.

"Thought we'd lost you for a second," Julia yelled.

"I was going to give you twenty minutes," Olga yelled back. "What now, Jeseph?"

"We move," Julia yelled.

"Agreed," Jeseph replied. "Julia's call and I agree. We have the GPS, we have the thermal imager. We can find them."

"Jeseph, you lead," Julia said. "I'll take the GPS. Olga, check me. Hold onto my pack, I'll hold Jeseph's. Let's roll!"

"I've got it, Ivar," Vanner shouted. "You just keep checking for the rest of the team."

"We could call," Ivar yelled.

"Not on your life!" Vanner shouted. "We'd have to *broadcast*. Now shut up and watch!"

Vanner had set up a dome tent before, but never on solid rock and in a howling blizzard. He'd gotten the damned thing unrolled but it had nearly been snatched out of his hands twice so far. If they lost it, it would have a number of bad consequences starting with the possibility of the Chechens finding it and continuing through "lack of shelter."

He finally managed to get one side tied off to one of the boulders that they were sheltered in. With that side tied off he could manage it better. One bit of ground would take a stake. Another tie-off. Finally he got all six points anchored and added a couple of anchors, groping through the driving snow, to make sure it stayed in place.

That done he started threading the poles. The snow was piling up so fast he nearly lost one of them but groping finally dredged it up. When the last one was stuffed into the loops and the tent up he grabbed his pack and tossed it inside then went to approximately where he recalled Ivar being.

"It's up!"

"I still don't see them," Ivar shouted back.

"They'll make it or they won't," Vanner said. "They've got gear for this, too. We need to get in the tent!"

Vanner got Ivar up and over to where he recalled the tent being. But it wasn't there.

"Oh, *tell* me it didn't already blow away," Vanner said then shook his head. He'd tossed his pack in it on purpose. It had to be here somewhere.

He and Ivar shuffled forward carefully and then Vanner sprawled on the ground, fortunately not taking Ivar with him.

"Found one of the tie-downs!" Vanner yelled. He felt along the tie-down and then saw the ghostly outline of the tent. "Here!"

When they were finally inside, Vanner let out a breath of relief. "Safe, by God."

"Sergeant," Ivar said, diffidently. "My pack is back where you found me. I only say that because it has my fartsack in it. I don't think you want to share."

"Fuck."

Jeseph saw the boulder before he hit it with his nose, but only just.

"What?" Julia yelled.

"I think we're there," Jeseph said, scanning with the thermal imagers. It seemed to him that the picture had gotten dimmer, but it might be the snow. "I don't see them, though."

"Move into them," Julia said, trying to look around through the spotty NVGs. "They have to be here somewhere!"

"They could have gotten lost as well," Olga noted helpfully.

They wandered into the rock pile and after tripping several times and nearly slipping off a boulder they hadn't even realized they were climbing Julia let out an exasperated sigh.

"Where *are* they?"

"I don't know," Jeseph yelled back. "But we have to do *something!*"

"We make camp," Julia said after a moment. "Try to find a reasonably flat spot! We'll put up one of the tunnel tents! We need to find somewhere to tie it off!"

"Where am *I* going to sleep?" Jeseph yelled.

"What happens on the mission . . ."

"The wind has died," Ivar said, nudging Vanner.

"I noticed," Vanner said, quietly. It was what had awakened him.

He and Ivar had taken two-hour shifts, sleeping and waking, hoping against hope that the rest of the team would show up. It was pre-dawn and the howling blizzard had finally started to die. Now if the rest of the team just hadn't. But, they were smart and had nearly as good gear. The only difference was they had the tunnel tents.

Vanner kicked at the front of the tent where he could see snow had mounded up and then stuck his head out. The snow was still falling thickly but mostly straight down. It had dropped about a foot and a half overnight, with more drifted up against the rocks. The tent had a drift up against the side and front that was nearly three feet thick.

Vanner looked around cautiously then ducked back in and pulled out his NVGs.

"Nothing," he said quietly.

"They might still be on the back trail," Ivar said, just as quietly.

Vanner sighed and shrugged on his heavy coat; he'd kept most of the rest of the gear on. The temperature had dropped precipitously but he left the balaclava and hood down. He needed his ears as well as his eyes.

He slid out of the tent, negotiating the snowpack, and stood up with the snow up to his waist. Another look around with the NVGs then he reached in and pulled out the thermals. Looking on the back trail he couldn't see any sign of the team.

"Fuck," he muttered. He did *not* want to broadcast.

He walked back the way they'd come, stumbling over Ivar's pack in the process. He'd dragged it over to the tent, gotten out the Keldara's sleeping bag and then left the ruck near the entrance. It was so covered in snow he hadn't seen it until he tripped over it.

"Found your ruck," he called, turning around.

"I was wondering when you'd look behind you," Julia said, grinning. She had a thermal imaging sight hanging around her neck.

"How'd you get past us?" Vanner asked.

"I really have no idea," Julia admitted with another grin. "But I'm just about standing on our tent. We're set up about three meters from each other."

"Our tent?" Vanner said. "Where's Jeseph?"

"Asleep," Julia said. "In the tent. With Olga."

"With . . ."

"Hey, don't ask, don't tell . . ."

Kacey drove the Hind down the twisting river valley so close to the surface that the rotors were kicking up spray on the banks.

"Hoo-rah!" she shouted.

"I don't think Dominick is keeping up," Marek said, a grin in his voice. "Drive it, girl."

They were in the second day of the ferry flight and, given that they were making good time, Marek had declared a one hour game of hide and seek. Kacey was given a box she had to stay in and a three minute head start. The kicker was that it wasn't Tammy driving the search bird, it was Dominick, the other IP.

"This is like flying a fucking Kiowa," Kacey said. "These things used to be pigs. This is *awesome*."

"We are low," Marek pointed out. "The air is thick. Higher . . . less maneuverability."

"Got that," Kacey said, glancing in the rearview. "I still don't have him."

"Twenty minutes until we're done with the exercise," Marek said. "But he's not necessarily following. He could have cut one of the bends."

"Yeah," Kacey replied, looking ahead. There was a fork in the river that went left. "Marek, what's the chart say about that turn?"

"Narrow," Marek said, tersely. "But still inside the box. Want me to take it?"

"My bird," Kacey said, banking into the tributary. She instantly recognized that it was *much* narrower than the main river: the trees that overhung it barely cleared her rotor cone. "Crap."

"As I said. Narrow."

Kacey pulled the helo into an in-ground-effect hover and looked forward. The damned channel only got narrower. Looking up she realized she'd drifted *under* the trees in slowing; the branches now extended *over* her rotor cone.

"Double crap. Marek?"

"Your bird, hotshot," the IP said, easily.

No way to go up. No way to turn around. No way to go forward. That only left two choices; ditching the bird in the river or backing up. Of course, the channel twisted slightly so it wasn't exactly *straight* back. Fortunately, Hinds had a rearview mirror.

She pulled back on the stick and tilted the rotor gently to the rear. The increased angle had her chipping some branch-tips, but nothing unsurvivable.

Backing down to the joining, she got enough room she could go up or turn around. So she carefully spun in place then looked at the main river. The other Hind had a five-hundred-foot maximum so they could run down the river at height, looking for them. But they couldn't just perch like a falcon.

Which gave her an idea.

"Kacey?" Marek said as the helicopter started sliding backwards. "Where are we going?"

"Under the trees," Kacey said. The trees were evergreens; there was some solid concealment to be had. With the gray-green camouflage of the Hind, they would be hard to spot.

"Okay," Marek said. "Your bird."

"And now . . . we wait," Kacey said as she reached the spot she'd been "stuck" in before. She could see the main river, barely, through a small gap in the trees. They were making a hell of a signature but that would be, partially, masked by the trees.

Sure enough, about ten minutes later, Tammy's Hind came sniffing down the river about a hundred feet up. But the trees and the camouflage of the Hind kept them from noticing the bird hidden two hundred meters up the tributary, despite the massive "signature" from their rotors. She'd have thought they'd notice the waving treetops at the very least.

"Very nice," Marek said. "I would have stayed higher."

"They probably did and couldn't see us," Kacey said. "This river was the only place to hide. So we had to be on it, right? Start at one end, go to the other and trap us at that end of the box. Nobody would be stupid enough to come up this tributary."

"If it's stupid and it works . . ."

"It's not stupid," Kacey said, sliding the bird forward.

The other Hind had continued up the river so it was out of sight when she got to the joining. She pivoted to look up-river and then popped up. Sure enough, there they were, just going around the bend to the right.

She dropped down and slid out into the main river, sidling towards the opposite treeline and then popping up again. The Hinds had a rearview but there was a solid blind spot at about four and seven o'clock. Only by craning way over could you see into it. As planned, she was right on Dominick's four o'clock. She pivoted again and flew along side them, keeping more or less parallel, in the four-o'clock position and sidling closer. When she was about a hundred meters away she pivoted again so she was pointed right at them and pushed the bird as hard to the side as it would go so that she had her nose pointed right at them as she came into peripheral vision.

Tammy, scanning left and right, was the first one to see her and she shook her head and said something in the intercom.

"Where in the hell did *you* come from?" Dominick said over the radio. The disgust was clear in his voice.

"I'm a woman," Kacey replied. "We're tricky. Ask any guy."

"I *still* want to know where you went," Dominick said, picking at his fish.

They'd continued down through Ukraine and stopped at a small airport near Yalta on the Black Sea. Tomorrow was the last day of the ferry, a short overwater hop into Russian airspace, one refueling in Russia, hopping down the Black Sea coast and then cut into Georgia near the port of Sokhumi. After that it was free-sailing.

"How's it feel to want?" Kacey said with a grin. "Seriously, I was hiding. If I tell you *where* I was hiding, it ruins the fun. And it was probably Tammy's fault anyway. She was the one that was supposed to be looking for us."

"Hey!"

"Ah then, I am satisfied," Dominick replied. "As long as my delicate pilot ego isn't damaged."

"You still got your ass kicked by a girl," Marek pointed out.

"Yeah?" Dominick replied. "Then tomorrow I will have you try to find Tammy. See whose ass gets kicked then!"

"Hey, Marek," Kacey said as the pilot opened the door to his room.

The Kildar had paid top billing for the training and hadn't stinted on the travel budget; the pilots didn't have to share. And the small seaside resort they'd found was more than willing to provide lodging; the hotel was practically empty.

"Kacey," Marek replied, raising an eyebrow.

"I was going to say that I wanted to go over something in the dash-ones, but why be coy?" Kacey asked. "Frankly, I'm really hoping you're straight. I didn't see a wedding ring and hard flying always makes me horny."

"No ring, no wife, please come in," Marek said, stepping back. "I am very much 'straight.'"

"You're a good cook," Gregor grunted, spooning up the stew.

"Thank you," Dr. Arensky said, scraping up the last of his and taking the bowl to the sink.

They had settled into a routine. Arensky cooked and cleaned. Gregor sat in the corner most of the time apparently asleep. But if Arensky went near the door, his eyes flickered open. When Arensky had to have a call of nature Gregor would lead him outside to the nasty, stinking, spider-filled outhouse that provided relief. The house at least had running water and a kitchen sink, but no indoor toilet.

They had been provided with food—cans of potted meat and vegetables as well as some old bread that had seen better days. Coaxing decent meals out of the stuff had been tough.

"Since my wife died, I've done most of the cooking for Marina and I," Arensky continued, slipping the bowl into the sink. He lifted the cloth cover on a bowl by the sink and nodded at the mess within.

"What is that stuff?" Gregor asked. "I looked at it the other day. It's . . . crap."

"It's not 'crap,'" Arensky replied. "Do you know what makes the alcohol in vodka?"

"No," Gregor admitted.

"Yeast," the microbiologist replied. "A microorganism that excretes alcohol as the same sort of by-product as urea, the stuff that makes the strong ammonia smell, in human urine. So what you're drinking is, in effect, yeast piss."

"Ugh," Gregor said, dropping his own dish in the sink. Arensky also did the washing up. "Thanks so much for pointing that out. I'm never going to look at another bottle of vodka the same again."

"But yeast is only the best known of many microorganisms used in food preparation," Arensky continued. "Cheese is produced from a mold, several strains in fact. It is, basically, spoiled milk. Yogurt is the same. These are similar microorganisms. I'm attempting to capture some of them for . . . piquancy. They can be used as a spice, in other words. The problem, of course, is spotting the right ones without special tools. Fortunately, I am very experienced in doing so. Hopefully, I can get a crop of fistanula going. That will add a dash of tanginess to the next soup."

"That is really weird," Gregor said, chuckling.

"I'm *bored*," Arensky said. "As your hands are your main purpose in life, my *mind* is mine. I have nothing to read, no TV to watch, no internet to surf and no experiments to conduct. So I find experiments where I can. This is the sort of thing I did when I was in grammar school. I made my first cheese, from a raw native culture, when I was nine. It's a way to pass the time."

"I guess that makes sense," Gregor said with a shrug. "No harm in a little mold . . ."

Chapter Twenty-Three

Mike leaned on the butt of his M4 and wondered how many hours he had in helicopters. A lot was all he could come up with. Of course, since Master Chief Adams had stayed in the teams longer, he probably had more by an order of magnitude. If either one of them had been flying, they'd both be master aviators. Which made him wonder if maybe he could get some bootleg time after the mission was over.

He was doing it again. Woolgathering. He could focus like a laser during a mission and during planning. But right now, he just wanted to think about something else. When they got the word they were almost at the LZ, his mind would kick automatically into gear. But right now . . . anything but the mission.

He wasn't sure it was a good thing. Probably real commanders thought about what might go wrong, what was supposed to go right, what the actions of each sub-team should be on landing, all the way to the LZ. It seemed like his team commander back when, that was how he thought. Hell, Nielson was probably that way. It was one of many things that Mike was unsure about. Because, basically, he was an NCO that just got caught up in the game. He'd never set out to be an officer or a commander. All he'd ever wanted to be a was a shooter on the teams and, maybe, buck for master chief. Not be a commander. Real commanders probably thought about what Lee should have done at Gettysburg at a time like this or who the weak link on the team was. All Mike could think was how good a beer would taste about now.

The Russian crewman held up a hand with two fingers extended and Mike was instantly in the game, beer, and doubts, forgotten.

"Game face!" he shouted. "Get it on!"

"FATHER OF ALL!" the Keldara shouted back in unison. In nearly the same unison they jacked a round into their weapons and placed them on safe.

Mike jacked a round then undid his safety harness. Last, he pulled down his balaclava. The LZ was almost certainly cold. Lasko would have called in otherwise. But you never took an LZ as guaranteed to be cold unless it was your home base. And only then if you got the word ahead of time.

He probably shouldn't be the first one off the bird, either. But be damned if he was going to let the Keldara lead. He took the lead in the door as the helicopter flared out and dropped to a soft landing.

As soon as the crewman yanked back the door he was out, running forward about half way to the treeline and then taking a knee, checking his sector. Clear.

He looked back over his shoulder as the last of the Keldara unassed the bird and took a knee. Catching Sawn's eye, he made two gestures with his hand and then turned and took his position in the teams. He wasn't stupid enough to take point.

The point team moved forward at Sawn's gesture and the trailer took a knee right at the edge of the woodline as the primary penetrated. After a moment the trailer stood up and moved in, followed by the rest of the Keldara and Mike.

Once inside the woodline, the point moved forward to the first high ground, cautiously, as the Keldara spread out in a cigar-shaped perimeter. It took about ten minutes for the point to reach a position where they could observe a fair bit of the route ahead and another five for them to ensure there wasn't anybody on the route and move out. As soon as they did, the teams got up and started moving forward to their previous position. When the lead of the team got there he took up the same spot, maintaining observation, as the team took a knee.

That set the pace. The point team would bound forward, find a good observation point and hunker down to check. When they were *certain* they weren't being observed, they'd move out again, slowly as if in a stalk. It was a slow, tedious, form of movement but very stealthy. And the mission depended *entirely* on stealth. Since it was the Keldara's normal form of movement, they did it so automatically they'd become damned near perfect.

The woods were deciduous, mostly, and pretty old growth so there wasn't a whole lot of understory. There was enough, though, that the Keldara had to maneuver through it. But they'd gotten used to that, too, and eeled through the brush as quietly as as many deer. Probably more quietly, deer could be noisy animals. The night was clear so at the second stop Mike flipped up his NVGs and let his eyes adjust. Plenty of light to go with Mark One Eyeball.

Mike paused at the third observe point and clicked his radio twice. A brief burst indicated that Lasko had received the communication and was moving out. The sniper team would bound far forward, probing for a good sniping point, one where they could observe both flanks of the teams. Mike would have liked to have another sniper team on their right flank, Lasko probably being on the left. But they'd arrange that after the first stop.

They had fifteen klicks, and a supply drop, to make before dawn. They weren't going to stop to deploy another team. If they did they'd have to *hurry*. Hurrying was *bad*.

Worrying was bad, too. He couldn't help but wonder what was happening with the other teams. He was with Sawn and Adams was with Vil. But that left Oleg, Pavel, Padrek and Yosif on their own. He had four other teams out there without "adult leadership." Now that he had time to think about it, he probably should have co-located with Yosif. Yosif was a great guy but if anything his team was the least . . . something. Motivated didn't quite fit it. They just hadn't seemed to find their niche, yet. All the other teams, while being all-around players, had sort of settled into a niche.

Oleg was a bull. Vil was a natural feint and flank guy; his team quite often totally screwed Oleg's in exercises by feint and flank. Sawn was slow, cautious and hated to attack a frontal position.

Padrek was the best Keldara at devices, including ones that exploded. Given his druthers, he'd hit a position with grenades and satchel charges and wait for the opposition to surrender.

Pavel's team actually had some climbers in it. When Mike had realized somebody *had* to have a totally screwed route, he'd chosen Pavel even over his own or Adams'. Pavel was the kind of guy who always had a spare rope and if he had the choice of going around a cliff or up it, he'd go up. If he'd grown up in a middle-class household in the U.S. he'd be on a climbing wall, or a building side, every weekend. Call his team "mountain ops" to a greater degree than any of the others.

Yosif, though, he didn't seem to have a niche. And he seemed to know it. His team just didn't have the same . . . oomph as the others. Mike should have put himself with Yosif. He realized, now, that he'd come with Sawn because at a level they were the most compatible. Sawn was a ghost.

If any team was going to blow the op, though, it had to be Yosif's. And he couldn't even check on their progress.

It was going to eat him all the way to the rendezvous, damnit!

Adams followed Vil out of the bird and took a knee in the middle of the V the Keldara had formed. As soon as the birds started to lift up he waved the point forward. When they gave the all clear he moved out.

The Keldara were moving well. They'd done this shit a thousand times already so except for the high alpine stuff they were dialed in. If any of the teams had problems in the high up, he'd find out at the rendezvous.

In the meantime, he let his brain go blank and soaked up the night. Thinking at a time like this could get you killed.

"I think this is good," Vanner said, looking at the cluster of boulders.

It had taken them most of the night to descend from their hide to the area of the op. The questions, once there, were: were they close enough to receive Katya and could they remain undetected.

They were practically on top of the town of Gamasoara; they could see it clearly from their position. But they still had about a thousand meters of elevation over it and straight line distance was nearly four thousand meters. Nearly three miles away. If they could find a good hide they should be golden.

And it looked to be a pretty good hide, a cluster of boulders with enough soil around them to dig in.

"Ivar, have a seat," Vanner said, lowering the Keldara to the ground. "And hand me your e-tool."

The entrenching tool was a folding shovel. This one was a German design with a larger, broader, head than the standard American one. But it was still a little folding shovel. Building a hide big enough for all five of them was going to be a stone bitch; Vanner hadn't done any serious digging since boot camp in Parris Island.

"Olga, see if you're getting anything from Katya," Vanner added, checking the time. They weren't going to finish the hide before dawn but they could build *something* for concealment. "And if you do, give her a tickle and tell her we're here."

For Katya, the burst ping was like a sudden flash of coldness in her brain.

The Amis had wired her for sound and video, literally. In an experimental operation they had installed implants in her head that picked up both whatever she saw and whatever she heard.

She could receive transmissions as well. But a conversation was a bit much given that the Chechens could have intercept capability. So the brief burst, no more than atmospheric static to any but the most sophisticated intercept gear, didn't even have any content. There was no "internal" for anyone to find. It was just the equivalent of "we're here."

Katya's transmission systems were even more advanced than those available to the Keldara, absolutely state-of-the-art in communications. It is said that anything in the commo field is obsolete before it's fielded but the only thing more advanced than the transmitters in Katya's mastoid bone were gleams in scientist's eyes.

Katya didn't know much about communications, but Vanner had admitted that, except with the gear designed to pick it up, he couldn't detect Katya's stuff even when in the same room. So she had no problem "opening up" the transmission, a mental exercise like moving a muscle that wasn't there.

"So, are you well?" Katya said, crossing her legs and looking steadily at the girl on the bed.

"What do you care?" the girl asked.

"Just checking," Katya replied. "If you die I suspect I will as well."

"I'm *fine*," the girl said. "I'd guess from your conversation with the Asshole-in-Chief that you, personally, could care less."

"More or less the case," Katya said. "Your exercise period is coming up. Be glad."

"I'd be glad if someone would read to me or something," Marina replied. "Even play some music. *Something*."

"Well, I don't have a book and wouldn't read it to you if I did," Katya said. "Nor do I have a music player. So I guess you're stuck."

"Okay, you can't know my name, but what's yours?" Marina asked.

"Katya," the agent replied after a moment.

"Hello, Katya, I'm the girl in the mask," Marina said. "I know you're a . . ."

"Whore, prostitute, hooker, streetwalker, take your pick," Katya finished for her.

"*Hetaera*," Marina said.

"A *what*?" Katya said, laughing. "Never mind, I've heard the term. And I am anything *but* a *hetaera*. I am a whore."

"Fine, be a whore if you wish," Marina said, sighing. "Why?"

"Well, unlike some people, I don't have a rich father to keep me," Katya said.

"Hah!" Marina snorted. "Rich. The Russian government pays as if it was still 1980 and true communism was just around the corner. Our rent was paid by the institute but much of the time we couldn't afford food. I had a vegetable garden in the summer; that was much of what we ate. Rich. Katya, will you keep a secret?"

"If possible," Katya said. "I'm not going to withstand torture to get it. And I can't guarantee that we're not being . . . bugged or something."

"Oh, I don't care what those men know or think," Marina said. "They're pigs. But I have been a whore. I have taken money to . . . do it."

"If you use a term like 'do it,' you have never been a whore."

"It was when I was at college," Marina continued. "Sometimes I would go to the bars and pick up men, Americans or Europeans of course, and ply them for money. I was using my body, screwed men, for money. That is being a whore, yes?"

"No," Katya said. "That's like saying that one of these Chechen pigs is a soldier. A whore is someone who is beaten twice a day by her pimp. Who is beaten until she pees blood but goes out to make his money anyway. A whore licks out toilet bowls because it is the choice of that or die. A whore has no *choice*. None. At *best* you were a prostitute."

"You have a point," Marina replied. "I guess being a whore is sort of a badge of honor for you."

"I hadn't thought of that, but, yes," Katya said. "It is what I am. If you do something for long you had better become proud of it or find a way, any way, to change."

"Katya," Marina said.

"Yes?"

"Don't take this wrong," Marina continued. "But I think you are probably a very good whore."

"The best you'll ever meet," Katya said. "And because we are such good friends you can call me Cottontail."

"That is a very strange name," Marina said nervously.

"I am a very strange person."

Chapter Twenty-Four

"Hey, Chief," Kacey said, stepping out of the Expedition. It was being driven by one of the older Keldara and she wondered how he felt about that. The Keldara women seemed more independent than some of the Third World types she'd been around but they were *definitely* second-class citizens. He had to be a bit put out chauffeuring a woman. But if he had an issue with it it wasn't apparent. On the other hand, the Keldara were pretty stone-faced. They'd make great poker players.

"Hey, boss," D'Allaird said, closing a hatch on the Hind.

"Everything good?" Kacey asked.

"Yeah, just looking at one of their junctions," Tim replied, grinning. "God *damn* those Czechs are some fine ass engineers. Call this a Hind if you want, but it's practically an entirely different bird. All the connections are better, all the systems are more robust *and* they're way better quality manufacture than anything I've seen out of the Russians. *And* they did all that without actually *changing* anything. Most of their parts can be switched out for standard without a hitch. The Czech ones are just better designed and made. Cool-ass shit."

"Glad you like it," Kacey said. "How are the Czechs working out?"

"Well, saying they speak English is a stretch," D'Allaird said. "But engineers all speak the same language, if you know what I mean."

"Good," Kacey said. "But, we've got another personnel problem."

"No crew," D'Allaird said. "No problem, I can toss supplies."

"I don't *want* you tossing supplies," Kacey said. "I want you back here making sure the backup bird is golden. And I want you ready to take care of anything wrong with this one when we land. We need a body. Two, really. Cause we're going to be unassing these supplies as fast as possible and I'd like to get people trained in so we can operate both birds."

"Uh, there's a personnel shortage, ma'am," Tim pointed out. "Most of the younger males are up in the hills, you know. I suppose some of the older guys, like your driver, could . . ."

"I was thinking something different."

"That's an interesting suggestion," Nielson said, rubbing his eyes. "I wish the Kildar was here to pitch it, though. I don't have a problem with responsibility, mind you. It's just the Kildar can say 'This is how it shall be done' and the Keldara, in general, just do it. He's the *Kildar*. That's big mojo. I don't have the same mojo."

"We need the bodies," Kacey said, ticking off the items she'd thought of on her fingers. "We're probably going to need them in the future. The older males all have day-to-day responsibilities, especially with the young men gone. That's not going to change. And there's nothing they can't do in the field. The U.S. military has, sorry, proven that over and over again. It's not field combat."

"Let's go talk to Father Kulcyanov," Nielson said with a sigh.

"Father Kulcyanov, thank you for meeting with us," Nielson said, nodding to the elder. He realized he was going to have to translate since Father Kulcyanov had damned little English and Kacey even less Georgian.

"You are the castellaine of the Kildar," Father Kulcyanov said, nodding. "In his absence, you are his Voice. I should have met you at the caravanserai. I am at your command in the absence of the Kildar. You honor me by your visit. I drink to you." He took a sip of beer and then lowered the mug. "May the Father of All give us wisdom in this council."

"The Father of All," Nielson said, taking a sip. "He just blessed this 'council' to the Father of All. I'll have to give you more background on the Keldara. They play Christian only when it suits them; they're actually pagans."

"I'm afraid I can't drink," Kacey said, uncomfortably. "Not before flying. But I, too, honor this . . . council by the . . . Father of All."

Nielson translated and then added with a wry grin: "And Captain Bathlick does not drink alcohol anyway."

"I shall call for water," Father Kulcyanov said, nodding and calling for it. "I did not know of your customs. My apologies."

"He said he didn't know your customs and apologizes," Nielson said. "He's getting you water."

"It is not meant to dishonor you in any way," Kacey replied, uncomfortably. "I just don't drink anymore. Also, it is very unwise to drink anything within twelve hours of flying. It requires very precise reactions. My co-pilot is a drinker but even she does not before flying."

"She no longer drinks alcohol and is prohibited from doing so before flying, anyway," Nielson translated. "Her co-pilot drinks but not before flying. And it is that which we must talk about. The pilots are taking up a supply run to the Keldara. They need someone to load and unload the helicopters."

"I shall tell . . ." Father Kulcyanov paused and sighed. "I am so used to having Oleg to do such tasks. But he is with the Kildar. We will arrange."

"He's tapped out for guys," Nielson said. "You wanna do your pitch. I'll translate it as you go."

"Sir, if I may," Kacey said as a young woman came up and set down a mug of spring water by her arm. "Thank you. Sir, if I could ask for something. We are going to need these crew on a regular basis. They don't just load and unload the aircraft. With training they take care of minor maintenance, respond to in-flight emergencies and man the door guns. They are *soldiers*, sir. However, there is nothing that requires great strength. In the U.S. military many of the aircrews are . . . women."

Nielson translated and then waited.

Father Kulcyanov looked at her for a moment and then gave a broad grin. And spoke at length.

"Let me see if I can do this verbatim," Nielson said, shaking his head. "I didn't even know he'd *been* in Stalingrad. Here goes:

"And you wish to use some of the Keldara women for this was how he started. I am one of only two of the elders who fought in the Great War in the army of the bastard Stalin. He was a godless communist and calling him a pig insults pigs, but he had some things to teach even one such as I. When I saw that women were in the army, even carrying weapons, I was shocked. I was a young man, and very easily shocked. But more than once, especially in Stalingrad, I saw the women fight with as much courage, and ability, as any of my fellow soldiers. Better. You, I think, maybe could have fought with those women, Captain.

"The other elders, none of them, even Devlich who also fought in the War, fought with women beside them. They are having a hard time seeing women as anything more than makers of babies and beer: women are for tending to the fires and warming a bed. But I have seen them fight. And I am no longer shockable. You shall have your girl, Captain Bathlick."

When Nielson finished translating, the young woman who had served the water said something to the elder and Father Kulcyanov answered with a shake of his head.

"Serena, I agree with Father Kulcyanov," Nielson interjected. "You're still sixteen. Give it a year or two at least. Seventeen or eighteen minimum. But preferably unmarried, which makes it tough. Not because of the danger, but because if the unit deploys they may deploy with it."

The young woman seemed to translate that from Kacey's perspective and then, with a very visible sign of screwing up her courage, said some names. Father Kulcyanov grunted and answered tersely without looking at her, at which the young woman ducked her head and went back in the back of the house.

"She suggested some of the girls and Father Kulcyanov pointed out that he didn't need an unbroached child to tell him who was who in the Keldara," Nielson said in a low voice. "And he said it that way, which I've never heard an elder say to an unmarried, or, hell, a married female before."

"Women's lib only goes so far, huh?" Kacey said.

"More like a very junior enlisted making suggestions to a general," Nielson replied. "Effectively he was just saying: 'Teach me to suck eggs, girl.' And the way that he said it was telling. He used the sort of language he'd have used with one of the militiamen. The girl doesn't realize it, but she just got a backhanded compliment in that insult. He's already put her in the category of warrior in his mind, even if he doesn't realize it. And Father Kulcyanov's opinion on that score is the *only* opinion that matters to the Keldara."

Father Kulcyanov asked something and Nielson answered in the affirmative. Then the old man spoke at length and to Kacey's ear somewhat ruefully.

"I'm trying not to smile," Nielson said. "And don't you. What he said was that when he thought of who would make good women for this position it was the same list Serena had suggested. But two of them are already on mortar teams and he doesn't want to lose their experience. So . . ."

"Gretchen," Father Kulcyanov spat.

Nielson looked at the old man and said something. The old man shrugged and said something back, looking at the colonel as an old sergeant might look at a new recruit. Oh, one with promise, but . . .

"And you have your crew-chief," Nielson said, frowning. "Gretchen's English is pretty good. Probably why he picked her. I *hope* that's why he picked her."

"What was that thing at the end?" Kacey asked. She'd heard the word "Kildar" in there and Nielson, at least, was clearly uncomfortable about her new crew-chief.

"Nothing that will interfere with your mission," Nielson said with a sigh. "Mine . . . possibly. But you have a crew-chief."

"Well, one thing I just realized," Kacey said. "I need to start learning Georgian, fast."

"Keldara," Nielson corrected. "It's as different from Georgian as Russian. But you'll learn. We all did."

Tim looked up and shook his head as Kacey got out of the Expedition followed by a girl in local dress.

"The good news is that she's a medium, so flight suits are covered," Kacey said. "Chief Warrant Officer Tim D'Allaird, Gretchen

Mahona. Gretchen, this is Chief D'Allaird. He goes by Chief or Gunny."

"Never could get over getting shafted into taking a warrant," D'Allaird said, shaking the girl's hand. He also was studiously trying to ignore her looks. "Do you speak English?"

"I speak fairly well," Gretchen said. "I am basic-trained in weapons, including machine guns. I can fire, strip and fix basic jam. Am strong. Work farm."

"That's a start," D'Allaird said with a sigh. "Boss, we're about to start loading. Can you scrounge the flight suits while I get started? While you were negotiating for crewmen I was finding some backs."

"Okay," Kacey said. "We'll be back."

For the time being all they had in the way of a ready room was a small shack but there was a crate of flight suits in it so that was the way she headed. The girl could change in there. It would be cold but she figured she could handle that.

"Captain, is a question okay?" Gretchen said as she opened the shed.

"The only dumb question is the one you don't ask," Kacey said. "That means if you have a question and we're not in the middle of something hot, ask it. Always."

"Yes, ma'am," Gretchen said. "Am I having rank?"

"You know, I didn't ask," Kacey admitted. "But, yeah, for now you're a buck private. We'll get the rest worked out later."

"Good," Gretchen said. "Thank you."

"Rank means a lot to you?" Kacey asked as she opened the shed.

"It means are soldier, warrior," Gretchen said. "If we die in combat, the Valkyr come for us. Are not condemn to Cold Land. Valkyr rarely come for women of Keldara."

"Interesting," Kacey said. "You're Asatru. Cool."

"I am not hear that name before," Gretchen replied. "And we do not talk much of our Mysteries."

"I heard you're like Norse or something," the pilot said. "I've got a couple of friends who worship those gods. The group's called Asatru in the States. About all I know about it. Can *I* ask a question?"

"Of course," Gretchen said. "You are commander."

"When you got picked by Father . . . Kulcyanov?"

"Yes, is Father of Kulcyanov family," the girl said.

"Nielson said something about the Kildar?" Kacey said. To her surprise, the girl blushed.

"Is nothing," Gretchen said.

"Is something," Captain Bathlick replied. "What is it? Specifically, is it going to affect the mission?"

"No," Gretchen replied, then paused. "Is problem with Ritual of Kardane. Kildar is . . . I am . . . Is hard to explain. Kildar . . . has feelings for me."

"The Kildar's got his eye on you?" Kacey asked. "Hasn't he got *enough* women?"

"Has many," Gretchen replied dryly. "There is ritual opening of Keldara women. Kildar has done this many times. Is *Keldara* ritual; Kildar has never been . . . happy with it. He has, however, participated in several such rituals. Called Rite of Kardane. I was last to be broached. He . . . He and I, though, developed . . . strong feelings for each other. Is under discussion if I should become Kildaran, the . . . wife of Kildar instead of my current intended. Will not be, Kildar will not interfere, but . . ."

"Oh," Kacey said in a small voice, her eyes wide. *Shit, she's potentially the boss's wife!* "I so have to learn not to ask questions. Case of suits in the corner. Grab a spare helmet. We'll fit those later. Somehow I'm sure you can figure out the zipper."

"I'm still not quite natural with this bird," Kacey said, banking the Hind down the narrow valley. "How's our clearance?"

"Good," Tammy said, watching the LIDAR. Technically, with the design of the Czech Hind, the pilot could do it all. And Kacey was risking glances at the instruments. But with her current comfort level it made more sense for Tammy to act as, effectively, a navigator while Kacey concentrated on not plowing the bird into the ground. "I think this is as low as we should go for now, but you're good. LZ is marked in about another klick up the valley. There's a ridge in the way you're going to have to negotiate."

"See it," Kacey said. The problem with the night vision goggles, though, was that they had virtually no depth perception. "Distance?"

"Six hundred meters, three hundred, start climb."

"I'm good," Kacey said, increasing power and touching the collective upwards. The helicopter lurched, not the smooth lift she was trying for but she was missing the ground and that was the important thing. She crested the ridge much higher than she would have liked but she could dial in her technique when she knew the bird a little better.

The LZ was clearly marked, fortunately, with what looked like cyalumes laid out in a Y formation indicating wind. She banked left then back to the right and settled towards the ground. The touchdown was smooth, if slow. Slow was still good in her opinion.

"Tell the lady to start a dumpin'," she said, breathing in relief.

Mike walked over to the Hind cockpit and waved in a friendly manner.

"Glad to see you ladies," Mike said. The pilots opened their canopies. He leaned up against the port side of the bird and grinned. "You said you couldn't fly one of these things. O ye of little faith!"

"This is very damned hairy, sir," Kacey replied, evenly. "This is high-skill flying, sir. I've got the skill but I don't have the time in the bird to feel really comfortable with it."

"Well, I'm comfortable with your skill, Captain," Mike said. "You're good or you wouldn't be here. You'll get comfortable. You know this mission wasn't precisely necessary, right?"

"No, sir," Tammy said, confused. "You needed the supplies, didn't you?"

"Sure, but only because we light loaded for the first movement," Mike said. "The main purpose to this mission is because the next one is tougher. You needed the experience and the Keldara have never operated like this with helos. They've flown in them but never been resupplied by them. I wanted both groups to get comfortable so when the shit hit the fan neither they nor you would freak. Tomorrow's mission is *way* more important. And if you have to supply us on the *other* side of the mountains, well, that's going to be hairy as shit. So get confident. Fast."

"Got it, sir," Kacey said.

"Looks like time for me to odie," Mike said. "I'll see you in a few days. Keep the faith."

"Yes, sir," Tammy replied, returning Mike's waved salute. "Is it just me or is that guy, like, charismatic as hell?"

"I've got sixty hours in this bird, as of this mission," Kacey said. "And I'm flying a night, tactical, NOE. You think I'd do that for just *anybody*?"

"So when are you going to nail him?" Tammy asked.

"I probably won't get the chance," Kacey replied. "Damnit. You know the blonde we got as load?"

"Yeah," Tammy said.

"Girlfriend."

"What?" Tammy snapped. "Doesn't he have *enough* women?"

"Long story . . ."

"Hello, Viktor," Gretchen said as she lifted the first box out of the starboard door of the helicopter.

"Gretchen?" Viktor said, surprised. He took the box of rations, though, and tossed it to the next man in line. "What are *you* doing here?"

"Somebody had to unload the helicopters, yes?" Gretchen said, tossing him another box. "The new crew-chief said we may be trained as crewmen. We are privates, now. The pilots are women, why not?"

"What does Father think of this?" Viktor asked, grinning.

"He sulks, what else?" Gretchen said, grinning back. "Women are for cooking and making babies and beer. Not for flying around in helicopters. Much less in combat. Father Kulcyanov has blessed us, though, and our mission. We are soldiers now."

"Are you going to be in combat?" Viktor asked, worried.

"The crewman mans the machine gun," Gretchen said, gesturing to the door gun. "You tell me."

"Hopefully not," Viktor replied. "I'd hate to be at your funeral. I would hate to have to deal with . . . Does the *Kildar* know about this?"

"I don't know," Gretchen said, shrugging. "But I think he likes strong women, yes? So this is good. As to funerals, I think I would hate to be at *yours*, brother. So I agree to take care and you do so as well."

"I'll try, sis," Viktor replied.

❖   ❖   ❖

"Damn."

Dr. Arensky looked at the rip in his shirt and shook his head.

"I wish they'd given us a *hammer*. There are nails sticking out all over. That's the fourth rip I've gotten in my clothes!"

"For a scientist, you sure are clumsy," Gregor chuckled from the corner.

Arensky had taken to walking up and down the small room whenever he wasn't puttering with his cultures or cooking. Both he and Gregor were putting on weight from the latter and he'd decided to fight it by pacing. Gregor hadn't argued or complained unless he neared the room's sole door. Unfortunately, there *were* several nails sticking out of the roughly constructed wall. And he'd managed to find *all* of them.

"Is there any way you could get me a needle and thread?" Arensky asked, fingering the tear.

"I'll see what I can do," Gregor said with a shrug. "Don't tell me you can sew as well?"

"Who else was going to fix our clothes?" Arensky asked. "Oh, Marina learned eventually. But I didn't get paid enough to buy clothes just because a collar was worn out or a sleeve ripped. This shirt is nearly ten years old, it's been mended, even rebuilt, many times. I suppose you can't even call it the same shirt anymore."

"You are a wonder, Doc," Gregor said, his eyes still closed. "I'll get you the needle. I need my socks darned."

Chapter Twenty-Five

"*Fuenf minuten!*" the load master yelled, holding up five fingers.

So much for "an English-speaking crew," Captain Guerrin thought. The *pilots* spoke English, but the only language he and the Ukrainian load master had in common was German. Guerrin had spent several tours in Germany in the course of his career and picked up the language readily. He should have concentrated on Ukrainian.

The good news was that the military attaché, who *did* speak Ukrainian and had been a Hercy pilot once upon a time, was along as a passenger. He'd smoothed things out quite a bit and been really helpful with figuring out the slightly different configuration on this bird.

The AN-70s were brand-new aircraft, the first new aircraft produced by Ukraine since the dissolution of the Soviet Union. So new the two the Rangers were using were the first the Ukrainians, themselves, had been able to afford.

The original design process had started back in the '80s, intended by the Soviet military as a replacement for the by-then venerable fleet of AN-12 Cubs. With the breakup of the Soviet Union and the accompanying economic disruptions, production of the first prototype was halted then started then halted several times. Finally, in 1995 a prototype was completed and entered testing. Unfortunately, on one of its first tests it collided with its chase plane and crashed, killing all seven of its crew.

However, the AN-70 was "the plane that wouldn't die." Antonov produced another prototype in 1997 and continued testing with the first production planes coming off the lines, finally, in 1999.

Produced primarily for short-range, high-capacity hauling in underdeveloped countries, the AN-70 was a turbo-prop, short-take-off-and-landing bird similar in many respects to the C-130 if considerably larger, with a maximum payload of 130,000 kilograms or 100 jumpers versus 20,000 kilograms or 64 jumpers. It also had one of the most advanced designs of any cargo aircraft in the world, with significant use of composites as well as a very high-end avionics suite.

Compared to even the newest generation of Hercules, it was a thoroughbred next to a cart horse. Among other things, it flew more like a fighter than a "trash-hauler."

There was also a shitload of room for the jumpers. They had a hundred and thirty jumpers with them. They could have, would have, cut a few if all they had were a couple of C-130s. As it was, if the mission hadn't been so high-level classified, they could have taken twenty or thirty "strap-hangers" and still rattled around like peas in a pod.

"STAND UP!" he shouted at the nearest jumper, flashing the same five fingers.

All through the aircraft the Rangers started struggling to their feet. Given that they had rucksacks over a hundred pounds in weight on their knees and parachutes on their backs, it wasn't the easiest maneuver in the world. On the other hand, they'd all done it dozens of times so they were up pretty quick.

"HOOK UP!" Guerrin shouted to the lead jumper, making a hooking sign in the air, then did so himself, albeit to the inboard cable.

Four cables ran down the interior of the aircraft, two about a foot from the skin, the "outboard" cables, and two about a foot apart running down the middle, the "inboard" cables. Jumpers hooked to the outboard cables, jump masters to the inboard.

Guerrin secured the cotter pin through his static line cable connector and then caught the eye of the lead jumper.

"CHECK STATIC LINE!" A sign of yanking on the static line.

Check to make sure you're hooked up, check that the opening was "outboard" so just in case it jumped open, against all reason, you'd still have your chute pull out of the bag and open. Check the pin, check to make sure the line wasn't around anything. If the static line got under your arm, for example, you would suddenly have a piece of nylon rope cutting into your biceps under pressure and screaming by at over a hundred miles per hour. In any airborne unit you saw the guys with "static-line arm."

Getting it around your neck was worse. You didn't see them much after the jump. Not even at the memorial service, which was *gonna* be closed casket.

"CHECK EQUIPMENT!" A pound on the chest like Tarzan.

He and the assistant jump master checked each other cursorily. Honestly, it was all Pentagon safety bullshit. You're jumping it, you'd better have checked it. But you had to make the show.

"SOUND OFF FOR EQUIPMENT CHECK!" Lean forward with hand to ear.

The cry was repeated then from the front of the bird the troops sounded off, coming down in a string. The last one, the lead jumper, Specialist Serris, leaned forward and gave him an "okay" sign and a big grin.

"ALL OTAY DUMPMATTAH!"

Christ, he'd told that joke *once*. Guerrin was prior service. He'd done time in the Rangers as an enlisted, then gotten out and gone civvie. It was only after 9/11 that he'd come back in, riding an OCS ticket, a few contacts and some luck into a Ranger commander slot.

But "back in the day" as they said, Eddie Murphy was still on *Saturday Night Live* and doing his Buckwheat routine. Thus the "accent." They did it all the time on jumps, just for shits and giggles.

He'd told a squad that just fucking *once*. So much for "opening up to the troops."

"DOOR CHECK!" he shouted at the Ukrainian load master, pointing at the door. The hell if he could remember the German for that.

The load master opened the door and the captain stepped to the opening. He took a good footing then grabbed the door edges and began his check. There were a lot of ways for a static-line jump to fuck up and airborne and Ranger units had managed all of them at one point or another. One of the real killers was having a rough or sharp spot on the door edge. On the leading edge, it meant a cut hand, no big deal. On the trailing edge, though, it could mean a cut static line. And then, well, you had your reserve but, bottom line, you were fucked. Pull your reserve, dump your gear and hope like hell you didn't hit *too* hard.

Modern "steerable" parachutes were designed to drop a standard-weight jumper at nine feet per second. The problem being that gear weights had gone up. So even if you dropped your ruck, you were still looking at thirty pounds over "standard" weights the chutes were designed for. Then there's the fact that "standard" weight, due to increases in size in the American public and the generally heavier nature of Rangers, were not "standard" in the Batts. And even nine feet per second was damned fast when it was you hitting the ground. About ten percent of the jumpers in any drop, even in training, got injured on impact with the cold, hard earth.

Reserve chutes dropped you at a "standard" *seventeen* feet per second.

He'd hit with a reserve once. It wasn't something he wanted to experience again. So he checked the *hell* out of the door.

But the Ukrainians, thank God, knew what they were doing. The molding around the door was as fresh as right out of the factory. Well, okay, it *was* darned near fresh from the factory. There wasn't *anything* wrong with the door.

Door checked, he leaned out and looked forward. There were still mountains in the way but he'd seen the approach maps; they were going to be looking at mountains right up until the jump. No problem. The Ranger motto is "The Whole World Is A Drop Zone." The area they were going into was actually *much* better than their usual training drops. The stone walls were going to be interesting, but that's why they had steerable chutes.

He could see an opening in the mountains, though. Probably their valley. Which meant they were *close*. He ducked back in and looked at the jump master, who held up two fingers.

"*ZWEI MINUTEN!*"

"TWO MINUTES!"

"WHOOF! WHOOF! WHOOF! . . ."

Guerrin shook his head again and leaned back out. The troops had also picked up that he was a UGA graduate. So it naturally became "Bravo Bulldogs." On a level he should be proud, it was a sign the troops thought well of him. But at moments like this it was a pain.

He could see the valley now. They were *high*. The birds were going to have to drop like a stone to get them down to anything jumpable. For that matter he noticed the air was pretty damned thin; it was a bit hard to breathe.

He popped back in and looked at Serris, hoping he could get this across.

"HANG ON," he yelled, suiting words to actions by grabbing a stanchion by the door. "WE'RE DROPPING!" He made a motion with his hand pointed down, like an aircraft in a dive.

Serris looked blank for a moment then nodded, grabbing at one of the folded-up seats with the hand not holding a static line and shouting to the guy behind him.

"*Dreissig Sekunden!*" the load master shouted.

"THIRTY SECONDS!" Guerrin screamed. "HOLD THE FUCK ON!"

Whether the word got back or not, Guerrin saw virtually everyone grabbing something just before the nose of the bird tipped over. And it was a *dive*, a hard one.

"HOOOOOO-WAAAAAH!"

The bird rang with the cry and Guerrin had to grin, even with what felt like his entire last month's meals coming up in his throat. He could feel his feet half leaving the ground. The pilots were really having fun, that was for sure. Oh, hell, face it, they were *all* having fun. Even if this was an admin drop it *felt* like combat, coming in in a "friendly nation's" bird, nose down and screaming at the DZ. It felt fucking *hot*.

Guerrin leaned out and he could see they were right on the DZ. Still diving.

"*Zehn Sekunden!*"

"Serris!" he shouted at the lead jumper. "Stand *in* the door!"

Fuck the new regs. The way they were maneuvering Serris *couldn't* just stand up. He was going to be lucky to make it to the door without sprawling on his face. He needed something to hang onto and the *old* way, standing in the door, grabbing the edges, was going to work better.

Guerrin took another look out and could see they were flashing over some small town stuck in a tiny valley. Just out the door, practically on the same level as they were jumping, was some sort of castle. Fucking *cool*.

He grabbed Serris' hand and practically *dragged* him to the door, slapping the hand onto the trailing edge as the bird leveled out, hard. Just as it did, the light flashed green.

"GO!"

Serris bailed followed by the stick but Guerrin kept his eyes out the door, keeping count at the same time. There were mountains in their way, coming up fast. He started to raise a hand and then did so as the red light came on.

"HANG ON!" he screamed, grabbing the new lead jumper's risers as the plane banked up. The jumper, a sergeant from Third Platoon, lurched into him but stayed on his feet.

"Stand by!" Guerrin called, pointing to the stanchion on the forward side of the bird's troop door and shoving the sergeant to it. There was no way he could just stand in the middle of the open area, any more than Serris could have.

Sixteen out on his side. They might get more on the second pass. Maybe less, probably more. Thirty-two jumpers, including himself, on his side, just like a Herc. One more pass, maybe two. He had to wait for the assistant JM to go. Probably no way he'd make it out on the second pass.

He'd considered having one of the, many, other qualified jump masters in the unit cover the drop. Technically he should have been the first guy on the ground. But the situation on the ground, according to everyone, was pretty together. He had been more worried about the quality of drop support. Thus the fact that he'd be the *last* guy out.

The bird had nosed up then banked, hard. The bank was right so he was looking at sky but looking through the other door, over his shoulder, it was apparent that the pilots were staying pretty low. Low enough that you could practically count the damned pine needles. He'd have been happier with a little more AGL.

Bank, level out, bank another of those screaming dives and . . .

"GREEN LIGHT! GO!"

The Rangers had been able to count, too. He looked over at the assistant JM and shrugged and nodded to him. Up to him to decide if he could make it out on this chalk.

The assistant, Sergeant First Class José J. Clavell, the Third Platoon platoon sergeant, just nodded and looked back out the door.

Last jumper on Guerrin's side and he had . . . a little room. Looking over his shoulder Clavell was . . . gone.

"*Tchuss!*" he shouted at the Ukrainian load master as he threw himself out the door, red light and all. The reason for the red light was clear since the bird lurched upwards just as he was clearing it.

He'd just started to count and then felt the one *hardest* separation he'd ever felt in his life. The ascending bird had practically *ripped* his chute cover off. He felt the chute open, though, and looking up he had a good canopy. Whew!

Looking down, though . . .

"Fuck," he muttered. Drop altitude was supposed to have been eight hundred feet, above ground level. And it probably *had* been. But going out late he'd ended up exiting over a damned at-least-two-hundred-foot *ridge*, covered in *trees*. This was really gonna suck . . .

First Sergeant Kwan hit the ground like a sack of shit, as always. He could instruct on a proper PLF, parachute landing fall, and had as a Black Hat in the Jump School in Benning. But he *always* hit like a sack of shit himself and so far, so good. He'd sustained injuries in jumps but only in cases where a good PLF wouldn't have mattered worth a damn. Like that one time he hit a fence post covered in barbed wire. That had really sucked.

This time, though, he could tell it was a good hit. Nice spot. Plowed field. Recently cut. Comfy.

He popped a riser, hit the quick release on his harness, got his LBE untangled, and rolled to his feet, scanning the area. No yells for medic, which was a *very* good sign. He was usually about the last guy down in a drop. If nobody was screaming for a medic it meant no major injuries.

He started to gather his chute and then paused as, through a break in one of the stone fences, he saw a cluster of locals headed his way. *Women* locals by the skirts and blouses, carrying sacks just about the size to pack a chute in.

He stood up and began bundling the chute as the women spread out, one or two towards each jumper. None of them were armed, so he didn't see a security situation. He wasn't sure about swarming Rangers with . . . damn, they were good-looking! women just after a jump, though.

"His" gal had reached him by the time he had the chute bundled, though, so there was no stopping it now.

"We take," the lady said in heavily accented English. "Clean, pack, give back. You go. Duty." She pointed towards a cluster of houses to the south. That *was* the designated assembly area.

"Okay," Kwan said, dubiously. "Take care of it. That's U.S. Government property."

"Clean, pack, give back," the gal repeated, grinning. "You go. Duty. Beer."

"Yeah," the first sergeant said, suddenly alarmed. "I'd better get going." They had *better* not be serving his Rangers beer already.

Guerrin swung back and forth, kicking his feet like a kid on a swing and working out the pain in his left arm. He'd taken a hell of a bang coming down through the branches of this . . . oak, by the look of it. But the canopy had caught on the upper part of the tree, leaving him dangling about twenty feet off the ground. There was a procedure to get down but, given that the ground was covered in scrub and rocks, he was already banged up and this was a *training* jump, he was planning on staying here till somebody came by with a ladder.

He looked up, though, at the sound of an unusual helicopter engine approaching. He couldn't see much through the trees but it sounded . . . Well, it wasn't a Huey and it wasn't a Blackhawk. Not a Eurocopter or a Kiowa, either, he knew those. Sounded big, though . . .

He looked up, though, as it came to a hover overhead, battering him with rotor wash. A fucking *Hind*? Guerrin had never been around for the Cold War days but things like Hinds still gave him the willies. They were the image of the Soviet war machine that was going to crush the U.S. Army given half a chance. Having one hovering overhead wasn't pleasing making. Neither was the way it was causing the branches above him to sway.

A guy was already sliding out of it on a harness connected to a cable, though, dropping towards him. So much for a ladder, apparently. He'd never been extracted out of trees by a chopper before. Something new every day.

He ducked his head against the wind and only lifted it as he felt more than heard a body come crashing through the branches overhead.

"Captain Guerrin I presume!" the helmeted crewman shouted. Guerrin couldn't see much past the helmet, visor and boom mike but the guy was clearly American by the accent. "Care for a ride?"

"Sure!" Guerrin shouted back. "How we going to do this?"

"Not a problem," the guy yelled. "Done it plenty of times!"

The guy said something into the mike then clambered around behind him. Guerrin felt something click onto his harness; then they both lifted for a bit. They paused again and Guerrin realized the maneuver had been intended to take the pressure off his risers. If they'd popped the connections to the canopy while he was dangling they'd have flown upwards under pressure and who *knows* what would have happened. Flying risers were no joke. With the pressure he reached up and disconnected one just as the guy on his back disconnected the other.

He felt another lift and ducked his head as they crashed up through the canopy.

"Don't sweat it, Captain, done this plenty of times!" the guy repeated.

"Who the hell pulls Rangers out of trees with a *helicopter*?" Guerrin shouted back.

"Who said anything about Rangers?" the crewman yelled. "I usually pull *pilots* out of trees!"

"You're a para-jumper?" Guerrin yelled.

"Well, actually, not in the last ten years! But it's like riding a bicycle . . . !"

Chapter Twenty-Six

"First Sergeant . . . Kwan?"

Most of the company had assembled on a flat open area near the houses of the locals. It was a flat spot slightly lower than the area where the houses were with a short bluff separating it from another open area directly in front of the houses.

Quite a few of the locals, ranging from some oldsters that looked on their last legs down to the usual gaggle of kids that swarmed around any American military unit, had come out of their houses to look over the new arrivals. And quite a few of them were *damn* fine-looking women. Most of the company had been around enough, the average was four trips to the sandbox, that they weren't gawking, much, except at the girls.

Kwan had at first worried about the gathering, not just because Rangers and women went together like iron and magnets, but because in the sandbox a gathering like that read "riot" or a car bomb taking out a bunch of locals. But these folks didn't seem hostile or worried. They didn't seem exactly *friendly*, either. They seemed to be more curious and even *judging* than anything else. Quiet. Even the kids were making quiet comments to each other, taking the serious tone they were getting from their elders. One of the oldsters, a big blond guy that was one of those who looked on his last legs, was standing at parade rest and observing them like a general on a reviewing stand. It was nervous making.

Kwan turned to the guy in unfamiliar digi-cam and paused. His nametag read "Nielson" but he was wearing some foreign rank the NCO didn't recognize. He didn't even know if the guy was an officer or a civilian advisor or what. But he had an air of authority and on the basis that a salute never hurt the first sergeant saluted.

"Yes, sir."

"Pleasure," Nielson said, returning the salute. "Colonel Nielson, late of the U.S. Army, currently operations officer of this little lash-up. Where's Captain Guerrin?"

"I don't know, sir," Kwan said. "We were just discussing that. He chose to JM the drop, sir. Sergeant Clavell said the CO told him to decide if he could go in the last stick and it looked good. But he came down fucking close to the treeline. He doesn't know if the CO went out or not or what."

"Oh, he's gone from the bird," the colonel said. "The Ukrainians confirmed all jumpers gone before they flew home."

"So the CO . . ."

"One jumper, at least, went down on that ridge," the local said, gesturing to the north. "He's probably in the trees. I've already sent a recovery team. Where's the XO?"

"Here, sir," Lieutenant Robert Imus replied.

"I'll need to hold most of this until your CO gets here," Nielson said. "But I'll give you the quick version. The locals are called the Keldara. They are superb mountain fighters with a tradition that goes back . . . well, very *very* far. I noticed your first sergeant giving the tall man the gimlet eye. First Sergeant, are you familiar with the term the Soviet Hero's Medal?"

"No, sir," Kwan said. "Not really."

"It was a general medal given by the Soviets, sir," Imus said. "It ranged in grade from something like the Legion of Merit up to the Medal of Honor."

"Yes, well that gentleman earned a Hero medal in WWII," Nielson continued. "Several, actually. They passed them out for everything from building more widgets to personally strangling Hitler with your bare hands. Because we have become close, he permitted me to read the citation for his highest one. He took out four German Tiger tanks with a fucking captured German rocket launcher, by himself, on foot."

"Holy shit," Kwan blurted.

"I tell you this because while Father Kulcyanov is *unusual*, he is not *abnormal* among the Keldara. They are a race of fighters, of warriors, par excellence. They also have been recently introduced to Western-style tactics and training by a group of people at least your equal as fighters and in many cases your superiors. Some Rangers were among their trainers but also former Deltas, SEALs and SAS. So the Keldara know 'good.' But you are one of the first American units they have gotten the opportunity to observe. So the Keldara are going to be judging you, every minute of every day, on everything from your tactics to your professional deportment. Until your CO gets here, ensuring that you hold up the high standards of the United States military is up to you, Lieutenant, and will *always* be up to you, First Sergeant. The Keldara asked if they could come out and serve beer, which is to them something like the inevitable green tea in the sandbox. I suggested they hold off. I have never seen a Ranger act with anything like professional decorum around a keg of beer. And I say that as a tabber myself."

"Yes, sir," Kwan said. "Thank *you*, sir."

"Have your men rest until the Bobbsey Twins recover your CO," Nielson said. "Then we'll settle you into quarters and get started on briefings."

"Sir, one question," the XO interjected. "I don't see any young males. Where are they?"

"In the mountains, Lieutenant," Nielson replied. "And that is all you are permitted to know. I'll be briefing your CO further."

"Are we going to be aggressing against them, sir?" Kwan asked.

"First Sergeant, for a senior NCO of a company in the United States Army you have remarkably poor hearing," Nielson replied, tightly. "I said, that is *all* you are permitted to know. So put a fucking cork in it, Top."

Kwan raised his eyebrows but shut the fuck up. His questions about whether the "colonel" was a PX Ranger were answered. No.

Guerrin flexed his knees as the Hind dropped him lightly to the ground, looking around at the company. The PJ guy undid the connection to his harness and then the Hind lifted up and away.

As soon as the rotor wash had settled he popped the quick release on his parachute harness and headed over to the cluster of senior NCOs and officers. One of the group, however, was unfamiliar.

"Colonel Nielson?" Guerrin said as he approached.

"The same," Nielson replied. "Tree landings suck, do they not? I had a friend in the unit who preferred them but I always thought he was high when he jumped, anyway. I've been giving your first sergeant and XO a brief précis of the local conditions. I'll catch you up later. The problem, at the moment, is figuring out quartering. There are . . . issues. May I make a suggestion?"

"Yes, sir," Guerrin replied. "I was told that you'd brief me in on our mission, so I'll take it as more than a suggestion."

"This *is*, however, a suggestion," Nielson said. "There are decisions to be made so having the troops pick out their bunks would be unwise at this time. Troops so grumble when they are moved and moved again. We do, however, have a very nice live-fire range and even a CQB facility. There is daylight to be had. I would *suggest* that you have your senior NCOs take the troops over to the range while we, that is yourself, myself, your first sergeant, XO and such others as you deem fit, figure out quartering. That way they're not sitting about. Idle hands and all that. When we figure out the quartering, then I can brief *you* in on the secure aspects of this mission while your people actually get them settled."

"Sounds good, sir," Guerrin said.

"It should," Nielson replied. "I've both had time to think about it and been at this game for a while. I will meet you in the middle house over there," he added, pointing to one of the local houses, "when you're ready. I'll have one of the Keldara join you with keys to the ammo bunker. I know you've brought your own, but it's a lovely day to be shooting."

"Gentlemen," Nielson said, nodding at the Ranger officers and one NCO. "I have asked Father Kulcyanov to sit in as a courtesy. Father Kulcyanov speaks and understands very little English. This is, however, his house and he is the senior, if not oldest, Keldara father."

Guerrin had wondered at the inclusion of the old man and come to much the same conclusion. Kwan had also given him an apparently verbatim report on what he'd been told by Nielson. So he took a chance.

"I understand, sir," Guerrin said. "Does Father Kulcyanov understand Deutsch?"

"*Bisschen,*" the old man said, nodding. "*Kennen sie irhen Feind.*"

"*Danke schoen . . . Fuer Seinem Haus verwenden.*"

"*Soldaten sind immer wilkommt zum Senke des Keldaren, aber nicht zum seinem Frauen. Seien gewarnt.*"

"*Ja Mein Herr,*" Guerrin said with a chuckle. "*Verstandet!*"

"Sir?" Kwan asked, confused.

"He said that soldiers are always welcome here," Imus translated, chuckling. "But keep your hands off our women."

"Yes, sir," Kwan said.

"Not 'sir,'" the old man said, making what was either a wet cough or an equally wet laugh. "I work."

"So now that we're acquainted," Nielson said when the chuckles had died down. "Here's the quartering issue. We have two useable sets of quarters, the barracks and the caravanserai up on the ridge. We can quarter all of your people under roofs and in beds. Barely. That's the good news. The bad news is that the barracks are open bay with the exception of two rooms per barracks that are private; you can handle that. But they are only big enough for two platoons. The other bad news is that the caravanserai is the personal home of the local landowner and warlord. He's an American, Mike Jenkins, who is currently out of town. It is also the quarters for his harem. And I mean that in every possible sense of the word. I will now entertain questions."

"Girls," J.P. said, wincing.

"Eleven of them . . . actually, make that about thirteen," Nielson replied. "Four of them are straightforward hookers who can be available to your personnel at your discretion. They're underutilized at the moment because most of the male residents are out of town. Then there's the harem manager, Anastasia, who is a former harem girl of a sheik in Uzbekistan and now runs Mike's. Whatever Mike may think, she considers herself monogamous to Mike. Daria, who is the operations executive assistant and bookkeeper. One hot blonde, as is Anastasia, who is unattached but equally unlikely to have a casual fling with any of you.

"Then there are five ladies who are Mike's exclusive, highly exclusive, harem. I don't have access so neither do you. One of them is, in fact, a virgin who is waiting anxiously to be popped. Looking forward to it more than he, unless I'm much mistaken.

"So, gentlemen, this is the problem. You can put all your troops in the barracks and all your senior NCOs, officers and such, up at the caravanserai, creating a huge impression of favoritism but reducing some potential problems, or you can quarter *some* of your youngsters with a bunch of incredibly fuckable little ladies, most of whom are equally incredibly off-limits. Oh, last problem, most of the rooms that are available are *in* the harem quarters. At the very least we're looking at senior NCOs quartered with seven nubile but off-limits young ladies and four very available hookers. Questions, comments, concerns?"

"Harem?" the XO said.

"Virgins?" the first sergeant added.

"Kildar?" J.P. asked.

"Harem," Nielson said. "Another thing to brief your personnel on is not running off at the mouth about conditions in this valley. While a large number of extremely senior people are aware of Mr. Jenkins' harem, it's not something for casual discussion down on River Street. If it becomes a subject of casual discussion the leaker will be punished under the full weight of the UCMJ. Guaranfucking-teed. Yes, virgins. Their history is complicated and not germane to the discussion. Kildar is the local term for Mr. Jenkins' position. The history is not germane, either. Having said that, it's an ancient term for the noble who commands the Keldara. They are a very feudal tribe with traditions that date back to the Byzantine Empire. I'll discuss it at length if we ever have time. It's quite fascinating.

"The Keldara girls are equally off-limits, as Father Kulcyanov pointed out," Nielson continued. "Unless you brought a chaplain, with the permission of the parents, which you're not going to get. Most of the girls are promised to guys who are currently . . ."

"Out of town," Guerrin finished. "Okay, fuck favoritism. I'll put it straight to the troops. How willing are the professional ladies?"

"You're speaking of the hookers?" Nielson said. "Anastasia considers herself a professional *lady* but that's besides the point. Quite willing. Enthusiastic even. And, as I mentioned, currently underutilized. Why?"

"First Sergeant?" Guerrin asked. "Girls in the barracks?"

"Ouch," Kwan replied.

"Let me add they had better get the *private* rooms," Nielson interjected. "And some decency. They're *willing*. That's not the same as interested in being trained or gang-raped. They've had that in their lives and we'd rather they not go back, thank you."

"If the senior NCOs were there to . . . manage things . . . Maybe," Kwan said. "But not if it's just the troops and junior NCOs, sir. Fights among other things. And the evangelicals would flip. Even if what happens on the mission, stays on the mission . . . I'd recommend against it. There's that new UCMJ reg, for that matter."

"Can you clear the harem quarters entirely?" Guerrin asked. "And is there enough room for a platoon there?"

"Yes," Nielson said. "It was one possible solution. Some of the girls will have to double-bunk in other rooms. They can handle that."

"With your permission, we'll do it that way," the CO said. "Second Platoon."

"Yes, sir," Kwan said.

"Next on the agenda," Nielson said. "Your mission is to perform local patrolling and positional defense training here in and around the valley. During patrolling phase there is a chance of encountering and possibly engaging Chechen convoys and patrols. I'll arrange a more thorough briefing on the local threat situation. But, effectively, you're here to protect this area while their normal protectors are . . . out of town. You will, in fact, arrange things so that it *appears* that you are here as aggressors against the Keldara, who are hiding up in the woods. The supposed notional mission is that you've captured a hostile town and are hunting for the hostiles up in the mountains. The Keldara are not, in fact, there but if you could shoot off some blanks from time to time as if you were engaging in raids and ambushes it would be nice. But don't get caught with blank adapters on if there are any Chechens around. They *will* mount your head on their wall."

Kwan started to open his mouth and then shut it.

"The question was, 'where are they?'" Nielson said.

"And I didn't bother to ask, sir," Kwan replied. "Not my business."

"Indeed," Nielson said. "I will discuss that with your commander and he will *not* be authorized to pass that on. I might add that that fact is a National Command Directive, not something thought up by some local asshole. You are here because someone in your chain of command found it wise that you be here, now, doing this mission. That is all any of you, save your commander, needs to know. As far as anyone outside of your command is aware, you came out, did some training missions with a local mountain militia then flew home. God willing, that is all that will happen, except the militia will not, in fact, be there. Is this clear?"

"It's a deception plan," Imus said.

"Correct. There are additional details but I will discuss those with your commander *only* for the time being."

"It's clear," J.P. said. "Top, get the quartering started. Colonel Nielson, we have *another* briefing?"

"And I need to get the girls moved," Nielson said. "Fortunately, Mike has good subordinates. They'll be moved by the time your guys get there."

"This is a nice fucking shoot house for some Third World yahoos," Serris said as he emerged from the smokey interior.

Lance Serris, six feet one inch tall, slender with short-cropped blond hair and an almost unnoticeable beard, was twenty, just, having joined the Rangers straight out of high school with only intervening steps at One Station Unified Training and airborne school at Fort Benning. Upon completion he hadn't gone far, just across the state to Hunter Army Airfield. There he'd passed the initiation rite known as "Ranger In Processing" or "RIP." RIP was a kinder gentler version of SEAL Hell Week, a weeklong test of endurance designed to determine if the candidate had what it took to be a Ranger.

He had assumed that when RIP was over things would get easier. What he realized within a month of joining 1st Battalion was that RIP wasn't a pointless test. There had been plenty of weeks in the Batt when RIP had looked like a day at the beach.

Rangers had an interesting role in the U.S. military in that, in many ways, they were neither fish nor fowl nor good red meat. Rangers were trained in much the same way as any standard light infantry outfit. Every light infantry company could patrol, every light infantry company could march, scout and do a basic entry. Delta Force, the primary "black op" unit of the military, was specialized for entry and killing or capturing targets. They could do a long-range reconnaissance quite well, thank you, but tended to work in shorter ranges and hard bursts of highly clandestine activity.

Rangers, though, trained in it all. They were better than any other light infantry company in the U.S. military, possibly the world, at patrolling, either in vehicles or on foot. They could march farther and faster, in worse conditions. They were, in general, much more stealthy in reconnaissance and their raids hit harder and faster. Their missions were always classified Secret and often involved, as in Mogadishu, "backstopping" Delta and doing much the same missions, just with lower-profile targets or less resistance.

Some units that had a bit of one skill and a bit of another but no real concentration tended to be underutilized. Not Rangers, though. Especially since 9/11, their operational tempo had been through the roof. Jacks-of-all-trades, close to masters of most, they were constantly going somewhere doing *something*.

Serris had started to wonder if it was worth it. If he transferred to the 82nd or, God help him, a leg infantry unit, he'd at least be more or less guaranteed of spending *some* time Stateside. Hell, he couldn't even find a *girlfriend* when he was out of town ninety percent of the time.

"No shit," Lane replied. "And those *women*."

Specialist Kevin Lane, five foot five, dark of hair and eye, had just gotten his specialist rank, whereas Serris was already on the list for the sergeant's board. But that didn't mean he hadn't seen a few shoot houses, or foreign women, in his time. And so far this mission was just fine by him. Among other things he was a "there's no such thing as a bad jump" parachutist who freefalled on his rare free time. The ride in and the jump had been a kickass start as far as he was concerned.

"That's because they ain't yahoos," First Sergeant Kwan said. "Get your ass over here!"

Apparently Top had gathered the rest of the platoon while the two had been doing their run-through and Serris and Lane hurried over to join the rest of the cluster.

"Gather round," Top said, shaking his head. "I don't know why the CO picked you idiots for this, but . . . While the rest of the company is being quartered in the local militia barracks, which I've looked over and ain't half bad, you yardbirds are going to be up in the castle."

"Hoowah!" Lane said. "That's *gotta* be cool!"

"Yeah, cool," Top replied. "Now shut up, fuckhead. Here's the first problem. You ain't gonna *think* it's a problem but if you give it some *small* consideration you'll see that it's a *hell* of a problem. Most of the rest of the residents of that castle, which is called a caravan surry or something, are women. *Fine* women from what I've been told. And you're all thinking 'Excellent' or 'Hoowah!' But I guess I need to explain in words of one syllable. If you touch one *single* woman in that house, if you look at them *sideways*, if you even *think* about talking to them, smelling them, kissing them or, God help you, *fucking* them, I will personally *bury* your ass in the ground. If you're *lucky*, you won't be *breathing* when I bury you. So you are going to be surrounded by good-looking women and you can't so much as acknowledge their existence. Now, Lane, you were saying?"

"Fuck!"

"No," Kwan replied. "No fuck. No look. No talk. That is the point."

"Top?" Serris asked. "What if they talk to *us*?"

"You smile," the first sergeant answered. "Politely. And then you *walk the fuck away*. Fast. Understood?"

"Understood," Serris said. "Fuck."

"Now, as to the nature of the quarters," Top continued, smiling. "That's the second problem. Some of the girls are being moved out of their rooms. Some of you will be *using* those rooms. They are, for sure, not going to be moving all of their stuff out. So if one of you *perverts* goes and jacks off on their underwear, or even opens a fucking *drawer*, the same thing goes. Understood? *Sound* off!"

"Clear, First Sergeant!"

"Don't try to game it, don't try to get around it and damned sure don't just fucking ignore me," the first sergeant said, tightly. "I'm starting to get a smell about this op. I don't know who this guy is who runs this place but he's connected. There's a very strong smell of high brass and seriously deep black ops to this place. If you piss off the owner, you are going to be head down in shit, deeply head down in shit, faster than you can say 'condom.' Now grab your shit and head up to the palace. This is going to be *so* much fucking fun I can't stand it. The good news is some of us are going to be training in 'positional defense' here in the area. *Others* of us, and I will permit you fine young men to think on who that might *primarily* be, are going to be doing heavy-duty mountain ops during our stay. Guess who's going to be doing *most* of them?"

"This way, Captain," Nielson said as they entered the great room of the castle. It was a hell of a place, that was for sure. "Big" didn't begin to cover it; it had a dome that was at least three stories high and the rug on the floor looked like an antique Persian. "I think I'd better take you to my . . . Anastasia!"

Guerrin froze and, frankly, stared. The woman that had appeared out of a side door was . . . Beyond hot. If she was one of the harem girls, his problems had just gotten worse than he could *possibly* have imagined. She looked like she should be in the *Sports Illustrated* Swimsuit Edition.

"Captain J.P. Guerrin, Anastasia Rakovich," Nielson said. "Anastasia is the Kildar's housekeeping manager."

"I run the house and his harem," Anastasia said, taking J.P.'s hand. She had incredibly fine hands. "I am given to understand you were to be briefed on the latter. Welcome to the home of the Kildar, Captain Guerrin."

"Thank you," J.P. replied, tongue-tied.

"Anastasia, we're going to have to quarter one of the platoons in the harem quarters," Nielson said. "I'd like to move all the girls out into the other rooms in the house. For the time being, *all* of the girls are off-limits. If we had the beds to do it the other way around, and put them in purdah for the duration of the Rangers' stay, I'd be happier. But we don't."

"It will be fine," Anastasia said, easily. "I will begin moving the girls. I would suggest, however, that Katya's room be placed off-limits."

"Well, she's not here to agree on its use so I can see that," Nielson said.

"It is not that," Anastasia said, exasperatedly. "The last time she went out of town she left some nasty surprises behind. I would guess this time they would be nastier."

Chapter Twenty-Seven

"Have a seat, Captain," Nielson said as they entered the office. "Coffee?"

After meeting Anastasia they'd headed straight to the colonel's office. It was a windowless room on the first floor and looked pretty secure with a heavy, soundproofed, door. And it would be hard to get a signal through the walls.

"Please, sir," J.P. said, taking a seat. "Black, sir."

Nielson poured two cups and handed one to Guerrin then sat down on the edge of his desk.

"Your stated mission was to engage in training with the Keldara," Nielson said. "Obviously, the Keldara militia, which is called the Mountain Tigers by the way, is out of town. Your higher, those who ultimately tasked you, knew they were out of town. So why are you here?"

"To cover their backs?" Guerrin asked, taking a sip of the coffee. It was excellent, big surprise.

"There is that," Nielson said, walking around the desk and touching a control on his keyboard. The computer flashed a map of the local area up on a whitewashed wall. "This is our AO. As you'll note, directly to our north curving to the east, is Chechnya. The Russians hold the lowlands. They've been unable to dislodge the Chechen militia from the highlands, the bit closest to us. The

Chechens had been using this part of Georgia as their personal fiefdom, a secure rear area, to supply their forces and provide safe areas, notably in the Pankisi Gorge." Nielson pointed it out with a laser pointer.

"Not far from here at all," Guerrin mused.

"No, it's not," Nielson admitted. "And I'll add that it's simply crawling with Chechen mujahideen. And muj from all over the world that didn't want to get their balls blown off in Iraq. Fighting the Russians isn't safe but it's a damn sight safer than fighting Americans, as the muj have started to notice. I'm not saying that the guys over there are cowards. Call them the wiser part. They've tried to hit us once and we handed them their heads. One team of twenty Keldara, straight off their first week on the range, took down a Chechen force of about two hundred."

"Not bad," Guerrin said.

"I think, at this point, the Keldara are probably close to the ability level of your Rangers," the colonel mused. "I'm not sure who is better and I don't think it matters. They are quite good. They've been running patrolling ops, shutting down Chechen movement in our AO, for the past nine months. This has made the Russians very happy because it has significantly reduced the supplies the Chechens are getting. It has made the American government happy because the Russians are happy and it's an American driving it, even if it's for his own reasons.

"The Keldara teams, twenty men per team, patrol on a cycle so it's not day in and day out. But they go out for a week or so, do intensive patrolling, scouting and ambush ops then come back. So far, they've taken light to no casualties while killing over fifty Chechens and bringing back several tons of supplies. They're good."

"Got that, sir," Guerrin said, nodding. "And based on the results, I'd say I agree. Not better than *my* company, you understand . . ." he added with a grin.

"Understood," Nielson said, smiling back and then becoming serious. "The following information is classified TS Code-Word Ribbon Blade. Ribbon Blade is an Ultra Blue classification, you may not discuss it with anyone without authorization from the person informing you of your portion of the mission or someone with National Command Authority clearance. Do you understand this classification, Captain?"

"National command authority level?" Guerrin said. "President, national security advisor . . ."

"Secretary of defense," Nielson said, nodding. "They are the only three persons permitted to open up the compartment. No one else. The code word itself is classed Top Secret as is its classification level. Nobody can ask you what you really did on this mission. Should your mission parameters change then you need to ensure that your men are made aware that the basic mission parameters can be considered open source but if there is a mission change it goes totally black. Are we clear?"

"Clear, sir," Guerrin replied.

"Your cover mission, the open source mission, is to train on mountain operations with the Keldara," Nielson said. "As I pointed out, they're gone. Your confidential mission is to cover their backs while they are out of town. Which gets to what they are doing.

"For a number of reasons, among others that the Keldara are *good* enough, they got handed one hell of a fucked-up mission. You'll note the nature of the terrain between Chechnya and here."

"High alpine, looks like," Guerrin said. "I saw the mountains on the way in. Nasty. You've already had a couple of snows I see."

"They are 'out of town' doing a penetration of Chechen-controlled Georgia for the purposes of a raid," Nielson said. "The area is one that even the Russian Spetznaz hasn't penetrated. It's been in Chechen hands for at least ten years. The nature of that raid is not in your need-to-know at this time. However, when they attempt to extract, on foot, they are likely to have every damned Chechen in the entire region on their ass. If they are in contact or being closely pursued it is likely that D.C. will authorize you to engage the Chechens to stop them from crossing into Keldara territory. At the very least you *are* authorized to keep them from taking this valley and its infrastructure. Do you understand the three-level structure of this brief?"

"Yes, sir," Guerrin said. "We play like we're doing training ops with the Keldara, we really make sure they've got a home to come back to and if they get dropped in the shit we screen them on their way out. The first is confidential, the second TS and the third absolutely black."

"The Keldara are using very out-of-the-way areas for their penetrations," Nielson said. "But the best egress routes are here, here and here," he added, pointing to three passes. "They didn't go in that way because the Chechens have outposts and patrols covering those routes. But those are the egress routes. They are also the primary routes the Chechens use to penetrate *our* area and the area that the Keldara do most of their missions."

"So if I ran my patrol ops up through there . . . my teams would be in position to support the Keldara," Guerrin said.

"Exactly. You're not quite a Go-To-Hell plan, Captain, but you're close."

"What *is* the Go-To-Hell plan?" Guerrin asked.

"Falls very strictly into need-to-know," Nielson replied. "There are . . . five people who know it. Including NCA in its entirety."

"I . . ." Guerrin started to ask a question then shut his mouth.

"Go ahead, Captain," Nielson said mildly.

"Is this some sort of CIA black op or something?" Guerrin asked. "I figure the answer is going to be NtN but I figured I'd ask."

"The Kildar is entirely an independent operator," the colonel said. "We are not employed by the U.S. government in any capacity. The Kildar does, however, often take on missions that require a high degree of deniability or that the U.S. government isn't willing to touch with its own forces. Even the extremely black ones. I will not detail the nature of those missions but suffice to say they are important enough that the rewards from the missions pay for . . ." Nielson just shrugged and gestured around. "I will say this: The Kildar is the only person I've ever personally met who has a direct line to the President on the speed dial of his phone. He rarely picks it up just to chat, but I've seen the opposite happen."

"You know, the first sergeant said this mission had a high-rank 'smell' to it," Guerrin said. "I guess he was right."

"But be clear, Captain," Nielson said. "This mission has a high priority due to the nature of the raid. Not because the Kildar can pick up the phone and talk to the President. More the opposite. We got the mission because the President knew we could do it and because Mike is on *his* speed dial. This was a mission that had to be black, it had to be politically correct in a very real meaning of the word—there were huge problems with the both the Georgians *and* the Russians but both were willing to trust the Kildar—and it *had* to be successful. *That* is why the Kildar was tapped. Because he hasn't failed in a mission yet. Let's hope this isn't a first."

"Oh, hoowah!" Lane said.

Serris, looking around the new quarters, had to agree. The harem quarters were two stories and circular, the upper balcony and lower rooms facing into a center atrium with a fountain in the middle. The fountain had a sculpture in it, probably marble, so worn by the water the original statue had faded into something that looked modernist. But there was enough left of the original shape to determine that it had been two forms, horizontal and superimposed. Murals depicting pastoral scenes, some of the tiles missing, covered the walls between the doorways.

The south facing outer wall was mostly glass with complex metal filigree supporting it. It took Serris a second to realize that the metal was both thick enough and closely enough spaced that it was, effectively, bars.

"I wonder what the rooms are like?" Lane said, leaning his M4 against the wall and dumping his ruck on the marble floor.

"Girl froo-froo," Staff Sergeant Gordon Keller their squad leader said, emerging from one of the rooms. "The one with hundred-mile-an-hour tape on it is off-limits. I have a reliable report that it may have one or more IEDs in it. The girl who uses it is *not* part of the harem and currently 'out of town' with the rest of the group. There's a half-dozen rooms that aren't occupied. Junior guys get those."

"So where *are* the girls?" Lane said, grinning.

"Lane, did you *hear* the first sergeant?" Keller asked. "If you so much as talk to any of them, you are going to have an Article Fifteen so fast it will make your head spin *and* you are going to be out of the Batt and up at Fort Bragg picking trash with the rest of the trash. Is that clear enough for you?"

"Clear, Sergeant," Lane said with a grin. "But it also didn't answer the question."

"That's it," Keller snapped. "You are official brass detail for the rest of the mission."

"Fuck."

"Just to keep you from getting too fucking curious, I've arranged a tour of the castle," Keller said. "Among other things, it will point out the secure areas and the no-go areas. Effectively, you're restricted to this area, the main foyer, the dining area and the living rooms. There are three offices on the first floor and the kitchen in addition. You are restricted from all of those areas. You are also restricted from the basement areas and the upper floors. You're going to be *shown* some of that, but you are otherwise restricted from entering those areas."

"When are we going to get the tour?" Serris asked.

Keller turned at a quiet knock on the door and opened it to reveal a very pretty, and *very* young, lady wearing a school uniform.

"Staff Sergeant Gordon Keller?" the girl asked in good, if accented, English. "My name is Martya. I was instructed to give you and your soldiers a tour of the facility. I am at your disposal."

"Hoowah," Lane said making damned sure it was a whisper.

"Are these quarters acceptable, Captain?" Anastasia asked, waving at the room.

The bedroom was about twice the size of the master bedroom of the house Guerrin had, until the divorce, shared with his wife. The floor was marble but covered in deep-pile throw rugs that looked handmade. The bed could best be described as "sumptuous," a king-size four-poster with those hanging things on the side. For that matter there was a desk and a small seating area and nice paintings—maybe originals, Guerrin had no clue—covered the walls. There were two doors on one side and through the open one he could see enough that it was apparent there was an attached bathroom that was on the same order as the room.

The one odd aspect was that the two windows of the room were rather small and deep, making it deeply shadowed. Then he had to kick himself. Duh. *Castle*.

"The only problem with them is the vague feeling that I shouldn't be living like this when more than half my company's in barracks," Guerrin admitted. "And this is a *guest* room?"

"This is one of the three Distinguished Person guest rooms," Anastasia said. "We occasionally have visits from distinguished individuals and the Kildar felt it wise to set up some rooms for their stay and left the details to me."

"You do good work," Guerrin said. "You can decorate my house any time. If I could afford it."

"If you know where to shop, and have a ready source of labor to do sewing, it is not so expensive," Anastasia said with a smile. "What kind of house do you have?"

"Had," Guerrin said. "Lost it in the divorce. Pretty standard two-story tract home. Liked it but not enough to stay. My wife liked a 3rd ID officer more than me."

"I'm sorry," Anastasia replied.

"Yeah, well, she got the cats, too," Guerrin said with a shrug. "So I looked at it as a fair trade."

"Colonel Nielson asked that you join him in the tactical operations center as soon as you were settled," Anastasia said. "When you're ready just step out in the hall. I will have a guide waiting."

Guerrin followed the young lady to the lower level then into the main foyer. As they reached the area the front door opened and two females in flight suits, one short, one a bit above average female height, walked in, the taller one chuckling about something.

"Hello," Guerrin said, looking them over. Both were wearing those unfamiliar rank tabs and he made a mental note to find out what the rank structure of the organization was and how to read the tabs. "I take it I have you to thank for plucking me out of the trees. Captain J.P. Guerrin, United States Army."

"Captain Kacey Bathlick," the shorter pilot said, walking over to shake his hand. "Glad to give you a ride, Captain."

"Captain Tamara Wilson," the taller added. "No problem. Any time."

"The young lady was showing me the way to the TOC," Guerrin said. "I guess we can touch base later. I'd appreciate a bit more background on this place. Nothing confidential . . ."

"We're new here, too," Captain Wilson replied. "But we were headed down to the TOC, too. We can show you the way."

"Okay," Guerrin said, turning to his guide. The girl couldn't have been a day over seventeen and had some of the best knockers he'd ever seen in his life. "I go with them, yes?"

"Okay," the girl replied, smiling and shrugging. "Go back to class."

"Class?" Guerrin said as the two pilots continued across the foyer.

"All the girls are taking classes," Captain Bathlick replied. "It may be a harem but apparently the Kildar would rather move them out with an education under their belt. Apparently he only took them in at first because nobody else would. It was that or dump them on the street to be whores. Concubines was a good second choice. Actually, the one girl we talked to saw it as a first choice if she'd had one. The Kildar's a big guy around these parts."

"More than around *these* parts," Guerrin said.

"You noticed?" Captain Wilson said, dryly. "We got recruited by some spec-ops unit that works in the Pentagon. Just came to our apartment in D.C. and told us to get on a plane to Georgia, don't worry about visas, it's taken care of. And it was. You got flown over here like a FedEx package: guaranteed delivery by nine AM. They even diverted a C-130 on a relief mission for a part of this package. The guy has got *clout*."

"How long have you been here, if I can ask?" Guerrin said as Captain Bathlick, the shorter one, opened an obviously heavy door. When it was open it was apparent that it was steel and about as thick as an armored hatch on a cruiser. Since it was covered in a thin wood facing—not veneer: very thinly sliced wood—the sturdiness wasn't apparent. Anybody trying to force the door was going to have to use some very advanced entry techniques. An oxyacetylene torch probably wouldn't even cut it.

"Not long," Captain Wilson answered. "We got recruited, flew over, agreed to the job, flew the same day to the Czech Republic, trained in on the bird and then flew it back. We only got here, again, a couple of days ago. We're still trying to catch our breath."

The door led to a narrow spiral staircase. Fighting down is always easier than fighting up but Guerrin would *not* have wanted to fight down these. At the base was a small landing, another heavily armored door, this one undisguised, then a T-intersection to a corridor lined with doors.

"Welcome to the dungeons," Captain Bathlick said. "To the right is the TOC, commo room, signals intelligence and commander's combat office. To the left is the humint area. Prisoner holding and interrogation chambers on the lower levels."

"Holy shit," Guerrin said. "This is a much bigger operation than I'd realized."

"Yeah," Captain Bathlick said. "When we got here we saw these, well, peasants running around with guns and thought 'what the fuck, over?' Then we started dealing with them and, well, the Keldara are *something*. I've barely had any dealings with the Kildar, mind you, but he's pretty interesting, too."

"Hmmm . . ." Guerrin said then grinned. "I'm coming up on my open resignation time. I wonder how you get a job around here?"

"You get *asked*," Captain Wilson said, chuckling. "And you have to be very *very* good at what you do." She paused and then grinned. "My, that sounded arrogant."

"Ladies, you plucked me out of some trees and dropped me out of a SABO with the smoothest skill in a helo I've ever seen," Guerrin replied. "And now you tell me you've only got a couple of days in the bird. I'm not going to knock your 'arrogance.' "

"Why Captain, I do believe that was a compliment," Captain Bathlick said. "Kacey," she added, holding out her hand.

"J.P.," Guerrin replied. "It stands for Jean-Paul. Long story."

"*Star Trek* fans?" Kacey asked, then shook her head. "Nah, that was Jean-Luc . . ."

"Tamara," Tammy added. "It's a short story. I'm named after a space hooker."

"Excuse me," J.P. said, blinking.

"Love it," Tammy said, laughing at his expression. "It's a character in a book . . ."

"Tamara Sperling?" J.P. asked. "Tamara Sperling was *not* a 'space hooker.' She was a *hetaera*. More like one of the Companions in *Firefly*. Very *high* status."

"My God," Kacey said. "The man reads Heinlein and knows about *Firefly*. There may be hope for the Rangers after all."

"I know," Tammy said, more or less simultaneously. "But I like 'space hooker' better."

"TOC's towards the end," Kacey said, continuing down the hall. "I'm not sure if you're permitted in intel or not so we'll just go there."

The door was steel again, undisguised this time. Not as heavy as the vault doors to get into the basement area but still solid. Take a good breaching charge to take it out. Inside there was a young woman in digi-cam at a computer station with Colonel Nielson leaning over her shoulder. There were several more stations, most powered down, and a conference table on the left with a large map of the area on the wall behind it. Another wall had six big plasma screens, three of them set to world news, the other three set to remotes somewhere in the mountains.

The major difference from any TOC Guerrin had ever seen was besides the usual coffee station there was a tea samovar and an espresso machine. Other than that, and the fact that every bit of equipment was state-of-the-art, it could have been an American TOC anywhere in the world.

"Captains," Nielson said, turning and nodding then turning back to point to something on the computer. He said something in a foreign language Guerrin didn't get.

"*Da*," the girl said, clicking the mouse. "Uploading." The latter was English.

"Welcome to Chaos Central," Nielson said, straightening up. "Captain Bathlick, we've got your LZs. Which to use depended on weather. There's some really heavy weather coming in. I'm not sure we can make the drop early this evening. It might be late tonight. And the winds may still be high."

"We'd better go get some crew-rest, then," Kacey said. "Brief later?"

"That works," Nielson said. "Brief at 2000 and liftoff based on weather?"

"Should work," Kacey replied. "One helo?"

"You should have lift for it," the colonel replied. "You're bringing in the body armor on this one, though. It will probably require three sorties. Touch and go. Just dump the shit out the door and keep moving. Don't stop. You're getting into the edge of Injun country on this one. The Keldara will be securing the LZ but that doesn't mean it will be fully secure."

"Okay, in that case I'm *definitely* gonna get some rest," Tammy said. "Night ops in a new bird in the mountains doing a drive-by. Sleep is a good thing. Captain Guerrin, catch up with you later."

"Okay," Guerrin said. "Later."

"Nice girls," Nielson said after they'd left. "Marines. They got involved in a hairy mission and the Marine brass freaked and yanked all their females out of any potential combat missions. So they went looking for work."

"The guy who plucked me out of the trees said he'd been a PJ," Guerrin noted.

"D'Allaird, the crew-chief," Nielson said. "He *was* a PJ once upon a time. Burned in on a jump and got too banged up. He transitioned to crew-chief in the Air Force and then, for some reason, jumped to the Marines in rank. Spent the rest of his career as a Marine avionics guy."

"Well, he seemed to know his shit," Guerrin said.

"While there are some that are learning the trade," Nielson said, looking fondly at the young lady at the computer, "we only hire people who 'know their shit.' There's a fairly tight job market for such people at the moment, admittedly. But there are perks to this job that working in the sandbox doesn't afford. Among other things, Georgia is just a prettier country than Iraq or Afghanistan. And you haven't had a chance to sample the beer, yet, but you're in for a treat."

"Sounds good," Guerrin, wondering, again, how one got a job working for the "Kildar." "What's up?"

"I thought we'd go over the local area and where you might want to operate in a bit more detail," Nielson said. "And I thought you should get oriented to where the TOC resided. I don't know if you're planning on going out with your patrols or controlling from here. We can maintain commo pretty solidly. Our top commo guy is, unfortunately, 'out of town' but we've got a distributed network for the area that we can hook your teams into. For backup, I'd say sat phones for each of your platoon leaders. We have plenty available. And I take it you brought your own commo."

"Yes, sir," Guerrin replied. "I'm planning on leaving Third Platoon in place and deploying First and Second. I'll centralize our heavy unit where they can move to support either team. And, yes, I'll probably stay here until there's contact. I'd like to move forward if we get in contact or if we have to support the retreat of the Keldara."

"That may depend on assets," Nielson said. "We've only the two choppers and two pilots. They are probably going to be in support of the Keldara. On the other hand, I could see them capable of dropping you on or near your units on the way by. We'll have to take that one on the fly. There's a road, vehicle capable, that runs to quite close to where I anticipate the Kildar retreating. Again, that part is going to depend upon enemy reaction. I would suggest, however, that you bring in your platoon leaders and such and brief them in sometime this evening."

"Yes, sir," Guerrin said. "1700?"

"Fine," the colonel replied. "Then we can repair to the bar to *really* discuss the mission."

"Gentlemen, welcome once again to the valley of the Keldara," Nielson said.

The Ranger officers and NCOs had been brought down to the headquarters room for their briefing and were looking around in interest.

"Sir, if I may," First Sergeant Kwan said, "when they said we were going to be aggressing against some Georgian mountain infantry, this wasn't exactly what I expected."

"The commander is an American," Nielson said. "What he was prior to ending up here you don't have the need to know. Frankly, I don't know the whole story. But when he moved here, he decided that he needed a militia. The Chechens had been using this area as their personal fiefdom and he chose to change that. Since he knew what good equipment, and training, could do for a militia, especially if they had the basic instinct to make good soldiers, he didn't stint on spending. As it turns out, the Keldara very much *do* have that special trait, in spades. Any of you gentlemen history majors?"

"Here, sir," First Lieutenant Mund, the Third Platoon leader, replied.

"The Keldara are a remnant of the Varangian Guard, Lieutenant," Nielson said with a grin. "Ring a bell?"

"Viking bodyguards of the Byzantine Emperors?" Mund said with a furrowed brow. "What are they doing up here?"

"Long story," Nielson said. "For the rest of you gentlemen, understand that the Keldara are mountain fighters from *way* back. And they've kept the tradition even while being farmers. They are . . . fierce. Like the Gurkhas or the Kurds they are warriors first and farmers a distant second. Not that they're bad farmers. However, you're likely to not deal with them at all. What you are doing is covering their back and *acting* as if you're fighting them. Captain Guerrin?"

"This is the Guerrmo Pass," Guerrin said, pointing to the map on the wall. "While Third Platoon stays in place with the Keldara, First and Second will move to this region and perform patrolling, carefully staying on *this* side of the pass. The other side is serious Injun country.

"As previously mentioned, they should take both blank and live ammo. From time to time they can act as if they have raided or ambushed someone using blanks. However, they should only load blanks, fire, then reload with live ammo. For that reason, don't actually have anyone in the kill zone. Just play act. We're supposedly aggressing against the Keldara. The impression is that we're an American unit which has taken a hostile town while the muj types ran to the hills. We're trying to comb them out. The reality is that the Chechens still, occasionally, try to penetrate the area. So keep your units hot at all times unless you're performing one of the deception missions. I'll give you each written op orders detailing your area of patrol. Third."

"Here," Lieutenant Pope replied.

"The Keldara women handle fixed defenses," J.P. said. "So your guys are going to have to interact with them. Rules on that are no male is to be present with less than two women at any time. Preferably work in groups at all times. But part of the defenses are bunkers and there are only so many who can fit in them. Make sure there's no hanky-panky and brief your men that if there are any complaints, they are automatically considered to be in error if there was any way there *could* be a complaint. Understood?"

"Yes, sir," Pope said.

"Full op order," J.P. said, tossing sealed manila envelopes on the table. "In those is a sealed envelope containing secondary missions and communications details. If you're told to open them, do so. In the event that you are in a position to be captured or killed, ensure the destruction of the contents. In the event that the carrier goes down, brief your personnel that destruction is paramount, even over survival. Clear?"

"Yes, sir," the group chorused.

"Yes, we're here as a deception mission," Guerrin said. "But in the event that the deception fails we have a secondary mission. You get briefed on that only if it goes off. For now, just go play in the hills. The weather should be great for it."

Chapter Twenty-Eight

The weather was preparing to suck.

The mountains were really steepening up. They'd gotten out of anything that couldn't be called "low" at this point and were well into the "high-up."

Between that and the decreased O2, Mike had slowed the pace. They weren't quite going at "mountain speed" yet, but close.

It was coming on towards dawn and what he hadn't seen, yet, was a good hide point. Hiding twenty people, above the woodline, was a chore. But they were going to have to go to ground. Soon. Like vampires, they couldn't be out in the light.

They were moving up a narrow defile with an ice and boulder-choked stream running down the middle. He could just have them disperse to the sides of the canyon in their bivvies, but he didn't like the looks of the weather. He also hadn't been able to check his BFT gear recently. There was a storm coming in, but it wasn't supposed to hit until late in the day. The way the clouds were building, it was going to be sooner. Given the storm, they might have to hunker down well into the night. The supply drop was going to be problematic.

They also hadn't changed into their really heavy alpine gear yet. The weather was still a bit too warm. The heavy alpine gear was for temperatures near or below zero Fahrenheit. Currently it was just a tad above freezing and the standard fleece jackets were plenty. Probably too much; he was sweating a bit.

But the temperature usually climbed just a bit before a big storm. It would drop as it hit and drop more as it passed. Changing gear was going to be a pain in the ass, but necessary.

Finding a good hide site was even more necessary.

The stream had petered out and they were really scrambling, now. The slope was about sixty degrees, not quite vertical but close. Easier to negotiate on all fours, even with the ruck on his back. The Keldara struggled in a line up the slope to just below the crest while the lead poked his head up. After a moment the lead turned and looked at Mike, pointing to his eyes.

Mike scrambled the rest of the way up the slope and cautiously poked his head up, turning it to the side to reduce the silhouette. Then he looked at the lead, Mikhail Ferani, and nodded, smiling.

Down below was a large cluster of boulders, probably dropped by the glacier they were headed for in its retreat. The teams could snuggle into the area, about an acre in size, easily.

The point had already made it up the next ridgeline but the trail was looking back and as Mike looked at him he pointed to the boulders. Mike gave a thumbs-up then turned to the lead and pointed at the boulders.

Their day hide was in sight.

There wasn't a *fucking* place to hide.

Adams didn't want to push the movement much more. They were marching along the side of a ridge, getting pretty close to the snow line and not having a great time of it. The damned trails were slick with ice in places.

And there wasn't a fucking place to hide. Mountains reared in every direction and he felt like an ant on a floor. *Anybody* could fucking see them as soon as the sun came up and it was already starting to get light.

The only choice was going to be to hunker down in their bivvies with netting over them and hope like hell nobody noticed them. It wasn't good tactics at *all*.

The point had already crested the ridge and getting him back was going to be a pain in the ass. And the weather was closing in;

the upper summits had already disappeared in clouds. It was about to either rain or snow, or maybe both, like a bitch.

Which would at least reduce visibility.

Finally he called a halt and signaled for the lead to go up and pull in the point. The damned sun was just about up and it was time to try to hide in plain sight.

He gestured for the team to spread out and then opened up his rucksack, pulling out his sleeping bag, which was already encased by a bivvy sack. Short for "bivouac," the bivvy sack was a water-proof covering that could have a slight stiffener emplaced to keep it off the face. Adams hated the damned stiffeners so he always left his behind.

He rolled the bivvy out and secured it to the thin soil of the hillside then yanked out a ghillie net and covered the sack. Last he slid his rucksack under the net and climbed into the sack.

Dafyd Shaynav, the assistant team leader, had followed his lead but now paused and made the gesture for "sentry."

Adams shook his head and gestured to get in the sack and freeze. Then he pointed to the sky.

Dafyd nodded then laid out his gear as the master chief had. But instead of immediately getting in the sack he began circulating, making sure everyone else was secure and camouflaged. That was his job.

Adams zipped the bivvy up, slid his hand out to pull up the net, then closed the bag all the way. He'd get out and look around in a minute, right now he wanted to check the weather.

He slid out of his jacket, got his weapon to one side and then pulled out the BFT satellite communicator. It was set to receive only but he could do a weather check.

Sure enough, the storm was moving faster than predicted. The satellite view showed it already raining at their location. This was so gonna suck.

When the sound of the Keldara getting into position died away he stuck his head out of the bag and looked around. It wasn't full light, yet, so he slid out and walked up the hill.

It wasn't as bad as he'd feared. Since he *knew* what he was look-ing for he could tell where the bivvies were. But the netting really *did* break up the outline. They didn't look like much of anything.

From the mountainsides around them they were probably invisible. And even close up they were going to be hard to spot.

He slid back in his sack but kept the top off his face. The lead and the point still weren't back. He wouldn't really settle in until they were.

A snowflake hit his face and he winced. They'd better fucking hurry.

Danes Devlich shook his head.

"They were right *there*," he said, pointing to the hillside which was rapidly disappearing in the snow. The snow was falling straight down, now, but he could tell by the taste of the air that it was soon going to be storming.

"There's a hot spot," Jachin Ferani, the point leader, said shaking his head. "But . . . Oh, now I see it," he added.

The sun was already up and they knew they were supposed to be out of sight. But they also didn't want to lose their team. Not with a storm coming.

"Where?" Tomas Kulcyanov asked. All three of the team were down on their bellies, just below the crest of the ridge. Jachin was using thermal imaging binoculars that could be switched for normal vision while Tomas and Danes were peering through standard range-finding binos.

"Right where Danes was pointing," Jachin said, chuckling. "In bivvies with their nets over them."

"Damn," Danes said after a moment. "That is weird. I was looking right at them . . ."

"We can make it down in about five minutes," Tomas said.

"If we hurry," Jachin pointed out. "We're not going to hurry. We're going to do the same thing. Right here."

It had been nearly an hour since the team had bedded down when Adams heard a double click in his headphones. The point was, presumably, nearby but not coming in. Okay, he could live with that. They probably didn't want to move in the light. He clicked once in reply. As he did, the wind started to pick up and the bivvy started flapping, hard.

"Well, this is gonna totally suck," Adams whispered as the blizzard descended in earnest.

✧   ✧   ✧

"Well, I think that Mr. Jenkins would say that this 'sucks,'" Colonel Chechnik said, his jaw working as he read the report.

Russia's intelligence agency did not have the technology or funds of its American equivalents. It made up for both by having much better spies.

The fall of the Soviet Union had released a flood of information related to the "spy war" between the U.S. and the Soviets going back to the 1930s and the returns were pretty much in: The Soviets had hammered the U.S.

The Russians had moles in most of the major defense and intelligence agencies not only in the U.S. but in all of the West. They had penetrated almost every communications department, most secure research and regularly had people with access to the White House. They'd managed so many disinformation operations that straightening out fact from fiction was taking careful work by historians. For example, the entire Vietnam "peace movement" had been KGB funded, as were many journalism departments.

After the Fall, they'd had a hard time maintaining those links. But they had managed to retain very good humint in other areas.

Notably Chechnya.

While, as with the U.S., it wasn't really helping them win the war, they often knew of movements before the Chechen high command. And when the High Command knew . . . well . . .

Chechnik looked at the document and sighed. He had placed a mid-level request related to the general area of the Keldara mission. And this was the result.

He looked at the phone, then the document then the phone. Finally, grimacing, he picked it up.

"I need to speak to the President."

"You wanted to speak to me?" Nielson said, looking up.

Kacey and Tammy were in their new Keldara uniforms rather than flight suits since, given the hairy-ass missions of the last couple of days, they were taking a well-earned rest day.

"Colonel," Kacey said, shifting uncomfortably in her new digicam. "Missions went fine. Clean in and out. How're the teams?"

"Now we're in blackout," Nielson said, shrugging. "Hell of a storm on the way in. If they get into serious trouble they'll call. But that's likely to blow the mission. You know the orders the Keldara have on injuries?"

"No, sir," Tammy answered.

"In the event that the casualty is anything but life-threatening and saveable by extraction, they are not to request evac. If the casualty is immovable, a broken leg for example, they and their partner will remain in place until after the mission and then be extracted if and when. We more or less anticipate Keldara being strung across the mountains until we can pull them out."

"Holy crap," Kacey breathed.

"That sucks," Tammy said. "I mean, really sucks. I can see the reason, but . . ."

"So I have no idea how the teams are doing," Nielson said, smiling thinly. "For all I know, they could have been wiped out in an avalanche. We won't know for . . ." He paused and checked his watch. "For four days and about twenty-one hours."

"Understood, sir," Kacey said. "And I notice most of the Rangers have moved out."

"Third Platoon is tasked with local security," Nielson said. "The other two platoons are up in the hills. I'd like you to coordinate with Captain Guerrin on any air support he might need. Doing at least one training mission with them would be wise to work out any bugs in methods or communication."

"Will do, sir," Kacey replied.

"And if that is all . . . ?"

"Actually, sir, we really came about something else," Tammy said then nudged Kacey.

"Sir, we were looking at our budget . . ." Kacey said.

"Just say it, Captain," Nielson replied with a smile. "I don't need a PowerPoint presentation."

"We'd like to do some . . . customization to our birds," Kacey said, walking over to his desk and sliding a sheet of paper onto it. "I think we can do it just by shuffling a few items in the budget around. We don't have two load masters and don't really need them. We used a couple of the Keldara girls, who are budgetable lighter, for the supply drops and that worked fine. At some point the chief can probably train them in on more complex tasks. So we can shift that portion of the budget around. And the chief has some assets for parts that can probably cut our anticipated costs there. Even with the mods we should be able to cut some out of the budget."

"I see," Nielson replied, looking at the calculations. "And these mods are . . . ?"

"Well, that's pretty hard to explain," Tammy said, nervously. "Here's a sketch," she added, sliding a new sheet of paper onto the desk.

Nielson regarded it for a second and then grinned.

"Who came up with this?" Nielson asked, still grinning. "You gals or Chief D'Allaird?"

"We were talking about force multipliers," Kacey said. "And I don't know who said it first but we all thought of it at the same time."

"The only thing I can't figure out is why the Kildar didn't first," Nielson said. "Approved. And you might want to add express shipping on it," he added with a grin. "It would be interesting to have it for the next series of missions."

"How will this affect the mission?"

Getting to speak to the president of Russia, even when you have hot intel in your hand, was not easy. It was late in the day and Chechnik had been told he had only ten minutes.

Fortunately, the president was a former spook, so they could cover the ground fairly quickly.

"If Sadim sticks to this time table, it will make extraction very difficult," Chechnik said. "Especially if they do not know about it."

"If they know about it they are likely to cancel the mission entirely," the president said, looking at the report again with cold eyes. "If I understand the timing, this should not affect the basic mission. They should be able to capture the package and destroy it long before this affects them. As long as they are not detected on insertion."

"Correct, Mr. President," Chechnik said, his face closed.

"What is the means?" the president asked. That information was not on the basic document.

"Dassam," Chechnik replied, frowning.

"So the only data that we have is from our highest-level source in the Chechen resistance," the president said, slipping the document back into its folder. "There are no intercepts, no lower-level confirmation?"

"No, Mr. President. Just this."

"The Keldara can complete the basic mission," the president said, handing back the document. "If they reacted on the basis of this it might reveal the source. They are not to be informed. The Kildar is resourceful. Let him figure out how to survive."

Mike paused, looking up at the front of the glacier and frowning.

The storm of the previous day had laid a blanket of snow that, while deep, wasn't particularly trying. But a night's full movement had brought them to the base of the glacier that was, from his point of view, their major obstacle. Just getting up on it was going to be a pain in the ass. The glacier had plowed out the valley it formed in, ripping away the hard rock walls and even if there had been "easy" ways up before it formed, thousands of years before, they were now gone.

However, he needed to get up onto the damned thing. The best route he'd been able to find crossed the glacier. While that had its own issues, they were minor compared with the problems every other route presented. The Keldara were fine at walking in mountains, even very steep ones. They weren't, by and large, quite so up on going up vertical faces.

The best approach seemed, based on both the satellite photos and his own eyeball, to be the left. But even that was damned near vertical. He'd planned on just tackling the face, about seventy-five feet and about a 3 face, maybe a 4. However, thinking about it there was an easier way.

The glacier was flanked on either side by ridges that stretched in a serpentine up to the two nearby summits. They were currently positioned on the shoulder of the left ridge and the ascent on that looked fairly smooth and the worst pitch was maybe 60 to 70 degrees. They could walk that. Once they were above the glacier they could just rappel down to the surface.

He signaled to the point to head up the ridge and started walking again.

They'd gotten down to "mountain speed," take a step, plant your ice axe, take a slow, deep breath, take another step. It was a slow way to move but the only way when the air got this thin. And the step-breath speed had several added benefits.

High mountains had dozens of ways to kill you.

The first and most obvious was just falling. The team was roped together so that if someone started to slip down on of the faces the rest of the team could stop their slide and recover them. But whole groups had slid off mountains before this. It was one of the things he was worried about with Yosif's team. The step-breath pace meant each member of the team had time to get sure footing before taking the next step.

More subtle was hypoxia. Air pressure fell off fast above ten thousand feet. They weren't in the super high, such as the Himalayas, but the air was *definitely* thin. At this level mild to extreme hypoxia was a real danger. Hypoxia occurred when the cells of the body exhausted all of their oxygen. Symptoms were headache, extreme exhaustion and nausea. At the extreme, convulsions or even death were possible as the body's tissues wrestled oxygen away from the nerve cells, which required one hell of a lot of O_2. By moving slowly and deliberately it gave the body time to move all the oxygen it could grab around to the spots that needed it. If they moved faster the big muscles of the thigh, the reason that runners had to breathe so hard, would start hogging the stuff.

And water was an issue. With the body needing more oxygen, the blood started to produce more red blood cells, thickening it. You had to drink and drink *a lot* to keep the blood from getting thick as molasses.

Another danger was sweating. Even as cold as it was, and it was *really* fucking cold, well below zero Fahrenheit since they were moving at night, if you moved too fast you could break into a sweat. That was just fine under normal conditions. But up here if you sweated at some point you'd slow down and stop being so warm. Then the sweat would freeze onto your body, just like the frozen snot in his nose that tickled like mad and crinkled his nose hairs. If that happened, the only thing for it was for the whole team to stop and get whoever had broken a sweat into cover. They'd have to strip off their wet clothes, put on dry and cool down. If they didn't, when the sweat froze it would suck every bit of heat out of their body, fast. The term for that was "hypothermia." And just like hypoxia, it was deadly. Once the body dropped below a certain temperature it started to shut down.

To keep from sweating, despite the temperatures the team had their jackets partially unzipped and most were only wearing a balaclava over their face and head. Gear-wear ran a knife edge as thin as the ridge they were walking up. If you wore too many clothes you got too hot and started sweating. By the same token, any exposed flesh was liable to frostbite.

Keeping an eye out for hypothermia, frostbite and hypoxia was the job of the assistant team leaders. Heck, it was everybody's job. When a person became hypothermic or hypoxic their judgment dropped to nil. And frostbite only occurred after a portion of skin had become so numb from cold you couldn't tell it was frostbitten. The only way to tell was to look. And it was hard to look at your own face.

The problem was, what with the exertion, fatigue and general malaise caused by the low O2, everybody was thinking slower and so worn all they could do was concentrate on the next step. Mike found he had to flog his brain to get it to work. It was worse than being awake for a couple of days.

The team paused to rotate the point and he was willing to just stop and breathe for a bit. The guys breaking trail couldn't take the added exertion for long. Mike had set a hard time limit of twenty minutes on trail-breaking and everyone, including him, took turns.

Just climbing up the slopes, carrying one heavy-ass ruck, with a quarter the amount of oxygen available in lower areas, was hard enough. But when you also had to stamp down snow on each step it became a nightmare. So they were rotating. Mike found himself only two back from the front as they shifted the safety rope back. The previous point was standing by the side of the trail, carefully balanced on the edge of the knife ridge, just breathing deep. Mike wasn't sure, what with the helmet, goggles and face mask over the guy's face, but he was pretty sure it was Sawn.

"Sweat?" he asked as he passed the previous trail breaker. He checked to see there was no exposed flesh but as far as he could see Sawn was covered from head to toe.

"Good," Sawn said, gasping. "Tired. Fucking tired. No sweat."

"Good . . . man," Mike gasped back, taking another step. Even conversation was impossible.

Three more days.

Pavel slid the piton hammer into place and triggered it, slamming one of the spikes into the rock wall.

Pavel had never taken rock climbing training. He had only recently begun, through the internet connections the Kildar had installed, to realize there were others like him in the world. For among the Keldara Pavel had always been considered strange; he liked to climb.

The Keldara would sometimes, when grazing was bad, run their sheep, goats and cattle into the high valleys. And while sheep were stupid, goats were canny. They frequently did not *want* to come back to the corrals at night. And goats could climb. My, could they climb.

Since Pavel was very young, he had followed the herds into the mountains. And since he was a child it was often Pavel who went searching for the recalcitrant goats. Because anywhere a goat could go, and more, Pavel could, and would, go. With a grin on his face. The higher, the stranger, the more brutal the face, the more he enjoyed himself.

Currently he was in heaven. The Kildar had carefully pointed out the "difficult" portions of the mountain crossing to him, the places where it would be necessary to climb. And the device in his thigh pocket said that this face would be about fifty meters. Because of the angle of the shot, nearly vertical, it was hard to judge how difficult the climb would be. But the Kildar, although an excellent fighter, was clearly not an imagery analyst.

It was more like a hundred and fifty, much of it about a grade five if he was capable of judging. It was night, the clouds finally cleared off and the wind howling. It was probably forty below zero in Celsius. And he was splayed across a rock wall, one finger stuck in a crack, his boots barely scrabbling to two more points and slamming in a piton with the biggest grin in the world on his mask-covered face.

This was the fucking shit, as the master chief would say.

He clipped a carabiner to the piton, ran his safety line through it and looked for the next set of hold points. Frankly, directly up there weren't any. But he'd seen an *easy* ledge off to the side.

He let go of all three points, holding himself only on the piton and swung sideways. For a moment he was suspended in the air, flying free as a bird. Then one hand slammed into the crack in the rock, the "easy" ledge that was a bare jutting of rock, and thumb and finger clamped to it like a limpet.

For a moment he hung, suspended, then the other hand came up, sliding a pair of fingers into the crack and clamping them in a knuckle hold. There wasn't anywhere to put his feet, but he could see another hold just a half meter or so up. He'd have to leave the fingers in the crack and lift himself on those to get to it.

This was assuredly the shit.

"How long we gonna be doin' this shit?" Serris asked.

They'd been out on the mountains for only a day and already he was ready to head back to the barracks. First of all, there wasn't a thing moving except them. You got a feel for an area pretty quick and all the animals they'd run across had that "undisturbed" feel. They'd sat on one trail in ambush positions all day and half the night and seen dick all.

Then there was the terrain. The area reminded him of Afghanistan except for the, often thick, underbrush and the trees. The vegetation was more like around Dahlonega, the Rangers' primary mountain training area. But the slopes were one *fuck* of a lot higher; Dahlonega was in the Appalachians not the fucking Alps. And they seemed steeper. They'd been slithering upwards towards the treeline for the last day, except for the ambush position, and they could quit any time as far as Ma Serris' little boy was concerned.

This was just stupid.

"Till we're done," Staff Sergeant Jordan Lawhon said. "Time to do one of our 'deception operations.'"

The Ranger squad had stopped on the east slope of a ridge, looking out over a small valley that had a trail running down the far side. Just to their north and west the valley funneled to a pass through the mountains, the source of the trail. The deciduous trees and choking underbrush of the lower slopes had given way to firs, mostly wide spaced. A careful visual check hadn't spotted anyone in view, though, so it seemed like a good place to do a "notional" ambush.

"This is such shit," Lane replied, flopping down and leaning back on a tree. He opened up the breach on his Squad Automatic Weapon and pouted. "I'm gonna foul the shit out of this, you know that? I'm gonna have to break it right the fuck down, clean it and *then* maybe I can load live rounds again."

"Quit the bitching," Lawhon said, frowning. "We're all gonna have to clean our pieces. Which is why only Alpha and Bravo team are gonna fire. Charlie's gonna stay hot."

Squads were broken down into two "fire teams." Each of the fire teams was led by a sergeant or corporal and had five men, the team leader, a SAW gunner, a grenadier and two riflemen. At least on paper. Rarely was a TOE, table of organization and equipment, filled.

"Fine," Lane sighed, pulling out his blank adapter and a case of blank ammo. "Let's get this over with. We gotta run and shout or what?"

"I think we just shoot the shit," the squad leader said. "Maybe do some shouting."

"This is fucking nuts," Serris said, readying his weapon. "Say when."

"Everybody ready?" Lawhon asked. "Charlie, do *not* fire."

"Got it," Corporal John Pitzel, the Charlie team leader, replied. "Team, check fire." Since the team was sprawled out on the ground in the traditional "rucksack flop," that was unlikely.

"Okay, Alpha and Bravo, open fire," Lawhon said and pointed his blank-adapter-covered muzzle in the general direction of uphill before pulling the trigger.

The blank adapter was required because without the backpressure from the round that normally traveled down the barrel, the weapon would only fire one time and the receiver wouldn't cycle the next round into the breach. With the usually red blank adapter screwed into the barrel the weapon would cycle normally even firing the blank ammunition.

The other problem with blank ammunition was that it was dirty as hell. The propellant was a less refined material than the usual propellant in live rounds and coated the weapon in carbon that was difficult to remove. You could fire thousands of rounds through an M4 before it fouled. You might get a couple of hundred blanks out before the damned thing jammed solid.

Despite those facts the Rangers had as much fun as they could.

"ARRRRHHH!" Lane screamed, triggering expert five-round bursts from his SAW despite having the barrel cover laid over his right knee. "TAKE THAT YOU DIRTY RAGHEADS!"

"EAT SHIT AND DIE, ISLAMIC MOTHERFUCKERS!" Serris replied.

"YOUR MOTHER WAS A WHORE AND YOUR FATHER A PIG!" Lane screamed, not to be outdone.

"I WAVE THE BOTTOM OF MY SHOE IN YOUR GENERAL DIRECTION!!!" Serris added then looked up. "SARGE! WE'RE TAKING FIRE!"

"CHECK FIRE!" Lawhon screamed, diving to the ground. He had been firing properly, weapon tucked into his shoulder, leaning into the nonexistent recoil and aiming. In this case at a tree over by the trail, but training was training. Now he dove to the ground and looked up. Sure enough, the branches overhead were being cut by fire. "Where the fuck is *that* coming from?" The rounds were *big*. Maybe a fifty-caliber. And now that the firing had stopped, he could hear the weapon firing, the dull thud-thud-thud of a heavy machine gun.

"Not in sight," Pitzel replied. "Sounds like it's coming from over the ridge."

"Serris, check it out," Lawhon said, instantly.

"Can I at least put live rounds in?" Serris asked, sarcastically. He already had the blank adapter unscrewed and was seating a mag of hot.

"Just get your ass up there," Lawhon replied.

"There you are, you fucker," Serris hissed. He'd pulled a ghillie cloak over his head and pulled up his balaclava to reduce the shine on his face then slid up the ridge to the crest. The top was a knife edge and by lying belly down, half behind one of the firs, he had a pretty good view of the far side. The valley they'd been in hooked around to the west and up at the head of it, right at the opening of the pass, there was a bunker. It was hard to spot, whoever built it had camouflaged the hell out of the damned thing, but Serris had spent enough time in the Stans to get pretty good at spotting shit like that. One of the reasons Lawhon sent him up. He also had "sniper eyes," the ability to pick out something from the background that others missed.

The bunker, though, was damned near two klicks away. They must have been firing at the sound. For that matter, thinking about the approach, the squad had never been in view of the guys, probably Chechens, in the bunker. The stupid fuckers had given their position away for *nothing*.

"Bunker up in the pass," he hissed over his shoulder to Lane. "Can't see anything in it. Probably a 12.7."

"Got it," Lane replied. "Here comes the sarge."

"What you got?" Lawhon asked from just down the slope.

"Bunker," Serris repeated. "Probably a 12.7. Maybe a 14.5. Nobody outside." He paused, bugged by something, he wasn't sure what. "Damn, make that two . . . no *three* bunkers. Any of them could have been firing."

"Could they see us?"

"Negative, wrong angle." Serris turned his head ever so slightly and verified that. Yeah, their whole approach had been out of sight. But if they'd gone another couple of hundred meters up the valley . . . "They're securing the pass."

"I called in," Lawhon replied. "We're to pull back. Our job is not to get into a pissing contest with them unless they come down from the mountains. Let's get the fuck out of here."

"Ay-firmative," Serris said, sliding ever so slightly backwards. "I don't want them taking my head off."

"Captain Bathlick," Colonel Nielson said. "Another familiarization flight?"

The pilot was just exiting her recently completed—there was still sawdust on the floor—ready room, helmet under her arm.

The first of the pre-fab hangars was in place. The structures were large versions of the venerable "Quonset" huts, large enough that the Hinds could be slid in with their rotors still on. They had come packed on dozens of pallets and the non-militia Keldara men had taken less than a day to get the first one up: the concrete holding up the curved metal skeleton was still drying.

Tacked onto one side was a small utility hut, the pilot "ready room." Kacey was pretty sure it was going to be cold as hell when full winter hit.

"Not plowing one of the birds on the supply-drop missions was luck as much as anything," Kacey said. "The more time we get in the birds the better. Especially at night."

"I agree," Nielson replied. "However, you might want to wait up a bit. The first thing you need to know is that we just found out the Guerrmo Pass is secured by heavy weapons."

"Damn," Kacey said, shaking her head. Guerrmo Pass was the lowest pass into the area of the Keldara operation. It was their primary route if they had to go in in support. All the other ways were much higher and, thus, they could carry less equipment in or casualties out. "That's bad news. How secured?"

"At least three bunkers with heavy machine guns at the opening," Nielson said. "Not sure what might be further in."

"The Hinds are tough, but . . ."

"But, indeed," Nielson admitted. "Not tough enough to take cross-fire from multiple heavy machine guns. So stay away from the opening to Guerrmo Pass. The second reason you might want to wait up is that we were just informed that there is a shipment from the Georgian military on the way. They said it was left over parts from their Hinds; they recently decommissioned them. You probably want to look it over. Chief D'Allaird as well."

"Great," Kacey said, grumpily. "DXed parts from the Georgians. These should be great."

"Never look a gift horse and all that," Nielson said, smiling.

"Oh, I'm not," the pilot replied. "But D'Allaird is going to have to fully cert them before they go in the bird. What are we going to do about the bunkers?"

"That is under discussion."

"Well ain't that some shit," Captain Guerrin said.

"I think we can take 'em out," Sergeant Lawhon offered. "They've got the pass covered. But if we swing up on the shoulder of the mountain we can come in on them from behind and above. Either hammer them from up there with Carl Gustavs or get a team down on top. I don't think they can fire at each other or back up the pass."

"And if they have supports further up the pass?" J.P. answered. "No, our mission isn't to take out bunkers. Certainly not yet." Guerrin paused and thought about the situation, both the "known" situation and the potential mission to support the Keldara. "But we need to keep an eye on them. Keep your squad up here. No more patrolling. Put in good security and keep a watch on that trail. Stay defiladed from the machine guns but if anything comes out of that pass I want to know about it."

"Yes, sir," Lawhon replied.

"I'm going to redirect the company in this general direction," Guerrin added. "So if you get in the shit, holler for help and we'll come a runnin."

"Well ain't this some shit."

Mike looked down the slope and wondered if he should have stopped earlier. He had been in the lead on the last stretch of the ascent so it was all his fault if they had. He unzipped his jacket all the way, feeling a bite of cold sink into his mid-layer of fleece pullover, and pulled out his rangefinders. The battery-powered range finders, along with *all* their batteries, had to be carried under their clothes to keep the power from being drained by the cold.

He looked through the binos and pressed the button for rangefinding. An invisible laser, good for about ten miles much less this short distance, lased the ground below and returned a range of nearly five hundred feet.

Fuck.

They had a couple of thousand foot ropes with them but he would have liked a bit more safety margin. However, this was as good as it was going to get.

He waved to Gregorii and Mikhail then dumped his ruck in the snow. The serious climbing gear was in an outside pouch and he pulled out the pre-rigged harness. Some climbers would have clucked in horror at the piton hammer and pitons he pulled out. However, at the moment environmental consciousness was the last thing on his mind.

He used his ice axe to clear away some of the snow until he found solid granite then looked for a crack in the face. The air-driven piton hammer would drive one of the stainless steel spikes straight into the granite. But a crack to start it was preferable. The *good* news was that it *was* granite. Feldspar or limestone, both prevalent in the area, both had the possibility of being highly friable. Friable rock had a tendency to shatter under pressure and release pitons. That would be *bad*.

He found a crack, finally, and loaded the piton hammer then laid the tip of the piton on the crack, leaned into the hammer, and fired it.

The sound rebounded across the rocks. If there were any Chechens around he'd just definitively given their position away. For that matter, he was lucky he didn't start an avalanche.

He punched in three pitons then connected caribiners to each of the pitons. The military called caribiners "D rings," a metal "ring," generally some form of oval with a sprung-loaded opening bale. Some people used them as key rings but they were originally designed for climbing. Finally, he took one of the ropes Mikhail handed him, uncoiled it and then recoiled it in two heaps. Taking the center section, he began tying it off. That was a bit complex. He didn't want to leave the rope behind so he had to put in a recovery knot. However, he also wanted to make sure that nobody fell, thus the three pitons. Putting in a three-way recovery knot was a pain in the ass. Finally, he managed it. The knot had a slipknot built into it that permitted someone on the ground to untie it by a hard yank on one of the two dangling ropes. The problem was that they could start to untie all by themselves under heavy use. The answer was to slide a pin of some sort into the loop of the slipknot until the last climber was ready to go down.

Finally he had the entire rig set up and stood up, groaning as his bad knee protested. One of these days that damned thing was going to go out entirely. Hopefully not today.

Mikhail looked at him quizzically for a second and then picked up the two coils and tossed them over the side. Both, fortunately, fell straight and true without tangling and the tips hit the ground, barely.

The reason for the quizzical look, Mike realized, was that he should have tossed the loops. His brain was *really* working slow.

Nonetheless, he pointed to Sawn and then at the rappel, at which Sawn nodded and stepped forward.

Everyone had already donned their climbing harnesses. These were padded nylon that ran around the upper body and under the arms. Earlier harnesses and those used for "light" mountaineering were a seat. But the upper body harnesses were necessary when you were working with rucks. Without them you tended to dangle upside down.

Sawn picked up the doubled ropes and attached them to his figure-eight. There were, Mike swore, as many ways to rappel as there were climbers. However, one of the simpler involved wrapping the rope through a doubled metal circle that looked vaguely like an 8 with one end much smaller than the other. They were only good for relatively short rappels, longer ones required a device called a "ladder." But Mike wasn't planning on doing any ten-thousand-foot rappels on this mission.

Sawn looped the ropes through the figure-eight, hooked it to his harness with a carabiner and stepped to the edge. He seated the ropes by leaning back on them while holding himself in place by the rappel line. The method of descent was simple. The tied rope ends, called the standing end, ran to the figure-eight then through a complex double loop. The untied end, the running end, then was held in the right hand of the climber. If he pulled the rope around his back it stopped him. Pulling it out to the side permitted the rope to slide through his hand. The left hand was placed on the standing end for stability. The important thing was to remember to bring the arm around rather than "grabbing" the running end. Grabbing didn't get you anything but a burned glove. The gloves Mike had ordered had leather palms specifically for rappelling but if the rope ran through the palm too fast or was gripped too hard it was going to burn through, anyway.

When he was sure the ropes were set, Sawn walked backwards to the edge of the cliff, looked down over his shoulder, placed his feet carefully on the ice-covered edge of the cliff and shook the rope slightly to keep it from binding. At the top of a long rappel the weight of the rope tended to stop the climber from descending due to friction across the figure-eight. Once his full weight hit, though, it would smooth out.

Finally, he was in an L shape, feet planted on the wall. At that point he began bounding slightly outwards from the cliff, falling a short distance on each bound, stopping when his feet hit the wall then bounding out and down again. He took it slow, which was good, but it meant the team was going to be rappelling when the sun came up. Bad.

Mike started putting in another set of ropes. Sigh. God he was tired. Hopefully something was going *right* on this mission.

"So far, so good," Rashid said as the Nissan pickup bounced down the potholed road.

Al-Kariya nodded but didn't answer, continuing to run a string of worry beads through his fingers.

The king-cab pickup was the third truck in a convoy of nine, each of them holding four to five handpicked mujahideen. Most of them Al-Kariya had known, off and on, for years.

Although he was now a "senior financier" he had not always had that job. After getting a degree in finance from Princeton he had disappeared for several years in the late 1970s. The first stop of his wide travels had been to the new government of Iran, where the Ayatollah Khomeini had recently overthrown the Shah and instituted Shariah law. This was a goal for which the Prophet, praise be upon him, decreed all good Muslims must strive. And the young Al-Kariya, then using the name Al-Dubiya, had reveled in the triumph of the True Faith over the secularism of that pig the Shah. Yes, Khomeini had been, in many ways, a blasphemer. The Shia branch of Islam believed that Mohammed had not been the last prophet, true blasphemy. But Khomeini had made much of the oil wealth of the nation available to any group that was willing to strive for worldwide jihad and the imposition of true Shariah.

Managing that wealth, stealthily, was difficult however. Moving the money was a pain when the Americans, French, Germans and Israelis were always poking in where they weren't wanted. Al-Kariya had seen his proper place in the worldwide jihad clearly. He knew the theoretical details of international finance back and forward. He knew the gaps, the hidden ways.

But you didn't just get handed a bunch of money no matter what your financial CV. You had to prove you truly supported the jihad. You had to be "made" in the fraternity of the mujahideen.

Thus, after a brief trip to the Bekaa Valley for training in a PLO camp, his next stop had been Afghanistan, where the war against the pig Russians was in high gear. There the Americans, for reasons everyone recognized as cynical, were pouring in material and funds. And there the young man with the soft hands and mind of a calculator had been "made," killing Russian conscripts patrolling in the mountains they feared and hated.

That was a long time ago, though. Now he remembered the smells, the fear, of those missions. It had been a long time since he had had his kidneys jolted out by horrible roads. A long time since he'd been surrounded by unwashed fighters.

Some of them, though, he knew from those long ago days. The fighters in this convoy were the best the jihad had to offer. These weren't human bombs or half-trained zealots that pointed their weapons in the direction of the enemy and sprayed their fire. Every member of this security detail had been on multiple battle-fields, fighting the Russians, the Israelis and, especially, the Americans in multiple countries. They had fought, survived and often triumphed. Most were older, though few as old as Al-Kariya. Haza Saghedi, though, the team leader riding in the fourth truck, he was an old comrade-in-arms from Afghanistan. Pashtun, raised in the fiercest of warrior traditions, he had even fought on the side of the Saudis in the war against Iraq. Then, later, he had been in Iraq fighting the Americans. He had taken the path of true jihad, fighting the infidels on every front and surviving. It was he who had picked most of the fighters in the convoy.

Al-Kariya assumed that if the Russians saw an advantage they would try to betray them. Piled next to him in the back seat of the truck was a king's ransom; any king you'd care to name. And the areas they were traveling through could not be considered "safe" by any rational human. Thus he had ensured that the very best were guarding it, and him. Yes, things were going well.

But all he could think as they bounced down the atrocious road was how much he wished he were back in his comfortable office, sitting in his two thousand dollar chair, with a glass of tea by his hand and clicking on his laptop.

Instead of having his kidneys jolted out.

"I'm getting too old for this" was his reply.

It was less than twenty minutes before first one, then two and finally *seven* tractor trailers made the sharp final bend into the valley. By the time the seventh was on the flats, a machine-gun toting GAZ, a Russian-made military SUV, had pulled into the newly laid helo-port in the lead of the first truck.

"Colonel Nielson," the captain said in crisp, faintly Brit-accented English. "Good to see you. My father-in-law sends his regards." He snapped a salute and dropped it at the colonel's reply.

"Ah, Captain Kahbolov, we've never met," Nielson said, shaking the captain's hand. "Captain Bathlick, Captain Efim Kahbolov. His father-in-law is the Georgian chief of staff. And he's a pilot as well."

"Good to meet you, Captain," Kacey said, shaking his hand.

"And you, Captain," the Georgian said, grinning. "I was originally trained on the Hind. I understand the Js are sweet birds. Hopefully these will help." He pulled an envelope out of the GAZ and handed it to Nielson.

"This is certainly generous," Nielson said, ripping open the envelope and sliding out the contents. He looked at the papers and then blanched. "Holy fuck, Captain."

"Which one?" Kacey asked, looking over his shoulder. However, the documents were in Cyrillic and incomprehensible.

"Thank your father-in-law, Captain," Nielson said, awe in his voice. He looked up at the trucks and shook his head. "Thank him very VERY much for us."

"They were going to be sold," the captain replied with a shrug. "My father-in-law thought that using them in the defense of the homeland made a better choice. Use them well, Captain. That will be worth the very long, very cold, ride."

"What?" Kacey asked, frowning. "What's the big deal about parts?"

"They're not parts, Kacey," Nielson said, handing her the documents while continuing to look at the trucks in wonder. "The lead truck is three complete gun systems for a Hind. The second has rocket launchers. The rest . . . is ammo."

The whole team was down, the sun was coming up and it was time for Mike to descend.

The view across the glacier was spectacular in the pre-dawn light. The blue pre-morning twilight reflected off the glacier and filled the valley with a glow quite unlike anything Mike had seen before in his life. It was something like being in the middle of a blue-white diamond. The figures of the Keldara below, rapidly setting up a camp and getting camouflage in place, seemed to walk through a mist of blue-white.

However, this wasn't a good time for sight-seeing; it was time to get down to business.

The only incident during the descent was that one of the Makanees ended up getting tangled halfway down the cliff. The guy was utterly unable to free himself so the next rappeller down stopped alongside and managed to get him free, mainly by cutting on his outerwear. That was gonna require patching. Then the two of them went down the rest of the way.

Mike had already tossed the second rope and now, with difficulty, yanked out the pins securing the primary. Storing those, he hooked up and stepped to the edge, pulling carefully on both ropes to ensure they were secure. So far, so good.

Someone was on belay below and he looked down and waved. The belay man was in place as a safety measure. If the climber descending lost control of the rappel, the belay man could, by putting pressure on the rope, stop him in place.

Mike stepped over the edge and got in a good L position, then bounded out. All good. It wasn't like he hadn't done this a thousand times.

However, about halfway down, the entire rig trembled and went momentarily slack, dropping him into freefall for a moment and then jerking him to a stop.

He'd done slack rappels enough times to recognize the signs. The primary slipknot had released. Whether it was the cold working on the ropes to make them more slippery or what, the slipknots were coming undone. If all three let go, he was going to fall three hundred feet onto solid ice covered in about an inch of snow.

The term was "splat."

As his feet touched the face he bounded instantly outward and threw his right arm out to the side, removing all pressure on the rope and falling, effectively, in freefall, the rope screaming through both hands with the smell of burning leather.

The fall, however, wasn't *quite* freefall: the friction of the rope running over the figure-eight prevented that. So in keeping with simple Newtonian physics, Mike was pulled back to the face in a long, slow swing. The arc of pendulum was very long, but inexorable. Thus about two hundred feet over the ice he had to slow, again, for a bound. As he did he felt the shock of the second knot giving way.

This time he pushed off, hard, and let loose of the rope almost instantly. He'd never really stopped at the bound and was falling fast enough it wasn't much different from a freefall jump. He wasn't sure whether he should do a parachute landing fall at the bottom or not. However, doing it with the ruck on his back was pretty much out.

He had one more, probably shaky, knot between him and splatsville. He had about two hundred pounds of gear wearing him down and nasty ice right underneath. And he was falling at about terminal velocity. Oh, and he was inexorably swinging in towards the face.

On the other hand, he had to admit that this was the sort of thing he fucking *lived* for. Adrenaline was pumping, the time seemed to slow and endorphins were riding high in anticipation of sudden and incredible pain. A degree of skill and one hell of a lot of luck were the only things between life a very messy death. Forget sex, forget gambling, this was life on the blade. The only moments better than this was the kill after a long stalk or being in the center of a fuckload of enemies, a larger number than a butt-load and just shy of a shitload, with several full magazines and a mild amount of cover.

Time had slowed and he expertly judged the distances involved. The arc of pendulum had opened out a lot on the last bound and he anticipated that, even with breaking, he shouldn't slam into the wall. He was going to have to brake, though, and that was where the luck came in. The variable was how long the last knot was going to last. Based on the previous two the answer was "not very fucking long, if at all."

He had two choices, brake slow and hope the knot held under the lighter, longer, pressure or brake hard. Hard was shorter time on the knot but more "pull."

In an instant he made the decision. Hard. Hell, he'd passed the point of "slow" anyway.

Fifty feet over the ground, and smokin', literally, he pulled the rope in and pressed it, hard, against his side and back.

Instantly he started to slow from a full freefall to something survivable. With luck. But he was still going pretty fast, maybe seven feet per second, when he felt the knot pop free with a shock.

The next moment his feet hit the ice and he rolled back onto his ruck. His kidneys did not enjoy that moment but he was alive to feel the pain. Pain was good.

"Nice," Sawn said from the belay as the rope started to fall all over Mike. "That was the most perfect rappel I've ever seen, Kildar. You didn't even have to undo the ropes."

Mike, from his position on his back, realized with a feeling of horror that Sawn truly believed it had all been planned.

"Yeah, well, that's why I went last," Mike said, as nonchalantly as he could under the circumstances. "When you've been doing this as long as I have you pick up a few tricks."

"You know," Kacey said, watching as the gun system was uncrated by a couple of the older Keldara men, "I think it's cool that the Georgians just *gave* us all this shit, but I just realized, I have no fucking *clue* how to use it."

Unloading had gone fast; it turned out the Kildar had, among other equipment, a field mobile forklift. All the crates had been pulled off and the gear stacked inside the hangar. The ammo had been carted off to the ammo bunkers.

"There is that," Tammy admitted. "I've never driven a gunship."

"Got a *partial* answer to that," D'Allaird said. "Problem being, we are on incredibly short time. You know the mission goes down tonight, right? You're going to have to be ready to fly."

"And I'd love to be able to fly hot," Kacey said. "But I don't even know where the damned buttons are for this shit. Much less how to shoot with it."

"Like I said, got a partial answer for that," D'Allaird repeated. "Would you ladies care to accompany me up to my room?"

"Chief," Tammy said, "I didn't know you cared!"

"Oh, I've always cared, honeybunch, but that's not what I meant," D'Allaird said. He'd scrounged one of the Keldara trucks and he now gestured to it. "I do think a trip to the caravanserai is in order, though."

"That's a very interesting place," Specialist Andrew Sivula said, gesturing with his chin up to the castle on the hill as an SUV approached the front gates. "We're not quartered up there, which is too bad. I'd love to take a look around."

"The home of the Kildar," Jessia Mahona replied, smiling. "I suppose it is interesting, but it has been there my whole life, you know? It just is. The Kildar, *he* is interesting. He has brought many changes. I never thought I would be allowed to handle weapons, much less my beauty."

Sivula had to admit that the 120 was pretty. With a tube nearly six feet long and nearly six inches across, the thing could throw a mortar round, set for proximity, instantaneous or delay detonation, 7200 meters. And it was pretty clear that the mortar team, all women, maintained it meticulously. The tube looked as if it had just come from the factory, but looking down the bore it was clear it had been fired. A lot.

However, pretty as the mortar was, it paled next to the mortar team leader. The girl was fucking awesome. Tall, about five foot ten and *stacked*, with pretty brown eyes and curly brown hair. Sivula was pretty sure he was in love. Her English wasn't bad, either. He *knew* he was in lust, but he was pretty sure it was love, too. He knew there was a hands-off policy, but he wondered who you approached about an honest offer of fucking marriage.

They weren't alone in the bunker, though. Four of the seven "man" female crew were performing maintenance on the tube while three more were showing the Bravo mortar team the ammo bunker while his AG tried to chat up one of the girls doing maintenance.

"I haven't played with 120s since I was in mortar school," the Ranger said in reply. It was that or "ubba, ubba, ubba." "We carry 60s. But I know the tune and I can dance a few steps."

"What?" Jessia asked, confused.

"Sorry, not a reference you'd get," Sivula replied. "I sort of know how to gun one. What I don't get is what you use for poles."

Normally, mortars were aimed using poles that looked a bit like surveyor's stakes and were drawn from the same background. The poles, technically called "aiming stakes," were about five feet long and, generally, red and white striped. Two would be put in, aligned so that when the mortar was at a central "rest" position the rear pole was occluded by the front in the sight. When a call for fire came in the angle was dialed in on the sight, then the mortar was slewed right or left in the direction it needed to point. By keeping aligned on the poles the mortar could be vectored to its direction of fire.

This mortar, though, was dug *way* into the ground. The bunker was one of the best he'd ever seen, deep with sandbag walls and a metal "splinter" cover that could be drawn across the top. There were three tunnels running off of it, one to a separate ammo bunker, the other two to the mortar battery command center and a personnel shelter, respectively. The personnel shelter, for that matter, connected to the next bunker in line.

Jessia was in charge of the 2 gun of the battery, the central gun that was used not only for calls for fire but for aligning all three batteries. That was generally a position given only to the best crew and Sivula had to wonder just how good she was.

"You don't need them with these," Jessia said, pointing to the wall of the bunker at some lines drawn on plywood boards. They were numbered in some code he hadn't been able to figure out. "The green one is the primary east aiming line. Lay the sight on the left side of that and you can slew through half the circle. The blue one is primary west."

"And the red ones?" Sivula asked, looking through the sight. Sure enough, it was laid on the left side of the green line.

"Those are presets," Jessia replied. "They refer to specific spots that are probable avenues of approach. If something is detected at one of those points, all we have to do is swing the mortar to it, adjust the elevation and fire. Like this . . ."

She snapped something in Georgian and the girls doing maintenance dropped what they were doing, literally dropped everything, while the girls who had been in the ammo bunker piled out. Four of them took hold of the legs of the bipod and lifted the heavy mortar into the air. Another, presumably the AG, caught a tossed round from one of the girls in the bunker and shifted with the mortar.

The team rapidly slewed the mortar and then Jessia fiddled for a second, not much longer, and called out again in Georgian.

One of the girls in the bunker hit a button and a loud siren started to sound. The girls who had slewed the gun stuck fingers in their ears as Jessia backed off the gun and the assistant gunner lifted the round over the opening of the tube.

"Holy shit," Andy snapped, sticking fingers in his ears and ducking to the side. "FIRE IN THE HOLE!"

A mortar does not "crump" at short range, it cracks, it slams, it explodes. It is like a rifle shot but infinitely louder, compressing the lungs for a moment and causing the head to ring even through earplugs or stuffed in fingers. Especially in the confined space of a mortar pit.

The team was already moving the mortar back into place and in another few seconds, fast enough, easily, to pass Mortar Square at Benning, the gun was back in action on its original azimuth.

"We just fired one round at a trail in the mountains, one that the Chechens often use. Our accuracy is generally within ten meters with first round. The round impacted well away from your patrols." Jessia smiled at him prettily. "Wouldn't want anyone injured."

"Lady, you are fucking crazy," Andy said, grinning. "I am going to get in so much trouble for asking this, but are you married or engaged?"

Jessia suddenly stopped smiling and her face set. Andrew knew he'd fucked up. Bad. He was going to get fucking killed by Top.

"Actually, no," Jessia replied. "I'm a widow."

It was Andrew's turn to freeze and blink.

"How *old* are you?" Andy asked.

"Nineteen," Jessia said. "My husband was killed . . . He was killed in battle. I . . . We don't talk about all the battles our men participate in but he was killed earlier this year. They didn't, couldn't bring his body home, though." She paused and shrugged. "He is in the Halls but . . . The women of the Keldara rarely remarry. There are too many girls to marry off as it is."

"So, you're just going to go to your grave without even the chance of getting another husband?" Andy said. "That sucks."

"I had my time," Jessia replied. "Endar was a good man and a fine warrior. As are you, Sergeant Sivula," she added, smiling.

Fuck, fuck, fuck, fuck . . . Andrew knew when the fickle finger of fate had fucked again. This was definitely love.

"You brought an Xbox?" Tammy said. "You love Halo that much?"

The chief's room was much better outfitted than either hers or Kacey's. Among other things it had a full stereo system, a plasma-screen TV and the game console. On a small desk there was a high-end laptop.

"I don't play Halo that much these days," D'Allaird said, slipping a disk into the console. "I found another addiction. And it turned out there were already a couple around."

It took a moment for the game to boot up, then he fiddled with the menu. Finally, they were looking at a very familiar view.

"It's a Hind combat simulator," D'Allaird said. "I ran across it a couple of months ago. Face facts, most engineers are guys who couldn't get into pilot training. This is the closest I get."

"Holy shit," Kacey said, sitting down in the floor chair in front of the TV. "But it's one of those controller things."

"Ah, no," D'Allaird said, pulling out a set of controls and sliding them over. "I've got two. You can split-screen and both pl—train at the same time. You can even work on coordination."

"These are pretty accurate," Tammy said, sitting down in an adjoining chair. "Why two chairs?"

"Oh, I've been playing with Colonel Nielson," D'Allaird admitted. "He's pretty good at Medal of Honor . . ."

"Gun position, left," Tammy yelled. "Fuck, I'm taking fire!"

"Got it," Kacey replied then paused. "Okay, actually I missed it, coming around."

"I've got a hot engine light! See ya! I'm down."

"I got the gun position, at least," Kacey said. "Try to land near the friendlies."

"There *aren't* any friendlies here," Tammy pointed out. "I'm going back to last checkpoint. I see you, coming in on your seven o'clock, low."

"There's another position on the other side of the ridge," Kacey said calmly, pulling back on the stick and then leaning sideways with another yank. "Scissor left."

"Got it."

"Directly south of that other position, one hundred yards. They're engaging me . . ."

"Got it. Smoked."

"Good," Kacey said. "You take lead, I'll take your right. I got dinged on that one . . ."

"Okay, wingman. You get the chicken."

"Hey!"

"I wonder if everybody on this op is having this much fun?"

"Probably not . . ."

Chapter Twenty-Nine

Katya sighed and lay down on the bed in her clothes, wrapping the thin blanket around herself and luxuriating in the aloneness. Soon the mission would be done and she could go back to her room in the caravanserai. She realized she had started to think of it as home and blanched. She *lived* "in the cold" as Jay would put it. There was *no*where in her world that was warm. She refused to allow the possibility.

But the thought of the walls of the caravanserai around her, the Keldara patrolling the mountains, the Kildar with his guns and his training, the lock on the door.

Crap. She was getting soft.

She stuck her hand under the thin, lice-infested pillow, felt her fingers touch paper and froze. She rolled over, pulling the blanket up more and slid the slip of paper out in one natural motion. Even if there was a video bug in the room it was unlikely anyone would see the motion. Unfortunately, there was no way she could read it in this light. She considered that for a moment then stuck it in her bra and got up.

The outhouse was cold as hell but there wasn't anyone around on a rainy and nasty night like this. Once inside, fearful of the results from the stench of the place, she struck a match and read the brief note.

"Switch for Marina tomorrow night."

Stuck to the paper was a small bit of plastic. Peeling it off she saw that it was a fake scar, identical to the one on Marina's chin. Fucking identical down to the slight hook at the base.

The note was signed simply: J.

"Oh. My. Fucking. God."

She realized there was no way she was going to be able to figure out which of the people in town the spy master was posing as. But just having him nearby gave her that warm feeling again. It was that, as much as the fact that he *was* here, that had caused the exclamation.

She was *not* getting soft. Not.

She touched the match to the paper and it flared briefly, with very little light, then disappeared into bare ash. She rubbed her fingers together, waved the match out and dropped it between her legs.

The scar went into her bra. Right by her heart.

The point paused at the entrance of the defile and looked in cautiously.

The weather, to most people, would fall into the category of "sucks." The clouds had dropped even more, filling the upland valley with fog mixed with rain, sleet and snow as if it couldn't figure out which way it wanted to go.

To Mike it was perfection. It was damned hard to see fifty feet, much less miles, which meant easier for the teams to stay out of sight.

The terrain wasn't bad, either. The clear uplands had been nervous making from the point of view of being spotted. And this side of the mountains was incredibly drier than just sixty miles away. The lowlands were mostly covered in tight, thorny thickets of scrub. Making their way through the tight-packed and dripping scrub had been a nightmare. Mike had figured about twice their movement rate and, with the sun well up, they were late to their rendezvous. But even that wasn't bad; they'd spotted two Chechen patrols before they themselves were spotted and let them waft right by. Tight scrub was pretty scrub in his view.

Now to find out if anybody else was going to make the show. God only knew when Yosif's team would make it. If any of them did. He'd half convinced himself Yosif couldn't find his way across a paddock, much less over the mountains and through this maze.

The designated rendezvous point was a narrow ravine packed with rhododendron. The stuff was normal in upland areas but on this side of the mountains it was only found in narrow clefts where there was sufficient water.

The area was large enough to hide all three teams, away from noticeable trails and, of course, good concealment given the nature of the vegetation. The only question was whether the Chechens had thought the same thing.

The majority of the team was on the slope of the larger valley the ravine intersected. There was a small stream running down the ravine, its waters still free of ice, and a larger one, fed by the glacier they'd crossed, running down the valley. To get to the ravine they'd have to cross the river but that wasn't the problem.

The point team, Ivan Shaynav and Mikhail Ferani, were cautiously observing the entrance from about fifty meters away. They apparently didn't like what they were seeing. Mike, peering through the underbrush in the way, wasn't sure what had them spooked.

Finally, Mikhail slithered forward on his belly to the juncture of the two streams and took up a position by a boulder. Back in his ghillie suit, over the heavy arctic wear they were all still encumbered by, he was hard enough for Mike to see. Probably any Chechen sentry wouldn't have noticed him, yet.

Mike saw him start, though, and then look around. Finally, clambering to his feet, Mikhail lifted one hand, middle finger extended in a rude gesture directed across the river.

A figure in an identical ghillie suit stood up, right at the edge of the open area, and threw back the hood of the suit. Then Yosif Devlich waved and tossed a rope across the stream.

Fucking Yosif had beat them to the rendezvous. Mike couldn't figure out why he'd ever been worried.

"Do we know the status on the Georgian mission?" the President asked. It was seven o'clock in Washington and about time for him to retire. Especially since he was planning on being up early. "And do we have Predators up?"

"We've got four on standby, Mr. President," the national security advisor replied. "Two will take off at midnight and two more just before dawn. All four are CIA UCAVs with Hellfire missiles. Just in case they can be useful. We do not have a status on the teams at this time. We caught a glimpse of what was probably one of them on a satellite pass last night. But the next pass we'd lost them. There has been no special movement noted in the Chechen camps on the last two passes."

"B-2 is on the way," the secretary of defense added. "Flying light. Two special munitions."

"Two?" the President asked, curiously.

"There is always a possibility that one will be a dud," the SecDef pointed out. "Probably not, but . . ."

"I don't want to use even one," the President said.

"Naturally," the SecDef agreed. "But you will if you must."

"If I must," the President replied with a sigh. "Early morning, gentlemen. I want you all to get some sleep tonight."

"And are you going to take your own advice?" the SecDef asked.

"As well as I can."

"Whatcha got, Lydia?" Nielson asked.

The girl had asked to meet him in the command room and had arrived with a couple of documents and a flash stick. She stuck that in the room's computer and brought up a mapping program that flashed the data on the wall.

Nielson was looking at intercepts. People had been transmitting and each of the transmissions was triangulated. There were probably more than were on the screen, the girls were constantly getting intercepts, but he was looking at quite a few already.

"I'm not sure what I have," Lydia admitted. "It might be butterflies in my stomach from the baby. But we have been picking up a large number of slowly moving intercepts. They break down into two types, medium-range radios and satellite phones. We, of course, don't get all the satellite phones, especially at this range, but we are picking up most of the radio transmissions, we think."

She keyed a command and most of the intercepts disappeared. Then, apparently in a time loop, they began reappearing. They seemed to march east to west across the map, staying mostly close to roads through the mountains between Russia and Azerbaijan that were effectively owned by the Chechens.

"What we don't have is internals item one," Lydia continued. "The transmissions are brief, frequency skipping and encrypted. That, in and of itself, is a data item. Whoever is transmitting has good communication security. There are seven satellite phones. There are about nine radios. They only transmit once to twice per day. They are color coded as you can see. We filtered for any that were fixed. Sat Phone 28, though, appears to communicate with Sat Phone 19, one of the ones pegged as Chechen Command, about once per day."

Nielson fiddled with the controls for a moment, then shrugged.

"Could you do something for me?" he asked. "Zoom in on one of the radios. Then follow it as it moves. Stop at each of the transmissions. I'll need to see the previous transmission at each point. I'd like to see approximate *road* distance between each of the transmissions."

He pulled out a pad of paper and watched as the girl expertly massaged the data out of the computer. Given that he'd been using computers for a few years and she had only been introduced to them about six months ago he should have been better than Lydia but there was no question who had the better tech knowledge. So he just watched. At each point he made a note and nodded for her to go on.

He looked at the pad when she was done then shook his head.

"Do it again," he said. "Zoom in close on the terrain on each."

After the third he nodded.

"Stop," he said, pointing at the screen. "River crossing. The previous one was a road junction. The one before that a pass."

"And that means?" Lydia asked.

"Phase points," Nielson replied. "It's a unit calling in as it passes each phase point in what looks very like a route march on foot. They are moving west, how far we can't know. But the Pankisi is the obvious destination. The sat phone communicating to headquarters is going to be the commander of the overall unit. Probably he checks in each day to give overall progress reports. But it's what we don't know that is important."

"Which is?" Lydia asked.

"How big the total unit is and where, exactly, they are going. Send a priority request through to Pierson for a satellite pass on anything they have. And send this package on to Colonel Chechnik along with my analysis. See if the Russians have anything. Good job. And, no, it wasn't the pregnancy hormones; I've got the same butterflies."

Chechnik looked at the communiqué and swore. That was confirmation, not that he really needed it; Dassam had never been wrong.

He still knew the answer, but he typed up a short report and sent it to the priority attention of the president.

Then he sent a reply to the Keldara: The Russian Intelligence Service had no knowledge of a Chechen movement through that region.

In other words, time to lie.

"You made good time," Mike muttered, stripping off the arctic parka and wiping his face.

Yosif, Sawn and Mike were huddled under a poncho "hooch," a temporary shelter made by stringing the poncho up to the rhododendrons, having a command huddle. Sawn was mostly out of the climbing gear while Mike was still working on his.

"Thank you, Kildar," Yosif replied, grinning slightly. "But I think we had the easier route, yes? Nonetheless, Dimi broke a leg dropping in a small crevasse. I left him and Pavilis behind, as ordered. They should be fine; plenty to eat and fuel and well hidden. We found a cave near the head of the ravine. Our excess gear is cached there. Perhaps we can retrieve it sometime."

"Not until the Georgians or the Russians or somebody combs the Chechens out of these hills," Mike said.

"We spotted two of their patrols since we left the mountains," Sawn noted. All three of them had their voices pitched low, but not whispering. A whisper would carry farther. However, one reason Mike had picked the spot was that the stream would tend to cover the inevitable sound of everyone getting out of the damned arctic gear and into something marginally more comfortable. It would also conceal the sound of quiet conversation.

He debated whether to strip out of the long johns; it was still cold as hell, and decided to leave them on. They were going to be here till dark and might as well be marginally comfortable.

"Get Sawn a guide to the cave," Mike continued. "Sawn, cache your gear and then get your guys bedded down. This might be the last rest they get for a while."

"Will do, Kildar," Sawn said, shrugging into his combat fleece.

"No sign of Padrek?" Mike asked.

"Not . . ." Yosif replied as a light birdcall sounded through the trees. "Not until just now . . ."

Adams watched as the point team entered the rendezvous point, a rhododendron-choked pile of boulders. They hadn't seen hide nor hair of anyone on their way down the mountains. In fact, they hadn't seen sign of anyone in days. It was like the Keldara were the only people in the universe at the moment. Which was just the way he liked it.

The point came back in view for a moment and waved, indicating the area was unoccupied. Which was good in one way and bad in another. It was nearly noon, the sun well up, and he had hoped the other teams had beaten them in.

He moved out with the group, scanning the area for signs of life. So far, so good. He had four hours to see who was going to make the show. Then it was game time.

Katya led Marina back into the room, ignoring the looks of the men. She'd taken to keeping her head down, her hood pulled up, so that there was less to look at. But the Russian guards hadn't had much in the way of women lately and had been guarding Marina for a couple of weeks. They had to be jacking off on a regular basis.

As always she led the girl to the bed for the evening. This evening, though, she slid the blindfold off and held up her finger to her lips.

Marina blinked at the dim light in the room. The flickering kerosene lamp was probably the first light she'd seen in weeks. She looked frightened, too. She had to know that if they were caught there would be punishment. And it was almost time for Kurt's evening check.

Katya gestured for her to take off her clothes and began stripping herself, fast. She'd checked, carefully, to make sure there were
no video pickups in the room. As long as they weren't heard they
could get away with the switch.

Marina's eyes widened in fear again and Katya paused and
shook her head. She gestured to herself then the bed. Then she
gestured to Marina and outside. Finally she leaned forward to the
girl's ear.

"Pull the hood up. Keep your head down. When you leave, turn
right. Down the street three houses is a long building. Almost
empty but some beds. Go in there and sit on the bed that has a
blanket on it. Someone will come for you. Now *strip* and take my
clothes."

Marina pulled back and looked at her wide-eyed again then
started to strip, fast.

The two changed clothes and, at the last moment, Katya
applied the fake scar. She didn't know what glue J had used but it
still stuck to her chin. She hadn't applied makeup on purpose. For
one thing, Marina didn't have any and for another she was afraid
the scar wouldn't hold if she did.

When both were changed she got in the bed, put on the blindfold and held her hands up to be shackled.

Marina had been tied up enough but she'd never done it. With
some coaching, conducted in gestures, she managed to get the
shackles on, tight but not too tight. Then she covered Katya with
the blanket and left.

There was a chance that Kurt would notice the deception, but
slight. He would expect to see the girl in the bed, as she always
was.

Katya lay there, unmoving, as the girl left. There was no outcry
so presumably she made it out of the building. Now to see if that
blond killer would notice the exchange. If so she put her life
expectancy as slightly lower than a snowflake in a fire. But that was
the nature of the job. If she wanted safe she should have stayed in
the caravanserai.

Marina kept her head down the whole way to the building. She
had been in the town for two weeks and never seen it but she
didn't look around. What she did know was the sounds and they

were normal. God keep that they stayed normal. This had been a nightmare. All she knew was that the men wanted her father to do something and that he had been cooperating. Given what he did for a living she could imagine what that might be.

She stopped at the door of the building she thought the whore, or the girl who acted the whore, meant. Opening it she saw that it *was* filled with beds and otherwise nearly empty. One had a blanket on it and she went over and sat down on it.

She wasn't sure what to feel. She wasn't tied up anymore but she also wasn't free. There was no way she could get out of the town on her own. All she could do was hope. But it was more hope than she had had in weeks.

It was a seeming eternity before the door opened and a hugely fat man came in. She recalled that wheezing breath from when the new whore had been brought to the house. He was the girl's pimp. *Her* pimp, now, for as long as she could pull off the deception.

"You've been sold," the man said, wheezingly. "And the German says that you aren't needed anymore. So come along."

"Yes, sir," Marina said, keeping her head down.

She followed the man out of the building to a nearly deserted café. There were only five men in the room, one a large, powerful looking man with the most evil face she had ever seen.

"This is the girl I told you about," Yaroslav said, settling into an overstressed chair. "She is beautiful, no? Ten thousand euros."

"I can barely see her face and nothing of her body," the man replied. "A thousand."

"It is a cold, wet night and I am tired," Yaroslav said. "Nine thousand or I take her back."

The haggling was brief. They settled at six thousand.

"No profit for me but I finally have these damned women off my hands," Yaroslav sighed, taking the money. "I think it is time to find a better place for business."

"Wherever you go you seem to find women dropped on you," the man said, standing up and taking Marina by the wrist. "If you try to run, bitch, I will pound you into a pulp."

"I won't run," Marina promised. Had she been released from the men holding her only to be sold as a whore? Was that why the girl had changed with her? But, if so, where had that fake scar come from?

Chapter Thirty

The President walked into the Situation Room carrying a fresh cup of coffee. He settled into his seat and just sat there, eyes closed, head down. Possibly praying, possibly just preparing his mind for the day. Or both. After a moment he looked up at the Air Force major in charge of Predator data.

"What's our status on the Predators?" the President asked.

"We have two . . . on station, Mr. President," the major said nervously. "We have one more on the way to the target area."

"I thought we had four?" the President said calmly.

"One crashed on the way to the target, sir," the major replied with a gulp. "There's a major storm in the area. We don't actually have observation of the target area. The Predators are flying blind. The pilots inform me they're just trying to keep them in the air, much less get a view of the operation."

"And if we push them down under the cloud cover, even if we could, we're likely to blow the operation," the secretary of defense pointed out.

"Mike will call, one way or the other, as soon as the mission condition is clear," the secretary of state said. She would not normally have been in on a situation like this, but not only did she have an excellent background in the field—she had after all previously been the national security advisor—she had been deeply

361

involved in missions involving Mike Harmon from the beginning. There was no way the President was going to deal with something like this *without* her in the room.

"So we have to depend on him to make the call," the President pointed out. "But without a clear view, how do we know where to drop if we have to?"

"It's not exactly a precision weapon, Mr. President," the secretary of defense pointed out. "Close counts."

The man dragged Marina outside and into a Lada that had seen better days. It started though with an unusually powerful growl and the man drove rapidly to the north.

"Call me Boris if anyone asks," the man said in a friendly manner. "And try to continue to act scared. My name, though, is Captain Illyan of the Russian Intelligence Bureau. We'll be through the first Russian checkpoint in about an hour or so. After *that* you can feel safe. Welcome back, by the way."

"What about my father?" Marina asked, relieved but still tense.

"That is up to other people," the captain sighed. "But they are very good. He will be fine."

"Fuck me," Vanner muttered.

"Did I just see what I think I saw?" Julia said, quietly. "Is that Katya in the bed now?"

"Roger," Vanner said. Shit, he was going to have to broadcast.

"Marina has been extracted, replaced by Katya," Vanner typed into the BFT system. "Repeat, primary hostage is extracted. New extractee is Cottontail."

He set the recording to hold then hit the send button on the transmitter. It was a risk but the most anyone was going to get was a brief electronic squeal.

This was precisely the *worst* time to get an update from Vanner but Adams held up his hand for a pause when he felt the vibration against his thigh. He pulled the device out and held it up to his eyes, cupped to see the data.

He paused, assimilating the information then tried very hard not to swear. *What the fuck was that girl playing at?*

Whatever. He'd get Katya and then figure out where the other bitch went. Why could women never stick to a *plan*?

The Keldara used equipment that, while not identical to U.S., was better than most units had, and was fully compatible with U.S. equipment. So as soon as Adams got the news, so did the President.

"Whatever does *that* mean?" the President asked, puzzled.

"Cottontail is the code name for one of Mr. Jenkins' agents," the secretary of state said, with only a glance at her notes. "She was inserted in advance to localize and protect Dr. Arensky's daughter. I've seen pictures of both and there is some superficial similarity. Apparently she chose to take the daughter's place and somehow managed to smuggle her out of the building."

"Mr. President," the Air Force major said, looking at his laptop. "We just got a communiqué from Russian intel. They report successfully extracting Marina Arensky out of Gamasoara. She is currently well away from the area of operations and, in fact, in Russian territory. In the event that there are any problems, a Spetznaz team is on standby for a hard extraction. But they indicate that they think they can extract her without issues."

"So the Kildar's agent took her place, somehow got her to Russian intel and they're pulling her out?" the President mused. "Brave girl. We ought to do something for her. Even if we got Arensky and the 'materials,' whatever they really are, if the Chechens still had his daughter it would be a big problem, right?"

"Yes, sir," the secretary of defense said. "That's why the double mission."

"Yeah, we need to do something for that girl," the President said. "That's a really selfless thing to do. Get her and Mike up to Camp David you think?"

"I'll look into it," the secretary of state said smoothly, shooting an unnoticed glance at the secretary of defense.

"And, yes, I know she's probably one of his hookers," the President said, trying not to smile. "But I'll make sure nobody mentions it."

"Actually, sir," the SecDef said. "The problem is that . . . Cottontail is also the girl we . . . upgraded to be a professional assassin. The Secret Service is going to . . . be somewhat less than enthused."

"I'll try not to let her kill me."

"And I'll try not to gibber," the SecState said with a sigh. She had seen Katya's *full* dossier. The thought of her having tea with the First Lady at Camp David . . . boggled. Then she had to smile. The image was just too funny.

Mike smiled in a driving rain: it was, as they say, "Great weather for SEALs and ducks." So far, so good.

The visibility absolutely sucked, of course. So the effectiveness of the snipers was going to be cut damned near to zero. But that cut two ways; he had been pretty sure that the Russians, at least, were going to be in overwatch with snipers. When they took the meeting down the snipers had been his biggest worry. With the rain and wind, that worry had been cut in half.

But the rain and wind, which if anything was increasing, would mask their movement to the target. Which, unless he was completely lost, was just over the hill.

Before moving out from the assembly area he'd sent a coded burst, just an alpha code, indicating that they were prepared for the mission and moving to final phase. He had received, in reply, three bursts. Vanner's team was in contact with higher and Katya, Adams' team was in position and prepared to move out and supports, such as they were, were in place. As soon as they'd performed the raid he planned to break radio silence and get an update from Nielson. However, his BFT indicated there was an armed Predator somewhere up above the muck. Which meant the boss was watching. They'd better get their shit straight on this one or they were likely to get a nuclear enema.

He slithered through the thorny scrub covering the hilltop and slid down a short ways on his stomach, not noticing the spicy scent of crushed vegetation, until he could get a glimpse of the target. The designated meet, assuming NSA had its shit together, was an intersection of two barely gravelled roads in a valley about half the size of the Keldara's.

The valley was a branch off of the Pankisi Gorge, a massive valley with sharp walls clawing up to the mountains on either side. Gouged thousands of years before by the very glaciers the teams had crossed, the Gorge was the center of Chechen resistance to the Russian forces holding the lowlands. Most of it resided in what was technically Georgia but all of it was controlled by the Chechens. The Keldara would raid and run, but they weren't planning on taking on the entire Chechen force. If Mike could avoid *any* contact, he would.

The Gorge had another strategic utility to the Chechens besides being hard as hell to assault; it was very near the border of three countries and the intersection was one of two major joining points between the three. One of the roads led to southern Chechnya and Azerbaijan through areas almost entirely owned by the Chechens. The main branch south led to government-held Georgia. If everything went well that was their egress route; ten miles or so down the road a Georgian mountain battalion was supposed to be holding the door open. The northern branch led to the frontlines of the war between the Chechens and the Russians. That was not an option given that there were about four thousand Chechen and foreign mujahideen holding those lines. That was, however, the direction of Adams' objective.

Steep hills on all sides were similarly covered in thorn scrub. He crawled cautiously to his left and found the narrow gully that he'd seen in the satellite photos. According to the photos it continued downhill, bending slightly left then back to the right, and opened up down on the flats about a hundred yards from the rendezvous. It should serve to mask the movement and assembly of Sawn's team until they were close enough to strike. That was the north fork of the pincer. They'd probably be hitting the Russians. On the south there was a solid hill that would mask Padrek's team as it approached the fedayeen coming to the rendezvous. Yosif's team was being split on security north and south as well as putting in blocking teams on the south road. Pavel's team was in reserve in the event things went completely south. If somebody took off to the north, they'd have to deal with Adams' teams.

Mike crawled back up the hill and then waved the teams forward. The snipers took up positions on the ridgeline, fiddling with the brush to get a better view and more camouflage.

As they did, Mike gestured for the four team leaders to rally on him.

"Okay, mission time," he said. "We planned this out with you guys in charge, Sawn in lead. Here's why. I'm going to take position right by the meet point. I'll initiate from there. The teams are going to be too far out to ensure the package is secure. My job is to secure the package. *Your* job is to keep me alive and make sure it stays that way."

"Kildar . . ." Padrek protested.

"As soon as I move, you move," Mike said, shaking his head. "This is my thing. All I've got to do is stay alive for fifteen seconds or so. I'm very good at that. You be good at getting my ass out."

"Yes, Kildar," Sawn sighed. "As you will it."

"The Father of All will be with us this day," Mike said. "Now move out. And when it starts, you'd better come a runnin' like hell."

She hadn't realized that Kurt spent the whole *night* in the room.

However, he apparently didn't talk to Marina. She had heard the door open, footsteps and then a hand checking her shackles. Then a scrape as he sat down in the same padded chair Marina used. After that . . . Nothing. She couldn't even hear him breathing over the sound of the rain and wind.

After a bit, though, there was sound from outside the door and a knock.

"Come." She heard the quiet cocking of a pistol. Then wheezing. Fucking Yaroslav.

"Has the girl been satisfactory?" Yaroslav wheezed. It must have been hell for him to just keep standing.

"Fine," Kurt replied. "What do you want?"

"I have a buyer. I wish to sell her on."

"That's fine," Kurt said. "Do you want your money?"

"I think we're paid up," Yaroslav said, nervously.

"I think we're a bit behind."

"If I get out of this room alive, I'll be happy for the experience."

"Very funny, fat man. You can go. The girl has never mentioned her name. You don't know it. And soon it won't matter. You may leave."

"Good night, then."

From the sound of the footsteps, and the slight bump at the door, Yaroslav backed out of the room.

As the door closed Katya heard the gun decock and a slight giggle.

Fucking insane. And she was trapped in the same room with him.

God damnit, Master Chief, where the fuck are you?

Hardly anything was moving in the town. Not surprising given the weather. The exterior guards on the target building were still out, but they were blinded by the rain and the light from the forward windows.

Just as Adams thought that, the door of the target building opened and one fucking obese motherfucker waddled out and across the street. He was out of sight quickly. Adams tentatively ID'd him as the pimp that Katya had been bought by, based on the description from Vanner. He wasn't sure what he was doing in the building at this time of night, but it didn't really matter. If he'd still been in the building when they hit it, he was a target. Everyone in the building was a target except the detainee.

Adams looked over his shoulder and gestured for the Keldara to take up pre-attack positions. Then he glanced at his watch. Fifteen minutes. Good time.

Now to wait in the pouring rain. It was a fine night for killin'.

Mike slid down the hill cautiously, watching for signs of enemy snipers on this ridge and hoping his camo was holding. The Russians would have access to thermal imagery for sure and the Chechens might. So he was wrapped up like a mummy to avoid thermal signature, long johns, fleece and Gore-Tex top and bottom, hands in thick gloves, coldweather mask over his face, balaclava and fleece-lined hood up with the hood drawn tight. They'd tested the outfit and while he still gave off a heat image it was muted and weak, a gray ghost rather than a blazing white beacon. However, even with the cold and lashing rain, all the gear meant he was hot as hell. At this point his gear was so soaked he couldn't tell where the rain left off and the sweat started.

There was a click in his headphones and he froze. Slowly he reached down and pulled up his data pad, shielding it so the glow from the plasma fusion screen wouldn't be visible beyond his position.

Three points on the far ridge were now highlighted with the icon of snipers. Their "team" was unknown but they were overlooking the rendezvous.

Mike enjoyed sniping and hated snipers. For all he knew, the snipers had already spotted him and would wait until he was in position, or the meet was already going on, before they fired. That's what *he* would do. Let the target think he'd succeeded and then fuck him at the last moment.

He clicked on the icons and upgraded their priority to first engagement then slowly slid the pad away. Gear stowed, he started his stalk again. He was just going to have to depend on the night, rain and coverage to avoid the snipers. He shunted all doubts aside and slid onward, belly down. But he kept as much concealment between him and the three snipers as possible . . .

He wondered, briefly, how the rest of the mission was going and then put it out of his mind. He had good subordinates. They all knew their jobs. He could, had to, depend on them.

They were good. He was good. Time to odie.

Vladimir Yaroslav waddled to the small room he had been renting and quickly stripped off his clothes. As he pulled off his watch he gave it a brief glance and then dropped it on the bed. He was on *very* short time.

The fat suit unzipped in seven places and was off in less than a minute. Finally. It was one of the *worst* disguises he had ever affected, but very effective. Nobody noticed anything but the fat. Getting the smell of rotting flesh from obesity necrosis had been tough but he'd finally found just the right mixture of scents.

Pulling off the mask, J stretched, his own self, whoever that was, for three seconds. Then he started getting his next mission face on.

Islamic clothes went on, then a false beard, the prophet being big on beards. The old wig came off and a new one, long, black, lanky, went on. Shoes with the backs pushed down. A different, cheaper, watch. A scar on one cheek. A small silver ring inscribed with the symbol of a crescent moon. But mostly it was the attitude. He was suddenly a person from an Islamic society. Maybe a fighter. Maybe the scar was from being in the wrong place at the wrong time. Many men in the region were scarred who had never held a gun.

A packet of perfectly forged papers went into a pocket, money bag around his neck and out the door he went.

Down the street a Lada, virtually identical to every other Lada in the former Soviet Union, was parked on a side street. A Chechen gentleman had purchased it for cash five days before and it had been sitting ever since. A couple of street urchins had been paid by a different man, a Russian, to ensure that it wasn't stripped to the frame.

Hadit Temiz climbed behind the wheel and with a brief prayer to Allah that the infernal machine would start turned the key. The Allah-cursed vehicle came to life and he pulled out into the wind and rain.

At the main road he turned right, south, and headed to his next business appointment, secured two weeks before, in Azerbaijan. He'd have to remember to take the unmarked left fork in the valley ahead.

He tried to put out of his mind that as he went through the intersection he was going to have guns pointed at him from every side. Hadit Temiz did not know that.

In moments the Lada carrying Hadit, a Turkmen vendor of sundry cheap plastic knickknacks a selection of which were in the trunk, disappeared into the rain and darkness leaving nothing behind of Vladimir Yaroslav but a fat suit lying on the floor like the shed skin of a snake.

Chapter Thirty-One

Mike stayed still in his hide as an out of tune Lada puttered to the south. From the sound of it, it took the fork headed for Azerbaijan.

But that wasn't what he was listening for. That was the sound of multiple engines coming from the north.

He'd found a nice little hide, a dug out portion to the streambank which was relatively flat and just about covered in bushes. First, he'd slowly laid out a heavy ghillie blanket then slithered under it, snuggling into the comforting mud of the bank. Once under that, he'd divested himself of some of his encumbering gear; the blanket was thick and lined with mylar to keep from letting loose any heat.

Once prepared, he settled in to wait. When the vehicles—they sounded like small trucks or SUVs—pulled to a stop, he still waited. He could hear the group deploying, quietly and professionally. They dropped into the streambed and walked down it, within a foot of his position at one point, without noticing that the pile of junk along the side of the stream was something other than a pile of junk. The night was still awfully dark and he'd have been hard to see in daylight much less under NVGs.

The fedayeen were, as normal, late. When he heard the second group of vehicles he pressed the transmitter and started the countdown.

The next was art rather than science. The other group of vehicles approached. Their lights would be on. Even if they were tactical lights they would partially blind the Russians. And as the Islamics deployed the Russians, even though they each had a sector they were supposed to be watching, were going to be casting quick glances over their shoulder . . .

Now.

He stood up and casually walked up out of the streambed, fiddling with his zipper as he did.

Over all the rest of his gear he had a Russian military-issue poncho. The weapon he'd chosen for the op was a BIZON submachine gun. The weapon was a favorite of Russian special operations groups, firing a 7.62x25 bullet from an integrally silenced barrel. Heavier and less accurate than the silenced M4, it was still a pretty good weapon.

As he'd guessed, the former Spetznaz were armed with a motley collection of personal weapons. He spotted two BIZONs before he was even up on the flat.

"You should have taken a piss before we left," one of the guards growled, turning back from a glance over his shoulder at the Islamics. The guy was just about covered in frag grenades. Personally, Mike hated the things. He used them when he had to but never carried more than one unless *absolutely* necessary. He'd seen too many people frag themselves. This fucker clearly loved the damned things. Stupid fuck.

"Tea," Mike muttered back. Over the last year his Russian had gotten perfect and while accented, the accent didn't sound American. That was because it was a Keldara accent. But the Russian would have to be quick as hell to notice that in the middle of an op.

Suddenly, Mike was just another of the Spetznaz guards. Several of them sported ponchos virtually identical to his. Same gun, same walk, same wariness.

Just one problem.

The two groups had stopped about sixty yards apart. That was fine; there were Keldara positioned on the far side of the engagement. The two groups would pincer the meet as soon as Mike initiated. But Mike had intended to get to the package and take it down, *then* initiate. It was the only way he could be sure there wouldn't be a nuke dropped on his head.

The problem was that the principals, and a select group of guards, were moving to the no-man's-land in the middle of the two groups. On the Russian side there were four guards, Sergei Rudenko and Arensky. Arensky was carrying what Mike presumed was the package, a briefcase. On the Islamic side there were four guards, these guys encumbered with bags but still with their hands on their weapons, Al-Kariya the Al Qaeda money man from the bulk and another guy, slimmer, nobody Mike knew about.

There was no way that Mike could approach that group. Too much ground to cover. Too open. Too obvious.

Fuck.

Mike wandered one way, then back, looking up at the woods where the Keldara waited, then stopped by where he'd come out of the stream. Three of the Russians had gathered there, not exactly taking advantage of the shelter of one of the Mercedes SUVs they'd come in but close. One of them was the guy who had challenged Mike's "bathroom trip."

Fuck. This was gonna suck.

As he approached the group his BFT device buzzed, once. Adams was initiating. Out of time.

He reached over, casually pulled a pin out of one of the frags on the guy's harness and then pushed the man, hard, into the group.

Two steps and he was rolling across the hood of the Mercedes SUV, hitting the ground on the far side on both feet and aiming into the group of principals.

"Lasko! Go!"

Lasko had been continually adjusting his aim based on his read of the wind and, ignoring the sudden crash of multiple grenades, his finger stroked the trigger as soon as he heard the "Go" command.

"Target down," Sion muttered. "Shift right. Sniper on ridgeline. Target down. I lost the third one."

"Jackrabbiting," Lasko said. "Back . . ."

There was a thud next to him and looking over it was clear that Sion was not going to be drinking any more beer. Or, what was worse, doing any more spotting.

He was already down as the next round cracked overhead.

"Right," Lasko muttered. "If that's the way you want to play it."

He had two more hides prepared. Time to play the game.

"Sniper teams, engage targets in valley," Lasko said, thumbing his throat mike. "I'll take the enemy sniper."

Mike triggered a burst into the group of principals, trying for the distant figure that he assumed to be Sergei. The man was next to Arensky, anyway. Arensky and Al-Kariya were easy to spot. Neither one of them looked as if they knew what to do in the firefight that was erupting around them.

What he got, instead, were the two guards who moved to place themselves by the principals. It was the right move but it cost them their lives.

Sergei snatched the case away from Arensky and picked him up by the collar, pounding towards the nearest vehicle as the mujahideen closed in around Al-Kariya and began firing at the Russians.

Suddenly it was a free-for-all. Both groups, highly suspicious of each other, thought that they had been betrayed. The Russians were laying down fire on the fedayeen as the fedayeen backed up to their vehicles. Rounds were cracking downrange in both directions as Mike leapt to his feet and began pounding towards the retreating Russian.

Mike had counted on that. He figured when things went south, especially if it was from fire within the area, they would start fighting each other.

Neither group noticed, until too late, that they were being attacked from behind.

"Back!" Rashid shouted, drawing a pistol out of his robes.

He couldn't see who had fired but the explosion looked as if it must have been a rocket launcher and some of the Russians were down. The pig Sergei Rudenko had dragged the doctor, and the smallpox, away. The Russians were clearly attacking them, it was time to run.

"Protect Al-Kariya!" Haza shouted at the same moment, dropping to a knee and firing at the Russians on the other side of the open area. The fire from the SK-74 was short, controlled bursts. He fired twice then rolled to the side towards the riverbed, up on a knee, two more bursts.

Rashid grabbed the money man by the arm and started backing away, firing his pistol in the general direction of the Russians.

"Come Haji Al-Kariya!" Rashid said but Al-Kariya had already picked up the hem of his robe and turned to the rear, breaking into a rather fast run for a man of his bulk.

The fedayeen guards were moving forward, their training in such a situation to be to counterattack then withdraw. They were having to fire around the principals but they were all more than capable of doing so.

Rashid made it to the relative safety of the first pickup in line and ran to the rear, dropping down and fumbling for a magazine.

"We must get the smallpox," Al-Kariya said. He had dropped into the mud of the road next to the younger financier and was panting heavily. "We must."

"The money is in the road back there," Rashid snarled. "We have to get *that.*"

"To the devil with the money," Al-Kariya said, hefting himself to his feet as the last of the fedayeen dashed forward. "The smallpox is what matters!"

"Haza will get it if it is possible," Rashid assured him. "I will go forward and tell him." The younger man had just seated the magazine, it was not a natural thing for him, and looked up into the barrel of a weapon.

"Tell him *what*, pray?" a camouflage-clad figure asked in passable Arabic.

Rashid carefully set the pistol on the ground.

"Uh, sayyidi, you might want to raise your hands. Very slowly."

Mike pounded across the open area, trying to look like a guard closing in to secure his principle. As he did, he started taking fire from the fedayeen, some of it *damned* close.

"Uh, guys," Mike panted, keying his throat mike. "I could use some fucking FIRE here! And be aware that I'm in the middle of this gunfight!"

"Move! Move!" Sawn shouted as the Keldara boiled out of the streambed.

They were practically on top of the rear Russian vehicles. The Russians were concentrated on their firefight with the fedayeen and at first didn't even notice the fire coming in from behind. Guys were dying in the rain. When a person's hit, they generally fall forward whether they're hit from the back or the front. And most of them had guys behind them firing past them. Most of them were snuggled into the dubious cover of the trucks, anyway. As were the fedayeen.

Sawn bounded forward and triggered a three-round burst into the broad back of a Russian crouched into the wheel well of one of the Mercedes SUVs. The fighter slumped into the wheel and his weapon fell to the ground out of slack fingers.

As Sawn moved forward, shooting in the back another Russian who had been firing around the next vehicle in line, Sawn's number two pumped another burst into the Russian, just to make sure.

Some of them seemed to notice the fire from behind them, a few turned around. But by then it was too late. The Keldara were bounding forward in two-man teams, spread on either side of the trucks, engaging targets with their backs turned who were concentrated on firing to their front. It was almost too easy. It wasn't a firefight, it was a slaughter.

"We are coming, Kildar!" Sawn replied, keying his own mike. "We are coming."

Lasko slid into place and scanned the far ridge. There were cooling forms in the thermal imager but the difference between that and someone heavily cloaked was hard to determine.

He had pulled a ghillie cloak up and pulled up both his balaclava and face mask. The combination was going to reduce his thermal image. The sniper on the far ridge *had* to be using a thermal imager; there was no way to pick someone out at *this* range in *this* blackness using an NVG.

There had been three pairs on the far ridge. He counted one, two . . . six cooling forms. Wait.

He fired without thinking, ducking at the same time to hear the enemy round pass overhead.

He rolled to the right, slid down the slope then up behind a tree, peering out again. Where the slightly hotter spot had been . . . Nothing. He needed a spotter, someone to check all the cooling targets for him but . . .

There. A sudden warm spot. Barely different from the background.

There was no time for careful measurement, no time for consideration. The rifle, again, slammed into his shoulder a surprise as it always was when the shot was good. He jerked back then, instead of moving, came right back up.

The hotspot . . . . was still there. But . . . cooler.

"That's for you, Sion," Lasko whispered.

Revenge is a dish best served . . . cooler.

Fucking blackasses.

Ivar Terekhov wished that there was some selective plague that would wipe all the blackass Muslims from the face of the earth. He had joined the Russian Army as a conscript but after his first tour in Chechnya he had reenlisted to join Spetznaz. One mission to "support" a convoy that had already been overrun by the fucking Chechens was all it took. One look at the mutilated bodies of his friends, his fellow soldiers, and the formerly laid back Moscovite had hated the blackasses with a burning passion.

Oh, he'd lost his innocence over the years, as mission after mission had been completely fucked up by higher command. He had come to understand that incompetence and corruption were the reality of his motherland, just as betrayal was the nature of the Islamic. He had quit, he had taken pay from the mob, he had even attacked the motherland on more than one occasion. But he still hated fucking blackasses.

Unlike a lot of his peers he had studied them, had read a translation of their Koran, had read Western papers on their culture. He wanted to know what drove their thinking. And the thing that he came to, over and over again, was that the Prophet, spit be upon his grave, had promised them paradise for every lie they told an unbeliever. They weren't just untrustworthy, they were the *definition* of untrustworthy. They would rather lie to an unbeliever than tell the truth. Betrayal, to them, was as natural as breathing.

This firefight proved it. How they had slipped into their midst and detonated Matvei's grenades Ivar wasn't sure. But they clearly had. Matvei and his grenades might occasion some joking among the "Group" but he *never* made mistakes with them.

Now he had the chance to kill fucking mutilating, betraying blackasses and he intended to send as many of them to meet their Prophet in hell as he possibly could.

Another moved across the open area in front and he targeted the figure, fired five rounds and dropped him. Fire was coming from the streambed that the muj had been headed for but even that was slackening off.

They were winning. Fuck these blackass motherfuckers. They would have the money *and* the biologicals. Hopefully, Sergei would just destroy the latter. Then they could all retire on a nice trop . . .

Tunnel vision has an evolutionary purpose; it permits the mind to avoid distraction and concentrate on the "prey." It is probably derived from early hunting necessity; prey in herds scattered and crossed, making it hard to concentrate on just one target. Tunnel vision permitted the early human predator to ignore those distractions and dial down on just one prey. But the problem with it is that sometimes a distraction is important. Such as the "distraction" of someone coming up behind you and putting two rounds through the back of your head.

Gena Mahona was getting a bit sick of this.

He was a fighter. That was what the Keldara were raised to be; they took it in with their first sip of beer which was usually administered in the nursery. A weapon was placed in their hand while the afterbirth was still extruding from their mother's womb. The highest calling was to die in battle, eyes broad and screaming defiance into the face of their enemies.

The American way of war that the Kildar taught was colder, quieter, in many ways more merciless. But this was just sickening.

The mujahideen they were fighting were very good. They were aiming, they were taking cover. But they *weren't looking behind them.* They had had a security force out to the rear. But as soon as the firing started, the security force had oriented towards the Russians. Most of them had run forward to engage the obvious enemy.

He was shooting people in the back. *A lot* of people. He had stopped counting at four kills.

Even the muj that had taken cover in the stream weren't paying attention to their rear. They were firing in short bursts, reloading, firing, all of it perfectly drilled and automatic. But they didn't seem to notice the sound of the Keldara sloshing down the stream, or even the occasional curse as one slipped on a slime-covered rock. When one fell they assumed it was from the fire to the front, even though *that* was slackening off.

There were only three he could see still firing. One was clearly out of rounds and turned to his fellow, saying something quick in Arabic. But that had caused him to look around, finally.

"Don't," Gena said, quietly, as the rest of the team started to gather to either side.

The fedayeen looked at him, wide-eyed, then at the trail of bodies faintly visible in the streambed.

"Just . . . don't."

The fedayeen cursed and reached into his robe as his companion started to turn . . .

It wasn't good fire discipline, but the nine Keldara gathered in the streambed expended over thirty-six rounds on the last three mujahideen.

Just sickening. It made you want to weep. The Father of All wasn't going to consider *this* a battle. This wasn't exactly going to get him to the Halls of Feasting.

On the other hand, there were a bunch of dead fedayeen and in the grand scheme of things he had to consider that a plus.

Sergei hurled Dr. Arensky into the front seat of the Mercedes then climbed over him into the driver's seat.

"Make one stupid move," Sergei threatened, turning the key. "Yakov! Dmitri? Fuck . . ." He put the car in drive and looked in his rearview mirror. He'd thought the fucking blackasses had hit them but now he could see camouflage-clad figures moving down the line of vehicles, firing into the unprotected backs of his men. "It's not the blackasses!" He screamed over the team circuit. "You're being hit from behind!"

It was clearly too late. The blackasses were firing to the rear as well, clearly they'd been hit from both directions. It was a total fuckup.

Time to get the fuck out, then.

The blackasses had pulled into the Georgian road, blocking it. Not that he wanted to go that way. The proper escape route was up into Russia. But the only road open was the one to Azerbaijan. Fine.

He put his foot down and peeled out, all four tires screaming at the wet gravel.

Time to fly.

"No, no, NO! FUUUCK!" Mike screamed up at the clouds. As rounds cracked over his head from *behind* him he ripped off the poncho and triggered a UV strobe on his shoulder. "Check fucking FIRE!" he screamed into his throat mike. "This fucking op is BLOWN! The package is in movement. Repeat, the package is ACTIVE! Lasko, stop that VEHICLE!"

"That is not good," the President said. "Is the B-2 on station?"

"Ready to drop," the Chairman of the Joint Chiefs said. He'd been brought in late in the operation but was fully up to speed at this point. "All the codes have been given. Literally, all you have to do is give the drop order."

"Minuet?" the President said.

"One minute," she replied.

"We don't *have* one minute," the secretary of defense pointed out. "Those things do have a limited blast range. It's *big*, but it's limited."

"Give me the Kildar," the President said.

"LASKO?"

"Negative, Kildar," Lasko replied. "The target is out of view."

Mike was already in one of the Mercedes and starting it. Fortunately they all had keys in the ignition. He jerked it into gear just as he felt thumps in the back.

"Sawn, Kildar, I'm in the back."

"We are so out of . . ."

"Mike, this is the President."

"Oh, Jesus, sir, not NOW."

"Mike, is the package in movement?"

"I can *stop* it!"

"Do you have any forces in the way?" the President asked remorselessly.

"I take it back!" Mike yelled. "I was JOKING. I can STOP it. I've never fucking FAILED, sir. I am not about to start now!" He took a breath as he hit the first curve. He could see the lights of the other Mercedes up ahead. The guy didn't have that much of a lead on him. "I can stop it, sir. I am in pursuit at this time. I am sending continuous coordinates. All that I ask is that if you drop, you drop on me and not my men. If you hit my position, at any time, you will destroy the target. If that changes, you'll be the second person to know," Mike added as the Mercedes skidded through another turn.

"Very well," the President said nervously. "I'm out of the connection."

"Thanks," Mike said. "I can concentrate on driving."

"Do we actually have track on him?" the President asked.

"Yes, sir," the major replied instantly. "His BFT pad is updating his location every second and a half. The B-2 has the same track point and should be tracking."

"Send them definite orders to track on that source," the President replied. "When the track point is four kilometers from the origin point, they are authorized to drop." He pulled a card out of his pocket and consulted it. "Code Alpha, Charlie, One, Five, Six, Bravo, Niner."

"Yes, sir," the major said, swallowing but tapping the orders into the B-2 link.

"Kurt!" Sergei said into his throat mike. "Kurt, can you hear me?"

"Is he the one guarding my daughter?" Arensky asked curiously.

He seemed awfully detached, almost catatonic. Some people got that way when things went bad. Sergei, though, prided himself on keeping a cool head.

"Just shut the fuck up," Sergei snarled. He just had to clear the area. But the road was a nightmare, slick, twisting and climbing up into the mountains. He'd barely gotten a couple of kilometers, maybe three, away from the firefight. He had to get farther . . .

"Things don't seem to be going very well," Arensky replied, glancing over his shoulder. "What, did you think the Russian government was just going to let you walk away with smallpox? They, and the American and the French and the Germans and the fucking *Nigerians* are going to be hunting you for the rest of your very short life. Give up now."

"Just shut the FUCK up!" Sergei screamed. "Or your daughter—"

"Is either dead or already rescued," Arensky said, evenly. "Either way, that threat has grown weary, no?"

"Then try this one," Sergei screamed, pulling out his pistol and holding it to the scientist's temple. "Say one more fucking word and you are going to be splattered all over that window."

Arensky raised his hands in surrender and then pulled on his seat belt to tighten it. As the mobster put his weapon away the scientist braced his feet and shifted in his seat, grasping at the seat handles. After a moment he checked his watch, then braced some more.

"What in the fuck are you doing?" Sergei ground out. He was definitely feeling ill about this. He was practically shaking. No matter *how* bad an op had gone, he never shook. He was iron. Everyone knew that.

"Just bracing myself," Arensky said. "Airbags aren't perfect. I'm glad you chose a Mercedes, through. Oh, and checking the time."

"Why?" Sergei asked, wiping at his forehead. He was definitely shaking. Damn. Damn this man. Damn this op. Damn those fuckers back there. Spetznaz probably. He'd probably *trained* some of them for fuck's sake!

"Because as you were bundling me about and threatening me I was slipping three small needles into your thigh," Arensky said. "You probably didn't notice the slight pain what with everything else. One of them was coated in a product derived of ergot. It causes a reaction called Saint Vitus' dance. Think of it as LSD. Psychotropic, hallucinogenic, very effective. You're probably already feeling the effects; it's fast stuff. If that didn't get you, the second was coated in a nasty little microbe that is found in sink drains worldwide. Very rarely kills anyone despite that; most people don't eat food they pick out of the sink drain. However, if it is cultured by an expert and then stuck into someone's thigh, it will spread through the bloodstream rather fast. Oh, it's not going to kill you for three or four days, but that one was *guaranteed*. The last was, I'm *pretty* sure, botulinus toxin. One of the tins of meat you left us was rather swelled and the resultant culture sure *looked* like botulinus. And botulinus is nasty. A teaspoon would kill a city. The amount I gave you would only kill, say, an elephant. By the way, that would have killed me if I'd eaten it. Such great care you took, too . . ."

Mike slowed the Mercedes as he saw the vehicle he'd been chasing suddenly swerve from side to side then roll off the road.

When he slid to a stop near the wreck all he could see was airbags. Frankly, he'd always thought Mercedes overdid the whole airbag thing. Sure, one in the front. Maybe ones on the sides. But that wasn't good enough for Mercedes, oh, no. They had them on both sides, front and back, top and in the middle. If you so much as hit a pole in a parking lot you were suddenly smothered in exploding balloons.

The Mercedes SUV was upside down in a ditch on the left side of the road, the driver's-side window pointed towards him. He and Sawn approached, weapons pointed forward, as the balloons slowly deflated.

The man hanging upside down in the straps was alive and, amazingly, unscratched from the crash. Okay, so maybe that many airbags had a purpose. On the other hand, he was having convulsions. It was clearly Sergei, though. He might be foaming at the mouth, but it was Sergei.

Mike considered putting a few rounds into his head and then thought better of it. The guy might have information they could use. Waste not and all that.

He ducked down and looked to the other side of the vehicle.

"And who are you?" Dr. Arensky asked.

"Mike Jenkins," Mike replied, head on the side to look through the vehicle. "I work for various people. Right now I'm getting paid to get you, and some stuff you're carrying, away from *bad* people."

"Oh, glad to meet you," Dr. Arensky said. "I seem to be stuck."

"Yeah," Mike said. "What's wrong with Sergei here?"

"Oh, that," Arensky said with a shrug. "Mr. Jenkins, can I call you Mike?"

"Sure," Mike said, trying not to giggle at the unreality. "Wait just a sec, though." He keyed his throat mike. "Hello, God on High. You still listening?"

"Go, Mike," the President answered, tensely.

"Got the package," Mike said. "Call off the flyboys. Arensky is alive as well. Getting out will be interesting, but the package *is* secure."

"Glad to hear it," the President said. "Good job. Tell me when the material is . . . fully safe."

"Yes, sir," Mike replied, unkeying the mike. "Just make sure you make the payments. Sorry, you were saying?"

"Mr. Jenkins, Mike, let me suggest something to you," Arensky said, smiling despite being stuck in the seatbelt and dangling upside down. "I know that you do a lot of hard things in your line of work. That you piss off a lot of people."

"That's a given," Mike said, tilting his head again.

"Mike, Mr. Jenkins, my friend," Arensky said, grinning. "Let me give you one piece of advice. Take it for what you will. Piss off terrorists, piss off mobsters, piss off your president if you wish. But never *ever* piss off a microbiologist."

Chapter Thirty-Two

The BFT device in Adams' thigh pocket buzzed just for a moment. Time.

The snipers were using .338 Whisper sniper rifles. The rifles were big as was the round, but it was subsonic and the silencers were integral, part of the mass of the rifle. The two guards at the front door, shielding their cigarettes against the wind and rain, never knew what hit them. They slumped straight down, red blotches staining the wall behind them where their heads used to be.

The strike team crossed the road fast and silently. Shota was in the lead but even before he reached the door two teams of two Keldara each split left and right down the side of the building. The rest stacked behind the leaders, spread to either side in two wings of heavily armed, and armored, figures.

Adams was two men behind Shota and prayed that the big Keldara was finally going to get it right.

The big man was wearing body armor normally carried only by demolition squads: massive torso armor, heavy leg coverings and a helmet with integrated blast-shield faceplate. In addition, extra heavy-duty ceramic "chickenplates" had been installed not only in the torso but also thighs, shins and cup over the crotch. The armor and plates would have slowed a lesser man to a waddle, but Shota trotted up to the door, stopped, pressed the shotgun against the lock and triggered one round.

The blast of the shotgun rang through the street like an alarm but it didn't even occasion a shout. Too many guns were fired for too many reasons in Gamasoara for anyone to notice a single shot.

That was about to change.

The Keldara, despite the fifty-pound padding on his leg, kicked the door hard enough that it was flung off its hinges, then . . .

Took one, two, three, four, FIVE steps into the room. At a good solid trot. Hallelujah!

Of course, while he was doing that he was being fired on from three separate directions. Three of the former Spetznaz guards had been playing poker at the table in the front room and did not react kindly to a large man blasting their door down.

The heavy duty body armor shrugged off even the point-blank rounds from AK assault rifles and before Shota could finish his trot, Oleg and Adams were through the door, leaning to either side and using his bulk, and armor, as cover.

Three short bursts, nine rounds of 5.56 high velocity bullets and the former Spetznaz were down and dead. They were wearing body armor, too. But there was a qualitative difference between theirs and Shota's. And 5.56, at these ranges, had the penetration to break anything less.

Not that either Adams or Oleg fired at their center of mass.

Shota shot one as he was falling. It seemed like the thing to do. Nobody had said you weren't supposed to shoot someone, just because their head had been turned to pulp by three 5.56 rounds. No women, no kids. Dead bodies didn't count as either.

"NEXT DOOR!" Adams shouted, pointing across the small entry room. As he said it, there was a "crack" of a grenade from in the building. "MOVE!"

Each of the rooms down the hallway had a window.

Each of the rooms was occupied by men, identified as Russian guards. Valid targets.

Each of the windows had simple panes of glass protecting the interior from the elements.

But like a baseball thrown by an overzealous child, which flies out and breaks mommy's plate glass window as the children who had been playing watch in horror and fascination, hand grenades have no problem breaking such panes.

Less.

"This hardly seems fair," Danes said, plucking another frag grenade from the pouch at his side and arming it.

"Says you," Jachin replied as the window two behind the current one exploded outward in fire. "They can always toss them back."

He pulled the pin and threw it through the window, hard and to the side, so that it was likely to hit the far wall and bounce around a bit. They might just reach it in time for it to explode.

Danes followed with his own, thrown up through the broken window, aimed at the ceiling. He could see forms moving in the darkness as men scrambled to throw on clothes, body armor, grab weapons, whatever was necessary to prepare themselves for a battle out of nowhere. If either of them noticed the breaking window, they were far too encumbered to try to find the grenade bouncing around in the dark room.

He moved on. He wasn't going to be by the window when his present exploded.

"Open it!" Adams yelled. "Just use the *knob!*"

Shota paused and turned the doorknob, opening the door politely. Rifle fire cracked down the hallway in a much less polite fashion.

"Back!" Adams yelled, throwing a flashbang into the corridor then pulling Shota back from the door. "You okay?"

"Fine," Shota answered. "I am good. I like this armor."

The flash-bang went off with a massive "crack!" and a flash of light and heat.

"GO!" Adams yelled, yanking the massive Keldara around and pushing him into the hallway.

Shota shot one of the screaming men in the hallway in the face as a door near the far end blew in, throwing a body into the hall.

"Forget them!" Adams screamed. "CHARGE THE FAR DOOR. GO! NOW! TAKE IT *DOWN.*"

Shota lowered his head and bulled forward, throwing the two remaining fighters in the hallway to the side as Adams stayed right behind him. He ignored the rooms to either side; the teams following him had them to deal with, and he could hear the cries of "CLEAR!" following him in a wave. There were occasional cracks of fire, one or two rounds, always followed by the "CLEAR!"

He was concentrated on the far door. That was the target, the only thing that mattered.

One more defender and they were done.

Katya wasn't sure what caused the chair to suddenly scrape but she could tell by the sound that Kurt was on his feet. A moment later there was the shot from a gun. It wasn't a rifle like the Keldara used, something bigger, booming through the building. She heard a click, something like a briefcase might make opening. Then sharp, rapid footsteps.

Before the second burst of fire from the guards in the front room, Kurt was at her side. She felt the shackles come loose and longed to use her special fingernails on the bastard. But with the blindfold still on she couldn't be sure quite where to strike. And she *knew* she'd only get one shot.

He grabbed her by the hair and dragged her across the room. There was a click of something again and a dragging sound. She slid her hands up to her head and flicked the blindfold up just as she was yanked forward again. She had just enough time to see that the fireplace in the room was false, a doorway that led to a tunnel. But the second yank forced her to stumble forward, completely off balance and held up only by her hair. For a moment the pain half blinded her; then she had her balance back again and prepared to strike. Before she could the light was extinguished again as the false fireplace slid back into place. Kurt let her go and all she could do was stand in stygian darkness.

"We expected some such stupid attempt by the Russian government," Kurt said, flicking on his flashlight. "The best of the Russian special forces leave for better opportunities. Such as this one. You will be coming with me. Don't think to try anything stupid."

"Why Herr Schwenke, why would you think *I* would do anything stupid," Katya said, flicking the blindfold off and sweeping her fingers up to rake at his face.

Schwenke was fast, credit him for that. The strike that should have taken out an eye, and pumped his eye socket full of neurotoxin, just grazed one cheek.

"It's the little Russian hooker," Schwenke said, springing back and flashing the light in her face. He gave a chortle. "How very . . . rich."

"Katya Ivanova at your service," Katya said, taking up a cat stance and mentally triggering the combat hormones held in a pouch under her left arm. She could feel the world slowing down and, to her, her speech blurring. There was a distant explosion but her ears automatically muted it, her vision focusing down to concentrate on the target. "Or, rather, in the service of the Kildar. You may call me Cottontail."

"The fucking Keldara," Schwenke said with a grin. "You switched, you little bi—" He had automatically reached for his gun and as it came out in an expert draw it slid from nerveless fingers to the floor. "Wha . . ." He swayed and nearly dropped the flashlight as well but seemed to draw strength from some inner well. "What did you do to me, you bitch?"

"You have your cocktails, I have mine," Katya answered, sliding forward gracefully, hands held in a panther strike position, nails forward and hooked. "In this case, a little neurotoxin, made from cobra venom or so they told me. Courtesy of the United States government. I have the antidote. It's in my *fangs*. You're welcome to sample it."

Schwenke sprang backward then carefully knelt and came up holding a smaller pistol from an ankle holster. But his hands shook so hard he was going to have a difficult time hitting even a target as relatively large as Katya. He clearly knew that.

"Who is the cobra and who the mouse, now?" Katya asked, swaying from side to side as the man backed away. "Can you hit me little man? Or can I pump you full of my little cocktail, first?"

She slid forward and sideways, striking at the gun hand. Kurt fired while backpedaling. Both missed.

"Katya, Vanner," the communicator in her head crackled. "Quit fucking around with him. Shota is down. Adams is going nuts. Get the damned door open."

❖   ❖   ❖

Shota hit the door like a human battering ram and the door splintered under the weight and speed of the big man.

Which just meant he was that much closer to the bomb Kurt had left behind when it went off.

Adams felt himself lifted off his feet and flung backwards from the explosion. Being blown up was bad enough. Having Shota land on him was worse. The impact drove the air from his lungs and he was pretty sure he felt a couple of ribs crack. Fortunately, his helmet kept him from getting either a broken nose or a cracked skull.

"Oof."

Another weight hit the combined pile, a heavy step unless Adams was much mistaken. Oleg, true to his training, was continuing the assault. You worried about casualties when the firing was over.

Adams managed to push Shota off and get a breath, wincing at the pain in his ribcage. To his amazement, the big man was moving as well. Slowly, but he was moving.

"Shota," Adams said, rolling over on his side then propping himself up on one elbow. "Shota?"

"I don't like doors anymore," Shota said, petulantly. "I don't like bombs."

"You're *alive*?" Adams asked. He propped himself up some more and shook his head. The massive Keldara's armor was peppered with holes. The bomb had apparently been something like a claymore. There were even projectiles, small little ball bearings, stuck in his face shield. But, amazingly, he didn't seem to be wounded at *all*. The armor had caught all of it.

"I'm alive," Shota responded. "But I wish I wasn't. That *hurt*."

Adams couldn't bear it, he had to laugh. He was still chortling when Oleg called him.

"Master Chief?" the team leader said from the door of the room. "There is no one here!"

"Fuck me," Adams replied. He hadn't forgotten that there was a hostage in the room that had just got all blown up. But it was, after all, Katya. He'd take ten Katya's over Shota. If she got blown up it was no skin off of his nose. But *missing*? That was another thing. The girl knew things. "VANNER!"

❖   ❖   ❖

What was driving him nuts was that Adams could *hear* them talking. Oh, it was muted, but he could hear Katya's tones, like ice. No, not like ice. She was playing with someone. It was the voice of a cat, one of the really malicious ones, that has caught a baby mouse.

"Vanner! Tell her to get this damned thing open or I'm going to blow the son of a bitch in!"

They hadn't been looking long but there was no obvious switch to open the fireplace. Vanner had apparently caught a flash of it as Katya was dragged out. Pity he hadn't noticed the booby trap in front of the door.

"She's pretty locked in on killing this guy, Master Chief," Vanner replied. "We're in movement to your location. Be aware that the Chechens in town are up and moving. You're about to have about two hundred shooters on your ass in no more than five mikes. Security teams are in place and we've got wheels but we need to unass. Now."

"KATYA! OPEN THIS *GOD*-DAMNED DOOR!"

Another swing and a miss. Another shot ricocheting off the rock walls.

"You're running out of time," Kurt said. He was to the stairs, now, sweating heavily but, if anything, the poison seemed to be wearing off.

"You're the one backing away," Katya replied. But she knew it was true. They had to run away—the Kildar preferred the term "egress"—before the entire Chechen force dropped on their heads. "And where are you going to be without your Russian guards?"

"Gone," Kurt said, putting away his pistol and holding up empty hands. "Disappeared. A ghost."

"One haunting me?" Katya asked, straightening out of her crouch cautiously.

"You're not a professional are you, dear," Kurt said and grinned as if he really found it humorous. "I won't waste my time. Oh, perhaps we'll meet again. We live in the same world, after all. If so, I'll remember your cocktails, little girl."

"And I'll remember yours," Katya said, smiling as she backed away. "Another day then. I don't suppose you'll leave me the flashlight?"

"No, I need it," Kurt admitted. "But the switch for the door is on the upper right." He turned off the flashlight and she could hear him moving up the stairs, fast if a little unsteadily.

And damn if the switch wasn't right where he'd said.

Chapter Thirty-Three

"How'd it go?" Mike asked as Adams walked up.

"No big problems," Adams said, casually. "Turns out J spirited Marina out before we hit. Katya took her place. No casualties. Very clean op. Got Katya back. Don't know where J is. Don't care."

One group of Keldara had secured the vehicles the Russians had been using. Those had been used to transport them to the intersection, their previous owners being unavailable for complaint. After sweeping the area for fugitives from the firefight, and finding none, the combined teams were now spread around the intersection on security. A small group was keeping an eye on the small remnant of prisoners, including Al-Kariya, who was due for a long spell in a prison in a U.S.-allied country.

"Yeah, I heard about Marina already being gone," Mike said, absentmindedly. He was watching some figures moving inside of one of the dome tents. "Just got a call from higher; they're fully in Russian territory. Marina will be in Moscow in an hour or so."

"Great," Adams said. "So why are we still here? Shouldn't we be unassing with some nukes?"

"Oh, yeah, those," Mike said, shrugging. "We've got something else to do, first."

"Uh, huh," Adams said. "Mike, just so you know, old buddy, we sort of stirred up a hornets' nest. There are about five hundred Chechens on our ass. And I suspect they're calling their buddies. And the buddies are calling buddies. So, whatever you're doing, do it faster."

"This is one thing that, no matter what, I'm not going to rush," Mike replied. "Got a question for you. Do you think this was too easy?"

"Easy?" Adams asked. "Mike, did you remember the five hundred Chechens?"

"In the plan," Mike said. "You delay them until we're done and then we drive down the road, hit a poorly manned position on the border and we're golden."

"Sometimes it works out that way," Adams said with a shrug. "So we're just going to sit here?"

"No, you're going to grab all the teams except Padrek's and Yosif's, and go back down the road," Mike said. "There you are going to do some good SEAL shit and slow the Chechens down."

"SEAL shit."

"Yeah. SEAL shit. You know. Blow shit up. Kill people. Shit like that."

"And what are you going to be doing while I'm doing 'SEAL shit'?"

"I'm going to be standing right here, worrying like hell."

"I hate destroying all these weapons."

While Padrek's team pulled security, Yosif's was sweeping the battlefield, collecting the weapons and any documents they could find. The haul was pretty good and normally they would have carried them back to the Keldara, arms for the second-line defenders of the valley.

In this case, however, space and weight were going to be at a premium. They had vehicles, now, but didn't know for how long. So the weapons were being collected into piles and before they left they would be set on fire with thermite grenades. There might be a few left useable, but not many.

The ammunition was being put in a different pile, a booby-trapped one. A kilo of C-4 would go off thirty minutes after the trigger was set or, if anything was moved, immediately. One of

Padrek's team was preparing the trap while Yosif's men made the pile.

"Grab those packs," Yosif replied, gesturing to four of the dead Islamics. The four had apparently been close-in guards for the main terrorist, who was now wrapped up in rigger tape like a mummy. The guards had not survived the attack. "They've probably got ammo but check them for documents."

Edvin Kulcyanov bent down and started tugging the bags off. They were heavy but . . . something told him the weight wasn't ammo.

Yosif continued down the line of Toyota pickups, making sure everything was being swept. You never knew where something would turn up. And intel was intel.

"Yosif," Dima Mahona said, pulling his body out of the back of one of the pickups. "Laptop."

"Keep it," Yosif replied. "Vanner might be able to get something off of it."

"Yosif!" Edvin called. "You had better take a look at this!"

Yosif walked back to where the cluster of dead guards lay on the ground and looked at what Edvin held in his hands. It was a bundle of large sheets of paper printed in a language he didn't recognize. They were hard to see in the NVGs so he pulled up the monocular and turned on a blue lens flashlight. They still didn't make any sense to him but he could see now that there was a person's face on them. They looked something like money but they were far too large to be conventional bills.

"What are those?" Yosif asked.

"I don't know," Edvin said. "I hoped you might. There are a bunch of them."

Edvin continued taking the bundles out and stacking them in the mud of the road. At the very bottom there was a cloth bag with a drawstring tie.

Edvin untied it and spilled some of the contents into his hands, a few of the rocks falling into the mud.

"Father of All," Yosif whispered. He wasn't sure what all of the gems *were*, but he recognized gems when he saw them. His mouth opened and closed but he couldn't think of anything to say.

"I think we just found the payroll for whatever we captured," Edvin said.

"Yes," Yosif replied, then keyed his throat mike. "Kildar? I think you need to see this."

"Bearer bonds," Mike said, squatting down and picking up one of the bundles. "Ten thousand euro bearer bonds. German issue. Each of these sheets of paper is worth ten thousand euros." He riffled one of the bundles. "Half a million euros, right here. I'd been told that the price for what we captured was sixty million euros. I *hadn't* expected the money to be on delivery."

"There are four bags, Kildar," Edvin said. He'd gotten up to check one of the others. "There are more of those . . . bonds in here. And some euros as well."

"Break it up among the Keldara," Mike said. "Give the gems to Vanner. If the money weighs us down too much, we'll dump the cash and burn it."

"Burn it?" Yosif asked. "But Kildar . . . there is *very* much money here."

"Do you fight for money, Yosif?" Mike asked, straightening up with a grimace. The weather was being hell on his knees. "I don't. Oh, I like it. Just about anyone does. And it has certainly helped the Keldara, yes? But the reason we're here, the reason that I am here, is in that tent over there. And I would not have come if it weren't for that shit. Not for a billion euros. We're getting paid for this op, paid well. This is just more weight to carry. If we have to run, on foot, then we'll have the entire Chechen force on our ass. We may end up in a battle with ten, twenty, forty times our number. Now, which would you rather have if that happens, another two hundred rounds or a half a million euros?"

"Two hundred rounds," Yosif admitted. He didn't even have to think about it.

"Just so. But I can actually think of something very important to do with it. Distribute it among the teams when they get back. Make up bundles of appropriate size. But tell them to put it somewhere they can dump it. Because if it comes down to ammo or money, we're going for ammo. And hurry. As soon as Dr. Arensky is done, we are *out* of here."

"Now that we have containment," Dr. Arensky said, his voice muffled by the gas mask, "we pour the material into the beaker.

Normally, it is best to pour the acid into a material. But in this case, it risks explosive exgassing. That would not be good."

"I understand," Padrek replied, calmly. "Whatever this is, it is very bad, no?"

"Very bad," Dr. Arensky admitted. "If any gets on us, I have asked your boss, Mr. Jenkins, to just shoot us through the tent and then pour all the acid on the result."

"That's bad," Padrek admitted. The Keldara team leader was the best of the Keldara when it came to mechanisms and, as the Kildar put it, "fiddly stuff." Which he supposed was why he was in this tent, breathing through a gas mask, covered in a rubber suit and helping this Russian destroy this white powder. Mostly he was holding the flashlight. Occasionally he poured some of the acid, what the Russian called "high molar sulfuric," into one of the beakers or test tubes.

The Russian had poured some of the acid into a flask, several of which the Keldara had carried on the mission, carefully packed in boxes. Then he had wrapped a plastic bag around one of the test tubes in the strange metal containers. The bag had been taped to the flask top with the test tube contained in the whole arrangement. Only then did he remove the screw-stopper, working from the outside of the bag, and carefully pour the white powder into the flask. As it fell it the stuff melted, releasing gases that puffed up the bag like a balloon. But well before it was ready to burst all the powder except a very small dusting was gone.

"Now it's done?" Padrek asked.

"No," the Russian said. "That dusting could kill the world, young man. Now it gets tricky."

The Russian carefully raised the flask and, with Padrek holding the plastic out of the way, poured some of the liquid into the test tube. This time the effect was almost impossible to notice. Last, he swirled the liquid around, poured it back into the flask, back again, getting every trace of the white powder.

"Now we are done," the Russian said. "How many flasks do we have?"

"Seven," Padrek said, pointing to the pile of boxes in the corner of the tent.

"Good, then we don't have to disassemble this and risk contamination," the Russian said.

"Dr. Arensky?" the Kildar called from outside the tent. Well outside from the sound of it.

"Yes?"

"How's it coming?"

"We have successfully neutralized one of the samples. There are four."

"Oh. Thought you should know. We've got most of the Chechen army bearing down on us. They're really pissed about something or another. Just an FYI."

"Then I shall endeavor to hurry," the Russian said. "Mr. Padrek, if you could get me another flask, please?"

"Just Padrek," Padrek corrected. "Padrek Ferani. But Mr. Ferani doesn't work either so . . . Just Padrek."

"Then if you could please give me a flask, Padrek," Dr. Arensky said. "And you may call me Tolegen since we're such good friends."

SEAL shit. SEAL *shit*. *SEEEAL* shit.

Adams was blanked. All he could do was look down the road towards the town. He'd pulled the teams down about a klick from the intersection, dispersed them on both sides of the road and at that point his mind had just gone fucking *blank*.

"Do some SEAL shit," he muttered. Oh, fuck, he was starting to think like a fucking officer, or worse a *trainer*, but it just might work.

"Oleg!"

"Master Chief!" the team leader called from the side of the road.

"We got about five hundred Chechens approaching this position," Adams said as the sound of vehicles started to penetrate through the rain. "You are required to delay them for twenty minutes and then retreat, preferably without any engagement. What is your answer to this test question?"

Mike looked over his shoulder at a series of cracks. But the sound of trees falling indicated that Adams was just putting in a roadblock. Good old Adams, he always came through.

"Is it well, Mr. Jenkins?" Dr. Arensky called from in the tent.

"Yeah, no problem," Mike yelled. "Just putting in a roadblock to slow the Chechens down. Where we at?"

"Down to the last sample," Dr. Arensky called back, cheerfully. "Padrek has been most helpful."

"He's a helpful lad," Mike replied. "What are we going to do when you're done? Anything else?"

"I would suggest burning this tent and our containment gear. Most thoroughly."

"Anton . . ." Mike said to Padrek's assistant team leader. He was personally blanking on starting a fire in the pouring rain.

"I'll go find some gas cans," the Keldara said. "Diesel rather. We have thermite grenades to start them. That should work even in this mess."

"Exactly," Mike said. "Vanner?" he said, touching his throat mike.

"Right here, sir," Vanner said from behind him.

"Jesus!" Mike said as he jumped. "I think that's the first time in fifteen years someone's snuck up behind me."

"I didn't exactly sneak, sir," Vanner replied. "I've been standing here for ten minutes."

"What's the update?"

"According to the girls," Vanner said, referring to the intel section back at the caravanserai, "there is one Chechen battalion moving in from the north. That's one of their heavier batts, about four to five hundred. They are assembling vehicles and sending forward groups as they get transportation. In addition, we're getting heavy signal traffic across the area. They know the op went down, we've been ID'd as Spetznaz, Delta and, worst, Keldara. General consensus is coming down on Keldara and they seriously want our ass. There are indications that a blocking force is going in on the road to Georgia. We can make it part of the way, but I'm not sure we'll have the correlation of forces to force our way through. Right now it's a small force, but there's a short battalion, about a hundred, making their way to the blocking point."

He'd pulled out a large pad with a plasma screen and now cycled it on. The screen was about the size of a sheet of letter-size paper and had a map of the area. On it the friendly units were designated by blue icons and enemies were marked with red. Where either were off the screen their direction and distance was marked with karats pointed to the sides. Mike took the pad, scrolled out for a look around and shook his head. Red icons were popping up all over the map. Most of them were already showing movement symbols towards their position. The main threat, though, was the Chechen battalion approaching from the north. However, the defenses to the south showed heavy weapons capability and dug in defenses. Then he noted the symbol at the opening of the Guerrmo Pass.

And none of that covered units that signal intercept *hadn't* picked up. Some units could have been contacted and told to move but didn't respond. The girls might have missed an intercept.

Mike hadn't planned on the destruction of the smallpox taking so long and he'd always known the mission was on a knife edge. Currently, the situation was headed towards true military FUBAR. Fucked up beyond all recognition.

"How very good," Mike said. "We still in contact with higher?"

"Affirmative," Vanner replied. "There's a Predator up, not that it can see or do anything. But we're looking at clearing in about six hours. I got a note that there was a satellite pass but I don't have that, yet."

"I'd like to be out of here in six hours," Mike pointed out.

"Unlikely, sir," Vanner pointed out. "The blocking force is heavy weapons heavy. We'd be trying to fight our way past bunkers blocking the road. And, sir, we have very limited heavy weapons, no air support . . ."

"I'm aware of the issues, Vanner," Mike said. "Okay, what's our secondary?"

"Guerrmo Pass," Vanner said. "We take the road up about five klicks then unass and head up through the hills. Unfortunately, we have recent reports from the Rangers that the Chechens *also* have a heavy weapons position, three bunkers ID'd, in the pass. On the backside, admittedly, oriented to prevent entry from the Georgian side. But there are forces there."

"Saw that," Mike said as sporadic firing started to the north. "Cross that pass when we come to it. Dr. Arensky?"

"Just done," Arensky replied. "Preparing to come out. I would suggest that you set two more sets of environment suits outside the tent. We will exit and change into those. Then we will torch the entire assembly, after breaking the flasks through the tent fabric. Padrek and I will remain in the suits for a few days as quarantine in case we have not been as successful in containment as I have hoped."

"Sucks to be you," Mike muttered. "Works. We've got cans of diesel and thermite grenades on the ground outside the tent. We'll just back off, shall we?"

"Please."

"Right, Vanner, call in the dogs. By the time they get here, it'll be time to run."

"Hold your fire," Adams said.

The Chechens had apparently sent out vehicles as fast as they could find them. Given that Adams had stolen most of their dedicated trucks, the lead group was one Toyota pickup, the mujahideen vehicle of choice, and a motley collection of Ladas, Paykans and various other small sedans. The Toyota was in the lead and one of the mujahideen in the bed had a light machine gun across the top of the truck.

That would have been a bright move if the driver had actually seen the first tree in time.

The Toyota slammed on its brakes but it was far too close to do anything other than cause it to slew sideways. Before it could start to roll from the turn, the right front wheel hit the poplar in the road. The vehicle launched upwards and over, doing a flip in the air before landing amongst the larger trees that made up the bulk of the roadblock.

"Now open fire," Adams said as the mujahideen who had been standing up holding the machine gun slammed across one of the trees with an audible "crack" as his back broke. It really didn't matter since his head hit another log at the same time, splashing brains and blood across the road in a spray.

The teams had loaded fairly light for this mission so most of the machine-gun teams, who usually carried NATO 7.62 M240s, were armed with M249 Squad Automatic Weapons which fired the lighter 5.56 round.

That didn't help the Chechens much. Before they could even begin to bail out of their vehicles the four teams opened up with a withering storm of gunfire, stitching the vehicles with rounds. The rifle Keldara fired in controlled three-round bursts, aiming for the shadows of men in the vehicles, the rounds cracking through windscreens and doors. The SAWs sounded very much like chainsaws, ripping off five-round bursts that stitched the vehicles with small, neat, lines of bullet holes.

Two of the Chechens made it out into that hail of lead, trying to reach the cover of the nearby stream, but they didn't even make it three steps before falling into the road. The movement had attracted several of the Keldara's fire and the two did a dance as the dozens of rounds stitched them.

"Check fire," Adams said over the team circuit. "Snipers. If you see anyone moving, finish them off."

"Master Chief. Vanner. Kildar says pull in the dogs."

"Belay that," Adams said. "Everyone get to the trucks. We're out of here. Oleg, arm the claymores. Sawn, drop a marker."

"Slow down," Commander Bukara said as the first vehicle came in sight. "Stop! Everyone out!"

Mikhail Ashenov had been a lieutenant in the Red Army when the Soviet Union broke up. But though he had a Russianized name, he had been raised a devoted Muslim. The Prophet had decreed it permissible, indeed recommended, that the faithful lie to the unbelievers. And under Communism, being an Islamic made it impossible to have a decent life. So the Ashenov family had worshipped in secret and held true to the ideal that, some day, Chechnya would return to the umah.

But even with the breakup of the Soviet Union, the fucking Russians had held tight to Chechnya. Chechnya with its oil fields and mines. Chechnya with its forests and powerful rivers supplying hydroelectric power.

Mikhail Ashenov had been one of the first recruits of the burgeoning Chechen resistance. At first distrusted, he had rapidly proven to be a decent fighter, combining the methods of the guerrilla with his professional training. For the last ten years he had gathered more and more fighters to him until he was a notable "battalion" commander with five hundred trained mujahideen under his command.

Make that about four hundred and seventy, now.

The Chechens had been fighting the Russians for a long time so they knew the drill well. The fighters piled out of the vehicles fast, some of them moving up the sides of the road and others fading into the trees.

"Damn them," Bukara said, walking forward. He'd hoped to catch this team before they faded away and were picked up by their helicopters. He assumed that it must be Spetznaz. As he walked up the line of stitched vehicles, bodies tumbled out on the ground he shook his head. He had gathered together as many men as he had vehicles for and thrown them ahead, hoping to pin the Spetznaz before they could escape. This was the result.

"They were slaughtered." Sayeed was his long-term driver and bodyguard. But Bukara could hear the tone in his voice. It was a very unhappy tone.

A Chechen "commander" could only command as long as he had the respect of his men. Although there was discipline in the army—any army had to have laws—fighters could desert to other commanders. The quickest way to become an ex battalion commander was to lose his men's trust and respect. And having a slaughter like this on his books was a way to lose that respect fast. This was a disaster.

Suddenly there was a massive crash from the front and he dove behind one of the vehicles as the air seemed to fill with bees.

"Directional mines," Sayeed said.

"Fuckers," Bukara replied. The blast had come from up by the trees that blocked the road. The fucking Spetznaz had assumed whoever came next would start to clear the trees. And they'd laid in mines to make that more dangerous. If the whole blockade was laced with explosives this could take hours to clear.

"Commander!" one of the fighters called, holding something up in his hand. It looked like a piece of cloth.

Bukara strode forward as men gathered around the wounded, pulling them back to the motley collection of vehicles he'd managed to gather in Gamasoara.

The fighter was holding what looked like some sort of patch. Bukara took it and shown his flashlight on it.

"Blood of the Prophet."

Bukara had fought his former Russian masters for over ten years. They came in several forms, the half-trained conscripts that were so easy to kill it was almost a crime, the better trained "elite" units that some of the divisions now sported and, worst of all, the

Spetznaz, those cold-eyed killers who slaughtered and then faded into the night and shadows. But though the Russians were powerful, they were not feared. Hated, yes, but not feared.

This enemy, though. They had been interfering with convoys for quite some time now and the one concerted effort to destroy them had been a disaster; the battalion of two hundred sent against them had been utterly destroyed. And the word that they got from several sources was that it had been by less than thirty of the pagans.

But their reputation went back further than that. The Chechens had sparred with them for generations and of all groups in Georgia they were the most feared. Ancient and powerful fighters, wielders of broad axes which could cleave a man to the waist. Warriors and reavers who masked as simple farmers. Pagans that hid their faith and played at being Christians. Drinkers of blood in secret rites under the mountains, they were rumored to sacrifice their captives to their black gods.

Now they had a new lord, a mercenary from distant lands as had always been the case. And fucking American spec ops of all things. Americans *were* feared among the mujahideen as perhaps the greatest threat to the umah since the Byzantines. And their spec ops, from what Bukara had heard, made the Spetznaz seem like child conscripts.

It had been long since the Tigers crossed the mountains, bringing fire and axe to Chechen villages, but mothers still used them to strike fear into the hearts of children. "Be a good boy or the Tigers will take you and eat your heart."

The scrap of fabric in his hand told the whole story.

The Keldara were back.

Chapter Thirty-Four

"There's another one," Greznya said, holding up her hand. She tapped a control and the electronic feed was automatically shunted to a computer program Vanner had "borrowed" from the National Security Agency. The computer chuckled over the intercept and then spat out a prediction. "Borana's Brigade. Approximate numbers nine hundred. Heavy weapons, 12.7 on trucks and 81 millimeter mortars. RPGs as usual. They're about seven hours away but rolling out now."

"That makes well over nineteen distinct units heading for the Area of Operations," Lydia Kulcyanov said, looking over her shoulder at Colonel Nielson. She looked about six months pregnant. Given that she had been married to Oleg for only four months, that made the child almost certainly the Kildar's. Not that anyone was going to note that or even care. But it would be nice to get her husband back so she could have one with him. With nineteen Chechen units, each of unknown numbers, closing on the hundred and twenty or so Keldara, it was looking more and more like Oleg was going to come home in a body bag. If at all.

The colonel just nodded and gestured with his chin.

"Update the board," he said.

✧   ✧   ✧

Kacey watched her dials as they came into the green and took a deep breath.

The back had been rigged for litters. Four of them. There were more casualties than that but she could loft a couple more bodies. If they used the Guerrmo Pass on the way back. Outgoing, with just herself, Tammy, Gretchen, some ammo and heavy weapons and the litters they would be fine.

She'd seriously considered asking the Rangers for one of their medics. The Ranger medics were 18 Deltas, trained at the Special Forces Medic School at Fort Sam Houston. Like Special Forces medics they were trained to do anything but "open the cranial cavity." All of them were EMT-qualified and could keep somebody alive just about as well as a first-class emergency room. But they were under the same stupid damned orders as the rest of their company. They could *not* cross the mountains under any circumstances. Washington was playing political games while people were *dying*.

So were the Georgians, for that matter. But they were in support. Captain Kahbolov had turned up with three Blackhawks, each with handpicked medics in the back. All *Kacey* had to do was get the wounded Keldara back to the base. Then the Georgians would take over, flying the wounded back to Tbilisi Military Hospital.

Six casualties to evac. And the Russian scientist. And "Katya," whom she'd never met but heard enough about. There was no way they were getting them all in one lift. Too much weight.

No. Fuck that. She'd seen that the Hind had more lift than even the Czech engineers were willing to admit. They'd pack them in like sardines if necessary.

Just pray the wounded survived the trip.

Especially given that, that loaded, she was going to have to fly right through the fire of the bunkers in the pass.

She pulled up on the collective and lifted off into the howling storm.

For once, weather was the *least* of her worries.

"Drop everything but ammo and water," Mike said over the throat mike.

Sawn was driving the Toyota pickup and Mike wished they'd changed places. But he couldn't run the op and drive at the same time, the reason that the military assigned drivers to officers.

Fuck, he really *was* brass.

"When we hit the stopping point, we are going to *run* not walk, to the LZ."

He was in commo with the team leaders and depended on them to pass the word to their teams. That was what the chain of command was all about.

"Strip to bare necessities," Mike continued. "Anybody who can't run goes on a stretcher. Detail teams to replace as we move. All the casualties go out as soon as we hit the LZ. Oleg, you're in charge of keeping Dr. Arensky and Katya with us. If either one can't make the time, dump somebody's ruck and *piggyback* them. Our one mission is to get to the other side of the mountains as fast as humanly possible. Get moving."

He switched frequencies without thought.

"Vanner."

"Kildar?"

"Tell your girls to drop all their gear," Mike said. "They only carry LCE and their weapons. They *have* to keep up."

"Got it."

"Padrek."

"Kildar?" The reply was muffled.

"Drop all your gear except weapon and LCE. Cross-load your spare ammo. You're going out on the bird if there's room. You're going to sweat your ass off in that suit and drinking through the mask is a bitch. If you start to get too overheated, hell, I don't know what we're gonna do. Put you on one of the stretchers or something. Keep hydrated as best you can."

"Yes, Kildar."

"We'll extract you as fast as we can."

Three of the Toyota pickups, loaded to the brim with Keldara from Team Yosif, were in the lead. Mike hoped the Chechens hadn't gotten an ambush team in ahead of them—he couldn't afford more casualties—but if they had the three pickups would hopefully spring it.

The entire group, using every functional vehicle, was barrel-assing down the road towards the Georgian lines. There was no way to fight their way through, the girls had confirmed that a group of over two hundred had crossed a mountain and were now in blocking positions—but that was also the way to the Guerrmo Pass.

The mountains *thinned* at that point. Whereas they had had to cross nearly a hundred klicks of nasty assed alpine terrain on the way in, at the Guerrmo the distance from their current valley to "safety" was barely thirty kilometers. He could run that in a few hours on the flat. But this was going to be going up increasingly steep ridgelines stretching up well above the woodline and into the snowline. The Keldara could make it, assuming more Chechens didn't cut them off. But the females both hadn't been in as much training as the fighters and . . . Well, there was a reason that men and women competed in different leagues in the Olympics. The Keldara were, at this point, damned near Olympic-quality athletes. They could carry their rucks at a dog trot all God damned day even straight up a slope. He'd worked hard to get them to that level of condition for *precisely* this reason.

The girls could maybe maintain a jog for three hours. Uphill, less. Even if they'd been in the same condition, they couldn't have hung with the boys carrying the same gear. As long as they were with the group the Keldara simply couldn't run as fast. And right now, the only thing that they could do, should do, was run like hell.

Getting them out was a priority right up there with evaccing the casualties and Arensky.

Freq switch again. This time it was to a connection that automatically routed the call through a satellite.

"Tiger Two."

"Go, Kildar."

"I take it the helo is moving?"

"On the way," Nielson replied. "They *have* to fly through Guerrmo, though. They can get higher but not carrying any sort of useable load. And Guerrmo . . ."

"I saw," Mike replied. "So, is that a permissible Ranger AO?"

"Negative."

"Fuck."

"Sir, with all due respect, this is crap," Guerrin said.

He'd set up a satellite call to SOCOM. Their operational control for this mission ran direct to SOCOM, bypassing the Ranger command group entirely. It wasn't unusual to get tasked to other units that had operational control.

But he didn't usually talk directly to the SOCOM commander.

"I'm in agreement, Captain," General Howard said, mildly. "However, I just got off the phone with the CJCS on this very subject. Relations in the area are very touchy at this time. The Georgians don't want you fighting at all. They certainly don't want it apparent to the world that they can't control their own territory. So the Keldara have to fight their way out on their own. If the Chechens *pass* the entrance to Guerrmo Pass, if in other words they come past those defenses, you are clear to engage. Among other things, at that point it becomes self protection and I was firm on that point. But until then you are to remain in place and *not* engage anyone that is in or beyond the pass. Is that clear?"

"Clear, sir," J.P. said. "I will comply. If the situation changes, though . . ."

"I'll inform you immediately," the general said. "And I hope it does. For your information, I'm told the mission came off without a hitch. The only hitch is that the entire Chechen force in the area seems to be determined to wipe these guys off the map. And, trust me, I know exactly how it feels to just be sitting there in the rain not able to do a fucking thing. But that is *exactly* what you are going to do."

"Sergeant Sivula?" Jessia said, sticking her head in the doorway to the barracks.

"Yes," the sergeant said, rolling off his bunk and glad none of the guys were naked when she burst in.

"We are moving the mortars," Jessia said, panting. "The Keldara are trapped on the other side of the mountains."

"We got the word," Sivula said, walking over. The panting was doing really interesting things to her chest but he tried to ignore that. "But we can't do anything."

"Neither can we," Jessia admitted. "But we are going to move our mortars forward to support when they are in the pass. *We* can fire into it."

"Damn, that's right," Sivula said, grinning. "Let me get with the LT. I guess you'd like some help?"

"We are strong," Jessia said, shrugging. "But they are *very* heavy. As is the ammunition. Yes, we would like some help. As many strong backs as you can muster."

"Fuck, yeah," Sivula said. "I'll be with you in a few minutes."

The President stared at the take from the Predator and sighed. It was, more or less, gray clouds and not much else. The pilots had admitted that they were steering well away from mountains and otherwise entirely on instruments. Nothing could pierce the storm in the area.

"This is very frustrating."

"We can permit the Rangers to move," the CJCS said. "General Howard says that they are chomping at the bit."

"Georgia says not only no but hell no," the Secretary of State said with a sigh. "The defense minister has stuck his nose in to the whole thing. He's not about to let anyone think that the Georgians can't control their own territory. Even if that's truth."

"So the Keldara are going to have to fight their way out on their own," the president said.

"Unless this clears," the secretary of defense said.

"Unfortunately, this is all the time I can spare to this," the President said. "Or perhaps fortunately. Keep me apprised if the situation changes. If the weather clears, turn operational control of the Predators over to Mr. Jenkins. Use them at his discretion. Make sure at least one is up, armed, at all times. The B-2 is on the way back?"

"Yes, sir," the CJCS confirmed.

"Then my purpose here is really served," the President noted. "Time for real work."

No ambushes.

That was the good news. The bad news was that the easy part was over.

"Out!" Oleg was shouting from the back. "Move it!"

Mike glanced at his BFT device as he rolled out the door. The Chechen unit holding the road up ahead still hadn't moved, according to the device. Reality might be otherwise. The group behind them, according to the intercepts, was still held up at the roadblock. Damn, Adams was good.

The rain had slowed, at least. It wasn't clearing, really, but it had settled down to a steady, soft, really fucking cold, rain. Good weather for running.

The Keldara were already fading into the woods. He'd made it clear, get a point out in front but none of this slow-ass dicking around. The point now was simply *speed*.

"Why hello, Katya," Mike said as he trotted into the woods. The blonde was distinct, her hair practically glowed even in the near total darkness. He'd have to get her a balaclava. Somebody had already given her a coldweather suit. "Fancy meeting you here."

"This is not what I signed up for," the agent spat. "Running in the dark in woods is for you caveman types."

"If you can't make it, I'm sure Shota would be happy to carry you piggyback." The Keldara had been stripped, reluctantly, of most of his heavy armor for the run. Mike had heard him protesting from the back of the truck that he could keep up with it on, really he could. But Oleg had been firm.

"I'll keep up," the girl said, stumbling over a root. "If I could just *see*."

Mike stripped off his NVGs and stopped, pulling the girl over.

"Here," he said, slipping the harness on her head and adjusting it. Then he flipped the monocular down. "Better?"

"Yes, Kildar," Katya admitted. "Thank you."

"I can actually see pretty well in this," Mike admitted. He'd always had cateyes. "Oh, wait," he added, pulling off his own balaclava. He'd find one somewhere and his face and hair didn't stand out as much as hers. He slid the overlarge head covering on, after taking off the NVGs, then put those back on and adjusted the whole assembly.

"Thank you, again," Katya said, pulling up the hood of the weather suit. "Now, I think we run, yes? I wish I'd brought running shoes. But at least I'm in flats."

"You're going out as soon as we reach the LZ," Mike pointed out. "You should do fine. Stick with me, kid."

"I think I will," Katya said.

"Up, Vugar," Yosif said, cheerfully, yanking up on the ruck of the Keldara sprawled face down in a stream. "No lying down on the job."

"Just getting a drink, Yosif," the Keldara said, blowing out a mouthful of mud. "Gotta keep hydrated or the Kildar will have us sent to the Cold Lands."

They'd been trotting through the pitch-black woods for the last forty-five minutes and *everyone* had sprawled at least once. Even the Kildar had ended up sliding, backwards, down a hillside. Adams had run face-first into a tree, smashing his NVGs. Two men were on stretchers from injuries.

But they were nearly to the LZ, a bare hilltop four klicks from the road.

Now if the chopper would just be there.

"LZ in sight," Tammy said. "I don't see our friends. BFT has them nearby, though. I think we're coming down lonely, though."

"Gretchen," Kacey said over the intercom. "Make sure the Gatling is armed. We're coming into the LZ lonely so we don't know if it's hot or cold."

"Yes, ma'am," the Keldara girl said. "I will keep any enemies off."

"Just fire if fired upon," Kacey said, sighing. The girl positively *wanted* to get in a firefight. It was the *last* thing Kacey had on her mind.

The ride in had, frankly, sucked. The storm seemed to be breaking up but that just meant that the winds were getting worse. Coming through the high passes in the mountains, fighting the now piggish Hind in high altitude, had been a nightmare. She'd nearly clipped a mountain three times.

Now she had no clue what the winds on the LZ were going to be like. And it wasn't exactly large.

"Tiger, Tiger burning bright," Kacey said over the radio. "This is Valkyrie. Status, over."

"Valkyrie, this is Tiger One," Mike panted. He pulled on Katya's arm to drag her up the slope while thumbing his throat mike with the other hand. The agent was clearly just about done and he was half tempted to just throw her over his shoulder. Take that for calling him a "caveman." "We are five hundred meters east of LZ. ETA one mike, over."

"Roger, Tiger. We are going to swing around and come back. LZ looks clear, but . . ."

"Confirm, Tiger. Be there in a minute. Out."

"Just another minute, Katya," Mike said. "Come *on*."

"I . . . can't . . . breathe . . ." the agent panted.

"Surely you're not going to let us *men* out-do you?" Mike snarled. "The *men* are doing just fine but you puny *women* . . ."

"Oh FUCK you!" Katya snarled, pushing off from a tree. "I'll fucking *race* you to the top you fucking *pig*!"

"That's my girl," Mike muttered, quietly, as Katya stumbled up the hill, actually passing one of the panting Keldara shooters.

The wind was whipping the light rain into his eyes as he cleared the woodline. Katya was down on her hands and knees ralphing into the scrub that covered it. All good.

"Valkyrie, Valkyrie, this is Tiger," Mike panted. "LZ is clear."

Somebody, probably Pavel, was already laying out a Y with chemlights, indicating direction of wind.

"Y is laid," Mike continued. "Winds are high, repeat, high. About seventeen knots from the west. Suggest vector from east."

"Roger, Tiger. See Y. Inbound. Clear the LZ."

"Clear the LZ!" Mike shouted, thumbing his throat mike at the same time. "Incoming bird."

He grabbed Katya's arm and dragged her to the north side of the clearing, over into the trees on that side.

"Just one more run," he said. "Let them dump the ammo then you run girl. Good girl. You're a trooper."

"Oh fuck you," Katya said, spitting out bile. "Fuck this. Fuck the Keldara. Fuck missions. Fuck everything."

"Honey, you never want to fuck *anything*," Mike said, grinning into the rain. "But I appreciate the sentiment. Welcome to the wonderful world of soldiers."

"Damn that's a nasty wind," Kacey muttered. It was mostly from the west, yeah, but it was swirling around like a bitch.

"Six meters, three . . . touch," Tammy said, watching the FLIR.

"We're down," Kacey said over the intercom. "Gretchen, start dumping! We got wounded to load!"

Chapter Thirty-Five

"Hi, Gretchen," Dafyd Shaynav said, scrambling into the helicopter and starting to toss the boxes in the bay out the door.

"Hi, Dafyd," Gretchen replied, hefting a long, obviously heavy, package and tossing it into the howling darkness. "Where's Viktor?"

"He's . . . on the way," Dafyd replied as he kicked the last box of ammo out the door. "On the first stretcher."

"Hi, Gretchen," Viktor gasped as the stretcher was dumped into the holders. He was looking pretty happy given that there was a bandage bigger than his head slapped over his stomach. It was already bright red.

"Brother, I told you to be careful," Gretchen said, her face working. The Ranger medic had shown her how to start an IV and she pulled out a bag of O-positive blood, hanging it from a hook and sliding the IV into her brother's arm even as another body was dumped on the floor.

The man wasn't anyone she recognized, a fat man in Islamic clothing, his hands, feet and mouth bound with rigger tape.

"Another passenger," Dafyd said. "You're going to be heavy loaded."

She felt of Viktor's pulse then looked at the next casualty. Piotr Mahona had taken a bullet through the upper thigh, breaking his femoral bone but missing the artery. He, too, was in pretty good spirits, courtesy of two ampoules of morphine.

Juris Devlich had a head wound and was unconscious. She'd been told that head wounds bled rather spectacularly and the bloody mess of bandage was dripping already and the floor of the helicopter was becoming slick. His pulse was weak and thready. She took down the automatic defibrillator and, pulling open his uniform top, attached the leads to his chest. If his heart stopped beating, it was supposed to automatically restart it. One of the Ranger medics had told her to do that for the worst of the casualties but she had *no* clue what the damned thing did.

Vitali Kulcyanov was unconscious, too, a big bandage on his chest. There was blood coating his mouth and it had run down his face and into his hair.

Varlam Makanee had picked up grenade splinters in his calf and lifted himself into the helicopter, sliding to the rear and propping himself on the back wall.

"Hello, Gretchen," he said, grimacing but trying to sound light. "Nice night for flying don't you think?"

Katya scrambled on after him, looking around and then sitting down in the crew-chief's jump seat. Apparently Gretchen was going to be standing up for the whole flight.

Suddenly a large rubber bag was slid onto the slick floor, causing Varlam to have to pull his feet up so it would fit.

"Sion," Dafyd said. "He is away to the Halls."

"Oh, *damn*," Gretchen said, shaking her head.

"Don't grieve," Dafyd said. "Grieve for us who are forced to endure this fallen world. He has gone to the Halls. Rejoice."

A small heavyset man in some sort of rubber suit slid on last, looking around and then sitting down by Varlam. He nodded at her but she was far too busy checking the casualties. She wasn't going to try changing any of the bandages on the trip but all of the casualties were bleeding. She was mostly running in whole blood. She hoped that the Blackhawks had brought more or would bring more. She was just about out of O positive; most of the Keldara were that blood type.

"Gretchen."

"Yes, Captain Bathlick?"

"We're lifting off. We were supposed to pick up two more Keldara girls and one of the team leaders but I don't think we can. We're way overloaded so we're going to *have* to go through Guerrmo. Stand by the guns on my command. How are the casualties?"

"All alive so far," Gretchen said, looking at Viktor again. "Some of them are . . . very bad."

"I will try to hurry," Captain Bathlick replied as the helicopter staggered into the air.

"What did our personal Valkyrie bring?" Adams asked. There was a list somewhere in his BFT box, but he had never gotten the trick of bringing stuff up quickly.

"5.56," Oleg said, flashing a red-lens flashlight on the pile of boxes. "Magazines and belt for the SAWs. 7.62, belted and match for the snipers. Frags. And . . . why in the hell did they send us *rocket* ammo?"

"Here," Dmitri Devlich said, happily. "Where is Shota?"

"In the woodline," Oleg said. "Pouting because we left his armor behind. Why?"

"I think he'll stop pouting soon," Dmitri replied, lifting a long box up out of the scrub. It was a case for a Carl Gustav rocket launcher.

"Oh, *fuck* yeah," Adams said. "HEY! SHOTA! FRONT AND CENTER!"

"Sorry, Julia," Mike said as the helicopter lifted into the darkness.

"It is not a problem, Kildar." The commo girl didn't actually seem that put out. If anything the opposite. "Next lift, perhaps. The wounded have priority, yes?"

"Yes," Mike said. They were still a long way from home. There were going to be more casualties. "Adams? Get 'em moving."

The President signed the next paper on the stack then picked up the telephone and, without looking, pressed a button.

"Major," he said, sliding the next paper over and glancing at the header, "status on the Keldara and the Predators."

"Weather is starting to clear, Mr. President," the AF major replied. "Keldara made their first extraction without incident. The birds are going to have to fly through some hostile fire, though. Dr. Arensky is onboard."

"Very well," the President said, hanging up without saying goodbye. He read the executive summary of the document, turned to the last page, signed it and then slid it to the side.

Engines up in that "over redline" zone that Marek had sworn was there, and bottom just about brushing the rocks of the pass, the Hind made it over the highest point of their flight.

The rocks had been more guessed at than seen. The front was clearing but that just meant that the clouds were choking the pass, making visibility in the area something in the order of arm's length. She'd done the entire upper pass on pure instruments, trying *very* hard not to look out the windows so she wouldn't get vertigo.

Despite the fact that they'd passed the toughest flying, and it was a stone bitch with the winds whipping through the pass, Kacey kept the bird redlined as she descended. Just around the corner was the exit of the pass. And the bunkers.

She was trying to claw for any altitude she could get but the fucking Hind was being a total pig between the thin air and the overload. As the altitude dropped they slid out of the clouds but she'd just as well get back up *into* them. However, the bird was only in the air due to "ground effect" and even though the God-damned things were only fifty feet overhead, the damned Hind was just *not* going to go any higher.

"Gretchen," Kacey said over the intercom. "We're coming up on the bunkers. There are going to be two out the port, the *left*, side. Orient your fire there."

She'd made sure the Gatling was on that side for a reason. She'd considered not taking it, and the ammunition, which was even heavier, but suppressing *some* of the fire was going to be better than flying through cold.

"Make sure you *hit* them, girl," Kacey added. She banked gently to the side, using the rotor to turn as much as anything. Just keeping the damned bird in the air was about all she could do and they weren't going much faster than a horse. This was truly gonna suck.

✧   ✧   ✧

"There," Baakr Al-Rus said, looking out the slit of the bunker. "There is the helicopter we have been hearing."

"Why is it going so slow?" Hanan ed-Din asked.

"I don't know," Baakr said, pulling back the charging bar on the 12.7mm machine gun. "But it's not going to fly much further."

Gretchen had gotten oxygen masks on the worst of the casualties, all the masks she had, and replaced the blood packs on two. The floor of the Hind was now awash in blood, deep enough that it was lapping up on her boots. The Russian and Varlam were sitting in it, which was worse.

Now, though, she had other things to think about.

She pressed the button that cycled the first round into the Gatling gun and took it off safe. The 7.62 gun was electrically driven with eight barrels that would fire an amazing four thousand rounds per minute. She had never fired one, but it was supposed to be much like the machine guns she had trained on. Just much more powerful.

She also had never fired from a moving helicopter, but Chief D'Allaird had told her "just lead them a little." He'd chuckled when he said it for some reason.

She would have to do her best.

However, although she should be seeing the bunkers, she couldn't pick them out. They were down there somewhere but camouflaged.

"Ma'am," she said, nervously. "I don't see . . ."

Baakr led the helicopter, slightly, aiming for the area where the engine must be. When he was pretty sure he had a good sight he pressed the butterfly trigger of the machine gun.

The rounds missed to the rear, sparking off the tail. He continued to fire, twisting forward . . .

"Never mind!" Gretchen shouted as first one then the other bunker opened fire. She depressed the trigger of the minigun and was startled to see what looked like a stream of fire come out of it.

The sound was like nothing she had ever heard in her life, like one of the chainsaws the Kildar had bought, but infinitely louder.

The worst part, though, was that she was missing. The rounds were striking forward of the bunkers and she twisted her body sideways, bringing them around . . .

"Prophet's Ghost!" Baakr swore as the bullets, what seemed more like a laser, swept across the front of the bunker. All of them had been high, chewing the sandbags of the top rather than striking through the narrow firing window, but he ducked nonetheless.

"Maybe they were going slow so they could hit us better," Hanan said from the floor of the bunker beside him.

"We took some dings," Kacey said. "I felt the strikes."

"Dings, hell!" Tammy shouted. "I've got a *hole* in my right window!"

"Gretchen, how's things back there?"

Gretchen stopped firing as soon as she couldn't twist the minigun any more to the rear.

"I'm fine," Gretchen said, keying her throat mike and turning away from the window. "I think . . ." She stopped and sobbed. "Oh, Father of All."

The stray 12.7 round had traveled upwards at over eight hundred meters per second, cresting the top of the armored door on the side of the helicopter and striking Viktor Mahona from underneath, passing up through his lower abdomen and then bouncing off the armored top of the squad bay to ricochet, unnoticed, out the troop door next to Gretchen.

The effect upon hitting Viktor's recumbent body had been something like a small grenade exploding in his midsection. The top of the troop bay was splashed with red that dripped on the other casualties, and pieces, mostly intestines, of her brother's body were scattered across the bay. Virtually his entire body from his lower rib cage to his hips was missing.

The straps, across his legs and chest, had kept those parts in place. And Viktor still had that happy, goofy, grin on his face she knew so well. He'd been hit too fast, and hard, to even grimace.

"We took one casualty," Gretchen said, trying not to let her voice break. "Otherwise we're fine." She reached up and plucked at something dangling in her view. It was green and dripping and otherwise she couldn't begin to place it. She just knew it was from her brother's body. She suddenly realized that her back was sodden with blood. She laid the dripping thing carefully on the stretcher. "We're fine."

Chapter Thirty-Six

Haza Saghedi raised himself out of the stream, hands up.

He had managed to kill several of the Russians before he realized they were not, in fact, the enemy. He'd heard the different tone of the firing to the rear and swept around to the side, shooting at least one of the camouflage-clad figures that was sweeping across the convoy of mujahideen.

However, he was, perhaps, the only survivor. He had hidden under bushes as the pig infidels had swept the area. With long experience of surviving under every circumstance he wasn't about to let these pigs get him. He had vengeance to enact.

The approaching group, though, was probably Chechens, mujahideen as he was. They weren't very good, their sweep technique was awful and they looked jumpy. But that just made it that much more important than he attract their attention from as far away as possible.

Despite the fact that he was in clothing acceptable to the prophet and had his hands up, the idiots fired at him. So he dropped back down and waited.

"Who is there!" a young voice called.

"I am Haza Saghedi Al-Rusht, Al-Kemar, Al-Abdullah, Sword of the Prophet, Lion of Kandahar and warlord of the Pasht and if you shoot at me again I will take that weapon from you and beat you as your mother apparently never did!"

"Haza Saghedi Khan," Commander Bukara said, nodding in respect. "Your name is far known. Can you possibly explain this debacle?"

"We were hit by a pincer movement just as the meet started," Haza said, wiping at his arm. One of the shots from either the Russians or the other group had hit him a glancing blow on his forearm. It would become only one of many scars. "I have no idea who they were. It was not the camouflage of the Spetznaz unless they use something very different here. It looked something like the new American, but still not that."

"Keldara," Bukara said, holding up the patch. "Georgians from over the mountains. They have a new warlord, an American. I was told a meeting was going on, but also told by some very senior people to stay out of the way."

"Perhaps that was a mistake," Saghedi admitted. "Several mistakes were made. I think the people I had on security were not looking the right way. But that is to be forgotten. Those Keldara pigs have captured a senior member of the Movement. They must be stopped."

"I have already lost many men just getting here," Bukara said, frowning. "They are running away. Let them go. We can deal with them in our own time."

Haza tried not to snarl at what he saw as cowardice. He suspected mentioning his opinion would get him nowhere, what was more. He had dealt with many similar warlords in many lands. But he also knew they all had the same weakness . . .

"Besides capturing Sheik Al-Kariya, these Keldara captured the money we had brought to this meeting." Haza tried not to gulp at what he was about to do. Facing American Delta Force would be smarter. "It was sixty million euros. If you destroy them, you can have half, to support your great jihad against the Russians."

"As I said," Bukara replied, immediately. "We must stop these Keldara from escaping. But they will not get far. The way they are trying to take out is blocked."

"Do you have a map?" Saghedi asked. "Show me."

❖   ❖   ❖

"Here is the road," Bukara said, tracing it on the map. "This is the furthest point of Georgian control, in the pass. Commander Sadim has a blocking force already in place, over two hundred fedayeen, in bunkers and with heavy weapons." He pointed to the spot and shrugged. "There is a gorge there. The Keldara will not be able to go around before we reach them."

"Sadim is here?" Haza said, surprised.

"I only recently got word he was coming to this sector," Bukara said, stone faced. "But, yes, his advanced units are already at the border crossing and the rest of his units are close behind. He may yet cut them off."

"They might also anticipate it," Saghedi pointed out, looking around the map. "They will get off the road . . . here," he said, pointing to where a small stream crossed it. "Destroy the vehicles. Perhaps booby-trap them. Then they will either move to flank your positions or towards this pass."

"Guerrmo," Bukara said, frowning. "We have a small force there. Really just a few bunkers to stop the Georgians from sending patrols through there. They are oriented to the south. They will be able to take those easily. When this happened Commander Suliman sent some of his men down into the hills in case they headed that way. But only a few patrols; the most they can do is sting them."

"Then we have to block them," Saghedi said. "Do you have any guides that *really* know these hills? I need them and . . . a hundred men if you can spare them. I hate to ask but they must be many of your best. In shape, capable of running in these hills and able to *really* shoot. We will take only light ammunition and water and go to . . . this point." He pointed to a hilltop at the north entrance of the pass. "They will have to pass this point. We will also take shovels, yes?"

"Can you beat them there?"

"*I* can," Haza said, straightening up. "Can your men keep up is the question? And you must contact Commander Sadim, now. Tell him to try to cut them off sooner. But get him moving."

"I see," Bukara said, nodding as he listened on the satellite phone. "Yes, I will do that."

He sighed as he hung up. Sadim was not going to like this.

"They want you to call Sadim directly," Sayeed said, shaking his head. "Don't they?"

"They do," Bukara replied, trying not to curse. "And they aren't going to send me any of his codes; even they are not so stupid." He picked up the phone and dialed a number.

"This is Commander Bukara," Bukara said, wincing. "I must talk to your commander."

"Sadim."

Gregor Sadim's white mustache was twitching furiously, a sure sign that he was agitated, and his aides politely turned away.

The entire march had been, from an electronic perspective, perfect. Although they might have been picked up by satellites, although there might have been a rumor of their passing, they had only used codes. No unit designators. And all of it highly encrypted.

The offensive out of the Pankisi was designed to catch the Russians off-guard, at a time when they were retreating to winter quarters. Although the Russians were, proverbially, good winter fighters, they had gotten used to the Chechens pulling back over winter. With luck the offensive, led by the Sadim Brigade, would catch them off-guard and roll them back.

That was probably blown now based on one damned phone-call.

"This is Commander Bukara," the man on the phone said. "And let me start by saying that High Command ordered me to contact you in this way. We have a situation."

Sadim was sixty-two and had attained the rank of major in the Red Army before retiring. Despite a membership from an early age in the Communist Party, he had, his whole life, been a believing Muslim. With the fall of the Soviet Union and the rise of the jihad he had left his country home and joined the jihad, one of the first trained officers to do so. Since then he had built his reputation, and unit, into one of the finest the mujahideen had. Disciplined, experienced and well armed, it was the Chechen's crack force, which was why it had been moved to this sector.

But he *was* well trained, and personally disciplined, so he controlled his fury.

"What is the situation?" he asked.

✧   ✧   ✧

"Oh . . . damn," Greznya said as the intercept popped up. The satellite call had been open-circuit and the voices were distinct even if both of them hadn't identified themselves. And she recognized the name.

"Colonel Nielson?"

Vanner's BFT started buzzing, frantically, and he paused to draw it out.

The Keldara were retreating at a trot but he was keeping up just fine. He'd never let himself get out of condition after getting out of the Marines and had worked on it harder since joining the Kildar. The girls were doing fine as well, especially since dropping their rucks.

In fact, the way things were going they should get to the pass by dawn and be *out* of here.

He pulled up the BFT, looked at the data and blanched.

They'd *better* clear the pass by dawn.

"Kildar!" he said, running up the hill. "Kildar! You need to see this."

"Command, this is Dragar Five."

The commander of the light reconnaissance vehicle looked at the cluster of cars and trucks then at where the roadbed had been beaten down.

"Dragar Five, Command."

"Command, the Keldara force has left the road at point nine-two-one," the LRV commander said. "Force size unknown. Path indicates a generally southerly route. Terrain is unsuited to pursuit."

"Four thousand," Mike said, his jaw working. "Fuck me. Fuck *us*."

"It's worse than that, sir," Vanner said, quietly. "Sadim's their varsity. Former Soviet officer, very professional one, school trained at Frunze which was their equivalent of the War College. His unit is considered their best field-combat unit. Lots of heavy weapons, tanks, the works. The girls started picking up signals a couple of days ago but up until just now we didn't know who it was. Or the size of the force. They were apparently moving over here to push this sector against the Russians. Maybe against us but the Russians are more likely. But now . . ."

"He's going to be on our ass," Mike said. "Well, we just have to run faster. Send a message to the Teams; we're trading stealth for speed. If we get hit by an ambush, counterassault and screen through. Fortunately, except for the bunkers the pass should be clear . . ."

Of the hundred that had started, barely fifty were behind Haza as he reached the top of the hill.

The area was high. It reminded him of his beloved Afghanistan, now under the boot of the Allah-Be-Damned Americans. The last few kilometers had been through low brush, covered in snow melting in the rain. And it was *high*. He could tell by the thin air, the cold clear wind of the mountains he knew and loved.

The rain wasn't like Afghanistan, though, still spraying in his face and the wind was rising. It was going to be a cold, wet, night. But they had beaten these pig Keldara to the Pass. And he intended that they not pass.

"Get up you sons of pigs!" he cursed, kicking the nearest Chechen, who had slumped to the ground as soon as he reached the top of the hill. "We have digging to do. Those Keldara you so fear will be here soon and we will give them a hot greeting."

Mike cursed as firing broke out to his front. Initially, most of the fire was from AK-type weapons, the familiar "back, back, back" of the relatively slow-firing AK. The response, however, was almost immediate as the higher, faster cycling, SAWs and M4s of the Keldara responded to what was clearly an ambush.

Team Sawn was in the lead, with the other five teams following. The area was still woodland but the underbrush, in most areas, was thick. He knew that the Chechens were going to know the trails and easy ways better than the Keldara, making them faster moving, but all they could do was bull their way forward, hoping for the best.

"I don't know where they came from," Vanner panted behind them. "Nothing on the intercepts."

"Just because it isn't on the map, doesn't mean it isn't going to be there," Mike pointed out.

The Keldara hadn't even stopped. Their orders were to bull through light opposition and Oleg's team had, apparently, already switched to point without orders. So Mike's command team soon reached the ambush site.

The majority of Team Sawn were coming back down the hill, most of them carrying weapons which were being tossed on a pile. Others carried bodies. Those, too, were dropped with the weapons.

"Ten," Sawn said as Mike walked by. "They tried to run when we counterattacked. None got far."

"I take it none tried to surrender?" Mike asked.

"I wasn't asking," Sawn replied. The pile of weapons and bodies was apparently complete and he tossed a thermite grenade on it. The white light definitely gave away their position but it also sent a message; this is what happens when you face the Keldara. For once, the smell of burning pork didn't give Mike a sick stomach.

Other members of the same team were putting bandages on the wounded while there was already one body bag zipped shut. One of the wounded, Stephan Ferani, one of the MG team assistant gunners, was pretty bad. The rounds had ripped in from the side through the armhole of his armor and he was bleeding like a pig. He was still conscious, though.

Mike stopped and took the Keldara's uninjured hand.

"Hey, Stephan," he said, grinning. "What are you doing laying out?"

"Just catching . . . a quick . . . rest, Kildar," Stephan replied, the words spotting bright blood on his face; the rounds must have hit the lungs.

"Well, the good news is somebody else gets to carry you back," Mike said. "Riding along like a king. Kildar Stephan, yes?"

"Yes, Kildar," Stephan said, grimacing.

"Hang in there, buddy," Mike said, getting up. "We've got another evac site up ahead. You get to ride in style."

Mike trotted to get back to his place in line, Vanner tagging along right behind him.

"Think he'll make it?" Vanner asked when they were past the ambush site.

"Not a chance in hell," Mike said. "What's the status on the birds?"

"They're back at base," Vanner said.

"At least they made it."

When the door slid back, a wave of blood splashed to the graveled helipad.

"Varlam and those three to the other choppers," Gretchen said, detaching the defibrillator. "Then give me a hand with this one," she said, gesturing at Viktor's stretcher.

All the available men and women of the Keldara were gathered at the landing pad. Which meant that both Mother Mahona and Mother Silva, their mother by birth, were present as Gretchen and three other girls lifted Viktor from the helicopter.

Father Jusev, the Orthodox priest from Alerrso walked over as Gretchen was unloading. She wasn't surprised, Jusev was a good man and . . . understanding. The Keldara turned up on Sunday for church, tithed of their food and handiworks and he ignored the fact that in the dark of night they performed other ceremonies.

What she was very surprised to see was Father Kulcyanov in his full vestments. A tiger skin was flung over his shoulders, pinned at the neck with a silver brooch in the form of an axe. In his right hand he carried a large battle-axe and in his left a golden bunch of dried mistletoe. She had only seen him dressed that way at the "secret" rites of the Keldara. She couldn't believe he was so dressed in front of Father Jusev.

"He was hit coming back from the mission," Gretchen said as Mother and Silva walked to the stretcher. Mother Silva was crying, quietly, but Mother Mahona's face was smooth and oddly serene.

"May the Lord Bless and keep this soul," Father Jusev said, sprinkling the body with holy water. He recited a prayer in Greek then looked at the body bag. "Who?"

"Sion," Gretchen replied. "He was hit in the battle."

As the Blackhawks lifted off, filling the air with dust, Father Kulcyanov bent on arthritic knees and took one of Viktor's flaccid hands, wrapping it around the hilt of the battle-axe.

"From these Fallen Lands you leave," Father Kulcyanov recited. "Into the Halls of Feasting you go. Raised up on wings of the Valkyr to battle and sing until the day of fire, the final battle, when you ride by the side of the Father of All and Frey. You have faced the fire and been unburnt, you have faced the Reaver and been unafraid. Clean of body, clean of soul, pure of heart. True Keldara. True Son of Battle."

As he spoke he brushed the boy's body with the golden mistletoe.

"Let the Mothers bear him up and prepare him," the old man said, using the hilt of the axe to help him to his feet. "Raise him up like the Valkyrie, though your son is gone. Know, though, that he lives ever in the Halls and that in the days to come you shall see him again, pure and glorious, a warrior born and eternal."

Gretchen bowed her head, trying not to shed tears in front of the Priest of the Father of All. She knew her brother was in the Halls of Feasting and was probably looking down at her in pity. But she was going to miss him. Did miss him already, terribly.

She'd known Father Kulcyanov her whole life but she'd never really seen him as he was now. This was the high priest in truth, not serving over a rite of spring but sending the souls of warriors to fill the hosts of the Father of All.

And about that she had one small doubt.

"Father," she said, touching his arm as he was going to perform the rites for Sion.

"Yes, my daughter," Father Kulcyanov said.

"Father, I have been given a rank," Gretchen said, biting her lip. "But . . . I am afraid. Not of battle, but . . . Women of the Keldara have never been spoken of as warriors."

"And you fear the Cold Lands if you fall in battle?" Father Kulcyanov said, nodding. "Fear not, Daughter. You are a warrior as much as any of these fallen. Does not your weapon even now smoke? Do the technicians not rearm it? Are those bullets I see being fed? Did you not engage in battle on this day?"

"Yes, Father," Gretchen said, then shook her head. "But I don't think I hit anything. I wasn't used to the weapon."

"It is the battle, not the ability, that matters," Father Kulcyanov replied. "But next time, send some enemies to the Halls to be your servants. However, you are missing something. You have never been through the rites. And I think now is too short a time to perform them. But the center of the rites is simply this." He reached into his shirt and pulled an old and tarnished silver cross on a chain from around his neck. The cross was odd in that it had only a very small upward extension and broad arms. It looked, in fact, very much like the axe he still carried in his hand. He undid the clasp one-handed and then handed it to the girl. "There. Now you carry the sign of the Father of All. And the Valkyries shall not miss you if you fall."

"Who are you?" D'Allaird asked as a man in a rubber chemical suit climbed off the bird.

"Dr. Arensky," the man said, muffled by the mask. It was in English, though. "I need somewhere to wait out of the way."

"Well, why don't you start by taking that shit off?" D'Allaird said with a chuckle.

"Because I don't know if I'm infected," Arensky said. "And I don't want to be contagious. Is there somewhere I could, perhaps, set up as a quarantine area?"

"I *so* don't want to know what you might be 'infected' by," D'Allaird said, backing up. "But I'll figure something out. In the meantime, why don't you just go over by the hangar and as soon as I get this bird out of here I'll figure something out."

"Thank you," Dr. Arensky said. "Hopefully I'm just being cautious. We'll know in a couple of days."

"Great," D'Allaird said. "See ya!" He continued to walk to the bird, shaking his head.

"Oh, it's worse than it looks," Kacey said, climbing out of the cockpit. "I had to redline the engines coming over the pass."

"The other bird is partially ripped down, being refitted," D'Allaird pointed out. "I hope like hell the damned engines hold. This is our *only* bird right now."

"The left supercharger was giving me an overheat light," Kacey said, shrugging. "Check that out if you can. Pull it if possible. But we need to get back."

"You're already being fueled," Tim replied. He'd briefed some of the Keldara girls on it and they were already dragging over the fuel line, watched by one of the Czech technicians. "Any of those dings do more than kill people?"

"One went right *through* my fucking window," Tammy said, pointing.

"I meant anything *important*," D'Allaird pointed out with a grin.

"Fuck you, Chief," Tammy said, shaking her head. "And for your information, it *bounced*, so the answer is 'probably.' I don't know where it ended up."

"I dunno," Kacey said. "Why don't you figure that out while I go have a case of the shakes. That was one hairy fucking mission. I seriously need a drink."

"You don't drink," D'Allaird pointed out.

"That's what I mean."

Chapter Thirty-Seven

"Boss, we're not moving as fast as the Chechens," Vanner pointed out. "I just got an intercept from barely two klicks back and some of the sensors I dropped show their points are closer."

"That's what I was afraid of," Mike said, trotting down the hill.

The Keldara were damned near exhausted. They were carrying a massive load of ammo, stretchers with the wounded and their already heavy load of body armor, weapons and other gear.

And the Chechens knew the area better. They knew where the trails were while the Keldara were spending half their time breaking brush.

They'd gotten up into the pine zone, out of the deciduous, but that was, in a way, worse. The slopes were getting steeper and the underbrush was a thick thorn that was really slowing them down. The Chechens were going to catch them well short of the pass.

"Anton," Mike said over the team leader net. Since Padrek was barely making it in that fucking rubber suit, Anton Mahona had taken over as team leader.

"Kildar?" the team leader called back.

"Set some traps on the back trail," Mike said. "We're being trailed and I'd like to slow them down."

"Yes, Kildar."

"If we could just get out of this fucking scrub," Mike snarled.

❖   ❖   ❖

"This damned scrub is slowing us down," Bukara snarled.

"We are still catching up to the Keldara," Sayeed pointed out.

They'd been forced to leave their vehicles behind. The local guides had known a path that was vehicle capable for part of the way but about ten kilometers back they had had to dismount and follow on foot.

However, they were also being followed. Bukara had been using his satellite phone lavishly and every commander in the area was now headed towards Guerrmo Pass to try to stop the Keldara.

If they could catch them. And then there was Haza. The old mujahideen was good, but could he cut the triangle fast enough to cut off the Keldara? And if so, could he hold them?

"Fuck," Mike said as firing broke out to the rear. They were, at least, getting out of the damned scrub. But that just meant they were high enough that breathing was becoming difficult. The whole group had slowed and now they were going to have to slow more.

"Anton?"

"No casualties," Anton replied. "Some of their point caught up to us. Can we speed it up, please?"

"Negative," Mike said as a stretcher team passed him. The Keldara were breathing so hard they sounded like winded horses. "Time to change tactics. Keep moving to the next hilltop then hold that until I tell you to move."

Mike took the larger BFT device from Vanner and looked at their position.

"Team Padrek, hold in place," Mike said, starting to sketch on the touch pad. "Oleg, take up firing positions in support of Anton. Adams to Oleg's position. Yosif, Sawn, you're stretcher bearer detail and command security. Pavel, keep pushing forward to . . . here," he added, pointing to another hilltop. "Take up security positions. We're going to have to shift to retreat under fire."

A retreat under fire is one of the most difficult maneuvers to effect. As one group slows the pursuing enemy the other groups have to get into a position to bring the first group's position under fire. And they have to move *fast*. They have to get into position before the pursuer can flank the rear party.

On command, the rear party evacuates their position, usually bounding all the way to the front of the overall unit. The unit behind them then takes their position under fire since the enemy they *had* been fighting would generally assault the position as soon as it was evacuated.

Then the group had to do the whole thing all over again.

Casualties, which were inescapable, added to the complexity. They slowed everyone down. But the Keldara weren't about to leave anyone behind. Not to the Chechens.

Anton crested the hill then turned around and flopped on the slope next to Oleg.

"This is fun, no?" he asked, gasping for air.

"I'd rather be heading *at* them," Pavel said. "I hate running away."

"Frankly, I'd rather be back at home, drinking a beer," Anton replied. "There."

One of the Chechen point men had appeared over the next hill. He was clear in Anton's NVG.

"Do we wait until they get close?" he asked.

"I don't think so," Pavel replied. He touched his throat mike. "Braon, take him," he called to the team sniper.

There was a crack from Anton's right and the Chechen dropped.

"Team," Pavel continued. "Fire as you bear. Snipers, try to find the commanders."

Bukara paused, panting, as fire broke out to the front.

"We have them," Sayeed said.

"Maybe," Bukara replied. "We have to move forward."

"Anton, Pavel."

"Go Kildar," Anton said, firing to his left. He could see some of the Chechens moving down on the side of the hill, trying to flank their position.

"Get ready to leave," the Kildar said. "Pull straight south. Oleg is to your southwest. Skirt the edge of his hill then check your pads. They have your positions. Move as soon as you are sure you're ready."

"Yes, Kildar," Anton said. He quickly switched to the team frequency. "Arminis, status?"

"All here," Arminis Ferani replied. The SAW gunner was number three in the unit and, therefore, had taken over as assistant team leader. "No casualties."

"We're good, too," Pavel said. "You go first."

"Right. Team Padrek, retreat to the streambed and form on me. We are *leaving*."

"Can I shoot, now?" Shota asked as the first Chechen crested the hill where Pavel and Anton's people had been. Pavel had almost passed their position but Anton's team, Padrek's really, was still at the base of the hill.

"One round," Oleg replied. "The new one."

"Yes!" Shota said, happily. He already had one loaded and the range to the hilltop. "Clear!"

"They're retreating under fire," Bukara said. "Doing it well so far."

They were in the streambed on the back side of the hill, just starting to ascend. It was clear that the Keldara had abandoned it.

"Perhaps Haza Khan will stop them," Sayeed said as the hilltop was enveloped with fire. "What in Allah's name?!"

"Fuck their mothers!" Bukara shouted, shaking his head to clear the ringing. The back of the hill was suddenly pelted by rock, dirt, twigs and wet things. "Thermobaric round! Send the rest of the men *around* the hill."

"Oooh! Pretty!" Shota said, pulling another round out of the rack on his side and sliding it into the rocket launcher. "Can I do that again?"

"No," Oleg said. "Not yet, anyway. Stay under cover. If they see that thing you'll be fired at by every Chechen. I'll tell you if we need it." He touched his throat mike. "Where are they?"

"Coming around both sides of the hill," Jitka replied. "They don't seem to like the top anymore."

"Fire as you bear," Oleg said, spotting one of the Chechen fighters on the east side of the hill. "Snipers, look for leaders."

Sveryan Shaynav was normally a spotter for Juris. But Juris had been hit by the fucking Russian sniper at the raid so now he was the boss man. He'd grabbed Gregor Makanee, one of the regular riflemen, and given him a very brief class in using a spotter scope. But it was the first time the kid had spotted for a sniper so Sveryan wasn't hoping for much.

"Left side of the hill," Gregor whispered. "Range . . . five hundred thirty-two meters. Guy waving his arms."

Sveryan swung the scope back and forth and finally spotted the guy he was talking about. Sure enough, he looked as if he was in charge of the group. He adjusted the scope for the indicated distance, took a breath, let it out, stroked the trigger.

"Target down," Gregor whispered. "Thirty meters uphill. Guy carrying a big gun of some sort."

"PKM," Sveryan said, stroking the trigger.

"Whatever . . . He's hit but not dead. You wanna finish . . . Okay. Right side of the hill, think it's one of their snipers. There's two rocks near the top of the hill. Just down from them. Range . . . four seventy."

"I've *got* to give you a class on spotting," Sveryan sighed. . . .

"Oleg, got your little pad thingy working?" Mike asked.

"Go, Kildar."

"Next position," Mike said. "How you doing?"

"Whisky, one," Oleg replied, indicating one casualty. "Mobile. Ready on your command."

"As soon as you're ready," Mike said. "Pavel is to your southeast. Head due south. Your next position is on the chart."

"Roger, Kildar," Oleg said, switching to the team net. "Team, prepare to pull out. Everyone mobile?"

"Yes," Dmitri replied. "Mikhail took a round through the arm, but he's good otherwise."

"Can I fire now?" Shota asked.

"No," Oleg said. "Save your rounds. I think we're going to need them. Team, pull out . . . Now!"

❖   ❖   ❖

The temperature was dropping again, the rain had turned to snow, but that was fine. It meant the fucking Chechens had to dig to stay warm.

Haza knew how to put in a defensive position. He had fought the Northern Alliance, off and on, for years. That had been a war of attrition and no-man's-lands towards the end, trenchlines that stretched sometimes for miles. Occasionally one side or the other, usually the Taliban, would get an advantage and the lines would shift. Then it would be time to put in another defense. He had done it over and over again.

He, therefore, wasn't just letting the Chechens dig shallow scrapes and be done with it. That seemed to be the way around here. But that wasn't good enough for Haza. He had had them build a zigzagging trench across the brow of the hill, with fields of fire in both directions and to the sides. Machine-gun teams had finally straggled in, nearly exhausted, and he already had positions dug for them with sweeping fire covering the front and sides of the hill. If the Keldara tried to pass to either side they'd be taken under a withering fire. And assaulting straight at the position would be suicide.

Haza could hear the guns, now. The Keldara were retreating under fire, that was pretty clear. And it was also clear they were heading right towards the pass.

Let them come. Then it would be much warmer.

"Thank you for coming to the White House," the President said, smiling at the president of Burundi and shaking his hand. The two men were turned slightly sideways so that the White House photographer could get a good picture of them.

"Thank you for your hospitality," the man said. "It has been my pleasure to meet you."

"And I you," the President said, ushering him out of the Oval Office. "I wish you well on your return trip."

"And many good wishes to you, Mr. President," the Burundan said. He was quite pleased with the visit. His country had picked up a bundle in aid, which would please his cousins no end since most of it would go in their pockets. Well, that which he didn't skim. He could probably buy that chalet in Switzerland he'd had his eye on.

The POTUS walked back to the Resolute Desk and slumped into his chair. He looked at the documents on his desk, pulled one over and picked up the phone at the same time, hitting a button with his pinkie finger.

"Keldara?"

"They're retreating under fire, Mr. President. Weather is breaking and the Predators are starting to get some observation. They're about fifteen kilometers from the Chechen side of the pass. However, their intercepts, and ours, indicate that somewhat more than four thousand Chechen fighters are closing on their position, many of them carrying heavy weapons such as mortars and heavy machine guns. If they are slowed much more, the main force will catch them. In that case, sir . . ."

"They'll be wiped out," the President said.

"Probably, sir," the major replied, unhappily.

"Major, you're a good man," the President said. "But I want someone with ground-combat experience to start answering the phone. I want someone who can make calls based on that experience."

"I understand, sir," the major replied.

"Call Office of Special Operations Liaison," the President said. "See if Colonel Pierson can come by."

"Tiger One this is Tiger Two."

"Go," Mike said, looking at the map.

The command group, with the wounded just ahead of them, were in movement to the next position and Mike was trotting while watching the pad and thinking about the terrain ahead.

"Valkyrie is inbound. We need an LZ."

"It's gonna have to be a flyby," Mike replied. "She got ammo?"

"Yes. And machine guns."

"Oorah," Mike said, tiredly. The first stars were visible in the sky at the same time as the vague light of dawn. The clouds were clearing off fast, though, and the temperature dropping. It was gonna be one cold, raw, day. And the Keldara couldn't exactly worry about sweat. Fortunately, the pass was low enough that, given that they weren't planning on stopping moving, they shouldn't have to worry about freezing to death. "I'll designate an

LZ. Tell them to drop the stuff and don't even fully touch down. We are not in a position to stop."

"I'll pass that on," Nielson said. "We just got a satellite pass. It looks as if it's clearing over there."

"It is," Mike replied. "It's gonna be a pretty, if cold, day."

"Gretchen."

"Go."

"The LZ is a long, open, ridge running east-west. When we get down, just start pushing the shit out the door. We're only going to pause for the wounded. Got it?"

"Got it," Gretchen said. She was holding on to the handles of the minigun, hoping to see some Chechen bastards.

"Then it's back through the pass," Kacey continued.

"I'm ready," Gretchen replied.

The Hind banked sharply to the right and she braced her feet, hanging backwards from the gun, as it dropped sharply. As it leveled out she could see some men running, but from their clothing they were Keldara. And several of them bore stretchers. More than they could carry.

As soon as the bird leveled out she slid back the door. The interior of the plane had been cleaned but there was still water on the floor from the cleaning. The water had frozen during the flight and the footing was treacherous. But she got behind the line of ammo boxes and braced her foot on the far, closed, door.

"Start dumping!" Captain Bathlick said, slowing the chopper to the speed of a walk.

Gretchen pushed with a grunt and once the boxes started moving they slid easily enough. She then grabbed the four machine guns and stood in the door, carefully dropping them in a line. Last, she braced herself again and shoved out another series of ammo boxes. All of it was belted 7.62. It seemed like a lot of machine-gun ammunition.

Leaning out the door she could see the stretcher bearers waiting. They were down on one knee and looking back over their shoulders.

She'd just noted that when she heard a "ping!" and looked up to see a tracer floating towards her. The thing was going so slowly it looked funny. Then she realized that one tracer meant five more bullets. And there were more tracers.

The line of fire went behind the bird but the gunner was *going* to correct.

Fuck that.

"Get them on!" she screamed, grabbing the handle of the mini-gun and swinging it towards the source of the fire.

Her first fire was very low, she hadn't realized the hillside was as far away as it was. But she walked the rounds up towards the machine-gun position and onto it just as the helo stopped to let the stretcher bearers load the wounded.

On the basis that a machine gun is rarely by itself, Gretchen continued to walk the fire across the hillside until she sensed out of the corner of her eye that the wounded had all been loaded and the stretcher bearers had unassed the bird.

"Go, go, go!" she shouted over the intercom. "They're all on!"

Four stretcher casualties and Gregor Makanee who had a bad wound in his abdomen but, somehow, was walking.

"Gregor, lie down," she said, pushing herself away from the guns and making her way to the Makanee. "You're going to need to lie down. I'll get you some blood."

"See to . . . Stephan," Gregor said, but he lay down on the deck, which was already getting slick with blood. "He needs . . . help."

The rear bottom stretcher was Stephan Ferani and she could see what Gregor meant. Stephan's left shoulder was swathed in blood-soaked bandages and he was bubbling bright red out of his mouth. Despite that, he was conscious.

"My own personal Valkyr," Stephan said, trying to smile.

"You better not die on me," she said, hooking a unit of O-positive blood up and pulling the IV he already had in. "It would ruin my record."

"Gretchen, I didn't know you cared," Stephan said then slumped.

She felt at his neck and couldn't find a pulse. Frantically, as the helicopter banked up and to the left, she pulled down the defibrillator kit. She didn't know if it was going to work but the Ranger medic had told her if anyone's heart stopped to put it on and step back.

Most of Stephan's blouse had already been cut away to get at the wound so she only had to find the right places for the three connections. She glanced at the chart and then hooked them up as fast as trembling fingers could work. As soon as they were in place she hit the big green "On" switch.

"Detecting . . ." the machine said. She hadn't know machines could talk. "No pulse detected. Charging. Stand clear of the patient. Charging. Stand clear of the patient."

Gretchen backed away from Stephan and held onto one of the other stretchers.

"Defibrillating," the machine said, and Stephan's body jerked. "Detecting. No pulse detected. Charging. Stand clear of the patient. Charging. Stand *clear* of the patient."

Another jerk.

"Heartbeat detected."

Gretchen touched her finger to Stephan's neck and there was a pulse. It was faint and fast, but it was a pulse. She reached up, wide-eyed, and squeezed the bag of blood. He definitely needed more blood. Definitely.

"We live in an age of miracles," Gregor said. "Now could I have some morphine, please?"

Chapter Thirty-Eight

"That was helpful," Oleg said, looking at the line of boxes. "We were seriously down on ammo. And I'm glad to have the machine guns finally."

"It's not going to last long," Adams said and then, as a bullet whistled overhead, turned and spit in the direction of the Chechens. "Fuckers can't shoot for shit. Let's get this stuff and didee on out of here."

"Master Chief," Mikhail Kulcyanov said, in a puzzled tone. "These are not the right machine guns."

The former SEAL walked over and shook his head.

"Fuck me!" he shouted. "These are the damned guns we got for evaluation! Where the fuck are the M240s!"

"We can use them," Oleg said, picking up one of the guns. "We'll figure it out. But we'll need help with all this ammo. And it's all 7.62."

"Another fuckup," Adams snarled. "Kildar, this is Tiger Three. We got a situation here . . ."

"They sent the 60s?" Mike said.

"Yeah, they're M60s. The new kind. Those four we bought to evaluate."

"Fucking Oorah!" Mike said. "Don't use them."

"What?" Adams snarled. "What the fuck do you mean 'don't use them.' We've been *needing* them!"

"I'd rather keep them for a surprise," Mike said. "I was going to surprise you with them. You haven't seen the video. But you're gonna fucking *love* 'em. Trust me."

"Kildar," Adams ground out, "Mike. We are up to our ass in alligators. If one of these things jams, you know how to clear it, I know how to clear it. The Keldara don't know how to clear it. We don't need to be switching out weapons in the middle of a *battle*!"

"Yeah, speaking of which, I want one. No, better to leave them with the teams since we've only got four. But I'm gonna get one as a personal weapon . . ."

"Mike . . ." Adams stopped and took a deep breath. "I am getting fucking sick of this shit. What the *fuck* are you babbling about?"

"You'll see," Mike said. "We are not going to use those things until we absolutely have to. You'll see why."

"Whatever," Adams said. "Tiger Three, *out.*"

He looked over at Oleg and shook his head.

"I think the Kildar is losing it," he said.

"I think not," Oleg replied. "You don't go on the internet much, do you?"

"I've got better things to do," Adams said.

"I was surprised, and upset I will admit, when I saw that these were not the machine guns we usually use," Oleg replied, placidly. "But I am going to carry one, myself, thank you. You would be well to grab one as well before the rest of the Keldara find out we have them. They have all seen the video."

"What *video*?!" Adams snarled. "He said that too!"

"You will see," Oleg replied, grinning. "For once, the pupil knows more than the master."

"I'm going to fucking kill Mike," Adams said. But he grabbed one of the machine guns. It was an M60. They went all the way back to the Vietnam War. The U.S. had ditched them for the M240 because it was, hands down, a better fucking weapon. Higher cycle rate, much harder barrel so you could get a couple of hundred rounds through it before you had to change the barrel, a bit less prone to jamming, tad lighter. The M60 was *old* tech in comparison.

What was the big fucking deal?

Katya walked in the entrance of the caravanserai and directly to the harem quarters, ignoring the gasp from Mother Savina, who had been passing through the front room.

"Katya?" Anastasia asked, her eyes wide. "Are you okay?" She started to hold her arms out then thought better of it and just stood there, not sure what to do.

Katya was covered from head to toe in drying blood. There were still pieces of Viktor stuck to her, especially in her hair.

She knew she didn't look all that great. A few of the Keldara had even shied away from her. For that reason and because she just could not ask those people for a ride, she had walked the long way back to the caravanserai, her eyes blank and staring.

She was cold. She knew that. "A deadly little bitch" was what the Kildar had called her once.

But having a person blasted into pieces in front of your eyes, and all over you and in your face, mouth and nose, that was something even the coldest person had a hard time with. No one else in the compartment had really seen Viktor vaporized. The wounded Keldara and Dr. Arensky both had had their heads down. The other wounded were mostly so doped up they were half or totally unconscious.

But she had seen every splash. She'd barely closed her eyes and gotten her arms up in time to keep from being hit in the face by a length of intestine.

"I'm fine," Katya said, still staring into the distance. "I just need a shower. A very long shower."

For perhaps the first time in her life she felt pity for someone. Because the helicopters were going to have to go *back* through the pass.

"Gretchen!" Kacey said over the intercom. "I've got a little more altitude, but you need to fire up the bunkers again!"

"Got it!" Gretchen called. She'd gotten blood into the three casualties that really seemed to need it and made sure Gregor was okay. Now it was time to do battle.

She pulled out Father Kulcyanov's axe and kissed it.

"Father of All, let me triumph this day," she said, arming the Gatling gun.

As she did she looked up at the ridgeline. There, clear as day, there was a tiger walking along the shoulder of the mountain. A young male from the looks of it. Not yet to his full growth but . . . magnificent nonetheless. The tigers had returned.

She knew Sion had said he'd seen a tiger, but nobody had believed him. She thought for a moment how happy he would be when she confirmed that she'd seen it, too. Then she remembered that Sion wasn't going to hear of it, short of her joining him in the Halls.

Circling over the tiger, though, was a raven. It was headed to the north, towards the battlefield. How did they always know? And would this one, the eyes of the Father of All, stay to watch her upon the field?

No, it continued on, riding the strong winds to the battle. The tiger disappeared over the ridge. In a moment, she was alone again.

She shook herself back to the present and leaned outwards. The bunkers were just coming into view.

"Welcome to the land of the tigers," she screamed. "Father of All hear my prayer! Let me slay this day!"

"I am going to fucking kill that thing this time," Baakr said, pointing at the helicopter.

"It's going faster this time," Hanan noted, holding the belt. "Lead it."

"I *am* leading it you pig eater," Baakr replied, as he opened fire. He was crouched down, but he just couldn't seem to get the fire high enough. "Help me! Lift this thing up!"

* * *

Gretchen held down the trigger of the minigun, walking the rounds into the nearest bunker. They were both firing but she ignored that. She just wanted to bring some servants to the Hall.

This time she managed to walk the rounds into the firing slit of the north bunker and let out a hoot as the machine gun stopped firing.

"Yes! I have slain this—"

✧　　✧　　✧

Gretchen hadn't realized she'd left her intercom on but Kacey wasn't about to interfere with the girl's moment. But when the scream of joy cut off she hit her mike switch.

"Gretchen?" Kacey shouted. The damned Hinds weren't open to the troop compartment so she couldn't even look back to see if the girl was okay. "GRETCHEN!?"

Oh, fuck.

"Oh, fuck."

Two groups operated Predators in the United States government, the United States Air Force and the CIA. And USAF Predators were not armed. The Air Force held the position that if anything was going to fly and be armed, it damned well better have a pilot in the cockpit and not just a bunch of wires.

The Predator system was, in essence, a model airplane on steroids. Capable of cruising for up to twenty-four hours in its most up-to-date version, Predators were launched from a remote location (usually within five hundred miles of a target area) then cruised automatically to the AO. Once there, a pilot, who through the wonders of satellite technology could be sitting anywhere in the world, took over and controlled their actions on-site. With standard visual, thermal imagery, and Synthetic Aperture Radar (SAR) available, a Predator could see just about anything, anywhere. Whereas satellites had limited time over a target, swooping across the sky on their continuous orbits, a Predator could park and allow the snoopy to *really* get a look at things.

And, best of all, those who were not just snoopy but violent as well could hang missiles on them and, voila! Suddenly you had an eye in the sky with a punch attached.

The Army was making a bid to get some armed Predators but the AF was using every bit of political muscle to prevent it. Going all the way back to the Key West Agreement in 1947, the Air Force had done everything it possibly could to prevent the Army from having *anything* with a weapon on it in the air. They'd failed with helicopters but they were standing firm on anything with a "fixed wing." Predators were fixed-wing aircraft and, therefore, the Army *might* be permitted some that *weren't* armed, but armed Preds were right the *fuck* out.

The CIA stood outside that particularly asinine turf battle. The Air Force had occasionally complained about various armed CIA aircraft and the CIA had invariably answered "what aircraft?"

So the CIA had Predators. And they were, by God, armed. What's the point, otherwise? And they used them in various ways, mostly removing high-value terrorists that, for other reasons, were hard to reach.

They really didn't give a damn where they sent their Predators, or the Hellfire missiles they mounted, because if anyone said anything about missiles, or the occasional crashed Predator, they just said: "What missiles? What Predators? We have no knowledge of any such aircraft or missiles."

The pilot of the CIA Predator was a former Air Force captain who had made something of a career in the Air Force flying Predators. The problem was, if you made it known you liked Predators and thought they were the future of air combat, your days in the Air Force were numbered.

After an Officer Evaluation Report that, in subtle ways, indicated that he might as well hang up his flight suit, the captain had reluctantly left the Air Force.

But before he could ever hit the exit door a nice man in a suit had offered him a job.

Flying Predators.

Armed Predators.

Gosh, the captain had thought, *wonder who he works for? Because everybody knows that nobody has armed Predators.*

So these days he flew armed Predators for about twice the pay he made as a captain. And the great part about it was, he never had to leave the Northern Virginia area. The Predator could be controlled, via satellite, from anywhere in the world. Oh, the *launch* teams had to get closer. This one was, in fact, based in eastern Georgia. But he was a *pilot.* He could do the job from his *bedroom.*

No more sleeping in nasty barracks in some Third World shithole. No more bad chow—the commissary in this building was, in fact, first-rate. And his commute to work was about twenty minutes.

This was the shit.

But some days were better than others.

This mission had some very high priorities. Predator video was routinely pumped to the White House. Sometimes the President watched, sometimes he didn't. But unless it was a U.S. ground force in action, he rarely got involved. Even then, the most they might get was an occasional minor retask to look at something in particular. This president, thank God, wasn't Johnson. Despite having a better ability to control things from the safety of the White House, he stayed hands-off.

Mostly.

This seemed to be an exception to the rule. He'd been told that this mission was a direct tasking. The fucking *Director* had called three times, asking when they could get some good video.

Video, though, had been the least of the problems. Flying a Predator was always an exercise in mind over instinct. You sure as hell couldn't "feel" the plane. All you could do was watch the instruments and the video and hope like hell you didn't crash.

And the last few hours of flying had dropped his hope level pretty low. Technically, the Predator was an "all-weather" aircraft, at least according to his new employers. It had GPS and night vision (night was considered a "weather" condition). It had instruments to figure out if it was upside down or not. Ergo, it was "all-weather."

But last night, Georgia time, had been anything but realistic flying weather. The Preds had been socked in all night. And flying them back, over the mountains, was a nightmare. Generally you just told them where to go and they went. But the conditions had been so bad he'd had to manual them the whole way back, the most pulse-raising ride he'd had since his last F-16 checkride.

Even now, with the weather clearing and the sun coming up, he was sweating bullets. The winds were hell. The Predator was neither overpowered nor particularly aerodynamic so at times it seemed when he turned into the wind he was going backwards. Flying with the wind was worse since he lost almost all control. Crosswinds had him flying at a slant. Updrafts and downdrafts were all over the place. Conditions just *sucked*.

But for six sweating hours he'd kept the damned thing on station. Just in time to spot this through a break in the clouds.

"Control, you might want to look at the Pred take," he said. "We have a situation on the ground."

✧ ✧ ✧

"Get them off!" D'Allaird shouted. "Move!"

The Keldara women were already unloading the stretchers, the ripped Keldara men stifling screams at the rough handling. There was no way they were going to scream in pain in the presence of their own people.

As Gregor was loaded on a stretcher, Kacey scrambled out of her seat.

"Chief?" she yelled, running to the rear of the bird.

"Stop," D'Allaird said, holding up his hand. "Just get back in your seat, Kacey."

"Fuck that," Kacey said, pushing by as Tammy came up behind her.

Gretchen was lying against the far door. She had been hit on the upper chest. The round had cut through her armor as if it weren't there and blasted her chest into ruin. Most of the girl was still held in place by the surviving armor but her head slumped to the side, connected only by a few strands of tissue.

Kacey turned around and threw up, puking up everything in her stomach and then some.

"Oh . . . fuck," Tammy said. "When we couldn't get her on the intercom we . . . hoped . . ."

"Ain't much hope there," the chief said, climbing on the bird and picking up the ravaged and remarkably light body. He had long experience of bodies ripped by everything from crashes to gunfire. And it always amazed him how much of the weight of the body was in blood. Gretchen was pretty much fully bled out.

"Not Gretchen!" Mother Silva screamed. She tried to compose herself but she just couldn't. She ran to her daughter and cradled the broken body to her breast. "Not Gretchen. Please!"

"Kari," Mother Mahona said. "You will not do this. We have to clear the helicopter. We go on. We continue the . . . the *mission*."

"Oh, gods, Julia," Mother Silva said. "First Viktor and now Gretchen!"

"And Sion and Ama were not alive," Mother Mahona said, pulling the woman away. "We are the Keldara. Our place is in battle. They rest in the Halls. We will join them at the end of all things.

They shall fight the final battle in our names and bring us honor as they honor us this day. But you must come away."

Kacey didn't know what the women were talking about, but she kind of figured the one crying was Gretchen's mom. As they carried the little body off she turned to D'Allaird.

"Chief, I'm done taking fire and not being able to do anything about it," Kacey snarled.

D'Allaird, watching the two women carry Gretchen over to the line of bodies by the hangar, nodded.

"Got *just* what you need, boss," he said, gesturing to the hangar. "She's tanked and armed. And it's got the 'special' package on it."

"I'm taking it straight to those fuckers in Guerrmo," Kacey snapped, heading for the hangar.

"*Fuck* yeah," Tammy said, starting to follow her to the bird.

"Alone," Kacey said, holding out a hand. "Chief, load up this bird. The Keldara are getting hammered out there. Tammy, head back as soon as the bird is loaded. Do the drop, do the dust-off. But I'm going *this* one alone."

"Kacey, the front position is *designed* for a gunner," Tammy protested. "Why do you get all the fun?"

"We've got wounded to pull out and ammo to deliver," Kacey said. "*Both* birds, Captain. Chief, get Valkyrie One in the air. Fast. In the meantime, I'm going to go deliver a message to the Chechens."

The wounded had been cross-loaded to the Blackhawk, which was already in the air. Most of the Keldara in the area, therefore, stopped what they were doing as Tammy and D'Allaird started tugging back the doors to the hangar. Everyone, of course, knew that the other Hind had been armed, and painted. But this was the first time that most of them had seen it.

As the two Americans pushed the Hind into view the Keldara started clapping and hollering. About half the women present ran forward to help push.

D'Allaird had been a busy man. Not only were the pylons of the Hind now loaded with two Gatling guns and two 57mm rocket launchers, but the front of the bird had been painted in a snarling dragon head. To either side, tusks on the flaming dragon, were two more fixed Gatling guns for a total of four of the brutal weapons.

Kacey already had the engines warming and as soon as the tail was clear of the hangar bay she started up the rotors.

"Tiger Base, this is Helo Two, designation Dragon One," Kacey said, plugging in the route she planned to follow on the terrain-avoidance system. "Mission change. Combat op to clear defenses along the Guerrmo Pass route."

There was a pause then Nielson's voice came back over the radio.

"Keldara Two: Confirm. Good hunting, Dragon One."

"I'm going to bring them the word of God, Tiger Base," Kacey replied. "These fuckers are going to face the flame."

Chapter Thirty-Nine

"If we don't get the go word, I swear to *God* I'm going to make a boo-boo and initiate on my own," J.P. said. "The Hind got seriously dinged on that last flight."

"I know, sir," First Sergeant Kwan replied. "But until we get the okay . . ."

"I do not fucking *care*," Guerrin said. "D.C. is playing fucking political games while the Keldara are getting slaughtered over there."

It was great weather for Rangers and ducks. The rain was pouring down, the wind was howling and it was cold as hell. Black, too. The night was like being inside the gullet of a snake. For a few minutes, there had been some clearing and he got a glimpse of dawnlight. Now it was black again. If they got the order to move he could take out those bunkers in no more than thirty minutes. He had the plan in place. All he needed was the go order.

The distant firing, while muted by the distance and the mountains, was clear. Just the fact that they could *hear* it was amazing; it meant there was one fuck of a lot of firing going on. What was happening on the other side of the pass wasn't a firefight, it was a fucking battle. According to their latest intel update the Chechens were throwing everyone they had in the area, and even drawing back forces that had been in contact with the Russians, in a bid to destroy the Keldara.

"Sir, if we move, your career is toast," Kwan pointed out. "And so is mine for not stopping you. We're also out-numbered and out-gunned. So please don't go running right into the fucking bunkers, okay?"

"I won't, First Sergeant," J.P. replied. "But we are going to *have* to do . . ." He paused and cocked his head. "Okay, who in the *fuck* is playing their iPod too loud?"

"I dunno," Kwan said. "I hear it, too . . ." The music was Spanish flamenco guitar, carried on the wind. He wasn't sure what direction it was coming from. Then he realized, just as the tune changed, that it was getting closer. "That's not an . . ."

"Holy fuck," Guerrin said as the tune changed to screaming heavy metal guitar. And it was getting louder. Much *much* louder.

"Sir!" Serris yelled. "What is that?"

"Music, Serris," Guerrin replied, sarcastically.

"I know that, sir," Serris said. "Where's it coming from!" The last was screamed as the guitars and drums muted for a singer entered screaming something about "riding to the fight."

"That's a . . ." Kwan started to yell as finally, overwhelmed by the screaming guitars, the "whop-whop" of helicopter blades could be heard.

The Hind was nearly invisible in the blackness of the night but it was easy enough to follow as the deafening music pealed across the valley. And it was *low*, the Rangers were pelted by branches thrown from the trees in its rotor wash as it banked up the ridgeline and crested with its belly brushing the treetops.

Guerrin ducked unnecessarily and then started laughing.

"I think that Miss Kacey got tired of being shot at," Guerrin yelled. "This I gotta see!"

Kacey keyed the music as she entered the final valley before the pass. The Rangers were occupying the upper portion of the valley and she intended to cross their position as a final checkpoint. That position, at the least, was secure.

She reached down and cranked the volume all the way up. The speakers were special designs, flush-mounted, and enormously powerful. The thunder of the drums rattled her teeth but Islamics tended to *hate* Western music. Great. Let them hate it as she sent the fuckers to Allah.

She banked up and to the side as the terrain warning system screamed at her she was too low. Too fucking bad. Low was good. She had at least six inches' clearance, what more did the Czech piece of shit want?

The positions of the bunkers were keyed in on her firing system and as soon as they came in sight the system D'Allaird had installed karated them in her heads-up display.

"Time to face the flame, motherfuckers."

"Holy fuck," Serris whispered.

The Hind had seemed to clip the ridge but as it crossed over them it dropped to skim the scrub between the ridge and the pass entrance. And spotlights on the front came on showing not only the paint job but the heavy ordnance on the bird. It was a deliberate taunt to the gunners in the bunkers, practically *asking* them to open fire.

The Hind dropped down to practically ground level and flew straight down through the kill zone of the three main bunkers as tracers started clawing towards it through the night. Most seemed to be missing but some were sparking off the front of the bird.

The driver of the Hind, probably Captain Bathlick as the CO had said, didn't seem to give a shit that she was taking fire. She flew hey-diddle-diddle straight up the middle—actually slowing down as the gunners got the range—until the singer screamed something about "through the fire and flames." Then the Hind seemed to explode.

Rockets began spewing out of both pods as the Gatling guns opened fire, sending a quadruple line of tracers that looked like nothing so much as a laser into first one then another bunker.

The bunkers were wide-spaced but the Hind didn't have any problem with that. It was flying in the most bizarre manner Serris had ever seen. It would slide sideways through the air and engage one bunker then pivot at lightning speed and engage the other, pivot again and engage, pivot, engage, still maintaining an almost straight line up the middle of the defended pass. There wasn't any dilly-dallying with "walking the rounds into the position." The thing was just striking back and forth like a snake.

As the Hind came opposite the interlocking bunkers, all three of which had stopped firing, it pivoted left then one hundred and eighty degrees to the right, flying flat sideways in what looked like an out-of-control spin, past the second bunker and on to the third. But even though it looked out of control, as each bunker came into its fire cone the rockets and Gatling rounds would flash out. It didn't do the maneuver just once but continued through spin after spin, a flaming top in midair. The helo looked like a dragon spinning on its axis and flaming in every direction at its enemies. It looked terrifying and glorious, war in all its horror and beauty. And it looked as if it was going to slam into a mountainside at any moment. The pilot had to be puking her guts out and blacking out from G forces.

Once it was past the now smoking bunkers, though, it straightened out perfectly, went to full power, banked up and over in what was nearly a loop-de-loop and came *back*.

There wasn't any fucking around, now. The bird came in from the rear and top, filling the air with rockets and machine-gun bullets. And whereas before it had been spinning in only two dimensions it now was rotating in midair, something he hadn't realized helicopters could do. And still hammering rounds into the bunkers.

It reached the front of the pass again in what looked one hell of a lot like a flip, which just *had* to be impossible, and hovered as the music screamed through the wind and the driving rain. Just . . . hovered as if waiting for something, as whoever the group doing the music was went through one long-ass guitar solo and the Hind balanced against the gale, lights still on, in full view of the smoking and shattered bunkers.

Finally, it got what it had been waiting for as sporadic fire started to pop up through the rain. But the bird waited, hung in the air, still, until it was clear at least two of the machine guns had, somehow, survived the attack. But the survivors had had to claw them out of the rubble of the bunkers to engage their tormentor. They were out in the open now.

Suddenly the Hind pivoted in midair and swept back around over Serris' position. It circled up and up into the storm, engine redlined and rotors screaming until even with the lights on it disappeared into the storm. But the screaming guitar was still booming over the gale.

Then, as the singing started again, it lined up and dropped. Slowly at first then faster and faster it swept down like a bird of prey, like the dragon painted on its smoking brow. It came down like thunder out of the storm, right on top of the machine-gun positions, the only thing still firing the laser-like Gatling guns, clawing across both of the guns, tearing the crews apart, ripping into the guns themselves, slaughtering everything and everyone in the area.

The Hind pulled out in a hover, inches off the ground, and spun in place, fast as the music crescendoed, laying down a flat fire, scouring the ground of not only the survivor gun crews but every stick every rock, smashing apart the very mountainsides in a tide-wave of fury and vengeance until all four of its guns were expended.

Then it stopped.

The music stopped, the lights turned off, the mountains and the rain muted the whop of the blades as the bird clawed its way back into the storm and disappeared. In moments the only sign it had been there was three smoking holes in the mountainside and the shredded remnants of bodies.

"Holy fuck," Serris repeated. "Remind me never to get that lady pissed at *me*."

Kacey was trying very hard to not throw up. After seeing Gretchen there wasn't much left anyway.

She didn't remember much about the last few minutes. The last thing she really clearly remembered was turning on the music. And she sort of vaguely recalled crossing the Ranger position, *way* too close to the top of the trees.

She'd apparently expended all her bullets and rockets, used up a *fuck*load of gas and really stressed the engines; there were warning signs all over her dash. And she sort of recalled something that seemed a hell of a lot like a crash, the world spinning and flame and smoke all around her. But she was still flying.

There was, however, one hell of a lot of lead in her armored windscreen. Quite a bit of it had gotten through, too. D'Allaird was going to be pissed.

She really wished she could remember *where* she'd picked up all that lead.

"Tiger Base, this is Dragon," she said wearily, watching her fuel state and caution lights carefully and flying well away from the ridges. "Return to base for bullets and gas. Tell the chief I think this bird is going to require an overhaul as well."

"Roger, Dragon One." The commo person was one of the Keldara girls by the accent. "Info request from Ranger One: What was the band? Meaning of code unknown."

"Uh . . ." Kacey frowned. "DragonForce, over."

"Roger, Dragon One. Rangers report target destroyed. Precise words: Fucking vaporized. Tiger Two states: Well done, over."

"Well ain't that some shit," Kacey muttered trying not to grin. The hell if she was going to let anyone know it was a fluke. "Understood. ETA two zero mikes. Dragon One out."

Now if the poor bird would just keep flying.

"Good girl," she murmured. "Good Dragon. Carry me home."

"We're getting ready to load the bird," Chief D'Allaird said. "In the Corps we'd want to take it down for a full rebuild. And you don't have a crew-chief."

"Yeah," Tammy said, looking around at the crowd of Keldara. There wasn't, currently, anything much to do. But it seemed like the whole tribe was gathered at the heliport. At least those that were still here, the women, the oldsters and the kids. Hell, most of the younger women seemed to be gone. Maybe they had been told to stay in the houses or something. "I guess I could ask for volunteers. Fuck of a thing to ask when you've just brought back a dead daughter: Who wants to be next?"

She walked over to the group and looked around.

"Uh, does anyone speak English?" she asked.

"I do," one of the older men said. "I am Father Makanee. You need help."

"I hate to ask," Tammy said, stepping closer and dropping her voice, "but . . . I need another crew-chief. To replace . . . Gretchen. All they need to do is kick out the ammo. Oh, and a couple of other things with the casualties."

"Pick," Father Makanee said, standing up straight. "I will go if you wish. But it should be one of the young ones, yes?" he added with a resigned sigh. "Someone, at least, with better eyesight than I still have. I can barely see you in truth."

"I don't know," Tammy said. "I guess. But, I mean, after Gretchen . . ."

"You think we fear?" Father Makanee said, his voice lowering and a slight smile playing on his lips. "That the Keldara are afraid of death? Afraid of sacrifice? Very well, I will ask."

He turned from her and backed up so that he faced the whole crowd then said something in a loud voice. He was apparently explaining the situation. He paused and spat out another sentence.

Apparently that was the call for volunteers. Every single hand went up. From kids that could barely walk to one old guy wearing a tiger skin who looked to be about a hundred.

"What the fuck have I gotten myself into?" Tammy asked, quietly. "Are these people insane?"

Apparently she'd spoken loudly enough for Father Makanee to hear. His eyes might not be the greatest but his hearing was apparently fine. He turned around and smiled.

"Yes, Captain Wilson, we are insane," the old man said. "We are the Tigers of the Mountains and we have the insanity of the warrior. Don't you?"

"Point," Tammy said. "Well, pick somebody and get her over to the bird. She needs to get briefed in and we don't have much time."

"Tiger One, Tiger One, this is Tiger Two."

"Go," Mike said. Pavel was back in contact, Oleg was forward and so far things were going . . . okay. Not great by any stretch, but . . . okay.

"Good news and bad news. The bunkers in the pass have been cleared. So the birds will be bringing in heavier loads. Bad news . . . look at your display."

Mike hunkered down and stuck out his hand. Vanner didn't even have to ask, he just slapped it into his palm.

Mike looked at it for a second and shrugged. "What?"

"Try dialing out," Nielson replied, taking a guess.

Mike zoomed out and stopped.

"Fuck."

"My first words as well," Nielson said. "The Predator got a glimpse through the clouds. You want to see the video."

"Yeah," Mike replied.

"Feed Two."

He switched over feeds and watched. The glimpse wasn't long but it was complete.

"Is that downloaded here?" Mike asked.

"Yeah, while we were feeding."

"Vanner," Mike said. "Show me how to replay and zoom."

Vanner took the device and looked at it for a second.

"Where is that?" he asked, frowning.

"Right in the entrance to the pass," Mike said.

"Fuck."

He zoomed in and panned across, holding it where Mike could see.

"Colonel, I get a count of about a hundred," Vanner said. "Looks like medium machine guns and light arms otherwise. A few RPGs."

"That's everybody's analysis," Nielson said. "Kildar? My professional opinion is that if you try to screen past you're going to get your ass shot off; they've got defilading fire from the mountain to the plain. You can try to charge it, but I wouldn't recommend; those are good defenses. You could try slipping out straight up . . ."

"Not enough time," Mike said, automatically. "We'd get caught completely in the open by the pursuers."

"*So* far, it looks like his mortars are way behind you," Nielson noted. "It's just medium machine guns and light arms. *So* far."

"What are you saying?" Mike asked.

"Just a suggestion, but . . . Sit it out. Do what that guy's done. Take up a good position and lay in. We've got one bird armed, by the way. We can work over those defenses in a little while. Let the Chechens come to you. Get a good position and let them attack. You'll take some casualties. They'll take *a lot* more. At some point there will be an opening."

"We're going to go bingo on ammo, fast," Mike pointed out.

"Got another load on the way," Nielson said. "Bigger one."

"And that's a shitload of Chechens," Mike added.

"Not really," Nielson said. "Combat multiples, Kildar."

"That's a nice theory," Mike replied. "But you're talking about around a hundred effectives at this point and around four *thousand* Chechens."

"I didn't say it was going to be easy *or* pretty," Nielson said. "But they're going to think it's a walk-over. And, when, not if, their mortars get there it's going to get bad."

"That an armed Pred?" Mike asked.

"Yeah. And we've got tasking."

"That's their priority," Mike said. "Find the mortars. Out here."

"You have got to be shitting me," Adams said. "Mike, buddy, we're talking about most of the Chechen army!"

He was still with Team Oleg, currently humping up a hill to set up another defense point.

"I know," Mike said. "Would you rather try to assault some serious defenses?"

"Now that you mention it," Adams said. "Yes! There's a hundred of them. There's a hundred of us. That's one to one. Not twenty or *forty* to one!"

"They're in fixed positions and have machine guns covering all their approaches," Mike said. "We don't have time to argue about this. We're going to point 487 right *now*. You guys stay in place and *slow* them while we get into place and start digging in. It's got some natural defenses on it and there are steep slopes covering our sides. There's effectively only one lane they can assault on."

"Fine," Adams said, swearing under his breath. "But when we come running, we're going to need some fucking cover."

"Gotcha covered, good buddy," Mike said. "Out here."

Mike grabbed one of the stretchers and continued up the slope. It was a steep motherfucker and the air was thin; the Keldara were barely able to make it at a trot.

The weather was really clearing, now. He could finally *see* what was going on. Behind him he could see Oleg's team settling in and Padrek's team in contact. Hell, in the clear air and gathering light he could even see the Chechens they were engaging.

"Tiger, Tiger, burning bright, this is Valkyrie."

It was the other pilot, the taller one . . . Wilson, that was her name.

"Valkyrie, Valkyrie, Tiger One," Mike panted. "LZ point 487. Winds . . . Oh, fuck, I dunno. South I think? Drop the shit and get ready to dust-off."

"Roger, Tiger. LZ Point 487. Inbound. I see your teams. Why don't you stop the stretchers. I'll drop the stuff at 487 and come back. You're in a good position."

"Got it," Mike said, stopping, holding up a hand and lowering the stretcher to the ground. "Thanks Valkyrie."

"Gotcha covered, Tiger."

Mike watched as the Hind swept in to the hilltop about five hundred meters away. It didn't even stop or really slow down as the ammo boxes were kicked out the door. Then it banked back towards their position.

They were on a hump in the ridgeline headed up to 487 with a clear view in every direction. Also completely in view of the Chechens but about two klicks away. If the Islamics had heavy weapons they were in trouble. They weren't taking any fire, though.

The Hind settled down lightly and Mike walked over to the pilot's cockpit as the wounded were loaded.

"Where's Captain Bathlick?" Mike asked.

"Hogging all the fun," Wilson replied. "The Georgians dropped off their left-over Hind armaments. She used them to take out the bunkers in Guerrmo. And she didn't just take them out, she fucking flattened them. I guess she's RTB for bullets and gas."

"I think I got all that," Mike said. "We're cut off. Watch the opening to the pass."

"Knew about it," Tammy said, tapping an instrument. "We shot it up as we passed. We'll shoot it up again on the way out. I don't want to lose another crew-chief."

"D'Allaird?" Mike asked. "We're fucked without him."

"No, sir, one of the Keldara girls," Tammy said, shrugging. She didn't think to mention her name. "Game as hell. Took some with her, I think, but she got hit by one of the 12.7s. Wasn't pretty."

"Damn," Mike said, sighing.

"Anything else?"

"Nope. Just thanks. Hell of a time, huh?"

"Wouldn't be anywhere else," Tammy said then shook her head. "You know, I just was throwing out a line but . . . I really *wouldn't* want to be anywhere else. Ain't that some shit? I just had my crew-chief blown all over the bird, I've got so many holes I feel like I'm flying a Swiss cheese and *I wouldn't want to be anywhere else. I'm insane.*"

"Captain," Mike said, gently, "why the *fuck* do you think I hired you?"

"Point," Tammy said. "I gotta go. We're loaded. Once more into the breach and all that."

"Unto," Mike corrected. "*Everybody* gets that wrong. It goes:

Once more unto the breach, dear friends, once more;

Or close the wall up with our English dead.

In peace there's nothing so becomes a man

As modest stillness and humility:

But when the blast of war blows in our ears,

Then imitate the action of the tiger;

Stiffen the sinews, summon up the blood,

Disguise fair nature with hard-favour'd rage.

"*Henry the Fifth.* Great play. Unrealistic as hell and bad history but some of the greatest propaganda ever written."

"Damn, sir," Tammy said, her eyes wide. "I hadn't expected to hear Shakespeare quoted in the middle of a battle."

"No better time," Mike said. "And no better writer. 'Less it's Kipling. Now get out of here before you get *your* pretty little ass shot off."

"We got another engine?" Kacey asked, as soon as her canopy was popped.

The engine was *smoking.* Every light on her board that wasn't red was yellow. Her engine temp was running in the red. Her hydraulics were shot. And she had holes all over her window.

"What the *fuck* did you do to my bird?" D'Allaird shouted.

"I took out the fucking bunkers that killed Gretchen," Kacey said. "Now, we got another engine?"

"You need more than an *engine,*" D'Allaird yelled. "You need your *head* examined! And a windshield. And a splinter shield. Probably control runs. And from the *smell,* a new *transmission!*"

"How long?" Kacey asked, pushing herself out of the seat and stepping out.

"That's *it*?" D'Allaird yelled. "*How long?* I ought to strap you up with rigger tape and throw you in the shed! I don't *know* how long!

Next *week*? There's gotta be *somebody* around here can ground you!"

"I need it in a couple of hours," Kacey said, walking towards the ready room. "If you want to use rigger's tape for something, I suggest you start on the holes in the blades."

"I . . . you . . . AAARRRGH! I got *two* Czech mechanics and a bunch of people who are willing and got no damned idea what to do! And you want this busted-up piece of what was once one damned nice flying machine *when*?"

"As soon as *possible*, Chief," Kacey said, spinning on her heel. "There are a hundred of these people's sons and daughters on the other side of those mountains with about a billion fucking Chechens hunting their scalps. They need three things: Ammo, dust-off and *close-air support*! We cannot do any sort of reasonable dust-off or resupply with the bird loaded for combat. So we need *two* birds, Chief. *Two.* One for dust-off, one for support. So Get This One Flying, Marine! Or admit that all that shit you spouted about being a fucking miracle worker with birds was so much crap and get the fuck out of my *face*. Because every second you are flapping your jaw, *Gunny*, is one more second this fucker is not in the air. Do You Understand Me?"

"Clear, Captain," D'Allaird said, his face hard. "Sorry, sir. I'll get to work on it. I cannot guarantee two hours, sir, but I will do my best."

"Just get it flying, Chief," Kacey said with a sigh. "It don't have to fly great, just fly. Just get me back in the air."

Chapter Forty

"Okay, Master Chief, now would be good."

Adams looked at the Chechens on the far hill, and the ones probing forward on either side, and sighed.

"Waited long enough," he muttered. "Oleg!"

"We're ready," Oleg yelled. "Team," he said, thumbing his throat mike, "prepare to retreat. Shota!"

"Now?" Shota called.

"Now," Oleg yelled.

Dmitri, the assistant team leader, was acting as a combination spotter and loader. He pointed to the hilltop and tapped the big Keldara on the shoulder.

Shota got up on one knee and sighted through the massive rocket launcher. Mostly by instinct and with bare use of the sight he aimed at a large rock some of the Chechens were using for cover and fired.

The range was such that he had to angle the launcher upwards nearly thirty degrees for the rocket to reach. Nonetheless, the round traced across the slight valley between the two hills and flew right to the rock.

The round was a thermobaric round that used overpressure rather than shrapnel for its primary killing effect. Better in an enclosed space than a hilltop it nonetheless laid down a circle of devastation that spread for fifteen meters around the rock that was its target. Even beyond that point, the pressure from the explosion hammered the Chechens so hard that many of them stood up screaming and holding their heads. The other Keldara were more than happy to pick them off.

"Left," Dmitri said, slamming in another round. "On the side of the hill, there . . ." he said, pointing.

Another TB round flew out, cutting a hole in the attacking Chechens.

"Last one!" Oleg yelled.

"Right," Dmitri said, slamming in another round and pointing.

Another round, another perfect hit and another Chechen squad gutted.

"Say what you will about Shota's counting ability," Adams said as they pounded down the hillside. "The motherfucker is a *genius* with a rocket launcher."

Commander Bukara stood on the hilltop looking at the dead bodies around him and shook his head.

"It doesn't matter," he shouted. "We have them cornered, now. They are trapped and at our mercy. We will destroy them and then we shall continue to their pitiful valley and lay it to waste once and for all!"

The men around him, though, did not look particularly bucked up by his speech.

"After we receive reinforcements," he continued. "There are thousands of our brethren on the way. We will wait until we can strike them in force. Yes. When our brothers arrive, then we shall assault."

"Is it just me, or do those Chechens look a little hangdog?" Mike asked as Adams walked *slowly* through the preparing lines.

The Keldara were warriors, yes, but they were also farmers. Good ones. And farmers do a lot of manual labor. Whereas your average American soldier looks upon a shovel as a foreign and terrible instrument, to the Keldara they were more familiar than guns. Far more familiar. And they knew how to wield them, oh, yes. There were tricks to using a shovel that only experience and training could impart. How much of what kind of soil to lift in each load, where, exactly, to strike—small tricks.

Which was why the hilltop looked very much as if a hundred really scarily large gophers were building nests. Fast.

The top of the soil was frozen and would have been nearly impossible to dig through. They'd solved that problem by chopping small holes with their axes then slipping in explosive charges. That broke the frozen crust quite neatly. They'd also used the C-4 they carried to break up boulders or free them from the ground. Rocks were being piled to the front into sangers and the snipers were digging nice little hides with tiny firing slits.

The Keldara might just be getting used to things like helicopters and night-vision systems but there wasn't *nothin'* their trainers could teach them about digging. All Mike had had to do was point out slightly better angles of fire.

Adams stopped and just stared at him for a few seconds. Balefully.

"Okay, are you going to let me in on the secret?" Adams said, hefting the M60E4.

"Nope," Mike said. "But if you want to use it, feel free. I'll give you one hint: don't bother to fire in five-round bursts. Just hold the trigger down. I've got the guys setting up pretty good positions for them. Oh, and we'll probably be getting some mortars dropped on our heads, soon. There's not much to use for overhead. See if you can think of anything."

"I'm missing something," Adams said. "If I just hold the trigger down, this fucker's gonna overheat. Fast. It's an M60. That's what they do."

"Trust me," Mike said, putting a pair of binoculars to his eyes. "Yeah. They're fucking hangdog. They've been chasing us for the last seven or eight hours, they've got us cornered and they're just sitting there."

"That's because there are about four thousand of their buddies coming up to help," Adams pointed out. "I'd hang back, too."

"Good," Mike said. "I wonder when Tammy can get back here with some more ammo?"

"Valkyrie, Valkyrie, this is Tiger Base, over."
"Go Tiger," Tammy said.

"Divert position 219. FAARP and transfer point established at that location."

"Roger," Tammy said, looking at her instruments. 219 was right on a road junction not far from Guerrmo. "Diverting at this time."

The position was only about five minutes' flight time from Guerrmo, cutting at least twenty minutes off the flight. However, she didn't recognize any of the people at the site; they looked to all be Georgian military. There was a Blackhawk off to one side, though, with a red cross on the side. And there was a fuel truck, by all that was holy.

Tammy flared out, set down on the road, and shut down. Then she popped her canopy, popped her belts, stretched in her seat and groaned. There hadn't been *a lot* of flying, but it was tense as hell.

"If I weren't married, you would force me to make an offer."

Tammy settled back down and looked at the Georgian officer standing by the cockpit.

"Oh, hi Captain . . ." Crap. She couldn't remember the guy's name. But she *did* remember he was the son-in-law of the Georgian chief of staff. So forgetting his name was a major-league political boo-boo.

"Kahbolov," the captain said, handing her a bottle of water. If he was offended it wasn't obvious. "We have ammunition for you as well as fuel. If you need anything to eat . . . ?"

"I'm good," Tammy said, opening the bottle and downing most of it. "Thanks for this, though. Is the Georgian military taking over support?"

"Quietly," Kahbolov replied. "My father-in-law sent us up here. I have some good ground-support people, experienced with Hinds. And some parts. But if you have problems you might wish to go to your own people, I would understand."

"I appreciate it," Tammy said.

"The Keldara are not members of the Georgian military but they are *Georgians*, whatever the defense minister might think," Kahbolov said. "And they deserve more support than this. My father-in-law wishes to send a battalion through the pass. The defense minister is, pardon me, cock-blocking him I think would be the term."

"It's perfect," Tammy said, chuckling. She finished off the water and stretched again. "Christ I feel like I've been hammered into dogmeat."

"You do not look it," Kahbolov said. He was looking at the ground.

"Sorry," Tammy said, honestly. "I take it there aren't a lot of female pilots in the Georgian military."

"None," Kahbolov said. "No women in the National Guard. Period. Another thing the defense minister and my father-in-law clash on."

Tammy looked at her instruments and was surprised to see that she was tanked up.

"Anisa, where we at?"

"We are loading ammunition, Captain," the new crew-chief answered. "We just got the bird cleaned out."

The girl was one of the intel and commo specialists who worked up at the castle. She was also, unfortunately, the only unmarried female around who spoke English. Tammy hadn't caught quite where the other girls had gone, but they weren't around.

So she'd been rushed down from the castle, rapidly briefed in on care of the wounded, and suited up. Unfortunately, she was larger than Kacey and a bit smaller than Tammy so the flight suit sort of hung on her. However, she'd turned up with a suit of clearly familiar body armor and an MP5 that had seen some use. Apparently she was an "out on point" intel specialist.

"Okey, dokey," Tammy said, hitting the engine start button. "Captain?" she said, handing him the bottle.

"Good luck," Captain Kahbolov said, shaking his head. "I wish I was in your seat. Hell, in your front seat."

"You'll have your day, Captain," Tammy said as the waterfall displays came into the green. She rotated her back, then tightened down her straps. "Let me have mine."

Mike really wanted to use one of the new M60s but he had, reluctantly, turned it over to Ionis Mahona from Sawn's team. He had other things to do.

One of them was arranging the defenses. He'd detailed four of the teams to the forward slope of the hill, arrayed to create interlocking fire on the main approaches. Once he detailed that to Oleg, Vil, Sawn and Padrek he'd let Adams handle the details.

The rear, though, was another question. They were pretty solid, there, but nothing was perfect. The ridge, after the little "hump" they were on, steepened out and about four hundred feet over their head went straight vertical for a while. Getting down on them would take some serious mountaineering. And there were small gorges to either side with whitewater streams cascading down them. The walls there were steep and slick.

However, all that was surmountable and the ridges to either side were, potentially, useable to emplace heavy weapons or snipers to enfilade them. The positions that could be used were a couple of klicks away but a heavy machine gun wouldn't have trouble with it and some of the Chechens were reputed to be pretty good snipers.

He'd pointed the problems out to Pavel and left it to him. Pavel's approach to combat was simple but had merit; height was power. He'd left half his team working on security positions on the rear of the headquarters and taken the other half straight up. They were up there, now, tackling the vertical face. He'd also taken two sniper teams with him and a Robar. Mike wasn't worried about snipers on the other ridges anymore.

The headquarters was pretty secure, too.

The Keldara had managed to create a sort of bunker using a boulder formation that was already in a tripod. They'd piled rocks into the gaps, dug some of the dirt out and packed it in and generally stiffened things up. It was pretty solid. And it wasn't like they could find any trees to make overhead cover up here.

The remaining wounded, those that were totally out of the fight, were secured in the bunker along with spare ammo. Mike wasn't worried about running it back and forth. As soon as the Keldara finished their individual fighting positions they had started to run trenches to each other and back to the command post.

The boys were digging fools.

"What we got, Vanner?" Mike asked, leaning back on a boulder.

"The girls say most of the radio traffic has dropped off the air," Vanner replied. "But that's because a pretty big force has gathered right about . . . here . . ." he said, pointing to a big red spot on the map. "Say eight or nine hundred. Sadim's unit, and some odds and sods are still making their way up to us. The question is whether the first group is going to attack before they get here."

"What's the pool?" Mike asked, closing his eyes. Fuck, *now* he was getting tired.

"Six to one says they attack first," Vanner replied. "They're really exercised about something. I think it's the money."

"Or that fucker we captured," Mike said. "Heavy weapons?"

"Mortars are out there," Vanner said. "They might be setting up. We think we've got coordinates. I sent them to the Predator guys. Sounds as if the heavy machine guns are still straggling forward. Might not make it before the other force. If then."

"What I wouldn't do for a Specter or a few JDAMs," Mike said, sitting up. He was *not* going to sleep. "Team leaders. Check in."

"Sawn." "Vil." "Pavel." "Anton." "Yosif." "Oleg."

"Guys, do not, say again, do *not* use the new machine guns unless we have to," Mike said. "We're probably going to get hit soon. There may be mortars. Try not to use them in the first attack. Snipers concentrate on leadership. All the rest of you guys, fuck them over good. But try to play like we don't have mediums. If they get right down to the line, open up. But not unless I say so."

"Tiger Base, this is Tiger One."

"Go, Kildar."

Mike liked that the commo people were all Keldara girls. It was just refreshing to hear a chirpy female voice.

"ETA on the next Valkyrie run?" Mike said.

"Twenty mikes, Kildar," Base replied. "5.56, grenades, rocket rounds. Water, food and beer."

"Oorah," Mike said. "Six casualties to go. Make Valkyrie aware that we are expecting an attack at any time. She should not, say again *not*, attempt to approach without my call."

"Roger, Kildar."

"Kildar, out."

"Pedar is pretty bad," Vanner pointed out. Julia and Olga had taken over tending to the wounded but Vanner had been giving pointers. "He needs some whole blood."

"And it would be pretty bad if the Hind dropped on us in the middle of a major firefight," Mike pointed out then keyed his throat mike. "Hey, Ass-Boy One. You see if they're moving into position, yet?"

"Negative, Ass-Boy Two," Adams replied. "Nada."

"Kildar, Lasko."

"You still hanging in there old man?" Mike asked.

"Yes, Kildar, I am," Lasko answered, coldly. "They are putting snipers in on Hill 357."

Mike looked at the map and shrugged.

"Snipers may engage at will," he said. "Keep them off our backs."

"Roger, Kildar."

Mike looked at the boulders stacked over his head and started counting.

"Seven, six, five, four, three, two, one . . ." There was a crack of a rifle in the distance and he smiled. "One sniper down."

Lasko had kept up, but barely. And he had been ashamed that Pyotar, from Team Yosif, who had taken over as his spotter, had done most of the preparation of the hide. But he had been totally worn out. So worn out all he could carry was his personal rifle and ammunition. It was left to Pyotar to carry the heavier Robar.

Now, though, he was back in his element. He didn't need the Robar at this range, just the beautiful Mannlicher.

There were three snipers setting up positions on the hill, probably thinking they were out of sight or range.

Fools, if the enemy is in range, so are you.

Of the three, one was taking the most cover, and care, as he prepared his position. He was barely visible behind a rock, rolling more rocks in the way for cover. Really, all that was visible seven hundred and twenty-three meters away was his head.

Stroke, crack.

Now he *had* no head.

Chapter Forty-One

The President looked at the clock on his desk, sighed and picked up his phone.

"Sarah?" he said, "I do believe it's quitting time."

"Yes, sir," his administrative assistant replied. "Schedule is now officially clear. No evening meetings."

"Good, good," he said. "Have a good night. See you tomorrow." He hit the disconnect on the phone and touched another key.

"Pierson."

"Ah, Colonel Pierson, I see they tracked you down. Status on the Keldara."

"They're pinned, sir," Pierson replied. "Predators detected a Chechen blocking force in the pass. The Kildar elected to take a defensive position and hunker down."

"What?" the President snapped. "That's *suicide!*"

"We've been monitoring their communications, sir," Pierson said, uncomfortably. "The Kildar is aware of the correlation of forces but he and Colonel Nielson believe it is possible to ravage the Chechen main force. I presume they believe that will force the blocking force to be committed to the battle. If they can sufficiently damage the main force and the blocking force they have the possibility of slipping out of the noose. Mr. Jenkins' main worry is mortars and other indirect fire and the Predator has been tasked to look for those."

"That sounds like more of a desperate wish than a plan," the President replied.

"The reason that they feel that this is, in fact, a plan and not desperation has to do with some fairly high-end battle theory, sir," Pierson said. "Do you want me to cover it?"

"I've got ten minutes free," the President replied. "Can you give me a summary in less than ten minutes?"

"Yes, sir," Pierson said.

"Come up."

The colonel had been in the Oval Office only twice before, but he knew the route. When he entered he went to the center of the rug, a presidential seal, and came to a position of attention.

"Colonel Pierson, reporting as ordered, sir."

"Would you prefer to sit or stand?" the President asked, waving to a chair.

"Stand, if I may, sir," Pierson replied.

"Go."

"Theory on the psychology and processes of battle has rapidly advanced over the last ten years or so, Mr. President," Pierson began. "Many battles in history had outcomes that defied conventional wisdom. Notable among those are Rourke's Drift, Crecy and Alesia. In each of those cases, numerically inferior units comparable in apparent capability with their opponents were placed in a situation where defeat was, apparently, inevitable. Yet they prevailed. Countervailing these oddities were the much more common experiences where numerically inferior units failed. A well-known example of the latter was the Battle of Little Big Horn.

"Various theories existed over time in classic warfare literature which tried to define the reason for these anomalous outcomes. Most of them came down to sayings: 'On deadly ground, fight.' 'The moral is as the physical by three to one.' And so on. But the mechanism was poorly understood and did not always stand up to tests. At Dieppe, for example, a unit that might have survived under other circumstances was killed or captured. Whereas in the same war, at Bastogne, another unit with comparable correlation of forces survived and beat their larger opponent.

"Recent theory of the psychology of combat indicates that certain forms of training are synergistic. That is, one method of training laid upon other methods, along with a functionality best described as 'esprit,' is capable of creating units that have a high 'true' force multiple in combat. A recent example was found during the entry phase of the Iraq war in which a heavy infantry company was cut off and surrounded by the near order of ten times their number. Despite that fact, they were able to not only defeat the attackers but ravage them. They killed nearly three times their number in attackers and suffered a single casualty, he only wounded.

"Recently, this theoretical form of battle, tentatively called 'unit form asymmetrical battle,' has been used in an ad hoc way, notably in Afghanistan. On several occasions our small patrols have been attacked by numerically superior Taliban units. On each of those occasions the small unit was able to not only defeat the numerically superior force but do so with casualties to their attackers that were higher than would normally be expected.

"It should be noted, here, Mr. President, that all such instances were unintentional. No one in the U.S. Army is willing, at this time, to test the theory in practice. The chance of failure is too high.

"Theory suggests that there are two sides to the psychology. The first is the psychology of the attacker. Seeing a small unit, trapped, unable to be reinforced and numerically far inferior, the attacker assumes the ability to defeat the unit utterly. They, therefore, press the attack to a much greater degree than would normally be the case. Call it the 'bully' mentality. They can beat up on a group that has been bothering them and anticipate little real difficulty in doing so.

"The other side, the combat psychology and ability of the defender, is arguably more important. The defenders must have several conditions to succeed. They must see no possible outcome but utter destruction and universal termination if they lose. Surrender must not be an option. They must have total confidence in their superiority. They must have capable leadership. And last but arguably most important, they must have a level of training that places their combat skills in a multiple over their attacker.

"In World War II, for example, the Japanese had three of these preconditions: unwillingness to surrender, confidence, and capable leadership. And during the early phases of the war they were superior in training. Thus they often were able to defeat opponents that were numerically superior. As time went on, however, and the level of training of American and British forces improved, they were unable to effect their earlier successes.

"Modern Western combat training has been tested and proven to create soldiers that have a combat ability that is unheard of up until recently. Modern American standard infantry soldiers find, localize, engage and destroy targets with a coldness and precision that was unthinkable only twenty years ago. The reasons are complex and involve both new methods of training and certain societally common experiences. But the effect has been proven, repeatedly, to be synergistic and give the individual soldier and unit a combat multiplier over any of our standard opponents on the near order of twelve to one.

"The Kildar is apparently banking that the combination of prepared defenses, which are normally gamed as being a three-to-one advantage for the defender, and the combat multiplier of the Keldara over the Chechens will permit him to survive the encounter. And given the psychology of the attacker, that the Chechens will press the attack hard enough that he will not just defeat them but devastate them. That concludes my lecture, Mr. President."

"Well done," the President said, smiling. "How many times have you given that lecture?"

"About three, Mr. President," Pierson replied. "I specifically avoided words like 'transformative' but I am in a small but growing community that believes that the really 'transformative' aspects of warfare don't lie in the cool gadgets or 'effects-based warfare' but in transforming the ability of the individual to bring death and destruction upon the enemies of America, in stressing the training and psychological preparation of the combatant. I was unaware that Colonel Nielson was a fellow traveler but that is apparently the case."

"So you think this will work?" the President asked.

"Sir, honestly, I don't know," Pierson admitted, slumping slightly. "Every case in which this sort of thing *has* worked it has been when units were more prepared and had better support. Even in Rourke's Drift one aspect often overlooked was that it was a supply base. They had virtually unlimited ammunition and were well rested and fed before the battle. The Keldara have been running all night, they haven't had anything to eat in nearly twenty-four hours and they're yellow on ammunition already. That is, they are below eighty percent of their standard ammunition load. They have little or no functional indirect or air support; a couple of Hinds just don't do it for the current situation and one of those is down. They also don't have a source of water immediately available; there are two streams nearby but when they are under fire they will be difficult to access. Last, but not least, the Kildar, while capable, is not a trained officer for this sort of engagement. He depends to too great a degree on Nielson's professional input. Nielson, being remote from the situation, inevitably will overlook items of importance. If I were the Chechen commander, I'd set in a ring of heavy weapons and emplacements and starve them for a couple of days. *Then* I'd attack. Fortunately, with the nature of the Chechen resistance, that is unlikely. They just don't have the cohesion."

"When will we know?" the President said with a sigh.

"Sir, I would anticipate that the battle will go on for most of the day," Pierson replied. "That will carry it well into the wee hours of our morning. Either that or, unfortunately, be over swiftly. In which case we will have lost a key ally in the black side of the current war as well as a friend."

Shota was not an expert digger. He just didn't have the mentality to learn the basic tricks of how much to dig up with each shovelful, the better angles to strike, the best way to cut through a root or move a rock so as to not wear himself down.

However, in his case, it didn't really matter. The guy could hurl a shovelful of the heaviest substance on earth a couple of hundred feet and keep going. Where other Keldara would roll a small rock out of the way, in Shota's case they kept their helmets on; rocks the size of small boulders were likely to go flying by.

But even the strongest man needs food to work, and Shota was wearing down.

Mike looked up in surprise as the front wall of the bunker started to disappear, the rocks and dirt flying upwards and to the side. In the case of some of the rocks they were flying nearly to the emplacements fifty yards away.

When he saw Shota's head start to emerge from the trench he understood.

A boulder the size of a small suitcase was in the Keldara's way. Unable to budge it with the small entrenching tool, the Keldara grabbed it in both hamlike hands, lifted it over his head, and tossed it out of the trench. Although more or less rectangular in shape, it rolled ten meters.

"Hi, Shota," Mike said as the Keldara started hacking at the opening, widening it. "How you doin', man?" Despite the cold the Keldara was stripped to his undershirt and still sweating. He also was covered in dirt. Mike wasn't sure how much of it was getting out of the trench. On the other hand, it was pretty good camouflage.

"Hungry," Shota replied, tossing the dirt out of the trench in fountains of dust. "Really hungry."

"We've got some food on the way," Mike said. "Don't know if it will be before or after the first attack. But it's on the way. I held back a package of crackers if that will help?"

"Food?" the Keldara said, dropping his e-tool.

"And I've got one bottle of beer left," Mike admitted, pulling out the package of MRE crackers and one of the plastic bottles of beer he'd gotten made and issued for the Keldara beer ration. "Have at it."

The big Keldara stuffed the crackers in his mouth and washed them down with the beer. The entire bottle disappeared in one swig. Then he belched.

"Better," Shota said. "Thank you, Kildar."

"Now head back to your position," Mike said. "Don't fire the rocket until Dmitri or Oleg tells you to."

"Okay," Shota said. "I go back now."

"You know," Olga said, "if he was smart, he'd be scary."

"Yeah," Mike admitted. "Knew a guy like him on the teams, once. But smart. Wasn't as big but I'd swear he was just as strong. And you're right. He was scary. There's a couple of Deltas like that. Big as a house and smart. Those guys are freaks of nature. How are the boys?"

"Still with us," Olga said. Her arms were red to the elbows with blood. "But they're losing a lot of blood no matter what I do. When can we get them out of here?"

"Valkyrie, Valkyrie, ETA?"

"Five mikes, Kildar."

"Stand by." Mike reached down and switched frequencies without looking. "Tiger Three, status?"

"Looks like a council of war. There are a bunch of guys scattered around on the hills just hanging out. Minimum of fifteen mikes if they move right now. Got some sniper fire. Lasko's picking them off as fast as they get in position, though."

"Roger, out." Another freq switch. "Valkyrie, Valkyrie, dust-off hot. Position will be marked with yellow smoke."

"Roger, Kildar. Inbound your position, three mikes."

"YOSIF!" Mike yelled. Team Yosif had set up secondary positions to either side of the command bunker, a combination final security team and reserve.

"Yes, Kildar!"

"Dust-off coming in! I need some bodies!"

Mike crabbed past the casualties, then crawled through the rear exit of the bunker—a narrow passage between the original boulders—and stood up in the area behind. It was on the reverse side of the small hill from the Chechens and, hopefully, out of sight of their snipers. He pulled a yellow smoke grenade off his harness and tossed it to the more-or-less level ground just as he heard the "whop-whop" of the Hind on its way in.

"Valkyrie, LZ is marked."

"LZ in sight," Tammy replied. "Anisa, we taking any fire?"

"Negative, ma'am," the crew-chief replied.

"Okay, the job is toss the boxes out as fast as possible then load the wounded. I'm not going to stop while you toss, just for the wounded. Got it?"

"I think I can handle that, ma'am," Anisa said, a note of humor in her voice.

Anisa Kulcyanov was seventeen, just. She had all the height and musculature of her Kulcyanov Family but was dark of hair and eyes, the latter showing the traces of some Tartar ancestor. Her first experience of a "real world" mission had been sliding down a rope into the offices of an Albanian-owned nightclub in Romania, in the midst of a hot firefight. Her job had been to pull every last hard drive in the room in no more than three minutes. She had managed to do it in two minutes and forty-eight seconds, slightly bettering her best time during rehearsals.

As the Hind slowed while passing over some boulders she released her grip on the spades of the minigun, slid back the troop door and started tossing boxes out of the helicopter. About half of the cargo was ammunition crates, which were heavy but nothing compared to hay bales; she picked up one in either hand and hurled them out the door. The rest were wooden boxes, gifts from the Mothers of the Keldara to their sons. Those, she handled with a bit more care.

The last thing out the door was a big rubber bag. That was the hardest to maneuver. It had to be rolled and there wasn't a good way to grab it. She finally lay down on the floor and pushed it out with her boots.

The bag held enough water to supply the company for a day. By that time the helo had come to a stop and she scrambled forward to help with the stretchers.

"We've got it," Yosif said, climbing into the helo. "Hey, Anisa. Where's Gretchen?"

"In the Halls," Anisa said. "Hit by the bunkers in the pass."

"Shit," Yosif said, shaking his head. He grabbed the next stretcher and put it in the rack. And the next and the next. Two were walking wounded, Karoly Makanee with a round that had punctured his body armor low on the left side and Pedar Shaynav hit in the upper right arm. The round had hit the brachial artery and he was half unconscious with blood loss. "She was true Keldara."

"As are you, Yosif," Anisa replied. She was already hooking Pedar up to a liter of whole blood. She wasn't sure which of the stretcher casualties, or maybe even Pedar, would need the defibrillator. The Ranger medic had started to explain it and she'd cut him off; she'd seen one before and the instructions were easy enough to read. Compared to circuit diagrams they were comical. "Aer Keldar."

As the helo lifted into the air she hooked up two more liters of blood then turned to the miniguns again. The bird would be crossing near the defense position closing the pass. She might be an angel of mercy on this mission, but she was more than willing to be an *avenging* angel.

The Valkyr were, after all, warriors.

"We are agreed, then," Commander Bukara said, trying to hold onto his patience.

The Chechen resistance had something resembling a high command but they were in the hills nearer to Grozny. They'd been sending suggestions, most of them idiotic, throughout the entire action. But here, Bukara was the seniormost commander.

That didn't mean he could just order the other groups around. Each of the Chechen "battalions," most not much larger than a traditional company, were groups controlled and kept together by individuals. And a bigger bunch of prima donnas it was hard to find.

"I still feel that if you wish to command you should *lead*," Commander Sorrano said, his face hard.

"My force has been *chasing* these bastards for the last nine hours," Bukara said, patiently. "Now, as the wolf pack changes members to drag down the deer, we shift over. There are six hundred of you with your combined groups. There are only a bare *hundred* of them, now that we have done cutting them down on the chase. I have taken nearly a hundred *casualties*. But if you're afraid of a few Keldara . . ."

"We are not *afraid*," Sorrano said. He was a big man, dark of face and hair, wearing bandoliers of ammunition for the PKM he carried across both shoulders and four gigantic daggers on his belt.

He probably thought it made him look fierce: to Bukara it made him look like an idiot. Some of the links in the bandoliers were clearly kinked; if he tried to use the ammunition, his gun was going to jam. And Bukara, who had been in more than one hand-to-hand battle, had never used more than one knife in his life. His experience of "hand-to-hand" was that you generally used the biggest, heaviest thing you could get your hands on, generally an empty rifle. Knives were weapons of absolute last resort.

"Then don't you think that over six *hundred* of you are capable of killing less than a sixth your number?" Bukara asked, patiently. "My men will be in support. We will establish a base of fire on the hilltop to keep their heads down. My mortars will be in support shortly. You should have fire from them before you reach the objective. All you have to do is run up a hill and kill them. What could be easier?"

"Hey, boss, we got movement," Adams said.

Mike lifted his head out of the bunker and looked down the hill. Sure enough, there were figures moving on the hilltop below.

"Guess they got done with their little colloquy," Mike said, pressing his throat mike. "Gonna get hot soon. Tell the guys as soon as they push back this attack we've got fresh food."

"Now that's motivation," the former SEAL replied. "It's cold as hell out here. And I are hungry."

The clouds were clearing off rapidly and the sky was turning a beautiful blue. Mike stopped as he saw some movement in the sky, wondering if the Chechens had gotten air support. But it was only birds. Ravens.

"How do they know?" Mike asked, slipping back into the bunker.

"The ravens fly?" Olga asked, smiling. "The eyes of the Father of All are upon us this day."

"The bird of wisdom," Mike said, frowning. "You know, I think it finally makes sense."

"What?" Vanner asked, not looking up from his pad.

"The bird of wisdom," Mike said. "You can just see it. There was some shaman who was teaching a kid the different animals. He gives them all attributes, just cause they're easier to remember that way, right? So the kid sees a raven. 'Hey, shaman dude, what's that?' 'That's a raven. He's the bird of wisdom.' 'Why's that?' 'Cause he never lands until after the battle is over.'"

"Sort of like lawyers," Vanner said. "The ambulance chasers of the animal world."

"They just turn up to pick the dead," Mike said, frowning. "Be damned if any lawyers are going to pick over *my* dead. What's the intel on this group?"

"I get a count of about one kay, boss," Vanner replied. "That's based on prior intel on the different groups that have arrived. There's about six. The main group is a guy with the code name of Commander Bukara. Former Soviet lieutenant went over to the Chechen resistance quite a ways back. Was in on the battle of Grozny and a couple of other major actions. *Had* about five hundred. According to the ladies he's been bitching on open channel about casualties in the pursuit."

"He don't know for casualties, yet," Mike said.

Chapter Forty-Two

Salah El Ezam was seventeen, born on a small farm in the mountains above Grozny.

Salah could write, barely, and read a bit. He had been taught some words of writing by the mullahs in the town's madrassa. But he knew the words of the Koran, and especially of the Hadiths, by heart.

From the time he was born he could remember men talking about the Great Jihad. To die in battle in the jihad was the highest honor a Muslim could attain. Such a martyr was guaranteed a place in heaven at the Prophet's side.

The Prophet, peace be upon him, had spoken Allah's will, that the entire world must be in submission to the will of Allah. All Muslims were slaves to Allah: the common name "Abdullah" simply meant Slave of Allah, and Islam, in Arabic, meant submission. Men were in submission to Allah and women in submission to men. It was through the men in their lives, their fathers when they were growing up and their husbands when they married, that women worshipped the True God.

Any who were not in submission to Allah were infidels. The only true submission was through the laws of Shariah being the highest law of the land, the laws of submission to Allah.

This was the jihad, the will of Allah, to place the world under submission. Some were called to preach but Salah had never been a great speaker. His calling was to place the world under submission through the gun, as the Prophet also had decreed in the Hadiths.

There was no fear in his heart as he crossed the hilltop and first saw the small cluster of boulders on the ridge above that protected the pagan Keldara. Allah had decreed that the world would be in submission to his will. They could not fail; Allah, the Victorious, the Beneficent, would not permit it.

"Okay, now that is an A-Number-One clusterfuck," Adams said with a sigh. The Chechens were coming, oh, yeah. Lots of the motherfuckers. But they were just straggling over the hill that the snipers had been trying to use for cover and heading up the ridge any old way. It was almost sad. He hoped they'd cluster up a bit towards the end or the Keldara weren't going to get enough of them.

"Teams," Adams said, touching his throat mike. "Let them get in close. Do not open fire until I initiate. Keep under cover during their approach then bugger the bastards when I give the signal."

There were two reasons for that order. The first was that it was the best way to break an attack. Letting a group close on you and then hitting them, hard, at the last minute, tended to break their will. Especially if you waited until they thought they weren't going to be fired on at *all*.

The second reason, though, sucked. The M4s that many of the Keldara carried had a problem. They were great weapons out to 250 meters. Beyond 250 meters, though, the muzzle velocity fell off, sharply. The upside was that you could carry a hell of a lot more of the rounds than, say, a 7.62 weapon for the same weight. However, in a situation like this he could wish they were all carrying German G-3s using NATO 7.62 rounds. Those fuckers were killers out to about a thousand meters. Hell, the Keldara could start picking them off from *here*.

But what they had were the M4s.

"Vanner," he said, after switching frequencies.

"Go, Tiger Three."

"Make a note for me to talk to Mike about our weapon choice when we get back."

"Will do," Vanner said, a note of humor in his voice. For sure he knew the reason, but what he was probably finding funny was the "after we get back."

Well, fuck that. Adams had been in some nasty clusterfucks in his time and walked out of every one. This one wasn't going to be any different. He did *not* intend to die on a ridge in fucking Chechnya.

The Islamics wanted to be martyrs and go meet Allah. He was here to give them their wish.

This wasn't Kiril's first battle by any stretch. He had had a small piece of the last Chechen attack to cross the mountains and threaten the Keldara. But, more, he had been on the teams that had assaulted the Albanian town of Lunari and fought four times their number of Albanian defenders to a bloody standstill. He bore scars from that, as well, and the memory of an interesting encounter shortly after the extraction birds landed with not only the Keldara but several dozen former sex slaves, many of whom were *very* happy to be out of Albania.

He wasn't planning on getting laid right after *this* battle, not given the ambiguous situation with Gretchen, not to mention not being married to her, yet. But he fully intended to survive it. While the Keldara felt that there was no higher honor than dying in battle—being a hero was, after all, the only way to get to the Halls of Feasting—they believed just as deeply that your status *in* the Halls depended on how many had preceded you. One of the DVDs that was played over and over was an American movie about one of the greatest of their generals, a man named Patton. It was one of the ways they practiced their English. There was one part where he was making a speech, presumably to some of his troops, and said in it: "No bastard ever won a war by dying for his country. He won by making the *other* poor bastard die for *his!*" Whenever that part of the movie came around the roars in the barracks were deafening.

Now he poked his head up, briefly, taking the chance that any sniper would get his MICH-2000 helmet, then dropped back down. The Chechens were coming in a straggling herd. Hundreds of them.

Good. The Keldara believed in making the other bastard die. They didn't even have the bare mercy for them the American had professed. The only good target was a serviced target. And it was going to be a target-rich environment.

Adams wasn't about to poke his head up; he had a small video camera set up on his position and was watching the take on his BFT pad.

The lead Chechens, who were slowing down from their run and puffing pretty hard, were about eight hundred meters out. He briefly considered engaging them with the SAWs, which had the range. Then he shrugged.

Let them come.

Salah tried to shout in triumph. They were barely five hundred meters from the line of rocks that marked the Keldara positions and still the cowards didn't fire. He held his weapon forward in one hand and triggered a long burst of fire from the AK, joined by dozens, hundreds, of others. They were going to completely overrun these cowards, these pagan pigs, and then they would go on to the valley that whelped them and wipe them out for all time.

Three hundred meters. As AK rounds cracked overhead Adams looked over at Oleg and winked.

"Wait till you can see the whites of their eyes, eh?" the former SEAL said, grinning.

"That one I'm not familiar with," Oleg admitted. "Patton?"

"You guys need to watch some other movies for God's sake," Adams said with a sigh as a spent bullet tumbled into the position. Two hundred. "Bunker Hill. Big battle during the American Revolution."

"I wasn't even aware you'd had a revolution," Oleg said. "I will study it."

"Do," Adams replied. One hundred. He keyed his throat mike and lifted himself up to just below the rock lip of the fighting position. "Teams. Prepare to engage."

❖   ❖   ❖

They were on them now! There was no way to stop them!

"Alahu Akbar!" Salah shouted with what air he could spare. "God is Great!"

"Open fire," Adams said, straightening up and searching for a target.

That wasn't exactly tough. As he'd expected between the rough ground to their front and the steep slope, the Chechens had both tightened up and slowed down. He targeted one of the screaming horde, a young guy holding his AK at his hip and just starting a "spray and pray" burst and fired three rounds into his upper chest. Then he tracked right to the next target.

Kiril lifted himself and poked the barrel of the SAW out of the trench, opening fire before he really aimed. From his perspective he might as well; keeping the barrel down there was virtually no way to miss.

He was searching for priority targets: RPGs, other machine-gunners, leadership. But while he did that with one part of his mind he was engaging lower-priority targets, firing short, controlled bursts from the SAW.

He'd ganged three of the ammunition boxes together in anticipation of a hot fight. Normally the ammo box of the SAW hung on a holder on the left-hand side. In this case he'd dug out a small shelf just before the opening of his fighting position and placed the boxes there. Now they emptied their linked 5.56 into the weapon without him having to worry about reloading. He had six hundred rounds and *way* more targets. The sky was clear, the thin air blew cold down the trench and the ravens, harbingers of battle, were in the sky; the eyes of the Father of All were upon them.

It was a good day to do battle.

The fucking Keldara bastards.

Sorrano was watching his command broken and he could not believe it possible.

The fuckers had waited until the last possible moment to fire and now they were slaughtering his men on the very edge of victory. It could not be possible. They were so *close* he could see their eyes, yet his men could not reach them.

To the right, though, they were getting closer. There didn't seem to be as much fire there.

"RIGHT!" he screamed, pointing and slapping some of the fedayeen in that direction. "GO TO THE RIGHT!"

"Left. Big guy with a PKM. Looks like a leader."

Lasko tracked to the left and saw who Pyotar meant. The man had bandoliers of PKM ammunition crossed on his chest. Lasko automatically targeted the X point where they crossed and triggered one round.

Sorrano grunted and looked down at the red welling in his lower chest. One hand raised to it in surprise. He couldn't figure out where the blood had come from.

Suddenly the hole began spitting crimson and he fell to his knees as his legs lost all strength. He tried to prop himself up with his weapon but that, too, fell from his hands and he slumped forward on his face.

He was looking at a boot. It was very worn. They needed to get the men some more boots . . . soon . . .

Fuckers never learned.

When a gun was fired, the barrel tended to track upwards from recoil. Depending on how cases were ejected it could be pushed to one side as well.

When an automatic weapon was fired, the barrel tracked up and up and up. So when firing on automatic, the only way to keep the weapon from tracking off the target, unless you had a very firm position, was to fire in three- to five-round bursts.

Professional militaries knew that and trained their people to either fire in bursts or, more often, individual rounds. But groups like the Chechens, and the Taliban he'd fought in Afghanistan and Al Qaeda he'd fought in Iraq and various tribal militias he'd fought in Africa, the FARCs in Colombia . . . Christ it was a long list . . . they never seemed to learn. They'd just hold the weapon at their side, press the trigger and spray. Even if the first round was anywhere near the target all the rest tracked up and, in the case of the AK, generally to the right.

It gave you a great feeling to just yank the trigger and spray. He'd done it a couple of times for the fuck of it. But you didn't hit shit.

He hadn't even heard a medic cry from their side and the Chechens were getting *slaughtered*. The rushing attack was broken no more than thirty meters from their position with hundreds of bodies scattered on the ground. Most of them were wounded rather than dead, the fucking 5.56 tended to do that, but not many of them were still trying to fire.

The rest of the Chechens, though, were still charging. He dropped the spent mag out of the well, slapped another in and fired three rounds at one of the screaming horde. The guy kept coming so he put another two in his head. That dropped him.

On the right the Chechens were heavier; the slope tended to push them that way. Some of them were making their way through the fire and were nearly to the trench. That was Sawn's sector. The Makanee kid was good; he could handle that.

Kiril fired upwards as the Chechen came over the lip of his position then dropped the empty SAW and drew his hatchet.

The Keldara practiced at throwing axes but that wasn't the only skill they knew. As the next Chechen tumbled into the position Kiril's axe darted forward, fast as a snake, struck the man in the side of the neck and returned to guard position. The Chechen grabbed at his throat as the carotid began spurting high-pressure arterial blood across the position. With his hands clamped on the wound it still squirted out, but now in a spray that turned to a sanguine mist in the thin air.

Suddenly there were more of the screaming Islamics in the position and it became a bloody melee. Kiril blocked an empty AK upwards and kicked the Islamic in the crotch then brought the back of the axe across his face, smashing his cheek in and spraying teeth across the trench. Swinging it back so fast the head seemed to disappear he sank it into the upper arm of another of the Chechens, nearly severing it as the sharpened blade broke through the humerus bone and severed the brachial artery.

Back again to strike the man with the smashed face on the side of the head, crushing his occipital bone in a spray of blood and brains, across to catch another on the throat, tearing out his windpipe, down in one continuous motion to bury it in the neck of the one whose arm he'd cut off.

The last Chechen dropped as Sawn suddenly appeared in the opening to the position. The team leader wrenched his own hatchet out of the back of the man's neck and looked around.

"What are you doing just standing there?" Sawn asked the panting and blood drenched SAW gunner. "Get the bodies out of here and get your gun back in action. This ain't no ice-cream social!"

"I *so* regret introducing you to *Red vs Blue*," Kiril panted. But the next moment he was heaving the bodies of the Chechens out of the position. Carefully, though. Master Chief Adams had pointed out more than once that there was very little cover *better* than a nice fresh body.

Salah wondered why he could not move. He kept willing his body to rise and nothing would happen.

He had tripped, that was all. And rolled onto his back. His head turned to the side and he could not even move his neck. All he could do was look up and to the side. There was another man next to him, he thought it might be Ibrahim Shatti by the clothing. For some reason, his head seemed to be pushed to the side, weirdly, his face broader and flatter and the back of his head was missing. Salah thought that it made him look better than usual. Ibrahim was not a very handsome boy. He still had the spots very bad and they had scarred his already misshapen face. It was more misshapen, now, and had two large spots to either side of his nose.

The firing had mostly stopped. They must have won. Allah, the Victorious, was victorious once again.

Chapter Forty-Three

Commander Bukara couldn't believe his eyes. The straggled remnants of the attack force were running down the hill, dropping their weapons, dropping their ammunition, dropping everything in a desperate race to escape. And it was a race they were losing as first one then another dropped to sniper fire. Barely a hundred had fled, initially, and that number had been dropped by half before they were halfway down the slope.

"Pagan fucks," Bukara snarled. Already ravens were dropping from the sky onto the bodies and distant shots, single, indicated that some of the wounded were being finished off by the defenders.

"They say that the raven is one of their totems," Bukara noted. "The eyes of one of their gods. He's certainly getting an eyeful today."

"There is no God but Allah," Sayeed replied.

"Well, I wish he'd send me a sign, then," Bukara snapped.

"Commander Bukara . . ."

The young Chechen was panting, clearly having finished running hard. He was still carrying his weapon, though, and had come from the rear. So he wasn't one of the cowards up on the hill.

"What?" Bukara snarled.

"Another group comes," the young man gasped. "A large group under Commander Sadim. And they have *reporters*. From Al Jazeera! The whole world will watch us destroy these Keldara!"

"You said you wanted a sign," Sayeed said, impertinently.

"Sergeant Sivula, what, pray tell, are you doing here?" Captain Guerrin asked.

Of course the answer was obvious since the sergeant, sweating like a horse, was carrying one end of a 120mm mortar tube.

120mm mortars are, technically, man-transportable. And over short distances, if you have enough bodies, they are. Of course, the tube alone weighs 110 pounds. The massive baseplate is even heavier at 136 pounds. And the bipod is no joke, despite weighing in at a comparatively light 70 pounds. Then there was ammunition, without which the weapon was useless. Each crate of three rounds weighed 40 pounds. And the more rounds the better.

There was no way that even all the young women of the Keldara could have carried the mortars the ten kilometers from the nearest road to the Ranger position. The women were strong but it would have taken four of them, alone, to carry the tube. Sivula and one other Ranger were currently carrying it, having traded off with the previous team a kilometer before reaching the Ranger position.

Sivula lowered the mortar to the ground and looked sheepish.

"Well, sir, our mandate was to work with the mortars," Sivula said. "And the ladies wanted to bring them up here."

Every female of the Keldara between the age of fifteen and about twenty, damned near a hundred of them, were in a long line behind him, carrying crates of ammunition, water and food. All of them had weapons, as well, mostly AKs scrounged from Chechens on various battlefields. The weapons and crates clashed with their bright tops and black skirts. It looked like the gypsy caravan from hell.

The one woman who was *not* young was right behind Sivula. She looked to be about two hundred but, despite her age and the weight of weapon and ammunition she was carrying, she was following along just fine, not even looking particularly bothered by the slope. The term that came to mind was . . . sprightly.

"You are the commander," the woman said in broken English as she reached Guerrin's commander. "I am Mother Lenka, brewmistress of the Keldara, Captain. I have brought your men some of my *personal* beer and in exchange I would ask for a favor."

"Well, ma'am," the captain said, uncomfortably, "my men can't drink on duty . . ."

"Even though you Americans have no legs for *real* beer," Mother Lenka snapped, "even *they* will not be made drunk by one bottle, Captain. And it's not as if they're having to fight."

Guerrin's eyes flared at that and he opened his mouth to reply but he didn't get a chance.

"We are here on a mission of mercy, Captain," Mother Lenka continued, more pleasantly. "There are, possibly, injured Chechens in those bunkers. We are here to provide aid to them. But we are but poor, weak women. So we would like to *ask* for a little help. Just, you know, toting things. I know you are under orders to not move forward but *surely* you can help us on a mission of mercy." The old woman batted her eyes coquettishly.

Guerrin was surprised. Despite looking as if she was two hundred, when the woman turned on her charm full force she actually *was* pretty good-looking. He'd never thought that was possible.

"Uh . . ." Guerrin said. "The *toting* you'd like help with, that would be, oh, mortars, baseplates . . . That sort of thing?"

"Well, we have to have weapons for self-protection," Mother Lenka said, still blue eyes wide and innocent in the face of the blatant lie. "And there may be poor, injured Chechens to bring back."

Guerrin had seen what Captain Bathlick had left of the Chechen position. If there was anyone alive over there he was a leg. But she had a point. A mission of *mercy*? Even *State* couldn't find fault with that.

"I can see that logic," Guerrin said, trying not to grin. The woman could charm the scales off a snake. "I'll round up some guys. Third Platoon looks a little worn out."

"Why thank you, Captain," Mother Lenka said, smiling. She dipped into one of her ammo pouches and pulled out a bottle. "Have a beer. But eat something with it. You Americans are weak drinkers."

❖   ❖   ❖

"Presents from the Mothers," Sawn said, dropping a package in Kiril's position.

Kiril had gotten the bodies arranged to his satisfaction, cleaned his SAW and reloaded it. He'd left one of the bodies, one of the less bloody ones, in the position. It gave him something to sit on.

"Blessings be upon the Mothers," Kiril said, opening the wooden box.

There were three meat rolls, beef and cabbage wrapped in bread, a small loaf of oatmeal cake, rich with honey and washed in egg and, blessed be, a bottle of beer stamped with Mother Lenka's *personal* rune. He'd only had Mother Lenka's beer on two other occasions; it was saved for holidays. The meat rolls were hot and the beer still cold, courtesy of the straw both were packed in.

"Blessings indeed," Sawn said. He had a load of other boxes in his arms. "I have to drop these off before *I* can eat. So I'm out of here."

"Go," Kiril said, his mouth already stuffed with meatroll. He cracked the top on Mother Lenka's brew and took a sip. Given that he'd been out of beer for days and hadn't eaten in nearly twenty-four hours, it was one of the best meals he'd ever had. "Go with blessings."

Mike opened up the box then looked over at the commo and intel section.

It was like friends told him about kids. They weren't getting into trouble until they were quiet. Before the food got dropped off they'd been happy-talking. Happy to be alive after the Keldara had beaten off the attack. Now they were quiet, and they weren't eating.

"What?" Mike said. "Whatever it is, I'm going to find out sooner or later."

Vanner looked up from the BFT pad and shrugged.

"Check the updated casualty report," he said. "Female."

Mike pulled out his own pad and keyed the casualty reports. He didn't need to sort it, the name leapt off the screen.

Mahona, Gretchen, Private, Crew-Chief. KIA.

Crew-chief. "*Game as hell. Took some with her, I think, but she got hit by one of the 12.7s.*"

Mike put the pad away then put his hand to his forehead, eyes closed. His jaw worked as he tried to get control but his mind was filled with the sound of laughter, flashing legs and the war in his head was one of chocolate mousse.

He could not do this right now. He could *not*. He had to bottle it away. And there was one other thing he *had* to do. Nobody else could do it. Nobody.

He wiped his eyes and took a deep breath as he stood.

"Keep the food warm. I've got to go over to Sawn's positions."

"Oh, shit," Pierson said as CNN broke in with a "special report from Chechnya."

Ever since the advent of the twenty-four-hour news cycle, every higher headquarters kept at least one TV tuned to one or more of the satellite news channels. Not only was it a necessity to see what lie was being perpetrated by the Mainstream Media today, quite often you could pick up intelligence that was otherwise unnoticed or unavailable.

And sometimes, you found out when an op had been blown sky high.

"This is Jack Sperman with CNN," the newscaster said. "We are receiving reports of a major battle going on in Chechnya at this moment. The region where the battle is taking place is called the Pankisi Gorge, an area long used by Chechen militants as a refuge in their resistance to Russian occupiers. Much of the area belongs to the country of Georgia but Georgia has been unable to stop the Chechens from using it. They have apparently sent a small force in for reasons at this time unknown and the force has been cut off and surrounded by the Chechen freedom fighters who are vowing to destroy them. We now take you to live video feed from the Al Jazeera satellite news service . . ."

The video was of an Al Jazeera reporter interviewing a big guy wearing the de rigueur bandana of "freedom fighters" everywhere. They were both speaking Arabic but there was a continuous translation overlaid on the voice track.

"Commander Bukara," the reporter said, "your first attack was beaten off. What are you going to do, now?"

"That was only a probe," Bukara said. "We were just finding where their positions are. Now that we know, we will attack in force and destroy the infidels, removing their stain. These are the lands of Islam and we refuse to let foreign crusaders, pagans and pigs set foot here!"

"You say they are pagans, yes?"

"Pagan eaters of pig flesh. They are not People of the Book. They are worshippers of false gods and will recant or die as the Prophet decreed!"

"You are confident, then?"

"Very. They are few in number and my men, after a long battle that left many of the pagans dead, now have them trapped. They are faithless, as well, leaving their wounded and dead behind. We have treated the wounded with care and the dead shall be buried with full Islamic ceremony, although they are pagans and thus doomed to hell. It shall not be said, though, that we are barbarians."

"You are acting in the best traditions of Islam, Commander. When do you plan to attack . . ."

"Somebody better tell the President," Pierson said with a sigh.

"Kildar, this is Tiger Two."

"Go."

Mike was just looking off into the distance. Telling Kiril had been harder than just about anything he'd ever done. But it wasn't that that had made a black place where his soul used to be.

"We're sending you a video on feed two," Nielson said. "Al Jazeera had some reporters covering the Chechen forces in the area. They've apparently caught up to your battle. Bukara is spouting bullshit but I thought you'd find it humorous."

"Fuck," Mike said, picking up his personal pad and hitting the control for feed two. Sure enough . . . Motherfucker. He could recognize their emplacements in the background. Just what he fucking needed.

He stood up and walked to the front of the bunker and looked down the hill then picked up his binoculars. Steadying his arm on the wall of the bunker he dialed in the digital zoom and spotted the group. Bukara had to be the guy waving his arms.

"Fuck. Is the President seeing this?" Mike said.

"Mike, it's satellite TV," Pierson replied. "It's being carried live on CNN, Fox, Al Jazeera and Sky News. Yeah, he knows. Hell, the whole *world* knows."

✧ ✧ ✧

"Mr. President," the Secret Service agent said, hand to his ear mike. "Sir, sorry to interrupt dinner, but Colonel Pierson says you might want to turn on Fox News."

"Sorry about this, honey," the President said to the First Lady, smiling slightly. He gestured with his chin and another Secret Service agent clicked the TV in the dining room on.

". . . Kill the Keldara pagans. Then we shall go to their homes and scour them. Their valley is a rightful part of Islamic lands, stolen from us long ago. Today is the day of reckoning against these infidel invaders . . ."

"Get me Colonel Pierson," the President said, his face hard. "Now."

"That's Michael isn't it?" the First Lady said, worriedly. "Honey . . ."

"Not now, Amanda," the President said. "Not *now*."

"Fuck."

Mike considered the group through his binoculars then hit the range finder. Two thousand seven hundred and ninety eight meters. Winds . . . pretty touchy. Mostly from the side but shifting . . . On the other hand it *was* downhill all the way . . .

"Hey, Nielson," Mike said, touching his throat mike and checking the time. "You'd better call higher and tell them if anybody's eating dinner they might want to turn off the video feed."

"Mike . . ."

Mike switched frequencies.

"Lasko, you'd *better* still have the Robar."

Lasko peered through the NightForce NSX scope of the Robar .50 caliber sniper rifle and considered the shot.

The target was barely a dot even at twenty-two times magnification. The winds were fifteen knots at his position but seemed higher in the air in between. Probably closer to seventeen. He leaned over and looked through the spotting scope then hit the built-in inclinometer. Two hundred and sixty-three meters below his position. And nearly three thousand meters. The height difference was the only thing that made the shot even vaguely possible.

The ballistics of a round is a simple function of gravity. Anything dropped in a gravity well has the force of gravity pulling it down. Once the bullet leaves the barrel of the weapon, it is continuously falling towards the ground and just as continuously accelerating, gravity being like that.

Thus the "parabolic" function of anything thrown in a gravity well, from a football to a CD chucked at your sister's head to . . . a bullet fired at a target nearly a mile and a half away.

In addition, rounds slow owing to air resistance. Winds push them around. A bullet fired from a gun pointed perfectly at a target even a hundred meters away tends to miss. Much less a mile and a half. Mile and a half just simply wasn't doable. Impossible. Unthinkable.

Lasko knew all this. He'd been a superb "instinctive" shot before the Kildar came along. Since then he'd studied and practiced constantly. The computations of advanced ballistics sometimes took him a while, he had, after all, barely been able to do multiplication before the Kildar, but he had technology to help out there. This shot, though . . .

Tricky, tricky. Winds . . .

Normally, Sion would be doing this but Pyotar had no clue how to really spot. So Lasko dialed back the zoom on the spotting scope, checking the winds. Winds seen through a scope at that distance made a "haze" effect similar to the mirage you got on hot days. You could *see* them rippling by and with practice could figure out direction and probable speed. The wind nearest the target was going to have the most effect because the bullet was going to be going slowest there. Hell, it might be going slowly enough to not have any effect on the target at all.

He checked six points going back, making notes on a pad at each point, then zoomed the scope back to the target. The fucker was still talking and standing nice and still for the cameras.

He pulled out his own BFT device, which had a program for long-range shooting calculations built into it. He plugged in the distance, elevation change and wind variables and hit the Enter key. The device in less than a second gave him numbers for elevation of the barrel and deflection off target. It also gave him the speed the round was going to be traveling, which, fortunately, was more than high enough.

Looking through the scope, he snorted. He'd adjusted his scope to the maximum hold-over, was at the bottom of the stadia on the vertical and still needed two mils. He shifted the rifle up and snorted again. *About* two mils was going to have to do. And the bullet was going to be breaking the sound barrier on the way. That, right there, was going to make this shot more luck than either science *or* art.

He also was firing with the scope at nearly maximum horizontal. The rifle pointed upwards and sideways at, apparently, thin air. Insane to even try . . . Oh, well. If he missed nobody was going to notice. Except the Keldara and, in a way, they were the only ones that mattered.

Shifting the rifle, he found the target again and wrapped his arm into the strap, getting a good solid seat. If he thought about the impossibility of the shot for even a second . . . he might not take it at all. So he just took a slight breath and squeeeezed . . .

"Colonel, we need to ensure that there is *no* discussion of our interaction with this," the President said.

"Yes, Mr. President," Pierson said. He was sweating. He'd *never* had an op go this far south in his life. The whole fucking *world* was watching one of the blackest of black ops on satellite TV. Mother-*fucker*! He shook his head as one of the commo lieutenants looked over at him, waving. "President!" he mouthed.

"I KNOW," the guy suddenly screamed. "Tell him to turn off the feed! NOW! Or at least get the First Lady out of the FUCKING ROOM!"

The bullet was a Hornady A-MAX, the round of choice for long-distance shooters. The sharp polymer cap over a more or less hollow center gave it excellent ballistic ability because it could knife through the atmosphere and maintain a solid spin over long distances. And the hollow point, well, that meant the round nearly exploded on contact with a target.

It started off at 854 meters per second and in a perfect spin, courtesy of high-quality manufacture in both the bullet and the rifle. But by the time the 750-grain round reached target it was going barely above the speed of sound and pointed nearly straight downwards. The edges of the sound barrier had caused it to begin "wobbling" and now it was tumbling as well.

It was that angle and wobble that did it as much as anything. The round entered Commander Bukara's chest going at slightly *below* the speed of sound, falling at a 75-degree angle and very nearly sideways, transmitting in one brief moment 1,804 foot-pounds of energy or nearly six times as much as the most powerful .45 pistol round.

At that point, hydrostatic shock took over.

The President watched, wide-eyed, as the man on the screen seemed to explode. His torso separated from his abdomen in a spray of blood and intestines. One arm was ripped off, spinning through the air and hitting the Al Jazeera reporter hard enough to knock him off his feet.

He just sat there for a moment, his mouth open, as the view from the camera became one of the ground, sideways, then started shaking and moving as the cameraman, smart man, crawled away. It suddenly terminated, showing an empty chair. From the sounds, the newscaster was throwing up into a wastebasket under the desk.

"Can we let the First Lady back in, now, Mr. President?" the Secret Service agent by the door asked.

"Sure," the President replied.

His wife still had her fork in her hand. When the Service got the word that the First Lady needed to "exit the room" they didn't mess around. This wasn't Hollywood. When the Service got the word to move a principal, they stopped being polite; the principal moved at the highest speed the Detail could run with him or her in their arms. Her feet had *not* hit the floor.

"What *happened*?" she asked, angrily.

The President looked at the fork and shook his head.

"Nothing," he said, grabbing at his mouth. "Excuse me!" he muttered, rushing out of the room.

The First Lady looked at one of the younger agents, who was throwing up in a wastebasket, the screen where the anchorman, green-faced, was just straightening up and then at her personal agent.

"I'm glad you picked me up, aren't I?" she asked.

"Yes, ma'am," the agent responded, stone-faced. He'd still been in the door, looking over his shoulder for the threat, when the guy made the shot and all he could think was "we have *got* to get that guy on the Detail."

"Vanner, what's the pool on Bukara's replacement?" Mike asked.

"Sadim," Vanner said. "He's the senior Chechen in the sector and most of the survivors are his men. He's not going to be as easy as Bukara, either."

"We'll deal with it," Mike said as his earphone beeped indicating that Nielson was on the other freq. "Go, Tiger Two."

"Kildar, do you think that was *wise*?" Nielson asked. "Pierson is fucking *fuming*. The President, along with several million other people around the world, is reported to be puking in the bathroom."

"No," Mike said, coldly. "But it sure was what *I* call quality television."

Chapter Forty-Four

"Lasko," Adams said over his throat mike. "You there?"

"Go, Tiger Three."

"You are now officially the most famous sniper in the world," Adams said, chuckling. He'd figured out how to get the feed just in time. "You know that was on satellite TV, right?"

"I was unaware," Lasko replied. There was, however, the slightest note of satisfaction in his normally toneless voice.

Lasko had no orders to engage the other targets and wasn't about to throw away a rep that high; another shot like that was not guaranteed. He would need a new screen name, though. 2782Robar sounded about right.

He picked up his meat roll and took a bite, chewing slowly and methodically. His beer was untouched. He wasn't about to have alcohol interfere with his fine motor control.

He continued to peer through the scope, watching the gathering Chechen force.

Come to the slaughter, pigs of Allah.

Serris hated fucking mortars. He hated being fired on by them because the bastards were worse in a way than regular artillery. He'd heard it was because their bursting charge was heavier than similar-sized artillery or something. He'd caught some regular artillery during Iraq and even one time in Afghanistan but mortars were worse. And all the fucking muj had the damned things; Iraq seemed to have more mortars than it had stray dogs. And Iraq had *a lot* of stray dogs.

But he hated humping the things even more than he hated being under fire from them. He'd cross-trained with the 60 guys and come away with the definite desire to *never* have to be fucking 11Charlie. Most of the time you couldn't see what you were firing at, you humped the shit around day after day and then most of the time everybody forgot to use you. It just fucking sucked.

But compared to these motherfuckers, 60mm mortars were like carrying around some spare sand in your boot. These fucking 120s . . . the guy who invented these motherfuckers should be *shot*.

He currently was holding one of the rope handles of the baseplate and not enjoying the experience one fucking bit.

"Jesus, Lane, lift up a bit," Serris snarled. "I'm taking all the weight!"

"It's not my fault I'm short," Lane puffed. "Try bending over or something."

"If I bend over I'm gonna get a hernia," Private Thomson said, his foot slipping out from under him. "Fuck!" the Ranger snarled, trying to hold up his end of the tube.

"Oh, son-of-a-bitch," Sivula said as more of the weight came down on him. "Don't hold yourself *up* with it, newbie!"

"Would you *please* quit fucking bitching?" Sergeant Simmons said, shaking his head. He had the bipod over his shoulder but still helped Thomson struggle back to his feet. "Jesus *Christ*! You're fucking *Rangers*. You're supposed to eat pain for *breakfast*. Those fucking *girls* following us have been carrying those damned ammo boxes for the last fifteen klicks and you're bitching cause you gotta carry a fucking baseplate maybe *two*? *We* can't even pass the bunker line! They're going up into the fucking *pass*. You know, where the motherfucking *enemy* is? So Would You Please Quit Fucking *BITCHING*?"

"Well, now that you put it that way," Serris said. "Can I just say one thing?"

"What?!"

"I hate fucking mortars . . ."

❖   ❖   ❖

"I hate fucking mortars," Adams said, ducking involuntarily as another salvo dropped across the Keldara position.

The Chechen mortar teams had finally gotten into position and they had apparently limitless ammo. Most of it was courtesy of the Russian Army, which had a terrible problem with securing its resupply convoys. How they'd humped all the ammo into position Adams wasn't sure, but they'd probably used mules. However they'd done it, they'd been hitting them for the last fifteen minutes and the Keldara had taken more casualties in that time than in the whole damned pursuit. Oh, most of them were light, just minor shrapnel, but a couple of guys in Padrek's team had had a round land right in their position. Two more body bags to add to the next Valkyrie load.

"They are quite unpleasant," Oleg said. He was pulled up against the side of the position, his head tucked down, but otherwise trying for the "totally imperturbable" look. He said it in English, Scottish-accented English no less, and Adams had to shake his head.

"Now you're sounding like a fucking Brit," Adams growled. "I never should have let McKenzie teach you guys. You're going to start talking about 'a spot of bother' and 'a dog's breakfast' next."

"Actually I was thinking more along the lines of 'a bit of a tiff.' As in 'well, this is a bit of a tiff, what?'"

"Oh Christ." Adams keyed the video feed on his BFT pad and shook his head again. "They're getting in position for another assault." He keyed his throat mike. "Yo, Ass-Boy . . ."

Kacey didn't have to look up, turn her head or otherwise move to fix D'Allaird with a stare when he opened the door. She'd been sitting in the hard wooden chair, the only seat in the "ready room" for the last two and a half hours with her arms crossed looking at the door.

"Your bird is repaired, ma'am."

The chief was just about covered in grease and hydraulic fluid. Forget being on his coveralls, being on his face, arms and hands; it was matted into his hair.

Kacey picked up her helmet off the floor and walked to the door, her face cold.

"I figure you've got the lift for a couple of gunner positions," D'Allaird said as they walked to the hangar. His face and tone were just as hard and cold. The two Czech contract mechanics were just walking out, clearly discussing in Czech just how soon they could get *out* of this fucking place. They, too, were covered in oil and hydraulic fluids. "So I mounted the last two Gatlings. The bird is armed and fueled. There are some yellow lights but nothing is critical. I won't certify it once you're in combat, though."

"Understood," Kacey said as she walked over to the Hind. She stopped and blinked, though, at the sight of the gunners. "What did you do, dig up the morgue?"

Father Ferani had, indeed, spent most of his time in the Great War safely behind the lines, much to his chagrin. But only "most." He had also been a member of the groups that ran weapons and supplies into Stalingrad during the siege. Those had been floated down on barges, often under direct and indirect fire from the Germans. It was not distinguished service but he'd had quite a few shots fired at him in anger. His biggest disappointment was that he rarely got to fire back.

When the call had gone out for people to man the guns on the attack bird, everyone had again volunteered. But this time, the Fathers interceded. Their argument went something like this. All of the young people were committed to the battle. Those of the middle age *must* stay to keep the farm going and, in extremis, defend it if all the others fell. And the job was not strenuous; all that the person need do was hold onto the gun and fire. Even the old women could do that. The elders were more than capable, thank you.

Everyone knew it was a lie. With the exception of Father Kulcyanov, none of the current crop of elders had ever had the opportunity to earn their Death Guard. Grapa Makanee, who had died two years before, was, except for Father Kulcyanov, the last survivor of the line combatants of the Great War. The Fathers wanted *one* chance, damnit, to earn their Death Guard.

So the rest of the Keldara humored them. Not only because, excepting only the Kildar, they were the final word in discipline amongst a disciplined people but because the way things were going, *everyone* was going to get the chance to earn a Death Guard. Had not Mother Lenka gathered all the young women to go to the battle? What was next, the Mothers?

Father Kulcyanov had excused himself. While he would have enjoyed one last whiff of cordite, he had a Death Guard, a big one that had been waiting many decades to be his servants in the Halls. And he knew that, with his heart, it was possible he would not survive even if he was not shot.

Then there was the matter of *which* Fathers got to go. None except Father Kulcyanov had been willing to relinquish the honor. Father Makanee had suggested arm wrestling. Father Ferani had countered with a hand-axe free-for-all, the traditional way of settling things that no one could agree upon in the Keldara.

Father Kulcyanov had forced them to draw straws. Father Ferani had been pissed. He'd been slowly developing the desire over *decades* to bury an axe in Father Devlich.

Father Ferani smiled at the young woman and gestured for her to get in the aircraft.

"Are fighters," he said in painfully bad English. "You pilot. Fly. Fight. Kill. We guard sides."

"Gunny," Kacey whispered, "I think that zombie just said something."

"Kacey, everybody else is committed," D'Allaird whispered back. "I found out when I was working on the bird that all the young women have gone up to the pass. All there is left is oldsters and kids. And this guy's apparently got some combat experience."

Another oldster, this one somewhat younger, leaned out the door next to the first and looked at her fiercely.

"Are going?" the man barked. "Battle waits!"

The first oldster looked at him contemptuously and spat something in a firm and angry tone. In a second the two were bitching away at each other in what Kacey figured was Georgian. They sounded like a couple of quarreling old women.

"The *really* old one is Father Ferani," D'Allaird said as Kacey climbed into the cockpit. "He was in the Russian Army in WWII. The other guy is Father Devlich. They're the bosses of two of the Six Families. So they're sort of muckety-mucks."

"Great," Kacey said. "Not only do I have a couple of corpses riding shotgun, they're *boss* corpses. Thanks, Tim."

"I was sort of busy fixing the bird, ma'am," D'Allaird replied.

"And you did one hell of a job, Chief," Kacey said. She sat up in her seat and gave him a peck on the cheek. "Thanks."

D'Allaird looked shocked, raising one hand to his cheek.

"Captain Bathlick!" he said after a moment.

"What?" she asked as she hit the engine start button. "You see an Equal Opportunity Office around here? Hell, if there was they'd probably be happy as hell. We've got equality of race, sex *and* age down pat. Black engineer, female pilot and two zombies manning the minis. Let's roll this puppy out, Chief. Like the man said, battle is awaitin."

As before people swarmed forward at D'Allaird's raised hand and pushed the Hind into the open. It wasn't nearly as spiffy as the last time; the bird was covered in holes that were patched with hundred-mile-an-hour tape, and all the hydraulic fluid hadn't been cleaned off. But, as D'Allaird had promised, while there were some yellow lights, none of it was critical. She wasn't going to need the FLIR for this mission.

But she wasn't going right away. Another oldster, the guy wearing the tiger skin, walked up to the front of the bird as it rolled onto the pad. He had that axe and mistletoe in his hands and he waved both over the nose of the bird, chanting something Kacey couldn't hear.

She wasn't particularly into mystic mumbo-jumbo but it seemed important to the Keldara so she waited. But then he stepped back and straightened into a position of attention and raised the axe in front of his nose just like a rifle salute.

Kacey looked at him for a second and then remembered who the guy was. This was the guy who'd picked up a "Hero's medal" for taking out four Tigers with a fucking rocket launcher. And been in Stalingrad, which deserved a medal all in itself. She was being saluted by the equivalent of a Medal of Honor winner.

Kacey slowly raised her hand and gave him the crispiest salute she'd *ever* rendered, warrior to warrior, the way it was *supposed* to fucking be. She wasn't saluting some guy who'd been promoted for honorable service as an ass-kisser in the Pentagon and she wasn't being saluted for being a flying truck driver. She was being saluted as a warrior by one fucking warrior par excellence: a pro.

She dropped the salute, fast, and hit the key to engage the props.

Time to go to fucking war.

The Pred pilot *knew* he should have turned over control before now. His supervisor had asked, twice, if he wanted to turn over the bird. But he'd been flying this mission through the whole last phase and he wasn't about to walk away now. He had a mission. Find those fucking mortars.

He'd been given a vague area to look and he was looking. But the area was chock a block with rock formations, and mortars, honestly, were pretty hard to spot during the day when they were firing. At night it was different, they put up one hell of a visual signature. But they didn't give off a lot of smoke when they fired. The biggest daytime signature was the dust from the baseplates when they slammed into the ground.

Finally, he caught a flash out of the side of the camera view and slewed the camera towards the flash. At first he wasn't sure he'd found them but then they fired again, throwing up those puffs of dust and, this time, he caught the slight smoke signature.

"Mortars spotted," he said. "I've got clearance to engage?"

"Stand by," his supervisor said, walking over. "Two more birds inbound in about ten minutes. I've got Tommy and Hank ready to rock on them. You about ready to take a break and let this one cruise back?" The supervisor bent down and peered at the screen, pushing his glasses up his nose.

"In a second," he said, lasing the target. There were three mortars and he'd been told there were more around somewhere. There, they weren't in one battery but they'd been clustered. There was a trail in the area and that was probably the reason. Three batteries of three mortars apiece. Looked to be the standard Russian 120s. And glory be . . .

"Stupid," the supervisor said, pointing at the screen. "They've got their ready ammunition stacked between the guns."

"I noticed," the pilot said, banking the Predator around to line on the positions. It wasn't strictly necessary, but it increased the ease of engagement. "Four rounds, three positions. Two piles of ready ammo and three guns per. How d'you want me to do this? One round to each position and one to finish off the wounded at one?"

"Wait," the supervisor said. "That's how I want you to handle it. Three positions, three birds."

"Yeah," the Pred pilot said. "I hope the guys who are taking fire can wait."

"Well, I hear they're in more trouble than mortars . . ."

"Good evening, Prime Minister . . ."

President Cliff, unlike his predecessor, was an "early to bed, early to rise" person. He liked a definite schedule and minimum possible interruptions in it.

However, he was more than aware that sometimes a president had to adjust such things. Such as when an international crisis of epic proportions, if very very quiet, was under way.

The problem was the files Mike had picked up in Albania. They contained blackmail information that could damage every major government in the world. Even when it was information that damaged an opponent, it was so inflammable that it was bound to blow back on the groups in power.

Since none of the governments had trusted the others with the information, Mike, as the easiest to erase if need be, had been chosen as the guardian.

And now the guardian was on international TV, apparently about to be wiped out by a superior force.

"I am happy that you were willing to take my call," the prime minister said. "It is very late for you, is it not?"

The Japanese never *ever* came to the point!

"Sometimes it is necessary to adjust your schedule," President Cliff replied. He could play the indirect game when he had to.

"Some issues do take precedence over personal comfort," the prime minister of Japan said. "I was, in fact, awakened from a quite pleasant dream by a senior aide when a particular name was noticed on television."

"I have had a very busy day," President Cliff replied. "But I have been watching some television this evening."

"I note a name, one I had not expected to see on CNN."

"As have I. Were you awake for his most remarkable . . . display? I was having supper."

"You have my sympathies," the prime minister replied. "I have seen the replay. He is . . . formidable. However, there is the issue of certain materials . . ."

"The materials are secure," President Cliff said, trying not to sigh in relief that it had only taken this long to get to the point. They must be really exercised. "This issue has had my attention for some days now. Perhaps I should have ensured you were informed but it was a private matter, some aspects of which have, unfortunately, become public. However, for many reasons but not least the security of certain materials I dispatched a Ranger company to secure the area. They are unaware of that portion of their mission but are under definite orders to ensure the security of the facility in question. I am also privy to certain details regarding close security and termination of the materials in the event of unauthorized access. I will ensure that you are given sufficient information to ensure your own peace of mind on that score tomorrow."

"I was, in fact, aware of the presence of your infantry unit," the prime minister said. "However, my advisors tell me that they are unsure of its ability to secure the materials in the event of attack by the forces in the area. And while we are equally aware of the 'trip-wire' aspect of even a small American force being in place . . . These are, after all, fedayeen and all the response in the world will not save the situation if they capture the materials."

The President looked around the Situation Room and rolled his eyes. The God-damned Japanese were telling him that a company of Rangers wasn't enough! God *damn* them!

He had one of two choices, tell them to fuck off or play their game. But the point was . . . *Was* a company of Rangers enough? Colonel Pierson's talk about war theory was all well and good but the operative word was "*theory.*"

"I apologize for this, Prime Minister, but could you hold for just a moment?" the President said.

"Of course," the prime minister said, politely.

The President of the United States put the prime minister of Japan, who was up in the middle of the damned night, on hold, and looked around the room.

"How fast can we get some B-52s on station?" the President asked. "In Georgia. The Japanese don't think that a company of Rangers can ensure the security of the Keldara."

"What do the Japanese care about . . ." the Chairman of the Joint Chiefs started to say.

"Not now," the secretary of defense snapped. "You're not in that compartment. They do. Leave it at that. How long?"

"We don't have any in Germany right now . . ." the Chairman replied. "England. Whooo . . . Nine hours? If we scramble them *right* now. If they can get off fast; they're not on pad alert . . ."

"B-1s," the secretary of state said. "Qatar. Tankers out of Iraq and Turkey, afterburner as far as they can on fuel. This morning's report had three mission-capable."

"Yes, ma'am," the Chairman said, shaking his head. So how in the hell did she keep up with all the changes she was making in her own department *and* read, apparently, his entire morning readiness report? "That's the answer, Mr. President. Four hours or so after they lift off."

"Start loading them with JDAMs," the President said. "Or whatever they should carry to support the Rangers in the event the Chechens enter the area." He picked up the phone and hit the release key. "Mr. Prime Minister, I apologize for keeping you on hold so long. We are dispatching aircraft at this time. They can be in the area before the Chechens can approach the facility. I will also call the president of Georgia and reensure that he is aware that I consider the valley of the Keldara to be a place worthy of defense. It might be useful if your government . . ."

"Said similar things?" the prime minister finished for him. "We will consider that with serious intent. Thank you for relieving me of this burden, Mr. President. Perhaps I can return to pleasant dreams. My best to your lovely wife. I hope she was not too discommoded by the images on the television."

"She was snatched out of the room just in time," the President said. "And I wish you pleasant dreams, Prime Minister."

"I've sent the orders to prepare the B-1s, Mr. President," the CJCS said. "I'll know in about thirty minutes how long it will take for them to get to the mission area."

"We've got calls from the Brits, the Germans, the French, the Russians . . ." the secretary of state said, ticking them off on her manicured fingers.

"If it's a prime minister I'll talk to them if I have to," the President said. "Otherwise, field it lower. But that's the party line. The area is secure, there are Rangers guarding it, we've got bombers on the way in case that's not enough and maybe they should suggest to the Georgians that they do some of their own damned jobs. It wouldn't kill them to push a battalion up into that pass!"

"I agree, Mr. President," the secretary of state replied, looking over at her aide who was scribbling notes. "Get that to the people authorized to discuss this issue."

"That's not many people outside this room," the SecDef pointed out. "Us, Pierson, who else?"

"Not me," the Chairman said, chuckling. He'd been watching the TV with half an eye during the discussion and now tried not to swear. "What the fu . . . Sorry, sir." The news had tuned back to "Special Bulletin: Battle for Chechnya" but this was a room preparing for a news conference.

"I've heard the word before," the President said, turning the sound up.

". . . the minister of defense for the country of Georgia," the announcer was saying, "on the subject of the battle going on in Guerrmo Pass where an elite group of Georgian mountain infantry have been trapped and are about to be overrun by Chechen freedom-fighters . . ."

"Why doesn't the guy just get a job with Al Jazeera?" the secretary of defense said.

"Doesn't want to get hit by a .50 cal?" the Chairman asked, rhetorically.

"Thank you *so* much for bringing that up, General," the President said, turning slightly green.

"Sorry, sir."

"Minister for Defense Vakhtang Gelovani," the Georgian spokesperson said, backing away from the podium.

Gelovani was a short, broad man who fit his suit like a stuffed sausage. He was also sweating under all the camera lights and whoever had done his makeup had given him raccoon eyes and lip gloss that was too bright.

"I wish to read a brief statement," Gelovani said in thickly accented English. "Then I will take questions.

"The current battle is taking place on territory which is internationally recognized as belonging to the country of Georgia. The Chechen terrorists who use this area are criminals who are to be dealt with as criminals should. The local militia currently operating in the area were on a mission without the support of the Georgian government when they were detected. At this time, the Georgian government has no plans to come to their aid. That concludes my statement. I will now take questions."

"The bastard is hanging them out to dry!" the Chairman snapped.

"So are we," the President pointed out. "Otherwise those B-1s would have another mission."

"Minister Gelovani, are you saying that this is a rogue operation?" The reporter was a Brit, probably print since he was taking notes on a laptop.

Gelovani leaned down for his aide to whisper in his ear and then straightened.

"No. The militia were authorized to operate in this region but were not specifically ordered to do so. The regular Georgian military was planning on a major offensive in the area this spring, after the passes were clear. By stirring up the nest they may have compromised this offensive."

"Oh my *God*," the Chairman said, shaking his head. "Is he *nuts*? You don't give away stuff like that on TV!"

"He wasn't planning it, anyway," the secretary of state said. "We'd know if he was. I think he just made it up on the fly."

"Minister, the group currently fighting, these are the militia called the Keldara, yes?" The reporter was probably Russian from the accent and obviously had been doing his homework.

"That is correct," Gelovani answered, starting to point to another reporter.

"Minister!" the Russian shouted. "On redirect. The Keldara, they are called the Tigers of the Mountains, yes? Is it true that they have an American commander? Is this an American operation?"

"NO!" Gelovani shouted, slamming his fist into the podium. "The commander of the Keldara is an American, yes. That is legal under an old law that is currently under review and will probably be changed. But this is *not* an American operation! We are *not* backside kissers of the Americans!"

"Hey, Minister!" one of the reporters shouted and caught his attention. "These Keldara people, are they the guys who make the *beer*?" The reporter had a pad of paper in his hand and a look that was somehow "former military." Since that was really unusual for the mainstream media, he was probably an independent, a stringer, blogger or both.

"Oh my God," the secretary of defense said, shaking his head as the defense minister bent over for another conversation with his aide. "This is getting into Twilight Zone. When is this guy going to just shut up and call it a day?"

"Yes," Gelovani answered. "The Keldara do make beer . . ."

"The Mountain Tiger stuff?" the reporter asked the clearly confused minister. "They're distributing it in the States and there was a little AP item on it where they said that part of the proceeds went to supporting the war on terror. Buddy of mine said it's pretty popular around military bases . . . Is that the same stuff?"

The minister bent down again and then came up, clearly trying to make sense of how things had gone so wrong.

"I think so," Gelovani replied. "I wasn't aware they sold their beer. But they are called the Tigers of the Mountains and they make beer. It is probably the same." He carefully picked his questioner this time.

"Minister Gelovani, you say that you are not sending any forces in support?" The reporter was European, probably German. "Then you are going to allow your own force to be overrun?"

"The Keldara are not members of Georgia's National Guard," Gelovani stated, emphatically.

"But they are from Georgia, *ja*?" the reporter pressed. "So you are going to let the Chechens kill a hundred of your people. Why?"

"They are not *my* people!" Gelovani shouted, pounding the podium. "They are Keldara! They live in Georgia but they are *not* Georgians! They have no business being in this country!"

"So are they immigrants? Are they Turks?" the reporter asked as other reporters jumped to their feet and started yelling their own questions. There was nothing a roomful of reporters love more than a senior minister who is clearly bleeding and just begging to be finished off. All of them had questions that were perfect to do that.

"Who *are* the Keldara?"

"Who is this American that is leading them? Do you feel it takes an American to fight the Chechens?"

"Do you think they are going to win? Is that why you're not sending forces, because they can win where 'Georgian' troops cannot?"

"Minister Gelovani, is it true to say that you're prejudiced against the Keldara?!"

"Minister, are you afraid to commit your troops to a battle with the Chechens?!"

"Do you think that you can ever recapture the Pankisi Gorge?!"

"Minister, is this a political move against General Umarov, the chief of staff? You're reported to be considering a run for the presidency; are the Keldara part of your opposition?! Are you trying to deliberately kill them off?"

"Would you say that the Keldara are trying to do your job for you?"

"NO FURTHER QUESTIONS!" Gelovani screamed, storming off the dais. There was not a side exit to the room so the cameras followed him in full retreat, at one point having to push a female reporter out of his way. The girl, who had been shouting questions while not actually looking at him, went over backwards with a scream of fear and landed on the lap of one of the male Russian TV reporters.

"Minuet," the President said, tears streaming down his face from laughing. He paused to catch his breath. "Minuet. Call the president of Georgia and ask him if he'd like any help from the American military. Of course, if he feels that that is backside-kissing."

"Yes, sir," the secretary of state said, but she wasn't laughing. "But there was one important question asked in all of that."

"What?" the president asked, wiping at his eyes.

"Who *are* the Keldara?"

Nielson had his head in his hands when Lydia touched his shoulder. He was trying to figure out if Mike had seen the casualty reports. Anger could be worse than fear in a commander. Given Lasko's sniper shot, it had to have been Lasko, he probably had.

"General Umarov."

Nielson picked up the phone without lifting his head and hit the flashing button.

"Colonel Nielson."

"The Zhoda Battalion is drawing weapons and ammunition at this time," Umarov said. "Some of them are coming by truck to the valley. Others are going to be carried to the pass by helicopter. But it will take a while to get them organized and ready. They will not be to the pass before nightfall. Sorry."

"Not a problem," Nielson said, still holding his head in one hand. "They won't get there in time to do anything but pick up bodies, but I appreciate the gesture."

"I'm sorry it took this," Umarov replied. "I almost feel sorry for the defense minister. Almost. But there was a reason that he was so off balance. Would you mind telling me why the President has been fielding calls from Japan, China, Russia, India, Italy, France, Germany and Great Britain, not to mention a call from your own secretary of state, about their interest in ensuring the Chechens do not capture the valley of the Keldara? They've all been quite polite about their calls but equally . . . intense."

"I dunno. They like our beer?"

Nielson heard the phone hit the desk and Umarov frankly snickering in the background. After a few moments the chief of staff apparently got himself under control.

"Thank you," Umarov said. "I needed that. Now would you like to answer the question?"

"Yeah. But I'm not going to. If you want to know the answer, ask the Germans, Russians, French, Indians, Japanese, Italians, Brits and Americans. If you can find anyone in any of the governments who can answer the question. Don't bother asking the people who expressed polite interest. They're just going to be obeying confusing orders. You might want to ask the prime minister, president or what have you, personally. They're about the only people that will know the answer for sure."

"Oh."

"Yes, sir. Oh. I'll put it this way, and don't take this as a threat. But if this valley looks to fall to *any* group or government, including yours, you're liable to find every major country on earth invading Georgia in force. Nobody will know why, it will probably be a scrambling clusterfuck, pardon my language, and liable to trigger

World War Three. But I thought you should know. Between friends."

"Does this have anything to do with your current mission?" Umarov asked.

"No comment," Nielson said. "Which actually means 'no comment.' Don't draw anything from it."

"Okay," Umarov said, sourly. "Anything we can supply right away?"

"Not unless you have a bomber in your pocket."

"We're quite low on aircraft. And given the conditions I don't see any of mine being of use to you at the moment. You really don't want the former defense minister's hand-picked fighter pilots dropping bombs anywhere *near* your people. Did my gifts help?"

"Very much," Nielson said. "Thank you. And might I suggest that you stop by for dinner some time. We can talk about . . . international relations."

"I'll do that," Umarov said. "You have a battle to run and I have people to scream at. And *many* to fire." The last was said with satisfaction.

"I guess this was a pretty good outcome," Nielson said, hanging up the phone. "But I'd rather have one damned girl alive. I'd rather have *all* of them out of that valley of death."

Chapter Forty-Five

The mortar missed Adams' position by barely a meter, dropping in the trench instead of directly on them.

That wasn't much of a mercy. The blast area of the 120mm mortar was nearly twenty five meters. At a meter, the concussion could kill you.

The walls attenuated the concussion, though, the angles funneling it to the rear of the position and away from the two fighters. They also caught most of the shrapnel. Most.

Oleg's left leg caught the rest.

The team leader let out a shriek of agony that morphed into a bellow of pure rage.

Adams was knocked nearly unconscious by the blast. His position was more in the line the concussion had taken and it threw him against the earth and rock wall, the combination of overpressure and impact slamming the air out of his lungs and causing his head to ring.

He shook the fog off like a horse flicking a fly and looked at Oleg. The first thing he saw was that the Keldara was either screaming or shouting. It took him a moment to track down to the leg.

It was a mess. Meat had been stripped away from the bone and Oleg's foot was lying across the trench.

Adams slid forward and pulled out a fast-tourniquet, slipping it around Oleg's thigh, low down by the knee. If they were lucky they might keep the upper thigh. There was no way that the best reconstructive surgeon in the world was going to keep the leg.

Oleg had his hand clamped around the thigh and Adams had to push it to the side. He slipped on the fast-tourniquet and pulled it tight then used the latch to cinch it down. The red arterial blood stopped squirting out at least.

"I gotta get you back to the bunker, buddy!" Adams shouted, sliding his arm under the big Keldara's armpit.

Oleg was shouting something at him but Adams couldn't catch it. He realized he was deaf as a post. It should pass; it had happened before. But right now he couldn't figure out what Oleg was shouting. The Keldara pushed him off and reached down to his belt, pulling out that tomahawk all the Keldara carried. He pointed it at the leg and made a chopping motion.

"No *fucking* way!" Adams shouted, shaking his head. He reached into his own harness and pulled out a morphine ampoule. The guy was clearly crazy with pain.

Oleg slapped it out of the master chief's hand and reached forward, grabbing him behind the head and dragging him down to look directly in the eye.

"I NEED TO LEAD!" Oleg screamed. "TO FIGHT! TOO MUCH PAIN! *ONE* LEG!"

Oleg took the axe and shoved it into Adams' hand, then pointed at the leg.

Adams understood. Oleg only needed one leg to stand in the position and fight the Chechens. He didn't need any to command his troops. But he couldn't do that with the pain of the ripped-up leg. Or on morphine.

There was just one problem. Adams looked at the axe for a second and then held up one finger, getting up in a crouch.

He went down the trench, hunched over, to the position where Dmitri Makanee was located. He gestured at the assistant team leader with one finger and the two went back to the position.

When he got there, Dmitri took in the scene in an instant then looked at the axe in the master chief's hand.

"I don't know how to use one of these fucking things," Adams admitted. He could probably have cut the leg off, but he knew one of the Keldara could do it better.

Dmitri took the axe and knelt by Oleg then stretched his mouth wide. Oleg opened his and Dmitri shoved the hilt of the axe in for him to bite. Then he drew his own axe and in one swift motion cut down.

The blow cut through the shattered bones of the leg just below the knee and through half of the meat. It only elicited a coarse bellow from Oleg. A second strike to cut through the remaining tissue didn't even get that.

Oleg, pale and sweating, pulled the axe out of his mouth and buried it in the dirt. Dmitri leaned forward and held up his own bloody axe, looking Oleg in the eye.

The team leader wrapped his hand around Dmitri's, the blood running down over both, then leaned forward and licked the axe head. Licked off his own blood and bone.

"Aer Keldar," Dmitri shouted.

"Aer Keldar," Oleg replied, pulling him forward to slam helmets together.

"*Aer* Keldar!"

"Aer *Keldar*!"

"AER KELDAR!" they screamed in unison, pounding their helmets in time with the chant.

"Fuck," Adams said, sliding down the side of the hole. "And I thought *Hell Week* was fucked up. What do they *feed* these guys? Oh, yeah. Beer."

"Pavel."

"Go, Kildar."

Pavel had a bird's-eye view of the entire battle. Unfortunately, it meant he was *out* of the battle. Mostly.

The Chechens were trying to get sniper teams up on the ridgeline to the north. They weren't having much luck, though, because Pavel was letting them get mostly set up and then taking them down. So far it was like hunting mountain goats; they never looked up. They seemed to think that the counter-sniper fire was coming from the defenses below. They would get towards the top of the ridge at a walk then drop to their bellies and crawl forward. The snipers on the mountain would let them get into position overlooking the main Keldara position then fire them up. They never knew what hit them.

It wasn't exactly sporting, but good tactics never were.

And there were compensations. The view from their position was outstanding.

"We're getting our ass mortared off down here and hunkered down. So we're kind of blind. What are the Chechens doing?"

"Trying to get snipers on the ridge and failing," Pavel said. "And it looks as if they are moving into pre-attack positions."

"Tell me when they start heading up the hill," Mike said. "And thanks for keeping the snipers off our backs. I don't suppose you can see the mortars."

"No, Kildar," Pavel said. "I can climb *higher*."

"Nah. You're good. Kildar, out."

Damn. The mountain above him had one face that had to be at least three hundred meters and looked to be somewhere between a four and a five with some nice overhangs. He really wanted to climb it.

War sucked.

"It sucks," Sivula said, "but this is as far as we can go."

There was no question of recovering any injured Chechens from the bunkers. What was left was mostly pieces and they had scattered a flock of ravens when they approached.

"It's all right," Jessia said, smiling and walking to one side. She set her box of ammunition on the ground and gestured to the other women to start piling in the same spot. "This is as far as *I* go as well."

"Huh?" Sivula said, calculating distances. He'd seen the map. They were still at the back side of the pass. There was no way they could range all the way to the entrapped Keldara.

"This is as far as *I* go," Jessia said. "But others will go further."

"Well," the sergeant said, sighing. "I hope I'm still around when you get back. I'd . . . well, this has been. Interesting."

"What you're trying to say is that you hope you see me again," Jessia said, smiling. "I hope I see you again as well, Andrew. But now you must go and I must lay in the guns."

"This situation *so* sucks," Sivula replied. "Look . . ."

"I left an e-mail address where you can reach me on your bunk," Jessia said. "Which, by the way, was very messy. I hope you guys clean the barracks up before you leave; we worked hard on them before you got here. Now . . . go. We can talk later. Talk much."

"We will sweep the infidels from our lands, yes, Mahmud?"

The older fighter just grunted. From his perspective there wasn't much to talk about.

Mahmud Al Hawwari had been a young factory worker in Grozny when the Berlin Wall fell. He had never cared much about the Berlin Wall, or international politics. All he cared about was getting paid enough to afford some vodka and a little partying on the weekends.

But as the Soviet Union collapsed the economy collapsed with it. The factory closed. All the businesses in Grozny closed. Where before there had been long lines for anything of any worth, now there was no money for even less goods.

He had found solace in one of the new mosques that opened in the wake of communism. At first he just went because the mosque served food, if not vodka, and gave him a place to sleep out of the cold. So there was a little preaching to be put up with, it was worth it.

But the longer he stayed in the mosque the more he came to realize how empty his life had been and how little he understood the world. He had always known that his family was Islamic, even if they had "Russified" their name. Some of the grandparents talked of the Prophet and the word of Allah. But until he came to the mosque for the free handout the Prophet had decreed, he had never understood the importance of Allah in his life.

And the mosque taught him more than just the importance of charity. Chechnya was a part of the Dar Al-Islam, Islamic lands that had been occupied for too long by the Russians. Whether godless communists or Orthodox Christian, both were sins in the eyes of Allah. Those lands that had once been under proper Muslim rule *must* be returned to submission to Allah. And there was a way. The path of jihad.

The battle for Grozny, though, had erased that long-ago furor. It was a miniature version of Stalingrad fought with not much more high-tech weapons. The Russians poured masses of half-trained conscripts into the machine and got out sausage. The Chechens fought a hit-and-run campaign that the Russians never quite got a handle on. It was a cauldron of blood and fire that seemed to go on and on.

But over time, quantity has a quality all its own. The Russians suffered ten times the casualties of the resistance but in the end the resistance was forced out.

Somewhere in that cauldron Mikhail Mihailovich Talisheva, aka Mahmud Al Hawwari, a onetime factory worker and current "freedom fighter," lost his faith in Allah, in the Dar Al-Islam, in Shariah and jihad and all the rest. He knew that there was no road back to the man he might have been. There was no road to vodka and chess on the weekends. Some of the factories were reopened but he couldn't go back to shoving parts on a line. Not after the things he'd seen, and done. Not with the price he had on his head. And the resistance did not take kindly to deserters. The umah did not take kindly to those who recanted their faith. The punishment for apostasy decreed by the Prophet, the Beneficent guy, was stoning to death.

The only road forward was the one he was on. And that road, currently, led up a hillside covered with the dead of a previous attack. The road led into a storm of mortar fire and an enemy that was whispered of by the men who were from these hills.

It led to another cauldron. One that, if Sho'ad walked out of it, might teach the young fedayeen a thing or two.

So Mahmud just grunted as the lines of fighters sprayed out on the hillside and shook into lines.

He pulled out a bottle of water and drained it, wishing as he always did that it was vodka, even the cheapest vodka. Then he opened his fly and took a piss. There weren't any trees around and he didn't really care. He'd lost that, too, the caring. He'd left it behind in Grozny.

"Piss," he said to Sho'ad.

"What?" the younger man said, surprised. A few of the other old fighters were pissing as well. It didn't seem very . . . right.

"Piss," Mahmud said, again. "Did you take a crap recently?"

"No," Sho'ad said, reluctantly drawing out his pecker. Showing it in public like this felt, no *was*, sinful.

"Then don't cry to me when you crap your pants," Mahmud said. "Crap before battle. Drink and piss *just* before battle. It's the only thing I can teach you. If we're both alive tomorrow, you might be ready to start to learn shit like reloading and aiming."

The company leader whistled and the group started moving forward in teams. Up ahead there were two units that Mahmud had never fought with. One of them was Bukara's old unit. He'd met Bukara one time and thought he was a blowhard. He was like one of the old commissars who'd come down on the factory floor and tell you how to do your job when he'd never been on the line.

There was a three-hundred-meter gap between them and the Sadim Brigade. Let those fuckers soak up the ammunition and hope of the defenders. Then the Sadim Brigade would descend on them like the afreets.

He began whistling a tune, a sad one that was best rendered by the balalaika. The Chechen fedayeen didn't like the balalaika since it was a Russian instrument. But Mikhail's mother had lulled him to sleep to the tune and he had listened to it often over the years in bars when he was young and happy in his vodka and chess. It was a common tune with many lyrics attached to it. But the refrain was usually the same.

"Tum bala, tum bala, tum balalaika," he half sang, half chanted in Russian. "Tum balalaika, play balalaika, laugh and be gay."

The words were drowned, though, by the thunder of the mortar barrage and the sound of the first wave of the assault opening fire.

"Tom and Hank are up and on station," the supervisor called. "You have the first position, designated Tango One."

"When?" the pilot asked. He'd been circling the damned thing for nearly half an hour. Ten minutes my ass.

"Coordinated fire," the supervisor said. "Tom and Hank are up."

"I'm up."

"Then five, four, three . . ."

"Adams, how's it going?" Mike asked.

"Pretty fucked up, good buddy."

Adams was screaming. He must have lost his hearing. Again. Since Mike's ears were ringing from all the concussions, he was pretty loud, too. Before long both of them were going to be deaf as posts.

"Had to cut off Oleg's leg," Adams continued. "Actually, Dmitri cut it off. We're cool otherwise. You?"

"What?" Mike screamed. "Is he okay?"

"Fine. Just fucking *peachy*. I gave him the last of my beer, so he's happy as a clam, cleaning his M60 and for some reason belting together one fuckload of 7.62. Was this a social call? Because I'm getting my fucking *ass* mortared off at the moment!"

"Well, be of good cheer. The Chechens are coming up the hill. As soon as they get here, the mortars will stop."

"Keep going!" Sayeed shouted. He had been chosen to lead the remnants of Bukara's force by default. Now he wished he'd kept as far away from the idiot as possible. He'd come to realize early on in his tenure as driver and bodyguard that Bukara wasn't nearly as smart or tactically sound as he'd thought. Now he was in the middle of an Allah-damned nightmare. And the men with him weren't interested at *all* in running into a hail of mortar fire. Or at the Keldara. Being a martyr was all very well to shout about in the mosque but when the bullets were flying and the artillery was hammering down, when the force before you was meat for the ravens, doubts had a way of creeping in. "We must close with them just before the mortars stop! Keep *going*!"

They were still two hundred yards away and the group was faltering. Fine.

He stepped to the rear and fired over their heads. A long burst that emptied his magazine.

"Go towards the Keldara or be cut down from behind you pig-eating cowards!" Sayeed shouted, reloading. "If I don't kill you, Sadim's Brigade *will*. Now *move*. And *fire* as Allah wills! To victory in the name of Allah! God is Great! Alahu Akbar! Yell it, you pig-eating cowards! Alahu Akbar!"

They were moving again. And yelling. Whether from fear of him or Sadim's brigade of killers or for belief in Allah he didn't care. Whatever it took. Whatever it took.

"Kildar," Pavel said. "There is a large explosion to the north. Several."

Mike frowned at the call and shook his head to clear it. The bunker had sustained several direct hits. Dust filled the air and his head was a fog from concussions. He tried to make sense of what Pavel was saying but couldn't.

"The Chechen first wave is closing," Pavel continued. "They are at two hundred meters."

"Okay!" Mike shouted, holding his head. God he wished the fucking mortars would just *stop* for one fucking *second*. "Pavel, go to full team freq. How far?"

"One hundred meters!" Pavel called on the other frequency.

"Teams, open fire at fifty meters," Mike yelled then stopped yelling. The mortars had stopped. That was early. They should have kept firing until the Chechens were right on them. When you were in an assault like this it was best to actually catch a few casualties from your artillery support rather than have it stop early. That way the enemy had to keep their head down until you were right on them. Either the enemy had fucked up, always possible, or . . . He wasn't sure and didn't have time to think about it.

"Seventy-five!"

"Prepare to open fire!"

"Fifty!"

"Mother Lenka, the mortars are laid in!" Jessia said, straightening from the mortar sight.

"Very well," Mother Lenka said. "Now, you must keep firing right up until we reach the lines! That is very important. I would rather we have some of the girls hit than the fire stop too soon. You understand?"

"I do," Jessia said, swallowing hard.

"Kalisa has given you the coordinates so start firing as soon as we move out," Mother Lenka said. "And keep firing until we are there. You have enough rounds."

"Yes, Mother Lenka."

"Good girl," Lenka said, smiling and hefting her AK. "It is many many years since I have held a gun. But I think I still know how to use one. And then there is this," she added, tapping the hatchet at her side. "Good for close quarters, you know. I personally always liked a sharpened shovel, good for burying your friends, too. But these axes are nice."

◆   ◆   ◆

"We should go to help," Kamas Al-Rakabi said to Haza.

The hill Haza had occupied was a relatively small drumlin, a bare sixty feet or so over the surrounding rocky terrain. But it was right in the mouth of the pass, less than five hundred meters from the saddle. From it, Haza had full control of entry and exit. It was where he wanted to be and he wasn't planning on budging.

"We *are* helping," Haza said, losing patience with the young man. He had been an excellent scout but he had no head for tactics. "We forced them to ground and now, by staying here, we prevent them from escaping. I won't say it again."

"You don't understand," Kamas replied. "I want to kill *Keldara*."

"What is so fucking important about the fucking Keldara?" Haza snapped, finally losing it. "Everyone has been whispering about these fucking Keldara! Tigers of the Mountains! Evil pagans! So what? They are just men."

"They are the *Keldara*," Kamas replied. "Did your mother not frighten you with anyone when you were a child? Did she not whisper that if you were not good that something would come for you in the night? They have not been back in generations and we are *glad*. Is there nothing that you, deep in your gut, fear, Haza Khan?"

"Ah," Haza said, nodding. "Now I understand. They are the djinn that come for bad children. Yes, we had the same stories, but about a people called the Gurkhas. But I have fought the Gurkhas. They are good. Very good. Better than your fucking Keldara, I am sure. But they are men. They die."

"The Keldara eat the dead of their enemies," one of the fedayeen in the trench whispered in reply. "They are pagans who perform sacrifices to their black gods. They cut out the hearts of their enemies and eat them. Raw. They say that that way they eat their souls."

"Stupid stories," Haza said with a sigh. "There are many such stories. The people that the stories are about support them and hope the rumors spread. They make you *fear*. They break the will. But they are, always, stupid stories. I have heard the same stories about the Gurkhas but I know from *experience* that they don't eat the hearts of their dead. In one war a whole battalion ran rather than face the Gurkhas, because they'd heard the stupid stories. We will not run from these fucking Keldara and we will not run *to* them. We will wait and keep them in place for the others to destroy. Then we can eat *their* hearts, or say we did, and thus start stories about *us*. Yes?"

"I just want to kill Keldara," Kamas replied, sullenly.

"The radio said that we will attack their valley after we finish off their defenders," Haza assured him. "Then you can kill Keldara. And have their women as prizes as the Prophet decreed."

"That will be . . ." Kamas stopped and looked up and back towards the pass at a whistling in the air. He didn't see what was causing it but he did see something he thought never to see in his whole life. On the west side of the pass, on the ridge above the saddle, was a tiger. A real tiger. It looked like it was not full-grown but it had to be big for him to see it at this distance. He stopped talking, widemouthed.

"INCOMING!" Haza screamed, grabbing the young idiot and dragging him down. Mortars. Fucking mortars. The only people around here with mortars were supposed to be the fedayeen! Where were they coming from?

"I don't have time to teach you bitches fire and maneuver," Mother Lenka said over the booming of the mortars. They hadn't reached the saddle of the pass, yet, but they were close. "So when we get out in the open just spread out and head for the hill!" The first rounds were landing and the slamming of the explosions was racketing down the snow-covered pass. Hopefully they wouldn't cause an avalanche. That would be seriously unfunny.

"But if you see something to shoot, take one knee and *aim*!" she screamed as they approached the saddle. "Do you understand me?"

"YES, MOTHER LENKA!"

"On target," Kalisa whispered over the radio. She had run ahead and was now hunkered down by a boulder, calling fire. "One hundred Islamic Jerry's Kids in open trenchline. Fire for effect."

"All guns!" Jessia screamed. "Fire for effect! High explosive, mixed contact and proximity, continuous!"

Gana Kulcyanov hefted one of the high explosive rounds and slid the end into the tube. She released the round and slid her hands down either side of the tube then turned and took another round as the firing round slammed outwards. The explosion of the round compressed her chest like a giant fist but she ignored it, counting time as she took the next round from Jelena Makanee and twisted through three dimensions to raise it to the tube.

The modern 120mm could fire sixteen rounds in one minute. But they were, potentially, going to be dropping far more than that and she didn't want to wear out the Kildar's barrel. So she was firing "continuous" speed, one round every seven seconds, the speed she had been told by her American Special Forces trainer that "saved tubes and broke armies."

"Six Mississippi, seven Mississippi," she muttered then let the round drop, sliding her hands down the tube and doing it all over again.

She wasn't sure what Mississippi was, but it must be a horrible thing if it was used as a mantra for the guns.

Chapter Forty-Six

"Oh, fuck," Kacey muttered as she approached the pass.

Helicopters and firing mortars do *not* mix. They have to occupy the same airspace and have a horrible tendency to occupy the same three-dimensional point at the same time.

There was room to the side for her to pass, but she assumed they were firing in support of the Keldara trapped on the ridgeline. If so she was going to be following the gun-target line the whole way. That was really gonna suck big donkey dicks.

However, as she crabbed by she could tell they were pointed away from the Keldara position. What in the fuck were they firing at?

The answer became clear as she crossed the pass. The mortars were pounding the shit out of the Chechens blocking the pass. And, what's more, a group of Keldara women were just shaking out in what was clearly an assault line.

"Uh, hey, Father . . . uh . . . Ferrari?" Kacey said, keying the intercom.

"*Da?*"

"Those women, they're attacking the Chechens. Should we help them?"

"*Nyet,*" the oldster replied. There was the loud chainsaw sound of a minigun from the left side of the bird as they passed the

Chechen position. "Mother Lenka . . . Bad fucking news, yes? To the other battle."

Kacey didn't know who "Mother Lenka" was, but if the old fucker in the back considered her "bad news" she really wanted to meet her.

And she had to admit that the conditions up ahead looked worse. The fucking Chechens covered the damned ridge.

Well . . . good.

The Dragon was hungry.

"Eugenius," Father Ferani said over the intercom.

"What do you want?" Father Devlich snarled. He hadn't gotten to fire at the Chechens and it rankled.

"Sion was right," Father Ferani said. "I just saw the tiger he was talking about. Up on the ridge watching over the women. They will succeed."

"And on this side are fucking ravens looking to eat your eyes," Father Devlich replied.

"The Father of All watches."

"Yeah, he's gonna watch you piss your pants when the Chechens start firing at us."

"Fuck you."

"You fuck goats, I fuck women. Who wins?"

"That's just because goats are too fast for you. You only fuck the old women that you need a crowbar to open."

"And you *still* fuck goats. I win."

"Yeah, well I fucked your mother."

"I fucked *your* mother which is how you got born. But the *good* part dribbled down her leg."

"I'm older than you, you jackass. How does that work? You fuck her before you were born? I, on the other hand, really *did* fuck your mother. And she was loose from other men."

"Oh, fuck you. How do you cock this thing?"

"You have to have a cock, first."

"I'm serious."

"Father of All, you never listen, do you? Fifty-seven years I've been watching you pay attention only to your own bellowings and I'm about sick of it . . ."

"Oh . . . go to Hel! And tell me how to *cock* this fucking thing, smartass! We're nearly there!"

Sayeed crouched behind a pile of bodies. They had nearly made it. But only nearly. The mortars had stopped too soon. The men had been too slow. Again, as they got close enough to throw rocks at them, the Keldara had opened up with a withering fire. How so many could be alive after the pounding of the mortars he couldn't imagine.

He lay prone, using the bodies for cover, and looked through the gap between the chest and mostly exploded head of one of the dead fedayeen. He would fire if he saw a good target. Otherwise, he was going to wait for Sadim's Brigade to finish off these Keldara fuckers before he was moving again.

Kiril threw his last two boxes of SAW ammo onto the ammo step and slid in a belt. He had a total of four but he wasn't going to bother belting them up. The next Chechen wave was already less than seven hundred meters away. This one wasn't just charging, either. Oh, they were running, but they were using fire and maneuver, running forward to cover then dropping and firing up the hill to cover the next group.

He ducked as rounds impacted his position then took a long swig from his camelbak. Ammo, Liquids . . . Damn. A—L—I—C—E Hum, hum . . . Casualties . . . It was in English and he still was struggling with that. And he didn't fucking care anymore. The only thing that mattered was ammo. He just wanted to see which ran out first, his ammunition or the fucking Chechens. When the ammo ran out, he was going to climb out of this fucking trench and take them the axe until the *oceans* ran with blood . . .

"Tiger Three."

"Go," Adams said, taking a swig from his camelbak and breaking down his M4 by feel. It had started to get "hinky" on him in the last fight. Not jamming just . . . hinky. Probably the gas tube was getting fouled; he'd put a bunch of rounds through the damned thing.

"The next group, engage with the 60s," Mike said. "But not until I say. And tell Shota to stand by."

"Roger."

"How's Oleg?"

Adams looked over at the Team Leader. He was discussing ammo cross-loading with Dmitri. There was a big red rag over his stump. Every now and then he'd wince then go on talking as if nothing had happened.

"Great."

"Make sure that there's plenty of rounds for the 60s. Belt them together and when the time comes make sure the gunners know to just go to full-scale rock and roll."

"Mike, that's going to burn the fucking barrels and we don't have any spares."

"It won't. Trust me. If we're still fighting after *that* long, we're not going to care."

"Jessia, Mother Lenka is at the gap. Go to white phosphorus now."

"Two gun! White phosphorus, traversing fire! Continuous!"

"Now they fire smoke?" Kamas asked as the white smoke drifted over the trench. Then he screamed as burning white metal fell on his skin and the white smoke started pouring from his shoulder and head.

White phosphorus is a chemical, mostly the metal phosphorus, that, once ignited, is practically impossible to extinguish. It carries its own oxidizer so it needs no oxygen to burn. Water will not quench it nor fire-fighting foam. Flesh, especially, will not put it out.

When it hits flesh, white phosphorus is drawn downward by gravity inexorably. It stops only when it hits bone and even then for mostly mechanical reasons. And it continues to burn. It is a poor killer for it cauterizes the flesh even as it burns it. Deaths from white phosphorus come from mainly mechanical issues, such as when it hits the throat and damages the trachea, or from shock. For white phosphorus is most intensely painful.

Much more common are blinding when it hits eyes, damage to the lungs from inhaling the freshly released smoke, which is extremely hot, and of course horrific scars. And it is frightening. It breaks the will more than it kills.

But for all its military utility, white phosphorus is considered a poor weapon. Steadfast units will take the horrific casualties and continue fighting. It does not, after all, *kill*. Not well.

The military value of white phosphorus lies mostly in its smoke. The burning metal releases clouds of the stuff. It's not inherently harmful; once it is cooled it can be breathed without serious short- *or* long-term damage. And it creates faster smoke than conventional smoke rounds with the added benefit of being, well, horrific.

It was for these dual purposes that most mortar "obscurement" rounds were made of white phosphorus. The ladies of the Keldara had not intended to kill Kamas, they just wanted to blind the unit in a cloud of white.

Of course, burning a fucking Chechen was always a good thing. Blinding one, in truth, was even better. Burning off balls would be happy making.

The Keldara mortar women *loved* white phosphorus.

Haza looked down the zigzag trench as more of the Chechens began screaming in pain. Many were already dead or severely wounded from the terribly accurate mortar fire; most of the fire had been dropping right *in* the trenchline. He could *hear* the fuckers; they were close. But the way that sound echoed in this damned pass, he couldn't place where the fire was coming from. It could be anywhere.

But he knew what the white phosphorus meant.

"Get up!" he screamed, lifting himself to the lip of the trench. "Get up! They are coming!"

He didn't know who was coming, he wasn't sure what direction they were coming *from*. But smoke only meant one thing. The infantry would be right behind.

Mahmud fired at the shape of a helmet behind a pile of bodies then darted forward as the group ahead of him went to ground to provide covering fire.

There wasn't much in the way of cover on this slope. He could see where rocks had been pried out of the ground and even the remnant of sticks that had been range markers. The defenses were well prepared which just made this assault that much more idiotic.

Sho'ad was running beside him, as he'd been instructed, yelling as much as the thin air would permit and firing his AK in long, unaimed bursts. Mahmud considered telling the young idiot to conserve his ammunition then decided he didn't have the air or the care. He'd started the same way, screaming and running at the enemy, firing bullets everywhere but at the enemy. If he lived, the young idiot would learn.

Mahmud sensed rather than saw the rounds and dropped to his face, lying behind a convenient body, as bullets, sharp-sounding, probably 5.56 from the enemy's squad automatic weapons, ripped overhead. He heard the thud of the bullets hitting something and then the thud of a body hitting beside him.

Looking to his right he shrugged. Sho'ad wasn't going to be learning anything.

He reached over and took one of the dead idiot's magazines. He was going to need the ammo and Sho'ad sure as hell didn't.

Kiril fired a burst at one of the Chechens but the guy dropped before he could have hit him. However, his partner was still on his feet, screaming at the Keldara lines and spraying and praying. Kiril fired a burst into his chest and sent him to Allah as he wished.

He tracked right and continued to fire at the charging fedayeen. They were getting close. On the other hand, they were starting to bunch up and the careful fire and maneuver that they'd used on the lower slopes was breaking up as the assault dissolved into a human-wave charge.

That was fine by Kiril. More Islamic fuckers to send to Allah. More souls for his Death Guard. Souls to share with his love . . .

Mahmud could hear the SAW even over the rest of the firing. It was firing in precise bursts. These Keldara might be ghosts to the local kids, but they were also *good.*

However, he could also tell, by the sound, when the machine gun tracked away from him. The note of the firing changed, became more muted, when it wasn't pointed directly at him.

He rolled up to one elbow and pointed towards the sound. He saw the SAW gunner immediately, just the shape of a helmet and an arm behind the weapon. But he was less than fifty yards away. sy shot . . .

❖   ❖   ❖

Kiril couldn't understand how he'd gotten into the bottom of the position. He could see his SAW above him, still hanging onto the edge of the position by its bipod feet. It was hanging down, though, not being fired. It had to be fired. It should be served.

Above him he could see birds. Ravens. Circling above the battlefield. The eyes of the Father in a red sky.

"Gretchen . . . ?"

Mike was firing, now, hunkered down against the right-hand side of the opening to the bunker. They were individual, aimed shots at the Chechens that were *at* the fucking trenchline. Some of them were jumping it, heading for the bunker.

He saw one of the fedayeen jump the trenchline, a young guy, screaming at the top of his lungs and pulling frantically on the trigger of an empty weapon. The image was there but it was filed away in some corner that wasn't in the present reality. The only present was the two rounds he put right into the screaming mouth and the automatic part that told him the tango was serviced, sir, you can move on.

Another part of his brain was waiting for something. He couldn't describe it but it was like art: he would know it when it happened. Battles don't just go to the best or the most numerous. Most battles in history had gone to the side that just held out the longest. The side that just refused to quit. The side that you could wipe out but would refuse to fucking quit. The side that committed its reserve the last. Who dares, wins.

Mike *felt* it, even as his earphone crackled.

"Kildar. They have committed their reserve."

"Adams! 60s!"

Sawn looked up and around. Kiril's SAW had stopped firing. They *needed* that firepower if they were going to hold on.

He stepped back and turned to run down the trench, M4 pointed down in a tactical carry. He could damned well run a SAW if he had to.

❖   ❖   ❖

Mahmud darted forward and jumped into the empty SAW position. They would have to clear the trenchline and from where he was it made most sense to move to his right.

He ignored the weapon—it would be picked up after the battle—and turned right, holding his AK forward and ready to strike. He had fought in trenches before and knew that an enemy could appear at any time. The thing to do was to move forward, fast. Strike with the barrel or the butt. Fire when sight lines made it possible but most of all move forward *fast*. Take the positions still trying to defend from behind.

The direct line on this trench was about four meters to a turn. He hurried that way and, at the turn, almost ran smack into one of the Keldara who was running down the trench. He had probably noticed the SAW was out of action and was going to see why.

Mahmud clutched at his trigger and fired three rounds, point-blank, into the man's chest.

Sawn grunted in surprise as the rounds hit him then struck out, a trained and reflexive reaction, the barrel of his M4 striking the AK upwards and to the right. He followed in with the butt of the weapon, smashing the fedayeen in the chest and knocking him backwards. The M4 was bent by the combined blows so he dropped it as his hand dropped to his belt, ripping out his axe as he darted forward.

The Islamic raised the AK, either in defense or to fire, but Sawn's axe cut down in a lightning strike, sliding along the barrel and taking the man's fingers off his left hand. A second blow laid open his head.

Sawn fell to his knees, suddenly feeling weak. Just combat reaction, he was sure. He had been trained in this, had read the book on it. The sympathetic nervous system, the part that controlled direct action in the human body, went into full overdrive during intense moments of combat. When they passed, the parasympathetic nervous system, the part that was in charge during sleep and ran all the automatic systems, came back with a vengeance. You felt weak and nauseous. Your hands shook. You wanted to sleep.

The briefing had never covered being cold . . . though. And he couldn't understand where the flood of bright red pouring out of the bottom of his body armor had come from . . .

❖   ❖   ❖

Adams slammed the butt of his M4 into the back of one of the fedayeen's head and watched it buckle. The head *and* the butt. Fucking M16-series weapons were *lousy* for close combat!

"Adams! 60s!"

Fuck! They were down to hand-to-hand in the fucking *trenches*. How in the fuck did Mike expect him to get the fucking *machine gun* into action.

Oleg, though, had heard the call. He left his axe in the face of the Chechen he had just killed and picked up the 60 off the ground where it had been hidden. Another Chechen tumbled into the pit but he ignored the fedayeen as he cocked the weapon.

Adams wasn't about to let Oleg outdo him. Stopping only to kick the Chechen so hard his *mother* was gonna bleed, he picked up his own and dropped the bipod into the firing position.

The target view was pure Chechens. So, taking Mike's advice against his better judgment, he pulled back the trigger and started firing continuous.

The M60 series of weapons was first developed in the 1950s as a replacement for the WWI-era .30 caliber machine gun. Air-cooled, the series had suffered throughout its existence with many problems. It tended to jam, it overheated quickly and when over-heated would tend to "cook off," fire continuously despite releasing the trigger as rounds were heated hot enough to "explode" when they touched the smoking breech. The barrels also tended to heat quickly to the point that they would "droop" and cause an explosion that destroyed the gun. Mixing "cookoff" with "droop" was a sure recipe for disaster.

The Army had eventually replaced the venerable M60 with the M240 series manufactured by the Belgian firm of Fabrique Nation-ale. Machine-gunners throughout the Army and various other users had breathed a sigh of relief because while the M240 had its problems, it was head and shoulders above the 60.

The M60E4 was the manufacturer's attempt to regain that vast market it had lost. Besides various improvements to make the gun more reliable, overall, they had paid tremendous attention to bar-rel and breech design, using a series of new materials to improve barrel life, barrel strength and cooling.

Adams knew, from too much experience, the sound, the smell, the *feel* of an M60 that had been overworked. And he knew right when that *feel* should start. He knew he should be firing in short, controlled, bursts. But . . . damn there were just too *many* of the fuckers. The 7.62 rounds were dropping them in windrows, but there were still *more*! He knew he had to let up on the trigger, that the fucking 60 was going to overheat, cook off, jam, fucking blow the fuck up at any moment. But if he stopped firing the fucking Chechens were going to *overrun* them. As it was, his 60, Oleg's and the two with Vil and Sawn had stopped them, butt cold. To even fire in bursts would mean they could move forward, maneuver, something. He had to keep firing, just holding the fucking trigger down. It was the only way to stop the assault!

And the funny thing was . . . the fucker was still rocking! He could feel it. Like driving a car, you can feel when the car is at its maximum, when you'd pushed it too far. He had that same sense with a weapon, especially the 60 which he'd had to fuck with for far too long in the teams. And this fucker, this bad boy, it wasn't having *any* trouble with continuous fucking fire! The screaming Islamics were being ripped to fucking dogmeat by this beautiful fucking weapon and it wasn't even giving a God-damned hiccup!

"YEAH!" he screamed. This motherfucker was ROCKING AND ROLLING! "EAT HOT LEAD THINLY COATED WITH COPPER YOU ISLAMIC MOTHERFUCKERS!"

The Kildar called it "the money shot."

Sniping is, essentially, just a normal form of infantry combat. The sniper fired at the enemy with a rifle. That was the essence of infantry combat. Oh, he might fire farther than normal, he might use more camouflage. But he was, really, just an infantryman with a few more tricks in his bag.

The big difference with the sniper over the regular infantryman was in how he chose his targets. The infantryman tended to concentrate on the men in front of him, similar in interests and actions, the riflemen and machine-gunners that were trying to kill him by direct fire.

Snipers, though, had another duty. Their purpose was to find and eliminate priority targets. Snipers were the reason that infantry platoon leaders had one of the shortest life expectancies of any position in combat. The enemy sniper sought out the leaders to disrupt the management of the battlefield.

With the Chechens this was especially important. Their leadership was very personality-based and extremely hierarchical. Take out the leaders, and the followers tended to not only lose morale but have no fucking clue what they should be doing. The Chechens, also, derived their mimetic combat background from societies that specialized in hit-and-run. If the first rush didn't work, they tended to retreat. Especially if they didn't have anyone behind them driving them on.

Finding the leaders, therefore, was the primary job of the Keldara snipers. And getting the big leaders, the senior commanders, ah, that was the money shot.

Pavel had been scanning the battlefield, keeping an eye on how things were going, for the entire battle. And he knew that the Chechens were at the trenchline, that they'd committed their reserve. He'd called both in. But he also knew that somewhere down there was the man driving them on. The main leader. The man the large brigade had gathered around for a thousand personal reasons but all related to his personality, his ability, his command skills. His charisma.

He finally found it. A cluster of people behind the lines. Radio antennas.

One man was in the center of that. Oh, not the precise center but a sort of psychological center of gravity that was felt more than analyzed. The man that people were looking at. A big man, graying hair, very serene expression.

Pavel hadn't even realized he'd fired until he saw that expression change as the round hit the center of the man's white mustache, which suddenly became crimson as brains splashed onto the ground behind him.

Again, Mike felt it, like a shock rippling through the enemy. It was time.

He keyed his throat mike and strode out of the bunker, ignoring the rounds that cracked around him.

"ARISE KELDARA!" he shouted, firing one-handed at a Chechen that had, somehow, made it through the fire and was about to jump into Adams' position. The Chechen flew back in a spray of blood. "UP YOSIF! UP OLEG! FORWARD VIL! UNTO THE BREACH, TIGERS OF THE MOUNTAINS! FORWARD THE AXE AND THE FLAME! KILL *ALL* OF THESE MOTHER-FUCKERS! LET NOT *ONE* ESCAPE!"

Shota was very unhappy. He had this beautiful rocket launcher and he hadn't been allowed to use it. One Chechen had even gotten to his position, which was just forward of the command bunker and to the right. Shota had picked him up by the leg and beaten him on the side of the position until he stopped squealing. They were all over the place and *still* he hadn't been allowed to shoot.

But when the Kildar called, he scrambled to his feet, grabbing the launcher and jumping out of the hole in the ground.

There were Chechens *everywhere*. He couldn't figure out where to fire.

"Target! Guy in the red shirt!" Yakov shouted, grabbing him by the shoulders and turning him. "Fire!"

Oh, that was *easy*. The guy was barely fifty meters in front of the trenches.

Shota didn't even bother to use the sights.

Adams ducked as a massive explosion went off to the front of his position then picked up the M60, cradling the remaining links in his arm.

"Oleg, see you in a bit," he said, frowning.

"I'll give you cover, yes?" Oleg said, hopping up one-legged onto a firing stoop so that he could see over the palisades of the position. He began firing, sweeping the M60 back and forth, still going continuously. The position was filling up with brass and links. They both must have fired over a thousand rounds *each* and the weapons *still* weren't giving a hiccup. "Take some of my ammo."

"Okay," Adams said, clambering out of the position he had occupied for so many hours. The Chechens were still trying to move forward but they were looking . . . weak. They were hardly firing; apparently most of them had expended their ammo and weren't in any mental condition to reload or scrounge if necessary.

The explosion had shaken them, and another to the left that almost knocked Adams into the trench again was worse.

Eamon Ferani, loaded down with ammo boxes, clambered up beside him and grinned.

"The Kildar wishes us to advance, Master Chief," the boy said. He drew an axe and waved it. "I will cover your sides, yes?"

"Oh, fuck yeah," Adams said, lifting the belt up a bit more and raising the machine gun to his shoulders. He clamped down on the trigger and started striding forward, sweeping the weapon from side to side. It was like shooting a God-damned fire hose. "OH, FUCK YEAH! I GOT ME ONE OF *THESE* YOU ISLAMIC BASTARDS!"

Over his screaming, and the continuous clatter of the gun, he thought he heard wings beating. It sounded like a giant bird, bigger than any bird, ever . . .

"THE DRAGON IS ON YOU, YOU BASTARDS!"

As she swept around to the east, Kacey triggered the speakers. A sound like satanic chanting filled the valley, resounding from mountainside to mountainside. Then she dipped down to come in right at ground level.

There wasn't any need for special flying and there wasn't much chance of missing the target. The Chechens were all over the ridge. Kacey targeted one group towards the rear and just let fly with everything.

57mm rockets dropped into the Chechen command group as thousands of 7.62 rounds scoured the ground. The whole group fell, blown to bits by rockets, churned to red mush by the fire of the Gatlings.

She swept around to point up the hill, flying through the dust and smoke of her barrage, and fired everything again, ripping a ten-meter-wide hole through the middle of the Chechen formation as she swept up the ridge, engine at overload, drums, guitars and voices screaming into the void.

Mike had lost it. At some level he knew that and didn't care.

He leapt the trench, running ahead of the Keldara, M4 tracking right and left and automatically engaging targets of opportunity, round after round cracking straight through a screaming mouth, behind fierce-slitted eyes, rounds cracking past him, ducking and weaving as some part of his mind anticipated shots.

Combat psychologists had determined that there were four broad states to humans in relation to combat, mostly definable by heartbeat and blood pressure. The lowest, white, was a steady state. This was a person unstressed by combat and the hormones and endorphins released by it. Heartbeat was steady and low, blood pressure the same. Above that was yellow, generally found in persons who were aware that combat might occur at any time but were still more or less steady-state. Heartbeat was slightly elevated as was blood pressure. Above that were the ascending orange and red, red being Shakespeare's famous quote regarding summoning up "the actions of a tiger." Heartbeat was generally in the high hundreds, blood pressure well over two hundred and while fine motor control was reduced the fighter was acting at what most warriors considered maximum capability. Time was distorted, hearing was distorted, the world was an unreal state. The tiger was on the back of the deer and rending.

But above red was black. Most combatants, entering the black range, lost effect. At the black range the heart was pumping so fast oxygen to the brain was reduced due to poor pumping action, blood pressure was so high that the fighter was seeing either a red cloud or the true tunnel vision of the brain slowly blacking out.

But some warriors, the most highly trained, could enter into black and function. By definition, they were some of the most deadly persons on earth. In black, the fighter's reactions were superhuman, their automatic training processes working at a level beyond gestalt, their shots so fast that even on single shot they sounded like a machine gun and every one was going to hit a target. A fighter who could ride the wave of the black could, would, never miss.

Mike was in the black. Time was slowed for him to such an extent he could see the bullets flying from the Chechens AKs, seeming to glide through the air towards him. He could see his own and know before they hit that they were on target. He felt as if he was moving in molasses and yet the Chechens, screaming towards him, were moving slower. The ejected cartridges from the M4 were as big as beer barrels, flying past him as slowly as snails would could they but fly.

The empty magazine, dropped, unnoticed and another was seated before the first living Chechen in view could target him and still Mike ran on, brow lowered like the gallèd rock . . .

"Mike!" Adams bellowed, turning the M60, still on continuous fire, to the side so that his *stupid* boss wouldn't run right into his cone of fire. "God *damnit*! Where the fuck do you think you're going?"

"ARISE KELDARA!" Oleg bellowed. "YOUR KILDAR LEADS!" He targeted a group of Chechens to the side of the Kildar who was pushing into a wedge of dead bodies, firing rounds so fast it sounded as if he was on full auto, but one Chechen after another was flying back with single holes, right through the fucking X ring. Oleg cursed the mortar that had taken his leg. He should be at his Kildar's side! "FORWARD THE AXE AND FLAME! ARISE TIGERS!"

Mike had reached the Chechen line but the fighters in front of him were having a hard time even lifting their weapons with dead bodies falling around and on them.

Some detached portion of him watched as the butt of the M4 shattered on a Chechen face, the head of the Chechen slumping sideways as the hard-driven steel crumpled not only his face bones but his skull.

The barrel bent across the side of another's head, wrapping into a half U at the impact, and brains splashed, slow as dropping feathers, out of the shattered skull.

The axe came up. The axe of the Kildar and Mike struck down and across, shattering a skull, up to slash through a neck, down to take off an arm.

The air was filled with a mist of blood, the sacrifices falling slowly, so slowly.

Vil was up and on the Chechens, screaming as he dropped to a knee and fired. Two Chechens, older ones, were maneuvering in to fire on the Kildar and he dropped both with two aimed bursts. But the Kildar wasn't slowing down, and moving forward by fire and maneuver *obviously* wasn't going to let him catch up.

"Damn him!" Vil shouted. "What's the point of training us if *he's* going to forget it?"

Lasko was so in his element he thought he might just have to kill himself. Never could he have another day like this.

He was a very good shot. Good enough that with his scope dialed to more or less the windage and distance, he had no problem instinctually adjusting.

He was covering the master chief's back, sweeping the field and spotting Chechen fighters that were targeting the machine-gunner and terminating them. He wasn't stressed, was in fact in "white," his heartbeat slow and regular. He was coldly finding and terminating his definition of priority targets.

But the pile of brass gathering around him told the whole story. Lasko truly was "one shot, one kill." Count the brass, take maybe three percent off, and that *was* his count. There was a *huge* pile of brass building up. He was going to beat *Hathcock's* record, probably sometime in the next fifteen minutes. And that was the killer app in the sniper world.

The last round of the mag blew a head open, he dropped that one, took a full one from Pyotar, loaded and went back to sniping.

There was, in Lasko's world, *nothing* better than a field full of Chechens and a full magazine.

Adams still had his finger clamped on the trigger, holding the M60 at his hip and sweeping it slowly back and forth like a fireman hosing down a fire.

Eamon was yanking belts out of the boxes and linking them together as fast as he could, while simultaneously holding them off the ground and keeping up with the master chief.

But as fast as Adams advanced he couldn't catch the Kildar.

"Gods Damnit," Adams shouted. "*Ghost*! Slow the fuck down!"

Somewhere there was an ending to the Chechens. If Mike had a thought in his head it was that he was going to carve his way to that ending and then turn around and carve his way back.

"Oh, fuck," Pavel said, lifting his head away from the scope. He'd been covering the Kildar's back, since he'd apparently forgotten the idea, and only glanced up for a moment to get a general look. What he saw was not the best vision he'd ever seen.

"Vanner! Vanner!"

Patrick Vanner was having one *hell* of a time. He was a Marine brat, both his mother and father were former Marines, the latter a retired infantry gunnery sergeant.

But despite all his years in the Marines, and his service with the Kildar, he'd never gotten a chance to fire a shot in anger. He'd never known if he had that special quality that let men excel when the bullets were flying around them.

No question now. He had moved forward, following the Keldara and targeting "leakers," guys who for one reason or another got through the Keldara line. Most of them were slipping around the side, which could be bad if they got in behind the Keldara. But they *weren't* because Patrick Adam Vanner was by God terminating their mujahideen asses!

A Chechen dropped, three rounds in the sweet spot in the upper chest, when his headphone buzzed.

"Vanner! Vanner! This is Pavel. The Kildar is about to be shot by his own helicopter!"

Kacey wasn't quite in black but she *was* seeing red. Lots of red. A good bit of it was on her windshield.

She'd dropped down to where the belly of the Hind was very nearly scraping the ground and flown, hey-diddle-diddle, straight up the middle of the Chechen formation, guns blazing.

The result was flying Chechen body parts and some of them had flown high enough to impact the windscreen. So Kacey was *definitely* seeing red.

She could see the formation breaking up ahead, though, and there were good guys up there. So she let up on her trigger and started to bank up and away.

The last few rounds from the helo cracked into the back of Chechens and she could, for some reason, watch as the last tracer lazed its way into a gap in the formation.

A gap filled by a blood-soaked Keldara, holding a hatchet in his hand and charging forward in a berserker rage.

She flew up and away on automatic, watching as the tracer tracked in to strike the axehead, through it and into the center of the screaming fighter's chest.

"Dragon! Dragon! Pull up! You're about to . . ."

"Blue on blue," Kacey muttered, banking towards a cluster of Chechens that seemed to be trying to re-form. "Fuck me."

". . . kill the Kildar!"

"Oh, double *dog* fuck me!"

"It was only *one* goat! I was thirteen! I was drunk! It was a bet!" Father Ferani triggered a burst from the minigun. The helo was banking to the side over a shattered group on a hilltop. There were a few alive, though, and that couldn't be borne.

"You're still a goat fucker," Father Devlich screamed over the guitars. The helo flattened out, nearly at ground level, and began continuous fire to the front. But to the sides there were Chechens, many of them looking towards him, openmouthed in surprise at the sudden attack from the rear. He just aimed the gun and held down the trigger, watching rows of the fedayeen tumble away from the laserlike fire. "What is that *damned music*?"

"Yeah, well I really *did* fuck your mother!" Father Ferani shouted. The group in front of him was looking at him stunned but he didn't care. Fucking Islamic goat . . . Send them all to the All Father. "And she screamed louder than that fucking singer!"

"At least I've never fucked a goat!" Devlich shouted back, finding another cluster to scythe down. "You know, I've always wanted to ask . . ." He fired again, cutting down a fedayeen who was screaming down the hill, dropping his weapon and stripping off his ammo vest. "And it's not like she can understand us. So, just between a couple of elders . . . What was it like?"

"You know," Ferani shouted, sweeping the gun across a cluster of fedayeen trying to escape over the side of the gully, "I don't honestly remember."

"You think you'd remember something like fucking a goat," Father Devlich said as the bird banked up and over. This time *he* was the one still looking at the battlefield and he found another group, this one trying to take cover and keep fighting. They weren't going to fight any more. Not churned to red butter.

"It was a *long* time ago," Father Ferani said. He was looking at the sky, gripping the spades of the gun and hanging nearly straight down. The sun was already behind the mountains and the slight clouds that had come in in the afternoon caught the light in waterfalls of pink. "And I hadn't had sex before."

"You popped your cherry on a *goat*?" They were banking away from the battlefield, now. He hoped this stupid bitch wasn't going home already. He had plenty of bullets left.

"I remember its ass was hairy," Father Ferani said, musingly. "I remember thinking its ass was very hairy."

"Its ASS WAS HAIRY?" Father Devlich screamed, laughing so hard he had to stop firing. "Its *ass* was *hairy*." He triggered the gun and waggled it back and forth, not really firing at anything; there wasn't anything worth firing at in sight. It was just that he wanted to giggle till he got that bad pain in his chest. Oh, no, there was a group to fire at. Hey, more red fucking Chechens on the ground. "Its ass was hairy."

"What can I say," Father Ferani replied. "Then I *really* popped my cherry on your mother."

"You keep *saying* that," Father Devlich said, shaking his head. Good, they were headed back towards the fight. Not that there was much fight left in the Chechens.

"It was spring festival, the same year," Father Ferani said, lost in memory. Not so lost that he didn't fire at a group of the fedayeen that had clustered on the back side of a hill, away from the former battlefield. They scattered, leaving three bodies on the ground. "I think she felt sorry for me that everyone was teasing me about fucking a goat."

"You are *so* lying," Father Devlich said. He didn't even have anything to fire at. *Fuck.*

"Nope," Father Ferani said. "Sorry, Eugenius. I really did bed Martya. It was in a bed of tiger-berry bushes on a night with a crescent moon. And, Eugenius, do the sums." A large group was forming up in the ravine to the side of the ridge and he fired at them, working the Gatling gun across the group. Tracers came drifting up through the air towards the Hind, the first fire they'd taken. "You're . . ." He grunted and stopped firing.

"You *have* to be lying," Father Devlich said, furiously. Now there were some running Chechens in view. He fired, missed, fired again. "I am *not* . . ." Something made him look behind him.

Father Ferani was hanging from the harness the black mechanic had had them wear. Blood was pouring out of his mouth and back. There were three large, red, holes in his back and Father Devlich could see right into the mess inside his body.

Father Devlich turned back to look out the window of the helicopter. A group of screaming fedayeen was running towards the north and he clamped down on the trigger of the gun, tumbling them to the ground. He continued to fire into the bodies, churning them to red mush, until they were out of sight.

"Oh double dog fuck me," Adams said, running forward. Mike was on his back with about a million screaming Chechens still around him. Adams just fired up the whole area as a round from Shota dropped off to his right, blowing pieces of fedayeen all over the battlefield.

But the fedayeen didn't seem to care about the fallen Keldara. Mike's berserker charge had shaken them, the continuously firing M60s had them wavering, the rounds from Shota were terrifying them and the tunnel of dead, not to mention the windrows to either side from the door guns, broke them.

They were turning and running back down the hill. And the Keldara, their Kildar apparently dead on the field, weren't about to let *one* of them survive. They gave a cry like a hundred hungry tigers and charged forward, guns firing into unprotected backs, axes sweeping down on necks and over it all the hammer of the drums . . .

Mike shook his head and rolled on his side, groaning. There was no moment of "where am I?" He knew exactly where he was, still on that damned hill. The last few moments were pretty much a blur, but he knew right where he was, even if he couldn't remember how he got there. And there was still firing going on around him; the battle wasn't over.

No, he thought to himself, *it's pretty much done.*

He could see where Shota's rounds had landed, the sprawled circles of dead Chechens. He could see the windrows where the machine-gun teams had pushed forward, laying down that incredible barrage the new 60s were capable of. But the part that really got him was the fucking *hole* churned right up the middle, stopping . . . well, more or less where he was standing. He could remember that, the sight of those rounds marching towards him. He hadn't realized that Nielson had scrounged *that* much fire-power for the Hind. And where in the fuck had those speakers come from? The valley was still ringing with the song even as the Keldara pressed forward, harrying the Chechens from defeat into rout.

The Hind was helping in that, sweeping back and forth, breaking up any pockets of resistance and now segueing into another song, something about dragons. The combination of the firepower at the trenches, the Hind and Shota had not just broken the Chechens, it had slaughtered them. If there weren't three thousand dead on this battlefield, he'd be very surprised.

The other Hind was coming in for dust-off as the sky turned pink washed with violet. They held this battlefield, but Mike was well aware that there was one more battle to be done on this day.

He tried to push himself up and realized his right hand *really* hurt. Really *really* hurt. Holding it up he saw that the skin of the palm had been stripped off and it looked as if a couple of the fingers and the thumb were dislocated. So much for using *that* hand for a while. Hell, he hurt all over; pains started to pop up across his whole body. Then the chest decided to report. Pain. Big pain. Chest. That was bad.

He looked down at the *hole* in his body armor. It was smoking. Using his left hand, he undid his battle harness and armor, then reached under it and pulled out the still smoldering tracer, wincing a little at the heat. Hmph. 7.62x51. Same kind the Hind had in its Gatling guns. It was horribly distorted from something.

Looking around he spotted his axe. The head, anyway, which was bent in half and had a *hole* in it.

"Adams, call in the dogs," Mike said, keying his throat mike while still lying on his side. He stopped to get some wind. His chest *really* hurt. He was pretty sure the sternum was cracked. And he could tell he was bleeding from a couple of spots. But he'd bled before and nothing seemed critical except his hand. He'd live. "Vanner, get ahold of that armed Hind and tell them to conserve some ammunition. We've still got to get through the pass . . ." He reached over with his left hand and grabbed his thumb, pulling it out and popping it back into position. Then he did the same with his forefinger, middle finger and pinkie. Right hand . . . call it fifty percent functional. Needed to get a bandage on it. Plug a couple of holes. Good enough.

He rolled to his left and got up on one knee, picked up a blood-covered AK, then straightened up, swaying on his feet.

Now to go kill the fuckers in the pass . . .

Above him, the ravens soared . . .

"AER KELDAR!"

Haza had fought just about everyone on earth at one point or another. He had mostly fought Americans but there were other Pashtun tribes, the Uzbeks and Turks of the Northern Alliance. He had fought beside and against Somalis and animalist Christians in Sudan. He had fought the Israelis and the Gurkhas. The British SAS commandoes and American Delta force. He had fought Spetznaz, Rangers and SEALs.

But if he survived this he was going to quit fighting *anyone*. For the trench had suddenly filled with women, big women, big blonde and brunette and redheaded women, screaming a terrible battle cry and swinging AXES for Allah's sake!

They had come in on top of the damned mortars. He had glimpsed one blown backwards in a spray of blood and guts, hit by one of her own rounds. More were spouting wounds from shrapnel. They didn't seem to care. They didn't seem to feel. They were wide-eyed and screaming in skirts and bright blouses, shooting AKs from their left hand and swinging those axes in their right.

They had dropped on the fedayeen before most of them had realized the mortars stopped, dropped into the trench hacking and screaming in a berserker rage that made the most Allah-enraptured fedayeen look like a child having a tantrum.

They had dropped in like ravens from the sky and begun hacking and shooting. Some of them had shot each other but even that did not seem to stop them.

The fedayeen had not had a chance. They were still trying to recover from being effectively and relentlessly mortared when these screaming harpies dropped on them and began slashing and hacking until the trench was a river of blood.

The axes made terrible wounds, cutting off limbs, slashing necks, crushing heads.

Haza had shot one, point-blank, blocked one of the axes then felt another sink into his shoulder. The AK dropped from his nerveless hands and suddenly he was on his back with an old woman, red dripping axe in hand, looking down at him.

"You are the commander, yes?" the woman said in badly accented Arabic. "Feel glad. You are being honored."

The woman dropped to sink both knees in his abdomen and Haza tried to wrench upwards. But three wide-eyed women were pinning his arms and legs. The fourth, a little slip of a redheaded girl he should have been able to toss off, had his arm in a bar lock and was watching quite calmly out of the deepest blue eyes . . .

"It is said we eat our dead. Not true." The woman raised the axe and chopped downwards, splitting his sternum. Chopped again, working her way from throat downward to get through all of the big bone.

The fedayeen screamed in pain and tried to writhe away but he was effectively pinned and couldn't escape. The women holding him down knew what they were doing, acted as if they had done it . . . before.

"The men, they are so besotted of the Father of All," the horrible old woman said, reaching down and ripping his chest apart. "But the women, oh we women know who holds the power. Power of life, power of death, the breath of the crops and the wind in the trees." A knife came out and descended.

The last thing Haza saw was the horrible woman raising his still beating heart and dribbling his blood into her mouth.

"Ay Sibelus!" the woman shrieked, holding the heart to the sky. "Bring back the spring!"

Captain Guerrin stood up on the ridgeline as the line limped towards him. Bodies on stretchers carried by men in battle armor and women in blood-splattered smocks. Men with women, too wounded to walk, over their backs. Men carrying the bodies of dead comrades. Smoke-stained and blood-drenched. But they were all there, every dead Keldara, man and woman. Some of the men carrying multiple weapons and still helping to lug the heavy mortars.

"First Sergeant, get the stretchers," Guerrin snapped. "Hell, get the whole company. These people are going home if we have to carry them on our backs."

Epilogue

Mike stood before the massive dun of the Keldara, head bowed, as the light wind from the north ruffled his hair.

The entire tribe stood behind him, more than half wearing bandages. That was, the whole of the tribe that was not in the hospital in Tbilisi or the much more modern and capable Landschein Hospital in Germany. The worst casualties, those who had lost limbs or eyes, the ones with really serious damage, were in Germany undergoing reconstructive surgery. The survivors.

Those for whom no surgeon could do anything lay on the ground in front of the dun. Twenty-one bodies, the ones that were even vaguely viewable dressed in their finest clothes, weapons by their sides, axe in one hand and a bundle of mistletoe in the other. Five were covered with sheets. Including Gretchen. He'd had to look, too. God *damn* him he'd had to *look*!

Twenty-one bodies. Fifteen male, including Father Ferani and, fuck, Sawn. Kiril, Gretchen . . . Six girls, Gretchen and five more from the battle in the fucking *pass*. The fucking girls of the Keldara. The fucking *girls* had broken them out. Broken the defenses in the pass he had chosen to avoid, to go to ground, rather than assault. He couldn't imagine ever taking another, Rite of Kardane or no. They were now, *all*, his troops. You didn't fuck your troops.

He'd always known the favoritism reasons against fraternization. What nobody ever mentioned was having your *soul* ripped out of your body when you hit the perfect storm. It counted as the twofer from hell when you fell in love with the *fiancée* of one of your troops—Rule one: Do not screw the dependents of subordinates—then said fiancée got blown away by a fucking 12.7—Rule Two: Do not fall in love with anyone you are in command of who is liable to get splattered all over a helicopter.

He'd lost friends before, he'd lost comrades before, he'd lost *Keldara* before.

But he could not face losing Gretchen. He wanted to scream. He wanted to throw himself on that broken body and howl like a mad dog. He felt as if he was going mad, that he finally understood the madness of grief of King Lear, the repeating images that his brain simply would not stop showing him. Flashing legs and golden hair and blue eyes that haunted his dreams. He felt as if at any moment he would scream to the skies, begging *God* to bring her back.

But he couldn't. All he could do was stand, as calmly as possible, and watch her be sealed away in a fucking tomb.

He wanted to lie by the side of his wife and his bride. But he couldn't. Because she wasn't, never could be. And because of the people behind him.

They were so few, now. Yes, they had broken the Chechens, broken them good and hard. The Georgian military was advancing in the Pankisi, virtually unopposed. The Russians were pressing forward from the north, catching the remaining formed Chechen groups in a pincer.

But there were a billion fucking Chechens. He'd kill every fucking one, drop smallpox on them, nuke them to fucking ashes, if he could just have one of those brave fucking girls back, if he could raise Sawn from the dead. If he could share one more beer with Father Ferani.

If he could have one more moment, just to look in her eyes, with Gretchen.

He'd kill the whole *world* for that one more moment.

Anastasia, wearing a thin blue dress far too cool for the day, stood with the girls of his harem, just behind him and to his left. Katya was among them though he wasn't sure that was quite right.

He thought she probably belonged with the staff, now. He also wasn't sure what had happened to the girl during the mission but she was . . . changed. Oh, she still had that hard side, but he'd actually seen her do *nice* things for the other girls in the house. Nobody was sure the change was going to hold, but he wasn't sweating having her at his back anymore.

Most of the Fathers were behind him and to his right. Including the new "Father Ferani," a relative youngster in his early fifties. In a line behind them were the Mothers. Mother Lenka was right there with them. He wasn't sure what that boded, but he could feel it boding something.

Then the team leaders spread in an arc behind him. Yosif, his head still bandaged and one eye covered by an eyepatch. Vil with a bandage around his arm and leg. Pavel, unscratched and clearly unsure about that. Gregorii Kulcyanov, the replacement for Sawn. Tall, slim and blond, Mike kept wanting to call him Sawn. Did they change the name of the team? Fuck. Dmitri Devlich, in place for Oleg. They were promising miracles for a replacement, but the bottom line was that his top team leader was now going to be missing a leg. For Mike, it was like missing an arm. His left, maybe, Adams being his right. Last, Padrek Ferani, also apparently unscathed. But his eyes were dark. Team Padrek, the best of their technicians, had taken the worst losses of any of the teams on the mission. They were going to miss that brain trust. Badly.

Then the staff. Nielson in his Army dress blues. Adams, just about covered in bandages from the final assault, wearing Keldara camo, and the two pilots, standing side by side.

They wore their flight suits and the new patches that had mysteriously appeared in their quarters only that day.

The short one, Bathlick, wore a patch on her right breast of a flaming dragon, breathing fire down towards the ground. Banked in a tight angle, the dragon's tail was pointed forward and shooting out what looked very like a laser beam. The ground below was littered with small figures that might have been bodies.

The taller, Wilson, wore a patch of a woman riding a winged horse. The woman had a wounded soldier cradled in her left arm and a sword that looked very much like a yellow light saber held above her head. The figure was not in armor, she wore only a smoke-stained flight suit. She was not blonde with plaited hair, but brunette, her hair streaming out from beneath a pilot's battered helmet. But it was unquestionably a Valkyrie, one whose face and figure looked very like the wearer.

The patches were, just as unquestionably, hand-embroidered.

Also standing there, not quite sure of himself, was Dr. Arensky. Marina had chosen to remain in Russia but, with Mike's permission, Dr. Arensky had asked to stay in the valley. He was, besides being a microbiologist, a trained physician. He had helped, immensely, with the recovering Keldara.

Then the rest of the Keldara, the team members mingling unconcernedly with the girls who had fought in the pass. It seemed that there was no end to the wounds. But there were a lot of hands being held, too.

Father Kulcyanov stepped forward and raised his hands.

"Father of All, the Far-Seeing, Lord of Ravens, raise these warriors, these Sons and Daughters of Tigers, these right hands of Fir, to your home. Let the Valkyr come for them and carry them across the shining bridge to the Halls . . ."

Mike tuned it out, looking at the fucking tombs the dead were going to be laid in. He didn't know where the rocks had come from. Maybe the Keldara kept several dozen slabs of granite around just in case their Kildar really fucked up. The slabs had been set up in a partial circle at the base of the dun, twenty-one small chambers, flush into the base, awaiting the bodies to be placed within. Closing slabs were laid before each of the chambers, the bodies resting on them in all their finery. On the completion of the ceremony of Going the bodies would be placed in them, the chambers closed and covered in turf.

Finally, Father Kulcyanov finished the invocation and the team leaders stepped forward. Together with the Fathers, they slid the bodies into the tombs; then more of the young men stepped forward, closing the chambers and beginning to cover them in earth.

The Keldara could dig like motherfuckers.

When the chambers were covered, the turf placed on them and the whole business done, the Keldara began to break up, quietly. There was no sobbing from grieving mothers but nobody was exactly partying. Later, maybe. Mike, personally, was planning on drowning himself in beer.

"Kildar," Father Kulcyanov said, walking over to him. He was still wearing that fucking tiger skin.

Mike wondered, again, if he should tell the old man about the tiger. Kulcyanov didn't have much time left in this world, he'd probably like to hear that the tigers were coming back.

"Kildar," the man repeated, laying his broad, spadelike hand on Mike's shoulder. "It is well."

"Yes, Father Kulcyanov," Mike replied. "It is fine. Thanks. I'm good. Thanks for asking."

"No, Kildar," the old man said, clenching his shoulder with amazing strength for his age. "You do not understand. It is *well*. Father of *All*, Kildar, try to understand that. For you and for the Keldara. For decades the Keldara had no chance to enter what you Christians would call heaven. Yes, we miss our sons and daughters. I had known Ivan Ferani most of my life, and all of his. I miss his gentleness and humor. And . . . everyone knows that you grieve, especially, for *one* who was laid here.

"We grieve but at the same time we live in joy. For the first time in *decades* we have added to the dun. We have lived in *shame* for a generation, for we could not add to the dun as our ancestors have for time immemorial. We weep not for these heroes, but because their light is gone from our lives. It is selfish. They have, all, men and women, brought honor to our clan such as we have not had in centuries. You, Kildar, have brought our honor back. Do not *fear* so. Missions will come to you and, for *our* honor, for *her* honor, you must not *fear*. Do not turn from the path of the warrior! Do not forsake us to die of old age and be buried in the dirt. If you do, you shame us before our gods and our ancestors. You will shame her memory.

"So understand this, Kildar. Know it in your bones, in your water, in your soul. It is *well*. Year upon year, century upon century, we build the dun. It is said that the final battle will commence when the dun of the Keldara reaches the roof of the sky."

Mike looked up at the massive hill, fully a hundred feet high and three times that at its base. Then he blanched.

"Wait," he said, blinking in horror. Each of the tombs was *maybe* two feet high and seven deep. "I thought this was . . . Are you telling me . . ."

"The dun of the Keldara is the graveyard of our heroes, Kildar," Father Kulcyanov said. "Those that die of old age, sickness and infirmity, they are consigned to the Cold Lands and buried in dirt. They die without honor. *These* are our honored dead. These rest with the heroes of *centuries*, Kildar. Rank on rank, circle on circle, layer upon layer, it is the home of our soul. It is our destiny."

The bar in Georgetown was nearly deserted. It was always pretty busy at lunchtime and got really busy after dark, but in the middle of the afternoon in "The World's Capital" the busy beavers of congressional staffers, White House staffers, congressmen, senators and the predators that circled them were all beavering away.

Which was why Pierson had chosen it for a quiet drink with an old "friend."

"We know they weren't nukes, you know," Pierson said, raising the glass of Bushmill's to his lips. If the bartender found it unusual that a full-bird colonel in dress greens was drinking in the middle of the afternoon he didn't let on.

"That became obvious rapidly," Colonel Chechnik said, shrugging as only a Russian could. He tossed off his vodka and poured more from the bottle on the table.

"I'm thinking smallpox," Pierson continued. "The SecDef is holding out for Ebola, but I think he's been watching too many movies."

"He has," Chechnik said. It was a virtual admission.

"We need verification that it's gone," Pierson replied. "All of it. Everything along the lines."

"What? You won't take my word as a spook?" Chechnik said, lightly. "I hope you do get it. But all I can say is that I've been told, personally, by our president, that all such research has been shut down and all samples destroyed. Whether that is true . . . I'm not sure even Vladimir could say."

"Fuck," Pierson said, knowing that thousands of hours of very quiet negotiations, personal talks at high-level summits and billions of reams of paper would come down to that, that even the *Russians* didn't know if everything was gone. The problem with infectious biologicals was that one fucking lab tech holding back one fucking vial could destroy the world.

"I understand that you're now persona non grata in Keldara Land," Pierson added.

"I'm sure that will pass," the Russian said with a shrug. "We both need each other too much to remain permanently estranged."

"'Estranged' is, I think, too mild a term," Pierson replied. "And the Keldara, not to mention the Kildar, have long memories. The Kildar, in particular, is taking this one really hard. I don't have all the details but . . . Don't expect to be invited to tea any time soon. In fact, I'd suggest that you, personally, stay as far away from Mike as you possibly can. He will figure out a way to fuck you. Somehow, some way, he will fuck you."

"Well, at least he got paid," Chechnik said, tossing off another vodka.

"Yeah," Pierson said, snorting. "I can't *believe* you guys just handed him three nukes."

"Well, we wished for him to get paid, no?" Chechnik said, grinning. "And otherwise, you would not pay him. He had suffered enough, and done enough good, that he should not be 'stiffed.'" He tossed back another vodka, set the shot glass down, poured another and then paused, his face suddenly going blank, the bottle suspended above the glass. The neck rattled against the lip, faintly.

"Wait. Did you say *three* nukes?!"

The tiger propped himself up, hips sprawled to the side, and looked down into the valley.

He'd recently caught a feral pig and was feeling pretty happy. His belly was full and while there weren't any female tigers around, hey, things changed. This area seemed to be simply crawling with pigs and deer, most of whom had forgotten all about tigers. He'd stay awhile.

He lumbered back to his feet and stretched in the dying sun then raised his head to the purpling sky. He coughed a couple of times and then tried out the roar. But his throat still wasn't full-grown, didn't have the broadness of a mature male's. All that came out was a halfhearted bellow. It was lost on the wind, carried away into the dusk.

Well, there were other days. He turned away from the valley and descended into the darkness of the ravine. It was time to find someplace to lay up for the coming winter. It was going to be a cold one. But spring would come around again. He could feel it in his bones.

Above the tiger, the ravens soared.

◇   ◇   ◇

Unto the Breach CD Playlist

"Holding Out for a Hero," Bonnie Tyler

"She's the One," Bruce Springsteen

"Silent Running," Mike and the Mechanics

"Kyrie," Mr. Mister

"Riding the Storm Out," REO Speedwagon

"The Final Countdown," Europe

"Through the Fire and Flames," DragonForce

"Winterborn," Crüxshadows

"Planet Hell," Nightwish

"Dark Chest of Wonders," Nightwish

"Eye of the Tiger," Survivor

"Immigrant Song," Led Zeppelin

"Paint It Black," Rolling Stones

"Heart of a Dragon," DragonForce

the following is an excerpt from
the sequel to VORPAL BLADE:

MANXOME FOE

by
John Ringo

available from Baen Books
February 2008
hardcover

"I'd only do this for Mom, you know."

Sergeant Eric Bergstresser adjusted the high collar of the Marine dress blues and shrugged his shoulders, again, trying to get the uniform to feel right. But since he spent most of his time in digi-cam or jeans, it never quite did.

"You've skipped out of it the last two visits, bro," Joshua Bergstresser said, shrugging. Josh, just turned sixteen and decidedly civilian given the earring he was sporting, was wearing Dockers and a polo shirt, as dressed up as he was going to get for church. "Besides, you look good. You're going to attract the ladies like flypaper. Maybe I should get a set of those."

Eric winced and then shrugged.

"Don't do it unless you're sure," Eric said, frowning. "As long as you're not in my outfit, Mom probably won't get two telegrams."

"Not a good way to talk, bro," Josh said. "You'll be fine. Tell me you'll be fine."

"Ain't gonna lie, bro," Eric replied. "Not something I can talk about. But I will tell you that on my last mission, we went out with forty-one Marines and landed with five."

"Are you serious?" Josh asked angrily. "That never made the news!"

"Yes, it did," Eric said, one cheek twitching up in an ironic smile. "Thirty-six Marines killed in helicopter crash. News at Six."

"That was out west somewhere," Josh replied, furrowing his brow thoughtfully. "That was your unit? Eric, crashes, well . . ."

"There wasn't a crash." Eric chuckled grimly. "They all died in combat. But a helicopter crash was a convenient cover. Among other things, it explained why most of them had closed casket funerals. Hell, there weren't even bodies in most of the caskets, just sandbags. We didn't lose them all at once and quite a few weren't recoverable."

"And that was your unit?" Josh asked.

"Yep."

"And you're going back?"

"Yep."

"That's insane."

"Yep."

"Eric," Josh said desperately. "You cannot go do . . . whatever it is you do, again. Forget what I said about the uniform.

De-volunteer or something. Hell, I'll hide you under my bed. With casualties like that . . ."

"Not much chance of believing I'll survive, right?" Eric asked, finally turning away from the mirror.

"YES!"

"Believe it or not, on the last cruise I started to get into Goth and heavy metal," Eric said, talking around the point.

"And I was happy, happy, happy," Josh replied. "Since I no longer had to listen to Hank Williams, Jr. What's it got to do with the statistical certainty you're going to die?"

"I still listen to Hank," Eric said. "But one of the songs I got into was called 'Winterborn.' You've never heard of Crüxshadows, have you?"

"Bit indy for me, man," Josh said. "What's wrong with Metallica?"

"Besides that they haven't had an album out in ten years?" Eric replied. "But this song, it's about the Trojans. There's a line in the chorus: In the fury of this darkest hour, I will be your light. You've asked me for my sacrifice, and I am Winterborn. I'm good at what I do, Josh. Very good."

"I didn't figure you got the Navy Cross for being incompetent," Josh said quietly. "But there's these things called odds."

"And if I didn't do it, somebody else would have to," Eric continued as if he hadn't heard his brother. "From experience, probably somebody who wasn't as good, who has less of a chance of coming back. You want me to put them on the chopping block, bro?"

"Hell, yes!" Josh said, his jaw working. "They're not my brother!"

"They're somebody's brother," the sergeant said, picking up his cover. "They were brothers and sons. Some lady just like Mom carried them in her womb and nursed them and loved them. And most of them we couldn't even bring home. There wasn't anything to bring. I've got a better chance than any replacement." He tucked his cover under his arm and curtly nodded at his reflection. "So, this is my sacrifice. As my first sergeant once said, if I was worried about where I was going to die, I never should have joined the Marines in the first place."

❖   ❖   ❖

Commander William Weaver, Ph.D., topped out on the climb and stood up on the pedals, clutching the saddle between his thighs as he coasted downwards to catch his breath. The roots on the trail were still slick from the morning dew that had yet to be burned off by the mid-morning Alabama sun. The canopy of oak trees and the dense green foliage around the trail would prevent that for several more hours. The rear wheel spinning and slipping on the roots had made the climbs more difficult than Bill was hoping and he was getting totally worked.

Leaning his center of gravity behind the saddle as the screaming downhill rushed up at him, he managed to keep the bike in control just long enough to hop over a small oak that had been dropped across the trail to prevent it from washing out. Bill looked at his heart rate monitor on the center of the handlebars—185. He was working way too hard for this part of the trail. The ride was fun and had let him take his mind off of, well, off of a lot of things, but his heart just wasn't really in it. The climb on the other side had severely kicked his ass. He should be able to get his heart rate back down to at least the 160s, but it was dropping slower than he'd expected and his heart pounded like a bass drum in his throat. He felt so out of shape. And the ride back up the mountain to the parking lot was going to be hell.

Eight years ago he would have kicked this ride's butt and been up for another lap or two, but eight years ago was . . . eight years ago.

Eight years ago was when he'd put his ass on the line to save the world. Eight years ago was before there was any concept of the *Vorpal Blade*. Eight years ago was . . . eight years ago when the world was a relatively simple place and a little slope like that last one wouldn't have bothered him one bit.

Eight years ago he'd been working for a defense contractor, fixing problems for the military and other government agencies with acronyms, mostly ending in A. DIA, CIA, NSA. Then an explosion blew out the University of Central Florida physics lab. Not to mention the rest of the university. Two hundred fifty-one times ten to the twelfth power joules would do that. Call it sixty kilotons and be done.

Subsequent to the blast that flattened UCF and a goodly space around it he'd been blasted into other dimensions, died he was pretty sure, resurrected he was absolutely sure and generally had a hell of a time running around saving the planet. The blast had opened up gates to other worlds, some of them inhabited by hostiles with seriously negative intent. Called the Dreen, they consumed organic matter to create more copies of themselves. They had conquered multiple worlds and Earth was next on the list. Weaver, with the help of a SEAL master chief and sundry others had managed to close the gates the Dreen used. But the anomaly where UCF physics department used to be kept pumping out more gates.

In time Weaver, among others, had figured out how to create gates on Earth, shutting down the gate forming bosons that were the culprits. Instantaneous teleportation from point to point was now a reality, with more and more gates being opened every day. The now defunct airlines had been less than thrilled. After almost ten years it was getting to the point that auto makers were less than thrilled.

The Dreen were not the only alien species encountered. One of their subject races, the catlike Mreee, had pretended to be friends just long enough to scout out the new human prey. The destruction of the Dreen gates had almost certainly wiped out the Mreee as well. Contact with them had certainly been cut off. But the survivor Mreee, part of the Dreen invasion force, had been less upset about that than many expected. They were a proud race that had seen themselves fall into slavery to masters who took not only their planet's resources but the very bodies of their citizens for conversion into Dreen. A clean death at the hands of an honorable foe was preferable.

One friendly race had been encountered, as well. The Adar were in advance of humans technologically but had nearly as much trouble with the Dreen. It was the Adar, though, who had passed on two items. One was a bomb big enough to shut down the Dreen gates. They hadn't used it themselves because the only way to crack the gates was for the bomb to go off very close to one. If it went off on the wrong side, the planet wasn't going to be habitable. The humans were desperate enough to use it and it worked, shutting down not only the gate that it was sent through but all other Dreen gates.

The second device, though, was in a way more useful. The Adar had found it on an ancient planet whose sun was just about dead. Nothing more than an enigmatic black box the size of a deck of cards, it had surprising properties. Any electrical charge caused it to release orders of magnitude more energy than inputted. Weaver eventually guessed that it was at least in part a warp drive. And he was right.

Using the box, which was not only a warp generator but a reactionless drive generator, the U.S. government had converted a submarine, the USS Nebraska, into a spaceship. It had taken seven years, and Weaver had jumped ship into the Navy early in the process. One of the problems he was having with this hill, admittedly, had been caused by too much time in a swivel chair redesigning a submarine to go where no man had gone before.

But Weaver, and a team of thousands, had eventually done it. And then Weaver, acting as astrogator, had gone out with the rechristened *Vorpal Blade*. Humans, seeing the first mirrorlike gates, had christened them Looking Glasses. The Adar found human thought process fascinating and had insisted that this ship be named in accordance with that thought. Since the ship was an Alliance spaceship, they'd had enough pull to push the name through.

Unfortunately, the Adar, while fine scientists and philosophers, had very little understanding of human humor or thought processes. So the acronym for Alliance Space Ship had slipped past their filters before it was too late.

On the ASS *Vorpal Blade*, Weaver, a crew of one hundred and fifty-four officers, NCOs and enlisted, forty-one Marines, and a handful of scientists had ventured forth on a local survey. They had limped back with five Marines, a couple of scientists and a hundred and twenty crew. But they'd found out what they were sent to find out: Space may be an unforgiving Bitch but She was nothing compared to landings. On the other hand, they'd also found allies and some interesting technology.

On a moon of a gas giant circling the otherwise unremarkable star 61 Cygni Alpha they'd encountered a race of rodentlike mammaloids. Named the Cheerick in the language of the country the Vorpal Blade contacted, they were similar in form to chinchillas or hamsters and at their highest level of technology were about at

War of the Roses level. In other words, they'd just started to press the edges of real science, climbing out of the darkness of alchemy. However, they also had records dating back thousands of years that indicated that from time to time, for reasons unknown, another race would rise up and destroy them. Dubbed "The Demons" they had begun to show up shortly before the arrival of the Vorpal Blade. The Blade had, fortunately, been forty light-years away at the time of their first sighting so it was innocent.

Eventually, through about half of their casualties, the scientists of the Blade had determined that the "Demons" were some sort of biological defense mechanism that targeted electrical emissions. By that time, the majority of the science team and a goodly number of Marines had bought the farm. But before they died, the science team had gotten a lock on the source of the Demons.

It was left to Weaver, Chief Warrant Officer Miller, USN, a handful of local Royal Guardsmen and a small team of the remaining Marines to stop the scourge. Fortunately, they'd been accompanied by the ship's linguist, Miriam Moon. Normally as nervous as a rabbit, Miss Moon had been the person who figured out how the system worked and, using a local, shut it down.

While Weaver was away on his forlorn hope, though, the ship had been under attack. Most of the "Demons" were ground mounted but there was an aerospace component as well, giant red and blue "dragonflies" with a very fast reactionless drive system and lasers that shot out of compound eyes. The Blade had been chased into space by them and ripped very nearly to shreds. The local who had taken control of the system, Lady Che-Chee, had had to tow the ship back to the planet using the same flies that had ravaged it.

Enough repairs had been enacted to allow the ship to limp back to Earth, but making it spaceworthy again had been a half-year process. Weaver had acted as the ship's executive officer on the trip back but gratefully turned over the job on arrival to a more experienced officer. Since then, though, he'd been deeply involved in the repairs and upgrades. Like, pretty constant sixteen-hour days involved.

This was his first real break, since the major repairs were completed and all that was left was details. He'd grabbed at the new CO's suggestion, more like order, to take some leave. The ship wasn't due to leave for its next mission for two months. So he'd headed down to his real home in Huntsville to visit friends and reacquaint himself with the trails, baby-head sized rocks, roots, boulders, downed trees, screaming downhills, and extremely rough and technical climbs of Monte Sano Mountain.

He pulled his left foot out of the pedal and planted it as he braked just before the whoopdie-doos. Just as he started down, his cell phone rang. The ringtone—"Welcome to the Jungle" by Guns'n'Roses—was barely audible over his pounding heartbeat. Bill welcomed the break, he was that fragged. He bit the tube hanging from the helmet strap in front of his face and sucked down water from his CamelBak between gasps for air.

Despite the fact that he was on leave, he was required to be on call. Since he not only had a deeper grasp of the science behind the drive but a knowledge of every bolt and system in the ship that was unsurpassed by even its commander and XO, sometimes there were questions that only he could answer. And it appeared that there was another one.

"Weaver," he said, panting for breath. The earbud he was wearing automatically activated at his voice.

"Commander Weaver, Captain Jeller, SpacComOps. You're required to report at the earliest possible moment to your ship."

"Shit," Bill muttered. "Uniform?"

"Whatever you're wearing at the moment, Commander," the captain on the phone said. "There has been an incident . . ."

Eric tuned out the priest as the sermon started. It was a new one since he'd left for the Corps, a woman of all things. His family was Episcopal but while Eric had heard there were no atheists in foxholes, he didn't recall praying much on the last mission. Mostly he'd been too scared spitless to remember any.

He spent most of the sermon checking out the congregation. It was pretty much the same faces he'd seen most of his life. He was born in Fayetteville, NC, when his dad was still in the Army, a "leg" who did something in logistics Eric had never quite understood. But Eric didn't remember North Carolina as a kid. His dad had moved to Crab Orchard to work in the, then new, plastic plant as a dispatcher. Josh had been born in the Arh Beckley Hospital as had his sister Janna.

Most of the people in the church had been born in Arh Beckley, those that hadn't used a midwife. And he'd seen the same faces every Sunday for as long as he could remember. So was it his eyes that had changed or the people around him?

Coach Radner had been a nightmare during high school. The head coach for the phys ed department and the lead coach for the Crab Orchard High School football team, the former paratrooper was missing two middle fingers from some industrial accident back in time. One time Bob Arnold had mocked him as the coach was instructing him on the fine point of the three-point stance of a blocker. Bob, thinking he was being funny, had taken up a three point stance with those same fingers folded back as if they'd been cut off. Radner, half Arnold's weight, had knocked the tackle flat on his ass with that same damaged hand. You did not cross Coach Radner.

Looking at him now, Eric saw a man who was relatively out of shape and on the back side of fifty. He looked satisfied with his life but not the demon that Eric recalled.

Bob Arnold was in the audience, too, with his wife Jessie. Jessie was one of the co-heads of the cheerleading team; Bob was the school's top tackle. It had been a natural match. Now, they both looked worn and washed out, with two kids already; Bob's muscle was turning to fat quick and Jessie wasn't exactly svelte anymore. Eric heard Bob was in construction framing down in Beckley. Eric had a hard time adjusting the picture of the two in high school.

Behind them were the Piersons. Mr. Pierson and Mrs. Pierson looked pretty much the same as they always had, a good looking couple. Mr. Pierson was the local veterinarian, Mrs. Pierson had been a legal secretary to one of the town's lawyers for years. But Eric stopped and blinked for a moment at the people with them. The Piersons had four children. Paul had been a year ahead of Eric in school and Eric heard he'd gone to college so he wasn't around. The youngest girl had to be Linda, but she'd really grown. She must be ten or so by now and had shot up. Then there was Hector. He was recognizable by the shock of white hair but that was about it. Where'd the pimples come from?

But the one that really caught him was the teenage girl with them. The other Pierson child would be Brooke but . . . that couldn't be Brooke. He conjured up a vague memory of a gawky

and awkward blonde girl who had just entered high school the
year he was graduating. She'd had a serious overbite that mildly
affected her speech and a mass of metal to go with it. Nice hair, a
mass of naturally curly blonde locks, but . . .

Jesus! It had to be Brooke Pierson. But the maulking vision in a
pink dress sitting with them couldn't . . . Same damned hair,
though. Shit, it was Brooke . . . She'd sure shot more than up.

He turned away as the girl in question looked his way, as if
divining that he'd been staring. It wasn't that, though. He'd caught
other looks from the congregation as the service had gone on. The
dress blues certainly stood out and Dad had told him that the dec-
oration had been written up in the local paper. Given that they
weren't, as far as anyone knew, at war, the award of the Navy Cross
had been big news in a very small town.

Looking away from the girl who . . . hell, she'd be seventeen,
which would get you twenty even in West Virginia . . . he saw
Coach Radner looking his way. The old paratrooper gave him a
respectful nod, one former warrior to the present generation, and
turned back to ignoring the sermon.

It was times like this that got Eric thinking. Looking around the
congregation he picked out the veterans. There were a bunch:
small towns like Crab Orchard had always provided more than
their fair share of soldiers and Marines. But they left quite a few
behind, too. The annual Memorial Day celebrations pointed that
out, the roads lined with crosses with names on them. More
crosses than there were people who lived in the town it sometimes
seemed. WWII, WWI, Korea, Vietnam, the aborted "War on Terror," the Dreen War . . .

Would one of those crosses one day say "Eric Bergstresser"? Or
would he be one of the guys in the congregation, running to fat but
there to see their grandkids? Would he sit around in the VFW hall
and tell stories about crabpus and Demons? Or would he be an
empty box in a grave, a guy people sort of recalled on Memorial
Day, but really nothing but a fading memory?

He shook his head to clear the thought as the sermon finally
droned to a close. The new priest, priestess, whatever, sure seemed
devoted but my God she was boring. There had to be better uses of
his time but Mom wanted to show off her Marine-hero son. Given
that it might be the last chance she got, he owed her that. It was

that that had decided him on coming. Not that he was going to put it to her that way.

Since he was in church he figured he ought to pray, some, for a chance to come back to it. But he was blanking on prayers. No, there was one.

> "For heathen heart that puts her trust
> In reeking tube and iron shard—
> All valiant dust that builds on dust,
> And, guarding, calls not Thee to guard.
> For frantic boast and foolish word,
> Thy Mercy on Thy People, Lord!"

"What was that, Eric?" his mom asked, as the congregation rose to do what Eric thought of as "the huggy" thing.

"Just a prayer, Mom," Eric said as the lady in front of him, whom he didn't recognize, turned around to get a hug and a welcome. "It's called 'Recessional.' "

CALIPHATE

by
Tom Kratman

available from Baen Books
April 2008
hardcover

Where now is the ancient wealth and dignity of the Romans? The Romans of old were most powerful; now we are without strength. They were feared; now it is we who are fearful. The barbarians paid them tribute; now we are the tributaries of the barbarians. Our enemies make us pay for the very light of day and our right to life has to be bought. Oh, what miseries are ours! To what a state we have descended! We even have to thank the barbarians for the right to buy ourselves off them. What could be more humiliating and miserable?

—Salvian of Marseilles, 5th Century AD

Grolanhei, Province of Affrankon, 12 Safar, 1527 AH (23 March, 2103)

"Wonderful strike!" applauded the man on horseback, slapping the stock of the rifle in the saddle holster at the horse's right. Mohammad was his name, though, as Mohammad was the most common name in Europe, this was less than significant, individually. "Wonderful strike, Rashid," he repeated. A third man, Bashir, agreed.

Bashir's rifle was in his arms. It was hardly necessary. The *Nazrani* were like rabbits and no man needed a rifle to ward off rabbits. Even so, the presence of the weapon, and its display, was a badge of the superiority of the faithful and the inferiority—the *helpless* inferiority—of the infidel. Virtually all of the masters carried them almost all the time they were in public. There was quite a lively trade in personal arms, too. Nearly every town with any numbers of the faithful had a shop full of shotguns, rifles, and even automatic weapons for sale.

Rashid, their companion, just nodded. Like Mohammad and Bashir, Rashid also sat astride a horse, in his case a magnificent white animal. In truth, Rashid's attention was not on the birds, nor even on their prey. Rather, he watched the little hamlet of Grolanhei, part of his personal domain as one of the tax gatherers for the emirate of Kitznen.

Grolanhei did *not* have an arms dealer.

All my little helpless rabbits, Rashid thought. *All you disgusting filthy Nazrani are my prey.*

As light skinned and blue eyed as the wretched heretics that peopled the town, still Rashid more resembled his hawks than he did them. His eyes were bright, keen and avaricious; his nose a beak jutting from his face. Inside, too, he resembled a hawk, all fierce and selfish appetite, all blood-lust and drive to dominate.

Every year, at tax time, Rashid made sure to collect a few children in lieu of the taxes he deliberately set too high. He received a direct bounty from the *bundejaysh*, the army, for the boys he collected for the Corps of Janissaries. The girls went on the market to whosoever might want a female child for service. Sometimes that service was domestic. Other girls, especially the prettiest ones, could be sold for other purposes.

But the bastard Nazrani *hide their women and girls now,* Rashid mentally cursed. *It's become altogether too difficult to tell which of their little bitches might fetch a decent price. Shameful for them to pervert the law like that. Bastards.*

"Stop being such a *girl*, Petra," the young boy said to his sister as the two watched the bird of prey swoop and strike.

Petra bint Minden, aged six, had shuddered at the swooping hawk's cry. She shuddered again, shielding her eyes with tiny hands, as the hare screamed out in pain and terror. Barely, she forced her fingers apart to see the eagle carry off its limp and bloody prey. Again she shuddered, pleased that *she* was not so small as to be the prey of a raptor.

Petra felt her brother tug at her arm. His voice commanded, "Come *on*. The masters are coming. And we're almost late for school."

Turning away from the pasture where the eagle had struck, Petra followed after her brother on little legs. It was hard to keep up, what with the enveloping cloth sack the girl wore that covered her from head to heel. The covering was whole, though her mother had spent long hours patching and mending it. For it wasn't the law that required Petra to be so enclosed; she was too young for it to matter.

Rather, she wore the burka at her mother's insistence. As the mother had said, "Some of the masters take a long view of things. You're a beautiful child, Petra, though you're too young to know what that means. Even so, no sense in letting them see you and put you on a list for when you've turned nine."

Behind her, Petra heard a horse neigh, the sound echoed by several more of them. Turning quickly, she spied a group of three riding across the bare and open field. Two held their arms out, she saw, as another twirled something overhead. Two great hunting birds came to rest on the outstretched arms, one of them bearing the corpse of the hare. Petra knew they must be from the masters; *Nazrani* weren't allowed to ride horseback.

"Come along, Petra," insisted her older brother, Hans. Hans was nine, big for his age and strong. He was her protector and the hero of Petra's existence. Like his sister, the boy was blond with bright blue eyes. Folk of the town were already whispering that he was sure to be gathered for the janissaries within a few years. Unlike their father, Hans was too young to have the bowed back of the *dhimmi*, those who submitted by treaty to the rule of the masters, their taxes, and their laws.

There were several *orta* of janissaries in the old al Harv barracks set roughly between the town of Grolanhei and the larger one of Kitznen. They sometimes came to the smaller town to drink forbidden beer or make use of the town's dozen or so whores. (For the janissaries were well disciplined and rarely indulged in rape.) Petra found their black uniforms with silver insignia strangely compelling.

"Come along," Hans commanded again, grabbing her by her arm and pulling her back to the town that edged the open field. "We don't want them to notice us."

Bad things, so it was whispered, sometimes happened to blond and blue-eyed children who attracted the notice of the masters. Petra shuddered again and followed her brother, stopping only once more to turn and peer at the magnificent horsemen.

The way to school, up the cobblestoned Haupstrasse, led past a fountain and a crumbling monument, a painted wall, which listed the names of the town's war dead going back centuries. No names had been added to the monument in over one hundred and fifty years. Few of those old names were visible now. The picture, painted on a wall over the town fountain, was of an angel lifting a fallen soldier to Heaven. It was part of the back of the Catholic church. As such, under the rules of protection imposed by the masters, the treaty of *dhimmitude*, neither it, nor the church, could be repaired.

It didn't really matter anyway. Petra couldn't read yet, though Hans was trying to teach her, no matter that the law forbade it. Left to the masters she would never learn to read. She was, after all, a mere female. In their view, her ultimate value was in her body, in the pleasure it might someday bring to a man, in the household work she would do, and in the children she would bear. For all practical purposes, she—like virtually all the females of the Caliphate, to include the Moslem ones—was considered to be not much more than a donkey who could speak and bear children.

Instead, her school taught her only basic theology—to include, by law, a theology not her own—and homemaking, as well as the rules under which she must live out her life. That last was a part of that theology not her own.

As she had nearly every day since she had learned to walk, Petra looked without understanding at the wretched and abandoned memorial, then turned and continued on her way. She expressly did not look across the street from the monument to the crude wooden gallows where the remains of two teenaged boys swung in the breeze by ropes around their stretched necks. The boys were dressed in girls' clothing, minus the hijab.

Petra had known both boys. Their names were—had been—Martin Müller and Ernst Ackermann. She, like the other women and girls of the town, had cried when the masters took the boys and hanged them before the crowd last Sunday after church. The dry-eyed Catholic priest had stood by and blessed the masters' work. The boys would sway there, if history was a guide, until the following Sunday, just before church. (For while the masters had firm rules for the timing of the burial of their own dead, *Nazrani* bodies could be left unburied for educational reasons.)

Petra remembered the pleading as the executioner had forced the boys onto the stools under the gallows' crosspiece, the tears on the boys' faces as they were noosed and then the flailing legs, the eyes bugging and the tongues swelling out past blackening lips. That's why she couldn't look; she remembered it too well.

She didn't know why the boys had been executed. They'd always seemed very nice to her, especially nice in comparison to most of the other boys of the town, her Hans, only, excepted. After the hanging, all the girls had agreed that, among a pretty rowdy lot, those two had been much kinder and more decent to them than were any of the other boys of the town. Indeed, they'd been so sweet that they might almost have been girls themselves.

There was too much in the world that Petra really didn't understand. Shaking her head, she followed her brother to the small schoolhouse where she would spend half her day before hurrying home to help mother with the daily chores.

At the schoolhouse, Petra and Hans split up, he going in by the front door, she walking around back to the girls' entrance. Inside, she doffed her coat and her confining burka, hung them on her own peg, and walked into the classroom. A set of solid and pretty much soundproof walls separated the girls, all in one room, from the boy's seven classes. That was not so bad, really. Though the classroom was overcrowded, a little, education for girls wasn't mandatory and so there were only about a fifth as many girls in the school as boys.

Sister Margarete, the sole teacher for the girls of the town, was old enough to have learned to read as a girl herself. What would happen to the girls, once she died, the nun didn't know. The masters had granted the church a local exemption to the strictures against educating Christian females, but it was at best a partial and limited exemption. Margarete didn't know if it stretched enough to provide a replacement for herself once she'd gone to her final reward.

Tapping a wooden pointer on the podium, Sister Margarete directed the girls to sit, then began with a review of the previous day's lesson:

"We must pay the *jizya* . . . we must submit to the Sharia . . . Slavery is a part of *jihad* and *jihad* a part of Islam . . . we must cover ourselves in accordance with the Sharia . . . We must submit to our fathers and husbands or any other masters the Almighty may decree for us . . . No one not of the True Faith may ride a horse or an automobile, except at the order of one of the faithful . . . " Petra knew what an automobile was but had only seen one occasionally in her life. She knew no one who had ever ridden one. . . . "No Christian may live in a house better, larger or higher than any lived in by a

Moslem . . . In a court of Sharia a Christian's testimony"— Petra wasn't too sure what "testimony" meant—"counts for only half that of a Moslem, and a woman's for only half a man's. . . . No Christian or Jew"—Petra had no clue what a Jew was, either—"may possess a weapon . . . If the masters demand silver we must humbly offer gold . . . If a master wishes to fill our mouths with dirt we must open them to receive it . . . "

Along with the others, Petra recited. Like the other young girls, she didn't understand more than half of what she recited meant. Maybe it would come in time; she knew she was only six and that older people understood more than she did. Besides, her town was entirely Catholic, for the most part ruling itself. The Moslems all lived far away in the provincial capital of Kitznen or with the janissaries at the barracks of al Harv.

"Okay, children, school's over," announced Sister Margerete as she stood near the door. "You older girls, don't forget your burkas. Though you are not of the masters still you are subject to the same rules as the Moslem women."

This only made sense. How, after all, was one of the masters to have any peace at home if the shameless Christian hussies had more privileges than their own wives and daughters? Even many of the younger girls, such as Petra, wore burkas for the same reasons Petra's mother had for forcing it on her daughter.

School got out early. School, for girls, *always* got out early. After all, most of what they needed to know in this year of someone else's Lord, 1527, they would learn better at their mothers' knees than in a school. Pulling on her gray covering, Petra filed out with the other girls. Since Hans would be several hours more, Petra walked home alone. She took back streets, dirty and muddy, rather than the cobblestoned main street. That way she didn't have to walk by the swaying and soon to be rotting bodies of Martin and Ernst.

As she walked, Petra chanced to look to her right, out into the open fields. A small herd of goats was out there, property of one of the masters in Kitznen, no doubt. The goats were eating the shoots from a field of barley.

Imperial Military Academy, West Point, New York, 26 March, 2106

"Knock it off on the Area!" the corporal bellowed. Immediately, some fifty-odd stamping cadets took themselves out of step and ceased their illicit, cadenced marching on the asphalt. Hours were punishment, to be walked alone and not marched as a group.

Fun while it lasted, for some constrained values of "fun," thought the gray-clad, overcoated, white-crossbelted, biochemistry major and Cadet First Classman John Hamilton. (Hamilton, despite being a first classman, was also Cadet *Private*, but that was a different story, an altogether sadder story, involving an illicit tryst in a little-used alcove down in the Sinks.)

Hamilton was a native of Maine. He'd had an ancestor, as a matter of fact, in the famous 20th Maine, during the Civil War—a Canadian who'd come south from New Brunswick to enlist and decided to stay on after the war. (Though one couldn't tell from his color or his eyes, he'd also had an ancestor from Toronto who'd enlisted in Company G of the equally famous 54th Massachusetts. That might have accounted for the wave in his hair.) For more than four centuries, in every generation that was called, Hamilton's generations had answered. He'd answered, too.

Coming to a halt a few yards from the stone wall of Bradley Barracks, Hamilton transferred his rifle—now, in an exercise in deliberate anachronism, a reproduction Model 1861 Springfield—from one shoulder to the other, turned about, and began walking in the other direction.

Already, Hamilton could hear the plaintive cries of "Odinnn!" arising from the surrounding barracks to echo off the stone walls.

Much like the empire it supported and defended, the school had grown considerably from its rather humble beginnings. For example, while its first class, that of 1806, had graduated and commissioned fifteen cadets, the current class, that of 2106, was more than one hundred times greater. The Class of 2106 was expected to send forth some fifteen hundred and twenty-seven newly commissioned second lieutenants, or roughly one-fortieth of all new officers accessed by the Army in this year.

❖　　❖　　❖

Or, thought the gray-clad Cadet John Hamilton, as he paced off his four hundred and seventy-seventh hour of punishment tours, *One-thousand, five hundred and twenty-six if I get too many more demerits. I must be a shoo-in for the Martinez Award by now. If, that is, I don't get found*—booted from the Academy—*on demerits.*

As West Point traditions went, the Martinez Award was, at about one hundred years since founding, relatively new. Like being the goat—the last ranking man or woman of the class—it was a distinction not avidly sought. Still, there had been a fair number of general officers who had, in their time, been recipients of the award, just as there had been through history a fair number of goats who rose to stars, George Edward Pickett (1849) and George Armstrong Custer (1861) being neither the least significant nor the most successful among them.

Hamilton, though, wasn't interested in stars. He wasn't really all that interested in the Army, certainly not as a career. If he ever had been, the Imperial Military Academy had knocked such ambition out of him. Instead, he saw it as a way to pay for school and to serve out his mandatory service obligation. Whether that service would see him on the coasts of the Empire's British allies, more or less comfortably, if chillily, watching the Moslem janissaries across the Channel, or hunting *Luminosos* or *Bolivanos* in the mountains or jungles of the South American Territories, or policing the Philippine Islands, or any of the dozens of other places across the globe where the Empire held or fought for sway, he couldn't predict.

Anything, Lord, anything *but freezing my balls off hunting Canadians in northern Quebec or Ontario, please. I'm too tall and skinny for the cold. Even Chechnya on the exchange program would be better.*

"Ooodddiiinnn!" sounded again from out the barracks windows.

Hamilton already had his branch assignment, infantry. Yet he lacked for a unit assignment yet, and that must depend on the latest casualty figures and some schooling. As a matter of fact, he wouldn't find out his first assignment until he graduated Ranger School—assuming he did, of course; many did not—just before reporting in for the Basic Course at either Fort Benning (Light Infantry and Suited Heavy Infantry Officers Basic Course) or Fort Bliss (Mechanized Infantry Officer Basic Course) or Fort Stewart

(Constabulary Infantry Officers Basic Course). And even then it might change if casualties in, say, Mindanao suddenly soared.

And the casualty lists are never short, Hamilton mused. *They never have been; not in my lifetime, anyway.* He stopped, again facing a stone wall, then transferred his rifle and executed an about face. *Then again, when you've got a population of your own in excess of five hundred million, and control more than another billion, what's a few thousand a month? Except that one of them, sometime in the next five years, might be me. Oh, well . . . buy your ticket and take your chances. And it isn't as if we've a lot of choice about fighting. Maybe once we had that kind of choice. Not anymore.*

Hamilton took a surreptitious glance overhead. Yes, clouds were gathering. The prayers were working. *Perhaps no parade tomorrow.*

"OOODDDIIINNN!"

One of the nice things about walking hours in the Area was that it gave one time to think, though the weather could sometimes be all that one was able to think about. Weather permitting though, and today was merely brisk rather than outright miserable, one could really do some interior soul searching and reflection. Hamilton wondered, sometimes, if he didn't court demerits just so he could have that time alone.

I wonder what it was really like here, before the Empire. The histories don't discuss it much, beyond showing the before and after pictures of Los Angeles, Boston, and Kansas City. I've read the Constitution, all through the Thirty-Sixth Amendment, but the words don't really give me a feel for what it was like back then. Different . . . it must have been different. Did Free Speech really mean people were free to criticize the wars of defense? To protest them in public? Did Freedom of Religion accept even the enemy here? Well, that was before the Three Cities. Was military service really voluntary? For everybody? How the Hell could they maintain the hundred divisions we need that way? Then again, did we need a hundred divisions the old way? But after we were hit here, did we have any choice, really?

Despite being at war, and having been at war—even if it wasn't always recognized as such—for over a century, the emphasis at the IMA was still more on "Academy" than on "Military." Even so, there was a fair amount of military training, some practical, some theoretical. Hamilton had signed up for several practical electives over the last two academic years. One of these was "The Fighting Suit," the basic equipage of the Suited Heavy Infantry. (And, yes, when Hamilton had been the roughly four-millionth to publicly note the convenient acronym that came along with Suited Heavy Infantry Troops, he'd been slugged with a whopping forty hours of walking the Area.)

In any case, the Exo wasn't really a suit, not in the sense that it covered its wearer completely. Rather, it was an exoskeleton to which some considerable degree of armor protection could be added, at a cost in speed, range and supplies carried.

"Remember, it's not a cure-all," the sergeant-instructor, Master Sergeant Webster, had told the cadets the first day of class. Grizzled and old, Webster was the color of strong coffee. He was, so far as Hamilton could tell, the platonic ideal of a noncommissioned officer as such existed in the mind of God: tough, dedicated, no nonsense, and with just enough sense of humor to be, or at least *seem*, human.

"The suit is a bludgeon, not a rapier. It can get you to the objective," Webster had added. "It can get you there reasonably fresh and well supplied, but without much armor. Or it can get you across the objective, with full armor and reduced supply. Or it can do both if, and only if, something else carries you to near the objective.

"It's also a guarantee that, if you wear it while setting up an ambush somewhere in the Caucasus, the enemy will smell it from a mile away and never come near you. So why bother? And if you think you can use it for a recon patrol, I'll also guarantee you that the enemy will *hear* it from half a mile away. So why bother?"

"Because with full armor and a winterizing pack it will keep me warm while hunting Canadian rebels in Northern Ontario?" Hamilton had suggested, one inquisitive finger in the air.

"Mister Hamilton," Sergeant Webster had answered, "there is no such thing as a 'Canadian.' There are Americans. Then there are imperial subjects. There are also rebels, allies, and enemies. *No* Canadians, however. Write yourself up for an eight and four: minor lack of judgment."

❖   ❖   ❖

Story of my life, Hamilton thought. *Ask a question; get some time in the Area. Try to think and—*

The thought was interrupted by the Area sergeant. "Attention on the Area. The hour is over. Fall out and fall in on your company areas."

Young Cadet John Hamilton, and many another, hastened to get on with something that passed for a more normal and fruitful life.

Why the fuck didn't I apply to Annapolis? I love boats. I grew up around boats. But nooo. Family tradition was Army and so I just had to follow along. Jackass.

"What will kill or take out an exoskeleton?" Webster asked rhetorically, after the class had taken seats. His finger pointed, "Mr. Hamilton?"

"Kill the man wearing it, Sergeant."

"How? Ms. Hodge."

That cadet, cute, strawberry blonde and—Hamilton reluctantly admitted—probably tougher than he was, answered. "Without armor, Master Sergeant, shooting the wearer in a vital organ is sufficient. Assuming armor is worn, however, the armor can be penetrated by a .41-caliber or better uranium or tungsten discarding sabot projectile. The joints are subject to derangement by large explosive devices or near-impacting heavy artillery or mortar fire. The power pack can similarly be fractured or penetrated. This will also contaminate the exoskeleton such that it cannot again be worn short of depot level decontamination. If the enemy is very clever, and the situation on the ground very bad, it can be worn out of power—"

"At which point," Webster interrupted, "you will have made a present of some very expensive gear to some very bad people. Very good, Cadet Hodge."

Hamilton leaned over and whispered in Hodge's ear, "Ass kisser."

"Better his than yours," Hodge whispered back. "*He* probably washes."

Webster, more amused than anything, let the byplay go without comment. He continued with the lesson, "The point is, however, that almost anything that will kill you in your bare skin *can* kill you while wearing the exoskeleton, even with maximum armor. It's just harder to do.

"However, unlike armored personnel carriers and infantry fighting vehicles, the Exo allows the member of a unit to take maximum advantage of small bits of cover and concealment. It does not, individually, present as tempting and lucrative a target as a tracked vehicle carrying nine to twelve men. This is true even though at half a million IND"—Imperial New Dollars—"each, nine Exos cost slightly more than one infantry fighting vehicle. Men are not potatoes, after all. Their lives matter."

Webster noticed Hodge fidgeting in her chair. "You had a question, Ms. Hodge?"

"Not a question, Master Sergeant, just an observation. Whatever the cost, whatever the risks and whatever the downsides, the Exo makes sense for me because I'm a woman. Nothing else allows me to be a full equal of men in combat."

"Not quite, Ms. Hodge," Webster corrected. "Because you're the bottleneck . . . not you, personally; I mean women are the bottleneck . . . in the production of the next generation, the Exo cannot *reduce* your overall value to that of a man."

"God knows, *I* value you, sweetie," Hamilton said, no longer in a whisper but at least *sotto voce*.

Webster's voice thundered, "Mr. Hamilton, write yourself up for another eight and four: public display of affection."

Grolanhei, Province of Affrankon, 2 Shawwal, 1530 AH (1 October, 2106)

"*Jizya!*" demanded Rashid, the tax gatherer, his fist pounding the old oaken table in the Minden's kitchen. But for his beak of a nose, the gatherer did not look noticeably different from the *Nazranis*. Rashid's ancestors had converted early and then married into the dominant group.

"But, sir," Petra's father began to explain, "the harvest has been bad this year. The early frost . . . the rain . . . "

."Silence, pig of an infidel!" The *jizya* is a head tax. It is flat. It is fixed." *Fixed by me.* "It makes no account of the piddling troubles Allah sends you filth to encourage you to give up your decayed and false faith."

Seeing that Minden was still minded to dispute the collection, the tax gatherer's lip curled in a sneer. Cutting off further discussion, he said, "You realize, do you not, that the *jizya* is what permits you the status of *dhimmis*? That without it, without the pact, the *dhimma*, we are in a state of war, of holy war, of *jihad* with you and yours? That your lives are forfeit? Your property forfeit?"

"But . . . please, sir . . . "

Being inside the walls of her own home, Petra was uncovered. Neither she, nor her mother, had anticipated the arrival of the taxman today. Indeed, they'd all been so distraught and overworked with the gathering of the very skimpy harvest, they'd not thought of much of anything but how they were going to eke out an existence over the winter. They had to hope others had had better luck this year. If it was a question of letting the *Nazrani* farmers eat, or taking the food to feed their own, the masters had no compunction about letting filthy *Nazrani* starve.

Though only nine, and though she feared hunger as much as the next, Petra was ashamed to see her father beg. She was ashamed of his *dhimmi* status, now that she'd grown and learned enough to understand what that meant. She was ashamed of her people who submitted to this humiliation. And, when the tax gatherer looked over at her—more accurately, so she saw, looked her over—she was ashamed of herself. She remembered something Sister Margerete had told her class:

"Mohammad consummated his marriage with his favorite wife, Aisha, when she was nine years old."

Petra hadn't quite understood what "consummated" meant.

"Mark down the boy for gathering to the janissaries," Rashid told the chief of his four guards. "Take the girl now.

"And next year, you filthy swine, when I come for our taxes and demand silver, you had best give me gold or you'll see yourselves joining your daughter on the auction block."

One of Rashid's guards went to Petra. He took handcuffs and a chain from a pouch that hung at his side. The cuffs he ratcheted shut around her wrists, tightly enough to make her wince. The chain he attached to the cuffs.

Hans lunged. "Get your hands off my sister!"

The guard with Petra ignored the boy; that's what the other guard was for. That other guard caught Hans halfway through his lunge, wrapping one arm around the boy's waist. He then put Hans' feet back on the floor, stood and slapped him across the face several times, hard enough to stun and draw blood. The guard then knocked the boy down as his mother wailed and his stoop-shouldered father hung his head in helpless shame.

Petra, who had begun to cry when the cuffs were put on her, screamed when she saw her brother hurt. A slap from Rashid—hard enough to hurt without damaging the merchandise—quieted her.

She was sobbing as they led her away for her first ride in an automobile.

A crowd gathered outside the Minden's hovel, curious but too frightened to help. After all, what help could they give in a country no longer their own?